THE
FOURTH
PROCEDURE

THE
FOURTH
PROCEDURE

STANLEY POTTINGER

Ballantine Books

New York

Grateful acknowledgment is made to PolyGram Music Publishing Group for permission to reprint an excerpt from the lyrics of "Honey," written by Robert Russell. Copyright © 1968 PolyGram International Publishing, Inc. Used by permission. All rights reserved.

LIBRARY OF CONGRESS CATALOGING-IN-PUBLICATION DATA
Pottinger, Stanley.
The fourth procedure / Stanley Pottinger.
p.   cm.
ISBN 0-345-38400-8
1. Washington (D.C.)—Fiction.   I. Title.
PS3566.0724F68 1995
813.54—dc20   94-34282 CIP

Manufactured in the United States of America
First Edition: April 1995
10 9 8 7 6 5 4 3 2

THE
FOURTH
PROCEDURE

Maizie wanted to cut a new deal with God, but so many things were happening between her legs she found it impossible to concentrate. She propped herself up on her elbows and looked down.

"Let me see it," she said. She waited, but the only reply she heard was the sound of labored breathing. The sweat on her forehead ran down the bridge of her nose into her eyes. She used her naked shoulders to wipe it away, turning her head to the left, then to the right, then tilting it back to relieve the ache in her neck. It didn't help. She looked over the yellow-stained sheet covering her midsection, down to the frizzy gray hair of the old woman's head. "It's not a coat hanger—is it?"

The old woman looked up. "Relax," she said in a gravelly voice, and horked out a smoker's rattling cough. Feeling the damp lung air on the insides of her thighs, Maizie jerked her knees together, digging the crusty edges of the leather stirrups into her ankles. "Cut it out," the old woman said, and went back to work like a plumber under a sink: cigarette smoke, squinted eyes, dirty shirt, tool in hand. Everything but a flashlight.

Maizie dropped her head back on the table and fingered a ring on a gold chain around her neck. A naked lightbulb hung at the end of a cord above her face. *Give me a sign, Lord. Flicker. Brighten. Dim.*

Nothing. She chased rainbow spots on her retina. *What do you want me to do, go blind?* She waited for an answer, staring. The bulb glowed steady as the sun.

Warm fingers penetrated her body—then something sharp and cold. Her back snapped into an arch; a grunt escaped her throat and her fingernails dug into a plastic daisy on the shower curtain covering the table. She struggled back onto her elbows, breathing hard, straining to keep her arms from splaying out on the sweat-drenched plastic.

"What . . . are you using?" she said.

The old woman stopped a moment and looked at her wearily, as if she'd heard this question many times before. Blinking slowly, she withdrew the instrument and held it straight up, like a lightning rod. Maizie's eyes widened. It was a stiff wire about a foot long with a slight banana-

3

shaped curve, one end hammered into a tiny spatula, the other wrapped in electrician's tape to form a handle. Its black paint had been worn off long ago, removing any sign that it once had, indeed, been a coat hanger. It was so bizarre, so unlike anything Maizie could imagine being inserted into herself, she thought it was meant for someone else.

"It's just a tool," the old woman said. "Now lie back and relax." She lowered the wire beneath the sheet and returned to work. "Listen to the radio," she said in the tone of a busy mother talking to a pestering child.

Maizie laid her head back and placed her forearm over her eyes. *Get me through this, Lord, and I swear I'll never have sex again.* She peeked at the lightbulb. No sign. And no surprise: she'd cut that deal a month ago.

She lifted the ring from her chest and looked at the crystal intaglio of an angel standing with her wings at rest, sword in hand, foot resting on the severed head of Satan. It felt like a hundred years ago that Mike had given it to her. She'd have to leave it as collateral until she could scrape together the rest of the two hundred, but lose it? Never. It was the only item of value she owned, the one thing she'd never let go.

She laid the ring in the hollow of her neck and touched it, eyes closed, wondering once again how she got into this mess. She'd already been over the causes a hundred times—an unlucky time of the month, her boyfriend Bobby's perpetual sexual motion, a broken condom, assuming he'd used one—but she was tired of this line of reasoning, sick of blaming herself. It was time to look at the big picture, the forces beyond her control.

Put that way, the answer was obvious: the Nazis. If it hadn't been for them, Mike never would have been drafted and gone ashore at Omaha Beach, or been killed on some muddy French road fixing a flat in a rainstorm, leaving her a widow at the age of twenty-four. If it hadn't been for Adolf, she never would have been fooling around with guys like Bobby, filling voids, satisfying urges, looking for a new husband, a job, anything with some hope attached. Amazing, wasn't it? A sawed-off German with a Charlie Chaplin mustache and one ball (so they said) had reached halfway around the world, taken away her husband, killed him, and now had placed her spread-eagle on a kitchen table. . . .

She felt something strange happening in her pelvis and pictured Uncle Tad building a ship in a bottle. Play a game, she thought. Guess which is worse—the physical pain or the idea of the thing. It didn't work. She took a deep breath and expelled everything inside her. Everything she could. *Adolf, nothing. You're the one who broke the rules, Maiz. You're the one who pays.*

She lifted her arm from her eyes and looked at the brown Philco radio on the kitchen counter, a coffee cup stuck to its top. Glenn Miller's "String of Pearls" started up. Well, what d'ya know. God's finally talking. It was the same song she'd heard over and over the night she'd gotten pregnant. Rubbing it in, but talking.

Another jab inside her pelvis, another phlegm-rattling cough over her midsection, another tightening of her thighs. She saw a Listerine ad in her head with mouth germs as big as centipedes. A wave of nausea rolled over her, stinging her throat with soured french fries and chocolate shake.

Another phlegm-soaked cough from the old woman spewed over her skin, but this time she didn't move. Funny, how fast a person gets used to things. She remembered her honeymoon with Mike at a lake in the Ozarks, the run-down room they'd paid for in advance and couldn't afford to leave. The first night she'd found a roach in bed she'd turned on the lights and sat up half the night reading old *Look* magazines. But after a week of swimming and sunbathing and making love, she found herself sleeping like a baby, flicking the bugs out of bed in the morning as if they were cookie crumbs. It had amazed her even then how fast people adjusted, learned to cope, handled whatever came up. Like her friend Annabelle, who turned tricks all night but still managed to fix her kids a hot oatmeal breakfast before passing out.

Dear Annabelle. If she can handle it, so can I. Alls I have to do is hang on a little longer. A few more minutes, and tomorrow morning I'll be making roly-poly and singing Winnie-the-Pooh songs to my sweet-smelling little girl.

She closed her eyes and pictured the kitchen . . . the ironing board, the radio, the black- and white-speckled oven. She could almost smell the sugar and butter and cinnamon baking. . . .

The old woman worked with intense concentration now; the critical moment was almost here, the moment when she'd find the canal to the uterus and carefully, steadily, push the rod into the pear-shaped womb. Once inside, she'd move the rod back and forth, rotating it as she went, scraping the lining with the little cobra head, hoping to hit the egg or at least create enough havoc and bleeding to wash it away.

The concept was simple; it was the execution that was tricky. Not all cervices and uteruses were alike. She hadn't done this for years, and at seventy-four her hands and nerves weren't what they used to be. She must have performed hundreds of these things before she'd quit, but the truth was, anatomically speaking, she had no idea what she was doing. She knew if you punctured the intestinal wall and contaminated the rod with feces, you'd give the girl blood poisoning. She knew if you scraped too much and scarred the womb too badly, the girl would never have children. She knew there was an artery in there someplace, but she'd never hit that before, and didn't plan to now. Oh, she'd heard rumors of problems cropping up now and then—some of her girls coming down sick, a few going to the hospital. But what doctor did better? Since she'd started in the twenties, she'd been arrested only three times, tried once, and convicted of nothing. No sir, she'd performed a valuable service and everyone knew it, including the police. All she wanted was to perform one more now. A pure-vanilla, get-the-bleeding-started, send-the-girl-home, garden-variety job.

She reached under her wooden stool and pawed the linoleum floor, nearly tipping over the shot glass. Keeping an eye on the girl's face, she knocked back the rest of a Seagram's Seven and wiped her mouth with the back of her hand like a cowboy. After setting the glass on the floor, she picked up a dishrag and mopped the sweat off her forehead. Her nose ran, so she wiped that, too, and drew the cloth over the back of her neck. The soothing feel of it reminded her of hot summer nights when her husband would take a pitcher of beer off a block of ice and rub it gently on the back of her neck. My, oh my, what she wouldn't do for a cold draft right now.

She dropped the rag to the floor, blinked away the fog, and pulled her wooden stool up a few inches. God, how she hated this part; if only there was a way around it. *Stop stalling and get on with it.*

A muffled cough, a tug at her bra strap, and she was ready.

Using her fingers as a speculum, she moved the steel rod slowly upward, toward the girl's canal to the womb, or where she thought it should be. Slowly, she pushed the rod deeper into the flesh. *Easy now . . . take it easy.* She pictured the protruding cervix as a compass: if the rod went deeper all around it, the center had to be the opening.

She decided to go north first.

She angled the tip of the rod upward and nudged. It sank a bit and stopped. So far so good. She pulled it back an inch, rotated it to the east, and pushed again. The rod sank farther there, too. *Good. Gonna be easy.* She drew it back slightly and went south. No problem. Then she drove it in to the west and—

It didn't go.

Hmm. Maybe she hadn't gone west far enough.

She pulled the tool out and lifted a Ray-O-Vac flashlight off the floor.

Spreading the girl with her fingers, she shone it into her passageway, hoping to see the cervix. No dice. She set the flashlight down and reinserted the wire hanger, pressed it toward the girl's right side, and started the probe again. "Keep going," she muttered. It didn't.

A bolt of pain shot up her sciatic nerve into her hip; she groaned and leaned back on the stool.

"What's the matter?" the girl asked.

"Nothin', sweetie. Everything's just fine."

She sat still a moment, waiting for the pain to ebb, wondering what kind of geography she had in here. She took a deep breath. No way to tell without going in to check. If she could.

She withdrew the rod. The girl lifted her head.

"Is that it?"

"Not yet, honey. Lie down."

The old woman made her right hand as small and round as possible, squeezing her fingers together until the bones and cartilage hurt. Then she inserted it into the girl's body.

The girl didn't react, but the old woman wasn't surprised. This far into the thing most girls were used to weird stuff going on down there. She pushed her fingers in farther—the girl's body tensed—then more—it squirmed—then the knuckles—

The girl screamed, "Oh, Jesus! What are you *doing?*"

The old woman knew if she could move past the pelvic bone into the soft, roomy center, everything would be fine. What the hell; she'd had girls who could take her whole hand without a whimper.

Not this one.

"Oh, my God! Stop!"

The old woman grimaced and gave a shove.

"Stop!" The girl screamed, grabbing the woman's wrists.

The old woman withdrew her hand and peeled away the girl's fingers.

"Oh, Jesus, that's it!" the girl cried. "That's gotta be it!"

The old woman found the dishrag on the floor and began mopping the girl's face. "Thought you said you had a kid," she said, making conversation. The girl covered her face and didn't answer. "Musta been cesarean," she said, seeing that it wasn't. She stared at the girl's midsection, wiping blood off her fingers like an auto mechanic staring at a muffler. "Got yourself into some real trouble here, didn't you, pardner?" she said, dropping the rag. "One thing I know, whoever done this to you sure's hell wasn't your husband." At her age, girls rarely went through this if they were pregnant by their husbands.

The old woman stood up, gently lifted the girl's hands from her face, and laid them next to her sides. Her eyes were wet and swollen, her cheekbones white from the pressure of her palms. She looked up at the old woman with pleading eyes.

"Is it over yet?"

"No, dear. Not quite."

"I can't do this anymore."

"You don't need to do nothin', sweetie." Using a corner of the dirty sheet, she wiped away the girl's tears and stroked her matted hair. "Just hold on tight and it'll be over in a jiffy."

The old woman took the girl's left hand and massaged it, then placed it in the loop of a leather belt, buckled it, and did the same with her right. The girl tried to lift her wrists, turning her head to see them. The old woman said, "It's just to keep you from grabbing me again."

"I don't want to be tied down," the girl said. "I can't reach my chain. It's twisted." Her ring had become trapped under her shoulder and the chain was cutting into her skin.

The old woman lifted it off the girl's neck, placed it around her own, and tucked the ring down the front of her shirt to keep it out of the way. "When I give it back, we'll be done," she said.

She shifted her weight on the stool, reached into her breast pocket for her cigarettes, and with the ease born of a thousand repetitions, jerked the pack downward, popping a cigarette halfway out. Her lips pulled it the rest of the way; she lit it, blew out the flame, and tilted her head back to exhale. After a second drag she reached under the stool and laid the cigarette across the empty shot glass.

Her shoulders slumped. There was no escape.

Holding the coat hanger, she pushed the girl's knees apart and once again guided the wire into her body. The cobra head bumped up against something she thought—hoped—was the cervix. She probed around it briefly, then returned to the place where she thought the opening should be. This *had* to be it. She'd been there too many times for it not to be.

She reached down, found the burning cigarette on the floor, took a final drag, and crushed it into the empty shot glass.

Then, exhaling smoke, she pushed the wire toward the womb.

She felt the girl flinch but heard no cry. *Good. I'm inside.* Carefully she pushed it in farther, waiting for the sensation of the tough uterus wall to be transmitted down the wire to her fingertips. One more inch, now half an inch, maybe just a little more and she'd feel the back of the womb.

Nothing.

She wiped the sweat off her forehead with the crook of her arm.

Never mind. Probably still a ways to go. She pushed the rod in more—she couldn't tell how much—but still felt nothing. She stopped anyway. She was in far enough. *Had to be.*

She started to scrape.

"That feels funny," the girl said.

"Almost done, sweetie."

She scraped for a few minutes longer, then withdrew the rod slowly. It was bright red, which was good. She watched to see what happened next.

At first it was a trickle, what she expected. Then it was more—maybe the girl didn't clot so good—then it was heavy—maybe she—

It was a flood . . . blood spurting out the girl's body in pulses to the beat of her heart.

Jesus.

The old woman wiped the sweat off her upper lip with her fingers, leaving a mustache of red under her nose. She mopped her forehead with the dirty dishrag and stuffed it between the girl's legs.

"What happened?" the girl asked.

"Nothin', sweetie. You're bleeding, but you're supposed to."

The old woman pressed the rag into the girl's center and held it there, feeling the heat of her body's liquid oozing through. After pushing the cloth inside as far as it would go, she stood up and walked to the bathroom, pulled the light cord, turned on the faucet, and lowered her hands under a stream of cold water, watching the girl's blood make red swirls around the chipped porcelain and disappear down the drain. A dirty glass caught her eye; she filled it with water and watched it tremble as she brought it to her mouth. She took a swallow, set the glass down, and examined her hands. They were pink and clean, the hands of a working woman. Hands she'd seen many times before, glistening as they cleaned celery or rinsed dishes or gave her grandson a bath. Maybe they were shaking a bit, but they were clean. Goddamn it, they were clean.

She looked into the mirror. The mustache of blood startled her; she wiped it off with her wet fingers and dried her face with a crumpled towel. Why the hell'd you agree to do this? she asked her reflection. You told her you hadn't done one of these for years, but she wouldn't listen, would she? Well, never mind. She's free, white, and twenty-one. You done your best.

She shook another Pall Mall from the pack and lit it, holding the first rich puff of sulfur and tobacco until the scars on her lungs ached. She exhaled slowly at the mirror, softening the lines in her face. *My God, look at you. You're so—old.*

The silence from the kitchen caught her attention; she lifted the spotted glass and carried it back to the table.

The girl lay chilled and quivering in a pool of blood, its edges spilling off the table onto the floor. Her head was turned to the side, eyes staring across the room. The old woman brought the glass to her parched lips, but she didn't drink.

"Ray," the girl whispered.

The old woman put the glass down and unbuckled the leather straps. "You're gonna be all right, honey. You just lost some blood."

". . . scared," the girl whispered.

"Now listen to me. There ain't nothin' to be scared of."

". . . want Ray," she said.

The old woman released the girl's hands from the straps and lifted her head to make her sip some water. "Who's Ray, sweetie? He the bastard that done this to you?" Water dribbled down the girl's chin. "Forget him. He ain't here." She wiped the girl's mouth. "They never are."

The old woman pulled the sheet up around the girl's neck and held her hand and felt her body begin to quiver. At first it was a tremble. Then it was a shake. Then the table legs creaked and popped as the girl's body sank deeper into shock.

The old woman grabbed her arms and was holding them down when the kitchen door opened and a face peered into the room—the face of a pretty little girl of six or so with freckles and red hair and large, anxious eyes.

"Mommy?" she said.

The young woman on the table rolled her head to the side.

"Ray," she whispered, reaching out.

The little girl stood next to the kitchen counter trying to comprehend what she was seeing, understanding nothing, fearing everything. Her lips parted as if to speak, but the old woman said, "Sssh, not now," and she stayed quiet. Seeing her mother's outstretched hand, she walked to it on tiptoes, like a ballerina, and laid her fingers in its palm. It didn't close. She looked into her mother's eyes, which were deep and brown and glycerine-shiny. "Mommy?"

This time there was no response at all.

The little girl's face begged the old woman for an explanation, for deliverance; finding none, she turned back to her mother, eyebrows lifted, waiting for a sign of life. Her mother's fingers remained limp. She tugged at the hand gently at first—*Wake up, Sleeping Beauty!*—then more firmly—*Mommy, stop playing!*—then frantically, shaking her arm up and down, pleading with her to come back to life. In a moment her freckled face turned elastic and she began to cry, still clinging to her mother's hand, refusing to let go of her lifeline even though it had snapped before her eyes.

The old woman dropped her forehead onto the young woman's chest and listened to the little girl begin to wail.

"Shit," she whispered to herself. "And my last one, too."

PART ONE

"Where's the chief?" The voice came out of a speakerphone.

"She's still in surgery," Dr. Chang said.

"Terrific," the voice said.

"We'll have to make do till she gets here," Chang said. "What's the patient's white count?"

"Too high," the voice said.

"I was hoping for a specific number," Chang said evenly.

"Sorry," the voice said. "Thirty thousand."

Dr. Phoebe Chang sat at a laboratory console in a darkened room at George Washington University Hospital listening to a colleague's disembodied voice report what was happening on an operating table at a distant location. Telephone lines transmitted the patient's condition to a series of monitors above Chang's desk: an EKG beeping his pulse, a blood pressure readout, a respiratory monitor, an oximeter, and a screen revealing the patient's medical file, which Chang consulted from a computer keyboard.

"Monitor says his temperature just hit 105," Chang said. "Can you cool him down?" She punched some keys and looked at her screen. "Blood pressure seems to be holding."

"At ninety over fifty, it better be," the voice said. "I'm checking his abdomen."

Chang waited. "Is it hard?"

"Like a rock," the voice said. "What do you think we should do?"

"We don't have a choice."

A nervous exhale. "I don't know if I'm ready to cut."

"Yes, you are," Chang said. "I'll stay with you all the way."

"Okay," the voice said, "but get Ray on the line, too, will you? She knows what's going on here."

Down the hall from Dr. Chang, in OR 14, huge surgical lamps flooded the area with light from all directions, illuminating a different patient's open body. Surgeons and medical technicians were gathered around it like green-clad monks at an altar—heads bowed, voices calm and unhur-

15

ried, nimble latex-covered hands at work—suction pumps and laser scalpels operating, science and the spirit moving toward one goal, the preservation of life. The object of their attention was a newly transplanted baboon kidney resting snugly in the patient's fibrous pouch, its color deepening to kidney-bean red from fresh, engorging blood.

"Nice job, everybody," Dr. Rachel Redpath said through her surgeon's mask. "Let's close him up."

She stepped back from the table, leaving younger surgeons to do the job, and walked to the scrub room. Standing at a sink, she peeled off her splattered gloves, dropped them into a foot-levered waste can, washed her hands, and sat in a wooden chair to rest. She'd been on her feet for the last six hours leading the transplant team, and she was tired. A large glass of orange juice waited on the armrest. She drank it and checked the clock on the wall. Ten-twenty. No time to waste. Everyone would be waiting.

She stood up, stripped off everything but her surgeon's cap, and headed into the shower, emerging two minutes later partially refreshed. As she walked to her locker she pulled off the cap and shook loose her red hair, then opened the metal door, dropped her towel on the floor, and began dressing. She was naturally trim, looking ten years younger than fifty-four—an elegant, handsome woman with a feminine, seductive face. But it was her personality that marked her most. Regardless of where she was or what she was doing—even standing in a bra and panties with a wet towel at her feet—she conveyed a sense of command and charisma. Friends and critics alike agreed she was a pathfinder, a woman to be reckoned with.

She pulled on a dress, brushed her hair a few strokes in the locker-door mirror, and winced at the puffs under her eyes. Surgery might be good for her patients, but at the pace she was going it was killing her. For a moment she considered canceling her appearance, then tossed the brush inside. Raise your energy, she told herself. Picture your audience, organize your thoughts. She took a deep breath and left the scrub room—forgetting to check the message window or battery power on her beeper, whose fading, urgent words read: TO LAB—CALL CHANG— TO LAB.

She walked toward the elevator with new life. George Pettibone, the hospital's deputy administrator, joined her on the run. "Congratulations!" he said, clenching an unlit pipe between his teeth. He raised his arm as if to give her a hug, and thinking better of it, squeezed her hand instead.

"Morning, George," she said. She waved hello to a nurse, who smiled and clasped her hands in a bravo gesture.

"I've got an advance copy of the citation," he said. He held a fax from a friend on the White House staff. She continued walking briskly, touching the shoulder of a patient who moved past in a wheelchair. They turned the corner and stepped onto an empty elevator. "Listen to this," he said. " 'For her extraordinary imagination in extending the boundaries of organ transplantation, and for the creation of new medicine in the service of all mankind.' "

"Sounds nice," she said.

"That's it? 'Sounds nice'?"

"I'm not very good with compliments, George." She checked her watch and punched the lobby button again for good measure. "Is that why you called this morning?"

The floor numbers above the door were counting down. "I hear you're thinking of boycotting the award ceremony."

"Boycotting? Not at all. I simply said I can't be there the morning they want to have it."

"What's more important than receiving the Medal of Freedom in the Rose Garden?"

"Nothing. Except surgery."

The elevator stopped and the door opened. She was the first one out.

"What kind of surgery?" he said.

She continued walking, focused on other matters. "A transplant, George. Something that's been planned for weeks."

He removed the pipe from his mouth to say something, but she turned the corner and headed for the auditorium. "Look, Ray," he said, barely keeping up, "if this medal had no impact on hospital funding, I wouldn't care if you accepted it from UPS, but how's it going to look when our very own local hero is too busy to shake hands with the president of the United States?"

She reached the auditorium door and smiled at him sympathetically. He had supported her more than most hospital administrators had, arguing for her budget, not being too nosy, offering moral support when she was at odds with the Internal Review Board over an experimental procedure or a new immunosuppressant drug. He was a hospital bureaucrat—too political, too nervous—but he was one of the good guys, and she knew not to treat the good guys badly.

She grabbed the door handle. "Don't worry. I'll work it out."

He tapped his pipe stem against his front teeth and smiled.

"And George—without making a big deal out of it, do you think you could get them to change the word *mankind* to *humankind*?"

She entered the auditorium and walked down the center aisle toward the podium. As her presence became known the chatter in the audience dwindled to a hush, and as she ascended the steps to the stage the residents began applauding. When she reached the podium, she smiled, and the room quieted again.

"Thanks," she said, "but for those of you who are students, I'm afraid it won't do you any good. I'm not grading exams this semester."

Phoebe Chang checked the EKG monitor. Forty beats per minute. "What's happening to his blood supply?" she said into the speakerphone.

"I've got four peripherals and a central running wide open, and I've just given him an eighth unit of O neg," the disembodied voice responded. "Where's it all going?"

"Are you inside him yet?" Chang asked.

"Almost." Silence. "I need a number six, Foster," the voice said to someone nearby. "How's he look on the telemetry?"

"He's holding on," Chang said, studying the monitors. She sat quietly, allowing the team at the other end to work without interruption.

"I'm in," the voice finally said.

"What's it look like?"

"Like someone poured a quart of currant jelly into him." The voice described massive hemorrhaging, then asked for sponges and all the suction available. "I can't see the problem yet."

The patient's pulse slowed to thirty-two.

"Jesus," the voice said, "there it is! Looks like a full-blown rejection. The whole organ's swollen and—"

"Careful!" Chang said crisply. "We're on an open line."

"Let's see, how should I put it? The organ has, uh—*ruptured*. Do you understand what I'm saying?"

Chang paused a moment. "Ruptured? You mean the insides—the contents are—*gone*?"

"That's what I mean. It's burst open and expelled its—cargo."

Chang tapped her finger on the speakerphone. "Don't linger over it. Clamp off the major vessels!"

There was a pause as the team worked. "They're clamped," the voice said.

"Pulse is twenty-eight," Chang said over the sound of a beeping alarm. "Blood pressure's too low for the monitor."

"It's sixty over palp," a voice on the speaker box said. Additional voices spoke more urgently. "We're doing everything we can to stabilize," the voice said. "Where the fuck is Rachel?"

A student in the auditorium raised his hand. "Now that you've succeeded in transplanting baboon livers into humans, do you see any limits on other animal organs that could be used?"

"Ethical or practical?" Rachel asked.

"Either."

"Let's take the tougher question first, the ethical one. The oath of the physician tells us to do no harm, which is as relevant today as it was two thousand years ago. The difference is that Hippocrates didn't have to deal with the consequences of modern pharmacology, biochemistry, genetic engineering, and medical technologies. Today, if we fail to risk harm to one patient and that places many others in harm's way, should that influence what we do? Are we ever justified in using patients as pioneers in order to advance medical knowledge? Are xenografts like the one I performed this morning objectionable? Never mind animal organs—should human organs be harvested, or is that merely a modern form of cannibalism? Questions like these are as difficult as technological ones, and having faced my share of both, I can tell you, the ethical ones haunt and vex like no others. As well they should."

Rachel saw someone hurrying down the center aisle toward her—not a student, but a nurse. She started to take another question, but stopped as the nurse climbed the steps and approached her. The woman whispered something into her ear. Rachel, looking surprised, touched her power-drained beeper. She looked up and addressed the audience. "Excuse me," she said, "I have something urgent to attend to."

"Is it the kidney you just operated on?" a student asked, but Rachel hurried out the door without answering.

"He's in bigeminal rhythm," Chang said into the speakerphone. She heard a knock at the door and opened it for Rachel, who stepped into the dimly lit room and locked the door behind her.

"What's the situation?" she asked, pulling up a swivel chair. Chang briefed her quietly as the team on the other end of the line continued to work. Rachel touched some keys, bringing up a monitor showing the patient's blood gas. "Oh-two SAT," she said. "He needs oxygen."

"We're hyperventilating him now," the distant telephone voice said.

"Hundred percent oh-two, max respiratory rate." They worked in silence, then—

"He's in V-tach!"

"We're losing him."

"Stay with him," Rachel said. She and Chang locked their eyes on the EKG monitor. The remote team worked quietly.

The monitor beeps stopped.

"Asystole!" the disembodied voice said. "Paddles! Three hundred joules—everybody stand back! Clear!" Electrical jolts shot into the patient's chest, prodding the heart and momentarily blipping the telemetry.

One jolt. Two. Three.

"He's still flat line!"

"Skip the protocols and go right to the epi," Rachel said. "Intracardiac."

There was brief commotion, and the voice said, "Epi's going in now."

Rachel and Chang pictured the long needle piercing the chest and heart muscle, and the epinephrine draining from the syringe. They waited, but there was no response. They listened to the sound on the monitor, the voices at the other end speaking in clipped syllables, attempting to resuscitate, employing one measure after another. The team worked for another twenty minutes, talking above the quiet clatter of equipment, struggling to hold on, watching each protocol fail. Finally, the only sound remaining was the monotone hum of an EKG pronouncing its benediction, reminding doctors that they were human, humbling them with their impotence. Rachel reached up for the control knob and switched the monitor off.

There was silence at both ends of the speakerphone. A voice at the other end of the telephone said, "Damn."

"You did everything you could," Rachel said. More silence. "Is everyone there all right?"

There was quiet discussion at the other end, and the voice said, "Yeah, we're all right."

"We've known from the start that this might happen," Rachel said. "What failed here is the process, not the organ or the concept. We had a similar problem in the seventies, with our first liver transplants. I'm not suggesting any of us take this lightly, but we can't throw in the towel, either."

"Let's talk later, Ray," the voice said, and the telephone line clicked off.

Chang sat watching Rachel light a thin, brown cigarette, which she did only in dire circumstances. She exhaled toward the monitors, blowing smoke at them as if they, too, were at fault.

"What do we do now?" Chang asked quietly, perspiration glossing her forehead.

Rachel tapped her finger against her cheek, thinking. "I'll call Rome and tell Delfina. After that, I'm not sure, except to follow rule number one."

Chang questioned her with raised eyes.

"Never let them see you sweat."

Congressman Jack MacLeod emerged from the bathroom wearing a jockstrap, a pair of gravity boots, and a small patch of toilet tissue stuck to a shaving cut on his left cheek. He stood in darkness, waiting to make sure he hadn't awakened the woman sleeping in his bed. Seeing her immobile, he took a step toward her.

Victoria was lying on her side, her long brown hair mingling with shadowed creases on the pillow. Even asleep, she looked lovely and smart, the girl from Ipanema with brains. He walked around the end of the bed, stepped over a stack of unread *Congressional Records*, and moved quietly to the table on his side of the bed. Keeping his eyes on her, he lifted a lidless jar off a book of Gary Larson cartoons, fished out a green olive, dropped it into his mouth, and picked up a can of Yoo-Hoo to wash it down. No response from Victoria. Knowing as he did what she thought of olives and Yoo-Hoo, no question she was asleep.

He set the empty can on the table, walked back to the bathroom door, and reached up and grabbed a steel bar across the jamb. After ten chin-ups, he lifted his ankles above his head, fixed the sponge-lined boot hooks onto the bar, and lowered his torso slowly, burning his abs until he was fully extended, upside down. He dropped his arms limply and let gravity pool blood in his head. When it became lead, he closed his eyes. For a moment.

What time is it? The clock next to Victoria glowed red with an inverted 4:35. This is crazy, he thought. Waking up in the middle of the night, losing sleep over ancient history. Worse, walking in his sleep. *It's been twenty-five years. It's dead and buried. Forget it.*

He closed his eyes again and told himself to picture the day ahead. He saw himself taking a taxi to the Hill, arriving at his office, reviewing the incoming mail that Ben Jacobs, his administrative assistant, had decided was priority. Then it was signing outgoing letters requiring a personal note, glancing at news clippings, reading memos, watching the rest of the morning news . . . returning yesterday's phone calls, meeting with constituents and lobbyists before the mid-August break, twisting people's arms and having his own twisted. At ten o'clock he'd head across the Capitol to the Senate side with one of his legislative assistants in tow, briefing him on the witnesses scheduled to testify before the House-Senate Joint Committee hearing that morning. Later he'd call what's-his-name, chairman of the Onondaga County Democratic Committee, accepting an offer to speak at the party's annual dinner. Upstate New York was a long way from his congressional district in Manhattan, but if he decided to run for the Senate in a couple of years, he'd need all the help from Onondaga County he could get. After all, Onondaga was Syracuse, and Syracuse was—*Syracuse?* Syracuse was where it had happened.

Fuck. There it was again.

He dropped the reins on his mind and let it wander where it wanted. The dream he'd been having the last few weeks floated past his eyes, repeating itself like a fugue: same theme, different variations. Tonight he'd dreamed the woman was standing on a dock above a swelling sea, the usual bundle in her arms, the same anguished look on her face.

It was Honey. It was always Honey.

Trying to reach her felt like moving through molasses, and when he finally came close, she stepped off the edge and disappeared beneath the waves. With the baby still in her arms.

He opened his eyes. The clock read 4:45. Summer light would soon be leaking around the edge of the drawn curtains, making it too late to go back to sleep. He reached up and grabbed the crossbar, unhooked his feet, and lowered himself smoothly, then removed his boots and climbed into bed, still careful not to wake Victoria. He breathed deeply and burrowed his shoulders into the sheets, looking for an hour of sleep before the automatic timer turned on the television set, bringing him and his fellow Washington news junkies their first fix of the day.

Closing his eyes, he relaxed and let himself float . . . drifting nicely toward a neutral shore where castaway memories were washed up, bleached by the sun, and forgotten.

He almost reached it.

It was six o'clock in the morning, December dark, but Jack still hadn't moved from his perch across the street from Robertini's Shoe Repair. He shoved his hands into his jeans pockets and hunched his shoulders under his football letter jacket. In the last hour he'd seen the drizzle turn to sleet, sleet to snow, and snow back to rain again; he'd seen delivery trucks with milk, doughnuts, and soda pass by. He'd watched newspaper trucks drop wire-wrapped bundles of the *New York Daily News* on the corner; he'd looked at buses go by too many times to count. Not one police cruiser, though. Not yet.

He stared across the street at the door and calculated the odds. He knew old man Robertini kept the box behind the register, but that had been an entire summer ago. What were the odds it was still there? He rubbed his arms. *Wrong question. Question is, do I break in to find out?*

He looked for signs of the police again. Nothing. The only car in sight was a red Pontiac parked across the street with its headlights on, no driver behind the wheel, battery draining. Nice car.

He continued arguing with himself. He'd consider it a loan instead of a theft. Maybe he'd win enough next week to pay it back right away. Maybe if Robertini knew the trouble he was in, he'd understand and forgive him. Maybe the old geezer wouldn't even know the money was missing until he found it in an envelope with an anonymous thank-you note. Maybe, maybe, maybe—shit. Maybe he should go home.

He blinked and made his eyes huge to stay awake, dancing from one foot to the other, recirculating his blood. If he got caught, it'd be all over. No college, no job, no future. High stakes, bad odds, wrong result. Just like the game he'd played at Luboff's. What had happened to his magic touch, anyway? All he'd needed were a couple of winning hands, which should have been easy, especially with Angus Brody at the table. Big wad, no talent. Trouble was, poker wasn't merely a game of skill. Luck, timing, surprise, the cut of the cards—everything counted. He'd been on a bad streak for a month of Fridays, and he knew a lot about streaks, both the good ones and the bad.

A bus approached, forcing him to make a decision. *Get out of here. Burglary isn't your game, and this damn sure isn't your night.*

He ran for the bus and slipped through the door just as it closed. As it started up he stood at the coin box fumbling for a quarter. He found it—then lost his grip and watched it hit the floor and roll under the driver's seat.

"Don't worry, son, I'll fish it out next stop."

Jack leaned down anyway, reached for it, and dropped it into the box.

"Thanks," the driver said. "God helps them that helps themselves."

Jack walked halfway down the aisle and sat down, cradled his chin in his hand, and stared out the window. The handful of people on the street walked slowly and bent, and the unopened stores appeared dreary and lifeless—dress shops and locksmiths, beauty parlors and dime stores, barbershops and tobacco shops—little places with big names like Paradise Café, Ideal Cleaners, Fancy This, or Famous That. Who did they think they were kidding? This was Brooklyn, the town that had traded the Dodgers for heroin and busted neighborhoods. Paradise? Sure it was. That's why he was getting out.

He checked his watch. Honey would be standing at the Greyhound bus station in—Jesus—an hour! Heat prickles covered his face.

The bus stopped to pick up a passenger and started up again.

Staring out the window, he saw his reflection and caught a glimpse of something that reminded him of his father—the mouth, maybe, or the chin. He pictured his old man as he'd seen him only a few hours before: asleep in his worn-out easy chair, suspenders off his shoulders, a Bible open on his lap, a half-played game of Chinese checkers on the nicked-up table in front of him. Jack had thought about waking him up and unburdening himself, asking advice about what to do. But then, knowing he couldn't, he'd set off for Luboff's Funeral Home and his regular Friday-night poker game. He and his father didn't talk about the kind of problem he had. He and his father didn't talk about much of anything, which always pissed him off until he remembered who his father was: a poor Scottish immigrant with five sons and a dead wife, a literate man who'd swapped his dreams of teaching for steady work in the Brooklyn shipyards and bread on the table. When Jack saw the big picture, he wasn't quite so angry. If he had to live his father's life, it would have made him a silent man, too.

Which was exactly the problem.

He pulled his money from his pocket and counted it again. Same fifty-five dollars. No loaves or fishes in Flatbush. *Damn.* If Freddy only hadn't come up short.

Freddy Anticoli. The thought of him made Jack's scalp itch. He'd seen him only a few hours before, standing in his waiter's jacket at Romano's, looking over his shoulder for the maître d', licking his lips, pressing his measly fifty-five bucks into Jack's hands, begging him to triple it. Freddy had looted the restaurant's cash register to pay rent on a one-room apartment he'd taken after his wife's father had kicked the two of them and the baby out of the house. Jack could still see Freddy standing in the restaurant foyer, begging for enough money to cover the till . . . enough time to find a second job sweeping the print shop or stacking newspaper bundles . . . enough money to buy Kimbies. *Diapers, for crissake.* Freddy told Jack he had no idea what it was like, being married at seventeen with a kid, but Jack got it. Everyone did. Once you got a girl pregnant, the rest was easy: you quit school, got yourself a shitty day job, rented a tux for a wedding the bride's old man couldn't afford, and died a slow death.

He saw Freddy as he'd seen him last, telegraphing Jack a Hail Mary for good luck. Pathetic and childlike. Fucked. No longer was this the Freddy Anticoli Jack had once known—the fullback who'd broken the school rushing record with a gob of liniment in his jock, the class stud with the million-dollar smile. In fact, if Jack didn't get hold of some money tonight, no longer was he looking at Freddy Anticoli at all.

He was looking at himself.

The thought lifted him out of his bus seat. He gripped the stainless-steel pole in the middle of the aisle and compressed the biggest decision of his life into two competing clichés: "Never try to fill an inside straight when the pot's heavy," his poker head told him, urging him to go home. "God helps them that helps themselves," the bus driver's words echoed, urging him to go back.

For a moment the two clichés hovered on a perfectly balanced scale. And then he pictured Freddy begging for Kimbies.

The decision wasn't even close.

It was ten to seven by the time he'd returned to his spot opposite Robertini's, sweating from the long run back, lungs aching. He caught his breath and assessed the situation. Wrestling with his conscience had already cost him his best chance to pull it off; now there'd be more people on the street, and morning light only a few minutes away. Still, it could be done. He'd filled inside straights before, which meant he could do it again, right now. Besides, he had one other important thing going for him. He had no choice.

He found a Good Humor stick on the sidewalk, picked a wet newspaper out of a trash can, and walked across the street to the shop, passing the red Pontiac with its headlights growing dimmer. The entrance was set back a few feet from the storefront between two windows displaying old shoes, rubber heels, and a faded cardboard advertisement for Kiwi shoe polish. The only way anyone could see him was if they were directly opposite the door; from the sides he was covered.

He opened the limp newspaper and slipped it under the door until there was only an inch showing at the bottom. Holding the Good Humor stick like a scalpel, he poked it into the keyhole and jiggled it until it pushed into nothingness.

The key dropped.

Slowly he began pulling the newspaper toward him, praying the key hadn't bounced off, begging the soggy paper not to tear. Only a couple inches remained and still no key—and then there it was, top of page ten, lying on a photograph of the police commissioner swearing in a new class of cadets. The sight of a police badge gave him a start, but not a big one. It was too late for superstition, his mission too important to be derailed by omens. He was in it now. He was committed.

He stood up and looked around. There was no one in sight—no buses, no police. He pushed the key into the hole, turned it—and the door opened. My God. What planet was Robertini living on? When this was over, he'd have to tell him the facts of life.

He slipped inside the store, closed the door, and waited, smelling leather and linseed oil. A few months ago he'd been a good employee here. No question what he was now.

A light—should he turn it on? It'd make him look legitimate if anyone passed by . . . or was it too early for him to *be* inside?

Leave it off. The street lamp was enough.

He went straight for the shoe box and found it where he hoped it would be. He opened it up, pawed beneath some yellowed receipts, and found what he was looking for: a mess of greenbacks, unstacked and unsorted. His luck hadn't run out after all.

After counting out a hundred in fives and tens, he stuck them into an envelope he found next to the unpaid bills and slipped it into his jacket pocket. After carefully placing the rest of the money back in the box, he returned it to the shelf. Collecting his thoughts, he went to the front door and stood quietly, waiting for an opening. There was still no one he could see.

He opened the door enough to squeeze out, which only made him look like the burglar he was, and closed the door behind him. After locking the door, he laid the key in the space at the bottom and gave it a small shove. Maybe old man Robertini wouldn't figure it out. Maybe he'd think it had fallen by itself, gravity's version of the virgin birth. Considering how absentminded—

Two headlights, approaching fast. Had to be cops.

He stood frozen and watched a blue Ford pass by with the driver hunched over the wheel, trying to clean the fog off the windshield.

Then everything went quiet.

He turned and walked down the street. As he passed the Pontiac with the dying headlights, his pace slowed and he came to a stop. Damn. *Don't do it, Jack. You've pushed your luck too far already.*

Even as he told himself not to he knew he would.

He looked up and down the street. Someone hidden under an umbrella was on one side; a few people walking to work on the other. If he did it fast enough, he might get away with it.

He walked to the driver's side and tried the handle. Lucky again; it was unlocked. Glancing in both directions, he opened the door, reached inside to the dashboard, and pushed in a knob, turning the headlights off. If the driver was lucky, there'd still be enough juice to get it started.

He closed the door and stood still, expecting a cop to grab him, find the stolen money, and send him to jail for life.

It didn't happen. One successful theft, one good deed unpunished. His bad streak was over.

He ran for the bus station. If he hustled, there was still enough time to get there before the bus to Harrisburg left.

The strangest thing about the guy was his new suit. Not that there was anything obviously forensic about it—no bullet hole, no knife's entry point. Still, Detective "Bazooka Joe" Wilson had an instinct. He asked the two attendants to weigh and measure the body fully dressed and let him and the medical examiner do the honors themselves, which suited them fine. It was after five, it was Labor Day weekend in the nation's capital, and they wanted to go home.

Detective Wilson opened the door to the autopsy room and saw a man standing on the other side, scrub suit untied, washing his hands. "Dr. Landy?"

The man turned and Wilson was surprised again. He always expected medical examiners to have something of a grisly edge—long hair, circles under their eyes, a hunched back—but they never did. This one looked as clean-cut as Clark Kent: midthirties, black horn-rim glasses, square jaw, moderate height, moderate good looks, and a red bow tie with small, tasteful, blue pin-dots. Maybe this wasn't the ME but an insurance adjuster, working on a claim.

Seeing the gurney roll to a stop next to the autopsy table, Dr. Elliot Landy looked up at a wall clock in protest. The attendants deposited the body on the table anyway and left.

"Tomorrow's a holiday," Landy said to Wilson. "Why isn't this guy in the cooler?"

"Something told me he needed to be looked at," Wilson said. "We found him behind a Dairy Queen on Wisconsin Avenue."

Landy lowered his eyelids to half-mast. "Well, that certainly makes it urgent, all right."

Clark Kent with an attitude, Wilson thought.

Landy walked over to the body. "What's so interesting here, Detective—?"

"Wilson. Joe. First glance, he looks run-of-the-mill homeless, but take a look at the clothes." He touched the jacket pockets, which were still sewn shut. Brand-new.

Landy touched the man's lapels. "You think people who wear new clothes don't die?"

"Something like that."

Lots of attitude.

Landy rapped his knuckles against the steel table, debating what to do. Reluctantly, he retied his gown, pulled on a fresh pair of latex gloves and sleeve protectors, and straightened his tools on a cutting board: a Stryker saw, scalpels, forceps, scissors, and a long, sharp butcher's knife. "All right," he said, "let's take a look."

Wilson bent over the body. "He's got calluses on his hands. Must have been swinging an ax or something."

Landy said nothing. He moved the man's right arm as if he were testing a sore elbow. The muscles were still tight from rigor. "He's been dead less than twenty-four hours."

The two of them removed the man's suit coat, and Landy loosened the necktie, pausing to check the four-in-hand knot. "This was probably tied left-handed," he said. He unbuttoned the man's shirt and jostled it off the deadweight of his torso, leaving him in a clean white T-shirt. Raising the man's arms, he poked and squeezed his biceps and other muscles. "He's been pumping iron, not swinging an ax." He felt the man's finger muscles. "Most likely right-handed." He switched on a portable Olympus tape recorder and began to dictate.

"White male, thirty to thirty-five"—he flipped up the manila tag tied on the man's shoestrings—"five feet eleven, hundred and eighty-two pounds. No apparent wounds to face, neck, or head." He set down the recorder and picked up a pair of scissors. Before starting, he said, "Ever seen an autopsy before?"

"Yeah, sure." Wilson looked down at his jeans and dirty white sneakers, preparing himself.

Landy placed the tip of the scissors under the man's T-shirt and began snipping it off from the neck down. "Did it bother you?"

"No problem." Wilson cleared his throat. He knew that even veterans who'd seen a hundred autopsies would sometimes inexplicably keel over, and he wasn't real good with dead bodies to begin with.

He watched the white cotton part. *Snip. snip.* In a moment something began to appear on the man's naked chest—a cut, not a scratch—a deep, serious cut—*snip, snip*—a long incision that ran from the man's shoulder to the center of his chest. Wilson leaned forward from a safe distance, as if peering over the edge of a cliff. "What's *that?*"

Landy kept snipping, saying nothing until the T-shirt had been removed. On the man's torso was an enormous gash in the shape of a Y—two incisions from each shoulder to the sternum, then one straight down, detouring briefly in a C-shaped hook around his belly button and disappearing beneath his trousers. The cuts had been sewn together with ordinary cotton string in a single, long baseball stitch. Landy squeezed the suture between his fingers and looked up at the roll of string suspended on a spindle above the table. "Interesting," he said to himself.

"What is?" Wilson asked.

"Looks like he's already been autopsied."

Wilson used his knuckle to wipe small sparkles of sweat off his upper lip. He checked Landy's face for an explanation, but Landy stood in quiet concentration, contemplating what he was seeing. Wilson loosened his psychedelic tie and unbuttoned the top button of his blue denim work shirt. He forced his eyes back to the cuts, wondering if he could stay on his feet and keep breathing.

The room went quiet, with only the hum of the surgical lamp filaments buzzing softly overhead.

After studying the cadaver a moment, Landy removed the man's shoes and socks, took scrapings from under his toenails, and unbuckled his belt and pulled off his pants. No shorts.

Landy dictated: no wounds to the lower extremities, an apparent autopsy incision continuing down to the pubic bone, a circumcised penis. He raised a camera and took full body photographs, then, with Wilson's help, turned the body over, photographed that side, and returned the cadaver to its back. Landy slipped a rubber block under the man's shoulder blades, raising his chest for easier examination. After positioning the surgical lamp directly above, he placed the tip of the gleaming scissors under the first stitch at the man's left shoulder. And snipped.

The skin loosened.

He cut the next stitch, then the next and the next, repeating the same on the right side until both incisions had opened up from the shoulders to the center of the body, creating a large V-shaped slab that had once been the man's chest. He grasped the point of the V and peeled it upward as if it were the flap of a large envelope.

Wilson's brain didn't like what it saw. "Christ," he muttered, eyes rolling away. His fingers and cheeks tingled from lost circulation.

Landy peered into the body. The junction where the sternum met the cartilage showed saw marks. He lifted the free-floating chest plate out of the body and leaned forward and picked up the recorder. "Diaphragmatic attachments have already been cut," he dictated.

He lifted his scissors again and reached into the chest cavity to cut the ligaments and vessels holding the heart in place. And stopped. The translucent white sac that cradled the organ had already been cut open and stapled back together. "Some strange kind of an autopsy," Landy said.

Wilson didn't respond; he was bent forward, his elbow on the edge of the table, chin in hand, staring away from the action toward the man's feet. Landy saw him but said nothing.

Using a scalpel, Landy made a parallel incision in the sac, reached in with both hands, and lifted out the heart. Wilson peeked at it; it resembled a large, uncooked chicken breast, covered with a layer of mustard-yellow fat. *Yellow?* The sight of it was disorienting, as if he'd just witnessed a mutation. If the guy's *heart* wasn't even your basic Red Cross red, what was coming next? He stood up straight and took a deep breath.

Landy turned the organ over in his hands. "Look."

Reluctantly, Wilson complied. There was a black spot on it. "What is that?"

"It's been singed," Landy said.

"What for?"

"To draw blood. The burn sterilizes the surface."

Wilson cringed, for a split second forgetting that the man had been dead when it had happened.

Landy pointed to a board at the end of the table and asked Wilson to lay it across the corpse's naked thighs. Once it was in position, he placed the heart on it and turned his attention back to the body cavity, pushing the overturned chest flap farther up on the man's face to get it out of the way. He repositioned the light, then dipped into the upper body to remove the lungs, which he also deposited onto the board. Using the butcher's knife, in one long motion he sliced the spongy gray organ in half. Then he kneaded the tissue with his fingers, feeling for abnormalities.

Wilson found his lip curling up like his four-year-old daughter's. "What're those?" he asked of the coarse black streaks in the lungs.

"Anthracotic deposits," Landy said.

"He's a smoker?"

"Or urban dweller."

"Is that what killed him?" The detective's tone said he hoped so.

Landy didn't answer. He returned to the chest, probed the aorta, and paused. "This is getting weirder by the second. The body's been exsanguinated."

"What's that?"

"Flushed out. His blood and body fluids have been drained."

He nuzzled the scissors against the man's bluish-white skin and began cutting the stitches on the last leg of the Y, from the sternum down toward the abdomen. Wilson scratched his nose, keeping his hand close enough to his eyes to block his vision as needed. Landy knew he was struggling. "Think of them as strings on a pot roast," he said sincerely, trying to be helpful.

After severing the last stitch, Landy leaned over the body, placed his hands on each side of the cut, and pulled the flesh apart. Rubbery pink and gray and tan organs jiggled in the light. He hesitated, perplexed, and searched under the rib cage.

"Uh-oh."

"What's wrong?" Wilson asked.

"The liver."

"What about it?"

"It's missing."

Wilson took a step back, away from the body.

Landy didn't look up. "Going somewhere?"

"Looking for an ammonia capsule," Wilson said, sweating.

Landy raised his head. "If they're not on that counter, they're next door, but if you can handle it, I'd rather you stuck around. I don't know what's going on here, and I'd like a witness."

Wilson returned, placed his outstretched hands against the side of the autopsy table, and hung his head down between them, as if pushing a car.

"If you're going to pass out," Landy said, "sit on the floor. Save your head some stitches."

"Right," Wilson muttered. Just what they needed. More stitches.

Landy reached into the body cavity, cut the tube connecting the small intestine to the stomach, and began withdrawing the long, tan-gray bowel, slicing the fat that held it in place until he'd coiled about eleven feet of it into a heap next to the body. Wilson observed with amazement, as if it were an impossible number of clowns piling out of a tiny circus car. He stood up straight and wiped a line of sweat from his temple, listening to Landy dictate his findings. When the doctor had finished, he laid the recorder on the table and checked Wilson's pallor. "Still with me?"

"Hanging in there." He reached into his coat pocket, pulled out a piece of his Bazooka bubble gum, tore off the wrapper and the Bazooka Joe funnies, and began chewing.

Landy detached more connective tissue and lifted out the spleen. Then he removed the pancreas and stomach as a unit and laid them on the board. Using a plastic bag as a receptacle, he snipped open the stomach, drained its contents, and held them up to the light, poking at them with his finger. Bile, slop, and an intact baby squid.

"At least we know he's an American," Landy said.

"Why?"

"Eats too fast."

He stripped the left kidney from its capsule and carefully placed it into a shallow metal pan dangling below a hanging scale. Then he did the same with the right. "You have to keep an eye on livers and kidneys," he said. "They love to slip off the scale onto the floor."

Wilson stared at the pan swinging under the light. Kidney pie? he thought. *Kidney pie?* The English were fucking crazy.

Landy was almost finished. As he prepared to sever the colon from the rectum, he lifted an area of the large intestine called the cecum, a large pouch in the organ. Something caught his eye. "Look at that." Running along the side of it was a line of sutures.

He opened the stitches with scissors and reached in with his fingers. And froze. "What in the world—"

Wilson stopped chewing, and his eyes widened.

Landy withdrew something unrecognizable, about the size of a large hand . . . something remotely human, with arms, legs, and a head. He held it up by its feet.

It was a doll.

A plastic doll.

"Are you kidding me?" Wilson whispered.

Landy turned the thing back and forth, pausing to examine a small black hole about the size of a peanut in the center of the doll's belly. He touched the opening with his little finger, then lifted the figure to his ear and shook it. Something rattled.

He laid the toy on the steel grid, picked up his crescent knife, and after making a clean cut around its neck, pulled off its head and tilted the body upside down. A small object fell out and bounced up against the metal splashboard. He lifted it with his forceps and examined it through a magnifying glass. "Looks like a piece of pencil," he said, "with the letters *EOD* printed on the side." He positioned the piece of wood in the hole in the doll's belly. It fit. "Looks like somebody used it to puncture the hole and it broke off."

He picked up the doll and turned it upside down again. This time, a red-and-yellow aspirin capsule fell onto the counter. He held it up to the light with his forceps and carefully pulled it apart. The powdered medicine had been replaced by a tightly rolled strip of paper about the size of a fortune-cookie message. He lifted the scrap out, unfurled it, and pinned it to the cutting board between his fingers. Something was written on it, some letters printed in pencil.

The two men bumped heads leaning over to read.

Keep it, the paper said.

The television's automatic timer turned the set on at exactly six forty-five, as if God, bowing to the power of the medium, had finally substituted coffee commercials and the morning news for roosters and the rising sun.

". . . and that's it for the weather."

"Here in Washington today, President Clay and his national security adviser . . ."

Jack blinked at the TV screen and slid his hand inside Victoria's T-shirt, onto her warm back. "Time to get up," he said.

She stretched like a rubber band. "I'm awake," she said, and recoiled into the same position. He sat in the middle of the bed, scratching his head, staring at the TV screen. A pretty, auburn-haired reporter in her midtwenties stood on the steps of the D.C. Police Department with a microphone in hand. Someone named Molly McCormick.

"Dave, yesterday a New York man was found dead here in Washington in what police are saying is one of the strangest cases they've seen in years. Melvin Shivers, a paroled convict who's been missing from a halfway house in Manhattan for the last six months, was found dead behind a Dairy Queen on Wisconsin Avenue last night. But what makes the case so bizarre, and a bit gruesome, is that during the autopsy it was discovered that his liver was missing—and that a plastic baby doll had been planted in his abdomen."

Victoria's eyes popped open. She sat up in the middle of the bed, pulling the sheet around her legs, squinting at the screen.

"So far, no one knows what it means," the reporter said.

"Any theories?" the anchor asked.

"Nothing official. A detective I talked to with the New York City police said Shivers was serving out a sentence for the bombing of an abortion clinic twelve years ago in Queens, New York. He and an accomplice were convicted of first-degree manslaughter for the deaths of a doctor and his teenage patient."

Victoria felt the top of the table next to the bed for her glasses, which she found lying on a legal brief she'd been reading the night before.

"Do the police have any suspects?" the anchor asked.

"Not yet. Detectives here and in New York are checking for leads."

Jack and Victoria followed the report with unusual interest. "What a strange story," she said.

Jack swivelled off the bed and headed into the bathroom. "What, a murdered clinic bomber?" He turned on the shower to warm it up. "Sounds like a case of what goes around comes around." She said nothing. "Don't you think?"

She walked into the bathroom, naked. And quiet.

"What is it?" he asked.

"What's what?"

"The silence. You think the story's about something else?"

"I don't know," she said blandly. It was her way of saying *Yes, but I'm not sure what.* He didn't like it. Her track record on premonitions was too good to like it.

"Oh, man, I feel like a zombie this morning," he said, stepping into the shower stall. "I was awake half the night."

She piled her hair on top of her head, barrette in mouth, then clamped it in place and followed him in. "Another dream?"

"Yeah." He put his face into the stream of water. "Must have been triggered by our discussion."

"If that's possible, *I'm* the one who would have had the nightmare." She lathered up her legs.

He squirted a blob of shampoo into his palm and rubbed it into his hair. "Why don't we try looking at this thing logically instead of emotionally?" he said.

"Which thing, the nightmare or getting married?" She pulled a blue plastic razor up her long leg. "Or is there a difference?"

"Very funny, V." He squinted as shampoo ran down his face. "We're still in love—"

"Do we have to talk about this now?"

"—and we're compatible. At least on the big stuff."

"What do you consider the big stuff?" she said.

"Whatever. Hard work. Sunny vacations. Politics."

"Men and women never have the same politics." She kept her eyes on her legs.

"We have a history together," he said. "We've lived together for, what—three years?"

"Four," she said.

"They haven't been that bad, have they?" They changed places and she moved under the shower. "I said, 'They haven't been that bad, have they?' "

"They've been great," she said with her face in the water.

"Careful," he said. "I heard that."

He stood at the front of the stall and admired her body. If he'd been a cartoonist, he would have drawn her as a female Plastic Man, all length and litheness—long arms and legs, long waist, long fingers and hair. Tall grass blowing in the wind. He pictured her naked in some of the situations he kept stored in his brain—lying in a down comforter in a canopied bed at the inn near Monticello; emerging from belowdecks, squinting, her small breasts tanned without lines; in Mexico, near the beach, getting a massage. She was a moving willow tree with a steel-trap mind. A walking contradiction, which had always been one of her attractions.

Had been? There he was, doing it again—thinking of her in the past tense. As if they'd already split up. As if he already missed her.

He stepped out of the shower, grabbed one of the large towels she'd laid on top of the toilet lid, and ran it like a shoe-shine cloth over his back. She turned off the water, stepped out, pulled on her terry-cloth robe, and drew a tortoiseshell comb through her hair. "Should I turn up the news?" she asked, walking into the bedroom.

"Sure." Standing at the sink, he beat a shaving brush around the inside of an old soap mug—his father's—lathered his face, and looked for his blue plastic razor. It was nowhere on the counter. He opened a drawer beneath the sink and pawed through the junk: a bar of hotel soap, a comb with half the teeth missing. "Where's my razor?" he yelled.

"In the shower, remember? I used it on my legs."

"Right," he muttered.

"I thought you already shaved," she yelled. "In the middle of the night."

He retrieved the razor and returned to the sink. Bending toward the mirror, he pulled the razor against the grain, wincing. "What about the sex?" he said through the open door. Whatever problems they had, sex wasn't one of them. In addition to the sheer pleasure of it, sex was their best form of communication, one of the few times they stopped working long enough to connect. No way she could rebut that one.

"That's no argument. You get that whether we're married or not."

She could rebut anything. "Maybe it's better when you're married," he said, drawing the razor around the cut he'd sustained in the night. That one she rebutted with silence. Lame, he told himself. Really lame.

He finished shaving and walked into the bedroom to see her folding her favorite T-shirt, a threadbare relic of the seventies. On the front was a drawing of an androgynous, smiling tuna peddling a two-wheeled vehicle along the bottom of the sea, a straw hat in one fin and a bamboo cane in the other. Beneath it were the words *A Woman Needs a Man Like a Fish Needs a Bicycle.* The thing irritated him so much he wished he didn't want to marry her just so he could use it as the excuse.

He dressed quickly and walked downstairs to the kitchen, turned on the TV set, and spread the morning paper on the counter. Inside the refrigerator he found his breakfast: a tube of anchovy paste, a bagel, and a fresh can of Yoo-Hoo. He scoured the headlines as he ate.

A few minutes later Victoria came down the steps and saw what he was eating. "Oh, Jack," she said, half-sympathetic, half-disgusted. She noticed the cut on his cheek and touched it lightly. "God, you really did a number on yourself, didn't you?" He didn't respond. "Come on," she said, "we're late."

He turned over the last page of the first section, tossed the uncapped anchovy paste into the refrigerator, and looked at Geraldo Rivera on the TV screen. "Gay men who undergo sex-change operations to become lesbian lovers, today on—" He hit the off button. They paused, following the rules of the game.

"I give it a six," he said, holding up his hand.

"Wasn't that bad. I'll give it a four," she said, holding hers up.

"Five it is," he said.

They touched palms.

It was a humid early September morning as their taxi moved through Georgetown and headed for Capitol Hill. They talked briefly, comparing their work days. He was cochairing a hearing on his bill; she was giving a talk to a section of the American Bar Association. As codirector of The Law Clinic—"TLC" as it was called—she'd been asked to discuss recent developments in the law governing battered women. She turned the pages of her speech and read silently.

He looked out the window and saw a group of kids standing on a corner waiting for a school bus, lunch pails in hand, hair combed, faces scrubbed. She had always been honest with him about not wanting children, a choice she based both on visceral instinct and observation for as long as she could remember. Not that she disliked children—at least not as a species, or when they were cleaned up and cute and sitting on your lap with dry pants. He'd watched her hold a newborn baby once and saw her face as flushed and maternal as the stereotype said it was supposed to be. Which made him wonder if, in time, under the right circumstances, she might change her mind.

"Give me one good reason we shouldn't get married," he said. She laid the speech on her lap. "It's simple, sweetheart. It feels like slavery."

"And living together doesn't?"

"Not really. For some reason, marriage magnifies the differences between men and women."

"But not between women and women."

She looked at him strangely. "Whatever made you say that?"

"Nothing," he said, sorry he'd let something slip out of the murk. He knew that Rachel Redpath was Victoria's best friend, but getting into that subject was the last thing he wanted to do. At least at the moment.

"What differences are you talking about?" he asked. He watched her tilt her head and look at him to see if he really wanted to know. "You brought it up," he said.

"Okay," she said. "You want examples, I'll give you examples." She paused to think. "Playing poker with Sticks Dickey."

"Come on, V, that's Washington. People on opposite sides of issues always fight like hell during the day and put down their gloves at night. It's called being civilized."

"It's called fraternizing with the enemy, if you ask me."

Ah yes, he thought. Men. "The enemy." The people she loved to hate and hated to love. Maybe that was going too far, but saying she regarded them with deep ambivalence wasn't. A complicated relationship with her father, Dr. Steven Winters, was part of the equation, but most of it came from her work. Fifteen years of watching women limp into her law clinic looking for help. Fifteen years of peering into the snake pits of angry marriages, witnessing punching-bag violence, knife-wielding rage. Fifteen years of working with female victims, seeing the public in general growing tired of them, guiltily offering them the sanctuary of the courts, like modern-day leper colonies, and wishing they'd disappear. Fifteen years of battered women's anemic self-esteem transfused into her own bloodstream. She loved Jack, needed and trusted him, and there were other men whom she respected, too, once she got to know them. But at a distance, in the abstract, in their *essence*, she saw men the way weary social workers regarded welfare payments: with suspicion.

Jack said, "Poker isn't war, V. It's a few guys getting together for some cards and a couple of laughs. Women should try it."

"Women know more about getting together than you think," she said with an edge. Her face flushed slightly—not with anger, but as if she'd suggested something she wished she hadn't.

He let it pass. "Got anything better than that?"

She looked back at her draft speech. "Your shoes." She said she never knew where he was going to leave them—next to the bed, in the bathroom—except that she'd step on them, twist an ankle, get annoyed.

"I'll pick them up."

"No, you won't."

"Why not?"

"Because it's a detail, and men don't pay attention to details."

He smiled at her. "This is chickenshit, V. What's the real problem?"

She looked at him seriously. "You really want to know?"

"I really want to know."

"Are you sure you can handle it?"

He squinted in mock pain. "I'll try."

"The toilet seat." She looked back at her speech and continued reading, hiding a small smile.

The toilet seat. Christ, how could he have forgotten? Nothing pissed off the highly evolved woman more than an erect toilet seat—the essence of male insensitivity, chauvinism, and arrogance, not to mention the perfect symbol of *the* biological difference between the sexes. As far as Jack was concerned, it represented the perfect example of overheated, antimale, female irrationality. Here they were—brilliant, gutsy women running for president, merging railroads, flying jets, firing M-16s— surgeons, housewives, teachers, steelworkers—and not one of them had the simple wit to look down at a toilet bowl before sitting on it?

And she had the balls to say men were blind.

"Be thankful for toilet seats," he said. "Without them, we wouldn't have anything to fight over."

She didn't look up, but this time he caught her smile.

He watched the Rayburn Building pass by. "Small stuff aside," he said, "if the big stuff bothers you that much, maybe we should call it off."

The cab pulled up to the curb in front of the Longworth Building. The driver stared ahead, pretending he wasn't listening. Jack dug into his pocket for the fare. Victoria laid down her speech.

"You don't really mean it, do you?" she said.

"What, that we should call it off?"

"No, that we should get married. You don't really want to put up with me the way I am, do you?"

"How are you?"

"Angry, overworked. Preoccupied with—things."

"What things?"

"I don't know. Things."

"For a lawyer, that's a little vague, isn't it? What's been bothering you lately?"

She didn't answer.

He rolled down the window for some air. "I'm not looking for you to quit working or worrying, V. I'd like a family, and I'd like it with you. I assume that means living with a certain amount of shit." She said nothing. "Ultimately, if it's not yours, it'll be somebody else's." He saw her flinch. Christ, why did he have to say that?

"I don't want to lose you," she said. "I just don't want to marry you."

"Or have a baby," he said, handing the driver a twenty. "I understand what you're saying, I'm just not sure you can have it both ways." Her crestfallen face made him feel worse. "Look, maybe we're making too big a deal out of this," he said. "Maybe we both just need to bend a little and see what happens."

"Oh, my God. You've been watching talk shows again."

"It's what people do to save their marriages."

She shook her head and closed her eyes. "What do you have in mind?"

"I don't know. Something simple." He considered the possibilities. "I'll give up playing poker with Sticks Dickey if you give up cigarettes."

She let out a sigh. "Poker and cigarettes. The first steps to a zipless marriage."

The driver handed Jack his change. He returned a tip and took a quarter and squeezed it into her hand. "Call me after your speech and tell me how it went." He jumped out of the cab and shut the door.

She looked at the quarter. "Not with this," she said, through the open window.

"What's wrong with it?"

"It's not a quarter."

He stuck his head in the window and gave it a closer look. It was a Susan B. Anthony silver dollar. "How come these things never caught on?"

"When you guys approved a dollar honoring a woman, naturally you made it too small."

The cabdriver turned around. "Not in my book, lady. I love 'em."

Jack pointed at the man as if he'd just proved his point—then heard him add, "Half the time they give 'em right back to you thinking they're a quarter."

Victoria smiled. *Res ipsa,* " she said, and rolled up the window.

Jack dropped the silver dollar into his pocket and climbed the steps to his office.

Elliot Landy was leaning on his elbows on a lab counter examining a book of color photographs when he looked up and saw someone walking toward him.

"Hello, I'm Molly McCormick," she said. "A reporter with WAPL-TV in New York."

He straightened up slowly, as if he were seeing an apparition he'd never seen before. She was about twenty-five, with full auburn hair, dark brown eyes, the face of a fawn. Her skin was clear and slightly tanned, with a faint dusting of freckles across the bridge of her nose, sand sprinkled on ivory. My God. For a forensic pathologist to be taken with skin, it really had to be something. As she approached he straightened his bow tie instinctively, the way other men smooth down their hair.

"Elliot Landy," he said, shaking hands. "Didn't I see you on television this morning?"

"I certainly hope so. I'm covering the Shivers murder."

"You mean the Shivers homicide."

"Homicide, right." She paused. "What's the difference?"

He smiled. "You said you're from New York?"

"Yes. When I'm in Washington, I work out of our affiliate, WWDC. A dead New Yorker found in Washington with a toy doll in his stomach is a story that runs in both markets."

"Have you ever covered a death before?"

"Um, no. Afraid not."

"Homicide means death at the hands of another person, whether it's a murder, an accident, or whatever. Right now we don't know how Shivers died, so the cause is classified as 'pending.' "

"What can you tell me that you *do* know?"

His focus oscillated between her eyes and her lips. "What I know is that I can't talk to the press about an active investigation."

"Okay, I can understand that. I have a proposition for you. Let me tell you what I've heard, and you can tell me if I'm off track."

He smiled. "You *are* green, aren't you?"

She looked hurt. "Did I say something wrong?"

"Not at all. It's just that it's an old trick."

"Good, then I won't be taking unfair advantage of you."

Persistent, naive, beautiful. God. All at once he was ten years old on his grandfather's backyard fence, arms extended at his sides, one foot in front of the other, trying to do a tightrope walk from the house to the garage roof. Trying, this time, to cross from lust to duty.

As usual, he fell.

"Just a second," he said. He walked to the door, closed it, and returned to the counter.

She pulled out a notepad. "According to the police," she said, "Shivers was a convict who was serving the last part of his sentence at a halfway house in New York. A place called Wings, on Forty-third Street."

"That's what I understand."

"Anything to indicate how he got from New York to Washington?"

"Not that I know of. He disappeared a couple of months ago."

"And they found him on Wisconsin Avenue."

"Right."

"In a new suit."

"Right."

She took a note. "What caused his death?"

He grinned at her. "That's not asking for confirmation of something you already know."

"No, I guess not," she said, looking caught. "I'm used to covering cheese fairs and yodeling contests. The ground rules aren't so picky."

"Mm." He took pity. "You have to sneak up on a question like that. For instance, try asking about something that's already a known fact, like the baby doll."

"All right. So tell me, Dr. Landy—"

"Call me Elliot."

"Okay, call me Molly. So, tell me, Elliot, did the toy doll have anything to do with the cause of death?"

"That's better. See, it gets me thinking in a direction that's fair game."

"I see. So what's the answer?"

"No."

"That's it? 'No'?"

"That's it."

"Geez. Too bad I lugged along my notebook."

He stepped to another section of the counter, with Molly trailing. "Truth is, I can only tell you certain things that didn't kill him."

"Like?"

"Coronary, stroke, cancer, gunshot—the usual."

"So, if you were to guess, what do you think it was?"

"As my old pathology professor used to say, 'Never guess when you have to be right.' "

"You don't have to be right," she said. "At least not yet." She reached out and touched the large three-ring binder of photographs. "I've never seen an autopsy before."

"Sure you want to start now?"

"Why not? Listen, I've got another proposition. Why don't I ask whatever comes to mind, but I won't report your answers unless you say so? Or unless another reporter gets the same information?"

He'd been on that fence before, too. On the other hand, those eyes . . .

"Let's start with these," he said, sliding the book of photographs in front of her. He opened it to a tab marked *Shivers, Melvin—DC/1501*, and turned the pages quickly. She saw indistinguishable flesh-toned shapes sail by until he stopped at one in particular. She examined it but had no idea what she was seeing.

"This is Melvin Shivers's abdominal cavity," he said. "See this?" He pointed to a pinkish strand of thick spaghetti. "This is the iliac artery. If you could see it in context, it'd be about the diameter of my little finger. Now look here. It's been cut."

"Cut?"

"Like hedge clippers through a garden hose. Straight and clean."

"Is that what killed him?"

"I doubt it. Probably was cut during the first autopsy."

"What first autopsy?"

He blushed slightly at having given something away. "Someone professional opened up the body before we did."

"That's very weird, isn't it? Who'd want to do that?"

"I don't know."

"Take a guess."

He reminded her of his pathology professor's dictum and turned to another photograph. "Whoever did it pumped water through him and flushed out his blood and body fluids."

"Why?" She added, "God, I'm beginning to sound like a parrot."

"I don't know why. Except what you can't find, you can't test."

"You mean you think someone didn't want you to test Shivers's blood?"

"Possibly."

She tapped her long, oval fingernails on the metal counter. "But if Shivers was murdered, why would the killer reveal the body at all? I mean, if you could kill somebody, autopsy him, and drop him off at a Dairy Queen, why not just bury the guy? No corpse, no crime?"

"Exactly," He turned to a new photograph. "The police think the killers wanted him found."

"Wanted?"

"In order to send a message. You know, if you bomb a women's health clinic, you die."

She scowled. "Do you buy that?"

"Possibly. Look at the coverage the press gave it this morning. And here you are, right?"

She leaned her elbow on the counter and put her chin in her hand, studying the artery. "So what do you do next?"

"Tests."

"On what?"

"Tissue. If something interesting was in the blood, it's still in the brain, the pancreas, or other organs."

"Like what?"

"That, unfortunately, is a tough question. We'll send tissue samples to Tox and see what they come up with, but without having some idea what they're looking for, they'll be shooting in the dark."

She turned a photograph. "What's that?"

"A close-up."

"Of what?"

"Uh, I'm not sure you'd want to know."

"Come on, Elliot, I'm a reporter."

"This is a little off the beaten track even for a reporter."

She looked betrayed. "I thought we had a deal. What is it?"

"Hemorrhoids."

"Oh," she said. She drew her hand through her hair.

"Want to see another shot of them?"

"Uh, no thanks."

"Autopsies aren't exactly cheese fairs, are they?" he said, tweaking her.

She hated being called chicken, but not enough to look twice at a dead man's hemorrhoids. "How soon will you get the lab's results?"

"Micro in a few days, Tox a little later."

She examined the next picture. "Do you mind?"

"Not at all," he said.

She turned the page and gave a start. "Good Lord, what's this?" It was a photograph of Shivers's open mouth, his lips pulled back by latex-gloved fingers, like a dog being examined by a vet.

"I'm holding his mouth open for the camera," he said.

She pointed at the space where his right eyetooth should have been. "Doesn't that strike you as a little strange?"

"What?"

"A grown man with a prominent tooth missing?"

"I don't know. He was a bomb thrower and a convict."

She laughed. "You think convicts don't care how they look?"

He adjusted his glasses. He hadn't thought of that.

She turned another page. "Mind if I keep looking?"

"Here, use the magnifying glass."

She turned the pages slowly, examining close-ups of interior sections of the human body, unable to tell what she was seeing. "I feel like I'm back at St. Michael's looking at the kids' stamp collection," she said, turning another page.

"Oh, my God." She straightened up. In front of her was a long shot of Shivers's entire eviscerated body—the whole pig instead of a pork chop. She looked off to the side until Landy had turned the page.

"Here's another tight shot," he said, inviting her back. She looked out of the corner of her eye. "You can see a cross section of the human sheath. This is skin, this is muscle. This layer here is fat—"

It finally got to her; sweat sprouted on her upper lip. "Mind if I have one of those?" She pointed at some tissues.

He handed her the box. "Why don't you sit down a minute? You look a little green around the gills." Didn't sound right. "Actually, you look good in green." Her skin was beautiful even when it was translucent.

"I'm fine, really. Maybe if we turn the page." She wiped the perspiration off her face. "Any other clues?" she asked, looking at her tissue.

"Several, I'm sure. We just have to find them."

"Like the missing liver?"

"Perfect example."

She sat still a minute, recuperating. He checked his watch.

"I think I've taken too much of your time," she said.

"Not at all. I wish you'd drop by again, give me a hand."

She glanced at the Stryker saw. "Smile when you say that, would you?"

He did, and so did she, forcing color back to her cheeks.

They walked to the door and shook hands, holding their grip a millisecond longer than called for. His dark brown hair dropped boyishly onto his forehead. Impulsively, she reached up and straightened his bow tie.

"Oh—thanks," he said, blushing slightly. "Was it crooked?"

"Not really. I just couldn't resist."

The moment she'd gone, he paged through a tattered telephone directory, lifted the receiver, and dialed. In a few seconds a voice answered saying, "New York Department of Corrections."

"This is Dr. Elliot Landy in the medical examiner's office in the District of Columbia," he said. "I'd like to talk to someone about the dental records of a former inmate named Shivers. Melvin Shivers."

She slipped the last key into the lock and opened the door to see him lying on the couch, the bluish tint of the television set flickering on his face. She set her Bible and key ring on the table and turned on the lamp.

"Sweet Jesus," she said, looking at the piles of fives, tens, and twenties stacked on the table. "Where did *this* come from?" As if she didn't know.

Levoyd Davis turned his bottle of vodka upside down. His wife, Zenobia, watched the bubbles rise. He lowered it and looked at her through watery, red-rimmed eyes.

"I'm workin'," he said. She shot him a look. "Well, shit, Zee, what d'you think?"

"I don't see you bringin' home any kind of money for months and then this? What d'you think I think?"

Levoyd leaned back against the arm of the sofa. "It's cash, girl. You don't want it, I can find somebody that does."

Zenobia wanted it, all right. But living in Park Manor Terrace, one of the poorest projects in northeast Washington, she didn't see this kind of money unless it was from drugs, and Levoyd knew how she felt about drugs. "What kinda job?" she asked.

He shifted his weight and raised his torso on one hand. "Goddamn, Zee, either take it and shut up, or don't take it and shut up. But shut up." He sank back down onto the couch and looked at the set.

"I don't take dirty money," she said.

"Jees-zus-krice," Levoyd said. "We livin' in this dump with a seven-year-old cripple, we get some hard-earned cash, and you don't *want* it?"

He lifted himself off the sofa and walked over to the table. Zenobia sat staring at the money, not yet able to bring herself to touch it. He put his palm on her hair and ran his hand down the back of her neck. She didn't move.

"Hell, girl, I thought you might be a little grateful."

"Don't sweet-talk me, Levoyd," she said, not as sharply as before. Maybe, just maybe, he was telling the truth.

"You know I don't sweet-talk you, baby." He smoothed his hand on her hair again. "You're my woman."

"Mm-hm," she said. "Me and a dozen more."

He looked hurt. "How come we can't jus' be *nice* to each other once in a while?" Zenobia said nothing. "Ever since we had the kid you been differ'nt, her bein' messed up and—"

"Be quiet!" Zenobia said back. "Nothin' wrong with that girl's soul, and don't be talkin' 'bout her so she can hear, you hear?"

"She ain't regular, Zee. We had a regular kid, you wouldn't be like this."

"Like what?" She stared at him, daring him to answer.

He smiled and rubbed her back and looked at the money. "You gonna keep it?"

Zenobia swallowed hard. Levoyd was around when it suited him, and he was gone when it suited him. She thought this much money earned honestly was nearly impossible, but sometimes he did come through, and sometimes she was too hard on him, she knew that. And Lord knows she could use it. Church janitor by day, studying for her GED at night, paying a woman downstairs to baby-sit Sarah. Yeah, she could use it.

She looked at the money and decided what to do.

"Back rent's three months. That's six hundred in all." She counted it out and put it in a pile and pushed the other four hundred across the table, out of the way, as if his was tainted and hers clean. Then she looked at him.

"Now tell me the truth, Levoyd," she said, hoping he wouldn't. "How'd you get it?"

He looked her in the eye. "I'm a hatch clerk at the Marine Depot, takin' home two-ninety a week."

She looked at him, desperately wanting to believe him.

And so she did.

He smiled and lifted her up and took her in his arms. It had been a long time since she'd felt that, too, and for a minute she let him hold her, let herself feel the secure, physical strength of a man.

"C'mere," he said, and turned her face up to his. She started to turn away, but he stayed with her until they were in a kiss—long and warm. He ran his hands down her back, pulled her to his midsection, lifted her off the ground, and laid her on the floor in front of the couch. In a few minutes her dress was up around her waist and his fingers were into her underpants, pulling them down.

"I can't," she said, breaking their kiss. "I'm ripe."

"Don't worry 'bout it, girl," he said. He straightened up and dug into his jeans pocket and pulled out a shiny foil package, holding it up for her to see.

She said nothing as he pulled down his pants. She heard the tearing of the condom package and felt him fumble a moment, then felt him cup her buttocks in his palms and lift her slightly off the floor. They had just started their motion together when they heard a small knock at the door. "Who is it?" she asked between breaths. No answer. They continued, and heard another knock.

Levoyd yelled, "Get the hell away from that door!"

"Shush!" Zenobia said. "You'll wake up Sarah!"

They went back to their lovemaking, and in a few minutes Levoyd rolled over, rubbing away the pain in his knees while Zenobia lay still, breathing hard. After catching his breath, he stood up and pulled up his jeans, walked over to the table, and picked up the four hundred dollars.

"I'll be back in a while," he said, running a comb through his hair and walking to the door.

Zenobia raised herself onto one elbow. "Where you goin'?"

She felt something warm between her legs, a small trickle. Glinting on the floor in front of her was the condom package with its top torn off—with the condom peeking out, still rolled up, unused. She looked at Levoyd standing at the door. "Damn you, Levoyd!" She heaved her shoe at him. He hunched down as it hit the door, then ducked out, slamming it behind. "Come back here!" she yelled, hearing the sound of shoe leather on concrete steps.

She rose to her feet, angrier at herself than Levoyd. God help her if she got pregnant.

She walked into the bathroom and took off the rest of her clothes. She was in the middle of washing herself when she heard a knock at the door. After drying herself quickly, she grabbed a robe off the hook and went to the entrance. "Levoyd? That you?"

"Yeah," she heard, and turned the lock.

"Well, let me tell you something," she said, opening the door, "that was—"

She looked into the ski mask of a stranger . . . black parka and jeans and boots and black gloves . . . eyes staring through holes in a knitted hood.

She pushed the door toward the jamb; he stopped it and shoved it open. She backed away as he entered and turned the lock behind him.

She pulled her robe tightly around her and stared at the man's mask, watching it pulse in and out with his breathing. She saw his hand disappear into a pocket and pull out something black, then heard a click and saw a glinting blade motioning for her to open her robe.

She drew the gown tighter and backed up, stumbling over a clothes hamper. He stepped closer. She sank to the floor with her back against the wall, saying, "No," her face buried in her hands, her body as small and tight as an egg.

The man stood over her, not moving, and for a moment she thought he'd changed his mind. Then she heard him unzip his pants. He dropped them around his feet and knelt in front of her, grabbed her ankles and pulled them apart, and drew her legs around him.

She screamed.

He hit her face and pulled hair and put the knife to her throat.

She stopped screaming.

He scooted forward on his knees and raised her midsection. Then he took her. Fear and pain oscillated between her head and body—hard flesh and foul words assaulting her everywhere until, at last, the venom that made him crazy had been passed on to her. They both lay still a moment, recouping. As if he'd become another person, he stood up, pulled up his pants, grabbed her six hundred dollars off the table, and left.

Zenobia rolled onto her side and pulled her knees to her chest, trying to control the unknown . . . measuring what had been lost, fearing what had been gained . . . petrified that the rabid dog that had attacked her had made her crazy, too. Suddenly a hand touched her shoulder. She screamed, jumped, and saw her young daughter stooped over her with a quizzical look on her face.

Zenobia grabbed her and hugged her and rocked her in her arms, sobbing softly.

"What is she trying to pull?" the president asked. He raised the twenty-gauge Remington to his shoulder, swept it in a practice move from left to right—lowered it, broke it—and slipped in a bright red, brass-tipped shell. "This thing has been investigated by every goddamn busybody from the special prosecutor to Sally Jessy Raphael."

"I don't know," Senator Dickey said. He reached into his khaki shell bag, withdrew a cartridge, and played with it between his fingers. "When she first approached me, I told her to get the hell out of my office, but then I figured maybe I should listen to what she had to say. You know, as your friend, in case she had some toothpaste that oughta be kept in the tube."

"She's got nothing on me," the president said. "If she says she has, she's lying." He raised his shotgun, pressed the stock to his cheek, and sighted down the barrel. *"Pull!"* he yelled, and a navy ensign standing ten yards away touched a button, launching a yellow clay pigeon from a wooden tower on the right. The president led the disk, fired, missed, and watched it sail to the grass thirty yards away and break up. He removed his foam earplugs and stepped off the concrete pad. "You're up."

Senator Lamar Dickey III—known as "Sticks" for the three vertical lines following his name—walked gracefully to the pad and prepared to shoot. As the senior senator from North Carolina, he was one of the most powerful figures in the Senate: twenty-seven years of seniority, second ranking on Finance, chairman of Judiciary—which, of course, cleared judicial appointments—chairman of the Democratic Senate Campaign Finance Committee, darling of the pro-life movement, cochair with his ideological opposite, Congressman Jack MacLeod, of the House-Senate Joint Committee on Reproductive Rights and Responsibilities (known by the staff as "Fetal Attraction"). As a Democratic senator, he enjoyed a close working relationship with a president of his own party, but as a Bible Belt conservative, he and the president occasionally viewed matters somewhat differently. Except when they were in a political crisis, in which case they invariably favored the same course of action: protecting their own asses.

Dickey stepped onto the pad and set his feet in position to shoot.

Like other successful southern politicians, Dickey had raised charm,

52

stealth, and power to a political art form. He was said to be so smooth he could bury a man six feet under without ever turning a spade of earth. North of the Mason-Dixon line he wore Pierre Cardin suits; below it, baggy pants and rolled-up shirtsleeves. When he was down home, he talked proudly of the small farmhouse he'd grown up in; when in Washington, he and his elegant second wife lived in a magnificent Georgetown house that had once been Thomas Jefferson's tavern, entertaining guests often and well. In North Carolina he enjoyed meeting voters under a shade tree; in Washington, he enjoyed good restaurants, riding horses, sex, and a lively game of poker—on a good day, all in the same day. As the tobacco industry's best friend, he had been responsible for saving more tobacco farmers and killing more smokers than any senator in history, although he himself, being a lover of life, never smoked or chewed. Unless, of course, the situation required it.

Doing what the situation required summed up Sticks Dickey nicely. A man of towering principles and ironclad ethics, he found it necessary from time to time—as the "situation required"—to make use of what unsophisticated voters and an inconsiderate press called "loopholes"— those highly maligned but often practical political gadgets that ranged in size from thimble to Mack truck.

On this particular overcast day at Camp David, he was driving an eighteen-wheeler.

"Trouble is," Dickey said, relaxing a moment, "I'm afraid the situation isn't that simple." He pulled a handful of papers from under his khaki vest and handed them to the president. "She says this is a transcript of a conversation you had with her when the two of you met in secret to discuss how to handle the, uh, situation."

"She says we *met?*" the president said, grabbing the sheets.

"Twice, during the campaign." He adjusted the choke at the muzzle of his Weatherby, narrowing the pattern of his shot, then sighted down the black metal barrel. "Apparently, she was wearin' a wire."

The president read the transcripts. Sticks swung his shotgun from right to left in a quick practice move, like a golfer taking a practice swing. He raised his gun to his cheek, elbow out, weight forward on his left foot, knees bent slightly, his yellow sunglasses almost touching the stock. *"Pull!"* he yelled, and the throwing mechanism ka-thunked, flinging a clay pigeon out of the tower—*BLAM!* Shattered. He broke the barrel, kicked out the smoking shell, and reached into his pocket for another. Then he repeated three more perfect hits.

"Whoever this is," the president said, handing back the transcript, "it isn't me." They moved to the next shooting station. "I never met with her, at least not secretly." He closed his breech. "Hell, Sticks, except for the abortion issue, Barbara was one of my strongest supporters. You know she owns the biggest baby food company in America. She raised a lot of money for me." He set himself, took aim, and yelled *"Pull!"*— fired—*POP!*—and missed again. Damn. He was looking rattled. Guilty. And just when he thought he'd put this miserable episode behind him.

The "miserable episode" he had in mind was the one that had made him president of the United States. Three years earlier, during the presidential election, rumors had surfaced that the incumbent president, Walter Stone—Republican, Vietnam veteran, and odds-on favorite to be reelected—had secretly participated in a 1968 massacre at the village of Dau Ninh while serving as a Green Beret adviser to the South Vietnamese Rangers. According to the rumor, he'd used the code name "Lieutenant Mockingbird" as a cover, but because no evidence was produced to verify it, the rumor was dismissed by the press as a predictable October surprise. But then, a few days before the election, the story exploded. Defense Department records stolen from confidential army files and leaked to *The New York Times* showed that before going to Vietnam, during war games at Fort Ord, President Stone had, indeed, once used the code name "Mockingbird."

The scandal engulfed the campaign. The sitting president's opponent, Democratic Senator John Clay of Missouri, won the election by a slender margin, but left himself with a large postelection headache. Before he took office on January 20, outgoing President Stone, enraged by what had happened, used the last days of his incumbency to prove that he had *not* been present at the Dau Ninh Massacre (despite what the stolen documents indicated about his use of the name "Lieutenant Mockingbird" at Fort Ord). He appointed a special prosecutor to investigate the entire matter, including the criminal theft of Defense Department documents.

Three years later, long after the special prosecutor had issued a report but no indictments, the controversy seemed to be headed for graduate-student theses and conspiracy-junkie paperbacks, out of harm's way. At least that's what President Clay thought.

Until today.

"Is there anyone out there who matters who really thinks I'd be party to the theft of a sitting president's confidential military records?" the president said. "Or that I'd conspire with this woman to do it?"

"That's exactly what she's saying," Sticks said. "She claims that being a Defense Department contractor gave her the access to the records, and being your close supporter was the motive."

"All of us running for office get desperate at times"—the president looked into Sticks's eyes—"but not that desperate."

"Did you tell that to the special prosecutor?"

"Yes."

"Under oath?"

"Of course."

Dickey waited for the president to catch his eye again. "I ask that because it's one of those things you wouldn't want to have slipped up on or—*misspoke* about, Mr. President." He removed his sunglasses and held them up to the light. "Leaking a stolen document to the press is small stuff," Dickey said, looking for fingerprints on the lenses. "It's got First Amendment defenses hangin' all over it. But lying under oath—that would be another matter." He looked at the president. "An impeachable offense. As you know."

The president looked down his gun barrel, saying nothing. *"Pull!"* he yelled, sending a pigeon into the air—missing for the seventh straight time. He kicked out the empty cartridge, reloaded, and fired again. Another pigeon, another miss.

They shot from the next station without talking, breaking their silence with commands to the ensign, the thumping of the throwing mechanism, the sound of exploding shells. The president stepped onto the next pad and, without looking at Sticks, asked, "What do you think I should do?"

Perfect ambiguity: was he talking about blackmail or his poor aim? Sticks decided to tantalize him by playing it safe. "It's all in how you see the pigeon. When it's coming at you, shoot above it; when it's going away from you, aim below."

The president practiced a shot, taking aim at an imaginary clay disk. He yelled *"Pull!"*—fired—and the target exploded. Three more times.

He stepped back from the pad. "So what's she want from me? A bundle of money?"

"Nope. No cash, no job, no media celebrity status, no revenge. None of the usual stuff."

"Well, she obviously wants something."

"Yes, she certainly does. Although considering she was a supporter of yours, you'd never guess what." Sticks stood on the pad without saying more, allowing what his daddy used to call the "learning moment" to sink in. He shot his last bird, then walked with the president to the next station. "The way I see it," he said, "there's a way to handle this thing without even acknowledging this woman exists."

If there had been a transcript of their conversation, at this point the president's silence would have revealed nothing. But live, in person, he looked like a trout ready to strike.

Being a pretty good fly fisherman himself, Sticks didn't miss it. "Imagine a situation that requires a tough presidential decision," he said. "Then imagine that the best decision you could make for the country just happens, coincidentally, to be exactly what this woman wants. Now you're not doing something wrong because she's blackmailing you, you're doing something right because of your sworn duty. Oh, sure, maybe somebody like me tells her in private that she got her way—you know, give her a little ego satisfaction, but so what? You're clean, she's happy. Case closed."

"Two birds with one shell," the president said.

"Where I come from, nobody ever complained about that."

The president stopped short of the concrete pad, his gun on his arm, and turned toward his shooting partner. "Just so there's no confusion here, Sticks, let me make myself clear. I'm not going to do anything, or say anything, or let you do or say anything that could even remotely be construed as dignifying this woman's allegations. Understand? No blackmail, no cover-up. Nothing."

"I hear you, John."

"Good." He flipped on his safety and set the butt of his gun on the ground, leaning the barrel against a wooden rack. After removing his sunglasses, he placed a lens in his open mouth, fogged it with his breath, and wiped it with a chamois. "I don't mean to get worked up about this, but for God's sake, we're talking about the presidency here, not some smoke-filled back room. I didn't accept any stolen papers from her, and I didn't leak them to the press. And that's what I told the special prosecutor."

"I understand." Sticks looked chastised.

The president put on his glasses. "I'll be damned if I'm going to let the presidency be compromised over *anything*, least of all a pack of lies."

"Believe me, Mr. President, I wasn't suggesting you would." He'd gone too far.

The president gripped Sticks by the arm and looked him in the eye. "Time for a swim," he said.

"Frankly," Sticks said, "when it comes to polluting water, I prefer Jack Daniel's to my foot, if you don't mind."

The president heard him but had already started up the gravel path toward Aspen, the weathered, wood-framed lodge that was the presidential residence at Camp David. Sticks stood his gun against the rack and followed. He could argue with a president about a lot of things, but swimming or having a drink wasn't one of them.

They walked back to the house and went directly to the locker by the pool. Sticks looked around for a pair of trunks as the president peeled off his clothes. "Nobody here but us chickens," the president said, stripping naked, intimidating Sticks into doing the same. The president walked to the edge of the pool without a towel or robe, dived in head-first, bobbed up, and yelled, "Come on in." Sticks did as he was told, disappearing below a circle of white foam.

That oughta do it, the president thought as the senator came up for air and wiped the water off his face. The only place he could be hiding a wire now was up his ass, and knowing what turned Sticks on, he doubted it. Now that he knew he was off the record, he could forget the pious speeches.

The two of them dog-paddled toward each other until they were a couple of feet apart, with only their heads above surface.

"All right," the president said, spitting water and treading. "So I've got a problem here. Stolen documents, a denial under oath. Impeachable offense. Let's cut the shit and get down to business. What exactly does Barbara want to keep this thing under the rug?"

"Abner Titus," Sticks said.

The president blinked.

"She wants him appointed chief justice of the United States."

"All rise."

The clerk's monotone brought the courtroom to its feet. Judge Abner Titus entered from a side door, climbed the riser, and smoothly lowered his three-hundred-pound frame into a large leather chair. Victoria watched, wondering what in the world this particular judge was doing in this courtroom.

She sat at the defendant's table and stared at Titus as he read her papers. His face was white, almost sallow, as if he'd been studying too long for exams, but it wasn't his physique that interested her. Appellate court judges occasionally sat as trial judges, but why would an appellate judge of his renown—a man of intellect, enormous ambition, and one of the conservatives' top candidates for the Supreme Court—choose to hear a cut-and-dried temporary restraining order in the district court? Something didn't compute. She looked over at Zenobia Davis, who was sitting next to her at the defendant's table, and gave her a confident smile, giving no indication of her suspicion that serious trouble was sitting on the bench.

When Zenobia had come to see her two days earlier, to tell her about a rape and pregnancy, Victoria naturally assumed she was there to arrange an abortion. Then she discovered that her client was already twenty-two weeks pregnant. Victoria asked why she had waited so long. Pained, Zenobia explained that she couldn't decide what to do. On the one hand, the thought of bearing a rapist's child kept her awake nights and made her sick to her stomach, but then the thought that it was Levoyd's wasn't much better. She couldn't afford to raise another child, especially alone—and who knew what Levoyd would do to her if he found out that the baby wasn't his? And yet how could she put money and inconvenience over the life of an innocent baby? Half the time she thought the pregnancy was an accident, half the time she thought it was God's will—most probably in satisfaction of untold sins, and most definitely for accepting Levoyd's drug money. "God sees everything," she said.

Victoria listened sympathetically, holding her tongue, watching Zenobia finger her Bible.

Zenobia said that after weeks of praying and worrying, a few days earlier she'd come to a different conclusion. If she was pregnant from the rapist, it was a horrible accident, not punishment, and if she was pregnant from Levoyd, it was meant to be—most likely to make up for their daughter, Sarah, whose retardation she blamed on herself, not God or bad luck or nature or her husband. But then she realized that trying to play King Solomon wouldn't work: she wouldn't be able to tell whose baby it was until it was born, maybe not even then. And besides, when she thought about the fate of the child, knowing who the father was once again seemed irrelevant. It was still a baby in there, wasn't it? And even if it was defective, what difference would that make? She loved Sarah, why couldn't she love another? And yet, didn't she have a life of her own, too? Or was that being too selfish? Lord, it was so hard to sort out, she was so confused. When she was calm and listened to the still voice inside her, she was sure of only two things: she couldn't stand being pregnant another day, and she couldn't stand to end it.

What had finally prompted her to ask for help? Victoria wanted to know.

Zenobia said that when she had awakened that morning, something told her to look into the possibility of an abortion before it was too late. Having said that, she reached into her canvas bag, pulled out some legal papers, and handed them to Victoria.

Victoria had looked them over: notice of hearing, a petition by her husband, Levoyd, and—what's this? A temporary restraining order prohibiting an abortion? Reading further, she saw that it had been obtained by Levoyd with free legal assistance provided by the Red Rose Society and was signed by Judge Francis X. McCarthy, a notoriously conservative district court judge. Victoria told Zenobia that the order was wrong as a matter of law, and that if she wanted an abortion, she should appeal at once and have it lifted. "What do you want to do?" she asked.

Apparently taking the question literally, Zenobia pondered a moment. "I'd like to end the pregnancy without killing the baby."

Victoria stared at her a moment, hearing the anguished sentiment of Zenobia's reply. She told Zenobia that if she wanted to preserve the option of an abortion, they had to get to court immediately. At twenty-two weeks the fetus was dangerously close to viability; after the twenty-fourth week an abortion would be against the law in the District of Columbia and virtually everywhere else.

Zenobia said that after twenty-four weeks she wouldn't kill a fetus anyway. In fact, she wouldn't abort a fetus at twenty-two weeks, either, unless the judge said she could—not only because she wanted to obey the law, but because she saw the restraining order as an indication of God's will. If the court permitted her to abort, it was a sign that she should. If the court didn't, it meant she shouldn't.

And so here they were, sitting before Judge Abner Titus. He was smarter than Judge Francis X. McCarthy, had better credentials, was more published and polished, a potential Supreme Court heavyweight— and yet, in Victoria's opinion, still not qualified to deliver God's will.

She thought about the last time she and Titus had crossed paths. He had roasted her during an oral appellate argument and had written a blistering dissent, distinguishing himself, once again, as the nation's leading antichoice jurist. How long ago had that been? Two years. She remembered because it was shortly before Titus had undergone surgery for a new kidney. She remembered *that* because of a crack she'd made to Rachel Redpath, who was Titus's transplant surgeon. Something to the effect that a convenient slip of the scalpel would have saved more women's lives than all the transplants she could perform in a lifetime. Tasteless it was, but not as bad as Rachel had made it seem at the time. As Victoria remembered it, she hadn't even smiled.

Judge Titus raised his eyes to find Victoria. "Miss Winters?"

Victoria rose at the counsel's table. "Your Honor, I think this can be quite short. It is clear as a matter of law that there is no basis for the temporary restraining order issued here, much less for a permanent injunction." She said nothing more.

The judge looked over his glasses. "That's it?"

"Unless we're missing something, Your Honor, that's all there needs to be. As you know, the District of Columbia has no husband consent statute, and even if it did, the constitutionality of those provisions has either been denied outright or placed in serious question."

Judge Titus turned a page. "And what do you say in response to the moving party's contention that the Constitution itself provides a father with authority to prevent the abortion of his child?"

"I say nonsense," Victoria said. "Respectfully, of course, but there isn't a case to support that position—"

"Well, Miss Winters, of course there can't be precedent for any proposition until precedent is created. The question is, why shouldn't it be created here?"

Victoria told herself to slow down; Titus wasn't going to let her and her client ice-skate out the door. "To start with, Your Honor, my client's husband, Levoyd Davis, has no standing to be in this court. What protectable interest does he have?"

"Miss Winters, I should think even an independent, women's rights advocate like you would concede that the father of a child has some interest in it."

"Certainly, Your Honor, but what kind of an interest? Communicating and discussing the pregnancy with his wife, of course. Using the courts to stop her from a legitimate exercise of her rights, no."

"And the child's interest?"

"There is no child here, Your Honor. There is only a fertilized egg."

The judge looked over at Zenobia. "Mighty big egg, wouldn't you say?"

"Well, there is a fetus, Your Honor, but at twenty-two weeks it's still in the second trimester. It's not yet viable."

"Isn't that begging the question, Counsel? Whether it is protected or not under the Constitution depends on whether it is already a life within the meaning of the Fifth and Fourteenth Amendments."

My God, Victoria thought; was Titus *really* thinking of ruling against Zenobia? Surely he knew she'd appeal and have him reversed, so what was the point? Whatever it was, better to stop it now. She could attack Levoyd's right to sue by pointing out that he might not be the father, but that would mean disclosing the rape. Understandably, Zenobia dreaded that.

She'd have to raise the subject and walk on eggs.

"Your Honor, even if a father has legal rights in a fetus—and we believe it is clear that he doesn't—there are extenuating facts here that cast doubt on whether this particular petitioner has any rights at all. As for the nature of those facts—"

"All right, I see where you're headed," Titus said, cutting her off. "You want an evidentiary hearing before I rule on the proposed injunction. I think that's appropriate."

That sure was easy.

"But, Counsel," he continued, "be prepared to address a constitutional question of interest to the court. The question of when life begins."

So *that* was the point. Titus had apparently searched the court's docket looking for a case he could use to define when life begins. He'd given her an evidentiary hearing so that he could build the record and change the law, showcasing his judicial philosophy and intellectual qualifications to sit on the Supreme Court. It was outrageous, but there it was.

"Mr. Bivens," Titus said to the clerk, "set a hearing within ten days. The temporary restraining order is continued until then."

"Your Honor, I'm afraid ten days is too long," Victoria said. "My client is already twenty-two weeks pregnant, which means we're getting dangerously close to the point of no return."

Judge Titus stared at Victoria over the top of his glasses. "You know what that suggests to me, Counsel? That suggests to me that you not ask for one of your usual extensions."

Victoria closed her file. "We'll do what's in our client's best interest, Your Honor."

"As you always do," he said.

Victoria lifted her briefcase off the table and left the courtroom thinking how nice a slip of Rachel's knife would have been.

Dr. Elliot Landy talked to Molly over the telephone.

"Remember Melvin Shivers's missing tooth?" he said.

"Yes?" She grabbed a pencil and her notebook.

"According to his dental records, it was abscessed but hadn't been pulled by the time he was paroled. He had a phobia about it, wouldn't let anyone touch it. Threatened a lawsuit if they did."

"Then how'd it get pulled?"

"I don't know. But I doubt it was pursuant to his wishes."

"You think he was tortured?"

"I wouldn't go that far. There's no sign of that."

Molly waited, doodling little stars on the page.

Landy said, "I think he was kidnapped for a medical reason."

"Kidnapped? What makes you think that?"

"It's a guess. Remember the photographs? A person doesn't submit to that kind of treatment willingly."

"You're making a *guess*? Elliot. You must be a nervous wreck."

"Certain things make me nervous, but guessing's not one of them."

She thought better of asking what did. "What makes you think he was kidnapped for a medical reason?"

"The tooth. Surgeons don't like to operate on someone with an abscessed tooth. Risks spreading infection."

"Elliot! That's brilliant."

"It might be if we knew what the operation was for."

"How do you know he was operated on at all?"

"Whoever did the partial autopsy made their incision directly on top of a previous surgical scar running from his sternum to his pelvic bone. You can see small suture scars on both sides of the previous cut."

"Maybe those are from the autopsy incision."

"I don't think so, Molly."

"Why not?"

"Dead people don't heal."

"Oh." Silence. "You sure can get picky. Is there any reason for making a cut on top of an old incision?"

"None that I know of. That's what makes me think they were trying to cover up the earlier surgery. They even went to the trouble of removing his internal sutures."

"I thought stitches inside the body melted away."

"Depends on the suture. Catgut in stomach lining metabolizes in a few days. Dexon takes longer. Nylon, which is used to close muscle—that stays in place indefinitely."

Molly talked to herself. "No internal sutures and an earlier surgical scar. So what kind of surgery did he have?"

"If I knew that, I'd probably know everything."

"I know," she said. "It was his liver."

"His liver?"

"His missing liver. They operated on him to remove his liver."

"Is this based on logic or female intuition?"

"Don't knock intuition, Elliot."

"Do you have any idea how big the scar is from a liver dissection?"

"Big enough to get it out, I suppose."

"Exactly. It's huge."

"Why couldn't they have taken it out through the scar you found?"

"They might have *removed* it that way, but they sure couldn't have put another one in."

"So?"

"How did he survive without a liver?"

"Hm. I may have to consult my Dr. Spock on that one."

He was silent.

"What are you thinking?" she asked.

"Something else entirely."

"What?"

"I want to take another look first."

"Come on, Elliot—what?" She waited. He waited longer. She said, "Will you call me if it turns out to be something interesting?"

"Afraid not," he said.

"What?"

"I said, 'Afraid not.' I can't call you."

"Are you serious?"

"Absolutely."

"But *why*? I haven't broken the ground rules. I thought we were getting along fine."

"We are. That's why I can't call. Next time we discuss the subject, it'll have to be face-to-face. Over dinner."

It was late morning when Jack barreled into his reception area, said hello to everyone, and walked into his office. Ben Jacobs, his administrative assistant, was waiting.

"What have we got today?" Jack asked, surveying the neatly arrayed press clippings and correspondence. It was mid-September and Congress was back in session, the Capitol dome once again a huge, white beehive where politicians stored pollen collected from the taxpayers and dispensed honey to their districts.

"District stuff," Jacobs said. "Late Social Security checks are down, letters are running high on the president's foreign aid package, you've got three scheduled meetings beginning in five minutes, and there's a woman holding on the telephone who wants her garbage collected."

"A woman wants her congressman to collect her garbage?"

"I told her to talk to the New York City Department of Sanitation, but she said, 'Gee, do you really think I have to go *that* high?' "

Jack rubbed his forehead. Jacobs stood with a blank expression, taking constituent lunacy in stride, as usual. Everyone in politics played the angles, looked for the hidden agenda, figured the odds, checked the wind, but not Ben Jacobs. He always flew straight and level, which made him mildly boring, enormously reliable, and as credible as a saint. Jack liked and appreciated him deeply.

Jacobs said, "Eli Graves has released the Red Rose Society's annual hit list of the top ten congressmen and senators they intend to defeat next year. Guess who's number one?"

Jack continued signing letters. "If you're on a list, always be on top."

"He's going after you, Jack. Big time."

"Is he planning the usual press conference?"

"Yeah, in a couple of weeks. And guess where? In front of your New York district office."

Jack looked up. "If he's going to all that trouble on my account, maybe I should make a guest appearance."

Jacobs tried to gauge whether his boss was serious; it was precisely the kind of stunt Jack loved and made Jacobs's palms sweat. "If you want to play games with Eli Graves," he said, "do it this afternoon at the hearing instead." He started for the door. "Senator Dickey called and wants to know if you're playing poker Thursday night."

Jack thought about his deal with Victoria. "Tell him I won't be able to make it."

"Are you sure?" The senator invited his guests carefully; once you declined an invitation, you didn't show up unexpectedly.

"I'm sure," Jack said.

"Also, Winston called back," Jacobs said. "He wants you to put in a word with the mayor on his latest funding proposal." Jacobs looked for a nod. "He also said he has an answer to the question you had me ask him about this dead guy Melvin Shivers."

Jack picked up the telephone as Jacobs left the room, punched in a number, and waited for Winston to answer.

Winston Jones had been his friend since their first fistfight at Flatbush High. Two years older than Jack, he had been held back in school twice because he was dyslexic, which meant being exiled to special ed, taught to run the school projector, and kept eligible for basketball. A tall, graceful black man, he and Jack had struck up a friendship based on their mutual love of sports, a similar sense of humor, and the general respect people slightly off center hold for one another. They'd never lost contact after graduation, even when Winston moved to California to play professional basketball, where he was the last to be cut from the Lakers' squad in 1972.

When Jack ran for Congress he'd asked Winston to run his campaign, which he did on condition that Jack promise to help him raise enough money to fund a halfway house, which Jack did on condition that Winston promise to locate it in Jack's congressional district, which Winston did on condition that Jack promise to run again after losing his first race, which Jack did on condition that Winston promise to manage all his campaigns, which Winston did on condition of something else, until neither of them could remember who owed what to whom, much less why it mattered.

When Jack was finally elected to Congress, his Manhattan district included East Forty-third Street, where Wings, Winston's halfway house, was located. Jack placed his New York office next door in order to be nearby. No one understood Jack's election district, or Jack, better.

Winston answered the telephone and, after they exchanged insults the way male friends do, said, "Ben says you're interested in this guy Melvin Shivers."

"What do you know about him?"

"Not much. He was always kind of moody and quiet, but no trouble.

He'd been here about six months when he disappeared, which was really stupid. Another month in halfway and he woulda been home free. The only guy who really knew him was Iggy."

"Who's Iggy?"

"Ignatius Pitt. A kid who used to live here. I got him a job as a bicycle messenger."

"What do you make of this baby-doll thing, anyway?" Jack asked.

"Nothing. Why?" Jack didn't respond. "You aren't turnin' weird on me, are you?"

"Just curious. Do you think you could find him?"

"Who?"

"Iggy."

"He still comes by, yeah. What do you want him for?"

"I don't know. Just an instinct."

Winston mumbled, "White folks."

"Considering where this guy Shivers comes from, maybe we ought to check things out," Jack said.

"Check what out?" Winston asked. "What the hell's eatin' you, man?"

Jack hated to admit it. "Brooklyn."

Winston gave his signature groan. "Aw, come on, not that shit again. Nobody's raised that in five campaigns. You were in high school, for crissake. Your little shoe-store caper isn't even on the record." That wasn't Jack's worry. It was the other problem, the reason he'd robbed the store in the first place that bothered him, and Winston knew it. "Jesus, Jack. You don't even know for sure what happened to her."

That was true. Some things he knew about Honey, some things he didn't. Except that for some reason, once again her memory had been haunting him. "Look into it anyway, would you?" he said. "See if somebody's been snooping around the old neighborhood?" He disregarded Winston's grunt. "One other thing. What do you think about me making an appearance at Graves's press conference in a couple of weeks?"

"I think it's the only thing that would make anybody give a shit what he says."

"Mm." *Mm* was Jack's favorite way of disagreeing.

"You know," Winston said, "this is one of those little things that burns my ass. There's ten doors in front of us, nine marked *Sure Success*. You pick the one marked *Disaster*, and they call you a shrewd risk taker. I pick it, and they call me a dumb son of a bitch."

"I don't get it. Which time are they wrong?"

"Fuck you."

"See ya this weekend."

"Forget about Eli Graves. Bring some of that federal money I never see and everybody says we're wasting."

Jack hung up and stared at a pile of letters. Winston was right; everyone in Washington was paranoid, himself included. He put Brooklyn out of his mind and got ready for his next meeting.

Jacobs came through the door. "Got a minute?" he asked.

"Sure, what's up?"

"Detective Norman Pulaski of the NYPD and Detective Joe Wilson of the D.C. police are outside."

"What about?"

"You know the piece of pencil they found inside the baby doll?"

"Yeah?"

"They figured out what the letters *EOD* on it mean."

"And?"

"It comes from the word *MacLeod*." He held up one of the blue pencils with white lettering Jack handed out to visitors as a courtesy. "It's yours."

Harley Moon sat staring at the noon news, his knee jiggling up and down, waiting for it to happen. The newscaster had introduced the segment as "The case of the baby-doll homicide," which really irked him. It was just like the goddamn press to hype it with a sexy name, wasn't it? He saw an old news clip of his pal Mel Shivers, under arrest, being guided into the backseat of a police car . . . then a clip of the clinic they'd blown up together . . . then—*uh-oh, I knew it; here it comes*—footage of himself, the infamous Harley Moon, accomplice of the infamous Melvin Shivers, entering the courthouse in handcuffs. Staring at the TV screen, he hardly recognized himself. He looked so young and earnest: coat and tie, hair combed, sideburns trimmed (his lawyer had made him do that). More like an Eagle Scout than someone who bombed abortion clinics for Jesus. The reporter said that Harley Moon was living in the New York area where he—*snap.* He turned off the set, shoved a Saltine into his mouth, and paced around the room.

"Take it easy, Harley," Winston Jones said from the doorway. As executive director of Wings, he had taken a special interest in Moon since Melvin Shivers had disappeared from the halfway house a few months before. If Moon had become jumpy when that had happened, he had turned absolutely paranoid when Shivers was found dead in Washington. As a condition of his parole, Moon resided at Wings except on special days when he was permitted to spend the night at home in Brooklyn. Today was one of those days, but he was balking.

"Why don't you hike up to the park?" Winston said, trying to calm him. "They're building a fireworks display for the concert."

Moon flexed his jaw muscles with clenched teeth, considering the advice. Without saying whether he would or he wouldn't, he headed for the door.

Outside, he breathed in the hot, fumy air and looked up and down Forty-third Street trying to decide what to do. Three kids walked by with ice-cream cones, and for a moment he thought he'd go to Central Park after all. Then he pictured the fireworks they'd show that night. The ten-pounders booming overhead. Gunpowder. *Explosives.*

His throat closed and he headed home.

He crossed the street and turned west toward Grand Central Station to catch the subway. Idling at the curb, also facing west, was a beat-up maroon van, blue smoke putt-putting out of its exhaust pipe, one of the rear doors slightly ajar. As he walked by, the van started to creep forward, keeping its distance a few feet behind. Moon reached the corner at Third Avenue, stopped, and stuck a cigarette into his mouth. After applying a match, he crumpled up the empty pack and tossed it toward a wire trash basket, bouncing it off the rim onto the sidewalk. He stooped to pick it up—a habit from his days in the slammer—and caught sight of the van. It stood in the curb lane, stopped for no apparent reason. He studied it a moment, then turned and continued toward the station.

He'd walked another half block toward Lexington Avenue when suddenly another jailhouse instinct kicked in. *Look behind you.* He did. The maroon van was still on his heels. Experience whispered in his ear: Locate the van's mark and get out of the way. Immediately, he spotted the van's target: a man wearing a white shirt who'd been walking in front of him for the last block.

Take a look behind you, fella. Somebody's got you in their sights.

He slowed his gait to put some distance between himself and the mark. The man in the white shirt continued walking, oblivious to the danger he was in. As Moon expected, the van continued moving forward, dogging its victim up ahead. Moon stopped walking and waited to see what happened.

The van stopped, too. Slightly ahead of him.

Moon watched the back doors swing open slowly. Two figures sat inside on wooden stools. He strained to see their faces but couldn't make them out. Then he saw why: they'd been erased by nylon stockings.

Not so the semiautomatic rifle.

One of the van's occupants pointed the gun between Moon's eyes.

Moon's mouth fell open, dropping his cigarette to a dangle from his lower lip. A second commando in the van wiggled a black-gloved finger at him, motioning him to get in. Moon's hand rose reflexively to his chest. *Who, me?*

"Yeah, Harley. You."

He stood frozen a moment, staring into the muzzle, wondering who was holding it and how they knew his name. Not wondering if the gun was loaded.

He got in.

There must be a note of harmony here someplace.

Jack stood in the anteroom to the Senate hearing room reading a staff-prepared profile of Eli Graves, preparing to take his testimony on the Guaranteed Choice Act, which Jack had coauthored. Knowing that Graves would oppose the bill, Jack was looking for something the two of them might have in common. Whatever it was, he couldn't find it, either in the text or between the lines.

It wasn't surprising: their differences weren't superficial. From the small to the large, from matters of style to questions of substance, everything about them was in conflict. Graves had gone to night school; Jack had gone to Yale, albeit with financial aid. Jack liked football and rugby; Graves hated contact sports. Graves found raw fish disgusting; Jack ate sushi for breakfast. Jack believed in Darwin; Graves in Adam and Eve. Graves thought poverty built character; Jack thought it highly overrated. Jack acted in spite of his doubts; Graves had no doubts to spite. Graves thought sperm was sacred; Jack thought it was human. Even their physical appearance suggested their differences: Jack was tall, lean, athletic; Graves stocky, strong, pugnacious. On and on it went—sex, politics and religion, oil and water, black and white—everything in polarity, all things opposed.

A committee staffer poked his head in the door and announced that the hearing was about to begin. Jack read a couple more lines about the Red Rose Society's enormous coffers—it had one of the largest political action committees in Washington, serious influence, and allies in Congress—and rolled the briefing paper into a paper baton, ready to do battle.

The Hatfields and the McCoys. The Thrilla in Manila. High Noon on the Hill. Graves and MacLeod.

"Thank you, Mr. Chairman," Graves said into the microphone. "As one who's been called to fight for the rights of the unborn, I'm pleased to have the opportunity to appear before your committee."

"Welcome, Mr. Graves," Jack said.

He listened to Graves read a statement condemning baby killers, god-lessness, and the Supreme Court—more or less in that order. Graves had spoken barely a minute before Jack felt their old antagonisms charging like an electrical generator. Jack repositioned himself in his leather chair and told himself to stay cool. Even a cobra and a mongoose were capable of crossing paths without fighting. He assumed.

He continued reading the profile his staff had prepared. As the thirty-seven-year-old president of the Red Rose Society, Eli Graves had become one of the most powerful pro-life figures in the country. Although he would have had difficulty making the grade in Washington's finer parlors (not that he had the slightest interest in trying), in the halls of Congress, where power ruled without regard to pedigree, he possessed serious access and influence. He had built the Red Rose Society from a storefront operation into one of the largest antiabortion groups in the country, which meant in the realm of Congress his coinage was good. He was telegenic, earnest, and a good speaker, and capable of motivating his supporters to donate what every political movement needed most: time, votes, bodies, and money, the mother's milk of the unborn as well as the born. He was volatile and humorless, but smart in a muscular kind of way—the intellectual equivalent of a guy who could lift a truck's wheel off a baby. A true believer, a missionary who pursued his calling uncluttered by paradox, ambiguity, or skepticism, he was capable of doing whatever it took to achieve his goals. It was a personality trait Jack understood well, considering the number of business executives, professional athletes, and Washington politicians he knew. Himself included.

Whatever antipathy Jack felt for Graves was returned in spades. As far as Graves was concerned, Congressman MacLeod epitomized everything he hated most about Washington: its politics, its weather, its inside baseball, its self-important people. He despised Washington so much he refused to learn how it functioned, preferring the thirst of ignorance to drinking from a poisoned well. Compromise, which was Washington's style, was definitely not Graves's, least of all when it involved his immortal soul, which included virtually all things that mattered.

Jack had almost finished reading the profile when Graves asked a committee member who was questioning him if he could address a question to Congressman MacLeod. Hearing himself targeted, Jack looked up.

"Tell me, Congressman," Graves said. "How would you feel about a woman aborting a fetus when she's already given birth to four badly diseased and congenitally crippled brothers and sisters?"

"I'd say that was an appropriate case for an abortion."

"That's what I thought you'd say," Graves said. "Well, congratulations, Congressman. You just aborted Beethoven." He sat back in his chair with Jeremy Hackett, his lawyer, sitting beside him.

Jack felt his cheeks tingle. The spectators, sensing a brawl, quieted.

"That would have been quite a tragedy," Jack said, sitting up. "Almost as tragic as the loss of Wolfgang Schwartz."

Graves held still, one dog sniffing another. "Sorry, but I'm afraid I don't know who you're referring to."

"I'm referring to Wolfgang Schwartz, the most brilliant composer of all time. The man who wrote circles around Beethoven."

Graves looked at Hackett, whose expression said, "Beats me." "I'm not getting your point, Congressman."

"No, I'm not getting *yours*, Mr. Graves. You seem to be upset at the thought of losing Beethoven's music, but not the least bit troubled that you've never even heard the far more brilliant music of Wolfgang Schwartz."

"It's hard to miss something you know nothing about."

"Yes it is, which presents a small problem here, doesn't it?"

"I don't think so."

"I do," Jack said. "Like Beethoven, Wolfgang Schwartz had older brothers and sisters, all painfully crippled. So when Mrs. Schwartz became pregnant with Wolfgang, she faced a tough decision—should she risk bringing another deformed child into the world, or were the ones she'd given birth to enough? Being the God-fearing person she was, not wanting to cause needless suffering, she aborted Wolfgang to avoid a human tragedy. Of course, the world never knew his music, but fortunately that wasn't a tragedy, either. As you point out, we never missed it."

Graves did a slow burn. "So you think this little story justifies aborting Beethoven?"

"By that do you mean, if Mrs. Beethoven had told me about her four deformed children and asked me whether she could abort the fifth—sorry, I didn't see that coming—would I have said the decision was up to her?"

"Yes."

"I would have said it was up to her."

Graves drummed his fingers on the witness table. "So you would have given her the power to kill Ludwig van Beethoven?"

"Someone has to balance the prospects of misery against joy, art against suffering. I choose her."

"And I think that decision was made by God when he made her pregnant," Graves said. "But since you'd give it to a human, Congressman, let me ask—what about Mr. Beethoven? Doesn't his vote count?"

"I sure hope so. But if he and his wife disagree, only one of them can decide. In my opinion it has to be her."

"But there are *three* votes here, Congressman, not two. As usual, you're forgetting about the fetus."

"And which way does it vote?"

Graves was genuinely surprised. "For survival, of course."

"Why do you say 'of course'?" Jack asked. "If we're going to pretend that a fetus is smart enough to vote, shouldn't we assume it's smart enough to understand what it's voting about? Not merely its own survival, but its quality of life? And that of its mother, and its family?"

"Ah, yes." Graves smiled. "The old quality-of-life argument. The biggest excuse for legalized murder in the world. Are you saying the quality of Beethoven's life wasn't worth his survival?"

"I'm saying it turned out great for you and me, but I can't tell you at what price it came to his mother and family. And in my book, if it's life versus art, life wins."

"But in your book life *doesn't* win. You would have let Mrs. Beethoven *kill* a life, not save it."

"I was speaking of *her* life, not his," Jack said.

Graves leaned forward, incredulous and angry. "Doesn't your conscience bother you about any of this?"

"As a matter of fact it does, but not half as much as it would if I were forcing a woman to have a child against her will." Jack stared at Graves. "Wouldn't that bother you?"

Graves glared at Jack. "That's not for me to say. That's up to God."

"Oh, come on, Mr. Graves. You play God all the time."

"Never."

"Do you vote?"

"Of course."

"*Res ipsa.*"

Graves looked perplexed. "How's that again?"

Jack squeezed his pencil. *Smart, Jack. Real smart.* "It's a bit of lawyerese. Means the matter speaks for itself."

"Well, thank you for that education, Congressman. I guess those of us who live outside the beltway have been too busy worrying about what you call quality of life to keep up with our Latin."

"I didn't mean—"

"While you study dead languages—which I suppose is appropriate for a baby killer—the rest of us have been studying life and learning human values. We understand something that apparently you don't, which is that once an egg is fertilized, there's a moral duty to respect it and leave it alone. Period. Or as you people from Yale would say, *Res ipsa.*"

Damn. Fucker nailed me. "Well, Mr. Graves, I'm afraid I can't agree with that position—legally, practically, or morally."

"Given your background, Congressman, I didn't expect you would."

The crack had an edge that took Jack by surprise. "There's certainly no secret about my record, Mr. Graves, but I suspect you know very little about my background."

"More than you think, Congressman," Graves said coldly.

Jack felt his blood pressure rise. He didn't know what Graves had in mind, but he had no difficulty recognizing a threat when he heard one. Pulling rank and gaveling Graves down would be a chickenshit move. Better to beat him at his own game.

"One more question," Jack said. "I see from the news that a convict found dead here in Washington spent some time in your neighborhood in Queens." He opened his folder. "Here it is. Melvin Shivers. Convicted of bombing a Queens clinic in 1980. Do you happen to know whether he was a member of the Red Rose Society?"

Graves's face reddened and his left hand curled into a fist. "I have no idea, Congressman. Nor do I understand the purpose of your question."

"The purpose of my question is simply to establish the facts. Tell me something, Mr. Graves. Would you go on record here and now as condemning the Shivers bombing, and the bombing of all abortion clinics?"

Graves's eyes began twitching. "I prefer not to be goaded into that, Congressman. The Red Rose Society has always deplored violence of any kind—especially the violence pro-abortionists perpetrate on defenseless embryos. And that, I assure you, is going to stop." He sat trembling, and then he added another thought: "The way I read the Shivers story, looks like the pro-choice fanatics aren't limiting themselves to killing babies."

This time Jack burned. "I was just about to ask if you had any information you could share with the committee indicating the cause of Mr. Shivers's death. For example, do you think he may have been killed by a pro-life zealot who was deliberately trying to make it appear to be a pro-choice crime?"

Senator Dickey, who'd entered the room a minute earlier, broke in. "If my esteemed colleague and cochairman will yield, I see that we have a vote on the floor. We'll resume in twenty minutes." He gaveled an end to the argument.

Jack picked up his briefing paper and went out the side door, through the waiting room, and across the street toward the Capitol. As he walked through the Rotunda he reached out and touched the foot of the statue of Andrew Jackson, the great warrior-president. It was a small superstition he indulged whenever a vote was nearing on a bill he'd sponsored, or when he found himself in some kind of trouble.

He entered the door to the House floor and smiled a hello to the assistant sergeant at arms. *Given your background* . . . he heard Graves's voice echo in his head. *I know more than you think.*

Maybe he did. But more what?

*J*ack saw Honey's hands clinging to the wing strut, her strawberry
hair whipped around her face by the wind. He held on to the side of the
airplane door and stretched out his hand as far as he could. Reach! She
did—just as her other hand slipped off. Watching her fall, he yelled at
her to pull the rip cord, then saw that she couldn't: it wasn't a parachute
on her back but a backpack, with a baby inside—its eyes fixed on him
as it drifted down toward a gray sea.

Jack woke up, once again standing at the bathroom sink, water running. He turned it off and headed back to bed. Victoria was asleep on
her side as he slipped under the covers. He closed his eyes and tried to
sleep, unable to shake his image of Honey O'Connor. She'd been his
first love, and he thought of her the way men remembered first loves
and first scars: tenderly, respectfully, with a mild ache reminiscent of the
wound's original pain. . . .

The clock over the Greyhound bus station entrance read exactly seven-
thirty as Jack ran through the door, letter jacket open, loafers flopping.
He reached into his pocket and pulled out the envelope of money he'd
stolen from Robertini's Shoe Repair, ready to show Honey he'd gotten
it after all. The buses waited on the angle, idling, ready to depart. He
jogged in front of them, listening to warming engines and the sound of
air brakes letting go, inhaling exhaust, checking destination signs above
the windshields.

He saw one reading Harrisburg.

The door was open; he leaped on board and moved down the aisle,
combing the seats with his eyes, checking faces. No Honey.

He bent down to look through the bus window, sure he'd see her running for the door. Instead he saw Jeanie Anders, her best friend, standing next to a metal newspaper box in the waiting room. He got off the
bus and walked inside.

"Where's Honey?" he asked.

"Jesus, you look like hell," she said. "She asked me to give you
this."

She handed him an envelope. He tore it open and found a handwritten note on pink stationery with little red roses around the border.

Dear Jack:
If you get this, which means you showed up, I'm sorry I'm not there. Jack, my parents found out. They're taking me to live with my great-aunt until I have the baby. When they heard I was on my way to Harrisburg, they had a fit. Mother screamed an abortion could have killed me, Father yelled he was going to kill whoever got me pregnant (don't worry), Mother said I would burn in the eternal fires of hell. Which doesn't seem too bad right now. I wouldn't say who the father is and I never will, I promise, although they suspect it is you. I miss you already. I love you.

Honey.

She had written *P.S.* at the bottom, but nothing followed.
Jack stared at the note. "Where is she?"
"I don't know. Honest to God." She saw the envelope in his hand. "What's that?"
"The money," he said.
She cocked her head and looked at the logo in the corner. "From Robertini's Shoe Repair?"
Noticing the logo for the first time himself, he stuffed the envelope back into his jacket pocket.
"Jesus, Jack—what did you do?"
"Where does her great-aunt live?"
"In Syracuse, but I can't—"
"Where in Syracuse?"
She rolled her eyes. "She said she didn't want you to contact her because it would only make things worse. She'll write you first."
Jack paced back and forth.
"It'll all be over in April," Jeanie said. "And she'll be back."
He looked at her as if it was her fault, and walked away.
"Get some sleep," she called after him. "You look like hell."

Snow. Piling up. Cold and deep. Slowing the bus to . . . a . . .
Stop.
The driver told the passengers to sit tight, another bus with chains was on the way. Jack looked at his wristwatch and felt his heart pound.

If he could have transferred his body heat to the road, they wouldn't have needed another bus.

Honey had left Brooklyn in December, and now it was February, the one month of the year that was eight weeks long. There was no way he could get through it without seeing her.

Not that they had been out of communication. They had established a Friday-night telephone routine: Honey called from the diner pay phone at eight o'clock, just before Jack left for his weekly poker game at Luboff's. Jack sent her cash to make the calls. They also wrote each other even though Honey's parents had forbidden any contact and had instructed her great-aunt to intercept any letters. Hadn't they ever heard of general delivery? "The only thing dumber than a dumb Scot is a smart Irishman," he could hear his bigoted uncle saying. Amazing, the things you called people when they had you trapped and desperate.

Despite their cleverness, bad luck battered Jack's and Honey's fragile linkage. His poker playing had turned so sour he'd had to borrow the money for his bus ticket. Served him right for returning Robertini's money the night he stole it. And now a snowstorm had stopped the bus near Apulia Station. He got off wearing his worn-out loafers and letter jacket and began trudging north toward the Blue Whale Diner in East Syracuse, worried that by the time he arrived she would have vanished. A snowplow slowed, took him aboard, and brought him within a half mile of their rendezvous. He walked the rest of the way.

He entered the diner, his face snow-burned and wet. Honey was standing next to a booth, pulling on her coat to leave. The sight of her made him light-headed, then surprised: she looked so—*pregnant.* Before she'd left Brooklyn she must have been holding in her belly.

She saw Jack and threw her arms around his neck and gave him an enormous hug—no kiss, which troubled him—then shed her coat and sat down in the booth. For some reason they'd become unexpectedly shy, talking about the snow and the saltshaker instead of the intimate and cosmic subjects they discussed on the telephone and in their letters. For weeks he had fantasized about their reunion, imagining soft-focus embraces, lying together on a beach, drawing their initials in warm, honey-colored sand. Of course he knew this wasn't possible at the Blue Whale Diner in East Syracuse in February, and yet, as with all people in love, the romantic dream refused reality's chill.

They sat in the booth and looked at each other across a Formica desert, eyes touching, souls apart. As they talked he searched for a bridge to the Honey he had known when she left, ultimately finding it in the most obvious place of all: the jukebox. He dropped a dime and punched in Bobby Goldsboro's "Honey." *And Honey I miss you,* the singer crooned, *and I'm being good . . . and I'd love to be with you . . . if only I could.*

Honey laughed with her mouth wide, lips soft and pink, churning his blood. Finally the ice had melted; soon they were talking about their old days together—what they called B.C., meaning Before Child. She wanted to know what was happening at school—was Connie Klepp still prowling the halls with her tits hanging out? Were the cheerleaders still big-dealing it? Was Winston okay? Jack answered with forced patience, longing for something more, something that was missing, although exactly what, he didn't know.

After three more plays of "Honey" and two pieces of coconut cream pie, she finally extended her hand across the table. He held it only a second before sliding into her side of the booth and kissing her. She broke their embrace quickly, once again sinking his heart until she looked over her shoulder and explained that they were too close to home for PDAs—Public Displays of Affection. He didn't like it, but he had no choice.

"Want to feel my stomach?" she asked.

Not really. "Sure." He gave her his left hand and let her lay it on a taut belly.

"Sometimes I can feel a kick," she said. Happily for him, there was none at the moment. The idea of his own child being that close was confusing, threatening their loyalty to each other, reminding him of Freddy Anticoli and a life he greatly feared. He told himself that once the baby was given up for adoption, neither of them would have to worry about it again. It was the only way he could leave his hand on her womb.

"It bothers you, doesn't it?" she said.

"The baby? I don't know if it exactly *bothers* me." He saw her expression. "Yeah, it bothers me."

She smiled. "Me, too."

The waitress brought them a piece of lemon meringue pie. Honey cut the tip of it with her fork and held it up for them to make a silent wish, and ate it.

"What did you wish for?" she asked.

"I wished you'd come home and everything would be the way it was B.C.," he said, "and that the year after next we'd both get scholarships and go to college together. What'd you wish for?"

"I can't tell you."

"Why not?"

"It's too disgusting."

"What is it?"

She checked his eyes to see how badly he wanted to know. "Rubbers," she said. She picked up her fork and dabbled at the pie, then looked at him. "I wish you didn't mind."

"If that's what you want, it's okay with me," he said.

"I'll use a diaphragm, too."

"At the same time?"

She smiled at him and cut another piece of pie, fed it to him, and ate another bite herself.

She was due back at home at six o'clock, but by seven they were still sitting in their booth, holding hands, touching, breathing air instead of fire, mending instead of tearing. It was only when she described the trouble she'd get into for coming home late that he allowed her to pry herself away.

They pulled on their coats and stood outside the diner door, shivering. Jack opened his coat and pulled her inside and huddled her against him with her head under his chin.

"I want you to come home with me," he said.

"I wish I could."

"I mean it," he said. "You could live at my house. Or with Jeanie."

She looked up at him. "You really miss me, don't you?"

"Yeah. I'm worried about you, too."

"Why?"

"I don't know. I feel like I'm supposed to be doing something, but I don't know what. Makes me—you know. Worried."

She nestled her head back under his. "That's nice." After a moment she said, "I have to go," and lifted her face for a good-bye kiss. She plunged her tongue into his mouth as if she'd had this in mind the whole time they'd been together—as if the sweet torture of making him wait would give their parting more power than anything else she could do. He didn't realize it until it happened, but it was what he'd been longing for, and missing.

She shivered and walked back inside the diner and turned to look at him through the door. He made a fist and touched his knuckles to the glass. She leaned forward, fogged the glass with her breath, and drew a small heart in it. When she'd finished, she smiled at him and mouthed the words *I love you.* Exactly the way she always did. It always drove him crazy, seeing her say those silent words.

"I love you, too," he said. Then to his surprise, he added, "I always will."

Up from the ground-floor hallway of white Georgia marble they moved, into the main-floor foyer, past the marine band, which played Gershwin like Gershwin, not Sousa, then into the wide hallway and left toward the East Room, everyone maintaining an air of cool preoccupation, no trace of awe in their faces, no sailors in Manhattan here. On they came in a slow, steady stream, pairs of handsome creatures among many handsome creatures . . . women in their full-length gowns and elbow-length gloves, men in black tie. When they reached the receiving line, they waited, couple by couple, standing in dignified poses, talking quietly, waiting to be presented to the most powerful man in the world.

A tall, handsome marine stood next to the president wearing blue, red, and gold, white gloves, a square jaw. He leaned forward at the waist and said, "Name, please," and received the information from the gentleman, who spoke in a barely perceptible voice, loud enough to be heard by the marine, no one else.

"Hello there!" the president said, smiling and pumping the hand of the next guest. "Good to see you again!"

Between guests he spoke to the first lady sotto voce, for her ears only, without looking at her. *"Chief Justice Brown is about to die."* He shook a hand, smiling. "Hey! Great evening, huh?"

"And?" the first lady responded quietly. *"Uh-oh, here comes Emily Johnson. She's loaded with powder and she likes to hug."* She shook a hand and smiled. "Jane, so glad you could come." Jane smiled and moved on.

The president said, *"Titus is looking strong."*

"What are you talking about? How are you Emily? My Lord, you look wonderful! *You're joking, right?* Hello, Jerry. Nice to see you. *You've got Emily Johnson's face powder all over your left shoulder."*

"I'm not joking. It's time to end the abortion litmus test. Hi, there. *Restore some political balance to the Court.* Jim, great to see you. I hear we have a winner in Ways and Means, is that true? *Titus is brilliant. Besides, all I do is appoint these guys. After that they're on their own."*

"Hello, Samantha. How's the baby? *But you know perfectly well how he's going to vote on abortion!* Oh, my, what a pretty rosebud!"

82

"No, I don't. Senator, great to see you. Mrs. Crandall, nice to see you, too. *Court's full of surprises. Look at Earl Warren—big Republican governor, big liberal judge."*

"You've lost your mind. Mr. Patterson? Excuse me, Peterson. Welcome to the White House. *Why are you telling me this now?"*

"He's coming through the line. Good-looking tan, there! *I need a little support, Maggie.* Jerry! Great to see you!"

"I'm the first lady, John—Hello, Senator, it's good to see you again— *not Mrs. Pontius Pilate."*

The marine turned and introduced Judge Abner Jasper Titus.

"Judge," the president said. "Welcome."

"It's nice to be here, Mr. President," he said, shaking hands.

The president said, "After dinner, let's spend a minute together."

"I'd be delighted."

The judge moved his three-hundred-pound body a step to the left and extended his hand to the first lady.

"Judge Titus," she said, smiling. "So good to have you with us."

" 'Pontius Pilate?' I've been called a lot of things before, but never Pontius Pilate." He threw his tux jacket over a wooden caddy and started undoing his tie, talking to the first lady through the door of his dressing room, into the large bedroom. Pontius Pilate my ass, he thought. Whoever made him the bad guy sure as hell never sat in the Oval Office. If a president hasn't got the guts to turn his back on a righteous cause now and then, he may as well not take the oath.

He started to untie his left shoe, impatiently pulled it off, lost his grip, and lofted it into the air. "I suppose you'd feel better if I was more like Crandall," he yelled into the bedroom. Senator Robert Crandall of Rhode Island was one of the Senate's unabashed, old-fashioned liberals. "Christ, you don't think he'd sell a seat on the Supreme Court to be president?" He unzipped his pants. "Damn right he wouldn't," he said. "Fucker'd sell the whole Court."

He stripped down to his underwear and walked into his bathroom. The mirror didn't like him tonight; a stubble was already making an appearance. He picked up his toothbrush, bit a piece of toothpaste off the end of the tube, and worked up a mad-dog foam in the mouth. Of course he'd take some heat for appointing a right-to-lifer, but so what? Titus was plenty smart and politically okay on everything else. Abortion wasn't the only issue in the country, and he was getting sick and tired of hearing that it was.

He spit a mouthful of suds into the sink.

It galled the hell out of him, the way liberals played politics with abortion. If they had the broad public support they said they had, why didn't they pass some legislation guaranteeing choice? Because they didn't have it, which made them phonies. Or else they *did* have it, which made them weaklings. Well, screw 'em. If they wanted to bet the ranch on one lousy Supreme Court appointment instead of their own legislation, that was their problem, not his. He had his own fires to tend to.

He looked into the mirror again and saw an expression on his face he didn't want to see on the evening news. The face of a president who's just received a subpoena . . . a special prosecutor standing at a bank of microphones . . . a senator at an impeachment hearing . . .

Shit. What was the point of debating the pros and cons of Titus's appointment? He didn't have a choice.

He dropped his toothbrush into a glass and toweled off his mouth. "You may not think much of Pontius Pilate," he yelled through the door, "but at least he knew the first rule of politics, which, in case you've forgotten, is survival." He turned off the light. "Even liberal do-gooders know they aren't worth a tinker's damn once they're out of office making I-used-to-be speeches on some sunny California campus."

He walked into the bedroom. All the lights were out except a small one next to his side of the bed. Maggie was on her side with her back to him, apparently asleep.

He turned out the light and climbed into bed and lay on his back with his hands behind his head. After a minute he turned onto his side and curled up behind her, one spoon fitted into another.

"Don't touch me," she said quietly.

He held on tight and didn't move away.

Neither did she.

Jack sat behind his desk with his face illuminated by the halogen lights and a copy of his bill, the Guaranteed Choice Act, at his finger-tips. Molly McCormick—reporter, interviewer, fresh new face—was pursuing a different subject. She looked up from her notebook to ask one more question.

"One of the hypotheses the New York City police are working on is that radical abortion-rights advocates may have killed Melvin Shivers in retaliation for the clinics he bombed. Do you think that's possible?"

"Not likely," Jack said. "People who favor choice don't kill, it's not their style. But I wouldn't put it past some right-to-life fanatics to try to make it look that way."

"Do you have anything to base that on?"

"Look at what's happening around the country. Right-to-life zealots shooting doctors, bombing clinics."

She looked at him a moment and said, "Thank you, Congressman." They shot reverses, and the lights died.

She unclipped the microphone from her silk blouse, and her camera-man began breaking down his equipment. Jack watched, momentarily fascinated with something about her—not her sex appeal, which was ob-vious, but something more elusive. A sense of familiarity, as if they'd met before, even though he was sure they hadn't.

She caught him staring.

"You know," he said, "if the politics of abortion is what you're cov-ering, I know a case you might want to look at."

"What is it?"

"A woman whose husband is trying to stop her from having one."

"Can he do that?"

"No, but he is. He's got a TRO and a hearing scheduled on a perma-nent injunction."

Molly opened her small spiral notebook.

"Call Victoria Winters at The Law Clinic," he said. "The case is *Da-vis* versus *Davis*."

Molly slipped on her shoes and stood up, pulled on her leather shoulder bag and stuck out her hand. "Thanks for the interview, Congress-man. Can I call you if I have a follow-up question or two?"

"Anytime," he said.

He stood, came around his desk, and shook hands.

"Oh, one other thing," she said. "I was reading the transcript of your hearing. In case it comes up again, Beethoven's mother had one child before Ludwig, not four."

"Really," he said. "How'd you know that?"

"Everybody in West Virginia knows that."

She broke their handshake and left him standing at his desk, staring a bit too long, saying not quite enough.

Victoria walked through the reception area toward her office, past the women sitting in bucket chairs with black eyes and broken hearts, past their children whining and pulling at their mothers' hands, unaware that the fingers they yanked had only the slightest grip on reality themselves.

She picked up a stack of call slips as she walked into her office. She lifted the telephone and called Rachel.

"Can you make it to the Zenobia Davis hearing?"

"I'm in surgery nearly every day, Vick."

"I need you on this one. Any chance you can find someone to cover for you?"

"I'll try. Did you see this morning's paper?"

"Not yet, why?"

"Chief Justice Brown isn't going to be with us much longer."

Victoria continued shuffling through her call slips. "Relax," she said. "There's no way the president is going to appoint a right-to-lifer. It'd be political suicide."

"Just a thought," Rachel said. "You understand why I'm asking."

Victoria ignored the comment. "I'll call you as soon as I have the exact time of the hearing." She hung up to interview her next client.

Sticks Dickey shoved the key into the lock of his hideaway, a private two-room office immediately next to the Senate chamber, and opened the louvered door, ushering Eli Graves and the Reverend Gaylord Jenkins, executive director of a powerful political action committee, inside.

There were a hundred members of the U.S. Senate, but not all of them had one of these special suites. Given Senator Dickey's seniority, he was eligible for the finest: a comfortable sitting room with an L-shaped sofa, overstuffed club chairs, a well-stocked bar, and two television sets—one transmitting C-SPAN continuously, the other plugged into a VCR—and a second room with a desk, a double bed, and a kitchenette. The cozy little rooms were perfect for conducting serious business—rounding up votes for a bill, organizing or defeating a filibuster, hammering out compromises on a budget—and tailor-made for lesser crimes such as drinking, napping, getting laid, and negotiating financial "contributions." Sticks had been asked by more than one lobbyist what made him think the hideaways were not bugged by the feds, to which he said the proof was as obvious as it was simple: most senators were honest, and as for those who weren't, how many did you see casting votes from Allenwood?

Dickey told the good reverend to help himself to the bar, which he did. After a few sips, Jenkins snapped on the TV and sat playing solitaire, watching *As the World Turns.*

Eli Graves joined Dickey in the next room. The senator opened the refrigerator, gave Eli a Dr. Pepper, and poured himself two fingers of Jack Daniel's. He sat on his desk. Two hours earlier he had brought Graves and Abner Titus together for lunch in the Senate dining room. The meeting had not gone well, and the reasons needed to be dealt with.

Graves paced the room. "Why are we here, Sticks? This feels like a trip to the woodshed."

"Relax. As my daddy used to say, sometimes a trip to the woodshed ain't nothin' but the easiest way to gather up wood."

"Why don't we cut the bullshit and get to the point?"

Sticks sipped his whiskey. "You came damn close to blowing it down there today. You understand that, don't you?"

"No, I don't. Maybe you should spell it out for me."

"All right. Let's start with you pushing Titus to say how he'd vote on *Costello*. He can't talk about specific cases and you know it."

"Why not? If he's the big pro-lifer he says he is, why can't he just come out and say he'll vote to overturn *Roe*?"

"If everybody knows he will, why's he need to?"

"Because I don't trust him."

"Why not?"

"He talks like a professor. He's too complicated."

"Jesus Christ, Eli. Far as you're concerned, anybody who speaks the King's English is too complicated. Abner Titus is our ally!"

"If I help get him on the Court, I want to know he's going to deliver the goods."

"What do you want him to do, sign a contract? Of course he's going to vote against *Roe*. Just watch what he's doing on the bench right now."

Eli put his hands on top of his head like a prisoner of war. "What else is bothering you, Sticks? Let's get it on the table."

"It's your style, Eli. It's too hot. Too obvious. Titus knows you could derail his appointment. You don't have to shove it up his ass to make the point." He took another sip. "And I'll tell you something else. If you back off and give him some room to breathe, he'll do more for you than you think."

"Such as?"

"Leave that to me."

Graves shook his head. More Washington doublespeak.

Sticks said, "And what the hell is this stuff you were saying about taking on sex?"

"What's wrong with that? If we could stop people from having sex out of wedlock, we'd solve abortion, AIDS, and pornography all at the same time."

"Lord have mercy, Eli. I thought you wanted to broaden your political base, not shrink it."

Graves was miffed. "I'm sure this comes as a shock to someone with your particular appetites, Sticks, but in my book sex is meant for procreation."

"Sex is meant for everything," Sticks shot back. "Open your eyes and look around, boy! Every song, every movie, every TV show—clothes, cars, food—you can't name anything in America that isn't about sex.

It's our obsession. So before you go charging around declaring war on it like some Puritan, you better think twice."

Graves paced back and forth, tapping his Dr Pepper can, glaring at Dickey like an angry spouse. "I think it's time we reassessed our relationship. I mean, what do we have in common, Sticks? Except for a game of poker now and then?"

"Coalitions," Dickey said. "One and one makes three. Nothing gets done without political coalitions."

"But coalitions for *what*?" Graves said. "What do you *believe* in?"

Sticks Dickey hadn't heard that question for so long it momentarily baffled him. The first answers that came to mind—"power" and "winning"—he knew would only piss Graves off. Graves was an idealist who believed that ending abortion was so important he'd do anything to achieve it, while Dickey cared about political process more than any particular ends it served. So what could he say? On what ground did they meet?

He considered what was at stake and decided to take a rare course of action, one he took only when the situation absolutely required it. He decided to be completely honest.

"Let me level with you, Eli. Truth is, I don't give a shit whether a woman has an abortion or not. As far as I'm concerned, the world has too many starvin' pickaninnies already. But I'm gonna support you down the line on this abortion business, because I see a great opportunity here for us both."

"You mean the money?"

"PAC money, sure, but more than that. Liberals have run things in Congress since the New Deal, especially in our party. Now we've got a chance to change all that, but we need a few hard-core issues to carry us, and abortion's one of them. Here you are a natural leader—young, fired up, standin' on the brink of changing America from people's bedrooms to the Supreme Court. You and your friends have beaten the ERA, you've put a political stranglehold on most of the statehouses, you make the president sing for his supper—there's no telling how much of Congress conservatives could own by the end of the nineties. It's all just sitting there waiting for us to take it."

Eli liked what he heard. "So what's the problem?"

"There isn't any. As long as you stay cool and don't blow it."

Graves grimaced and tossed his empty can under the sink. "I gotta tell you, Sticks, I really get tired of hearing that. You want to lecture me on how to become an effective hypocrite in Washington, fine. But we're in a war, okay? We're battling to save lives and the other side's winning. When you're fighting a war, you don't have anything if you don't have troops, and to keep the troops moving I have to communicate, and I can't do it with tea-party manners the way you guys do it up here. I gotta keep my people fired up. I gotta harness the hate people have for baby killing. Far as I'm concerned, nothing's more important than that. And I mean nothing."

Dickey looked at him with a mixture of awe and contempt: awe because he knew it took this kind of zeal to change the world, contempt because he knew that, misdirected, it could bring down the house. He needed Graves—his followers, his money, the votes he could deliver—but he also knew that if Graves didn't learn how to conduct business more cautiously, he'd become more trouble than he was worth. He poured himself another whiskey and leaned back against his desk.

"I grew up on a farm in North Carolina," he said. "You ever live on a farm?" Graves shook his head. "Well, let me tell you a little farm story."

Graves rolled his eyes as if he'd already been fed enough corn to stuff a hog. He longed to be back in New York City, where a guy spoke his mind and made his point, assuming he had one of either. Sticks saw his impatience and shoved a fresh Dr Pepper into his hands.

"When I was a kid," the senator said, "every Sunday we had chicken, but instead of taking a fryer out of the henhouse and ringin' its neck, my brothers and pals and I played a game called straight arrow. Ever hear of it?"

"Can't say I have."

"Well, here's what you do. Everybody has a bow and arrow, see? And you go into the middle of the barnyard and throw a little corn around your feet, and pretty soon the chickens come waddlin' over to feed, and while their heads are jerkin' up and down, everybody draws back an arrow and points it straight up and on the count of three lets go." He picked up his glass and let the image sink in.

"Now you got six, seven, maybe eight arrows sailin' into the sky, and in a few seconds they're gonna turn around and start coming down, so naturally you got to get the hell of out of there, but you can't just cut and run or you'll scare away the chickens." He waited for Graves to ask the inevitable.

"So what do you do?" he asked.

"You tiptoe away, real carefullike."

"Yeah? And then what?"

"Most of the time you don't hit anything, but if you're patient and play long enough"—he snapped his fingers—"chicken stew."

"How do you know whose arrow hit the chicken?"

"That's the whole point. You don't." He looked at Graves to see if he got it. "The object of the game is to kill the chicken, not figure out who did it." Dickey took a sip of whiskey and kept his eyes on Eli. "You understand what I'm saying?"

There was a knock on the door. Gaylord Jenkins stuck his head in with a serious look on his face. "There's a pretty young lady at the door, Sticks. Says she has an appointment to see you."

Dickey looked at his watch; he'd forgotten the time. "Bring her into the living room and ask her to wait a minute, will you, Gaylord?" He stood up and turned to Graves. "I've got a little personal business to attend to, if you don't mind."

Graves's brow remained furrowed. "Why don't you give me the lesson in plain English?"

"There isn't any lesson here, Eli. We're just a couple of good ol' boys swappin' stories." Graves looked more frustrated than ever. Dickey checked his watch again and leaned against the desk. "Look, son," he said. "Take the JFK assassination. People are still runnin' around like bumper cars trying to figure out who was behind Lee Harvey Oswald."

"You mean you don't think anyone was?"

"Hell, boy, I don't think anyone was, and I don't think anyone wasn't. All I know is if somebody put him up to it, ain't nobody going to find out who."

"Why not?"

"Because whoever did it was playin' straight arrow!"

Graves looked lost.

"Let's say it was somebody in the mob," Dickey said. "The first thing the boss asks himself is, How am I gonna kill the president without getting caught? Answer? Straight arrow. He locates a few crazies without their knowing it—you know, guys who hate the president, guys with Christ complexes who think they're going to save the world, fellows with a loose nut but smart enough to know how to function."

"Then what? He brainwashes them?"

"No, no, no, that Manchurian candidate stuff is for the movies. Too dangerous, too many tracks. The guys he picks are *already* disposed to kill the president. All he does is make sure they have what they need to get the job done—a gun, a scope, a plane ticket—stuff they could get on their own with a little money and the right push. Stuff with no finger-prints. And that's it. He's fired them into the air. Now all he has to do is tiptoe away."

"But how's he know one of them is going to kill the president?"

"He doesn't." He took another sip. "Hell, he can't even be sure they're going to try. Maybe they'll chicken out, or maybe they'll try and fail. Maybe they even get caught, but so what? The boss is safe because nobody can trace it to him. He's swapped control for insulation."

"Sounds pretty hit or miss to me."

"It is! That's the beauty of it! Most of the time it doesn't work, but what if one of your boys gets lucky? Scores a hit instead of a miss? Then what have you got?"

"Oswald. With no tracks."

Dickey smiled. "Even if the police had rubber-hosed the hell out of Lee Harvey, they never would have found the mob or Castro or anybody else in the picture because Oswald himself didn't know who else was in the picture. He was just an arrow who'd been shot into the sky by nobody-knows-who."

Dickey recognized the same look on Graves's face he saw when he'd convinced a fence-sitter to vote for him. He patted Graves on the shoul-der. "Titus is flying up to New York this afternoon. I want you to sit with him and get to know him better, understand?" Graves looked sul-len. "Now let's check out the reverend," Sticks said. "One thing I learned long ago is never leave a preacher alone with whiskey and a beautiful woman."

"Wait a minute," Graves said. He stepped in front of Dickey and placed his hand on the senator's chest, spilling a splash of Jack Daniel's out of his glass. "Who am I in this game, anyway—an archer or an arrow?"

The veins stood out on Dickey's forehead; a United States senator was not used to being manhandled, least of all in his own hideaway. He brushed the booze off his tie. "You say you're in a war," he said, his voice a register lower. "Well, let me tell you something. In every war you lose a few good troops." He stared through Graves. "Whether you're one of them or not depends on whether you learn how to play the game."

He raised his forearm and pushed Graves aside, letting him know who was boss, and walked into the sitting room, restoring his famous grin as he greeted his lovely appointment.

Eli watched him go through the door. "Don't forget to zip up when you're done," he said, loud enough to be heard.

Eli Graves settled into his shuttle seat and paged through an airplane magazine. "How to Make a Better Aspic" . . . "Winter Tennis in Bermuda" . . . "How to Improve Your Golf Swing." He closed the cover, disgusted that so much ink was spilled on trivia when life-and-death issues abounded.

He turned toward his seatmate. "So," he said, interrupting Titus's reading. "I understand my friend Jeremy Hackett is representing a husband who's trying to keep his wife from aborting."

"*Davis* v. *Davis,*" Titus said.

"How's it look?"

"Unfortunately, I can't comment on a specific case."

Graves looked as if he'd sucked on a lemon.

Titus shifted his weight and laid down his book. "Tell me a little more about the Red Rose Society," he said. "What's on your long-term political agenda? Besides premarital sex?"

"Passing the Right-to-Life Act and overturning *Roe* v. *Wade.* Everybody says it can't be done, but I know it can. Get enough Americans upset about baby killing, you can stop it."

"And how do you do that?"

"Not easy," Graves said. "People are so used to abortion they're becoming immune to it. You practically have to blow somebody's head off just to get anyone to pay attention."

"What about symbolic acts? Fetuses in bottles and things like that?"

"Forget it. The networks and the press won't show them."

"Why not?"

"They say they're in bad taste." He laughed derisively. "Liberals are amazing. They show every form of slaughter known to man in the movies and on TV, but they won't show the biggest form of real mass murder there is. They keep whining about how their precious First Amendment is in danger, but they're the biggest censors of them all."

"How about doing a documentary?"

"We tried that with *The Silent Scream.* Remember? Everybody said it was 'too explicit'—which in my book means too good. The only people with the guts to show what it feels like to be ripped apart by the suction machine are your TV tabloids. Even then, you'd have to give them something sensational."

"Such as?"

"I always thought if you could catch a fully formed third-trimester baby being aborted, they'd find it impossible to turn down."

"Why haven't they done it?"

"Can't get it on film. If it's a put-up job, nobody will show it because it's staged, and if it's the real thing, who's gonna invite in a camera? Abortionists don't like to be on videotape murdering viable fetuses."

"But if a tabloid had it, you think they'd air it?"

"Yeah. They'd probably put a blue dot on some of it, but they'd keep enough to show what it looks like. Don't you think?"

Titus said nothing.

Rachel Redpath entered the operating room on time, scrubbed up and ready to begin. The rest of her team, lagging under the pressure of a relentless schedule, was still draping the second table, adjusting the overhead lamps, positioning the rows of hemostats on the sterile tray, preparing for surgery. She looked around the room. There was no dog or lab attendant in sight.

"Where's the patient?" she asked. Everyone looked around, but no one answered.

Annoyed, she checked her watch, snatched the requisition slip off the wall, and walked out of the operating room, down the fire stairwell to the floor below, and up the hall to the hospital's animal pound. She stood still, catching her breath. *Slow down. You're pushing everyone too hard, yourself included.*

She surveyed the room. It was eerily quiet, as if all the kennels had been vacated. She lifted a muzzle from a hook by the door and found the cage number indicated on the slip. Peering through the wire mesh, she saw an ordinary dog with a brown-and-white coat and sleepy face, rising to his paws to see who'd come to visit.

She opened the kennel door and extended her hand to his nose. Preparing to slip the muzzle over his head, she remembered why she herself never retrieved her experimental subjects, why she always had one of the younger staff put them to sleep before she entered the operating room. Lab animals were always the sweetest, most affectionate beasts of them all. Here she was, staring into the mutt's black, trusting eyes, watching its body move in counterpoint to its wagging tail, feeling its warm, smooth tongue lapping her hand. Sinking her heart.

In spite of herself, she knelt down and held the dog's head between her hands. Although it wasn't a breed she'd ever owned, it reminded her of one she'd had as a girl. One in particular.

The dog pushed his snout forward, straining to lick her chin; she sat back on the floor and let him step forward into her lap. Talking to him softly, she pulled his body against her chest and stroked his coat, reassuring him, letting him comfort her. Soon she was catching glimpses of lost, tender moments from her childhood . . . sitting on a cracked linoleum floor playing with her beagle . . . feeling the warmth of a speckled oven . . . smelling the roly-poly cinnamon crust baking.

She saw a pair of smooth calves standing at an ironing board and heard a brown radio beaming the voice of Don MacNeil and his Breakfast Clubbers across the ironing board. She saw her mother's fingers sprinkling fabric with gentle shakes of her hand, like a priest blessing a baby, then laying on the iron . . . the vapor hiss, the smell of lightly scorched cotton. She caught a streak of sunlight slanting through a window on a sleepy afternoon . . . the picture of the father she never knew, in uniform . . . a pattern of hydrangeas on her mother's blue housedress . . . a worn velveteen sofa . . . a little girl snuggled up against her mother's side, listening to Winnie-the-Pooh poems. She saw her own small hand reach up for . . . For what? What was it? What image was trying to break through?

She held the dog closer, pushing her senses until the last veil fell, clearing a path to the memory of the soft, cool underside of her mother's upper arm, her favorite spot in the whole world. She saw herself clinging to it as long as possible, eyelids drooping with warmth, listening to her mother's voice lull her to sleep . . . waking later, magically transported into her own bed.

She rested her cheek on the dog's back and rocked him gently, letting the tears roll, unsure exactly for whom, or for what, she was crying.

Eli Graves walked off the shuttle, bought a newspaper for an umbrella, and grabbed a taxi to his office on Queens Boulevard. As the cab pulled up in front he reached into his pocket for the fare and saw a small headline: QUEENS ABORTION PROTESTERS JAILED.

Ninety-five protesters were jailed today following their arrest for unlawful trespass and disorderly conduct at a Queens abortion clinic. The protesters, who identified themselves only as "Baby Jane Doe" and "Baby John Doe," are being held without bail pending their agreement to disclose their true names and be fingerprinted. Arnold James, an attorney for the group, said they "preferred jail to betrayal of the unborn."

Graves looked up to see the driver's hand offering him his change. "Keep it," he said, and ripped the article from the paper.

Graves entered his office and stood behind his desk, raincoat still on, pawing through a stack of mail to see if he'd received a delivery of one of the manila envelopes. None today. He drew a key from his pocket, opened a locked desk drawer, and lifted out a black three-ring binder filled with green notebook paper. Opening it to the last page, he began reading. His general counsel, Jeremy Hackett, came into the room and closed the door.

Graves spoke without looking up. "I've been thinking about MacLeod. Getting my thoughts together for the press conference. Any more green sheets arrive while I was gone?" He continued reading. Hearing nothing, he looked up.

"Nothing new," Hackett said.

"I'm looking for another delivery before the press conference."

Hackett looked pained. "You're making me nervous, Eli."

"A good lawyer is always nervous," Graves said.

"I'm serious. You have to consider the consequences of defamation

97

here. You're talking about making public charges against MacLeod on the basis of anonymous stuff that's coming in over the transom."

"Not *'stuff,'* Jeremy. Facts. MacLeod's life."

"So this source says."

Graves closed the notebook and flopped into his chair with his raincoat spread open around him like a robe. He put his feet up on the desk. "It doesn't matter who Greensheets is," he said. "What matters is what he's digging up. Everything he's given us on MacLeod has turned out to be true. So far so good."

"That's what the guy who fell off the Empire State Building said as he passed the fortieth floor," Hackett said.

"Relax. I'm not using anything we haven't checked out. Have you got a handle on the MacLeod funeral-home story yet?"

"I haven't been able to locate the guy Greensheets says was there when it happened. Somebody named Angus Brody." Hackett wiped his balding forehead with a handkerchief.

"Find him before Monday, will you?"

"Sure," he said sarcastically. "The story is twenty-five years old, Eli. Even if I find him, you gotta check out what he says."

"Just track him down. What I use or don't use is my problem."

"As your lawyer I'm telling you—a congressman is a public figure, but he can sue the hell out of you if he can show reckless disregard—"

"Jeremy," Graves said, holding up his hand. "Just check it out. Okay?"

Hackett shook his head and turned for the door. "I'll do what I can, but I'm not taking responsibility for any of this."

Graves watched him leave. "What lawyer ever does?"

He picked up the telephone and hit a button. "The lawyer who represents those jailed Baby John Does. What's his name? . . . Arnold James. Have you reached him yet? I want an appointment with him as soon as possible."

He hung up and found the article he'd torn out of the newspaper. What better place could you find a straight arrow than in a bunch of people who'd rather go to jail than give the police their names?

Molly McCormick and Elliot Landy sat in a Wisconsin Avenue restaurant at a small candlelit table with a red-checkered tablecloth, the last couple in the room. In the eyes of the waiter, they were merely another young, handsome couple resting on the ladder of success after a day of heavy climbing. Two Washington professionals deeply in love with politics, ambition, and careers, but not each other.

On the other hand, the way this guy poured wine for her, and looked at her across the table . . .

Molly said, "How do you know somebody didn't try to transplant a new liver into him then take it out to cover it up?"

"It's what I told you before. The signature scar of a liver transplant is a large inverted T, which he didn't have. Besides, there's no evidence that there was anything wrong with his own liver."

"If it was gone when you opened him up, how do you know?"

"No yellow sclera—"

"Sclera?"

"The whites of the eyes. He didn't have jaundiced skin, either. Tox didn't turn up glucose imbalances indicating liver damage, and his heart wasn't enlarged or scarred from serious alcohol use. His veins weren't unusually clean, either."

"I don't follow."

"Alcohol is a solvent. Large amounts tend to dissolve plaque. It's also a vasoconstrictor, which breaks small veins. That's why drunks have red noses."

"Are you serious?"

"That's the way it is," he smiled.

"So what happened to his liver?"

He shrugged his shoulders. "Someone took it."

She considered the possibilities. "That's too creepy for words."

"I called every hospital in Washington that does liver transplants, and the donors are all accounted for. I even called the National Donor Registry to see if they might have an anonymous donation. Nothing came in unaccounted for."

"So let's think. What would you do with a stolen liver?"

He looked at her plate. "How was the Stroganoff?"

She rolled her eyes. "Thanks, Elliot. First you tell me I'm drinking antifreeze, then you tell me I'm a cannibal."

He loved getting under her skin.

She sat back and bounced the tip of her knife on the table. "What happened to the blood tests?"

"Everything fell within normal parameters except for a chemical compound we can't identify."

"What could it be?"

He shook his head. "A very small trace of something. It's not that unusual."

"Can't they do more tests?"

"Sure, but as I told you, without having some idea what you're looking for, it's a crapshoot. You can test for specific compounds and either confirm or eliminate them, but you can't start from nowhere and tell what you've got. So far, the lab can't tell if it's natural or synthetic."

"So use your imagination. What do you think?"

"If I use my imagination, I think it's time to pay the bill and go dancing."

Eli Graves tore the check from the voucher and blew on the ink to dry it, then handed it across the paper-strewn desk to Arnold James. The lawyer read it and looked up with a smile. "This is right nice of you, Mr. Graves."

"Sure it's enough?"

"Absolutely. It'll post bail for every Baby Doe on the list. They're brave people, but it's time they got outta jail and went home. Now, what can I do for you?"

Graves stood up. "Nothing," he said. He shook hands and started to leave, then stopped as if he'd had a second thought. "Actually, there is one thing you could do." He unfolded a sheet of paper from his pocket and handed it across the desk. The lawyer took it and put on his glasses. It was a piece of Red Rose Society stationery, with large typed letters:

LICENSED DEMOLITION WORKERS WANTED

To assist in clearing site for construction of the new Red Rose Society national headquarters in Queens, New York. Applicant screening 8:00 P.M., Friday, September 20, at Red Rose Society office, 1622 Queens Blvd.

Pro-lifers welcome!

"Give this to your clients, would you?" Graves said. "Who knows, maybe one or two of them can use a job."

"**S**top a minute, okay?"

"Okay."

"Here, Harley. Wipe off the sweat and turn over on your back. How are you feeling?"

"Nervous."

"Still not sleeping?"

"Not much."

"Some of that's from the nicotine withdrawal."

"That's not the problem. What's keeping me awake is—"

"Don't talk for a minute so I can hear your heart. . . ."

Silence. "That's cold."

"Sorry . . . How long have you had a heart murmur?"

"Since I was a kid. Rheumatic fever."

"Any problems with it?"

"Uh-uh. Listen, when are you going to tell me why you kidnapped me?"

"Lie still a minute. I want to feel something. . . . Does that hurt?"

"Not really."

"I want you to work your abs more. Understand?"

"Okay, but why?"

"Let me see your hands. . . . How'd you get these?"

"I always get blisters when I first start working out. Then they turn to calluses and everything's fine."

"I want you to scrub them up and use gloves tomorrow. . . . Open up. Say *ah*. Any unfilled cavities or abscesses?"

"Uh-uh."

"We'll take another look when we do the X rays. . . . Looks like you've got some pretty nice veins here."

"They're from working out. Listen, I want to know something—"

"Make a fist."

A sigh. "What do you need blood for? Did you take blood from Mel? I bet he took one look and passed out, didn't he? Is that what killed him?"

"We're not talking about Melvin Shivers, remember? Now relax.

Couple more tubes and we'll be finished. Why don't you tell me a story while we're waiting."

"What kinda story?"

"Whatever you want. Something about your life."

"Nothing to tell. Me and Mel grew up in Brooklyn, lived on the same block, went to the same church, chased the same girls. We did everything together."

"Including bombing the clinic."

An exhale. "I thought we dint have to talk about that." Silence. "Is that why you kidnapped me?"

"Hold still a minute."

"I served my time, you know. My corrections counselor says I don't have to talk about the bombing if I don't want to."

"Your corrections counselor is right." Silence. "I'm just curious about one thing."

"Uh-oh, here we go. Which one is it? How big was the bomb, or did we know somebody was inside when it went off?"

"I'm curious about why."

"Why we did it?" Silence. "We thought it was the right thing to do. The idea of all those innocent babies being killed . . . you know? It's against God's laws."

"You mean you killed someone for God?"

"Yeah, sort of. But not the way you make it sound."

"Why, how do I make it sound?"

"You make it sound like me and Mel were like, *totally* wrong."

Silence. "Okay, we're all set, you can sit up now. Hold that cotton on your arm a minute, and you can take your shower."

"And then what, more TV?"

"You can do anything you want. TV, videotapes, the library—this isn't a prison."

"This place is spookier than a prison. At least there you know what you're in for. Can I take a walk on the path again?"

"As long as you stay off the fence, sure. Are your wrists okay?"

"Yeah, they're okay. It's my butt that hit the ground."

"So now you know what a couple hundred volts feels like. I'll be back at six. Want anything special for dinner?"

"I don't know. Got any more corn on the cob?"

"Sure."

"When I was growing up, I was the only kid I knew who liked fresh vegetables. I don't know why."

"Maybe that explains why you're in such good shape. Physically. Just don't forget those abs, okay?"

"Wait a second! I answered your questions, now you gotta answer mine."

"What?"

"Just a simple yes or no, okay?"

"Harley, what's the question?"

"Are you people gonna kill me?"

Silence. "Look at me, Harley. . . . No, not there, up here, in my eyes. Now tell me. Do I look like somebody who wants to kill you?"

"**H**ow many of you have had experience with dynamite?" Graves was perched on the front edge of a table in a room at Red Rose Society headquarters. Of the seven men sitting on the folding chairs in front of him, four raised their hands. "Then you know it's dangerous."

"Not if you handle it right," a lanky man in the front row said. He sat in a slouch with his head cocked slightly to the side, an arm slung on the back of the chair next to him, his tan work boot bouncing up and down.

This guy was a possibility.

"What kind of experience have you had?" Graves asked.

"Me and my blaster's assistant here"—he nodded to a man in a checkered shirt—"we've probably worked ten demo sites."

"Least ten," the man in the checkered shirt said.

Graves looked at a third man, a short young fellow in his midtwenties with a light brown beard, horn-rim glasses, and a Dodgers baseball cap pulled down low on his forehead. He looked back at Graves but said nothing.

Graves handed the group some pamphlets and watched them read. "The contractor's name is printed on the back," he said. "A. J. Lyman Demolition. Won't hurt you to be pro-life, so take along one of these pamphlets when you apply. And don't forget. We're protesting at the Women's Health Center on Atlantic Avenue tomorrow afternoon, two o'clock. Come on out, give us a hand, pick up some literature, and show Lyman Demolition you were there."

The men stood up and meandered out, leaving behind the man with the beard, horn-rims, and Dodgers cap. He leaned forward in his chair with his forearms resting on his thighs and his hands between his knees. His fingers touched at the tips, expanding and contracting like a shark chewing chum.

"Any questions?" Graves asked him.

The man continued reading the pamphlet, as if he hadn't heard.

Graves walked toward him, curious. When he came within a few feet, he caught the musky-sweet scent of patchouli oil—a whiff so faint an ordinary nose might not have noticed, but to Graves's nose, as powerful as a jolt of electricity. His skin tightened as the smell shot him back to childhood San Francisco . . . a house stinking with patchouli . . . and a few years later, standing at a perfume counter in Macy's—smelling it—remembering the things Maxi, his so-called guardian, used to do to him—losing control—sweeping all the perfume bottles onto the floor.

Graves caught himself. "Enjoying the pamphlet?"

"I've been reading your stuff for some time," the fellow said. "I think I can be of help."

"Good," Graves said. "So we'll see you at the protest tomorrow?"

"Yeah, but that's not the kind of help I had in mind."

Graves looked confused.

"Remember Arnold James?" the young man asked. "The lawyer?"

Graves snapped his fingers. "You're one of the Baby John Does we bailed out of jail."

"Some of us still haven't given our names to the police."

"Good for you," Graves said.

This guy was a *definite* possibility.

"All of us made a pact not to tell," the fellow said. He put out his hand to introduce himself. "The name is—"

Graves raised his hand and stopped him. "Bad luck. Don't break the pact." He looked into the man's eyes to see if he'd put him off. The guy didn't blink. *A straight arrow.* Launch him and get out of the way.

He took the man into his office and called A. J. Lyman of Lyman Demolition to say he was recommending a demo man for a job—didn't know his name, but he couldn't miss him—midtwenties, beard, horn-rims, and a Dodgers cap. Lyman asked about his qualifications. Graves said he didn't know those, either, but he assumed they were okay, and even if they weren't perfect, he could be trained. One way or another, he wanted the guy on-site. He hung up. "You're all set."

The young man and Graves headed for the door. When they reached the bulletin board, Graves stopped. "Here's where we post upcoming demonstrations," he said. "What's happening in Congress, want ads, things like that." He watched as the man squinted to read the notices, scratching his beard. "Feel free to wander in and take a look any-time. You might find some things of interest. You know, some targets of opportunity." The phrase *targets of opportunity* made Graves blush; he was being too obvious about what he was soliciting. He waited for a reaction, but nothing registered on the man's face. He hadn't been too obvious. He'd been too subtle.

The young man finished reading the notices and walked to the door.

"Hey," Graves called after him. "Why don't you drop by a press conference I'm having a week from Monday?"

"What's it about?"

Graves decided to be more direct. "I'm announcing our list of the top ten baby killers in Congress. The guys we'd like to see destroyed." Not *destroyed at the polls.* Just *destroyed.*

"Who's on the list?"

"The guy at the top is the biggest problem we've got. Congressman Jack MacLeod. Know who he is?"

The young man nodded. "I've heard of him."

Graves waited for him to say more, wondering whether he understood what was wanted of him . . . wondering whether the two of them were brothers under the skin, gears in sync, archer and arrow. The man looked back at him, but Graves couldn't tell. His response was hidden under his beard. Either that or Graves didn't know how to read him.

It didn't occur to Graves that this straight arrow might have launched himself and was already in flight.

"I'll be there," the man said.

The young man reached his car, closed the door, and sat in the dark. After a few minutes he turned on the ceiling light and looked at himself in the rearview mirror. He scratched his beard and removed his baseball cap and glasses, placing them in a tattered leather briefcase on the passenger seat. Then he pulled out a three-ring binder and opened it up. It was bulging with green sheets of notebook paper, each filled with handwritten notes dating back for several years. He turned to a clean page at the back, wrote something, closed the binder, and placed it in the briefcase on top of newspaper clippings and press releases, all of which had one subject in common: Congressman Jack MacLeod.

Victoria sat at the counsel's table on the defendant's side, waiting for the hearing to begin, watching her pencil eraser tap up and down on a yellow legal pad. She glanced at her watch and took a deep breath. The air felt dense and spongy, absorbing everything in the room: a man's cough, a lawyer's twanging briefcase latch, her client's spirit. Everything was drawn upward and away, as if in Abner Titus's courtroom not even the laws of gravity could be trusted.

She stopped tapping. Zenobia was sitting next to her in a plain cotton dress and wire-rim glasses, looking older than her thirty-two years as she peered down over her fetal paunch at an open Bible resting in her lap. Her lips moved slightly to the words of the Twenty-seventh Psalm: " 'The Lord is my light and my salvation; whom shall I fear? The Lord is the stronghold of my life; of whom shall I be afraid?' "

Two of the answers sat across the aisle at the plaintiff's table: Jeremy Hackett, knight errant in shining armor for the pro-life movement or, as Victoria saw him, a balding hired gun in an iridescent suit. He doodled on a pad while his pro bono client, Levoyd Davis, slouched next to him in an open shirt, arm slung back, head cocked toward his wife. Like her, he, too, prayed for something he wanted—that the judge would force her to give him the "normal" child she'd failed to give with their retarded daughter.

A young woman—late twenties, sandy hair, serious face—entered from a side door, walked to the center of the courtroom, and took a chair in front of the judge's bench. Victoria shook her head and said something under her breath. Sitting behind her, Rachel leaned forward and whispered, "What's wrong?"

Victoria leaned back. "Know who that is?"

Rachel seemed momentarily startled by the question. "Why do you ask?"

"It's Titus's favorite law clerk, Pepper Loomis."

"Yes? So?"

"She's bad news."

Rachel sat back without saying anything.

The door at the front of the courtroom opened. "All rise!" a man's voice said, and everyone stood.

Judge Titus entered, black-clad and hulking. His face was large, his complexion sallow, his large eyebrows naturally furrowed, giving him the visage of a judge even when he was not judging. He lifted his tent-sized robe like a woman lifting a coat at a puddle and climbed the steps to his chair, lowering his imposing frame into his seat. The clerk of the court said, "Court is in session!" and everyone sat.

"Good morning," Titus said. He focused on a file Pepper Loomis handed up to him.

"Your Honor," Victoria said. "May I approach the bench?"

"There's no jury here, Counsel. Speak up."

"What I have to bring to the court's attention is highly personal and sensitive. If I may."

Titus motioned her forward. She and Jeremy Hackett walked to the bench as the court stenographer laid her hands in her lap and sat back in her chair.

"Your Honor," Victoria said, "this entire proceeding is based upon Mr. Davis's claim that he has certain rights as the father of the fetus. If it were not for that, we wouldn't be here."

"Go on," Titus said.

"We have an issue of fact that may make Mr. Davis's petition moot."

"What is that?"

"We don't know who the father is."

Hackett looked surprised. "What are you talking about?"

Victoria said, "The night she became pregnant, my client was raped. We don't know whether the father is her husband or the rapist."

Judge Titus turned to Hackett. "Do you know anything about this?"

"Nothing," Hackett said derisively. "If Mrs. Davis is claiming she was raped, why is she bringing it up at this late date? I don't believe we're obliged to buy a pig in a poke that's been lying in the weeds all this time."

"So to speak," Titus said.

Hackett looked at Victoria. "When did you say this supposedly happened?"

"This *did* happen the last time they had sexual intercourse," she said. "On April fifteenth. Tax day. When he failed to use a condom."

"Your Honor, may I have a moment to confer with my client?" Hackett said.

"I wish you would."

Hackett returned to his chair and talked quietly with Levoyd Davis while Victoria returned to hers and explained what was occurring.

"Oh Lord," Zenobia said. "Does this mean I have to talk about it?" Victoria put her hand on Zenobia's arm. "I can't do it," Zenobia said. Victoria saw Hackett walking to the bench and joined him there.

"Your Honor," Hackett said, "my client knows nothing about this alleged rape, and before his rights are to be denied on the grounds that he is not the father, I think we have a right to examine the witness."

"And ask her what?" Victoria asked.

"He says he was home the entire night in question. As for the condom, he says it broke."

"This is ridiculous," Victoria said.

"Then put your client on the stand and let her say so," Hackett said.

"Your Honor, I'm not going to allow my client to take the stand and be raped all over again. It would be unfair under any circumstance, but given that she has the right to abort regardless of who the father is, it'd be outrageous."

"That's not true," Hackett said. "My client is suing not only to protect his own rights, but the rights of the fetus regardless of who the father is. We believe the fetus is a person who can't be killed no matter who sired it."

Victoria pulled out her pocket calender. "Today is September twenty-second, which means April fifteenth was exactly twenty-two weeks and six days ago. The law gives her the right to abort until the twenty-fourth week."

"Your Honor," Hackett said, "we don't believe the question of when life begins has been settled. We think it begins at the moment of conception, but even if it's at the point of viability, medical technology is changing, making viability earlier and earlier." He paused. "We intend to show that this fetus is legally viable right now."

Titus looked at Victoria. "If you recall, I did ask you to address the question of when life begins, Ms. Winters."

"And I'm prepared to do so, but not without the cooperation of Mr. Hackett's client in determining paternity. Because if he's not the father, this case is moot."

"What do you want?" Hackett asked Victoria.

"A blood sample," Victoria said.

Looking burdened, Hackett pushed away from the bench and walked to his counsel's table to confer. Victoria stood at the bench until he returned.

"He doesn't want to do it, Your Honor," Hackett said.

"Why not?" Victoria asked.

"He says it would be an invasion of his body."

Victoria looked at the ceiling.

"I doubt there ever was a rapist," Hackett said, "but even if there was, it's immaterial."

"Immaterial?" Victoria said. *"Immaterial?"*

Titus held his hand up to Victoria and addressed Hackett. "I think you have to give up something here."

Hackett played with his pencil, thinking. "All right, all right. You can have your blood."

"And you waive any objections to my witness?" Victoria said. Hackett was aware that Rachel Redpath had given Judge Titus a new kidney and continued to monitor his health. He could have claimed a conflict if he'd wanted.

"No problem," he said, returning to his seat. He didn't want to disqualify Rachel Redpath. He wanted to destroy her on cross-examination.

Titus turned to Victoria. "Call your witness, please."

With her right hand in the air, Rachel was sworn to tell the truth and took a chair on the witness stand.

Speaking from memory, Victoria spent the next few minutes qualifying her as an expert. First in her class and summa cum laude at Washington University in St. Louis; top of her class at Chicago Medical School; a surgeon on a transplant team at the University of Pittsburgh, where she'd assisted in performing animal-to-human organ transplants, known as xenografts. In addition to her formal training in physiology, anatomy, and neurology, she had instructed herself in biochemistry, pharmacology, and molecular biology, applying her knowledge to the development of immunosuppressant drugs. While working in Pittsburgh, she had met Dr. Phoebe Chang, an expert in FK 506, the powerful immunosuppressant that prevented the body's rejection of transplanted baboon kidneys, among other organs. Together they had built a team of surgeons and researchers at George Washington University Medical Center. In addition to the experimental use of animal organs, in recent years they had focused on organs donated from anencephalic babies—infants born without their brains—which qualified her in fetal brain-stem development, making her the expert Victoria wanted on the question of when life begins.

Their friendship had started ten years earlier in an unlikely place for two workaholics: a spa in Arizona. The trip had been a thirtieth birthday present from Victoria's parents, while for Rachel—forty-two years old at the time, working too hard, and smoking too much—it had been a heal-thyself prescription from her personal physician. Although the two women both lived in Washington, D.C., they had never met until their first day of vacation when, lagging red-faced and wheezing on a mountain hike, they'd stopped to sit on a rock and rest their aching, out-of-shape bodies. Within minutes they found themselves swearing off all forms of poison—cigarettes, coffee, sugar, buttered bagels, dirty air, chocolate, computer screens, compulsive work—and then, having caught their breaths, ex-changed who-are-we-kidding looks and cracked up. They had liked each other instantly.

In the warm, surreal atmosphere of the spa, their friendship blos-somed easily. At the Wake-up Stretch for Novice Stretchers they dis-cussed where they'd grown up and what kinds of work they did. At Power Walking for Intermediate Walkers they discussed men and poli-tics. At Body Sculpture they talked about women and their bodies, and lying covered in volcanic-ash mud, they talked about law, judges, and face-lifts. At Incredible Abdominals they discussed medicine, diets, and estrogen, and during yoga they considered God's gender and Victo-ria's long nails, which Rachel, sporting a surgeon's short manicure, en-vied. But it was not until the sauna, sitting naked and sweating, that they finally opened up on the subjects that measured true friendship: their se-cret ambitions, their private lusts, their fantasies about how to make a difference, their terror of cellulite. After that, it wasn't long before they were able to finish each other's sentences as easily as an old married couple.

On the last day of the week, feeling rested and strong, they decided to conquer the mountain trail that had defeated them on their first day. Around noon they found the rock where they had first dropped out and, feeling satisfied with themselves, decided to return to the spa by hiking directly down the mountainside. They got lost. An hour later, having reached the desert floor, they stood in the suarho and bramble bush, tired and dusty, legs scratched, unable to see the building or, for that matter, anything else except twisted scrub trees and red earth.

Rachel had brought a small plastic bottle of Evian water, which they had shared as they wandered in the heat, cursing their urban ineptitude, whistling in the graveyard with not-so-funny one-liners, looking for scorpions, speculating whether rattlesnakes really gave warnings, be-coming fatigued and dehydrated. Finally, at about four o'clock, they cleared a space and sat on the ground, sunburned and weary. And a little worried. If they couldn't find their way back before nightfall, who knew what trouble they were in? Dangerously low temperatures, meat-eating scavengers, poisonous things that stung—they were not pleased with the possibilities.

Rachel held up the plastic bottle of Evian and handed it to Victoria, who drank one swallow and handed it back. Rachel drank the last mouthful and the two of them sat with each other, lost in the desert.

Resting in the shimmering heat, they talked long and personally. Finally, eager to get back, they estimated their position and once again began trekking, using the sun as a compass until they had made their way to the spa.

They arrived in time for the six o'clock sitting, which they skipped in favor of showers and naps. Later that night, sore but satisfied, they met at a large map in the hallway and reconstructed their circular hike. Afterward, sitting in the lounge with the first wine they'd had in a week, they congratulated themselves on their self-rescue and celebrated their friendship. After returning to Washington, they promptly lost track of high-fiber diets and low-impact aerobics, but not of each other. Now, some ten years later, they remained the best of friends, neither of whom saw an Evian label without remembering their desert walk.

Having finished qualifying her, Victoria stepped back to give Rachel a moment to collect herself. She found her to be a formidable witness, particularly during cross-examination. (A hostile lawyer, giving up in defeat, was once heard to say, "Her opinion seems to count more than other people's facts.") Her only weakness on the stand was a tendency to become flippant, especially when she was tired. Unfortunately, this morning she had been awake for twenty hours, engaged in a transplant. Knowing that Rachel should have been home asleep, Victoria had thanked her warmly—and warned her about her impatience when she was tired. Both assumed the problem was under control.

After a brief pause, Victoria asked one question: "When does life begin?"

"Human life begins when the brain stem is sufficiently formed to regulate the brain and the rest of the organs of the body." She spoke in a dignified, restrained voice. "This usually occurs in the twenty-fourth to twenty-sixth week of pregnancy."

Victoria hovered silently a moment, dramatizing the authority with which Rachel had testified. Then she turned, walked to her chair, and sat down. "Nothing further, Your Honor," she said.

Rachel leaned forward to rise from her chair, but Hackett reached his feet first.

"Before you step down, Miss Redpath, I have just one or two short questions. If you don't mind." He laid his yellow pad on the table and, with a pencil in hand, walked to the witness stand as slowly as he could without being absurd.

"Now, Miss Redpath—"

" 'Doctor' will do fine," she said.

"Very good. Now, Dr. Redpath, would you mind telling us once more your opinion of when life begins? It was such a short answer."

"Human life begins with the formation of the brain stem, which occurs in about the twenty-fourth week of pregnancy."

"You say *human* life begins then. Is that to be distinguished from other animal life?"

"Yes."

"And you make this distinction for what reason?"

"It's my understanding that this case is about humans, not animals." Hackett smiled but said nothing. "On the other hand," she said, "if you want to talk about primates, I'll be happy to do so. I work with them all the time."

"Thank you for that permission, Doctor. Now, why do you look to the brain to decide when life begins? Why not, say, the heart?"

"The heart is a pump, that's all. Most organisms have a pump—dogs, cats, snakes, lizards. Even lawyers." She heard someone in the audience snicker but didn't move, fearing Victoria would catch her eye. She could feel her glowering.

"Don't be too sure about that," Hackett said coldly, and Rachel straightened up. He paced a moment, and stopped. "What's so special about the brain?"

"The brain is what distinguishes us from the algae we evolved from," she said. "It is the most important among many unique features of human beings. It not only regulates basic body functions, but our behavior, our morals, our creativity, our spirituality—everything that makes us special among living organisms. In biblical terms, it is what infuses us with a soul."

Hackett pulled his lips down at the sides in a skeptical look. "Then why do you suppose we've venerated the heart instead of the brain throughout recorded history, including in the Bible?"

"I suppose the people who write books are like everybody else," Rachel said. "They prefer romance to science."

"Really," Hackett said, bouncing his pencil in his palm. He walked to the empty jury box. "And is that one of your expert opinions, too?"

"No," she said. "It's merely an observation. But wouldn't you agree?"

Rachel had a way of asking questions of cross-examining lawyers and getting away with it.

"I think we were talking about the heart," Hackett said.

"Yes. Well, it has enormous literary value, but if you're undertaking a medical or scientific exploration of life, the heart doesn't do much that's uniquely human. That lies in the brain."

"And before the brain forms, what status do you assign to the fetus?"

"Before that the fetus is an unformed organism like any other unformed organism, unable to think, control itself, or survive without its host."

"In other words, not yet 'viable.' "

"That's right."

"Which you say arises in the twenty-fourth week of gestation."

"After the twenty-fourth week, right."

"And until then, it's no different from, say, a dog or a cat?"

"That's correct. Except for its potential."

"Its potential?"

"It has the potential of becoming a human being, where a dog and a cat do not." She appeared taken with another thought. "At least not yet." She blushed slightly, as if once again she'd said something she shouldn't have.

Hackett hovered a moment, looking as if he might pursue a glib answer. He let it pass, and Rachel looked relieved.

Hackett said, "Wouldn't you say that this potential for human life defines the fetus as something important even before the brain stem forms? Before it is viable?"

"Absolutely."

"And shouldn't this potential to become a human being be protected so that it might ultimately be realized in a birth?"

"Certainly," Rachel said. "As long as one condition is met."

"And what is that?"

"The mother agrees."

Hackett walked back to his table with his eyes on the floor, mind churning. He stopped and turned back to Rachel.

"You say the mother must agree. But what about the fetus? What would it say if it could speak?"

"That begs the question, Mr. Hackett. If the fetus could speak it would be viable, which means its life should be protected. Before then, the mother decides the fetus's fate, just as she decides whether or not to become pregnant in the first place."

Hackett walked to the front of the bench. "Perhaps we'll come back to whose decision that really is, Miss Redpath. Right now I'm still interested in why you wouldn't protect all life, even *potential* human life. Could it be that you think there's just too much of it?"

Rachel sighed. "Well, it's true that overpopulation is a problem."

Victoria tried to catch Rachel's eye with a frown to tell her not to let Hackett lead her down an irrelevant path, but Rachel was staring at Hackett.

"Tell us how, in your opinion, there is too much potential life?"

"It's the way the species evolved. Eggs are plentiful. Sperm is plentiful. You probably have enough right there"—she pointed at his crotch—"to make forty-five million babies right now."

Someone in the audience laughed, interrupting another comment Rachel mumbled but Hackett didn't hear.

"How's that again?" he asked.

"Nothing," she said.

"Please. Tell us what you said. I couldn't hear you."

Rachel hesitated. "I said, 'Then again, maybe not.' "

Hackett reddened as he looked at his pad. "You were right to characterize that crack as 'nothing.' "

"Your Honor—" Victoria said, but Titus waved her down.

Hackett folded his arms and continued. "So you think there is too much potential life on earth."

"Let me put it this way," Rachel said, staring at the ceiling. "At the rate we're making babies, by the end of the next century the earth will look like a football stadium on Super Bowl Sunday."

"You don't believe that by 2100 there will be space colonization?"

Rachel leaned forward. "Actually, I've never thought that much about it. But now that you mention it, maybe you've hit on a solution to the entire abortion controversy."

"And that is?"

"If you'll support a woman's right to abort until we set foot on Mars, I'll support antiabortion laws the day it happens."

Hackett smiled and dismissed her answer with a shake of his head.

"Dr. Redpath," Judge Titus interrupted, "the judicial system is not the place where deals are made."

"Sorry, Your Honor. Whatever you call plea bargaining and settling cases is what I had in mind."

Titus popped a small pill into his mouth.

"Your Honor," Rachel said kindly, "that's the second time I've noticed you taking something. May I ask what?"

"No, you may not," he said.

"I've been noticing your skin tone, too," she said.

"Thank you, Doctor," Titus said. "I've scheduled an appointment for a checkup."

"If I were you, I'd keep it," she said.

"May we continue?" Hackett said. "So to summarize, you feel that potential life is unprotected because there is too much of it, that human life is going to overrun the planet, and that abortion is the only way to save the world?"

"Those are your words, not mine," she said.

"Would you summarize your position in your own words then?"

"Prosecuting a woman for aborting a fertilized egg is about as sensible as prosecuting a man for having a wet dream."

Hackett stopped beating his pencil against his palm.

"Tell me something, Doctor, what is it in your background that makes you so all-fired concerned about mothers?"

Rachel shifted in her chair. "I'm a doctor, Mr. Hackett. I've seen all kinds of death and suffering and as far as I'm concerned, forcing a woman to stay pregnant is as outrageous as forcing her to nurture a cancer. It's as if society and the fetus conspire to take her hostage, not just for nine months, but for life. If she were a prisoner somewhere in Beirut, we'd do everything we could to set her free, including killing the kidnappers if we could find them. In fact, I suspect some of your pro-life clients would be happy to pull the trigger themselves. But when it comes to a pregnant woman, we calmly sit here and debate her survival as if the hostage takers have all the rights and her only chance of freedom is to risk her life on a butcher's table. It's barbaric."

Hackett stood in front of her and smiled. "Well, that's all very dramatic, Dr. Redpath, but the question remains, is it accurate?"

"You've never been pregnant," she said.

"That's true," he answered. "Have you?"

The question took Rachel by surprise. "Let's just say I know it's accurate." Her cheeks remained flushed.

Victoria rose to her feet. "Objection, Your Honor," she said. "We're going well beyond the bounds of expert opinion."

"We went well beyond the bounds of expert opinion a long time ago," Titus said. "I'm inclined to give a lot of latitude on this, but I think it's time to draw some lines."

"Your Honor," Hackett said, "the witness brought up the subject of personal pregnancy, not me."

"True, but since she can get pregnant and you can't, her comment was rhetorical, while yours is probative. The question is irrelevant. Objection sustained."

Hackett flapped his arms at his sides again and returned to his table. "Your Honor, could we take a five-minute break?"

The audience rustled, and Rachel stepped off the witness stand to join Victoria and Zenobia. They walked out of the courtroom into the hallway.

"I told you not to get cute," Victoria said without looking at Rachel.

"Lighten up," Rachel said back.

"What's all this mean?" Zenobia asked. Her question reminded Victoria and Rachel that they still had a client here.

Victoria said, "Eventually, Judge Titus or another judge will obey the law and give you permission to abort."

Zenobia looked confused. "How can a judge not obey the law?"

"Do you have a few hours?" Rachel said. She turned to Victoria and said, "What *is* the answer to that?"

Victoria needed to construct one. She looked at the Bible in Zenobia's hands. "How could David disobey God?" she asked.

"Very *good*," Rachel said. She touched Zenobia on the arm lightly, then, looking serious, drew Victoria out of Zenobia's earshot. "Is Titus going to give you a decision today?"

"I doubt it. Not today or tomorrow."

"When?"

"Not until he knows it's too late."

The jeweler looked over his shoulder to make sure no one was watching. "I could get in trouble for this." He lifted a fine gold chain with a coin twirling at the bottom and laid it on a black velvet pad. "Is this what you had in mind?"

Jack picked up the silver dollar he'd received from the taxi driver a couple of weeks before and examined it under a magnifying glass. To the right of Susan B. Anthony's cameo profile, next to her lips, the jeweler had engraved the letter *V*, as if she were saying, "Victoria." The coin had been polished and framed in a thin, gold rim with a small loop for a chain.

"That's it," Jack said. He wrote a check while the jeweler found a velvet box.

"You sure you don't want a diamond ring?" the jeweler asked. "I can tell you from experience, Congressman, most women prefer a diamond ring."

"I know," Jack said, picking up the box. "That's the point."

He stood in the middle of the parking lot with his hand shading his eyes like Christopher Columbus standing on deck, searching for land. On one side of the asphalt he saw the rear entrance to the Atlantic Avenue Women's Health Center; on the opposite side, fifty yards away, were the backyards of small frame houses circled by rusting chain-link fences and tall, dying weeds.

He pulled off his glasses and lifted his Dodgers baseball cap, wiped his beard with his sleeve, and headed toward the clinic . . . past clumps of people assembling for the rally, past the flatbed truck that would serve as a temporary stage. When he was twenty feet from the clinic's rear entrance, he stopped, pushed up his cap, and looked up at the roof.

Help me, Lord, he prayed. I can't do this alone.

He took a step backward to see the vent pipes on the roof and a voice yelled, "Hey!" Looking down, he found himself standing on the word MURDER, next to ABORTION IS, on a hand-painted sign. A man in his midtwenties, on his knees, was nailing it to a stick. The man in the Dodgers cap stepped off the poster, saying, "Sorry."

"No problem," the other man said. "You here for the rally?"

"Yeah. Sort of."

The sign maker stood up and extended his hand enthusiastically. "Billy Bannister," he said.

They shook hands. "Benedict," the man in the Dodgers cap said. "Alfred Benedict."

"So what do they call you? Alfred or Al?"

"Neither," he said. "They call me Eggs."

Bannister thought a moment, and smiled. "How'd you let them get away with that?"

Eggs Benedict shrugged.

"Where you from?" Bannister asked.

"Everyplace. And no place. What do you do for a living?"

"Construction," Bannister said. "When there's work."

Eggs nodded sympathetically.

The rally got under way with Eli Graves climbing onto the truck and welcoming everyone through a squealing sound system. The crowd set-

120

tled down and listened. Eggs Benedict and Billy Bannister continued talking about jobs, families, and abortion, discussing their mutual mystification about how any civilized society could permit it.

The crowd roared, capturing their attention.

"This murder factory," Graves said into the mike, pointing at the clinic, "is open for business right now. We can talk about the evils of baby killing all we want, but in the end it comes down to what we're willing to *do* about it!" Everyone cheered. "So—what are we gonna *do* about it?"

People joined hands and started to sing, forming a line around the building.

The pro-choice counterdemonstrators behind the barricades went wild.

Police bullhorns blurted their warnings to the pro-life picketers that obstructing access to the facility was a violation of the law.

Eggs and Bannister watched from a distance. "Hey, let's join 'em!" Bannister said. He started for the picket line, but Eggs grabbed his arm, stopping him. "What's the matter?" Bannister asked.

Eggs's eyes wandered over the crowd. "I've already done the protest thing. I just got out of jail. Let's do something that'll make a real difference."

He pulled Bannister away from the demonstrators. When they reached the far edge of the asphalt, he turned and walked along the parking lot perimeter until the crowd noise had faded in the background. Something in one of the adjoining backyards caught his eye.

He stopped opposite a little swing set and plastic swimming pool gathering fall leaves and gazed at them wistfully, as if his nose were pressed against an imaginary window. What was it like to live here? he wondered. What child took his afternoon nap in one of these little houses, safe and secure, soothed by the drone of a passing airplane, the wheezing of bus brakes, the rhythmic clacking of dishes being washed and dried in the kitchen? He longed for it so much it made his throat ache. What mother stood in the living room ironing a shirt, watching a soap opera, listening to the melodrama drift like a blanket over her sleeping child? What father dozed on Sunday afternoons, snoring in a threadbare easy chair with the sports section spilling from his lap, serenaded by the voice of a football announcer and the cheering of a stadium crowd? What was it like to be safe? What was it like to be wanted? What was it like to be loved?

The skin under his beard itched so badly he could hardly stand it. Heat blossomed on his cheeks, giving off his trademark scent of patchouli.

"What are we looking for?" Bannister asked.

"You need a job, right?" Eggs asked absentmindedly.

"Yeah?" Bannister said. "So?"

Eggs didn't answer. He started walking again, continuing along the edge of the parking lot until he found something else he was looking for: a narrow path between two small houses, a neighborhood shortcut running from the sidewalk in front to the parking lot in back, and from there to the A&P located next to the abortion clinic. Eggs's eyes followed the footpath out to the street. Then he turned and squinted across the parking lot at the clinic.

"Ever done any demolition work?" he asked.

S itting against a wood-paneled wall and partly hidden by a plant, Abner Titus dined alone at a table for two. His second plate of pasta—he ate no meat, his concession to good health—had been covered with a pesto sauce containing more fat than a sirloin steak. Around him were couples chatting, dealmakers dealing, people eating, drinking, connecting. Feeling like a loner at a grade-school dance—not quite part of the party, but not unwelcome, either—he enjoyed being near the noise and the laughter. Having finished his dinner, he was reading a book under a small table lamp with its shade tilted back like a cocked hat, spreading a triangle of yellow light onto the table. He lifted the tome and drew it near, careful to hold its tattered leather jacket in place. *A History of the Common Law in the Victorian Age, Vol. II*, the cover read.

He peered at the words through his reading glasses, as engrossed in the book as if it were a suspense novel. A waiter approached with a high-stemmed martini glass on a tray and set the drink down quietly, out of the way. Without looking, Titus said, "Thank you, Dallas." The man said, "Judge," and left.

After reading another page, he turned the book facedown and pulled his drink closer. He gazed into the pool of gin and vermouth—he preferred his after-dinner martini not too dry—stirring it lazily with a speared olive, a boy poking at a summertime puddle with a stick. After a moment he lifted the olive to his mouth, pulled it off the toothpick, and chewed it slowly, imagining the conversations he saw taking place around the room: over there, a husband and wife celebrating an anniversary; over there, a lawyer plotting strategy with her client; in the corner, a bureaucrat leaking secrets to a reporter; across the room, a father soothing the brow of an anxious son. *An anxious son.*

He washed down a salted almond with a gulp of gin and pulled his father's ornate gold watch from his vest pocket, flipped it open, and closed it with a snap. He reached for his book.

The waiter returned and said, "Anything else, Judge?"

"No, Dallas, I'm going to finish my drink and go home. It's getting late."

"Only for us old married folks," the waiter said, smiling.

"How *is* your family?" Titus asked.

"Fine, Judge, just fine. And yours?"

Titus patted his book. "This is my family. This and Blackstone. But he takes care of himself like a good cat."

The waiter peered at the imposing leather book jacket. "Mm, mm, mm," he said. "How many years does it take to understand a book like that, Judge?"

Titus blushed. "It's not as difficult as it looks."

The waiter walked away, leaving Titus with his martini and his treatise. As he lifted the book to turn it over, it slipped out of its jacket and landed on the floor, a few feet away. He pushed his chair back and reached for it quickly, reddening his face with the effort. After returning it to the table, he placed it back in its cover.

He pulled his vest down over his stomach, touched the knot on his tie to be sure it was straight, and opened the lemon-scented towelette Dallas had left on the table. Dabbing it on his forehead and cheeks, he cooled and composed himself. A glance through the palm leaves at the other patrons, and once again he felt dignified, judicial.

After a swallow of gin, he opened the leather jacket and continued reading his book, *The Shining* by Stephen King.

Victoria set the telephone receiver into its cradle and looked at Rachel. "That was the lab. They completed the blood typing. Levoyd's not the father."

Rachel slumped.

Victoria stood up and laid her shoulder bag on the desk, getting ready to leave. They were in Kathy Keenan's office at the Capitol Hill Women's Clinic, where Rachel was conferring with someone on a medical matter. "Not only that," Victoria said, "but I found out half an hour ago that the clerk's office lost my appeal papers."

"Has that ever happened before?"

"Yes, but something about this one reeks." She tossed her telephone directory and diary into her bag. "I've decided to go get Zenobia and bring her back here for an abortion."

"Sit down, Vick," Rachel said. "I'm not letting you risk a contempt citation over this." Victoria leaned her back against the wall. "Just sit down and think this through a minute."

"I have," Victoria said. "I'm not going to let Titus get by with this. I'm tired of watching this woman be destroyed. She can't work, she's depressed, her daughter's scared to death and doesn't know why. And for what?"

Rachel rested her hand on Victoria's arm. "You need a vacation," she said. Victoria closed her eyes. "Wait a few more days, Vick. If the court hasn't ruled by then, fine. We'll figure out something."

She looked at Rachel. "What if Titus rules in favor of Levoyd?"

"Now that we know he's not the father, how can he?"

"In loco parentis. Hackett says he's representing the fetus, regardless of who the father is. Titus didn't say he wouldn't entertain that."

"It's nutty," Rachel said, "but it's still not the end of the world. You'll reverse him on appeal, Zenobia will 'have her abortion, and Titus will have handed us an outrageous opinion we can use against him if he's ever nominated to the Supreme Court."

"Very strategic, Ray."

"I think so," she said earnestly. "Unless you prefer to consider alternatives."

Victoria glared at her a moment, then looked away and opened the door. "Sorry, Ray, but I've made up my mind. Tell Kathy I'll have Zenobia back here in an hour."

Zenobia Davis opened the door to her apartment. Victoria was shocked at the deep circles under her eyes.

"Miss Winters, what are you doing here?"

"Good news," Victoria said, trying to sound honest. "The judge ruled you can have your abortion. Pack your things for an overnight. We're leaving now."

"Lord, I'm not ready. Sarah's not back from school yet. Why don't you come in and sit a minute?"

"We don't have time," Victoria said. She saw more confusion on Zenobia's face.

"When did this happen?" Zenobia asked.

"Just a while ago," Victoria said, avoiding her eyes. "Now hurry."

Zenobia stood still. "What made the judge change his mind?"

Victoria stepped inside the door and closed it. "We got the results of the blood test back, Zenobia. Levoyd's . . . not the father."

Zenobia's face fell and her arms embraced her stomach. She backed up to a stuffed chair and sat down. Victoria went to her and laid her hand on her shoulder. "It just makes the decision that much easier." Zenobia said nothing. "Why don't you pack your things?"

Zenobia rose slowly and disappeared into her bedroom. Victoria walked downstairs and arranged Sarah's overnight stay with the baby-sitter, making sure the woman said nothing to anyone about Zenobia's whereabouts. In a few minutes Zenobia came down the steps carrying a canvas bag of toiletries, a cotton dress on a hanger, and her Bible. Victoria looked around the area to see if anyone was watching, another concession to guilt. Then she walked Zenobia to the car.

They turned into the Capitol Hill Clinic garage and parked next to a cement column. Victoria left the car first, looking around cautiously, and escorted Zenobia to the basement elevator. Once they were in the building, they took the elevator directly to the first floor. Rachel was there waiting—with an unhappy face.

"There's been a small development," she said.

"What?"

"You know Titus's law clerk? Pepper Loomis?"

"Yeah?"

"She just called."

Victoria looked puzzled. "About what?"

"She said if we're thinking about helping Zenobia Davis obtain an abortion before the judge rules, we should remember the penalties for the willful violation of a court order."

"You're kidding." Victoria was stunned. "Who tipped her off?"

Rachel shrugged. "She didn't say."

Victoria looked dumbfounded. "How'd she know to call here?" Rachel glanced toward Zenobia as if to tell Victoria that she needed to tend to her client.

Zenobia said, "I thought the judge already said I could have the operation?"

Blushing, Victoria took her by the arm and walked her to a waiting-room chair and eased her into it. "I'll get to the bottom of this," she said, and returned to Rachel. "Jesus, I just totally blew my credibility with her."

"Not necessarily. I'll talk to her."

Victoria shook her head in disbelief.

Rachel said, "How do you think Titus found out?"

"I don't know. But I'm awfully suspicious."

"Could he have guessed?"

She exhaled. "I've had clients who've aborted while they were under an injunction, yeah. Maybe he suspected the same thing was going to happen here and made a call." She sat down. "I don't know. God, I'm sick of men interfering in women's lives."

"Then why not do something about it? Something meaningful."

"All right, Ray. Stop."

Rachel watched her fume a moment, then sat down beside her and put a hand on her knee. "Sooner or later you're going to have to stop avoiding me on this."

"I'm not avoiding anything. I know what you want, and I love you dearly, but this is *not* the time or place to talk about it."

Rachel raised her eyebrows, took a breath, and let out a sigh. "All in good time."

Victoria looked over at Zenobia, who rose slowly from her chair and picked up her canvas bag, dress, and Bible.

Rachel walked over to her. "Don't let any of this scare you," she said. "And don't blame Victoria. She was only trying to help you do what the law says you have the right to do."

Zenobia shook her head, disappointed, slightly stooped, dry-eyed. "I want to go home."

Rachel placed her arms around her and held her—and whispered in her ear. "I have a way to solve everything. Just be calm and trust me when I call, okay? And don't tell anyone. Not even your lawyer."

Victoria lay on the sofa in the living room, mildly attentive to the eleven o'clock news, talking to Jack through the kitchen door. He had come home a few minutes before, loosened his tie, and was prowling through the refrigerator assembling dinner. Herring bits in mustard sauce, Cinnamon Snax cereal, a handful of Hershey's Kisses, and for nutritional balance, a raw carrot, slightly dehydrated and unwashed.

Victoria knew what he was up to, but she was too tired to object. She told him what had happened in court with Zenobia Davis and said she would probably have to file another interim appeal in the morning. Then she scrolled through other news of the day—a staff change; a trial that her codirector, Sylvia Kingston-Brown, had won; a telephone call from her father in California.

Jack walked to the living-room sofa with a can of beer in hand, lifted her leg to sit, and laid her feet on his lap. Touching her muscles, he could feel the tension; another night of preoccupation and depression lay ahead. Another night when he, too, was too tired to do much about it.

The *Know Yourself* segment on the news talked about cholesterol.

"See that?" she said. "If you don't do something about your diet, you're going to croak from clogged arteries."

He set the can down and massaged her feet. "I'll cut back on the carrots."

She groaned. "I'm going to make an appointment for you to have your blood tested, okay?"

"When?"

"I'll ask Kathy Keenan to draw it at the Capitol Hill clinic. You can walk over during a break."

"Whatever," he said, massaging her ankles.

They watched the program in silence. He worked his massaging hands up to her calves with the local news, reached her knees with the football scores. No response. In the old days, they would have been upstairs before the weather report, but not tonight. He continued massaging anyway.

"This business with Titus has really got you down, hasn't it?" he said.

"This case, that case. They're all becoming the same."

"We need to get away for a few days," he said.

She didn't object, but didn't agree, either.

"What did your father want?" he asked.

She took a breath, instinctively fortifying herself. "He wants to have dinner when he's in Washington next week." A car commercial appeared with the automobile moving sideways, in slow motion, through a puddle of water. "Is that all right with you?"

"Fine," he said. "How about you?"

"Sure. I'd like to see him."

In a few minutes the news ended and he squeezed the top of her thighs. He stretched and said he was heading upstairs to the horizontal bar and bed.

She said she'd be up in a minute, and closed her eyes.

He turned off the television set and all but one lamp. Even though she said she was coming shortly, he pulled a cotton quilt over her, tucked it in, and gave her a long kiss on her neck. She smiled and ran her fingers through his hair.

After he'd gone upstairs, she opened her fingers and searched for a small rise in the palm of her hand. A smoothness, a hardness. Whatever sign remained. There was nothing there. It had been too many years ago.

She turned onto her side and snuggled her head into the sofa pillow. *Try to remember Daddy the way he was when you were both innocent . . . sunny days at the beach when you were a ten-year-old and he was a colossus who strode the earth.*

Forget graduation day. Try to remember that.

Victoria stood in front of her full-length mirror practicing her high-school graduation speech one last time.

"And so, in this time of turmoil in America, from body bags in Vietnam to the smoking ruins of Watts, we, the Class of 1972, have a golden opportunity."

She paused to check her cap and gown and the dress beneath, deciding black was right after all. Other class speakers would be wearing white and giving sentimental talks about coming-of-age, fun stuff laced with inside jokes and class-clown anecdotes. That was fine, but as valedictorian she had an obligation to speak with a gravity appropriate to the times. Black helped. She looked down at the text, found her place, and faced the mirror, continuing the speech from memory.

"Fate has made us a phoenix to rise from the ashes and restore our lost principles of peace and equality."

She glanced at her watch; almost time to go. Hurry through the last few sentences.

"And so, my fellow classmates, let us dare to be different. Let us follow Mahatma Gandhi and Martin Luther King and eschew violence and hate even when they are used against us. For if we remember that the end can never justify the means, we will be the class that began the *real* revolution that helped create a new world."

She looked for a pencil, struck out *eschew*, and wrote in *give up*. Then she underlined *the end can never justify the means*, the point of her speech, the heart of her philosophy. She checked her hair, grabbed the speech, and ran out the door, robe fluttering. In a moment her mother followed her down the marble staircase, high heels clicking on the steps.

"Where's Daddy?" Victoria asked, dancing anxiously in the foyer.

"He's finishing up with a patient. He'll come in his car."

Victoria went slack-jawed and rolled her eyes. A plastic surgeon in Beverly Hills was always with a patient.

"Stop worrying," her mother said. "We've got a whole hour before the ceremony begins. He wouldn't dream of being late for this."

Victoria stuck her arm inside her mother's and walked toward the three-car garage. Hurrying along, she stepped on the hem of her gown, tearing it loose. She told her mother to go ahead, she'd find a roll of tape and meet her at the car.

She ran down the palm-lined breezeway to her father's three-room clinic. The back door led directly into the examining room; she knew not to use it when a patient was there, but today he'd understand, considering the circumstances.

She knocked gently. No answer. She knocked again and cautiously tried the knob. The door opened—he hadn't locked it after she'd been there that morning, looking for cotton balls. She stuck her head inside. The lights were on.

"Daddy?" she said softly, but there was no answer.

She walked in. Everything was quiet. He must have been attending his patient in the adjoining office.

She laid her speech on the counter by the door, pulled a strip of tape off a roll, and hemmed her gown. As she replaced the roll, she saw a scalpel on a stainless-steel tray. She picked it up and looked at its blade gleaming under the light. It felt good. Powerful. She remembered how he'd taught her to hold it in her fingers and make the first cut, applying it to skin the way a painter applies a brush—deliberately, decisively.

When she was ten he'd showed her pictures of various operations and helped her practice her technique on chicken breasts, a dead squirrel, the Thanksgiving turkey. She'd taken to it instantly, fascinated with the beauty and the gore, imagining a day when she'd become a surgeon, too, just like Beverly Hills' most prominent one, the "face doctor to the stars." He'd always be a giant in her eyes, a rich man who didn't count money, a heavyweight who saved children from burning houses. Missing him would be the hardest thing about going to college.

She looked at her watch; her mother was waiting. She hurried back to the door, laid the scalpel on the table, pulled the door shut behind her, and with one hand on her mortarboard, ran down the hall to the garage. The Mercedes was waiting, engine idling.

She jumped in and they drove around the tree-lined driveway to the street. As they headed toward the auditorium she practiced her speech in a quick, monotone mumble. Hesitating over a phrase, she looked down at her lap for help.

"Oh, my God. I forgot my speech!"

Her mother looked unconcerned. "Sounds to me like you don't need it."

"Yes I do!" She checked her watch. "We have to go back!"

Her mother made a U-turn at a filling station and headed back. When they pulled onto the garage apron, Victoria jumped out, ran into the house, and bolted down the breezeway to the examining room. She grabbed the doorknob and entered.

And froze.

Her father was standing at the end of the examining table with his back turned three quarters toward her, his hands in front of him, holding something. He lifted his head to see who'd come in, surprised, mouth open. The expression on his face confused and frightened her.

"Daddy?"

She took a step forward and saw a young woman in front of him on her knees, head at zipper level, her mouth connected to something pink by a crystalline strand that sagged in the middle like a suspension bridge. The woman looked up at Victoria with eyes more glazed than surprised, lips pale and puffy, hair disheveled by the hands of the world's greatest surgeon—the perfect, loving hands that held his wife in bed, had cradled his daughter as a baby, bathed her as a child, hugged her as a girl. The woman turned her face away.

Victoria looked at her father. His face was turned down, red and sweating; he fumbled to tuck in his shirt and zip up.

She felt the shock of it roll in, drying her mouth and heating her cheeks. A steel plate clogged her throat, holding down an eruption. She stood perfectly still, transfixed by the Jekyll–Hyde transformation taking place before her eyes. The giant she'd always known was shrinking to someone small and weak. A rich man counting pennies, a heavyweight shooting dope.

Then came a moment as unexpected as the first.

All during her childhood the words had been right—*sugar and spice, everything nice, Daddy's little girl*—and yet, somehow they had always seemed slightly insincere. *Suspicious.* There were even moments during adolescence, slightly crazy ones, when she fantasized that she, alone, had been chosen to understand some vast, awful secret—a diabolical plot that affected little girls, someone poisoning the milk they suckled at birth and the air they breathed at puberty, contaminating them with a pink, sweet organism that insinuated itself into their heads on the wings of insincere, loving words, oozing a message into their brains so dark and powerful she knew it had to have been authored by God Himself: *You are defective. You are inferior. You are a female.*

Now, standing there seeing her father, she realized that she'd been viewing the world upside down. The defect wasn't in being a *woman*, but in being a *man*. Suddenly vile pinkness wasn't female, but male; the proof was right there in front of her—this disgusting thing, exposed for what it really was—a little Napoleon, a pathetic Wizard of Oz, ruling the world from behind a curtain of trousers, deflated and small, spoiling everything it touched, even her father's love.

It was an outrage. *He* was an outrage. She wanted to fling the mud back on him, tell him exactly what he was, but in the turmoil she couldn't find the words.

Her eye caught sight of the scalpel.

She grabbed it and cocked her arm to throw it—and felt a sharp pain, and something warm on her wrist. She lowered her shaking hand before her eyes, opened her fingers, and dropped the knife. Blood ran from a slice in the center of her palm. The sight of it was like a slap in the face, a sobering cold shower.

She looked at her father again, and in one clear moment the words she'd been searching for rose from someplace inside her—not from the mind or the heart, not even from the soul, but from a place darker and more distant than any she knew existed.

"You prick," she said in a stone-cold voice she'd never heard before. "You fucking little prick!"

Overwhelmed, she burst into tears and ran from the room.

"**W**here are we now?"

"In a room."

"Who's playing the guitar?"

"Lou Reed. Do you like it?"

"Never heard of him."

"Just relax and enjoy it."

"Have you got flow? Good. Hello, Harley."

"Who's that?"

"A doctor."

"What doctor? I thought *you* were the doctor. Take off the blindfold now, okay?"

"We're hooked up."

"How about over there?"

"All connected."

"Who else is in here? I want to see what's goin' on."

"You will. Right now I want you to breathe deeply, like you're working out."

"Why? What's going on?"

"Breathe."

Huuuuuh . . . whoooosh . . . huuuuuh . . . whooosh

"Perfect. Just keep that up and relax."

Huuuu . . . "What was that?"

"What was what?"

"That voice."

"Which one?"

"The one next to me!"

"There's nobody next to you, Harley—"

"Yes there is! Right here!"

"Put your arm down—"

"I just heard her say something! She said she was ready to—wait a minute—"

"Harley—"

"Holy Shit!"

"Harley—"

"You gotta be kiddin' me!"

"Lie back! Harley—"

"You people are crazy! I want outta here!"

"Tighten the restraints!"

"Ouch! Christ! You're cutting my wrists!"

"The chest! Tighten the chest!"

"Harley, listen to me—"

"Start the Pentothal!"

"Calm *down*, Harley."

"Let me go!"

"How much Valium did you give him?"

"Twenty milligrams."

"*You're* the ones who need the Valium, not me!"

"For God's sake, Harley, calm down!"

"Take that thing off! I can't breathe!"

"Yes you can! It's just a mask, that's what it's for! Now breathe in, nice and deep."

"I can't . . . breathe. . . ."

"Thaaat's it . . . nice and easy. Nice and easy . . . Harley? Can you hear me?"

". . . can't believe . . . you're gonna do . . ."

"Keep talking to me, Harley."

". . . you fuckin' . . . can't . . ."

"Can't what?" Silence. "I couldn't hear you, Harley. Can't what? . . . Harley? . . . He's under."

"All right, let's get started."

"When do you want the electrodes, before dissection or after?"

"After." Silence. "Scalpel, please."

Silence.

"Just for the record, Tar, he didn't say, 'You fuckin' *can't.*' He said 'You fuckin' *cunt.*' "

"Mm-hm." Silence. "Respirations look good."

Tell me about the kid who knows Harley Moon and Melvin Shivers," Jack said. He was sitting in Winston's office at Wings, waiting to meet the young man.

"His name's Iggy Pitt," Winston said. "Midtwenties, shy, kind of a loner like most of the guys around here. He was homeless until he started working for a messenger service. He roomed with Moon for a while."

There was a knock at the open door. Jack looked up to see a young man with light brown hair, a sorrowful face, and cheeks so smooth they didn't even show peach fuzz. At first glance he looked to be in his twenties, as Winston had guessed. But then again, with a bicycle clip on his pant leg and a shoulder bag on his hip, he also looked adolescent, a kind of urban Huck Finn. Except for the eyes, which were older, deep set, and electric. Jack felt them burrow in—nervous and curious—driven by a small tic in his left lid.

"This is Iggy Pitt," Winston said. "Iggy, this is Congressman MacLeod."

Jack stood and extended his hand, but Iggy didn't move. Finally he pulled his hands from his jeans pocket and waved timidly, his eyes still lasered on Jack's.

Jack sat at Winston's desk, and Iggy sat in a chair in front. Speaking in a friendly tone, Jack said, "I understand you knew Harley Moon."

"A little," Iggy said.

"What can you tell me about him?"

Iggy was quiet. "What d'ya want to know?"

"Whatever. Who were his friends?"

"Far as I could tell he didn't have any, 'cept me."

"How about Melvin Shivers?"

"They didn't talk to each other after they got out of prison."

"Was he upset when Shivers disappeared?"

"Yeah, sure."

"How about when Shivers was found dead?"

"I don't know. I suppose so."

Jack leaned back in his chair and put his hands behind his neck. "Do you know who Eli Graves is?"

Iggy turned to Winston, looking for guidance.

Winston said, "Being a messenger, Iggy's on the street a lot. I asked him to check in at the Red Rose Society, see if Graves has something special planned for his press conference." He nodded to Iggy to proceed.

"He's a right-to-lifer who hates you," Iggy said.

"So I've heard," Jack said. "Can you think of any connection between him and Harley Moon? Or between him and Melvin Shivers?"

"What kind of connection?"

"Any kind. Like, did they know each other? Were they friends?"

Iggy shook his head. "Not as far as I know."

Jack studied him a moment and decided to lay off. Obviously, he knew nothing. "Thanks, Iggy, I appreciate your help."

Winston patted Iggy on the back of his arm.

"Is that all?" Iggy asked.

"That's it," Winston said.

Iggy went out the door and headed for the men's room.

Jack tapped his thumb on the top of the desk.

"What's eating you?" Winston asked. He pushed away from the wall toward the desk. He was tall but not lanky, and moved with the fluid grace only athletes possess.

"Too much coincidence," Jack said. "A clinic bomber named Melvin Shivers is found mutilated in some screwball way that makes the police think it was done by a pro-choice nutcase, and inside the guy's stomach is a piece of pencil with my name on it."

"You've handed out those pencils to everybody in your district. Never mind Connecticut and New Jersey."

"And if that's not enough," Jack said, ignoring him, "the bomber's accomplice, Harley Moon, goes AWOL while he's living next door to *my* district office in a halfway house operated by *my* campaign manager—which is the same halfway house Melvin Shivers lived in when *he* disappeared. You get the drift."

"That's what it is, my man—drift. You're goin' paranoid on me."

"All Graves has to do is make me look bad, Win. Get the police to ask questions, leak it to the press. A smear is easy."

"Aw, c'mon, Jack. The police haven't said anything to the press about you or the pencil."

"They showed up in my office to interview me."

"So what? You've got all kinds of people sitting in your reception room. Were they in uniform?"

He shook his head.

"Forget it." Winston lifted himself off the edge of the desk. "So what about the press conference?"

"I'm thinking about it."

Winston stroked his trim goatee. "I told you, if you show up, all you're gonna do is give it more attention."

Jack consulted his instincts, which, as usual, told him to fight. He stood up, his decision made.

Coming out of the men's room, Iggy saw them walking out the door and joined them.

They stood at the back of a group of sidewalk listeners—ordinary New Yorkers and pro-lifers bussed in from Queens—watching a man in a black, skintight suit with a skeleton painted on it holding a scythe with a sign that said ABORTION, THE GRIM REAPER. Jack scanned the crowd of a hundred or so, looking for the press. To his left was a TV reporter and a cameraman, and next to them two pencil reporters. To his right, standing with her cameraman, was Molly McCormick. Beyond her—

He felt a switch in his brain flip over. His eyes moved back to Molly. There it was again. That spooky, unexpected attraction.

Graves was standing on a pine coffin, bullhorn in hand.

"Now," he said, "let's get down to business. We're here today to announce the top ten congressmen whose actions contribute most to the continuing slaughter of the unborn. Considering where we are, it should come as no surprise who's number one on the list."

A sustained *Boo!* went up from the crowd.

"That's right! Congressman John MacLeod, cochairman of the Joint Committee for Reproductive Rights, author of H.R. 111, the Guaranteed Choice Act, fund-raiser for abortion causes, untiring proponent of the silent scream, and unless we stop him here and now, a future candidate for the U.S. Senate."

"Booooo!"

"Congressman MacLeod," Graves said, "wherever you are, on behalf of generations yet unborn, the Red Rose Society pledges its heart, soul, and coffers to your defeat!"

As they applauded, Graves's eyes wandered over the crowd in search of a man with a beard, glasses, and a Dodgers cap. To his surprise he found Jack MacLeod instead, standing at the rear of the audience, arms folded, Winston on one side, Iggy Pitt on the other.

The instant their eyes met, Jack felt the hate. Graves's first, then his own.

"Ladies and gentlemen," Graves said, "I'm pleased to see that the congressman has joined us today." He pointed at Jack. The crowd, and cameras, turned in his direction. Jack unfolded his arms.

"Congressman MacLeod wants to pass a bill that says murder is approved by the Constitution," Graves continued. "Well, I'll tell you this—innocent, unborn babies may have a hard time standing up to legalized murder, but when the congressman picks on someone his own size, he's gonna find out we're not so easy to sweep into the garbage. Are we?"

"Noooo!" the crowd boomed. It was growing in number.

Jack listened, reacting quietly. *Give it your best shot, Graves. Because when you're finished, I'm going to take one of my own.*

The applause died down and Jack waited for the next wave of antiabortion clichés.

What he heard was something else.

"I want to tell you something," Graves said, and the crowd went silent. "And no matter how sick it makes you, I want you to know there isn't an exaggerated fact in it. Not one." He waved a black three-ring binder above his head as though it contained the irrefutable authority of King James. "In fact, I'm so sure of what I have to tell you, I'm announcing here and now that I'm waiving my legal defenses to any slander suit the congressman wants to bring against me. All defenses except one—the truth. If he sues, I won't say I made a mistake. If he sues, I won't claim absence of malice. In fact, I *want* him to sue, because I want to repeat under oath what I'm about to tell you. And I want him under oath, too, admitting to the stench of his life—or denying it, so I can prove he's a perjurer in addition to the rest! Because now we know how the honorable Mr. MacLeod arrived at his pro-choice, pro-abortion, pro-death philosophy!"

Jack could hear mumbling and see more faces turn toward him. He glanced at Molly and saw her tap her cameraman on the head to start the videotape rolling. Graves played out the moment.

"You see, Congressman, I *know* that just a few years ago, right across the East River, you got a teenage girl pregnant."

Graves surveyed the crowd. It remained attentive, more passersby accumulating at the edges.

"At first it was the usual story—sex before marriage, the fruits of fornication. It happens, we all know that. But instead of making it right with the Lord by marrying the girl and having the child, what did he do?" He looked at Jack. "He committed a felony! That's right! He robbed a shoe-repair shop—owned by the man who had hired and trusted him. And why?" He made Jack sweat. "So he could pay for a death! That's right! Using the stolen fruits of another man's labor, he *forced* his teenage girlfriend to have a late abortion!"

A man near Jack looked at him over his shoulder, at a distance.

Graves continued. "But it was too late in the pregnancy to do that, wasn't it, MacLeod? Any God-fearing person would have known that— but that didn't stop you, did it? That didn't stop you from committing the greatest mortal sin there is." He looked over the crowd. "And you know what that was? You know what he did?"

Jack's jaw muscles crushed his teeth together.

Graves looked into the face of a woman in front of the crowd. "How many times have we heard the proabortionists give their number-one excuse for baby slaughter? That it supposedly saves the mother?" He waited for a nod of agreement. "Isn't that what they say?" He waved his hands at another listener. "That it *saaaves* the mother? So, did this pro-abortionist *save* the mother? No, God help him. *He killed her!*"

Every head turned to stare at Jack's face.

"That's right!" Graves yelled. "In his effort to kill their love child, he sacrificed the mother's life!" He lowered his bullhorn a moment, cleared his throat, and continued. " 'Choice,' they call it. But what kind of choice is death?"

Winston turned to Jack. "This is ridiculous, man. Let's walk." People had closed in behind them, listening.

Jack stood glaring at Graves, who stood glaring back, looking for a sign of weakness—a curl of the mouth, a twitch of the eye. Jack gave him nothing.

"Now, I know what you're all asking," Graves said. "I can see it in your faces, and believe me, I haven't forgotten. You're all asking the big question." He cupped his hand behind his ear and leaned forward to hear the crowd.

". . . baby . . . what happened to the baby?"

"Right." He chopped the syllables with his hand as he spoke: "What—about—the baby? When the mother died, what happened to the child? Well, let me tell you." He paced back and forth with his index finger at his lips. "*I* know what happened to the baby, but I think it would be more interesting if we heard it directly from the congressman, don't you?"

The crowd turned toward Jack and parted, leaving an invisible beam of charged particles between himself and Graves.

"So, Congressman, what about it? *What happened to the baby?*"

Jack stood still, trying to assemble a reply. At one time or another he'd been called everything a politician could be called—it went with the territory—but this struck deep and opened veins wide.

He started to step forward, but Winston grabbed his arm. "You don't have to answer this shit."

"No sweat," he said, not having the foggiest idea what he was about to say. Suddenly New York was so quiet there seemed to be no noise at all—no cars or trucks, no garbage cans or sirens—nothing but the quiet whir of a three-quarter-inch camcorder picking up the details of his dry lips, damp forehead, and the mangy little secrets of his teenage life.

He took a step forward and stopped. "Ladies and gentlemen," he said, his voice surprisingly clear. "Some small part of what this man says is true, but most of it is a lie, and I don't answer lies standing in a gutter on Forty-third Street. Seeing the decency in your faces, I don't believe you expect me to."

The crowd stood still, listening.

"But there is one thing I do want to say. Because what counts are not the sins of a seventeen-year-old boy from Brooklyn. Lord, even if my teenage life were laid bare, the only person who wouldn't yawn would be me, and I'm not so sure about that." He hoped for a few chuckles but heard none. "No, what counts is where I stand on matters that affect your lives here and now, including where I stand on the subject so dear to Mr. Graves's heart."

Graves raised his microphone to speak, but Jack cut him off.

"There is only one person who can ever decide the fate of the unborn, and that's the person who is pregnant. That's not selfish or uncaring. That's moral! That's right! That was true twenty-five years ago when I was a boy in Brooklyn, it's true today, and no matter what you hear about me from this man, it will still be true tomorrow!"

Winston knew when Jack's speeches were finished before Jack did; he grabbed his arm and dragged him toward Wings. Loud boos and a small smattering of applause followed.

"That's no denial!" Graves screamed into the bullhorn. "That's a confession! Sue me! I'm begging you! *Sue me!*"

Jack and Winston pried their way through the crowd—emerging into the snout of a camera on a large man's shoulder.

"Is it true?" a reporter asked, pushing her mike into Jack's face as they walked. "Did your girlfriend die in an abortion?"

"Is this why you're a champion of abortion rights?" another reporter yelled.

"Who's this girlfriend, Congressman?" They were gathering like birds.

"What's her name?"

"Are you going to sue?"

Jack saw a camera moving backward in front of him and imagined how he'd appear on the news, a Mafia don crucified for silence instead of answers. If he'd had any.

"Do you have a child?" a reporter yelled.

"Where's the mother today—is she still alive?"

"Was it a boy or a girl?"

"What happened to the mother?"

"What happened to the child?"

Looking over his shoulder, he saw Molly McCormick giving chase with her cameraman, now just one more face among others who were asking the same haunting questions he'd asked himself for twenty-five years.

What exactly did happen to the mother?

What happened to the child?

"**C**ome on, chickenshit. Cut for it."

In the kitchen at Luboff's Funeral Home were five big-time poker players: Angus Brody, Jack MacLeod, Bozo, Jimmy, and Harris Luboff, the mortician's son. Brody, a beefy twenty-year-old with a seriously large wad of money, was staring across the table, daring Jack to shove his chips into the pot and cut the deck, high card takes all. The offer was tempting. Honey's baby was due in a month, which meant Jack needed enough cash to buy a round-trip bus ticket to Syracuse, three nights in a cheap motel, and a dozen long-stemmed roses. He was playing well for the first night in months. It was the start of a streak, and he believed in streaks.

He checked his watch. Nearly ten-thirty, the time they'd set this particular Friday's collect call. How nice it would be to tell her he'd won four hundred dollars.

How shitty to tell her he'd blown it all.

"Forget it," he said. "Deal some five-card." He picked up a Bic ballpoint pen and fluttered it between his fingers.

Brody shuffled the cards. "Tell you what. I'll make it so's you can't lose. You win the cut, you got my two hundred. You lose, you keep your two hundred."

Jack stared at him. "What's the kicker?"

"No kicker. I win, you keep your cash. All you gotta do is come downstairs and have a little fun, which means you can't lose."

Jimmy hummed the first four notes from *Dragnet.*

"He's just kidding," Harris Luboff said, rubbing his nose with his palm.

Jack stared at Brody. "Cut the shit and deal."

Brody looked at his pal Jimmy in mock surprise, raising his open palms. "What is this? The guy nuts or what?" He turned to Jack. "All right, tell you what. I'll throw in another hundred for laughs." He dealt five twenties onto the table next to the two hundred in chips he'd already shoved in.

Jack looked at the pot and felt the beams beneath his principles creaking. "And if I lose, you want me to do what again?"

"No big deal," Brody said. "Just a little bachelor party downstairs."

"Hey, guys, come on," Harris said, but no one paid attention.

Jack fluttered his Bic pen between his fingers, calculating but refusing to give in.

Brody shook his head. "You're killing me, MacLeod. All right, one last bump. You want to get your nigger friend Winston out of a jam, right? You make the bet, I'll throw in his marker, too."

Winston had taken money from Brody in exchange for promising to throw a basketball game with St. Julian's, but when the time came, he couldn't bring himself to do it. Sinking a jump shot at the buzzer, he'd won the game by two points. Jack had known nothing about the fix until he was walking toward Winston's house one afternoon and saw him lying on his back, Brody straddling him, his goons standing by. As Jack started running toward them he saw Winston suddenly go crazy— yelling, writhing, blowing snot out his nose—but by the time he reached him, Brody was on his feet, snapping on his black satin jacket and heading for his candy-apple-red Chevy with its sixteen coats of hand-rubbed paint, the automotive pride of Flatbush. Winston brushed himself off and told Jack about taking money to fix the game, but refused to say what had made him go berserk a few minutes earlier.

Jack talked across the table to Brody. "Remember that day you had Winston pinned to the ground? What'd you tell him that made him go nuts like that?"

Brody looked surprised. "I just had to educate him that you don't welsh on a deal with Angus Brody. Especially when you're in his shoes, if you know what I mean."

"No, I don't know what you mean."

Brody looked at the cards with raised eyebrows. "I reminded him we both had granddaddies from the South, but before he thought that made us equal, he needed to remember that my granddaddy had his grand-daddy's skull sitting on the mantelpiece."

Jack felt his face burn. He jammed the ballpoint pen into his shirt pocket. "Make up the deck."

"It's made, asshole."

Jimmy cut the cards and pushed them to Jack, who spread them in a perfect rainbow. Brody kept his eyes on Jack and pulled a card from the center, keeping it facedown in front of him. As Jack reached for a card Brody grabbed his wrist and stopped him. "Look at me when you draw, Jackson."

Brody let go, and Jack drew a card from two o'clock on the arc. He pulled it in front of him, facedown.

"Come on, guys," Harris said. "This is supposed to be a friendly game."

"Shut up," Brody said, and the table fell silent. "Me first, asshole." Without looking down, he turned his card. It was the six of diamonds. Jack spread his nostrils and aired out his lungs. The odds were with him and everybody knew it.

"I haven't got all night," Brody said. "Roll it."

Jack turned his card and saw Brody's eyes widen. It was the four of spades. Groans and whistles filled the air. He swallowed and checked Brody's face, hoping to see it expand. It didn't.

"Follow me, Jackson." The room rumbled with the sound of chair legs vibrating on a hardwood floor.

"Okay, guys," Harris said nervously, "if my old man comes in, we got real trouble, know what I mean?"

Brody pointed a finger at Harris and instructed Bozo: "If he wants to be tied up so's it dissolves him of responsibility, tie him up." He turned and led everyone down the steps to the morgue. Harris held up a hand to stop Bozo and bobbed along behind the others.

Brody opened the steel-lined door to the morgue. The smell of formaldehyde hit Jack's face like dentist's ether, making him slightly dizzy. Brody turned on a hanging lamp and let it swing back and forth over a stainless-steel table in the center of the room. Everyone stood still and watched.

Brody walked to a wall of drawers and rested his hand on a handle, and suddenly Jack got it: when he pulled it open there'd be nobody inside. He decided to be a good sport, act nervous, play along, wipe his forehead, say, "Wow, Brody, you scared the shit out of me—I'd rather lose the two hundred than go through *that* again." Everybody'd have a laugh, turn out the lights, punch each other on the shoulder, and go play cards.

Brody pulled open the drawer and Jack saw a sheet covering the unmistakable form of a human body—feet splayed at one end, the shape of a head at the other. He waited for it to sit up and yell, "Surprise!" It didn't.

"Come over here, Jackson," Brody said. "It's not polite to fuck somebody you haven't met." He bent his knees slightly and grabbed his crotch. "Even if you are getting sloppy seconds." He let out a single laugh.

Jack turned to the guys for help, but they'd become corpses themselves. He turned back to Brody and waited for him to burst into his high-pitched laugh, point at Jack, fall on the floor, and tell everybody, "What a look!" Instead, Brody walked to the other side of the steel table and wiggled his finger at Jimmy and Bozo.

They went to the drawer, lifted the corpse in their arms, and carried it, covered, to the table under the hanging lamp. Like pallbearers at a grave, they stepped backward and waited. Harris watched in horror. The room became stale and quiet.

Brody pulled out a cigarette and lit it, exhaling across the shrouded cadaver. As the smoke spread he closed his lighter with a loud clack, piercing the moldy air.

"Payback time, Jackson. Drop your pants."

Jack still didn't quite comprehend what was happening. His head perceived a dream, an expectation that any second an alarm would sound, the cavalry would ride in, the joke would end. Finally he understood that if anyone was going to save him, it would have to be himself.

He looked up at the lamp cord. Out of reach. He looked around the table for an undertaker's tool. Nothing. He waited to hear Harris's old man come down the steps, but they were silent. He looked back at the guys, hoping they'd get a grip on themselves, but they were hiding in the shadows, tasting adrenaline, peeping at a strip show like three drooling old men.

It was just himself and Brody.

Brody motioned with his finger for Jack to get up on the table. "That was the bet, Jackson. You played it, you pay it."

Jack looked at him quizzically. "What's the point, Brody?"

"You lost the fuckin' bet!" Brody yelled. "That's the point!"

"This isn't about the fuckin' bet!" Jack said. "This is about something else! What is it?"

"I don't know!" Brody barked, punching the air. "It's who you are! All pretty and perfect!" His eyes narrowed. "You piss me off!"

Jack felt his face boil. "You want to make something out of who I am, come on over here and try, you chickenshit bastard!" He pointed at the corpse. "But leave this out of it!" He made two fists and raised them, surprising Brody, who was bigger and had more experience with brawls. Then Jack's left eye began to twitch, and Brody knew he had him.

Jack held his ground a moment, thinking he'd managed a standoff. He lowered his fists and looked at the corpse. The sheet had slipped off one of its feet; he reached out and pulled it back, respectfully. He looked at Brody. "You sick fuck," he said, and turned around and walked toward the door.

Brody snapped his fingers.

Jimmy and Bozo stepped in front of Jack.

Without hesitating, Jack swung his left fist, hitting Jimmy in the face and knocking him to the floor.

Bozo jumped behind Jack, grabbed him by the arms, and wrapped a leg around the front of his knees.

Jimmy picked himself up and punched Jack in the stomach. Then he grabbed Jack's belt and started to unbuckle it.

Harris yelled, "Hey, guys, come on!"

Jack freed a leg from Bozo's grip, raised his foot to Jimmy's stomach, and kicked him backward against the stainless-steel drawers. Then he twisted his body wildly, trying to free himself from Bozo's grasp.

Brody stood calmly on the other side of the table, humming the classic stripper's tune, pulling the sheet off the cadaver in small, tantalizing jerks, from the feet up.

Bozo slipped his arms under Jack's armpits, locked his hands on the back of his neck, and crunched his face toward the floor in an excruciating full nelson. The hold was too much to break: Jack was now a walking crucifix—head down, arms extended at his sides—forced to go wherever Brody wanted. Which was toward the table.

Jack tried to lift his head to see what lay ahead. Bozo pushed Jack's neck down harder, confining his view to his own feet and fly, which Jimmy was unzipping. Jack flattened his feet against the floor, but it was useless. With Bozo pushing and Jimmy pulling, they moved him forward at will.

The body on the table began coming into Jack's view. First a pair of feet and ankles . . . bluish-white legs, a light brown triangle . . . a long vertical cut on the stomach that had been stitched together and painted with yellow antiseptic . . . soft breasts that fell to each side above a small midriff—a slender neck—strawberry hair—a beautiful face—

Honey's.

Jimmy recognized her at the same time. "Jesus," he whispered. Bozo looked over Jack's shoulder, recognized her, and released his grip.

Jack stood perfectly motionless . . . mouth open, eyes fixed. His spirit left his body, floated upward, and viewed the room from a distance; his mind told time to stand still, which it did, then commanded it to go backward, which it did not. His disembodied hand rose toward the body and touched it, confirming it wasn't a mirage.

"Jesus Christ," Harris whispered.

"What?" Brody asked. He'd never heard of Honey O'Connor, had no idea who she was. "What, what, what?"

Jack's fingers touched the cesarean cut.

"Hey, don't let the slit bother you," Brody said. "She's got a smaller one between her legs, and trust me, it ain't sewed up."

Brody's words penetrated Jack softly, from a distance, like his mother's voice after his tonsillectomy, when he was finally coming to. He looked at Brody and felt his spirit return to his body. Bloodless and cold. Smoking and hot. Freezing and scalding. A chunk of dry ice.

"I'm going to kill you," he said calmly.

Brody looked surprised. "You and whose army, asshole?"

Keeping his eyes on Brody's face, he walked slowly toward the end of the table and around to the side where Brody was standing. "I'm going to kill you."

"What the fuck is this?" Brody said. His pals stood in the shadows, watching.

Jack stopped six feet away, with nothing between them.

Brody's forehead sprouted small beads of sweat. He'd seen this sort of madness before, knew that it carried a peculiar strength of its own. He dropped his cigarette to the floor and stepped on it, then pulled his sleeves up to his forearms. This wasn't what he'd come for, the gesture said, but what the hell: if MacLeod wanted the shit kicked out of him in a funeral-home basement, why not?

Jack took another step forward.

Brody shifted his weight onto one foot and looked over at the peanut gallery. "What is this?" he asked with his New York shrug, palms out. He hoped Jack would look away long enough to deck him with a sucker punch.

It worked the other way. Jack took a small step and kicked Brody between the legs so hard it sounded as if he'd punted a football.

Brody keeled over, sucking air in a reverse scream, eyes bulging, veins popping, hands grabbing his crotch. He fell to his knees and rolled onto his side; Jack leaped onto him, grabbed a fistful of hair, and yanked his head back with one hand. With the other, he pulled the Bic pen out of his shirt pocket, removed its cap between his teeth, and rammed the metal tip into Brody's right nostril. Everyone froze. Jack spit the plastic top out of his mouth, bouncing it off Brody's forehead.

Brody lifted a shaking hand to his nose and gripped Jack's wrist. Jack yanked Brody's hair back harder and pushed the pen in deeper. Brody's spine went rigid and his hand trembled. The quaking hand of the supplicant, weak and afraid.

Bozo reacted first. "What the fuck—"

"Shut up!" Jack yelled between breaths.

Jimmy put his hand on Bozo's chest to stop him. Except for the sound of two animals panting, the room fell quiet again.

Jack leaned down and put his mouth next to Brody's ear, talking between breaths. "Did you have—old man Fisher—for biology?" Brody didn't answer. Jack yanked a fistful of hair.

"Eah," Brody said. The *Y* was lost to the missile that plugged up his nose.

"Remember when—he pinned a frog—to the table?" Jack whispered.

"Eah," Brody's voice cracked.

"Remember its little legs—twitching and jumping?"

"Eah."

"Remember what he did next?"

"Uh-uh," Brody said.

Jack swallowed and caught his breath. "No wonder you're so stupid. You never paid attention in school." Brody didn't respond. "Doesn't matter," Jack said, " 'cause I'm gonna tell you anyway. Old man Fisher took a hat pin and put it between the frog's eyes and pushed it up until it touched its brain. You know what happened then?"

"Uh-uh."

Jack exhaled. "Its little legs stopped twitching."

Brody let out a hoarse squeal and tried to push Jack's hand away from his nose, but Jack pulled his head back and drove the pen in deeper. Blood spurted out his nostril and ran down his cheeks into his ears. "Cut it out," he yelled, "or I'll turn you into a fucking little frog right now!"

Brody lay still, gurgling blood and phlegm.

Jack felt the power in his hands spread through his body. He thought of the cockroach he'd killed on the bus that brought him here, how he'd squashed him, how good it would feel to squash Brody, too. He blinked away the sweat so he could see Brody for the vermin he was.

Then he remembered Honey. "Put her back!" he snapped. The three others hustled to the table, threw the sheet over her, and carried her to the drawer. "Now get away!" Jack said.

"Come on, man," Jimmy pleaded.

"Get back!" Jack shouted, gripping the pen in his fist.

Jimmy took a step back. "Brody didn't know she was your girl!"

Jack heard the words and hesitated. The guy had a point.

"Yeah," Bozo said, trying to clinch it. "She was dead before he fucked her!"

Before he— Point gone. The muscles in Jack's neck stiffened as he placed the heel of his hand on the bottom of the pen and aimed it toward Brody's brain.

And shoved.

Brody screamed—back arching, head snapping—blood gushing from his nose and mouth. The tip of the pen hit a gristle barrier, diverting it long enough for Brody to jerk his face to the side, claw at Jack's wrists, and knock the heel of his hand off the bottom of the shaft.

Jack grabbed the pen in his other hand and held fast. Brody held tight, too, gulping air, eyes watering—a weasel in a coyote's jaw seeking one more moment of grace.

Jack squeezed the sticky pen tighter in his fist. He'd do it right this time. No deflection. No reprieve.

As he focused on the pen, calculating the best angle to penetrate, inexplicably, weirdly, a piece of the weapon disappeared from sight. He raised the back of his bloody right hand to his eyes, wiped away the sweat, and looked again. Now the side of Brody's head had disappeared. In its place were fuzzy neon worms, vibrant blind spots Jack had never seen before. He tried to blink them away, but even with his eyelids closed they hovered in the air like paisley helicopters.

His concentration was broken, his rage dented. His senses began functioning again. He heard the sound of human breathing, smelled human sweat, sensed human fear. As the blind spots grew, his blood was becoming less molten, his heart less deadly, his head less certain of his cause. In a matter of seconds he found himself teetering on a narrow ledge. Balancing. Deciding. Weighing what to do.

He pulled the pen out of Brody's nose.

Brody covered his face with his hands and rolled onto his side, drawing his knees up into a fetal position. Jack saw splotches of Brody's face between the opaque spots. He stood up and walked toward the door. Bozo and Jimmy ran to Brody's side. Bozo offered him a shirttail, but Brody slapped it aside.

"You're a dead motherfucker, MacLeod!" he yelled in a harelip voice. "She was better on that slab with me than she ever was with you!"

Jack was already climbing the steps two at a time, hearing Brody's words fall behind him like spent bullets. He walked through the kitchen, grabbed what he could see of his coat, picked up his money, and knocked the back door open with his fists.

Striding into the parking lot, he felt his body begin to shake. He saw Brody's Chevy out of the corner of his eye. He walked to it, leaned over the hood and vomited, then lowered his head next to the fender and caught his breath. In a few minutes his blood carried the blind spots away, leaving the excruciating pain of a migraine in their wake.

He felt something in his left hand. It was the ballpoint pen. He raised it to the side of the car, dug the brass tip into the sixteen layers of mirror-smooth, hand-rubbed candy-apple paint, and ripped them open from the headlights to the gas cap. *Just like her belly.* Then he threw the pen down and started running, teeth chattering from nerves, and coldness, and the pounding of his feet on the pavement.

Jack's taxi took him to the Onondaga County Democratic Central Committee headquarters in downtown Syracuse. He was there to meet Fritz Olsen and his wife, Ginger, to discuss his possible Senate candidacy and an upcoming speech he'd be giving at the committee's annual dinner the next month.

He was also there on a private mission.

Regardless of what brought him, he was happy to be out of New York. It was the day after Graves's sidewalk press conference and he hadn't yet shaken the image of himself on the evening news, walking down the sidewalk after Graves's speech, trying to grin away his guilt. Jesus. Now he understood raincoats pulled over the head.

The meeting at the committee headquarters went reasonably well, considering that a hint of scandal was usually death to politicians. Fritz Olsen said Eli Graves's charges would sink of their own weight; Ginger Olsen pooh-poohed big city media; Fritz said it was a one-day story at most; Ginger said Jack would get some bad mail, so what else is new? Jack nodded his appreciation, knowing that ultimately their opinions would depend upon how the story turned out.

He stood up and shook hands, eager to get to his next stop. Ginger Olsen said, "And you'll be bringing your wife to the dinner?"

"I'm not married," he said.

"Oh," she said, and her expression changed ever so slightly.

Fritz came to his rescue. "Jack lives with one of the most beautiful and talented lawyers in Washington. Will Victoria be here?"

"I'm afraid not," Jack said.

"Oh," he said, and his expression changed ever so slightly.

Jack smiled. "Thanks for the help, folks. See you in three weeks."

Nothing had changed since the days of Noah's ark. It was still pair up or drown. He left the building and headed for his rental car.

The small frame house in East Syracuse was located in what had once been a neat little postwar neighborhood, but was now as old and worn as its residents. Ida O'Connor was Honey's eighty-seven-year-old great-aunt, her grandfather's sister. Honey had lived with her during the pregnancy, which made the old woman the only link to her he could find. He'd come to the house many years before, after a client's deposition in Syracuse, but no one had been home, and after returning to New York City, he'd buried his curiosity once again. Or so he thought.

He checked the address on the piece of paper one more time and knocked on the scalloped storm door. An inner door opened a crack, revealing the worried face of a shrunken, white-haired woman.

"Mrs. O'Connor?" he said through the glass.

"Yes?"

"My name is Jack MacLeod."

"Who?"

"Jack MacLeod," he said louder. "I went to high school with your niece, Honey. In Brooklyn."

"Mary Theresa?"

"Yes, Mary Theresa. May I come in?"

"Mary Theresa's dead," she said. He waited, and she opened the door anyway.

He walked into the living room and unbuttoned his jacket. The shades were pulled against the Indian-summer sun, leaving the room shadowed and musty. The sofa and easy chair were covered with worn, chocolate-brown velvet, with a shine on the seats and white lace doilies on the arms. The oak floors were polished smooth; at the foot of the high-backed rocker was a small Persian carpet resembling a sleeping pet. He sat on the edge of the sofa while the old woman lowered herself into her rocker.

"Do you know where Honey's parents are?" he asked.

"Oh Lord. Honey's mother moved to Florida years ago, right after her husband died."

"Her husband's dead?"

"Hit by a truck comin' out of a diner in Tucumcari, New Mexico. Killed on the spot."

"What was he doing in New Mexico?"

She went blank. "Who?"

"Her husband. Mary Theresa's father, George."

More confusion. "George wasn't in New Mexico. That was Larry."

"What happened to George?"

"Died of pneumonia. Let's see, when was it?" She stared at the ceiling.

As she thought about it, Jack looked around the room. He pictured Honey living here in exile, sitting in this very spot reading his letters, watching clocks, counting days. Both of them seventeen. He'd once looked up Honey's death certificate, which listed the cause of death as acute hemorrhaging during a premature birth, but mentioned nothing more about it. Or the baby. Checking with the Office of Vital Statistics had revealed nothing of a child under any surname he could imagine— hers, his, her great-aunt's, her middle name. All he had to go on was what her parents had told him at the time, that the baby had died, too. It had all been so long ago, and yet, sitting here, he could feel her in the room.

"Tell me something," he said loudly.

"Don't need to shout," she said. "My hearing's fine. It's my mind that's goin'."

"I'm trying to find out something about Mary Theresa when she lived here. You know, when she was pregnant." Ida rocked in her chair— staring blankly. "I don't want to pry, Mrs. O'Connor, but—"

"It's Miss. Never married, thank you."

"Smart woman."

"What's so smart about it?"

Her mind wasn't totally gone. "Can you tell me what happened to Honey's child?"

"You mean Mary Theresa's?"

"Yes. Mary Theresa's."

"Don't know nothin' about that." Suddenly her face brightened as if she remembered after all, giving Jack heart. Then she said, "Care for some horehound tea?"

Last thing on earth he wanted was a cup of bitter, medicinal tea. "Sure," he said.

"Nobody makes real tea anymore. Not since I was a little girl."

She rose from her rocker and headed into the kitchen, rattling on about rose-petal tea and dandelion soup, leaving Jack in the living room to shout answers she couldn't hear despite her good hearing. After a few minutes she returned to the living room carrying two teacups, one for him, one that she held on her lap in the rocking chair.

"So, you don't remember Mary having a baby?" he asked.

The old woman looked at him with narrowed eyes. "Why do you ask?"

"She was a very close friend of mine." He took a sip of tea and looked at her over his cup.

She rocked gently, spilling neither tea nor information. "Her mother never wanted anyone to know."

"Know what?"

"Her mother moved to Florida several years ago." He'd already heard that. She fondled her teacup. "Never writes."

"Was it a boy or a girl?" he asked.

"Don't know," she said.

"You don't know?"

"Don't know." She waited. So did he. "Never saw the child. Her mother said it was stillborn." She picked a piece of fuzz off her gray sweater and held it out and dropped it on the floor. "Never saw such pills on a new sweater. Just got it Christmas, and look at it." Her face clouded. "Or was it my birthday? Lord, I don't know." She looked into her teacup and rocked gently.

"What do you think happened?" Jack asked.

"About what?"

"The baby."

"What baby?"

"Mary *Theresa*'s." Christ. "Was it stillborn?"

She picked at some more fuzz. "Couldn't say."

Jack's cheeks flushed. "You mean you think it wasn't?"

She dropped the fuzz ball, lifted her teacup, and brushed her lap. Then she looked him directly in the eyes. "Think what wasn't?"

"Stillborn. Honey's—Mary Theresa's baby."

"You think her baby was stillborn? What makes you think it was stillborn?"

He took a deep breath and repositioned himself on the edge of the couch. Time to show his hand. "I was the baby's father," he said.

Her eyes widened. "*You* were the father? Heavens to Betsy!" She let out a howl.

Now *he* was confused. "Did I say something funny?"

"Either you did or the other fellow did. You can't both be the father."

Jack caught the distinct whiff of a dead rat. "What other fellow?"

"The young fellow that come by to see me a few days ago. Or was it a few weeks ago? Let's see, it was right before Edna brought me the cinnamon rolls with pecans." She leaned forward to speak confidentially. At last, something that mattered. Jack leaned forward to listen.

Whispering, she said, "Doctor says I'm not supposed to eat nuts."

Jack nodded. That he understood. No nuts.

He leaned back and watched an image of the "other father" form in his mind. "What was his name?" he snapped.

"Doctor . . . oh, what *was* his name?"

"Not the doctor, the other fellow who said he was the father."

"I told you, I can't remember. Didn't I say that already?"

Jack wanted to take the lovely old lady by her scrawny neck and twist it into a licorice stick. "Do you remember *anything* about him?" he asked.

"Well, of course I do. He was just here."

"What do you remember?"

She tilted her head back and clasped her hands together in front of her nose. "He had the prettiest brown eyes." She compared Jack's. "Just like yours."

Three billion people on earth with brown eyes, but Jack saw only one pair: Eli Graves's.

"He was sweet as could be," she said. She looked over her shoulder at an empty table. "Now where is it?"

"Where's what?"

"The flower he brought me. Prettiest red rose you ever did see."

A *red* rose? The thought of it made Jack's neck ache. "What did you tell him?" he asked.

"Same thing I told you. He said he was the father of Honey's child, but frankly, I didn't think he hardly looked old enough to *be* Honey's child." She finally took a sip of tea and put down the cup. "But he was the father, all right."

"How do you know?"

"Looked just like her. Same nose, same coloring. Knew things about her, too. Like where she went to school. She was a cheerleader, you know."

"Yes, I know." Jesus, where was Graves getting this stuff?

"Let's see." She looked at the ceiling. "He told me how she loved Coney Island, and playing cards. Do you play cards?"

"Sometimes." The guy knew *a lot.*

"When your mother lived here, we used to play canasta pert near every night," she said.

"You mean Mary Theresa's mother."

Fog drifted across her face. "What about Mary Theresa's mother?"

Jack sat on the sofa and stared at her with eyes nearly as spiraled as hers. Then he sat back and relaxed.

"Miss O'Connor?"

"Yes?"

"Mind if I ask a favor?"

"What is it?"

"Could I have some more horehound tea?"

Jack hung upside down in the bathroom doorway, warding off a migraine and watching a *Wheel of Fortune* rerun, which didn't help. Victoria lay on the bed doing a crossword puzzle.

"What did you find out?" she asked. She had become nearly as curious about Honey as he was.

"Nothing, except somebody's out there digging up my life."

"Who?"

"I don't know. Eli Graves, I think. Or somebody working for him."

"What's a five-letter word with an *R* in the middle for 'acted human'?" she asked.

He was raising himself at the waist, straining and puffing. On the television screen Pat Sajak said, "Yes, there are three *M*s," and panels lit up to a clanging bell and applause.

Jack spoke between puffs. "You think . . . there's gonna be . . . a lot of fallout . . . from Graves's press conference?"

"You won't know until the next election. Unless he comes up with something more."

"What do you suppose . . . that could be?"

She was concentrating on the puzzle. "What's a six-letter word for frustrate?"

Jack continued doing abs until he'd completed fifty. He lowered his head and stretched out, groaning lightly. After a moment he said, "Vanna White looks different upside down."

"Most people do. What's the answer to my question?"

"Thwart?" No answer. "Outwit?" Still no answer.

On screen a hefty woman with glasses said she wanted to buy a vowel, an *A*. More panels, more applause.

"How do you know it's Graves?" she said. "Maybe it's a reporter." She paused. "The word for 'acted human' is *erred*."

He unhooked himself from the crossbar and drew a towel over his chest. Standing at the sink, he took a plastic bottle of aspirin from the medicine cabinet. There were only four pills left; he popped three and put the bottle back on the shelf. "I've had enough of Honey and Eli

Graves," he said through the door. "I've been too preoccupied with the whole subject. You realize I missed a vote today? Interviewing a senile old woman in Syracuse?"

"What's another word for 'faithless'? Seven letters."

"Does it go down or across?" he said.

"Across." She looked up. "What difference does that make?"

"I do better with words that go up and down," he said.

She smiled. "My mistake. I just noticed. It goes up and down."

He turned on the shower and walked back into the bedroom. "It does? Let me see." She shook her head no, daring him to do something about it. "Now *that's* an error," he said, and climbed onto the bed. She pulled the puzzle back against the headboard, smiling a challenge. He leaned forward and grabbed her wrist.

"No fair," she said, shoving him away with her other hand. He corralled both her hands and pinned her down. She tried to wriggle free. Getting nowhere, she gave up and lay still, breathing hard. He held her a moment, let go, and kissed her. She dropped the newspaper and wrapped her arms around him and kissed him back. He positioned himself over her and slowly began pulling up her robe. When it reached her thighs, she broke the kiss.

"The shower's running," she said.

"Come in with me. We can do two things at once."

"You can't even hang by your heels and do a crossword."

"Sure I can," he said. "Hinder."

She looked puzzled.

"Your six-letter word for 'frustrate' is *hinder*," he said.

She pushed him away. "How did you figure that out?"

"Don't look so amazed." He leaned down and kissed her neck.

"Are you always solving crossword puzzles when you're making love to me?"

"All the time. Want to hear a few of the words?" He waited. "Let's get in the shower."

She raised her hand to his face and pushed his hair off his forehead, considering the offer. Weighing it.

Finally, escaping it.

He rolled off the bed. "Okay," he said, heading for the bathroom.

"This isn't my last chance ever, is it?" she asked.

"Sure is," he said, closing the door. In a moment it opened and he stuck his head out. "One more chance," he said.

•   •   •

"Do you remember me?"

"Of course I do. How are you?"

"Fine. I hope I'm not calling too late."

"If you find me at the station, it's not too late," she said.

"How are your knees?" he asked.

"Scabby, but much better than they were when you saw them. Thank you for helping me, Iggy."

"Be sure to change the bandages every day."

"I will. Is that why you called?"

"Yeah, I wanted to make sure you were okay."

"That's sweet of you."

"Molly?"

"Yes?"

"Watching you at that sidewalk press conference Monday got me to thinking. I'd really like to get into television if I could."

"Watching *me*?" She laughed. "What grabbed you most—seeing me chase after Congressman MacLeod with a microphone, or falling down and skinning my knees?"

"I'm serious. I'm a hard worker, Winston Jones will tell you that. So will my dispatcher down here at Ace Messenger."

"What do you want to do?"

"Anything. Need another cameraman?"

"Sometimes, but that's a union job with a long waiting list. You need experience, training."

"If you help me learn, I'll do it for nothing."

"Lesson number one is never to say that again."

"I would really."

"There's an intern program here at the station called Talent Development, which is a fancy name for letting people hang out, carry equipment, and see how a television crew operates. They don't pay you anything."

"Okay with me. I can keep my messenger job and go with you when I have time."

"I'll talk to my producer about it."

"Thanks, Molly. Really."

"No problem, Iggy. Thanks for the first aid."

Eggs Benedict stood in a puddle of water in the dimly lit basement, hands flattened over his ears, eyes fixed on a jackhammer as it bashed its shaft into the building's foundation. Long after the noise had stopped, it still rattled in his head.

"Holes are ready," the driller said. He pushed his plastic safety glasses up and wiped his face on his forearm, then propped his jackhammer against a cement column and headed for the steps. "Time for lunch." A. J. Lyman Demolition was behind schedule, but lunch was lunch. Workers needed muscle to destroy buildings.

The driller and his assistant stepped over a box of bits and headed for the stair. Billy Bannister looked at Benedict, who hung back, straightening the red and green wires leading from a silvery, pencil-shaped blasting cap. He waited for the other two workers to disappear before talking. "Still with me?" he asked Bannister, not looking up.

Bannister licked his lips. "Hey, I'm ready."

Benedict set the blasting cap in a box and turned to a yellow, shoe-box-sized device with an ignition switch. "You don't sound ready," he said, separating the wire leads.

Bannister shifted his weight from one foot to the other. "I was just wondering how we're gonna steal this stuff with those drillers breathing down our necks."

"It'll work if we stay cool and do it the way we practiced."

Bannister looked over his shoulder toward the stair steps. "Maybe we oughta run through it once more."

Benedict looked at him impatiently, then reached down and grabbed the inside seam at the knee of his pants and yanked. The Velcro tape parted, making a sharp ripping sound.

"Jesus," Bannister said. "It's too loud."

"I'll fix it," Benedict said. He pulled the seams wide apart, reached through the opening to his bare leg, and withdrew an eight-inch wooden dowel from a woman's knee-high nylon stocking. The dowel had been cut from a curtain rod, wrapped in brown paper, and stippled with a felt-tipped pen to show a date-shift code and the words EAGLE EXPLOSIVES, PATTERSON, PA. Plastered on the end was a mixture of oatmeal and

159

Elmer's glue holding two wires in the center, one red, one green, exactly like the wires of a blasting cap. Without careful inspection, even an experienced demo man wouldn't have noticed that it was a dummy stick of dynamite.

Benedict handed it to Bannister, turned his back, and faced two holes drilled into the base of a load-bearing column. With Bannister standing behind him, he stooped down, reached back over his shoulder, and swapped sticks, just as they would a real one. "Don't wait so long," he said.

Bannister looked at him, sweating. "I don't know," he said. "If I was standing close, I think I could tell what we were doing."

Benedict stood up and resealed the Velcro strips on his knee seams lightly, reducing the noise they'd make when he pulled them open.

"How we gonna make the switch twenty times?" Bannister asked.

"We only have to steal one out of every eight sticks we slap in, not every time. Once we move out of this area to the other side, it'll be easier. It's darker. If you yak as much as usual, only thing the driller will be thinking about is how to shut you up."

Bannister licked his lips and looked at his watch. "Let's get some lunch. I need some Pepto. My stomach's killing me."

They reached the top of the debris-strewn stair and squinted at the sun. Benedict saw that Bannister's face had become tense, his gab gone. "Still with me?" he asked.

Bannister thought about it a moment. After tossing a pink tablet into his mouth, he smiled and punched his pal on the arm.

Jack studied Victoria over the votive candle and waited for her answer. She picked up her butter knife and beat a small tattoo on the padded white tablecloth, looking for intervention—a spilled tray, a waiter, whatever. They had been over this ground so many times he knew what she was thinking: maybe his perseverance was stronger than her resistance after all. She pawed through her purse for one of the brown cigarettes she still carried for emergencies. He lifted the candle to give her a light and watched the tip glow red.

"If it's a child you want, why pick on me?" Her words emerged with exhaled smoke.

"You'd be a great mother."

"I'd be a terrible mother and you know it," she answered. "I'd put the kid in a drawer and forget it was there."

"Not with me around."

"Oh, right. I forgot how much time you have."

"I'd make time," he said. She didn't respond. "If we had a girl, she might turn out to be president," he said.

"She might also turn out to be a psychopath."

"They're not incompatible."

"With my luck, she'd probably be a lawyer," she said.

"God. Forget the whole thing." He saw her smile. "Think the gene pool could be that bad?"

"Mine are for sure." She drank some red wine. "I've been a rabble-rouser since birth. When the other girls were playing house, I was down at Howard Johnson's counting ice-cream containers, checking to see if they really had twenty-eight flavors, which, of course, they never did. Boy, did I love giving them hell."

"I can picture it," he said.

She straightened her silverware. "Why are marriage and kids so important to you?" she asked.

"I don't know. It seems like a fairly normal thing to do."

"Nothing wrong with normal, it's just not me. And no offense, sweetheart, but it's not you either."

"Even abnormal people get married, V. How else can they hold up their end of the national divorce rate?"

A smile flickered in her eyes, and disappeared. She drew on her cigarette and coughed. He handed her a glass of water; she drank it and dabbed a napkin to her eyes.

"What's wrong?" he asked.

"I inhaled too much," she said.

"I mean what's got you so depressed?"

She ran her finger along the edge of her empty plate. "Frankly, I'm not sure I like myself anymore."

"Are you kidding?"

She hesitated. "I overstated it. I'm just having a difficult time with a decision I have to make, and certain things about it make me feel lousy."

"Something about us?"

"Yes and no."

"What's that mean?"

She looked down without answering.

He shifted impatiently. "I don't remember when we decided to stop talking to each other," he said. "Remind me."

She raised her eyes. "Look, Jack, I know I'm sounding mysterious, but bear with me for a while, would you?"

He reached for the saltshaker, played with it a moment, and looked across the table at her. "Anything I can help with?"

She reached for the pepper shaker and played with it. "Just be patient and don't ask."

"Right," he said. He pushed the saltshaker aside. "Mind if I ask something else?"

"Off topic A?"

"Way off."

"Fire away."

"Can you imagine *any* circumstance where you'd have a child?"

She sighed. "God, you are persistent."

"Can you?"

"Only one," she said quickly.

"Really." He was intrigued. "What is it?"

She sat quietly, obviously wishing she hadn't said what she'd said. He observed without speaking. What the heck was eating her?

The waiter appeared and handed them two enormous menus. She opened one and hid behind it as the man informed them of off-menu items and said he'd return in a moment to take their orders. They read in silence, negotiated the entrées they'd share, and tried to start over again.

"Here's an easy one," Jack said. "If you could have anything in the world you wanted, what would it be?"

The sides of her mouth lifted slightly. "Realistically, or fantasy time?"

"Anything. Your wildest dream."

"Mm, fantasy. That makes it a serious question." She thought a moment. "You know me. I'd like to change a few things. For the better."

"Jesus, V, you're a bleeding heart. You're practically killing yourself as it is. What more can you do?"

"*That's* what I have to decide."

He looked at her curiously.

"Don't ask," she said before he did.

He leaned forward with his elbow on the table, rolling his knife over and back again. He couldn't complain about her wanting to improve the world; the problem was, she wanted a better world for everyone but herself. There'd be no personal life for her—no wedding cake, no diapers, no PTA, no mortgage, no kids. She'd chosen a different course, and even when she doubted the wisdom of it—which she did now and then, even without pressure from him—all she had to do was see a pregnant client with her back killing her, or her hair falling out, and like a rubber band she reverted to form. If she could have had an eighteen-year-old child delivered by a gigantic stork—no diapers, car insurance paid up, SATs finished—she might have gone for that. Maybe.

Jack knew all this, as he had from the start. But like women who loved men, he thought he could change her. What he didn't understand was something new: her depression, her lost sense of humor, her emotional distance and antipathy toward the world. Or toward him. Or someone. Gone were the days of Saturday-night movies, the Sunday *Times*, the never-made bed. It was all disappearing, and he didn't know why.

"I can't change the world for you," he said, "but I can give you some love and respect. Regardless of our differences."

"If we had no differences, life would be boring."

He liked the answer.

The waiter reappeared, took their orders, and left them drinking their red wine from large glasses.

"What is it about marriage that bothers you most?" he asked. "Being tied down?"

"Maybe a little. Not a lot."

"Everyone expecting you to behave like a married person, whatever that is?" he said.

"It is a little irritating, don't you think?"

"How about the law?"

"The husband's superior rights? It rankles, but in time it'll change."

"Are you worried about the sex going stale between us?"

"Yes, but more for what it would do to you than to me. Look, sweetheart, there's no silver bullet here. The thought of being married just makes me feel vaguely dishonest. You know, sort of the way a nun must feel about civilian life—it's fine for everybody else, but not for me. I see clients in my office every day and I want to help them make it, but when I see what 'making it' actually means, I don't want it for myself. All these women in curlers, killing themselves cleaning floors and wiping noses, worrying about Pop-Tarts and whether their husbands are going to cut off their allowances for the third time in three weeks. Jesus."

She fiddled with the pepper shaker. "Pretty hypocritical, isn't it? Not wanting to be like the people you help?"

"Marriage is like every other adventure. The best and worst of it are in your imagination."

"I'm sure all marriages aren't nightmares. I'm just afraid mine would be."

"I'll give up Pop-Tarts."

She smiled at him. "I could handle it if it weren't for children. You want them profoundly, and I profoundly don't. It doesn't leave much room for compromise."

"Maybe in time you'll change your mind."

"I'm forty, Jack. There isn't much time left."

"So, we get married and see what happens."

She smiled and took a nervous last drag on her cigarette, which he took as a good sign. "If determination counts, I should have married you a long time ago," she said. "Do we have to decide this tonight?"

He nodded yes. They'd been at this for months; a decision was long overdue. His internal hourglass told him it was time to stop treading water and get on with it. At some point even a procrastinator ran out of sand.

A flicker of Molly McCormick's face crossed his mind, irritating him with its bad timing, like an intruding waiter.

Victoria reached her hand across the table and laid it on his open palm. "Are you really sure you want to do this?"

"Absolutely," he said.

"I've been saying no for so long. What would you do if I said yes?"

He pushed his hand into his pocket and felt the Susan B. Anthony between his fingers. "I'll show you." He started to pull out the coin—just as the waiter intruded, telephone in hand.

"Excuse me, Miss Winters. You have an urgent call."

She pulled her hand back from Jack's. "Who in the world?"

"It's a Dr. Redpath," the man said, placing the phone on the table.

Jack shoved the Susan B. Anthony back into his pocket and killed the waiter with his eyes.

"I told her you were in the middle of dinner," the man sniffed, "but she said she was a *doctor*."

Victoria picked up the receiver. "Hello?"

"You won," Rachel said.

"Won what?"

"Titus is announcing his decision in the morning. He's lifting the injunction against Zenobia's abortion."

"How do you know?"

"A friend at the courthouse saw his opinion. It's a long diatribe about how *Roe* v. *Wade* is unconstitutional, but says until it's overturned, he has no choice but to lift the injunction."

Victoria covered the mouthpiece and whispered to Jack, "We won Zenobia's case." She fingered the telephone cord and smiled as Rachel continued.

"I'm out at the farm. I've been trying to call Zenobia for hours, but her line's busy."

"That's strange," Victoria said. "I was there an hour ago and no one answered the door."

"Maybe the phone's off the hook. I hate to interrupt dinner, but I wanted you to know. Titus is issuing his opinion first thing in the morning. We'd better find her as fast as possible."

"The minute Hackett gets the decision he'll run to the court of appeals and try to get a stay," Victoria said.

"How long would that take him?"

"Couple of hours, assuming he can find a judge who'll give him one."

"I wouldn't take the chance," Rachel said. "If we get her to the clinic and prep her, Kathy can do the procedure first thing in the morning."

"I'm on my way." She hung up and looked at Jack. "Sorry," she said, "We have to go."

"What is it?"

"Tell you in the car."

• • •

They climbed the steps of the apartment house, trying, and failing, to separate oxygen from the smell of urine. On the sixth floor, Victoria knocked on the door and paced back and forth, waiting. Jack was preparing to knock again when it occurred to him to try the doorknob. He turned it. The door opened.

He flicked on a light switch as Victoria closed the door. The room was in perfect order—the afghan folded neatly on the arm of the sofa, the rag rug unwrinkled, the leaves on the schefflera shiny and green.

Jack walked to the kitchenette and saw a fresh dish towel hanging neatly on the handle of the refrigerator door. Victoria went to a bedroom door and knocked gently.

"Zenobia?" She listened for an answer. "Zenobia, it's me, Victoria. Are you there?"

She waited a moment and opened the door.

Instantly her body went rigid and her hands rose to her mouth.

Jack walked up behind her and saw Zenobia lying in a white flannel shift, arms folded peacefully across her chest, her body lit by a small bedside lamp.

He slipped past Victoria and walked to the bed and laid his fingers on Zenobia's neck. It was cold. He touched her abdomen to see if the fetus was still alive. Her belly was flat. The fetus gone.

"She's had the abortion," he said.

Victoria dropped her hands from her face and walked to the living-room couch and sat down slowly, an old woman in pain.

Jack reached for the telephone on the nightstand and called the police. As he hung up, he saw Zenobia's Bible with a white piece of paper between the pages. He opened it and found an envelope from her church, Zion Baptist. Beneath it was a passage she had underlined in the Book of Psalms: *Have mercy upon me, O Lord, for I am weak.*

He placed the envelope back in the book and was about to close it when he noticed something written on one end. Holding it under the lamp, he saw the words *Denied clinic midnite 555-3273* written in black ink. He studied it briefly, turning it over and back again. She must have received a telephone call and jotted a note.

He considered the situation a moment. Logic said leave it there. Instinct said keep it.

He stuck the envelope into his inside coat pocket.

• • •

It was eleven-fifteen when Jack and Victoria pulled up in front of their house in Georgetown. After explaining to homicide what had happened, Jack asked a couple of questions of his own. Where had Zenobia been operated on? And what had killed her? The cops had no idea.

He drove Victoria home. Sitting at the curb under a street lamp, he turned off the engine and waited for her to make the first move. Finally she reached for the door handle.

"It's going to take a thousand years," she said, and got out.

They entered their second-floor bedroom using the hallway light to navigate. He had seen her this depressed only once before, three years earlier in Tijuana, the night he'd picked up the scar over his right eye. If what had happened then had taken her three days to recover from, God only knew how long this would take. He watched her light a half-burned candle on the nightstand as he stretched out on the bed, hands behind his head. She sat on the edge of the mattress, unbuttoning her blouse.

"I know what you're going to say," she said softly, "but this was my fault."

He raised his hands into the air as if he were reaching for an invisible trapeze. "What more could you have done?"

"I could have gotten her an abortion."

"How?"

"All she wanted was permission. I could have figured it out."

"Come on, V. You explained the law, you lied to get her into a clinic—" He pictured the word *clinic* on the envelope. The instinct that led him to pocket it nagged him. "You weren't—you didn't try that again, did you?"

"Try what?"

"To arrange an illegal abortion?"

"I wish I had. She couldn't have come out any worse."

"Be serious, V."

"I am. Whatever trouble I'd have gotten into, at least she wouldn't have lost her life to some back-alley butcher. God, I can't tell you how much I hate Abner Titus." She rose off the bed and headed for her walk-in closet. "Remember what you once told me? A litigator's not worth a damn unless she's always on the verge of contempt? You were right. It's all about nerve. Nothing happens unless you're willing to take risks."

She sounded as if she were lecturing herself. "What else is bothering you?" he asked. "Besides her death?"

"Isn't that enough?"

"Yeah, but you've been through this before. Remember the fifteen-year-old girl who died a few months ago? Why's this one hitting you harder than that?"

She hung up her skirt. "I think that's the problem. They accumulate until one of them is the last straw and you finally get the point."

"Get what point?" She didn't answer. "Goddamn it, V, talk to me. What the hell's going on?"

The telephone rang. She answered and heard Rachel's voice.

"I just got in and heard your message on the answering machine," she said. "Dear God. Are you all right?"

"Yes," Victoria said. "Sort of."

"You don't sound like it. Want me to come into town?"

"No." She covered the mouthpiece and said "Rachel" to Jack.

Using the remote control, he turned on the television set and headed for the bathroom, leaving the door open a crack to listen to the news.

Rachel said, "You really took a double whammy tonight, didn't you?"

"Yeah," she said reflexively. Then she said, "What do you mean, double whammy?"

"Zenobia and Abner Titus."

"What about Abner Titus?"

Rachel digested the question. "Oh, my Lord, Vick. You haven't heard."

"Heard what?"

"Justice Brown resigned tonight. The president's nominated Abner Titus to be chief justice."

Victoria's face fell.

Rachel said, "I think it's time we had a heart-to-heart talk, don't you?" Victoria still said nothing. "It's now or never."

"We'll talk tomorrow," Victoria said. She hung up and looked at the television set. On screen, behind an anchorman, was a photograph of Abner Titus.

"You prick," she said softly. "You fucking little prick."

Jack found the toothpaste in the drawer beside the sink, lying on top of Victoria's birth-control pills. He bit off a piece and stuck his toothbrush into his mouth. Brushing away, he glanced through the partly opened doorway toward the TV set and noticed Victoria standing across the room, undressed, examining herself in front of the full-length mirror on her closet door. Her head was cocked slightly to the side, her fingers spread apart on her bare abdomen as if she were holding a volleyball. Or imagining a pregnancy. She picked up her fish-on-a-bicycle T-shirt and pulled it onto her upper arms, turning it into a straitjacket. Then, instead of lifting it over her head, she turned her back to the mirror and slid into a sitting position on the floor. And cried.

Jack left the bathroom wrapped in a towel and walked over to her, turning off the television set as he went. She looked up at him, her face lined in the flickering candlelight, and extended her hands. He pulled the T-shirt off her arms and sat facing her with his hands wrapped around her back.

"I don't know what to do," she said. "I'm so burned-out I can't think straight."

He held her until she stopped crying. After a few minutes she turned her face up to his. Her eyes were red, the subtle makeup she wore streaked.

"I love you," she said in a cracked voice. "Don't forget that. No matter what happens."

He looked perplexed. "Why, what's going to happen?"

She looked at him the way she had at dinner—preoccupied, as if she wanted to tell him something but couldn't.

It was time to cut the crap and get serious. "Listen, V—"

She placed her puffed up lips on his, cutting him off. Then she raised herself to her knees and pushed him down on his back.

"What are you—"

"Shh," she said.

She pulled off his towel, kissed him, and swung her leg over his midsection, straddling him. Holding the kiss, she made him ready. And then she guided him slowly, surely, into the seam of her body.

She sat up, arched and willowy, and began her elliptical motion. Elegant and smooth. Purposeful. *What brought this on?* Her face became flushed and her muscles elastic: soon her sweat-covered skin was pebbled with gooseflesh, glowing in the candlelight like orange peel bathed in oil. Whatever it was, he didn't mind. Suddenly they were back in the old days once again . . . living in the present . . . unconcerned about the future . . . lost in each other.

It hadn't been that long ago; he knew exactly what to do. She liked him to paint pictures of hidden places behind her eyes . . . places like a sweltering, summertime attic where he could lay her on cotton batting and peel off all her clothes, stripping her down to her skin and her fantasies—not just the ones she knew about, but better still, the ones she didn't. Once he'd probed deep enough, he knew he'd find another person inside her—an uninhibited, erotic Victoria, hiding and compressed like a genie in a bottle. He knew what it took to release her, too—the right words, the right friction—and once her spirit was free, how to conspire with it and corrupt her with her own appetites . . . dizzying her in her own senses . . . convincing her she was so light and graceful and powerful she could do anything she wanted—*anything*—even fly. Once she trusted him, he'd take her to the edge of an imaginary cliff, close her eyes, and slowly, carefully, turn her inside out . . . emptying every fear and thought she had until there was nothing left of her but breath and heat and a core of pure, undiluted self. Then, at the first quiver of her muscle, he'd spread her wings . . . kiss the warmest, dampest feathers . . . and fling her over the side, into her dreams . . . down canyon walls through clean, blue air in one exquisite, concentrated, moment of self-love.

Not tonight.

Her eyes were closed and her face in pain, her voice external and strained even as she went through the motions. "No," she said as if she were talking to someone else. "I can't."

Can't what? "Don't think," he said.

She opened her eyes and looked at him blankly, as if she'd just discovered he was there.

"Let go," he whispered. "Do what your voice is asking."

She stared at him, absorbing permission. Once again she began moving in smooth, purposeful strokes. "Forgive me," she whispered.

"Nothing to forgive," he said, but she was already beyond the thought.

She increased the pace, driving herself forward, driving him on his back until the top of his head was bumping up against the bottom of the full-length closet-door mirror.

He looked up at it and remembered her words. . . . *don't like myself anymore . . .*

He placed his hand on the nape of her neck and drew her head forward, forcing her palms against the mirror to keep herself from toppling over. She bowed her head and let her hair fall down as if she were washing it under a pump, but he lifted her head upright. Pushing her hair aside, he startled her with her own reflection.

She stopped moving and studied her face . . . the moist lashes and small rivulets of sweat on her lips. Reckless eyes radiating agony mixed with pleasure.

He drew her head forward and spoke in a carnal language only the two of them understood, penetrating the last membranes of her resistance. He'd drawn her face so close to the mirror her breath fogged it in disappearing puffs. Then he told her to give in . . . open up . . . bridge the last inch . . . and complete the touch.

Her lips met her own lips on the glass. She held it as if it were her first kiss ever.

With a small tremor, she dropped over the edge of the cliff.

She turned her cheek against the mirror, framing her face with her outstretched fingers, expelling her lungs and throat with music. Her body expanded and released; he pulled her face into the crook of his neck and pressed his palms against the small of her back, telling her to rest. Instead, she gathered her strength and sat upright, looking back at him from the distance she'd fallen.

"Not yet," she said.

She moved on him smoothly, a kite flier striding in a field of grass, string in hand . . . raising him behind her in the wind. Finally, feeling him tugging to go free, she spoke the two magic words that snapped his line, sending him bursting into the air, gravity free—everything broken, everything expelled—leaving nothing inside him but a cool, electric wind roaring through the empty space that had once housed his brain.

A few moments later they lay side by side on the bedroom floor, two paratroopers dropped from separate skies, back on terra firma at last . . . collecting themselves, checking for damage, plodding toward each other in heavy, earthbound steps. Joining forces once again.

They were almost asleep when Jack lifted himself off the floor, grabbed a down quilt from the bed, and covered Victoria, who was lying on her stomach with her hair covering her face.

"You awake?" he whispered.

"Yes," she said.

"Marry me," he said.

Her silence was like a wounded giant, large and helpless. "I can't."

"Why not?"

She reached out and laid her hand on top of his. "It wouldn't be fair."

"To who?"

"Anyone."

"Who else is there?"

She said nothing.

"That's it?" he said. "Your final answer?"

"Yes."

"Even though it means—"

"Don't say it. I know what it means."

This time the helpless silence was his. "We're going to miss each other, V."

"I know," she said. "I already do."

PART TWO

He'd been through breakups before and knew what they were about. First you spent your time looking at the bright side of things—no more of this, no more of that, a new world is waiting, anything is possible. Then you spent your time fighting the gloom that came from realizing there'd be no more of this, no more of that, a new world was waiting, anything was possible. The whole process was irritating as hell.

As he approached the street corner near his office building, a four-year-old boy stepped off the curb against a red light only to be yanked back by his mother, who proceeded to scold him severely. Before she'd finished, the boy's chin was trembling and his eyes were brimming with tears. The light turned green, and as Jack walked past them it struck him that Mother Nature was truly perverse, making humans tough, resilient, and intelligent—conquerors of worlds, adventurers into the universe—yet completely vulnerable to the most ordinary ailments on the planet: the common cold and the loss of love.

He pictured the human ego as an enormous elephant perched on a fine-spun crystal stem, waiting for the slightest emotional jiggle to bring it crashing down. How else could you explain a mother's ordinary criticism of a daughter—"Why can't you be more like your older sister?"—growing in the girl's brain like a malignant tumor for fifty years? Or presidents bedding every woman they could lay their hands on, satisfying insecurity so bottomless it compelled them to risk the most powerful office on earth? How else could the loss of a little boy's pill-covered blanket, picked each night as he went to sleep, wound him so deeply that forty years of biting his nails couldn't mend it? What was it about the psychic cocoon—so small people couldn't find it, so strong it dictated their happiness, yet so frail it could be crushed by a whisper?

Jack walked into his reception area, said hello to his secretary, Faith, and entered his office. He sat at his desk and began reading the mail. Before he'd finished the first letter, he reached for a frame on his desk—a snapshot of Victoria sitting on the beach in Baja, Mexico. After holding it a moment, he opened his desk drawer and placed it inside.

Facedown. It had been only three days since they'd split up, and her image was an unwelcome hook, suspending him in a sea of sentiment. As did certain other grabbers, like his secretary's oval fingernails, or someone's long, light brown hair, or the faint fragrance of Victoria's perfume on the old terry-cloth robe he'd retrieved from their bathroom.

He turned back to the pile of mail, read three letters, and once again found himself staring into space. *Snap out of it. You're a congressman; do what they do best. Cut a deal with yourself.*

He opened the desk drawer and turned the picture faceup, but without placing it back on the desk. A compromise. Closing the drawer, he hoped he'd fooled himself long enough to get back to work.

A knock at the door and his secretary entered to discuss his schedule. Was he planning to attend Senator Dickey's poker game this week? No, he said, distracted, reading. Had he remembered to tell Victoria about the Democratic Founders Club dinner on Ellis Island? No, he said, he'd be taking someone else. Excuse me? Did he say he'd be taking someone else? Yes, he said, he'd be taking someone else.

He felt a cold, murderous stare and, without looking up, heard footsteps and the door close with a special thunk.

And they say women don't bond.

After a morning of meetings and committee hearings, Jack canceled lunch and grabbed a taxi for Georgetown to pack up a few more things and move out. With a couple of telephone calls he had arranged temporary quarters in a town house on Capitol Hill, the home-away-from-home for three California congressmen. The place was large and only two blocks from his office, a convenience he appreciated.

When he was living with Victoria, he ordinarily flew home to New York on Fridays. Now, except when the legislative calendar was especially crowded, he decided he'd take the shuttle to New York on Thursday afternoons, as soon as Congress adjourned for the week, and catch the first shuttle back on Tuesday mornings when it reconvened. A six-pack of Yoo-Hoo in the refrigerator, a few tins of sardines in the pantry, and he'd feel right at home.

After packing some clothes, a dozen files, toilet articles, and a biography of Abraham Lincoln, he grabbed a cab to his new quarters, dropped off his suitcase, and returned to his office. Sitting at his desk, he reached into his coat pocket and withdrew the envelope he'd found in Zenobia Davis's Bible. He studied its handwritten words: *Denied clinic midnite 555-3273.* What did this stuff mean? Was *denied* an indication that someone had called Zenobia to tell her the judge had denied her husband's petition? Did *clinic midnite* refer to a back-alley abortionist? And whose telephone number was 555-3273?

He picked up the receiver and punched it in.

"Hello?" a woman's voice answered.

"Hello," he said. "Is this—I'm sorry, who is this please?"

"This is a private line. Whom are you calling?"

He faked it. "The clinic."

"Sorry, I'm afraid you've reached the wrong number."

"This isn't a women's health clinic?"

"No, it's not," the woman's voice singsonged.

"Hmm. That's strange. Is there someone there who can help me?"

"I'm sure if you call the information operator—"

"See, the problem is I'm at a borrowed telephone and—"

"Sir, you've reached the United States Courthouse, not a health clinic."

United States Courthouse? "Oh, of course, what am I thinking?" *Take a shot.* "This is Judge Titus's line, isn't it?"

"No sir. You're coming in on the private line of his law clerk, who's in court right now, and I really must go."

Titus's law clerk? "Sorry." He placed the receiver in its cradle.

He stared at the envelope. He knew nothing about Titus's law clerk, except that Victoria had described her as a pain in the ass. But if a clerk wanted to communicate with a litigant, why would she violate court rules and call her directly instead of calling her lawyer, Victoria? And why would she tip off Zenobia Davis about the judge's decision before he announced it? Or discuss a "clinic" with her? At "midnight"?

More to the point, why assume that because the call to Zenobia had been made on the law clerk's line, it had been made by her instead of her boss?

What was Titus up to? Could he really have had a hand in Zenobia Davis's death?

They stood at a counter in the examination room looking through the folder of photographs of Zenobia Davis's autopsy.

Landy said, "Pretty specialized beat you've got, abortion-related homicides. How'd that happen?"

Molly shook her head *who knows*? "First they ask you to find out what Melvin Shivers ate for breakfast, then when his pal Harley Moon disappears, they assign you to cover that because you're supposed to know what clinic bombers eat for breakfast. Then it's Eli Graves's press conference, and before you know it, if it's got anything to do with the subject, it's yours. But I've got no complaints. It's a step up from microwavable cake batter." She removed her shoes and wiggled her toes. "So, did she die from a back-alley abortion?"

"If she did, it must have been a pretty fancy back alley," Landy said. "She had a hysterotomy."

"A what?"

He showed her a photograph of a cut running from above Zenobia's navel to her pelvic bone. Molly took it in without sweating.

"Looks like a cesarean," she said.

"That's what it is. Not exactly something you do with a coat hanger."

"Why would someone abort her with a cesarean?"

"The fetus was probably too big. According to the police report, she was at the end of her second trimester." He paused. "But that's not what killed her."

"It isn't?"

"She died from a disseminated intravascular coagulopathy. DIC for short. A form of massive bleeding."

"That sounds back-alley to me."

"Not necessarily. Sometimes during surgery the blood simply stops clotting, and in a matter of seconds all the vessels are oozing."

"Really."

"Yeah. I saw it happen once, during my residency. This woman came in with an ectopic pregnancy, and when they—you know what an ectopic pregnancy is, right?"

"A pregnancy outside the womb, isn't it?"

178

"Yeah, usually in the fallopian tube."

"Usually?"

"Occasionally a fertilized egg escapes the fallopian tube and migrates to someplace inside the abdomen, like an intestine or the abdominal wall."

"How can it stay alive outside the womb?"

"Once it attaches itself to a blood supply, far as it knows it *is* in the womb."

"Amazing. So who needs wombs?"

He laughed. "They're a big help. If an ectopic tears loose, it opens up blood vessels. If it's bad enough, the woman will bleed to death fast." Molly winced. "Anyway, this woman I saw had an ectopic, and when the surgeon went in to remove it, she began major-league hemorrhaging."

"God."

"He tried to find the source of the bleeding, which was like trying to fix a pipe in the bottom of a tub of tomato sauce. The woman was bleeding so heavily they couldn't suction it out fast enough to see where it was coming from."

"Sounds awful."

"It's pretty dramatic. The surgeon called for help, and pretty soon three of them were clamping and suturing every vessel they could lay their hands on—nurses pumping her full of blood and plasma, everybody scrambling like mad."

"Did it work?"

He shook his head. "They packed her with gauze, but she was gone in thirty minutes."

"What a nightmare. And that's what happened to Zenobia Davis?"

"Not an ectopic pregnancy, but the hemorrhaging, yes."

"How can you tell?"

"The lab found no fibrinogen in her blood, the stuff that makes it clot, and high levels of thromboplastin, which thins it out. Classic footprint of a DIC."

"Did you see anything in her autopsy that looked funny?"

"No," he said. "Not really."

His tone of voice gave him away. She stopped turning photographs. "What do you mean, 'not really'?"

"Nothing. Just 'not really.' "

"You're holding out on me, Elliot."

He touched his bow tie again.

"You're a rotten liar, Elliot. Give."

"I can't go into it."

"Why not?"

"I have to talk to homicide first—"

"Elliot!"

"—I absolutely can't. Not yet—"

"I won't use it, I won't say a thing—"

"No way, Molly." Silence. "Sorry."

She turned pages of photos again.

"You're awfully quiet," he said.

She pulled on her shoulder-bag strap. "I'm mad at you." She pushed her feet into her pumps and looked at one more photograph, a shot of Zenobia Davis's abdomen taken immediately after she'd been brought to the morgue, before Landy had removed the abortionist's sutures.

"This is sort of interesting," she said.

"What?"

"The suture. It's a baseball stitch. Just like Shivers's."

Landy took a look. "That's a standard closing stitch when a patient dies during surgery."

Molly gave up with a sigh. "Okay, Elliot, you win. I'm out of here."

"Have a cup of coffee and relax."

"Believe me, there's nothing I'd rather do than hang out in a morgue drinking coffee, but now and then I have to convince my producer I'm out here gathering news."

He touched his bow tie, spreading his fingers from the knot to the edges. "Next time I'll be able to tell you more."

"Next time, right." The only way she was going to get this story was to take it.

His tie was still crooked, so she reached up to straighten it. "I'm not really mad at you," she said. "You're just doing your job, that's all." She patted it in place and smiled at him. "Which is exactly what I'm going to do myself."

In any other city, the four players assembled around the felt-covered poker table would rarely have found themselves in the same ballpark, much less the same card game. But in Washington, where the veneer of democracy and the reality of ambition blurred class distinctions, the gathering was as normal as politicians at a Fourth of July picnic.

"Congratulations, Abner," Sticks Dickey said, lifting his glass to Titus. The other players, Eli Graves and Reverend Gaylord Jenkins, followed.

Titus riffled a stack of chips in his fingers. "I still have to be confirmed."

The paneled game room in Senator Dickey's sprawling Georgetown house was the perfect place for conducting political business. Graves's prickly, visceral reaction to Abner Titus worried Dickey enough to try to bring Titus and Graves together in a comfortable, informal setting. If Titus's confirmation hearings built up a head of steam, no one would stop it—hostile liberals, disaffected conservatives, both groups put together. But in a close, controversial hearing, Eli Graves's clout could help tilt the decision either way.

"Nothing's a slam dunk in the Senate," Dickey said, "but once a president sends up a judicial appointment, he usually gets what he wants."

Titus stopped playing with his chips, sipped his martini, and folded his hands in front of him. "So what do you think?" he asked Dickey.

"Other than the abortion issue? Piece of cake."

Graves said, "What do you mean 'other than abortion'? I thought that's the reason he was appointed."

Dickey scowled, and Titus said, "What am I in for?"

"A dollar," Gaylord Jenkins said, his eyelids slightly droopy. Titus ignored him the way imperious judges knew how.

"It's too early to tell," Dickey said, "but you know what the women's groups are going to say."

Graves looked disgusted.

"What about this woman who died?" Dickey asked.

"Zenobia Davis?" Titus said.

"They'll try to use that against you," Dickey said. "I'll open for fifty cents."

Everyone checked his cards and considered the pot. And Zenobia Davis.

The doorbell rang. Dickey looked up, surprised. On poker nights his wife was out and the housekeeper off. He laid his cards facedown and walked down the hall and opened the door. It was Jack MacLeod, in a jacket, jeans, and loafers.

"Jack! What the hell are you doing here?"

Jack looked confused. "It's Thursday night, isn't it?"

"Yes, but your office said you were going home to New York."

Jack finally heard his secretary asking him if he was going to play, and his own reply, no. "Jesus, Sticks. I forgot."

Dickey reached out and grabbed him by the arm. "Come on in." He pulled him through the door into the foyer. "We need a fourth."

A fourth? Dickey usually had six or seven, never less than five. Jack wondered who had canceled out.

Dickey led him into the living room and pointed toward a sofa. "Have a seat and I'll be back in a city minute."

Dickey walked into the study and closed the door. "It's MacLeod," he said. "We can poll him on this Zenobia Davis business right now." He looked at Graves and pointed toward the kitchen. "Take the servants' stair and make yourself scarce awhile."

Graves didn't like being told what to do, but he got up anyway. Jenkins stacked his friend's chips and handed them to him as he left. Dickey surveyed the room, motioned for Jenkins to get rid of Graves's beer mug, and left.

Dickey found Jack standing at the fireplace examining a photograph of the senator's wife on the mantelpiece. Putting his arm around Jack's shoulder, he pulled him toward the hallway.

"I hope you brought cash," he said, grinning.

They entered the study and Jack saw Abner Titus first. "Congratulations, Judge," he said, extending a hand.

Dickey introduced Jack to Reverend Jenkins, whom Jack knew by reputation but had never met. Then Jack sat down in Graves's chair, which had cooled enough for him not to notice. "What's the game?" he asked.

"Five-card draw," Dickey said, picking up the deck. "A buck to play."

Jack reached into his pocket and withdrew a small fold of bills, swapped them for chips, and anted up.

The group played the hand stiffly, a slightly inebriated Reverend Jenkins mumbling to himself about how the game of cards resembled the game of life, full of risks and uncertainties but surmountable with faith.

Dickey won the hand after a single round of betting.

"That girlfriend of yours," he said to Jack as he raked in the pot, "now there's one hell of a lawyer."

Ex-girlfriend, Jack thought, hating the *ex*. "That she is," he said. "Although she's not too happy about her profession at the moment." He glanced at Titus.

Titus drank his martini and took the deck from Jenkins. "Her client's death was a real shame," Titus said, "but it wasn't her fault. If Davis had been a little more patient, she would have been fine."

Jack pictured Zenobia Davis's dead body and felt his cheeks redden.

"What's the story on this woman?" Dickey asked Jack. He opened the betting with a dollar.

"I don't know the whole story," Jack said, "but it wasn't a lack of patience that killed her. If anything, it was the opposite." He checked his hand again, saw a pair of tens and a queen, and ponied up his dollar. He considered keeping the queen, but tossed it away with two other cards and held the tens.

"How'd she have too much patience?" Titus asked. He dealt everyone three new cards and arranged his hand.

Jack focused on his new cards: a useless seven, an equally useless deuce, and a queen that would have paired nicely with the one he'd just tossed away. Right move, wrong result. He'd have to play his tens.

"I'd say the system worked just fine for her," Titus continued. "She won. A few more hours and she would have had the abortion she wanted."

Sticks opened the betting with two dollars.

"Wasn't that the first cliché they taught us in law school?" Jack said. "Justice delayed is justice denied?"

"I like that," Jenkins said, pushing four blue chips into the pot. "Up another two. 'Justice delayed is justice denied.' That's good."

Jack added his four dollars and said nothing. Dickey squinted at his cards, laid his unlit cigar on the beige felt, and tossed in two dollars and called. Everyone had a pair, but none as good as Jenkins's kings. He raked in the pot.

Jack shuffled the deck, glancing across the table at Titus, watching him glance back.

"Well, you're right," Titus said. "Justice delayed *is* justice denied. If the Supreme Court had written a decent opinion when it wrote *Roe* v. *Wade*, a lot of this upheaval could have been avoided. Zenobia Davis's baby would have been born and she would have been alive tonight."

Jack cut the deck and pushed it to Jenkins, who dealt. "I think she felt her life was threatened by staying pregnant," he said.

"Nonsense," Titus said.

Dickey intervened. "Jack, you and I take enough testimony on this subject when the sun's up to keep goin' at it after dark."

"This isn't serious, Sticks," Jack said, picking up his cards. "Not compared to what it'll be like with fifty million Americans watching on the evening news." His comment caught Titus in the middle of popping a blood pressure pill. Titus hesitated before washing it down with a gulp of his martini. Just long enough for Jack to notice.

Dickey saw his opening. "How big a factor you think this Zenobia Davis thing's gonna be?"

Jack separated his cards with his thumb and looked at his hand. A pair of aces. He opened with two dollars.

"Hard to say," he said. "Maybe the press won't see a connection between the judge's late decision and her death."

"I should hope to kiss a pig they won't," Dickey said. He saw Jack's two dollars.

"On the other hand," Jack said, looking at Titus, "I'm sure you can expect a few surprises."

Titus looked down at his chips and said, "I'll see your two and raise five." He pushed a stack of seven into the pot.

"This is gettin' rich fast," Jenkins said, scowling. In most Washington poker games, the money wagered was inconsequential compared to personality, ego, and conquest. Who one-upped whom, who played with style and skill, who gave no quarter and expected none, who won and who lost—these were the real stakes; money was merely the proxy.

"What do you think, Gaylord?" Jack asked. "You're on the Hill all the time."

"Oh, I'm the last person you should ask about women," he said. He pushed seven blue chips into the pot.

"Why is that?"

"My views on women and politics are too basic for this town. Who wants cards?" Jack and Dickey asked for three, Titus only one. "Yeah, my views come straight out of First Timothy two-eleven." Jenkins dealt out the cards and scripture with equal smoothness: " 'Let a woman learn in silence with all submissiveness I permit no woman to teach or to have authority over men she is to keep silent for Adam was formed first then Eve and Adam was not deceived but the woman was deceived and became a transgressor yet woman will be saved through bearing children if she continues in faith and love and holiness with modesty' dealer takes two." He laid down the deck. "Besides," he said, "the only time liberals ever pay attention to born-again Christians is when one of us gets caught screwing a hooker. Then it's one TV network after another telling the world what hypocrites we are." His eyes darkened as he sipped his whiskey. "You guys ever looked closer, you'd find a reason or two to take us seriously."

Dickey's temperature dropped twenty degrees.

"Believe me," Jack said, "there isn't anybody in Congress who doesn't take you and FUNPAC seriously." FUNPAC was the acronym for the Fundamentalist Political Action Committee, of which the Reverend Gaylord Jenkins was executive director.

"I wasn't talking about money," Jenkins said.

Dickey gritted his teeth. "Ease up, Gaylord."

"Tell me something," Jenkins continued. "Everybody's so all-fired upset about this Zenobia Davis woman, but what about this fellow they found mutilated with a toy doll in his gut? And his missing partner?"

"I don't know anyone who excuses that," Jack said, "but you can hardly compare those guys with Zenobia Davis. Not when you consider what they did."

"Why? What'd they do?" Jenkins asked.

Jack looked at him incredulously.

"Bombing clinics isn't nice," Jenkins said, "but sometimes it's the only thing you can do."

"The only thing you can do to do what?" Jack asked.

"Protect life."

Dickey sank into his chair.

"You're interesting, Gaylord," Jack said. "A Christian minister who thinks Christ is irrelevant."

"Oh, I'm not saying Christ is irrelevant. I'm just saying He was here two thousand years ago and a lot has happened since. Like suction machines and RU-486. After two millenniums, it's only natural Christianity's bigger than Christ."

"And the Bible?" Jack said.

Jenkins laughed. "I always get a kick out of nonbelievers who use the Bible to preach to believers."

"Who said I was a nonbeliever?"

"Come on, Jack. You liberals believe in the Lord about as much as I believe in *People* magazine." Jenkins brought his shot glass to his lips and turned it bottoms up.

"How about some poker?" Dickey said.

Jenkins ignored him. "The Ten Commandments are like everything else. You have to put them into the context of today's world to figure out what they mean."

"The man has a point," Titus said to Jack. "All he's doing is arguing against a strict construction of the Old Testament, which is exactly how liberals think the courts should interpret the Constitution." He smiled at the irony and examined his cards.

"Listen to that!" Jenkins said, pointing at Titus. "Don't you just love how he talks?" He fanned his cards in front of his nose and laid them facedown. "Truth is," he said, "when it comes to killing, we're all hypocrites. Heaven knows, you liberals have dropped more bombs to protect the American way of life than all us conservatives put together. FDR and World War Two, Kennedy and Johnson in Vietnam. Harry Truman in Hiroshima. Now there's a guy who killed more people in sixty seconds than all the abortion-clinic bombers could kill in a hundred years."

"You think that's the same thing?" Jack asked.

"In the eyes of the Lord, killing is killing," Jenkins said.

"Really," Jack said. "You think old Harry made it to heaven?"

Dickey said, "Pity the devil if he didn't."

"You've got me all wrong," Jenkins said. "I don't blame him for bombing the Japs. I would have done the same thing. And I would have bombed Hitler, too, like those rebel German officers tried to do. I'd bomb wholesale killers of the innocent any day. And you know what?"

"No, Gaylord, what?" Jack said.

"So would you."

Jenkins poured two fingers of Wild Turkey.

"Come on, fellows," Dickey said. "Let's play while we talk."

Jack studied his cards: a useless five, a useless deuce—and his third ace. He glanced quickly around the table. Dickey was examining his cards and chewing an unlit cigar. Titus lifted his martini to take a sip. Jack tried to read his face to see if he'd drawn the card he was looking for. He couldn't tell.

"I'm folding," Jenkins said. Dickey turned his cards over, too, leaving Jack and Titus in the game.

Jack looked at his three aces and considered Titus's hand. Had he filled a straight or a flush, or converted two pairs to a full house? Titus didn't have a habit of bluffing. On the other hand, good bluffers never did. Besides, they were no longer simply playing poker.

Jack counted his chips with his fingers. "Your five and up seven more," he said, betting all he had left.

Titus looked at his cards again.

He's taking too long, Jack thought. If he filled his hand, he has to bet it, not think about it.

"I'll see your seven dollars," Titus said, shoving a stack of three blue chips into the center of the table, "and raise you one." A blue chip landed in the pot with a thud.

What a weak bet. Must be trying to sucker me into raising him so he can kill me big. Except that's the oldest trick in the book, and he knows I know it, which means he wants me to fold, then he'll turn over a rotten hand and show everybody how he bluffed me out.

Like hell.

"I'll call," Jack said—and suddenly he realized he had no more chips. Now he understood Titus's bet: it was small enough to keep Jack in the game, force him to go light, and borrow a dollar from Titus in order to stay in the game. A clever way to win the ego game that counted, even if it meant losing the card game that didn't. No way he was going to owe Abner Titus anything. Not even a buck.

He reached into his left pocket and found the Susan B. Anthony. Pushing his thumb against it, he popped it out of its gold frame and slid it into the pot.

Titus laid his cards down and said nothing. Jack didn't see a single number on them. He didn't need to: they were all black and all shaped like little clubs. He'd filled a flush.

"Nicely done," he said, and meant it.

Titus raked in the chips and Jack watched the Susan B. Anthony disappear to the other side of the table. Titus picked it up and turned it over and back again, examining it curiously.

"These things never caught on, did they?" he said.

"Too small," Jack said.

Titus held it up. "Want it back?"

Jack saw it glinting under the Tiffany lamp. Taking a gift from Titus was as bad as owing him something. Besides, since he'd broken up with Victoria, the loss seemed fitting. "No thanks," he said, and Titus dropped it into his vest pocket.

Jack pushed back his chair. "Fellas," he said, standing, "I know it's early, but I'm calling it a night."

"Come on, Jack," Dickey said. "Your credit's good here." Jack patted him on the shoulder. Dickey protested, "How we gonna play without a fourth?"

"What about Eli?" Jenkins blurted out.

Dickey nearly freeze-dried him with a stare.

If Jack considered the comment at all, he assumed that Gaylord was proposing to call Graves on the telephone.

He said good night and left.

Jenkins left the room and brought Graves downstairs. Dickey was leaning back in his chair with his hands on the arms, chewing his unlit cigar.

"Look at this," Titus said, squinting at the silver dollar. "It's been defaced. It says *V*."

"Let me see," Jenkins said, reaching.

Graves looked at it, too. "*V* for Victoria Winters?"

"I'm sure," Titus said.

"She's a tough cookie," Graves said, staring at the coin. "I'd keep her in my pocket, too, if I could." He handed it across the table.

Titus raised his hand in a stop sign. "Federal judges don't carry defaced legal tender," he said. "Keep it."

Graves put it into his pocket. "What'd MacLeod say about the hearings?"

"Hope for the best and prepare for the worst," Dickey said, pushing the deck to Graves.

" 'Hope for the best and prepare for the worst,' " Jenkins repeated. "I like that."

Dickey laid his cigar on the table. "Gaylord?"

"Yeah?"

"Shut up and deal."

Molly stood in the shower with her head tilted back, water beating on the front of her neck, a bar of soap in both hands, between her breasts, as if in prayer. She turned her shoulder to the stream and lathered her body carefully, everywhere, trying to wash away the remains of a three-year affair.

She stepped out of the shower and wrapped herself in the Washington Hilton's oversized, white terry-cloth robe, then ran a wide-toothed comb through her hair. After slipping on a fresh pair of underpants, she turned to the fogged mirror and cleared a small spot with her sleeve. Leaning forward, she pulled down her lower lids and examined red fracture lines in the whites of her eyes. One more reason to do what she had to do. She snapped a rubber band around a ponytail and walked into the bedroom.

Jesse was in bed on his side, asleep, unaware that the light from the bathroom was dissolving over his body. The room remained musky with the scent of warm flesh and damp sheets, none of which pleased her. She climbed onto the bed and walked toward him on her knees, threw her leg over his hip, and sat on him. He didn't move. She looked at him a moment, lowered her lips to his ear, and kissed it.

"Two things," she said. "The shower's free, and I'm leaving."

He turned onto his back and looked up at her. He'd seen her this way only an hour before, without the robe or the somber face. "What're you talking about?"

"I'm finished," she said. "With the bathroom, and with us."

She started to climb off, but he placed his hands on her thighs and held her still. She relaxed. He moved his hands up under her robe to the top of her thighs—she didn't move—up the inside of her thighs—still holding—up to— His face fell. *Underpants?*

"Fun and games are over," she said. She swung her leg off him, bounced off the bed into a standing position, and picked up her jeans and pulled them on under her robe.

"Come on, Molly, let's talk about it."

"We've talked." She zipped her fly. "This time I mean it."

He sat up in the middle of the bed with his legs crossed, a sheet gathered in his lap, watching her pull on her socks and boots. She turned her

189

back to him, dropped her robe, and slipped on a bra. As she reached back to fasten it, he pushed aside the sheet and reached for her. Sensing him coming, she took a step forward, hooked the back, and pulled down her cotton sweater. When she turned and faced him, suddenly she was fully dressed and he was naked as a field mouse.

He retreated behind the rumpled sheet in the middle of the bed.

"Is it Linda?" he asked.

She dropped her hands to her sides. "Listen, Jesse. Yes, it's your wife. Yes, it's because we have no future. And yes, it's—I don't know. Wrong." She felt no need to acknowledge the positive side of the ledger—that they had once been in love, had once made plans with each other, had helped each other the way lovers do, even at a distance. A simple roll in the hay would have been easy to contend with—no blood, no foul—a small, pop-out dent in a woman's self-esteem. Superficial relationships always polished themselves off easily. It was the death of true love that left scars and took time, like the glue in an old piece of furniture . . . drying out slowly until the joints finally popped. She'd known that was happening months ago, which prompted her to leave West Virginia. But while an airplane could take her away at the speed of sound, her heart still had to follow at the pace of a sad-eyed beagle. She looked down at Jesse, sympathetically. "If we stay together, I'll be messing up something that's important to me."

"You referring to sex?"

She rolled her eyes. "I was referring to my *life*," she said, walking back to the bathroom. "Leave it to a horny professor of ethics to confuse the two."

She picked up her satin cosmetics bag, tossed her overnight things inside, and walked back into the bedroom. "There's nothing new in this, Jesse. Except this time I'm going through with it. I'm glad you came up to see me, really I am. But now you have to let go." She pulled on her raincoat.

"What are you going to do up here?" he asked.

"I'm a reporter. I'll report."

"Assuming you don't trade it in to get barefoot and pregnant." For a moment he'd forgotten that she couldn't. Not a good slip. "Sorry," he added.

She picked up a glass paperweight, shook it, and watched the snow swirl around a little Capitol dome they'd bought in a souvenir shop the day before. She threw her arms around him and held him one last time. "You're going to be fine," she said. "And so am I."

She got off the bed, grabbed her bag, and left.

He swept the long stick from side to side, tapping and feeling the ground as the street-smart pigeons waddled out of his way, always a step ahead, never allowing themselves to be touched. The old man was working his way along a Lafayette Park sidewalk in the direction of the White House, toward the sounds of a bullhorn and the crowd. "Bless you," he said to the passersby who dropped quarters into his paper coffee cup. "Bless you," he said to those who complimented him for the hand-painted sign on his back, BORN BLIND, and the one on his chest, LIFE, WHAT A BEAUTIFUL CHOICE. Fuck you, he thought to those who ignored him altogether. Behind his exterior he felt private and protected, hidden beneath baggy clothing, a scraggly gray beard, a fedora pulled low on his face, and dark glasses that blinded the world's eyes to his.

His stick continued to sweep from side to side until he touched something and stopped. No response. He jangled his cup of quarters: Hello there? Still no answer. He moved the tip of the stick around the object as deftly as a finger. This one was easy: a shoe. The tip came upward to an ankle, then lifted the heavy cuff of a man's trousers. "Excuse me, brother," he said, but the man didn't answer. He was asleep in the sun with his hands folded on his stomach, his head tilted back, a sheet of newspaper covering his face.

The blind man moved around the sleeping man's feet and stood in front of the empty bench seat next to him, preparing to sit. He reached down to feel the bench and stopped, uncannily, as if he could actually see the glob of pigeon dung on it, or the glob on the sleeping man's callused hands, or the glob on his brand-new pants, some of it long-dried, some of it still fresh and gooey. How long had this guy been asleep?

The blind man held still a moment, considering what to do. He turned his head slowly to the side as if he were looking over his shoulder. The sidewalk was empty; the crowd had gathered at the other side of the park for the rally.

He turned back to the sleeping man and leaned over him until their faces were mere inches apart, separated only by the classified section. Then he raised his finger to his dark glasses, pulled them down the bridge of his nose, and gently lifted the newspaper to peek underneath.

191

The first thing he saw was the man's open mouth—cracked lips, a tongue swollen and protruding—then the nostrils, caked and dry—then a pair of open eyes—dried, dead corneas staring straight up into a Help Wanted column.

The blind man stood up with a jerk, spilling his cup of quarters into Harley Moon's lap.

Molly and Dr. Elliot Landy stood on the mezzanine floor of the Air and Space Museum, leaning on a waist-high wall, looking down on the *Spirit of St. Louis* that hung in the main gallery.

"Moon's death looks a lot like Shivers's," Landy said. "The immediate cause was pneumococcal pneumonia instead of a stroke, but the rest of it was the same—a prior autopsy, a toy doll in the abdomen with a *keep it* note inside, exsanguination, a severed artery, a missing liver."

"The liver's the key," Molly said.

He didn't want to get started. "Tox and Micro are doing their best with tissue samples."

He opened a briefcase and pulled out a large manila envelope, which he set on top of the balcony wall. "I brought a few key photographs."

"Did you include close-ups of the hemorrhoids?" she asked.

"He didn't have any."

"How disappointing."

He began unwinding the string clasp. "Moon had the same calluses on his hands that Shivers did, and his right arm was superior to the left, which means he was probably right-handed."

"What's the significance of that?"

"Nothing. Just a fact. We did find a couple of new things, though." He opened the envelope. "We still operating on the same ground rules? Nothing disclosed without an okay from me?"

"That's the deal. Although—"

"Although what?"

"Nothing. My producer is on my case to come up with something. But no more than I am."

He withdrew a set of eight-by-ten color glossies. She held her breath. "Don't pass out on me, Molly. You'll draw a crowd."

"Thanks, El."

He showed her a human mouth with lips held apart by latex-covered fingers. "This is Harley Moon." She flinched but kept her eyes open. "See how the gums are growing down between the teeth?"

"Just like they did on Shivers," she said.

"Right. It's called gingival hyperplasia."

"What causes it?"

"Could be phenytoin. It's a drug used to control epilepsy."

"They both had epilepsy?"

"There's no indication either one did. Nothing in their records."

"What else could it be?"

"I'll tell you in a minute."

He showed her another photograph, which she examined out of the side of her eyes, cautiously. "This is the abdominal cavity, right?" she said.

"Very good. Melvin Shivers's to be exact. Keep this up and before long you'll be teaching this stuff." He pointed to some white strands. "See these things? They're called flimsy adhesions."

"Looks like pizza cheese."

"That's funny. That's what the interns call it." He shuffled the photographs. "Which reminds me, I'm getting hungry." He looked for a reaction but her eyes were closed tight. "Now, here's a similar adhesion inside Harley Moon's abdominal cavity."

"What causes these things?"

"They're the remains of something adhering to the abdominal walls." He flipped to another photograph. "Look. Two more."

"Like what? The toy doll?"

"No. Whatever it was had to be there a few weeks before they died. Besides, the toy dolls were in the intestine, not here. Look at this." He placed the first photo on the bottom of the pile and showed her a tight shot of a small white lump.

"What's that?"

"A granuloma in Harley Moon's abdomen. They grow around an irritant, sort of like an oyster grows a pearl around a piece of sand."

"Oh, sure. I can just see a string of these things on basic black."

"I dissected it." He showed her the next photo. "What's that look like to you?"

"A tiny knot?"

"Exactly. It's a suture."

"What's it doing in there?"

"I don't know, but he wasn't born with it. What gets me is what it's made of."

"What is it?"

"Black silk."

The image stopped her. "Black *silk*?"

"Yeah. Two-oh-gauge black silk."

Molly shivered.

Landy said, "It's unusual to find black silk here. It doesn't dissolve the way internal sutures normally do."

"So why would somebody put it in his stomach?"

"Only reason I can imagine is that whoever did it wanted it to last. And it wasn't in his stomach, Molly, it was in his abdomen. The anterior wall, behind his belly button. The granuloma had already grown around it by the time he died. Whoever cleaned him out during the partial autopsy must have missed it."

"Did you see signs of more than one?"

He shook his head. "But that doesn't mean more weren't there before his first autopsy."

She stood with her chin in her hand, watching the people on the floor below admiring the huge rotary engine on Lindbergh's airplane. "I still think the key to this thing is the missing livers," she said. "They were removed to hide what they're using them for, or who they're using them on. Something like that."

"The abdomen is a long distance from the liver, Molly."

"Can't be that far." She stared ahead. "Maybe somebody is developing a special liver."

He gathered up the photographs. "For what purpose?"

"Something weird and unnatural. Like, for somebody who can't live without one."

"Who? Superman?"

"Now, don't be ridiculous. Or do you think I am?"

"No, no, no, not at all. You made a guess. That's the thing about guesses. They're always so—*imaginative.*"

"You're humoring me."

"No, I'm not."

"Elliot."

"I'm not, really. I don't need to. You're doing a good job on your own."

She shot him rubber daggers. "All right, I gave it my best. What's yours?"

"I prefer facts to hypotheses. Look at this." He showed her a picture of Harley Moon's face, front and side views, and did the same with Melvin Shivers. "Notice anything unusual?"

"Yeah. They're both dead."

"Look at the hair growing out of their noses and ears."

"I see men like that all the time."

"Maybe in their sixties and seventies, but in their thirties?" He shuffled the photos of Shivers. "Look at this hair below his sideburns." He turned to Moon's photos. "And the hair encroaching down his forehead, right here."

"Mm."

He turned to a photograph of Moon's upper back and pointed to a slight rise just below the base of his neck. "See this? I think this is the beginning of something called a buffalo hump. Now, look at this." He turned to a photograph of Shivers's back. "Shivers had the same thing, even more pronounced." He turned to an exterior shot of Moon's abdomen. "Look at these bluish streaks in his skin. Very unusual. Like something is making his skin thin out."

"What's all this point to?"

"Steroids."

"I *told* you somebody's building a super liver!"

"No, Molly. Not anabolic steroids. These are glucocorticoids. Like prednisone."

"So what are they used for?"

"Lupus, multiple sclerosis. Many things."

"Any sign of those diseases in these guys?"

"No."

"Geez, Elliot. Why do you keep telling me what they *didn't* have?"

"That's the nature of the mentor–student relationship."

She rolled her eyes. "What else are steroids used for?"

"Transplants."

That surprised her. "What kind of transplants?"

"Any kind. Gingival hyperplasia and encroaching hair are signs of cyclosporine. A buffalo hump and thinning skin are indications of steroids. Both drugs are used to suppress the immune system to keep it from rejecting a transplanted organ of some kind."

"A transplant." She thought about it. "Maybe somebody planted livers in these guys, cultivated them, and took them out."

"Molly."

"I know you think it's crazy, but I haven't heard something better from you."

"Anything is better than that. How do you explain the stitch?"

"The stitch in the stomach is—unrelated. A minor detail. Or related somehow."

"The stitch in the *abdomen*."

She shook her head. "Abdomen, stomach—you've got to stop getting hung up on the trees and take a look at the forest, Elliot. They transplanted livers into these guys, then harvested them like melons in a hothouse. When they took them out, the men died, of course, so to mislead everyone they stuck plastic dolls inside them and made it look like it was a political vendetta against abortion-clinic bombers."

"Molly?"

"Yeah?"

"You still haven't explained why somebody would want to create a super liver."

"Well, Elliot, that's certainly a fair question. And as soon as you find the answer, we'll know who did it."

"Molly?"

"Yeah?"

"What do you say we take a break? Catch an exhibit or two?"

"Okay by me. What do you want to see?"

"Considering your analytical frame of mind, how about a space capsule?"

She gave him a pissed-off smile, picked up her notebook, and began scribbling.

"I mean, you're full of creative stuff, but . . ."

She continued taking notes, ignoring him, light years ahead of him.

He leaned his elbow on the railing and watched her. "Want some lunch?"

She finished writing and looked at her watch. "Sure, why not?"

"Italian okay?"

"Fine." She raised her head. "As long as it's not pizza."

Jack pushed the buzzer and stood waiting, a bottle of champagne in one hand, a yellow rosebud in the other. He had planned to catch a seven-thirty launch to Ellis Island, but he was late, as usual, and it was already seven-fifteen. If this thing weren't a fund-raiser, he never would have—

The door opened, stopping him midthought. Molly stood in the doorway, tying a red ribbon in her hair, her head bent slightly forward, exposing the nape of her neck. Stunning him. "Come in," she said.

What a nice idea. He entered.

In the few days since he had broken up with Victoria, and Molly with Jesse, the two of them had encountered each other at a couple of Washington receptions—*rat fucks*, they were called—that politicians and reporters hated but routinely attended. Soon they found themselves chatting and smiling . . . sharing bad hors d'oeuvres . . . comparing notes on their recent breakups, flirting and raising small hopes, body temperatures, and, ultimately, the same unspoken, troubling questions: How can I be doing this so soon after splitting up? What does this say about me? What does this say about the deathless affair that just died?

"You look beautiful." He handed her the flower. He had asked a taxi to wait in the drizzle, but after seeing her, he forgot about it.

"Back in a second," she said. "Make yourself at home."

She glided off to the bedroom, ribbons fluttering. The dinner invitation had read *Black Tie or Immigrant Original*. Feeling more immigrant than formal, she had gone to Trash and Vaudeville, an antique clothing store on St. Marks Place, and found a 1920s white cotton dress with lace insets in the ankle-length skirt and a fitted bodice with buttons down the front. Except for a small rust stain that she'd covered with an antique mother-of-pearl heart, the dress was in good shape, and at fifteen dollars the price was right. She'd purchased a package of red satin ribbon, which she wove through the lace around the waist and tied in a bow at the front, letting the tails fall to her feet.

Jack wandered into the living room and looked around. It was furnished with a slipcovered sofa, two easy chairs, and a paint-chipped rocking chair near a pine coffee table holding two candles, a pitcher of flowers, and a bowl of unshelled pistachios. Centered on the wall was a small fireplace with a white enamel mantelpiece and white bookshelves on either side.

He set the bottle of champagne on the coffee table and crossed a kilim rug to the bookshelves. Paperback novels, an out-of-date encyclopedia, bowling trophies, two stereo speakers, photographs of Molly with a group of kids under a sign that read ST. MICHAEL'S HOME FOR CHILDREN. Even with the fireplace unlit, the room felt warm.

She reappeared wearing an old, deep-blue Salvation Army cape with red trim. He grabbed the bottle off the table, and they headed for the door.

The boat chugged through the black waves. Jack and Molly sat on the upper deck, breathing salt air, drinking champagne and watching the lights at the tip of Manhattan. After one glass Molly stood up and walked stiffly to the railing.

"Are you all right?" he asked, following.

"Couldn't be better. Why?"

"You look as if you're walking in pain."

She stood with her back to the railing, ankles together, and lifted her dress to her knees. On one was an enormous scab, on the other a large bandage.

"How'd you do that?" he asked.

"Chasing you last Monday." He looked puzzled. "At the end of Graves's press conference, when everyone was running after you trying to get a comment. I tripped."

"What a bad thing."

"Not for you. You don't know what I would have asked you if I'd caught up."

"Yes I do. It doesn't mean I want to see you bleed." A couple of other reporters he knew, maybe, but not her. "How bad is it?"

"It's nothing. I used to get strawberries like these all the time."

"Doing what?"

"Playing ball." She bent one knee, tenderly. "Gets a little stiff now and then. Your friend Iggy Pitt was a big help, by the way. Picked me up and took me next door to Wings. He and Winston Jones cleaned up the scrapes and bandaged them."

"Iggy did that?"

"Yeah. He was very sweet. For a small price, of course. He wants to break into television."

"Oh, yeah. The world is waiting for that. Does he know the odds?"

"No, but don't worry. I'm not going to let him give up his day job."

Jack felt sympathy for him anyway. "So, the knees are my fault, and now I owe you something."

"An on-the-record interview will do fine."

"Sorry, can't do. Now that we've dated, it'd be a conflict of interest."

For a second she thought he was serious. "Forget it," she said. "Takes a lot more than a glass of champagne to immunize you from me."

He broke into a grin. "Ever been caught between a story and a personal relationship?"

"No, and I don't intend to be." She exercised her other knee. "Anyway, you can relax. I'm off duty. I spent enough time on this stuff yesterday."

"Doing what?"

"Chasing the baby-doll story down at the D.C. medical examiner's office."

"Find anything interesting?"

"On a different case, yeah. I discovered Zenobia Davis."

He leaned both arms on the railing, trying to appear uninterested, hoping she'd volunteer more. She didn't. "What about her?"

"Nothing I can talk about."

End of that, at least for the moment. He turned back toward the Brooklyn lights. "That's where I grew up."

"And met your mysterious high-school sweetheart, who according to Mr. Graves died because she was pregnant, and who either did or didn't have your baby."

He said nothing.

"How *did* she die?" she asked.

"Graves wasn't completely off base. Something went wrong during a cesarean delivery. At least that's what they told me at the time. I thought you said you were off duty?"

"I'm not looking for a scandal. At least not tonight." She leaned on the railing. Close to him. "Tell me about Brooklyn."

"What do you want to know?"

"Do you miss it?"

"Yes and no. My parents are dead and my brothers have scattered to the four winds."

"I see." She squinted at the lights. "I love going home to West Virginia."

"West Virginia's closer than Brooklyn."

She turned her head. "What makes you say that?"

"Home is a state of mind. Some things you love to remember, some you'd just as soon forget. Depends on the day."

"Hmm. Tell you what. I'll make you a deal."

He groaned. "You're in New York two months and already you're making deals. What is it?"

"You show me yours and I'll show you mine."

Sepia-toned images floated in his head. "Last time I did that I was a ten-year-old in an attic with Frannie Altschuler."

"Our homes. We'll show each other where we grew up." The wind whipped her hair against her face, forming a veil.

"I guess Frannie wouldn't mind that," he said.

"What a relief. And how about Victoria Winters? Have you got any second thoughts?"

"A few lingering first ones, but no second ones, no. How about you?"

"Jesse? None. Minute it was over, I realized I'd been praying over a dead body for some time." She pushed the hair out of her face. "So, it's a deal?"

He placed his arm around her shoulder and escorted her toward the cabin. "Deal."

When they walked in the door at Ellis Island, Molly felt more like an immigrant than she had imagined. The room was full of well-coiffed women in designer gowns—very few in costume—and men in tuxedos, all of them standing, drinking, and talking in small groups. Waiters circulated with silver trays of champagne, white wine, and caviar, and a string quartet played Mozart. Linen-covered tables dotted the room but no one sat; everyone huddled in conversation or studied pictures and artifacts along the walls.

At the side of the room was an elaborate buffet of roast beef and ham and honey-glazed chicken, whole poached salmon with dill sauce and fresh lox with lemon slices and capers, creamy potatoes and French green beans, and baby vegetables in steaming stainless-steel trays. On and on it went—layer cakes and crumb pies and napoleons and a variety of sherbets sculptured into bananas and apricots and every other fruit she'd ever seen. Molly knew the party wasn't about food, but at the moment it was the most impressive thing in the room. She pictured Homer in his pickup truck, bringing donated watermelons and hot dogs and deep-fried hush puppies back to the orphanage for the Labor Day picnic. The thought of his seeing her here made her slightly embarrassed, like a boy in a drugstore getting caught peeking at a skin magazine.

"Sure these are Democrats?" she said. "Looks pretty Republican to me."

"Where do you think all these people come from, anyway?" Jack asked.

"Not West Virginia."

"You'd be surprised." Someone caught his eye. "I have to do something for a minute. Do you mind?"

"Of course not."

He disappeared into a group of black-suited men holding drinks and slender cigars.

She walked around the empty tables and chairs, wondering why rich people always seemed to stand when they ate. She remembered the time as a kid when two itinerant workers appeared at the orphanage door after a hot day of painting gutters and downspouts, looking for something to eat. Dinner was already on the table, but Betsy invited them into the kitchen and told them to take off their paint-speckled hats and wash up in the big enamel sink. After drying off, they stood at the worn maple countertop waiting for a plate of food, but Betsy wouldn't have it. "Nobody that works has to eat standing up," she said, and waved them into the dining room, where the kids scooched their chairs together and made room for two more. The first thing Molly had noticed when she came to New York was that everyone ate while walking, running, standing, leaning—anything but sitting. Soon she was doing the same, although she thought there was something slightly sick about it.

Someone touched her back.

"I've been watching you," a man in a tux with a velvet bow tie said. He took a step backward and looked her up and down, drink in hand. "Do you suppose your great-grandmother looked as beautiful as you when she arrived here?"

"I wonder." She tried to imagine who her great-grandmother was, whether she had come through Ellis Island, whether she had stood in this very room. How strange, she thought: rarely did she wonder who her biological ancestors were, and yet on this night, in this place, with Jack MacLeod and these people . . .

"Do I detect a slight southern accent?" he asked.

"Hillbilly more than southern. West Virginia."

"How cute. And I always thought the only good thing to come out of West Virginia was an empty bus." He yukked at himself and she forced a smile. "So, what do you think?" he asked, sweeping his arm to the side as though he'd built the place. "You look unimpressed."

"Not at all. It just seems ironic, all these well-dressed people laughing and drinking where immigrants once stood." She focused on a picture on the wall.

"We're their sons and daughters," he said.

"I know. Do you think we deserve to be?"

"I'm just as happy that I don't have to answer that." He took a swallow of vodka, then lifted his glass, waved tootle-oo with three fingers, and joined a group of happy drinkers.

Molly moved on, her reporter's ear picking up snippets of conversation as she went. ". . . first sign of frost I'll be out of here," ". . . the great thing about Jewish shrinks is they talk back and give advice," ". . . he doesn't use cortisone, and his elbow feels great," ". . . so much makeup, if you ran over her face with a Jeep you'd have to put it in four-wheel drive."

She wandered to a computer that held the names of thousands of immigrants who had passed through Ellis Island. The instructions invited the visitor to enter a family name and see if it appeared. A group of partygoers stood with champagne glasses in hand, laughing and entering names, oohing and ahhing when they appeared, entering new names when they didn't. When they finally departed, still talking about grandfathers, aunts, and uncles, she stepped to the keyboard. Finally she typed *McCormick*, her adopted name. The only one she knew. Ancestors? Hardly.

Instead of pressing the Enter key, she touched the End button and walked away.

Back in the main room, she looked around, amused and put off, entertained and bored. Jack found her looking at her Timex.

"Having fun?"

"Sure," she said. Her expression betrayed her.

"You'll make a poor politician unless you learn how to lie better than that."

"I'm just a poor sport. It's a great party, but for some reason I'm in a pissy mood."

"Good. We've been here an hour. Let's go."

They left and rode back on the chartered ferry, then hailed a cab and headed up the West Side toward her brownstone. It was only ten-thirty.

"I enjoyed it, really I did," she said. "But I'm just a hick at heart. I keep thinking rich people should be more interesting."

"You're just now figuring out that the emperor has no clothes?"

"Oh, I've known *that* forever," she said. "I just didn't know how skinny his legs were."

Jack laughed. "So what kind of people interest you?"

"You really want to know?"

"Sure."

She leaned toward the cabdriver. "Forty-second and Eighth," she said, and looked at Jack. "I'll show you the real Ellis Island."

The cab delivered them to the Port Authority. Molly led them to the bus terminal, where they sat on a bench. "Everybody here is an immigrant," she said. "Or at least an emigrant."

"What's the difference?"

"I'm not sure. According to our anchorman, emigrants come from New Jersey."

They watched people standing in line to buy tickets, and people stepping off buses carrying nylon duffel bags. There were children rubbing their eyes and whining, babies sleeping despite bright lights, public-address announcements, and commotion. Everyone seemed too hot or too tired, too fat or too skinny, but she enjoyed watching them anyway.

"Look at her," she said, nodding toward a woman with stringy brown hair and a pair of red pants so tight you could see the dimples on her bottom. "Check out the husband." Standing next to the woman was a lanky fellow with dirty-blond hair, heavy lids, and a droopy mustache frosted with powdered sugar from a doughnut. His Adam's apple bobbed up and down inside a chicken neck, and a patch of weedy hair stuck out the top of his chartreuse T-shirt.

Jack looked around and took everyone in: the forty-year-old man with the worn-out craggy face; the twenty-year-old in his beltless, cutoff jeans; the unshaven bushy-haired guy with his belly sticking out under a shrunken T-shirt that said *Sex Instructor—First Lesson Free.* As if somewhere there was a woman tasteless enough to take him up on it. And maybe there was, right here at the Port Authority.

"Even that jerk," Molly said. "If I'd fallen off the ferry tonight, I think he would have jumped in to save me faster than most of the people at the party."

"I'd jump in for you," Jack said. "Soon as I got my shoes off, folded my pants, hung up my coat—"

She pulled her mouth to the side, smiling. "The rich and powerful come to New York through La Guardia or Kennedy. The huddled masses arrive here."

"You're a better politician than I thought," Jack said.

"Not really. But they interest me."

"They interest me, too. They're all potential voters."

She pushed him on the chest, stood up, and walked toward the door. As he followed, something across the room caught his attention. He walked a few yards to the side and lifted a plastic baby rattle off the floor and handed it to a man carrying a sleeping baby on his shoulder. Then he rejoined Molly.

"That was a nice thing to do," she said as they walked outside. "Maybe you're not such a bad egg after all."

"Either that or I've got you fooled."

Jack left Molly's brownstone and raised his hand for a taxi. It rattled to a stop; he piled into the backseat and closed the door, overlooking an old Ford across the street with someone behind the wheel. Even if he'd noticed, it would have meant nothing to him.

It wasn't until he was well out of sight that the figure in the driver's seat removed his baseball cap, lifted a binder of green notebook paper, turned on a dome light, and began making notes.

"You'd better go out the parking lot entrance, Judge. The press is all over the front of the courthouse."

Pepper Loomis handed Titus his suit coat and placed his black robe on a wooden hanger, still amazed after almost two years on the job at how much of a judge's power and dignity disappeared into the closet with it. "I'll check to see if the coast is clear," she said, and started out the door.

Titus stopped her. "I want to tell you something. Assuming I'm confirmed, I want you to go with me to the Supreme Court."

Pepper smiled. "Thanks, Judge, but can I have a few days to think about it?" She walked to the door. When she looked back, she saw a worried look on his face. "Oh, please," she said, "you know I accept."

He smiled, stuck some papers into his briefcase, and walked into the reception area to talk to his secretary, Daisy Gibbs, about his confirmation hearing schedule. He looked at his watch. A few minutes had passed. Where was Pepper? He sat on the edge of Daisy's desk, hearing her talk but not listening, playing with the handle of his briefcase. Instead of biting a fingernail, he opened a packaged towelette and wiped it over his face.

Pepper finally returned and motioned for him to follow.

He picked up the briefcase and donned his fedora, pulling it low on his forehead, as if he thought it would disguise the only three-hundred-pound judge in Washington.

When they reached the steps outside the door, he saw his car halfway across the parking lot. Good. No one around. He'd made it.

Then all hell broke loose.

"There he is!" a woman screamed.

He and Pepper turned, startled, and saw a small group of women coming around the side of the building toward them with signs bobbing up and down in their hands. REMEMBER ZENOBIA DAVIS! NEVER AGAIN! IMPEACH JUDGE TITUS!

Titus froze.

Pepper grabbed the keys from his hand and ran ahead to unlock the car door. He came to his senses and followed, running with the gait of a moose in galoshes, trying to beat the crowd.

Pepper reached his car and nervously poked the key toward the lock. Before she could find it, a woman wearing a purple headband with white and gold stripes appeared out of nowhere and hit her arm, knocking the keys to the ground.

Pepper looked the woman in the eye, and the two of them momentarily held each other in their gaze, almost as if they knew one another. Pepper bent down for the keys. The woman swept her foot to the side, knocking them under the car. Pepper stared at her again, then dropped onto all fours and peered under the muffler. The keys were just out of reach.

Titus arrived behind her, panting. "What . . . are . . . you . . . doing?"

"The keys," she said, reaching.

He put his hand on her shoulder, pushed her aside, and dropped onto his hands and knees, jowls hanging low, eyes bulging. Pressing his sweating face against the asphalt, he looked under the chassis and reached.

The crowd of demonstrators arrived at the car, pushing against Titus's enormous butt, rocking the vehicle back and forth to chants of "Choice yes, hangers no; laws that kill have got to go! Choice yes, hangers no . . ."

He touched the key ring with one finger, pulled it toward him, and gripped the whole cluster in his hand. Pushing himself up onto all fours, he felt an object press against his right buttock, like a hand or a foot. Then he felt a sharp sting, as if someone had pinched him, or jabbed him with a hat pin.

Or stuck him with a needle.

He turned his head to see who it was, but the crowd was pressed in too close. With the keys still in hand, he reached for the car door handle and struggled to his feet, dripping with sweat, his lips dry and white. He loosened his tie and turned toward the center of the crowd. Women screamed at him, demanding that he leave them alone even as they pushed and shoved themselves against him.

Pepper stood next to him, facing the mob. "Back up!" she yelled.

"Traitor!" the woman with the headband yelled at her.

Titus craned his neck, a head taller than most of the pack. Another group was coming around the side of the building, this one carrying videocams, microphones, and all the fearsome equipment of the press.

He turned back to the car. His shaking hand poked the key toward the keyhold, missed it, then found the mark. He drove it in—twisted it—

heard the snap of the bolt, and lifted the handle. The door came open about an inch before it was smashed shut by the weight of the crowd.

"Judge Titus!" A television reporter stretched his arm over the shoulder of a woman protestor, trying to position his microphone within range of the judge's mouth, poking it into his ear instead. "Judge Titus! Do you think you'll be confirmed?"

Titus turned and knocked the mike away. As he glared at the reporter a woman's hand appeared from his blind side and reached for his face, fingernails touching his cheek. He grabbed her wrist and turned to find a face to go with it. It was Pepper Loomis. For a moment he didn't recognize her, she looked so—*angry*. As cameras flashed he eased his grip and let go. She picked something off his cheek and held it up for him to see—a cigarette butt—and brushed away some asphalt pebbles stuck to his skin.

"Are your views on abortion going to kill your confirmation?" a reporter yelled over the chants.

"Titus, Titus, make our day; quit the court and go away! Titus, Titus, make our day . . ."

Titus composed himself and reached into his pocket to pull out a clean white handkerchief. Unnerved by the filth of the cigarette and pavement debris, he drew the cloth across his forehead to the *zit-zits* of the automatic rewinds.

"Judge Titus!" another reporter yelled.

". . . hangers kill, abortions save. Titus, Titus . . ."

"Please, everyone!" Titus yelled, holding up his hands. "I'll make a complete statement to the Senate Judiciary Committee! Until then, I'm not able to comment!"

No one listened. Questions poured out with the chanting. He reached for the car door again, this time yanking it open hard enough to squeeze into the front seat. The engine started on the first try; he shifted into reverse and quickly placed his foot on the brake. Christ. All he needed to do was run over a protester.

The car crept back slowly. In a few moments he shifted into forward and moved through the demonstrators, picking up speed until only a few of them remained, running alongside, yelling and smacking the hood and fenders of his car with the flats of their hands. Finally the car bolted out of the lot and onto the street.

Several blocks away he wondered about Pepper, quickly concluding that she was safe. After all, regardless of her conspicuous loyalty to him, there was always that one, critical fact that would save her even from a mob as crazed as this.

She was one of them. A woman.

.   .   .

Titus was in bed, sleeping, when suddenly he sat up, heart pounding, sweat dotting his forehead, fogged by a fever. He regained his bearings and lifted the clock off the nightstand, holding it close to his nearsighted eyes. Two thirty-five. He set it on the table and lay back on his pillow. "Ouch."

He sat up again and turned on the light. Pushing back the covers with one hand, he pulled down his silk pajama bottoms with the other and searched for the point of pain. Under the skin on his right buttock, where he'd been stuck with something sharp, was a marble-sized knot. He kneaded it between his fingers a moment, wondering what it was, and patted his damp forehead with a fresh tissue.

As he reached for the light switch he saw a chocolate-covered cherry on the nightstand. He lifted it and popped it into his mouth. After turning off the light, he settled into bed and fell into a feverish sleep . . . drifting down a set of stairs.

To Chicago.

Christmas.

1952.

Descending the steps from the third floor, Abner stuck his bare foot into the darkness, found the second-floor landing, and shifted his weight onto it, sending a crack echoing through the house. He stood frozen, clutching the birdhouse against his pajama tops, waiting for a sound from his parents' room nearby. The library clock below struck twice, and the house went quiet. He waited a moment, then tiptoed another flight down to the ground floor.

The reflection from the snow outside cast a faint bluish hue in the hallway, lighting his way to the enormous Victorian living room. Near the fireplace he could make out the gigantic Christmas tree, a towering black ghost with glinting tinsel eyes. He plugged in the lights, flooding the room with colored bulbs, ornaments, and stacks of wrapped presents, stunning himself with the moment that was unlike any other.

He examined the birdhouse one last time before setting it in its special place. He'd painted it red and white and mounted the front wall on tiny brass hinges so that in the spring he could open it and see the baby robins inside. To demonstrate its unique design, he'd cut straw from the shop broom and built a model nest, placing a blue marble in the center as an egg.

He set the present on the floor in front of the others, like a drum major leading the way. Then he stood back to admire it. This Christmas it would be *they* who'd be swept away by the magic—

Thump.

His heart jumped. He pulled the light cord from the socket and listened. A door opened upstairs—to his parents' room!

He scooted across the hearth, grazing the brass fireplace tools, and came to rest under the Parsons table behind the sofa. Drawing his knees up to his chest, he wrapped his arms around his shins, closed his eyes, and waited.

Footsteps. His father's.

They moved into the darkened living room, across the Oriental carpet to the antique table by the tree. The sound of a decanter clinking. Brandy splashed into a glass. The sip of a drink and the sound of crinkling leather, his father's favorite chair.

Silence.

More footsteps coming down the stairs. The click of a lamp switch, lighting the room. The sound of his mother sitting in a chair. Quiet.

He heard the silver cigarette box, the schick of steel against flint. His mother's long exhale.

"How many times have we been over this, Herb?"

Silence.

"I'm not going to leave you and Abner behind, and that's final," his father said. "Washington is lonely. I'd miss you both."

"Oh, please. Spare me."

Crinkling leather from his father's shifting body. "Give me *some* credit, Helen. I haven't been that bad a father."

Another exhale of smoke. "I suppose not. Particularly since you didn't want to be one in the first place."

"Me? What about you?" Silence. "It was your decision, not mine."

"My decision? What choice did I have?"

"Oh, come on. The doctor was all lined up."

"That guy in Evansville? He wasn't a doctor. He was a butcher."

"Nonsense, I checked him out myself." A pause. "Considering how you got pregnant, I'd have thought you would have been willing to take a risk or two."

A long, black silence.

"You bastard," she whispered.

The sound of the brandy glass on the antique rosewood table. The rattle of the crystal ashtray against wood from a cigarette being tapped out.

"It's after two," she said. "I'm going back to bed."

A pair of footsteps. Another clack of the brandy snifter on the table, the lamp light off . . . more footsteps . . . the distant thunk of the bedroom door.

Nothing but the sound of falling snow.

Abner sat perfectly still, listening to his pulse. It was all a dream, he told himself. He'd seen absolutely nothing, heard nothing that made sense. Only words. An argument. Adult talk. Gibberish.

For a second he thought he'd made his escape—then the words hit him like a searchlight: *didn't want to be a father . . . not a doctor, a butcher . . . considering how you got pregnant . . .* Panic engulfed him— the same familiar dread that had haunted him before . . . the ghost that came whispering to him at night, saying, *You're not wanted. You shouldn't be here. They don't love you.*

He gripped his shins and rocked back and forth on his bottom, crying. After a few minutes, he crawled out from under the table, hobbled on pins and needles to the tree, picked up the birdhouse, and headed for the stair. When he reached the landing, he was struck dead with yet another horrible thought: the entire time they'd sat there in the light, his parents hadn't even noticed his gift.

He trudged up the steps to his unlit room and crawled under the covers. After staring at the ceiling, he looked down at the floor and saw his masterpiece resting in the murky light. The pride of his life only minutes ago was now cold and distant, mocking him for his stupid, misplaced love.

He rolled out of bed, picked up the birdhouse, and smashed it against the wall, making a crash he was sure would wake them. That was fine with him. He *wanted* them to come in and see what had happened. He *wanted* them to get angry and ask what he was doing. He wanted to tell them he knew their dirty secret—to make them feel guilty and say they were sorry—then, when they begged his forgiveness, he'd tell them he was leaving home and never, ever returning.

He waited, but they didn't come.

He felt something sticky on his palm and turned on the bedside light. There was a cut on his finger, blood on his hand.

Reaching for a Kleenex, he saw a glint inside the cardboard box. He lifted it and looked closer. There, stashed and forgotten, were the bane of his chubby body, the soothing, forbidden poison he loved so much: six foil-wrapped, chocolate-covered cherries.

He picked them up, turned out the light, and laid his head on the pillow. Then, sniffling back the tears and mucus, he ate them slowly, one by one.

Crossing the East River, Jack felt himself moving backward in time and space. For Molly, a trip to Brooklyn was something of an adventure, a place she'd never seen. For Jack, it was something more ambivalent, the exploration of the egg's abandoned shell.

From the Brooklyn Bridge he drove down Bedford and Ocean Avenues into a black neighborhood in Flatbush. After winding through a checkerboard of well-kept and run-down frame houses, he pulled to the curb and stopped. On Molly's side of the car was the old Victorian he'd grown up in: peeling green paint, the steep roof with a few missing shingles, patches of brown November grass and dried summer weeds—everything had changed and nothing had changed.

"Who lives here now?" Molly asked.

"I don't know. It was sold twelve years ago when my father died." He put his hand on the door handle. "Let's find out."

They walked onto the wooden porch and rang the doorbell, and in a few seconds a black woman with gray hair looked out a small window. She sized them up and opened the door a crack.

"Sorry to bother you," Jack said, "but I grew up here many years ago. We were in the neighborhood and—"

"Congressman MacLeod?"

"Yes?"

"Well, do come in." She pushed the door open. "The neighbors said this used to be your house."

He stepped into the foyer, looked around and momentarily lost track of himself. Everything was so familiar, yet shrunken.

"I'm Molly McCormick," Molly said, shaking hands.

"Would you two like to look around?" the woman asked.

"Would you mind?" Jack said.

"Go right ahead. My husband and I did the same thing in Georgia a few years back, just before he passed on." She said she had something to do in the kitchen, which wasn't quite true, and told them to make themselves at home.

Jack stepped into the living room. He could almost hear the tick of the pendulum clock, almost see his father in his easy chair next to the oak-paneled fireplace, working a crossword puzzle, his feet on the needlepoint-covered ottoman, the Chinese checkers on the scratched-up table next to him.

Molly watched, saying nothing.

"I'll show you my room," he said. Leading the way, he climbed the oak staircase with the ease of a nag returning to the barn. When he reached the top of the stairs, his hand moved as naturally onto the banister's wooden ball as if he'd never left.

They reached his room and saw a teenage girl's bedspread and paraphernalia, momentarily disorienting him. But then he imagined his brother's neat bed, his own messy one, his mother's hand-sewn quilts, the model airplanes hanging from the ceiling, the walls covered with pennants, posters, and album covers.

He turned toward the light switch by the door, half expecting to see the old photograph of Piper Laurie still stuck in the frame of his mirror. What a love affair that had been. All the times he'd touched her cheek before turning out the light, certain that if she knew how much he loved her, she'd wait for him to get out of Flatbush and marry him.

He thought of Honey, and their dream of escaping Brooklyn and going to America . . . getting married and having children and a dog . . . a golden retriever with brown eyes and a pink tongue that hung out the front of its mouth, not out the side the way a Brooklyn dog's did. And a station wagon, with wood on the sides, sitting in a circular driveway framed by stately oaks shedding fall leaves . . . blue smoke rising from a fieldstone chimney. It was a life straight out of the magazine ads. And they wanted it.

Funny. The part about the kids he still did.

He remembered the moment he'd given up Piper Laurie for Honey, during a baseball game his junior year. Crossing home plate, he'd seen her standing in the front row, clapping and smiling and catching his eye with her silent words, *I love you!* No matter how many times she did that, it startled him and made him crazy with desire. More than anything he'd ever known. Maybe, he thought, more than anything he ever would know.

He recalled the snapshot of his mother, her strawberry hair radiating energy, her warm smile still competing with his last image of her lying in a coffin . . . her cancer-ravaged cheekbones like tent poles under canvas, the full lips that had kissed him good night shrunken to thin lines of gray.

"Knock, knock," Molly said.

He caught himself and gave her a squeeze on the arm. They found their host sitting at the kitchen table drinking coffee and reading the newspaper. After a few minutes of chatting, they thanked her and left.

Jack's next stop was Flatbush High. He pulled to the curb and described what he remembered best: Mrs. Young's English class . . . the locker room where the guys snapped towels and smeared Red Hot in Bobby Dickinson's jock . . . the dances, the fistfights. And the POWs: a buddy sent upstate for stealing one too many hubcaps . . . a guy flipping hamburgers to support a pregnant wife . . . somebody sawing off a finger in machine shop, someone flunking geometry for the third time. Whatever.

Molly asked him about Honey. He remembered the day she'd told him she was late, and the day she'd said she was pregnant.

"What did you do?" Molly asked, but he didn't answer.

He started the car and drove past stores and churches and little shops, pausing at Robertini's Shoe Repair, which was now the Good Life Sewing Center. He described how he'd robbed the store—to no avail; Honey's parents had already taken her away—and slipped the money back under the door that same morning. It hadn't fooled Robertini, although he'd never pressed charges.

With that part of the story finished, they headed west. He said he'd played poker in a regular game at a place called Luboff's Funeral Home, which was still standing, but since there was nothing much to see, there was no reason to stop. She said they had stopped at the school without seeing much either. "True," he said, but kept driving.

They reached Coney Island and walked the beach, arm in arm, Molly with a scarf, Jack with his collar turned up. He told her about Freddy Anticoli and Romano's Fine Italian Restaurant, and how he had tried to triple Freddy's stake in a poker game, only to discover that Honey had already died. He didn't tell her how, or where, he had discovered Honey's body, or what Angus Brody had done to her. That part of the story was still too sacred and too profane, even now.

As the story ended they entered Romano's for dinner, replacing nostalgia with pasta and Chianti and laughter. When dinner was over, the waiter brought the *tombala*, a dried gourd filled with numbered tokens, and told Molly if she picked out the number she guessed first, dinner was on the house. She said, "Eleven," then reached in and drew out number twelve.

"That was close," Jack said.

"Close doesn't make it. We'll have to keep trying till we get it right." The way she said it made his veins swell.

On the way to the front door, they passed the private room where people were eating and dancing to an accordion, trumpet, and drums. Jack pulled Molly inside, took her in his arms, and danced. When the tune ended, he said, "I always wanted to do that."

Everyone else returned to their tables. Jack stood still and kissed her. When it ended, he looked over her shoulder and saw an old couple sitting at a table holding hands behind bottles of Pellegrino and red wine, smiling at him.

"Let's go home," he said.

"Not yet," she said, touching his lapel. "First I want to hear the part you skipped over. The part about you and Honey and the funeral home."

Of course. Always the reporter, listening for what is not said, filling in the blanks. He'd already confessed a burglary—what more did she want? "Not tonight," he said.

They climbed into the car and headed for Manhattan, saying less than before, as if they'd exhausted their conversation. The silence took its toll. He turned off Coney Island Avenue onto a side street, turned some corners, and stopped in front of Luboff's Funeral Home. It was the first time he'd been there in twenty-five years.

He sat staring, engine idling. Of all his high-school haunts, like death itself this one seemed to have changed the least. He checked his watch. Twelve-thirty.

He turned off the engine and told her the whole story of himself and Honey. Or at least all of it he knew.

By the time they arrived at her brownstone, it was one-thirty in the morning. Jack took off his jacket, loosened his tie, and leaned back on the sofa. She fixed him a drink and sat next to him with a glass of wine and her bare feet on the coffee table. He slipped off his shoes and laid his feet next to hers. She drank some wine and wiggled her toes. He moved his foot onto hers and massaged it gently, holding feet instead of hands, not knowing that in this part of her anatomy he'd found her Achilles heel, the path that led straight to her heart.

She turned toward him, put her palm on his cheek, and kissed him lightly. He dropped his feet to the floor, took her into his arms, and eased her back onto the sofa. In time, he worked his palm up her leg . . . over her thigh . . . crumpling her dress around her waist, touching the crease at the top of her legs, running his hand up to her stomach and down to her panties . . . holding a moment, then slipping his fingers under the elastic.

She broke their kiss. "Sorry," she whispered. "I'm not ready."

She pushed him off, stood up, smoothed down her dress, and walked out of the room, leaving him staring at a bowl of pistachios, longing for the seventies. He couldn't blame her; first time was never easy. He reached for a nut, shelled it, and popped it into his mouth. By the time he'd shelled the fifth one, he heard a creak in the wooden floor behind him.

He turned toward the hallway and saw Molly standing in an open robe, naked beneath, her eyes fixed on his, daring him to look at her— and when he did, daring him to stop. Her breasts were full and wide, creating crescent moons outside the profile of her torso. Her midriff and waist were small, with gentle curves of muscle around her belly, smooth and firm like the hills and valleys on the palm of a hand. Beyond that, it was less what he saw—velvet and porcelain—than what he felt. Never had he seen a woman so unselfconscious about her body, and the effect was wild.

She walked to him and knelt on the sofa, wound her fingers into his hair, and pulled his head back, tilting his face up to hers. Saying nothing, she kissed the side of his mouth, where his lips joined.

"I thought you said not now," he said.

"I did. But that was then."

She kissed him point-blank.

He peeled off her robe.

She unzipped his fly.

He kicked off his jeans.

She ran her hands under his shirt onto his chest, down his stomach, down his hips to the top of his thighs, moving her body downward as she went until her lips hovered so close to him he could feel her breath on his skin. He unbuttoned his shirt and peeled it off, turning the sleeves inside out, watching her hair billow over his midsection like waves of windblown, auburn wheat. He pulled her up and joined them together, slowly starting a rhythm between them . . . giving and taking, taking and giving . . . giving and taking until, in a blurry heat, neither of them could tell who was giving and who was taking.

"Oh, my God!" she finally sang out.

"Sweet Jesus!" he said in his own final amen.

Then, going the way of all flesh, their moment of revival came to an end.

"Any minute now," he said.

Eggs Benedict and Billy Bannister sat in Benedict's green Ford staring down an unlit footpath between two houses. Across the asphalt parking lot was the back of the clinic. Benedict lifted his wristwatch and shone a tiny flashlight on it. Five minutes to one.

They pulled on their black gloves, turning themselves into part of the night—Benedict in a black turtleneck and sweatpants, Bannister in a midnight-blue jacket, jeans, and a black knit cap.

Benedict trained his binoculars on the clinic's back door. In a few seconds the light from the windows next to it went out, and a man emerged carrying a plastic bag of trash on each shoulder. He walked to a Dumpster, tossed in the bags, climbed into an old red pickup truck, and started the engine. It coughed and rattled as it did when they'd seen it before. Accustomed to the sound, no one in the neighborhood stirred.

With one headlight out, the truck dropped into gear and disappeared from view. Although they could no longer see it, they had watched it from other vantage points enough times to know exactly where it was: once on the side street, it would chug to the stop sign at the corner, turn right onto Atlantic Avenue, and disappear down the empty thoroughfare.

"Let's go," Benedict said.

They jumped out and opened the car's back doors. Benedict lifted a folding aluminum stepladder and walked quickly between the two houses toward the clinic. Bannister grabbed a black parachute-cloth bag and ran to catch up.

When they reached the building, Benedict climbed to the eaves and quickly hoisted himself over the edge onto the flat roof. After lifting the black bag, he gave Bannister a hand.

They surveyed the scene. The vent pipe was a few yards away, rising three feet above the roof. Bannister set down the bag, unzipped it, and withdrew a two-foot galvanized pipe. Benedict shone his penlight on a kitchen timer taped to the end of the device and dialed it to the fifteen-minute mark. After turning off the light, he lifted the cylinder and slipped it into the vent pipe like a shell into a casing. When it disappeared below the top of the vent, he continued lowering it by an attached wire until it touched something and stopped. He stuffed the remaining wire down the hole, tapped Bannister—it's done, let's go— and they retraced their steps to the ground.

They jogged to the car, stowed their gear, and sat in the front seat, waiting. Except for the sound of their own windpipes, the air was quiet. Finally Benedict gripped the top of the steering wheel and straightened his arms, driving his shoulders into the back of the seat. "We did it," he said.

"Let's get out of here," Bannister said. He popped an antacid tablet into his mouth, then pulled off the knit cap, wiped the sweat off his face, and laid the hat on his lap.

Benedict started the car. Keeping the headlights off, he pulled into the street and moved forward . . . creeping past the house with the chipped aluminum siding.

Bannister suddenly grabbed the dashboard. "What's that?"

Benedict hit the brakes.

"Back up!" Bannister said.

Benedict dropped the car into reverse and moved backward until they could see between the two houses.

There was a light in the clinic window.

"Somebody's in there!" Bannister said.

"Can't be," Benedict argued. "We saw him leave."

"I'm telling you that light just came on!"

Benedict shoved the gear into park and lifted his foot off the brake pedal, extinguishing the tail lights. They sat in the idling car, staring between the houses. "Maybe it's one of those automatic jobs," Benedict said.

"Then why didn't we see it before?"

"Maybe we always left before it came on."

"We've been here later than this."

Benedict paused, thinking. "Nobody ever came out after the janitor left before, so why would somebody be in there now?"

Bannister licked his lips, feeling the panic creep over him. "I don't know, but we gotta check it out."

Benedict sat still. Bannister stared ahead, expecting the car to move. "What're you waiting for?" he asked.

Reluctantly, Benedict turned on the headlights and drove around the corner to the clinic parking lot, turned off the lights, and drove in. The car crawled to a point opposite the clinic's back door, made a U-turn to face the street, and stopped with the engine running. Both of them stared at the light, trying not to believe their eyes.

"I'm going in," Bannister said. He opened the car door and stuck his right foot onto the asphalt.

Benedict grabbed his nylon jacket. "Are you nuts? The thing's gonna blow!"

"There's enough time!" Bannister said.

"Like hell there is!"

"But somebody's in there!"

"It's too late! Even if we hustled them out, how you gonna explain why you're here when the bomb goes off?"

Bannister hadn't thought of that. He sat back a moment, car door open, right foot dangling above the asphalt, Benedict gripping his jacket. Then he made his decision. "I'm going to pull it out of the vent."

"You can't!" Benedict said. "I shoved the wire down! You'll never reach it!"

"I gotta try!" Bannister started out the door.

Benedict yanked him back and floored the accelerator. The rear wheels spewed pebbles and smoking rubber as the car fishtailed toward the street. The forward jolt slammed the front door on Bannister's shin; he pulled his leg inside and grabbed it with both hands, bent over in excruciating pain.

The car hit the exit ramp, showering yellow sparks into the air. Benedict turned left onto the street; the centrifugal force swung Bannister's door open again—smashed it into a signpost—and slammed it closed. After careening around the corner, they roared down Atlantic Avenue, past a realty office, a car wash, and a Sunoco station where a red pickup truck with a rusty tailgate and one dead headlight sat with a gas nozzle in its tank.

Four minutes later they heard the distant explosion.

By early morning, the crime scene was finally under control. Law enforcement people and favored members of the press had traipsed through the clinic—city police, bomb squad, firemen, photographers, federal ATF. NYPD Homicide was still picking through debris, checking for clues. Behind yellow police tapes, disaster junkies stood shivering in robes and T-shirts, teeth chattering. Everyone seemed to be there. Everyone, that is, except Julia Rodriguez, who had stayed inside the clinic to finish her husband's cleaning and use the bathroom while he drove to the Sunoco station to gas up. What was left of her was in a green body bag on its way to the morgue.

The detective in charge sat in the front seat of his unmarked car writing on a clipboard. A silent Mr. Rodriguez sat in the back, head in his hands. A policeman knocked on the car window; the detective rolled it down and saw something in the officer's hand.

"One of the guys found this in the parking lot," he said, sticking a black knit cap through the car window. The detective took it and examined it under the light. On the outside, in orange letters, was *St. Ignatius Tigers.* Inside, faithfully sewn by Billy Bannister's wife, Doris, was the name tag of their sixth-grade son, Kevin.

The detective laid the cap on the seat next to him and continued writing.

The morning light slipped through the sides of the shades, tickling Jack's eyelids the way his brother used to wake him with a pillow feather. Lying on his back, barely conscious, he blinked at an unfamiliar ceiling. He wasn't with Victoria. He was somewhere else.

He turned his head and saw Molly lying on her side, her cinnamon hair covering the freckles on her nose, coal-dust lashes outlining her eyes. Propping himself on his elbows, he looked around. Sometime during the night she had pulled the sheet down to her waist and laid one leg on top of the covers. Exactly the way he did. The coincidence intrigued him, but then the curve of her leg raised images from the night before, displacing the thought. He glanced at the clock next to the bed—seven-thirty—and felt his blood continue to go south.

So, I'll be late. It's Saturday.

The air in the room was cool; he pulled the sheet up to her neck and smoothed it lightly on her back. She turned onto her other side with her eyes closed. Moving up behind her, he wrapped his arms around her and gently placed his hand on one of her naked breasts. She reached up and, with equal gentleness, removed it. Her voice was soft gravel. "If you need a hand warmer, use your own."

His feet hit the floor. *I wonder what she likes for breakfast?*

"Toast and coffee," she said. He stood watching her trail back into a semisleep, wondering what kind of a psychic twin he'd found here.

He pulled on his pants, walked barefoot to the kitchen, and prowled through the cupboards and tiny refrigerator. "You're out of coffee," he yelled. "Want some tea?" She didn't answer.

Working around the kitchen, he assembled a tray of orange juice, huevos rancheros, slightly burned toast, and butter and jam. And tea. On his way back he stopped in the living room and picked up a flower.

"I hope you like Mexican eggs," he said, entering the bedroom. She turned over and looked at him bleary-eyed. "You're out of coffee, so I fixed some tea. Okay?"

She rolled out of bed, still too sleepy to talk, and walked into the bathroom. A few minutes later she returned and stood at the end of the bed, checking the tray. "What, no coffee?"

"Hello. You don't have any! Do you want some fuckin' tea or not?"
She walked around to the side of the bed and leaned over and kissed
his ear. "Yes. But you can hold the tea."

He pulled her down on the bed, and in a few minutes the Earl Grey
was sloshing onto the sheets along with the eggs and strawberry jam,
which were running under his elbows and her back.

They hardly noticed.

The telephone rang. Reaching for it with a slab of butter stuck to her
palm, Molly answered in the husky voice of someone who'd just run a
mile or had sex. "Hello?" It was her producer, Tim Benton.

Jack scooped cold eggs off her hip and fed them to her while she
talked. She motioned for him to hand her a pencil from the bedside
table—"Somebody bombed a clinic last night," she explained—and
scribbled notes onto the edge of a day-old newspaper. She took a bite
of toast and licked the butter off her hand. Waiting for her producer
to return, she covered the mouthpiece and whispered to Jack, "All
the world's problems could be solved with a little more butter and
sex."

Jack stuck a piece of toast into his mouth and lay back on the bed.
Lifting the remote, he turned on the television set and went channel
surfing—cartoons, cereal, cartoons, toy commercials—finally stopping
on a sports channel showing highlights of the previous week's football
games. Molly talked to her producer with one eye on the TV set.

"Have I got a camera?" she asked. "See if you can get Al."

" . . . then Ohio State tied it up going into the last two minutes," the
sports commentator said.

"Okay, give me the address." She scribbled it down and looked up at
the TV screen.

" . . . one of the best fakes you're ever gonna see . . ."

She continued watching the football play unfold.

" . . . a textbook, play-action fake . . ."

Her face dropped. "Hang on a sec," she said into the phone. She lowered the receiver to focus on the TV set.

" . . . and with the linebackers going for the tailback, he lofts a small
pass over their heads, and bingo. Touchdown."

She remained transfixed a moment before lifting the receiver. "I'll get
there as fast as I can, Tim. I have to make a call. Ask somebody to call
Iggy Pitt . . . yeah, the intern. Tell him if he wants to see some action,
this is his chance."

Holding the receiver with her shoulder, she paged through her leather phone book, hit the switch hook, dialed, and waited for an answering machine greeting to end.

Beep.

"Elliot, this is Molly. I hate to admit this, but you're right about the missing livers. They were removed from those guys to draw attention away from what's really going on, whatever that is. I just saw Ohio State do it to Texas A&M." She started to hang up, then raised the receiver. "So you were right and I was wrong. What else do you want me to do? Don't answer that. And where the hell are you, anyway?"

Beep.

She hung up the receiver and unwound the cord, thinking of Elliot. Not professionally, but personally. Momentarily missing him . . . feeling a twinge of betrayal, even though she had not, in fact, betrayed him.

She hopped off the bed. "I gotta get a move on," she said. When the heat was on, she tended toward West Virginia–speak.

Jack gathered up the dishes and carried them to the kitchen while she pulled off the sheets and threw them into a pile on the floor. "Not bad for a rookie, huh?" she yelled after him. "Covering two homicides, Eli Graves's hit list, and now this?" She headed for the bathroom and stopped, suspended by a thought. "Hey. You don't think they're connected, do you?"

He sat on the sofa pulling on his shoes as Molly slipped on her coat. She opened the door, picked up the morning paper, and dropped it next to him. "Here. See what you can do when you take your mind off sex."

"Very little," he said, tying his laces.

"I have to run. Just pull the door closed when you leave." She lifted his face for a good-bye kiss, and stopped. "What's wrong?" she said.

"Nothing, why?"

"Something's bothering you, I can tell."

He leaned back on the sofa. "Do you get these insights all the time?" he asked. "I was just thinking about our difference in age."

"Come on, we're not *that* far apart."

"Seventeen years? I got sneakers older than you are."

She leaned forward. "You're ancient," she said, placing her cheek against his. "Old enough to be my father. It doesn't bother me—does it you?"

He put his hand under her dress and pulled her thigh toward him.

"Something does," he said, but she pushed herself away and went out the door.

Jack tightened his tie as he read the metropolitan section, checking for news in his district. Finding nothing above the fold, he flipped it over and saw a headline: BABY-DOLL DEATHS BAFFLE POLICE. He scanned the column.

> The police are still pursuing a piece of pencil found in the Shivers doll. Detective Norman Pulaski said, "We know where the pencil originally came from, but that doesn't tell us who put it inside the doll. But we're working on it." He refused to identify the original source of the pencil.

Jack put down the paper and heard Molly's question: *You don't think they're connected, do you?*

Like feathers on a tar baby. And I'm the baby.

"**H**ello, Mr. Brody?"

"Yeah?"

"Is this the same Angus Brody who went to Flatbush High twenty-five years ago?"

"Maybe. Who wants to know?"

"My name is Ignatius Pitt, and I work for Channel Six in New York. I'm calling about Congressman Jack MacLeod. Did you know him when you were in high school?"

"He wasn't a congressman in high school. What do you want?"

"I have a few questions, Mr. Brody. I won't take more than a few minutes of your time."

Jack stood in Molly's living room next to the bookshelves, waiting for her to come out of the bedroom. Touching the book spines, he paused on a paperback edition of *A Tale of Two Cities*. Instinctively, he pulled it out and opened it:

It was the best of times, it was the worst of times, it was the age of wisdom, it was the age of foolishness . . . we had everything before us, we had nothing before us. . . .

He closed it. He didn't need omens or clichés. Least of all those that stuck like a jingle.

Too late. He had Molly before him, he had Victoria behind him. . . .

He returned the book to its slot. Molly before him? Maybe. Victoria behind him? Not yet.

He sat on the sofa, considering the concentric circles that made up his life. It had been less than two weeks since he and Victoria had said good-bye, and already he was shifting focal points, or at least trying. When he was with Molly, he put away his shoes, found the butter dish without asking, even lowered the toilet seat. Transitions were like that, prompting self-examination and attention to detail. Like taking care to call Molly "sweetheart" instead of "Molly" so that he didn't call her "Victoria" by mistake, which would have been embarrassing under any circumstances, and disastrous under certain ones. For some reason women had this overblown fear that men considered them fungible commodities, especially in bed. He didn't think of Molly and Victoria as interchangeable. Far from it. It was just that he still had one foot in Victoria's world, and old habits died hard. Fortunately, Molly understood perfectly. So well, in fact, that she had asked him in advance to forgive her should she ever inadvertently call him "Jesse" instead of "Jack." Which she did. That night. In bed. Giving him a deeper appreciation of why women didn't care to be considered fungible commodities.

He checked his watch and twirled the small globe sitting on the coffee table, watching the continents spin by—America, Asia, Europe, America. Only when a relationship broke up were its building blocks finally revealed. Like Victoria's bony ribs, which he missed. And her fingers,

226

long and slender. And her neck, and her female paraphernalia—cotton balls strewn around the floor near the bathroom wastebasket; the smell of freshly applied fingernail polish; the candle that she lit as her unconscious mating call; her legal briefs spread around the room, unopened, waiting to be read; the newspaper clippings she insisted on keeping even as they yellowed with age; the half-finished crossword puzzles; the acerbic one-liners that made him laugh even though he was the straight man who set them up. But most of all, her. All together, not in pieces. Just her. V.

But then, there were also things about her that he didn't miss. Like her depression and her insularity, her refusal to tell him what was bothering her, always stonewalling the question or blaming it on her bone-wearying job. No question her work was part of the problem, but it was the undertow dragging her out to sea, not the specific shark that was eating her. Still, she refused to say what it was, so he settled for what he knew, or suspected. Like her aversion to marriage. And Rachel Redpath.

Dr. Rachel Redpath. Somehow she always figured into the picture, although exactly how he wasn't sure. He speculated, of course, but speculation was different from knowledge. Speculation was inconclusive. Unworthy. A shadow that raised suspicions he couldn't justify even in that part of the brain that required no evidence. So he stopped thinking about Rachel and Victoria—as best he could, with about as much success as a teenage boy stops thinking about sex.

Breaking up was teaching him other lessons about himself and Victoria, too. He knew that in many ways they were not meant for each other, that it was right for them to be apart. Being with Molly had already made that clear. She was like a new song played on top of an old one he had been hearing every day—at first clashing with what he knew and preferred, but in time becoming distinct and sweet on its own, until it was the only one he wanted. That's what was happening to him—he was falling in love with one person and out of love with another, both at the same time. Freeing himself from Victoria but not yet disconnected; drawn to Molly, but not yet joined.

What a drag. Here he was, a poker-playing, fly-fishing man's man— trekking unshaven in the woods, building fires, peeing on trees—and what was he thinking about? Romance. Relationships. *Dating*, for God's sake. He needed to climb a mountain, pass a bill, slay a dragon—forget about marriage and children for a while—forget about women—Jesus, *especially* women—

"Hello."

He looked up. Molly was standing at the sofa wearing an ecru silk blouse, a suede jacket and skirt, black tights, and boots to her knees. Her hair was full, her smile a magnet, her doe eyes so alluring they froze him like a pair of headlights.

He stood up, kissed her cheek, and inhaled her perfume. They chatted a moment—"You look great!"—"Where are we going?"—"How was your day?"—"Tell you in the cab." In just that much time, he was following her out the door—*What was that last thought I had?*—feeling as smooth and cool as a slab of Philadelphia cream cheese.

It was the best, and worst, of times.

Pepper Loomis threw her long slender leg across Abner Titus's body, straddled him, and leaned down and placed her open mouth on his. She exhaled firmly, surprised at how difficult it was to fill his lungs, then lifted her mouth for a breath, blew life into him again, and laid her ear at his lips. Except for the smell of garlic from the two plates of pasta primavera he'd eaten at the Barrister's Club, nothing.

"Breathe!" she said in a whisper, and took another breath herself. "Come on, Judge, don't do this to me. *Breathe!*"

She was in the middle of her next transfusion of air when Daisy burst through the door with two paramedics pushing an aluminum stretcher loaded with equipment—a jump kit, a drug box, an oxygen cylinder, and a defibrillator. They immediately took charge.

"Yo! Can you hear me?" one yelled, shaking him by the shoulder.

The other questioned Daisy and Pepper. "Any idea what's wrong?"

"He had a terrible pain in his stomach," Pepper said. "He stood up, keeled over, and started gasping for air. And stopped."

"He has only one kidney," Daisy said. "And he eats too much for lunch."

The first paramedic placed his ear by Titus's mouth. "He's breathing. Looks like he hyperventilated." He pressed his finger on Titus's neck under his chin, along the trachea, searching for the carotid artery. "We have pulses," he said to his partner. After administering oxygen through a football-shaped ambu bag, they rushed him into the ambulance and off to GW Hospital.

Titus was sleeping with an oxygen cannula in his nose, Pepper hovering at his side, when Rachel, Phoebe Chang, and a nurse came through the door. Pepper shook hands with Chang and extended her hand to Rachel, who, appearing distracted, didn't extend hers. After discussing Titus's condition with Chang, Rachel left without saying good-bye.

"A real Florence Nightingale," Pepper said sarcastically.

"Actually," the nurse said frostily, "Florence Nightingale was a nurse, not a doctor." She followed Dr. Chang out of the room.

Pepper turned to the judge, pulled the sheet up around his neck, and gently stroked his hair away from his face.

"Don't fade on me now, Abner," she said with an edge, knowing he couldn't hear. "Your big day still lies ahead."

J ack stopped Molly in the middle of the doorway as they were leaving her apartment for the evening.

"Let me ask you something," he said. "Are you wearing underpants?"

She wrinkled her forehead. "That's a highly personal question, isn't it?"

"It's meant to be."

"Yes, of course."

"Take them off, will you?"

She did.

They left.

During the last half of October the two of them turned New York into their private urban playground. He caught the shuttle from Washington to New York every night, and she did her best to keep her news beat in the city. She wanted to see the New York she'd always heard about, so they took in the places native New Yorkers rarely visited: the Empire State Building, the Statue of Liberty, Radio City Music Hall, the Circle Line. They laughed at stand-up comics at the Comedy Club and danced a polka at the New Lone Star Café, even though there was no dance floor. They ate eggs at midnight at the Brasserie, and rubber chicken at fund-raisers, leaving early to hear Bobby Short at the Carlyle. When Ella Fitzgerald sang "I'll Take Manhattan," she sang it to them, and if they heard a song they liked at twelve-thirty on Saturday morning, they prowled the cassettes at Record World, then taxied to Fulton Street for fresh oysters and vodka so cold it poured like syrup. They met Winston and his latest girlfriend for dinner in Brooklyn, and joined them in the Village for front-row tables and good jazz. They worked all day and played at night as if sleep were an afterthought. If it hadn't been for lovemaking, they might never have gone to bed at all.

Although they had a dim idea that they weren't the only two people in the world, they acted as if they were. They stared at each other during dinner and didn't flinch when a waiter dropped a dish nearby. Jack called her "sweet pea" and she called him "babycakes," both within earshot of adults, without shame. They saw great signs in the small things

231

they had in common, like hot pastrami sandwiches and toothpaste tubes squeezed in the middle, and turned a blind eye to the things that separated them, like forgetting birthdays, snoring, and—perhaps—having children.

They touched each other everywhere they went. Squeezes on the elevator, kisses in the Egyptian wing at the Met, a groping hand on line at the movies, another once they were seated. They sneaked into a dressing room at Saks Fifth Avenue and emerged fifteen minutes later, she with a charley horse in her thigh, he with a crick in his neck. He took to carrying extra handkerchiefs, and so did she.

One Friday night, half a block from a Soho restaurant, she sat on a darkened loading dock, wrapped her legs around him beneath his oversized raincoat, and took the full measure of him. After that, she started wearing thigh-highs and stopped wearing underwear altogether, which wasn't a problem before making love, but was occasionally inconvenient after.

They did these things with no planning or discussion, no postmortems or acknowledgments, as if their sexual personas had become juvenile delinquents, indulging themselves without even so much as a passing bow to discretion or good taste. The more outrageous their lovemaking and the riskier the locations, the more blasé they became.

One night, coming home from a late fund-raiser, they hailed a cab with a scratched-up Lucite divider between the front and back and within minutes were taking each other face to face, playing with the cab's undulations over the asphalt moguls, feeling each other in ways they'd never felt before. In the middle of an openmouthed kiss, the cab hit an enormous pothole, smashing their front teeth together.

Molly's were undamaged, but Jack's took a half-moon chip. It didn't matter—he could have lost them to the roots and still held on to her flanks, which was what he did as they crossed Fifty-ninth Street on their way to Columbus Circle. Once they reached her brownstone, the crunching sound of his teeth cannibalizing one of their own was too much to ignore. When Molly saw the missing chip, she was horrified, but not him. It was Sunday night; he'd have it repaired the next morning.

Before taking the shuttle back to Washington on Tuesday, he met Molly for breakfast to show her the restoration. Relieved, she said they'd have to be more careful in the future. He disagreed, although he did become more fond of stationary surfaces for lovemaking, like desktops, tabletops, and beds.

He followed the same routine for the next two weeks, taking the early morning shuttle to Washington, trekking back to New York at night, working in his Manhattan district office, appearing at receptions in the evening, dumping his briefcase at his own one-bedroom apartment, and meeting Molly for the evening.

Slowly, they found themselves going out less and staying in more until, without realizing it, they'd turned her bedroom into a bunker. Ordinarily she kept the room neat, but with Jack around, the sexual wreckage had become too much to contend with on a daily basis. On any given morning the chair in her bedroom was draped with debris that had been flung there the night before: blouses, neckties, bras, shirts. There were high-heeled shoes in front of it, cocked sideways, half-covered with stockings; there was a tortoiseshell barrette and a pair of elbow-length red gloves hiding behind a potted areca palm. The bedside tables were cluttered with books stained with pomegranate juice, an antique alarm clock that didn't work, and a quartz model that did, conveniently turned face down.

On top of the telephone answering machine were two empty glasses with the fresh-bread smell of stale tequila, and next to them, small bottles of bitters, grenadine, and vanilla, their tops hiding from the carnage or missing altogether. Cinnamon and crushed cloves remained in a mortar with a solitary tangerine peel, and under the table sat a mixing bowl with the drying moonscape of the previous night's egg whites. On top of the bookshelf were opened jars of watercolors—red, orange, and black—standing next to a brandy snifter half-filled with pine-scented oil above a warming candle.

There was a sliver of honeydew melon rind lying on the shower-stall floor, a spent tube of caviar paste lying twisted beneath the bed. Stacked on top of the stereo were music cassettes of all kinds—classical, jazz, and enough pop to create a television promotion for the World's Worst Love Songs Ever. Across the room on top of the TV set were matchbook covers with song lyrics and bad poetry written on the edges; a soft boar-bristle paintbrush; and two dead batteries drained from a love toy, which was the only artifact either of them had the decency to put away before leaving for work.

On top of a walnut chest of drawers was an old-fashioned pitcher and a porcelain basin half-full of water, steaming only hours before, now cold and quiet, a washcloth hanging possumlike over its edge above a pile of crumpled towels. Next to the basin, in a crystal ashtray, were the melted remains of a large white candle, its burned-out wick and wax drippings standing in mute memorial to the events witnessed in its buttery light the night before.

And when they wanted to remind themselves that they'd lost all boundaries, there was always the eight-foot-long black feather boa with its plumes stripped clean on a three-foot stretch in the middle. They'd loved the dickens out of that thing.

It was the best of times.

Eggs Benedict sat slouched behind the wheel of his green Ford, his eyelids nearly closed under his Dodgers cap, his mind lulled by the blended sounds of the city. He pulled the bill down over his forehead, folded his arms, and was making himself comfortable when Jack and Molly emerged from her brownstone and stepped off the curb to hail a cab. One glimpse and he was wide awake. He lifted his camera and clicked off a few frames as they piled into a cab and pulled away. Then he started his engine and followed.

Their taxi turned east onto Thirty-eighth Street, entered traffic, and slowed. He remained a few cars behind, patient, cautious. He switched on the radio, and in a few minutes heard the news he was waiting for: "Police arrested a suspect today in the Queens bombing of an abortion clinic. More on that now from WINS News reporter Leslie Page."

He turned up the volume and stayed on the taxi's tail.

"A Queens man was taken into custody today in connection with last week's bombing of an abortion clinic on Queens Boulevard. Police say Billy Bannister, an unemployed carpenter, was arrested at ten-thirty this morning at his home on Hodges Avenue and charged with second-degree murder in the death of Julia Rodriguez, a janitor at the clinic. Police are seeking an accomplice."

Benedict turned off the radio and scratched his beard, flaring his nostrils, inhaling the smell of patchouli oil.

The taxi turned right onto Park Avenue and stopped. He pulled into an opening next to a fire hydrant on Thirty-eighth Street and watched.

Molly and Jack emerged from the cab, crossed the street, and headed across a large open plaza toward the building's entrance. Benedict turned off the engine, jumped out, and ran across Park Avenue, dodging traffic. Entering the building, he saw his quarry disappear behind a closing elevator door. He walked to a stainless-steel panel and watched the lighted numbers indicate the location of the elevator cab—six, seven, ten, fourteen—and back down.

Benedict walked to the building directory. The name opposite six, the elevator's first stop, read *Park Avenue Women's Clinic*.

No need to look further.

He took the next elevator to the sixth floor, stepped off, and looked around the corner. Across the hall was the door to the clinic with a window at eye level. He walked to it and looked inside. Congressman MacLeod and Molly McCormick were talking to a receptionist behind a desk. McCormick held an open notebook as if she were preparing to interview someone; MacLeod looked official, as if he was paying a visit to a constituent. Benedict backed away, pulled his camera from his fatigue jacket, snapped a couple of shots through the glass, and moved down the hall, around the corner, out of sight.

Fifteen minutes later MacLeod and McCormick came through the clinic door and headed for the elevator. She stopped to jot something in her notebook while he waited.

Neither of them saw the camera or heard the click of its shutter.

Sitting behind the wheel of his car, Eggs Benedict removed his baseball cap and glasses and wiped the perspiration off his face. He opened his beat-up briefcase, removed a three-ring binder, and thumbed to a clean page in back. Holding the opened book on his lap, he reached up to the visor for a blue pencil with *Jack MacLeod, Congressman, 19th District* printed on the side.

He filled an entire sheet of green paper with notes.

The weather was doing its late-October seesaw: bright and beautiful one day, cold and drizzly the next. The off-election year gave Jack a certain amount of freedom, and when he discovered that Molly, like himself, was a creature of the weather, the idea of sunshine became irresistible.

After circling La Guardia for two hours searching for a hole in the cloud cover, the 727 finally landed and rolled to the gate. Jack wasted no time. He took a taxi to a travel agency and bought two tickets to St. Thomas, then went to his New York congressional office and spent the next hour canceling meetings, rearranging appointments, apologizing for receptions he'd miss, and cajoling his staff to cover dinners and fundraisers for him. He called Molly, who arranged leave from the station, and three days later they were on a rented sloop, beating windward to Jost Van Dyke, dropping anchor at White Bay, eating melons drenched in island limes, soaking up the Caribbean sun.

At the end of their second day they anchored at Road Town on Tortola and went ashore for steel drums, island food, and dancing. Sitting at a bamboo table, drinking strawberry daiquiris, they studied the sunset as if they'd never seen one before, which, in a sense, they hadn't. It struck Jack that they'd been together most of the last month but hadn't tired of each other, at least not yet. It also occurred to him that fresh love would soon be tested.

"There's nothing like spending a few days together on a boat," he said. "If a couple can survive that, they can survive anything."

He spoke from experience. Cramped quarters, no privacy, always on top of each other hoisting sails, choosing a destination, navigating coral, dropping anchor. Even at night there was no place to hide, and when it rained, the best you could do was sit belowdecks trying not to get seasick, playing cards stuck together by water dripping from leaky hatch gaskets.

Molly listened to him describe what they were in for. Unfazed, she took a sip of her daiquiri.

"How're we doing so far?" She reached across the table and put her hand on his cheek; her fingers were cold from holding her drink. He held them up to admire them and saw that the tip of her middle finger was unusually white.

"Frostbite," she said. "Lost my mittens one day. It turns white when it gets cold. All it takes is a glass of ice water."

"How do you get it back to normal?"

She shrugged. "Put it someplace warm."

He felt his blood stir. Opening his mouth, he stuck her finger inside, expecting her to pull it back. Instead, she left it there, waiting to see who'd chicken out first. The West Indian waiter approached the table. "First aid," Jack said with her finger between his teeth.

The waiter put two menus on the table with a grin that said, If that's first aid for her, mon, I love to see how she give first aid to you.

She retrieved her hand.

"Bring me a box of cigars, would you please?" Jack asked the waiter.

Molly grimaced; she hated cigars. "There goes your goodnight kiss."

The waiter returned with a humidor. Jack examined a variety of shapes and sizes and chose one. As the waiter left, Jack slid the red-and-gold cigar band off the shaft, as if preparing to light up.

"Before dinner?" she said.

He slipped the band onto his little finger. It fit perfectly. Then he reached for her hand and slipped the band onto her ring finger. It fit perfectly there, too.

He stopped a busboy and handed him the cigar. When he turned back, her hand was outstretched, waiting to caress his cheek.

They ate fresh lobster tails and turtle-fin soup and cold creamed corn and danced until the place closed at two. After an easy stroll to the dinghy, they rowed across the moonlit harbor to their boat. A while later, lying in their bunk, Jack reached for the lamp switch and saw one of his blue office pencils on the counter, the word *MacLeod* printed boldly in white. All at once he realized that he'd managed to shed the pit of his stomach somewhere between New York and San Juan. The sinking feeling was gone. Melvin Shivers, Eli Graves were gone. Paranoia was gone. Victoria was . . . gone.

He turned off the light and stroked Molly's hair, admiring her skin in the reflected light. After she'd fallen asleep, he whispered, "I love you." The words sounded strange to him, he used them so rarely. Not really since high school. Not since Honey O'Connor.

He pictured Honey standing inside the Blue Whale Diner in East Syracuse, drawing a heart in the fogged glass, forming the words *I love you* on her lips. Those mind-bending, heart-pumping silent words. What had prompted him to use them now, with this particular person, with images of Honey dancing in his head, he had no idea.

A blue-and-white NYC Department of Corrections rally wagon turned off Ditmars Boulevard onto Grand Central Parkway with the driver drumming his fingers on the steering wheel, pretending to listen to his partner complain about a celibate sex life after twelve years of marriage. Sitting on a bench in the rear in prison denims, handcuffs, and leg restraints was Billy Bannister, on his way, at last, to a bail hearing in Queens Criminal Court. His lawyer, Jeremy Hackett, had called that morning to tell him that the Red Rose Society would post his bond. After several days in prison he was sick of the smell of sweaty men and antiseptic hallways, and he missed his son and wife, whose daily visits helped and hurt in equal proportions. He wanted to go home.

After traveling a few miles on the parkway, the van slowed at an exit and turned onto the half-mile access road leading to Queens Boulevard. On the left side of the road were trees and bushes screening it from the highway; on the right were small single-family houses, a synagogue, and red-brick apartment houses. It was a cold fall day in a quiet suburban neighborhood, with few cars on the access road and no one in sight.

The rally wagon was moving uneventfully down the street when the driver saw a small maroon van pull away from the curb and stop, brake lights glowing. The police wagon slowed to a crawl.

"Go around him," the driver's partner said. As if hearing, the maroon van pulled to the left, blocking passage.

The rally wagon stopped dead. The driver was pissed—then stunned. "Jesus Christ!"

Three commandos wearing combat boots and carrying assault rifles jumped out of the maroon van and ran toward the wagon, their faces veiled by nylon stockings. They opened the wagon's doors and motioned the deputies to get out.

A man driving a Toyota pickup pulled up behind the rally wagon and came to a stop. Seeing guns, he threw his truck into reverse and raced backward toward a side street. Before he reached it, the driver of a Plymouth approached from behind and, unable to see the kidnapping, stopped and laid on his horn. In a moment a half-dozen drivers sat motionless, wondering which New York screwup *du jour* was tying up traffic.

By now the prison deputies were facedown on the pavement, hands on the backs of their necks. A few feet away Billy Bannister was being lifted out of the back door of the police wagon by two of the kidnappers. "Close your eyes!" the first one barked at the deputies, and they did as they were told. The other two dragged Bannister at a run back to the maroon van while the first commando remained standing over the officers. A moment later the van roared backward, gathered up the remaining kidnapper, and with the rear door swinging shut, headed up to Queens Boulevard and lost itself in an anonymous stream of traffic.

High above the street where the rally wagon sat empty, a man leaned out his apartment window, cupped his hands to his mouth, and yelled down at the two deputies on the pavement, "You can get up now!"

Inside the van two masked figures rode quietly on wooden stools, Bannister seated on the floor between them, hands shackled in his lap by a plastic restraint.

"Who are you guys?" he asked, but no one answered. He leaned forward and squinted at one of his guards as if he recognized him. "Eggs? That you?" Still no answer.

As the truck turned onto the Long Island Expressway, the centrifugal force rolled Bannister off balance, prompting a commando to place a rifle butt under the hostage's arm to keep him from falling.

"Thanks," Bannister said, regaining his sitting position. His worried smile turned painful and he pulled his hands in against his midsection. "Any you guys got some Pepto? I got a serious problem with my stomach."

"We'll check it out," a muffled voice said.

Bannister actually took comfort from the offer.

It was a red-and-orange, late-October Saturday. Jack had rented a Pontiac and packed a large bag with the frankincense and myrrh of Brooklyn: bagels, Italian sausage, olives, and a jar of borscht. The distance to Rich Hill, West Virginia, was five hundred and forty miles, which meant that, assuming no delays, they'd arrive in time for a late dinner. They stopped along the way from time to time to gas up, eat chicken-fried steak and coconut cream pie, swap places at the wheel, walk around, and loosen up. By late afternoon they were on the road again, with Jack driving the home stretch.

"What's the sleeping arrangement tonight?" he asked.

"I don't know. My parents aren't prudes, but with all the kids, we'll probably have separate rooms. Why? Is that a problem?"

"No problem at all, as long as I know where your room is. I sleepwalk, remember?"

Molly's expression said, Give me a break. "You need a shrink."

"No way. You couldn't get me on a couch if my life depended on it."

"I've already had you there. As I recall, it wasn't that difficult."

She unbuckled her seat belt and dug her fingernails into his thigh.

His blood dropped. A Rest Area Ahead sign whizzed by; he swerved onto the turnoff, forcing Molly to cushion her hand against the dashboard. The car hit gravel, spun forty-five degrees, and came to rest in a cloud of dust that drifted toward a semi with a sleeping driver.

He unbuckled his seat belt.

"You're crazy," she said.

They looked at each other, and suddenly both of them were upping the ante: her shoes, his shoes, her top, his shirt. His first thought was, If we get caught, this is seriously not good for a congressman's image. His second was, I wonder how we do this with a console between us?

"Wait!" Molly said. "We can't do this."

Saved.

"We have to get into the backseat."

Saved again.

When it came to politics, Jack had the convictions of a statesman, and when it came to sex, the convictions of a politician.

She crawled over the top of the seat saying something about how everyone in high school had done this but her, and she wasn't going to go to her grave without trying. Jack climbed over the seat, too. In a few minutes the steam on the windows created a screen against truckers and the fading autumn light.

By the time they reached Rich Hill it was eight-thirty, and dark. Named at the turn of the century for its rich veins of coal, Rich Hill was now a gold mine of poverty: lightbulbs without lamp shades, rickety barns held together by cobwebs, fundamentalist snake handlers who thought Ronald Wilson Reagan was the devil because his names contained six letters each, scratch farmers who'd given up on politicians long ago and wouldn't go to the polls if their lives depended on it, which, in fact, they did.

Survival was the town's number-one industry, and yet as much as it promoted hardness and greed, it spawned tenderness, too: farmers who let hungry kids steal a few ears of corn at dusk; thrift stores that sold skirts for a dollar and blouses for a quarter, and then on credit; Baptist ministers who dispensed canned beets and pickled turnips as much as hellfire and damnation. Life in the town was a lot like the hard black coal that had brought folks there in the first place. It drove them into the ground, but it also burned quiet and warm, and with very little waste.

Homer and Betsy McCormick were probably as good as anyone in the county. Homer was a typical American who hated to pay taxes, never wrote thank-you notes, and although he had navigated a B-17 over Berlin, couldn't read a You Are Here map, as he put it, "irregardless." He avoided movies that advertised themselves as "enchanting," found vacations at the beach boring, and had never, to his knowledge, been charmed by a wine's bouquet.

Betsy was Homer's ideal complement, restive with the chores of life but endlessly patient with human foibles. It drove her crazy to stand in line at the salad bar watching people pick through buckets of chickpeas as if they were rubies, but she waited anyway, without complaining. She hated to cook but loved to watch her children eat; hated cleaning house, but took the duster from the hands of a sleepy ten-year-old and finished the job herself. No matter how busy she was, she could hold a child in her arms and with the simplest gesture—combing a girl's hair with her fingers, cleaning a dirty smudge from a boy's cheek—complete the human touch.

When Molly and Jack arrived, it was like any other homecoming. She bounded out of the car and onto the porch as Homer and Betsy came to the door. Then it was hugs, kisses, and kids piling out of the house and surrounding her like elves, yelling, "What'd you bring me?" and talking over each other.

They entered the house, and Jack gave Betsy his gifts from Brooklyn and listened to her talk about sausages. In time they moved into Homer's and Betsy's small sitting room with the fake wood paneling, a real fireplace, and an ironclad rule that no children were allowed to enter without a knock and permission.

The four of them sat and talked while Betsy worked her needlepoint and Homer lit a pipe. After stoking the fireplace, he settled into his easy chair with a shot of bourbon in a coffee cup. The conversation started on Jack—questions about where he grew up, the usual questions about Washington, Congress, and the economy. Jack handled them all with honesty and deference, making Molly proud.

Jack wanted to hear about Molly's childhood, so Betsy recounted how she and Homer had adopted her.

"It happened with the tulip," Betsy said, referring to the leaded-glass flower laid into the orphanage's heavy oak door. Facing east, it glowed brilliantly in the morning sun.

"Molly just loved that thing," Betsy said. "She'd be scolded for something like taking off all her clothes—which she did every time it rained, Lord knows why—"

"I was three years old, Mom," she said. Sitting barefoot.

"Whatever, the tulip was her special friend. Anyway, all the orphans were taught to call me 'Aunt Betsy,' but Molly kept calling me 'Mom.' I told her I loved her like a daughter, but someday a lucky couple would adopt her and then she'd have a real mother. But she wouldn't listen.

"Well, one day when she was five years old, she climbed up to a cabinet above the sink, looking for some baking chocolate. She slipped and everything came down—glass, sugar, molasses—Lord, what a mess. By the time I got there, she'd cut her finger on a broken jar of preserves.

"I whisked her into the bathroom and stood her on the toilet lid, and while I was cleanin' her cut she said, 'I'm sorry, Mom,' or something like that, because I remember thinking this was the perfect time to tell her once and for all she had to stop calling me Mom. But before I said a word, she looked up from the bandage on her finger and said, 'Mommy, you're as pretty as the tulip.' And that was it. She was mine."

Molly looked astonished. "I didn't know that. I don't remember any of that."

Jack asked for more stories and heard about Molly the Tomboy who climbed trees and got into fights and learned how to make a pivot at second base and bat a solid three hundred. He heard about Molly the Doctor, who forced perfectly healthy kids to lie in bed with thermometers in their mouths, and Molly the Reporter, who published a muckraking orphanage newsletter, and a dozen other stories. He fell in love with her a little more with each one.

They heard a stampede of feet, and a little boy entered the room, giving his obligatory knock on the door as an afterthought, his wide eyes made even wider by the thick glasses he wore.

"Hey, Molly! It's a commercial!" He waited for her to respond the way a dog waits for a stick to be thrown.

Molly jumped up. "Apples!" she yelled, and ran out of the room and toward the back door.

Jack stood up and followed them into the backyard to watch the ritual harvest. He lifted a six-year-old high enough to pick one. After the last kid had wobbled back through the door, apple in hand, Molly positioned the tip of the clothesline pole at the stem of a Jonathan.

"If you catch it—" She didn't finish the sentence before lifting the pole. A large red apple broke away and crashed through the leaves, hit a limb, and fell into Jack's hand. He held it up and smiled.

"Not bad," she said, "for a New York boy."

"If I catch it, what?"

She took the apple, rubbed it on her side, and put it to his mouth and told him to take a bite.

They walked inside and hung around the kitchen until the hour was late and the children were in bed.

Betsy stuck her head through the kitchen door and said she and Homer were going to bed, everybody would be up for church at nine. "I put Jack in Freddy's old room," she said, and left.

Molly leaned against the red maple countertop, legs crossed at the ankles, arms folded. "It's a long way from Freddy's room to mine, and if you didn't notice, Homer took the shotgun off the mantel."

"I'm telling you, I walk in my sleep."

Molly pushed herself away from the counter, smiling as she passed him. "Pump it back in the horse, Jack." She turned off the light.

Sunday afternoon Homer and Jack drove fifteen miles to the Blackridge County Mall to go bowling. They asked Molly and Betsy to come along, but Molly wanted to hang back and watch a football game with little Pauly, her favorite ten-year old. After the kickoff, she slipped out of the

Big Room and joined Betsy by the fireplace in the sitting room, where she sat working on her knitting.

"He's very nice," she said to Molly without looking up. "Is this serious?"

"Serious fun." Betsy responded with silence. "I don't know yet," Molly said.

"Looks serious to me. Does he want children?"

"Definitely."

Betsy straightened the yarn. "Does he know?"

"Yes."

"Does it matter to him?"

"Of course not." After a defensive pause, she said, "I don't think so." Another delay. "We haven't gotten that far."

"You will. Soon."

Molly picked up an apple and bit into it, making it crack even though she knew it drove Betsy crazy. "Mom?" she said with her mouth full, another offense. "What do you know about my birth parents?"

Betsy kept sewing.

"Does it bother you to talk about it?" Molly asked.

"I can't imagine why it would, I've already told you everything I know."

Betsy had explained Molly's history several times before, and Molly had never questioned her sincerity. Molly always assumed that what she didn't know didn't matter, a simple policy that had worked fine for the last twenty-five years. Until now.

"Tell me again. Everything you remember."

Betsy laid her knitting in her lap. "You were two years old, and the only thing we knew about you were the clothes you had on when Sister Helen brought you in."

"And where'd she say she found me?"

"I told you. She said a man brought you to the church."

"The man without a name."

"I'm sure he had a name, dear. He just didn't give it. Sister Helen said he put you in her arms and walked away."

Molly had been told this, too, but she wanted to hear it again, hoping a new clue would appear.

"Didn't she ask him who he was? Or who I was?"

Betsy looked mildly exasperated.

"What'd he look like?" Molly asked.

"I don't know, sweetheart. Really."

"Geez, Mom, didn't she find out anything? How could she not ask anything?"

Betsy rested her knitting needles, and suddenly Molly realized she was harassing her mother for information she couldn't possibly know. Molly stood up and paced around a moment, then sat down in her father's favorite chair and picked at some loose threads on the arm cover. "Mind if I see the blanket?" she asked.

Betsy left the room and after a few minutes returned and sat on the arm of the chair, holding a small scrap quilt about three feet square.

Molly took it and opened it up. It was a tiny crib-sized blanket of square patches of hand-me-down clothing, dishcloths, quilt remnants, feed bags, whatever had been handy to its maker. The only link Molly had to her birth.

Betsy said she had to check on one of the children and left.

Molly looked at the size of the blanket, wondering how she ever could have been so small. She laid it on her lap and smoothed it out, examining the patches. After a few minutes she folded it in half, respectfully, like a flag from a soldier's coffin. As she made the last crease her finger caught a corner of fabric that had frayed loose at the stitches—a double-layered square cut from a flour sack. Tucking it in, she saw printed letters. She held them up to the lamp, pulled the cloth from under the patch, and squinted to read. The letters were faint but unmistakable: *Onondaga Flour Mills, E. Syracuse, NY.*

Her heart raced. Had it been sewn by her birth mother? What were the odds of that? She felt something strange inside her stomach, a set of roots planting themselves in soil.

She heard the door slam and instinctively folded the quilt over the patch.

"What's up?" Homer asked entering the room. Jack and Betsy were close behind.

"Mom and I were just talking," Molly said. To her surprise, the word *Mom* sounded slightly tinny to her ears.

Homer and Jack lied about their bowling scores and talked about the woman in a spandex suit who'd bowled next to them—Cindy Crawford's twin, who had asked them to give her bowling lessons—these and other soft pitches Molly ordinarily would have knocked out of the park, but not now. She remained uncharacteristically quiet the rest of the day.

Jack and Molly had to be on the road early the next morning, so they called it a night. Jack reached for Molly's arm as she climbed the steps. "Are you all right?" he asked.

"Of course," she said, irritated with the question.

"I like your family," he said. "Wouldn't be so bad to turn out like them."

"They brought me up," she snapped. "Why wouldn't I?"

He looked surprised. "I think that's what I meant." He looked at the tulip across the hallway on the front door. "I didn't realize how nice an orphanage can be."

"Don't get carried away," she said.

She looked at him and her face softened. Then she cupped his cheeks in her hands and kissed him good night. "Some days I can't tell what makes us who we are," she said, holding on. "Knowing who your birth parents are at least gives you a clue."

J ack stood at the sink in Victoria's bathroom searching through the drawer for a bottle of aspirin. He'd taken an afternoon shuttle from New York and stopped by the house on his way to Capitol Hill to pick up his mail, grab a clean shirt if there was one, and find a memorandum he needed for his six P.M. meeting with the Leadership Coalition. Even though Victoria had told him to make himself at home whenever he wanted—after all, he was still half owner—he felt uncomfortable being there. He had decided to pop a few aspirin to cut short a headache, which might have been the first tickle of a migraine.

Pawing through bars of hotel soap and used emery boards, he found a new bottle of aspirin and took it out of its box, which he tossed toward the waste basket. It dropped onto the floor among Q-Tips, tissues, and Victoria's usual bathroom trash. He'd forgotten: she was the liberated woman who hated picking up her junk because it felt too much like women's work. He pulled the cotton stuffing out of the aspirin bottle and tossed it toward the wastebasket. And missed. Now *he* was littering.

He washed down four aspirin and began picking up the trash—the aspirin box, a cotton ball, a piece of cardboard packaging, mascara on Kleenex . . . Cardboard packaging? He lifted it out of the wastebasket and saw a piece of white-and-lavender cardboard with the letters *PT* on a torn label. Letters he'd seen somewhere before, although he couldn't remember where.

The waiting taxi's horn sounded. He tossed the piece of cardboard back into the wastebasket and checked his watch. Five-thirty. He was late.

He sat in the backseat of the taxi opening his mail—junk on the left, bills on the right, rip and read, save and toss. For no apparent reason, the letters on the cardboard package popped into his head: *PT*. Then another letter appeared. An *E*. The *E* that had been torn off the label.

EPT. *Early Pregnancy Test.*

The taxi stopped at a traffic light. He stared out the window and saw a telephone booth. "Be right back," he said, and got out. He jogged to the phone, dropped a quarter, and dialed Victoria's office.

"Brenda, it's Jack. Is Victoria there?"

"No, she's not."

"Do you know where I can find her?"

"I think she's still at the clinic."

"The clinic?"

"The Capitol Hill Women's Clinic."

"What's she doing there?"

"I have no idea."

"What time is she due back?"

"She said she'd be there all afternoon."

All afternoon? A visit, sure, but what was she doing there all afternoon? "Thanks," he said, and hung up.

Normal business hours had ended and the receptionist had stepped into the ladies' room when he walked through the door. He headed for the office of the director, Dr. Kathy Keenan, but no one was there. He closed the door and began striding down the corridor. A surprised counselor appeared in front of him.

"Congressman MacLeod," she said.

"Where's Victoria?" He knocked on the first door he saw and opened it. The room was empty.

"Congressman, what in the world are you doing? We still have procedures going on here!"

"Which room is she in?" he asked.

"Congressman!"

He opened the next door and saw Victoria's long brown hair. She was lying on a table, dressed in cotton, covered by a tent over her midsection. She and Kathy Keenan, who was examining her, looked up.

"Jack!" Victoria said. "What are you doing here?"

"Have you done it yet?"

"Done what?"

Kathy Keenan dropped a speculum into a stainless-steel tray. "Jesus Christ, Jack. This is outrageous."

He paid no attention. Victoria propped herself onto her elbows and looked down at Kathy. "Can we take a break?" she asked.

Kathy turned out her light, lowered the stirrups, and pulled off her gloves and tossed them into the foot-levered trash can. Victoria sat up on the edge of the examining table as Kathy left, muttering she'd be down the hall in her office.

Victoria pointed at her purse which hung on a hook on the back of the door. He handed it to her and sat down on a plastic chair. She opened her bag and pulled out a matchbook and a pack of brown cigarettes, lit one, and blew smoke toward the ceiling.

"How'd you find out?" she asked.

"Cleaning up your bathroom."

She took another nervous drag on her cigarette. "I need a minute to think about this, okay?"

He looked at her and tried to imagine what was going through her mind. After a long minute she raised her head and looked at him.

"I'm sorry you found out," she said. "And pissed."

"Are you still pregnant?"

She leaned on her elbows and looked at him. "Yes." He shifted his weight in his chair, relaxing. "It happened the last time we made love," she said.

He sat looking at her, wondering which of a dozen things to ask first. "Why didn't you tell me?"

"Jesus, Jack, I've only been pregnant since September." She drew on her cigarette, nervously.

"Aren't you supposed to quit smoking when you're pregnant?"

"This is the first one I've had in weeks. It's so stale it hurts." She tapped the ash into an empty specimen cup, gathering her thoughts. "I thought what you didn't know wouldn't hurt you," she said. "I know what a big deal marriage and kids are to you, and I didn't think you needed to cope with something like this."

Jack crossed his ankle over his knee and rubbed it. "What are you planning to do?"

"Well, considering where you found me, it shouldn't come as a surprise."

He lifted an eyebrow and cocked his head to the side. "I don't get it. Did you stop taking the pill?"

"Yes."

"Why?"

She paused a long time, once again looking as if she were making up her answers. Something wasn't right.

"When I had my physical in August, my gynecologist told me I'd been on the pill too long and fitted me for a diaphragm." She squinted at him through smoke. "If you'd dug around the drawer long enough, I'm sure you would have found that, too."

"So why didn't you use it?"

She laughed. "Do you remember that night?" His look said yes. "*Res ipsa.* When it comes to sex, smart people aren't any smarter than the people they think aren't so smart."

At last, a statement that rang true. "So when are you having the abortion?"

"It's scheduled for tomorrow morning."

"Does it have to be that soon?"

"No. But why not?"

He stood up and leaned on the back of the chair. "I want to ask you for a favor. Postpone it long enough to give us a chance to talk it over."

She smashed her cigarette into the cup. "Lord, I knew this would happen."

"The decision is yours, obviously. I'm just asking for an opportunity to discuss it."

"What's to discuss? I'm forty, unmarried, and not interested in being a mother. Nothing's changed."

"You could always give the baby to me."

He expected an "Oh, Jack, please," but didn't hear one. She opened her purse and pulled out another cigarette, stroked it between her fingers, and laid it next to her on the examining table. He sat down and leaned the chair back on two legs, inaugurating a long silence. Finally he dropped the chair onto all fours. He decided to try a different tack.

"Maybe you're right. Maybe I'm one of those guys who cares more about having kids than raising them. God knows, given the kind of lives we lead, it's hard to imagine doing it right."

"Actually, you'd be a good father," she said.

What made her say that?

"You know how I feel about a woman's right to choose," he said. "But this feels different."

"Of course it does. You have a personal stake in this one."

Another tilt in his direction.

He stood up. "Sorry I barged in, V. This obviously isn't the time to talk."

She tapped her fingers on the examining table. "I suppose a few more days sounds reasonable."

The more I back off, the more she comes forward.

She said, "We haven't exactly been close lately. I understand you've been seeing someone. A young television reporter from New York."

"Well—"

"Are you in love?"

Jesus, where did that come from? Never mind that—what's the answer? Yes, he was in love. But now there was this. A major complication and no time to assess it or make comparisons. Was it a simple equation, or apples and oranges? *Are you in love?* The answer could mean everything.

"Whatever it is, it shouldn't be confused with this," he said. It was borderline and incomplete, but as far as it went, it was honest. Enough to get by. For the moment. "How about you?" he asked.

"Am I in love?" she asked. "Yes, with the same lover I've had for a long time." He pictured his favorite candidate, Rachel, but Victoria pointed at her briefcase. "Whoever said the law was a jealous mistress forgot to mention the ball and chain that goes with it." She picked up her unlit cigarette, played with it—and stuck it back into its package, pulling out a stick of cinnamon chewing gum instead. "I'll think about it. But no pressure, all right?"

As a litigator, Jack knew that the moment a judge ruled in your favor you got out of the courtroom as fast as possible. He put his hand on the door handle. "One other thing," he said, pushing his luck. "Is it a boy or a girl?"

"Too early to tell."

"What do you think?"

She paused. "If I had to guess, I'd say a girl."

He smiled at her. "With your premonitions, I wouldn't bet against it."

He went out the door and walked down the hall, smiling. *I'd say a girl.* She never would have said that if she wasn't going to keep it.

He opened the front door to the clinic and headed into the street. Whether she meant to or not, she'd shown her hand the moment she returned her cigarette to the pack and pulled out a stick of chewing gum instead.

He raised his hand for a cab. *And another thing. It's not A girl. It's MY girl.*

In the examining room Victoria was already on the telephone. "He wants me to keep it."

"What did you expect?" Rachel said. "You shouldn't have told him."

"For God's sake, Ray, he found me in a pair of stirrups, what could I do?"

"Well, I don't know. Nothing, I suppose."

"Frankly, I feel better that he knows."

"Not me." A pause. "Does this have any impact on our—vacation?"

Victoria took a breath. "I don't know yet, and Jesus, Ray, when we're talking privately, can't we cut this vacation crap and call a spade a spade? Referring to something this personal as a 'vacation' really makes me—"

"Ah-ah-ah—we're on a telephone, remember?" She waited a moment. "You're just a little edgy. All things considered, it's understandable."

Victoria sighed. "Right. So, the moment I want to take a *vacation*, I'll let you know."

"Which has to be soon, if you're going to do it. I'm ready and waiting, as you know. You also know I'll love you either way you go. It's your call."

"As if I need to be reminded."

He stood at his bathroom mirror with a cotton ball saturated with spirit-gum remover, holding it against his sideburn. He pulled the hair outward, grimacing, and watched as it began separating from the skin. Dabbing the solvent downward, he continued peeling away the false beard—both sides, chin, and neck—until it rested in his hand, collapsed and lifeless.

He placed it inside a black parachute bag on the toilet seat, dropped in his bottle of patchouli oil, and finished removing the patches of glue that had held the beard to his cheeks. After washing and drying himself with an old towel, he leaned forward and checked his face in the mirror.

It looked good. Not a trace of Eggs Benedict anywhere. Only the person he really was.

Jack pushed the button under Molly's mailbox and waited to be buzzed in. He'd considered the situation for days—Victoria, Molly, the baby, himself—bouncing between points of logic and emotion like a pinball in a pizza parlor. The ache he'd felt for days hit him once again—the surprise he knew he'd see on Molly's face when he told her—the likelihood he'd never see her again. . . .

The buzzer buzzed. Holding cellophane-wrapped flowers under one arm, he shoved the door open and entered the hallway.

Molly had already stepped out of her apartment and was leaning against the door with a smile. Twenty feet away he could see the whole of her: one of his white shirts with the sleeves rolled up and the shirttail out, a tan suede skirt, a pair of pumps and her usual black stockings, no doubt topped off high on her thighs. Her auburn hair was everywhere, her face warm, eyes bright. All together, looking exactly as he'd hoped she wouldn't.

She kissed him hello and they went inside. She unwrapped the flowers, saying "How nice, what's the occasion?" The small table with the folding leaves had been opened and set with blue and white china, linen napkins, and silver candlesticks. The room was filled with the yellow halos of candlelight, the sound of guitar music, the smell of roast chicken, the crackle of burning logs. The air was so full of expectation, Molly so beautiful and unsuspecting, only a fool wouldn't have chickened out of this mission.

He opened a bottle of wine and poured while she placed a golden bird on a platter. He lit the candles on the table, stirred the logs in the fireplace. She made a joke. He forced a laugh. She said everything was ready at last. He helped her with her chair. She touched his arm in appreciation. He took his chair and sat. She smiled at him and raised her glass. He lifted his in return. She toasted their happiness.

"Well?" she said, holding her goblet.

"Well what?"

"Aren't you going to make a toast, too?"

"Oh, yeah," he said. He had to thread the needle: say something that was warm and loving, but make no mention of the future. Something that would make her hate him less, even if it made him hate himself more. If that was possible.

She looked at him curiously. "You're awfully preoccupied tonight, aren't you?"

"Am I?" He pulled his napkin off his lap and laid it on the table, as if he'd finished eating.

She looked worried. "What is it?"

"There's something we have to talk about. About us."

She looked confused. "What?"

"I'm afraid it's not going to work out."

Now she was *very* confused.

"It's nobody's fault," he said.

"*What's* nobody's fault?"

He placed his chin in his hand. "Ultimately, when you get down to it, it's the age problem."

"What age problem?"

"Before you know it, you'll be pushing me around the park with a blanket on my lap, wiping the drool off my chin and facing me toward the sun."

"Good grief, Jack. We haven't even made plans for the weekend."

He looked at her quietly, long and hard. Speaking with his eyes.

She turned pale. And flushed. "If you want to break up, why don't you just say so?"

"I don't want to break up. I have no choice."

"Why?"

"Circumstances."

"What circumstances?"

She brought to mind a detective in a 1940s movie—a tough guy with one foot on a chair, a fedora pushed up her forehead, eyes cutting through a pyramid of smoke, waiting for the suspect to spill his guts.

So he did.

"There's been a development."

"So . . . you said."

"With Victoria."

Victoria? "What about her?"

"She's pregnant."

Her face turned pale again. For a brief moment her eyes betrayed her, telling him she wished he hadn't confessed after all. She moved her finger lightly around the rim of her wineglass. Finally she stopped and looked up, tears spilling.

"I thought the flowers were a little unusual."

• • •

Jack came down the steps from Molly's brownstone and walked toward the corner, tapping the garbage-can lids as he went, trying to scare up some vermin—a roach, a rat, it didn't matter, he felt a close kinship to them all. After telling her of the pregnancy, the rest of the conversation had been a parlor scene at the end of a whodunit. He said Victoria had gotten pregnant accidentally the night they broke up. She asked how that was possible. He said it had been an unusually distracting night— Zenobia's death, Titus's nomination to the Supreme Court, his marriage proposal. She looked unconvinced, so he tried again. When it came to sex, he said, even smart people weren't always so smart.

She said if the pregnancy was an accident, why didn't this champion of choice abort? He said she'd wanted to—immediately regretting his answer since it required him to explain the one thing he wanted least to admit—that it was he who didn't want the abortion, not her. Could she understand that? he asked. Knowing his particular pathology? Yes, she said, of course. And it wasn't pathological, either. Considering how much she herself wanted a child, it made perfect sense.

All at once she was being magnificent. Then she added that considering she wasn't able to have a child of her own, to have him walk out on her for a pregnant woman—someone he was no longer in love with, at that—or was that not true?—made her feel more inadequate and damaged than anything she had ever felt in her life.

He said nothing. She said nothing.

He said he was deeply sorry. She said what a waste, the time they'd spent together. He said it hadn't been a waste, every minute had been genuine. She said funny, but right now it felt less like love than garden-variety fucking. He said come on, you don't mean that, to which she said yes, she did, but she didn't want to talk about it, to which he said obviously she *did* want to talk about it or she wouldn't have brought it up, to which she said thanks for the insight, but she could do without his playing amateur psychiatrist and fucking her mind as well.

He said this must be the fun part.

She said she wasn't trying to make a scene, merely trying to be honest. He said he was trying to be honest, too, to which she said she'd eventually thank him for that, although at this particular moment she couldn't imagine thanking him for anything.

More silence.

Finally he cranked up the courage to cross the Sahara that lay between himself and the door. With one hand on the doorknob, he said he'd call her in the morning. She said no, that wasn't necessary, she'd call him instead. He opened the door, but she stopped him. She said she couldn't let him go without confessing a lie. What lie? he asked. She said to be perfectly honest, she had no intention of calling him the next morning, or the next day, or in her lifetime, and if he'd be kind enough to do the same, she would have something to thank him for after all.

He looked at her lovely face, searching for an exit line that would link them forever. Unable to find it, he left quietly, pulling the door closed a bit too firmly, as if hitting a pinball machine a little too hard.

Tilt. Game over.

"I have no idea who'd want to kidnap Mr. Bannister or bomb a clinic."

Eli Graves spoke across the desk in his Queens office to Detective Norman Pulaski, NYPD, and Detective "Bazooka Joe" Wilson, who was there for the day from Washington. Pulaski was the senior member of the pair, a twenty-five-year veteran of the homicide division. One of the few detectives without a nickname, he was sometimes referred to as "Gorby" because of a physical resemblance to Mikhail Gorbachev: stocky build; benign earnest face; and a small birthmark on his forehead, which occasionally made him slightly self-conscious. He didn't mind the name, though; he only wished he had Gorbachev's suits. Today he was wearing his best baggy brown one, while Wilson was attired in sport coat, jeans, a colorful, undetectivelike tie, and sneakers.

"Do you have a suspect in mind?" Graves asked. "Maybe with a name or two I could help."

Pulaski rubbed his forehead, finished reading his notes, and looked up. "Bannister said he was working with someone named Alfred Benedict who goes by the nickname Eggs. He said they met at one of your protest rallies. I thought it might ring a bell."

"Nothing comes to mind," Graves said.

Pulaski jotted a note on his pad. "I understand you're clearing a site to build a new office building near here."

"That's right."

"Anybody come to mind in that connection?"

Graves shook his head. "Should it?"

"Just a hunch," Pulaski said. "The dynamite used in the bomb was the same type of stuff your contractor uses."

"I see," Graves said. "Maybe you should talk to him."

"We have," Pulaski said. "He says you sent him a demolition worker a few weeks ago."

Graves opened a file drawer in the bottom of his desk, pawed through some papers, and found the Help Wanted ad he had posted to recruit demolition workers. He handed it to the detective. "We advertised for help. I recommended a guy to Lyman, yeah."

258

"Did you take his name and address?"

"No, but I'm sure he did."

"There's no Benedict in his files," Wilson blurted. Pulaski froze him with an angry glance, momentarily stopping him from chewing.

"Do you remember anything about the guy?" Pulaski asked. He positioned his pencil on his pad and waited for Graves to answer.

"Not really," Graves said.

Pulaski closed his notebook. "Okay, Mr. Graves," he said. He and Wilson stood up, handed Graves their cards, and left.

"What do you think?" Graves said into the receiver.

"Beats me," Lyman said. "Maybe the dynamite was manufactured by the same company as the stuff we used, but our inventory checks out. The records are clean."

"Just out of curiosity," Graves said, "did you hire the guy I sent over?"

"Yeah."

"Did you give the police his name?"

"Sure."

Don't ask, Graves thought—then caved in. "What was it?"

"A guy named Benedict. Everybody called him Eggs."

Graves felt his pulse in his ears.

Lyman continued: "Benedict recruited the guy they arrested, Billy Bannister. The front office has Bannister's personnel file, but when they looked for Benedict's, they couldn't find it."

"What could have happened to it?"

"No idea. Nobody upstairs remembers hiring anyone named Eggs or Benedict."

"Maybe he gave them a different name."

"That's what the detectives think."

Graves asked about progress on construction, chatted a moment, and hung up. He picked up the Susan B. Anthony from his pencil tray and spun it on the top of his desk, watching it flicker, heads and tails blurred into a perfect sphere. Eggs Benedict had done it exactly right: a phony name with no trail of bread crumbs into the forest. Sticks was right, too. All you had to do was find a guy with the right attitude, put him in the right situation, and get out of the way.

The twirling dollar rattled to a rest on the desktop. He picked it up and spun it again, mesmerized by the flutter. He could see Eggs strapped to an arrow, drawn back on a bow, and released—*whoosh!*—up into the blue, hanging on the apex, turning toward the earth with Jack MacLeod standing below, head lowered, feeding like a chicken, oblivious to the silent death bearing down from above.

So that's how they got JFK, he thought. . . . Whoever *they* were . . . if, indeed, there was a *they* at all. Which was precisely the cool, elegant point of it all.

No one could tell.

"**A**re you comfortable?"

"Guess so."

"You don't look it. What's wrong, stomach still bothering you?"

"Yeah, but that's nothing new."

"What is it, then?"

"I still don't know who you guys are, or why I'm here."

Silence.

"Does it hurt when I press here?"

"Ow! Yeah, that hurts."

"How long has it been that way?"

"It's been getting worse in the last week or so."

"Even when you take antacid?"

"Yeah. Listen, when am I going to see my wife and kid?"

"We'll know in a couple more days."

"Why? What's happening in a couple of days?"

"Get some sleep, Billy. You'll know when the time comes."

Their taxi turned out of La Guardia and headed for the city.

"When are you going to tell me what's going on?" Victoria asked.

"When we get there," Jack said.

"Get where?"

"You'll see."

Thirty minutes later the taxi pulled up at the municipal building and the two of them stepped out and climbed the steps. Jack led the way, nodding to employees who knew him, waving to one of the hangers-on who populate city halls everywhere, escorting Victoria to a wooden seat in the hallway.

"Wait here," he said. He took a step and stopped. "I like your hair up. You look beautiful."

He turned away and walked down the hall to the clerk's office. A man behind a Lucite window, obviously expecting him, pushed a large manila envelope through the opening. Jack picked it up, waved thanks, and walked back to where Victoria was sitting.

She looked at him quizzically as he sat down next to her.

"All right," he said. "What's your decision about the baby?"

"We came all the way to New York for this?"

"Maybe. What's the answer?"

"Well, sweetheart, I've thought about it a lot."

"And?"

"I'm going to keep it."

His face crinkled into a smile.

"But you've got to understand something," she said. "The doctor says at my age the chances of a miscarriage are high."

"Don't worry, you're not going to miscarry."

"So what are we doing here?"

"Getting married."

He pulled a license from the envelope and handed it to her. His signature was on the bottom, next to a space with a red check mark for hers. "Before you say anything, I need to tell you a couple things to keep you from going into shock. There won't be any 'for better or for worse,' marriage vows. Just 'I now pronounce you.' "

She closed her eyes. "I'm not that bad, am I?"

"Worse. Second, I had a lawyer draw up our divorce papers—separation agreement, consent decree, joint custody of the baby. I've signed everything and I'm putting them in your hands. Anytime you want out, all you have to do is file them down the hall." He handed her the envelope. She laid it on her lap and fingered the edges of it tenderly.

"One other thing," he said. "I don't want you to think I'm proposing to your womb instead of you. Naturally, the baby had *something* to do with it, but I wanted to marry you before you got pregnant. If you recall."

"My God," Victoria said. "You've really thought this out."

The look on her face reminded him of the time he'd drawn her a hot bath, scented it with oil, lit candles around a stack of Turkish towels, and guided her into the tub with a glass of champagne and a huge sponge. To which she'd said, "Why do I have the feeling you've done this before?"

He stood up, put his arm around her waist, and led her toward the marriage license window, where his friend, the clerk, was helping another couple.

"Jack, this is insane. I mean, I'm bowled over, but we're talking about *marriage* here." She started to pull a cigarette from her purse, but shoved it back. "You're making me nervous and I can't smoke here."

"I'm the one who's supposed to get the cigarette and the blindfold," he said.

She wrapped her arms around him. The applicants ahead of them disappeared, and Jack and Victoria found themselves standing in front of the clerk. The man leaned on his elbows and listened.

"This is crazy," Victoria said.

"What's the answer?" Jack asked.

She looked back over her shoulder and saw three couples waiting. "We're holding up the line," she said, pleading.

He tapped the divorce papers in her hands.

"I hate to push you folks," said the clerk, "but you want to take the plunge, or not?"

Victoria looked at Jack and reached up and touched the Mexican scar over his right eye. He kissed her forehead and pulled her into an embrace. She took a deep breath.

"I do," she said. Hearing the phrase *I do* come out of her own mouth gave her a start. "But you'll have to wait a little bit longer."

"How long?"

She stood still, thinking. "First week in January."

"Two more months? Why not now?"

"There's something I have to do first."

"What?"

"Something I have to tell you."

He backed away, holding her arms. "Like what?"

"I can't tell you now."

He looked her in the eye. "Listen to me, V. Unless it's truly earthshaking, there's nothing you have to tell me."

"It . . . probably is. Maybe."

He pulled her into an embrace. "You're such a complicated mess." She held on, tightly. "So we'll do it the first week in January," he said. "Before Congress reconvenes." Looking over her shoulder, he told the clerk, "We'll be back."

"I know, I heard. Two months. Just don't wait till the last minute, folks. New Year's Day, the chapel's closed."

The grand old Senate Caucus Room—site of hearings on the *Titanic*, Pearl Harbor, Army-McCarthy, the Vietnam War, Watergate, and Iran-Contra—was once again packed with lobbyists, journalists, television crews, Senate staffers, law clerks, and even a few members of the public in whose name they had all allegedly gathered. Everyone was there except Abner Titus and his family—Titus because he would be testifying later that day, his family because he had none.

Victoria took a seat at the witness table, placed a copy of her testimony on the green felt cover, and turned around in her chair. Jack was sitting in the second row; she smiled at him and looked at the battery of television cameras and platoons of reporters around the room, seeing people she saw every night on the evening news. Molly McCormick stood between her cameraman and a crew assistant, Iggy Pitt. Curiosity tempted Victoria to linger on Molly's face; pride told her to look away.

The Senate Judiciary Committee had heard from all the opposing witnesses except for the women's groups. The Leadership Coalition's strategy had been to save the abortion testimony until last, bringing it up just before Titus testified so that it would frame his appearance and give him less time to prepare a response. Victoria had been chosen as the groups' primary witness because she was articulate, motivated, and photogenic. They hoped she'd provide the hearings with some badly needed zing.

Sticks Dickey tapped his microphone and leaned into it. "Will the room come to order," he boomed, and in a few minutes people found their places and settled down.

"Thank you, Mr. Chairman," Victoria said, and proceeded to read a three-page, reduced version of her written testimony.

" . . . and if confirmed, Judge Titus, by his own admission, will do his utmost to return women to forced pregnancies and maimed bodies—perhaps even the cold slabs of the morgue. The Leadership Coalition urges the committee to vote against his confirmation."

She lowered her text and pulled the microphone closer. "Mr. Chairman, there is another reason this committee must vote to disapprove Judge Titus's nomination." Her hands were folded in front of her without notes. Dickey looked at her and the room quieted. "A few months ago I represented Mrs. Zenobia Davis, a woman residing here in Washington, D.C., who chose to have a safe, legal abortion, as she was entitled. Instead, she died from an underground operation she'd been forced to seek because of unconscionable delays imposed by Judge Titus." She paused. "Delays which, in my opinion, make him at least partly responsible for her death."

The room stirred with whispers and the clatter of television equipment, camera shutters, and reporters suddenly finding their leads for the evening news.

Sticks Dickey flushed but remained calm. He opened a file and removed some newspaper clippings and a memorandum. Her testimony had obviously come as no surprise.

"This is a serious matter," he said, "but as far as I'm concerned, an unsubstantiated charge of this kind at this late hour—a charge that can only be classified as conjecture—raises questions about the credibility, ethics, and motives not merely of one witness, but of the entire proabortion movement." His strategy was instantly clear: he was not only going to defend the nominee; he was going to take the torpedo Victoria had fired, turn it around, and try to sink her and the whole armada of women she'd brought with her.

"Miss Winters," he said, "what evidence do you have to suggest that Judge Titus knew Mrs. Davis would harm herself?"

"Senator, when a man gets drunk and drives a car ninety miles an hour down Pennsylvania Avenue, he may not know he's going to hit someone—he may even intend *not* to hit someone—but he has to know he's *likely* to hit someone. This was Judge Titus. He knew of the rape. He knew of Mrs. Davis's desperate condition. He knew she had a right to abort. He knew that she wouldn't have the operation until he gave her permission. He knew that he was playing with her life. He was as reckless as a drunk driver on Pennsylvania Avenue, and her death was as predictable as if she'd been crossing the street at the White House. The Senate cannot put someone this irresponsible behind the wheel of the United States Supreme Court."

There was more commotion in the audience.

"This is all very stirring, Miss Winters," Dickey said, "but a judge can't be held accountable for all the quirks and puh-culiarities of the litigants who come before him. Surely you're not suggesting he's responsible for overcrowded dockets or the time it takes to render thoughtful opinions, are you? Or the strange things people choose to do to themselves in the middle of the night?"

"Senator, I—"

"So I ask you again—what *evidence* do you have that Judge Titus had any notion that Mrs. Davis would endanger her own life?"

"I believe it's up to him to explain how he failed to see that she would harm herself."

"Did you?"

"Did I what?"

"See that she would harm herself?"

"I thought she was capable of doing something desperate, yes."

"Then why didn't you stop her?"

Victoria sat up straight. "I did everything in my power as her attorney to see her safely through this ordeal, Senator. Unfortunately, she was not of a mind to tell me where, or when, she would react to the court's delays. I didn't live in her apartment."

"Neither did the judge. What actions did you take of a general nature to prevent her from hurting herself?"

"I sought to get her a legal abortion."

"And you were successful in that effort, weren't you?"

"Only technically. As a practical matter I was too late."

"Only by a matter of hours, according to the press." Dickey held up a newspaper clipping. "If you were worried that she might have hurt herself during those last few hours, do you feel you should have done more to keep her company or protect her somehow?"

Victoria turned red. "Senator, I have been wondering since she died what more I could have done, and I'll probably continue wondering for a long time."

"With all due respect, Miss Winters, you're misunderstanding the import of my questions. I'm not *condemning* you, I'm praising you. Your efforts were entirely reasonable, maybe even he-roic, and yet a tragedy occurred. But it wasn't your fault, Miss Winters. And if it wasn't your fault, neither was it Judge Titus's."

"Will the senator from North Carolina yield?" Senator Boone asked.

Sticks was happy to end his examination while he was on the attack. "The chair recognizes the senator from Montana."

Senator Stuart Boone launched into a well-intended defense of Victoria, hoping to appear to be a champion of women's rights, and soon the members of the committee were wrangling with each other, posing for the cameras, belching clichés, and obscuring the facts in a cloud of familiar hot air.

Dickey picked up his gavel and looked at his watch. "The committee will break for lunch and return at free. Excuse me, three."

Everyone stood except Victoria, who leaned back in her chair with the palms of her hands still on the green felt table. As friends and reporters closed in around her she stood up and caught Jack's eye, knowing he could read what she was thinking. He gave her a smile normally reserved for the bereaved. Abner Titus was about to become the next chief justice of the United States in time to hear the *Costello* case and put the knife to legal abortion in America.

Jack had barely left the hearing room when he felt Sticks Dickey grab his arm.

"I can understand your lady's emotionalism on this Zenobia Davis business," he said, "but unless she insists on saying more, I think we've covered it, don't you?"

"You have to take that up with her, Sticks, not me."

"Well, now, excuse me for thinkin' you might have something to say about your better half. I always thought the little woman didn't get to wear the pants until the honeymoon."

"I've met your wife, Sticks. She seems to have a mind of her own."

"That she does, that she does." He squeezed Jack's arm. "You got a great future up here, Jack. You're one of the few who could go all the way. I know you represent a bunch of liberals, and hell's bells, we all got to keep an eye on the folks back home. But it's downright silly to pick a fight you can't win."

"I'm not so sure about that."

"Titus's confirmation is a brick wall. Don't break your lance on it." For a split second Dickey's face was menacing. Then it turned into an engaging smile, and he walked off.

Jack found Victoria and walked with her toward his office.

"Dickey left me hanging," she said. "What do you think I should say after lunch?"

"Nothing."

"What do you mean 'nothing'?"

"I wouldn't go back. I'd leave it alone."

"How can I?"

He stopped outside his office door and faced her. "What else can you say? The target is Abner Titus, not you. Let someone else bang away on him for a while."

Her lips tightened. "I'm not giving up."

He ran his fingers through his hair and took her arm and drew her aside, away from the doorway. "I'm not giving up, V. I just don't want either one of us to be a kamikaze."

Her mental calculator summarized the situation. "You're right. When you get right down to it, this isn't your fight. It's ours."

He felt a veil fall between them. The one that, once it dropped, separated all men from all women. Actually, she was right. He loved a good fight, but he didn't need to join the Female Foreign Legion to find one. This was women's revolution. *Our* revolution, as she put it. They both knew it, which was why she'd let him off the hook.

So then why did he feel like a deserter?

She turned to leave but he stopped her.

"V?"

"Yes?"

"The night we found Zenobia—were you in her apartment earlier that day?"

"No, why?"

"Neither you or Rachel had any contact with her? Nothing to try to coax her to go to an abortion clinic that night?"

"Of course not."

"You'd tried it once before, if you recall."

"What are you driving at?"

"I just need an answer."

She stared at him a moment. "The first time I knew she was permitted to abort was when Rachel called me at the restaurant."

"So, if someone were to take a closer look at how she died—where she had the abortion, what time of the day or night—that wouldn't trouble you in any way?"

"Not at all."

"That's all I need to know." He looked at his watch. "We'll talk later."

Jack stood behind his desk fingering through call slips. After a moment he opened his desk drawer and pulled out the envelope he'd found in Zenobia's Bible. Ben Jacobs walked into the room.

"What do you think?" Jack asked.

Jacobs shook his head. "I can't see anything that's going to take his confirmation off track. The committee wants to finish up Monday, vote Tuesday, and get the nomination to the Senate floor Wednesday so we can adjourn before Thanksgiving."

"What about Titus's testimony?"

"He's in Dickey's office, waiting for the hearing to resume."

Senator Philip Canada, a liberal Democrat from Minnesota, was expected to be Abner's toughest opponent on the committee. A first-rate television interrogator, he was known for his ability to raise dust storms in living rooms across the country, reshaping the political winds in Washington and convincing senators with wet fingers in the air how to cast their votes. He smiled down at Titus from the dais, welcoming him to the hearings in an imperious tone, making it clear that he was now the judge, Titus now the witness.

Titus sat alone in an oversized wheelchair with a document bag at his side and Pepper Loomis in a chair behind him. There were no lawyers to whisper in his ear, no advisers to act as crutches—only the lights and cameras clicking around him at every move or twitch he made. Jack watched carefully from the back of the room, wondering how long a man of Titus's fastidiousness could stand the sweat on his forehead. As if he were thinking the same, Titus sat back in his wheelchair, closed his eyes, and drew a towelette across his pale white face, bringing the cameras to life like a swarm of crickets. Seeing him, Jack felt pleasure and pity alike. In real life wiping a brow looked completely normal. As a TV sound bite, it would look shifty as hell. And frozen on the front page of a newspaper, absolutely criminal.

Canada was already off and running.

"If a woman's right to choose is overturned, Judge, what are they to do?"

Titus shrugged. "Abide by the law of the land."

"And bring more children into the world who are unwanted, unloved, and uncared for?"

"All children are loved and cared for if given a chance."

"They are? You and I must be reading different newspapers."

"I said if given a chance, Senator."

Canada picked up a pencil. "But the world has changed, hasn't it, Judge? Today we recognize that mothers should be given a chance, too, don't we?"

"Of course we do," Titus said, "but that doesn't mean they shouldn't live wholesome, healthy lives and help their babies do the same. As far as back-alley abortions are concerned, I think those days ended after World War Two."

"Not entirely. Wouldn't you agree that without legal abortions, women would still be endangered?"

"History shows that people are endangered by many things, Senator, including drugs and murder. That doesn't mean we solve the problem by making drugs and murder legal."

Senator Canada shifted in his chair. "Judge, you're a smart man. Do you really believe that aborting a fertilized egg is the same as murdering a living person?"

"Yes."

"Do you see *any* distinctions between the two?"

"None that matter."

Canada played with his notes. "I'm wondering something, Judge. This is a bit off the beaten path, but if you had to guess what has shaped your views on this subject most, what would it be?"

Titus looked surprised. "You mean as a child?"

"As a child, an adult, whatever."

Titus touched his fingertips together and studied them. "I don't know that there was ever a single event, Senator. As far back as I can remember, respect for human life and protection of the innocent were basic values I was taught. In school, in church—even in the street."

"What about in the home?"

"And in the home, yes." He fingered the wet napkin nervously. "I didn't mean to leave that out." He wiped his face.

"One more question, Judge. Can you imagine any set of circumstances in which you might support a woman's right to choose? Other than in rape or incest, of course."

"First let me say that I would not want my silence on the subject of rape or incest to be construed as consent to your point of view—"

"Just a moment. Are you saying you *wouldn't* allow abortions in the case of rape or incest?"

"I'm saying I would rather not address those issues at this time, that's all."

"But how can you leave the door open to forced pregnancy in those circumstances?"

"Senator, I'm not leaving the door open or shutting it. I'm just not addressing it."

"I recognize that, which I find astonishing."

Titus folded his hands in front of him, pausing to slow the colloquy and regain control. "As you may know, certain writings point out that most of the physical and psychological damage done in rape or incest is done prior to conception, which raises the question whether *after* conception the rights of the innocent child outweigh the inconvenience of the pregnancy."

"Inconvenience? A girl who's raped is *inconvenienced* by pregnancy?"

"I was not using the word as a term of art, Senator, I was only suggesting that—"

"And what writings are you referring to? The Marquis de Sade?" Chuckles dotted the audience.

Titus looked down and smiled, letting the comment pass before continuing. "Now, with regard to the basic question you pose—whether I could envision supporting choice generally—let me say that while judges learn never to say never, no, I cannot envision circumstances in which abortion on demand would be permissible. With one exception, of course."

"What is that?"

"A decision by the Supreme Court that it is the constitutional law of the land."

"But, Judge, that decision exists right now."

"That's correct. Let me rephrase my answer to say a reaffirmation of that decision."

Canada bent his microphone into a new position. "Well, Judge, you certainly have been candid. I still don't know the reason for your views, but they are heartfelt, I'll give you that."

"Senator, it is not a matter of being heartfelt, it's a matter of justice. Someone has to protect the unborn, and if not us, who? Since *Roe* v. *Wade*, more than twenty-three million children who could have lived normal, healthy lives died before they were born. Who knows how many Nobel laureates were among them, or how many discoverers of the cure for AIDS? Who knows how many senators or justices of the Supreme Court? Even if they had turned out to be ordinary citizens—ballplayers and Girl Scouts, factory workers and housewives—they had a right to live."

"And Adolf Hitler, Idi Amin, Attila the Hun?" Canada asked. "Not to mention serial killers and common criminals who turn to violence from childhoods of neglect, poverty, and abuse? You're happy with their lives?"

"I think that's irrelevant," Titus said. He felt the camera lenses breathing on him.

Sticks Dickey interrupted. "I believe the gentleman's time has expired," he said, and moved the questioning back to the Republican side of the committee. "If we move this thing along, we can finish up today and get the nomination to the Senate floor vote by Wednesday so we can all go home and enjoy some turkey."

Stowing his gear for the rest of the afternoon session, Molly's cameraman, Al, said, "Where the hell's Iggy?" Molly looked around and spotted him near the front of the hearing room, next to the witness table, talking to someone sitting in a chair. Not just someone—Judge Abner Titus.

What was he doing?

She watched. Titus and Iggy chatted a moment, then Iggy patted his chest for a pencil and handed it to Titus, who jotted something on a piece of paper and handed it back. Iggy smiled, shook the judge's hand, and stepped away as reporters and well-wishers moved in.

Iggy stuck the piece of paper into his coat pocket as he walked back to rejoin Molly and Al.

"What was that all about?" Molly asked.

"I got his autograph," Iggy said, and gave Al some help.

Jack walked back to his office and stood by his desk talking to Ben Jacobs and Georgia Brimmer, his press officer.

"They just wrapped it up," Jack said. "It's all over."

Jacobs said, "Titus has at least twenty votes to spare."

Jack picked up a rubber band from his desk. "You know what our problem is? We're doing too much instead of too little." His staff members' faces went blank. "We've been trying to defeat his nomination, but that's not the point, is it? The point is to keep *Roe* from being overturned."

He started pacing around the room. "If we can't beat Titus, what if we delay him? What if we keep him off the Court until after *Costello* is argued? If he isn't sworn in by December fourteenth when the case is argued, he'll be disqualified from participating in it even if he's confirmed."

"What about the rest of the Court?" Georgia asked.

"That's the whole point. It takes a majority of voting justices to reverse a case on appeal. If Titus is disqualified, the Court will remain split four to four, which means they can't overrule *Roe*. It'll probably be at least a year before they take another case suitable for that, and anything can happen in a year. A conservative justice quits or dies, the president finally comes to his senses and appoints a pro-choice replacement, Justice Handelman changes his mind about being a pro-lifer—who knows? The point is, we live to see another day."

"But how are you going to delay the confirmation?" Georgia asked.

Jack sat on the edge of his desk. "Thanksgiving is the day after tomorrow and everyone is dying to go home. That's the leverage Sticks is using to ram this thing through. If we toss a monkey wrench into the process, everyone will throw their hands in the air and go home and reconvene in January. In the meantime, *Costello* will have been argued in December without Titus on the Court."

"What monkey wrench?" Jacobs asked.

Jack looked at his watch. It was three o'clock. "Georgia, round up everybody who's covering the hearings for a press conference tomorrow morning."

"What's the hook?"

Jack opened his center desk drawer and pulled out the envelope he'd found in Zenobia's Bible.

"This."

He stood in front of the cameras waiting for the last sound man to tape his microphone to the bundle and slip back into the pack of reporters. When everyone appeared ready, Jack began.

"Ladies and gentlemen, I regret to say that I have evidence that may link Judge Abner Titus to the death of Zenobia Davis."

He waited for the *zit-zits* of the cameras' automatic rewinds to end and the pencils to stop wiggling.

"As you know from testimony in the hearings, Mrs. Davis died while she was waiting for Judge Titus to acknowledge her right to an elective abortion. You've heard testimony about how he delayed his ruling, ultimately forcing her to resort to a back-alley abortion that resulted in her death. But what you have not heard about is this."

He held up the envelope while the cameras whirred and clicked again.

"This is an envelope I found in Mrs. Davis's Bible the night she died. If you look carefully, you'll see three handwritten words on it—*denied, clinic, midnite*—and a telephone number. If you call the number, you'll find it rings in the office of Judge Abner Titus. The desk of his law clerk, to be exact."

He paused as heads tilted down to scribble on pads.

"As reluctant as I am to draw this conclusion, I believe the evidence points to the possible involvement of Judge Titus in this woman's death. Not merely by the cynical lateness of his decision, although that alone could easily have accounted for her decision to abort. The evidence also suggests he or his clerk—or someone with advance knowledge of his ruling—may have had a personal conversation with her shortly before she died. Contact of that kind would have been highly irregular even under innocent circumstances, considering it was an ex parte communication between a litigant and a court sitting in judgment of her. But this case is far more troubling than that.

"Now, certain questions become obvious. Who other than Judge Titus would have known that Zenobia Davis's husband's petition was about to be denied? Why would he or someone privy to this information tip Mrs. Davis off to it in advance? Why would he or his law clerk tell her to go to a clinic? And why so late at night? Mrs. Davis was already a patient

275

at the Capitol Hill Women's Clinic, which isn't open at midnight. So what clinic was she directed to, and why?

"When I say that the evidence raises these questions, I mean just that. I don't know that something sinister occurred. All I have here is an envelope, but the questions it raises must be answered before Judge Titus is confirmed to the most powerful seat on the highest court in the land. And let's make no mistake about it—if the answers are damaging, or we are left with substantial doubts, the Senate must decline to confirm." He paused. "Now, if there are any questions—"

The room exploded with words.

Jack pointed to a reporter.

"What are you saying here, Congressman—that Judge Titus killed Mrs. Davis?"

"I'm saying that the evidence should be investigated."

"Investigated for what? What's your theory?"

"I have questions, not a theory."

"The judge is a public official," a reporter said. "What makes you think Mrs. Davis didn't get his telephone number out of the phone book?"

"This one isn't in the book. It's a private line."

"Given the judge's views, why would he want to direct her to an abortion clinic?"

"That's exactly what the Senate should investigate. Knowing she'd be free to abort as soon as he ruled, did he have some reason to suggest a clinic or a doctor other than her own? So far, no one's been able to identify where she had the abortion that killed her."

More hands and voices. "Congressman, why did you wait to raise these questions until the Senate is about to vote?"

"Frankly, I didn't want to raise them at all. I had hoped the committee would reject his nomination on the basis of his record."

"Shouldn't you have turned this envelope over to the police?"

"The night I found Mrs. Davis I didn't connect the envelope to her death, much less to Judge Titus."

"Then why'd you take it away?" someone asked. It was one of a dozen shouted questions. One he chose not to answer.

As he pointed and talked he saw a network reporter peel out of the group with her cameraman, move into the hallway, and do a stand-up for the nightly news. The moment her camera lights went out, he knew the damage had been done.

He answered two more questions, then stepped through the middle of the group to head back to his office. Keeping his eyes straight ahead, he saw a young man with a beard, glasses, and a Dodgers baseball cap standing at the back of the room taking notes on green notebook paper in a three-ring binder. As he approached, the fellow looked into his eyes and stopped writing, then turned and left the room. For a moment Jack thought he looked familiar, but he had no time to dwell on it.

Moving forward, he caught sight of Molly McCormick sitting on a chair on the other side of the room, notebook closed, hands folded, staring at him without expression. He tried to find something familiar in her eyes—anger, sympathy, forgiveness, acknowledgment. If it was there, he couldn't see it.

He walked out of the room and returned to his office.

Ben Jacobs was sitting on the edge of Jack's desk, waiting. Jack sat down, put his feet up, and covered his face with his palms.

"You sure you know what you're doing?" Jacobs asked.

About Molly? About Victoria? About my so-called personal life? Absolutely not.

He leaned forward. "Don't look so worried," he said, reaching for a rubber band. He stretched it onto his finger and shot it across the room. "The fireworks are just getting started."

Molly stuck the receipt from her airplane ticket into the bag at her feet and made herself comfortable in her seat. "Where's Iggy?" she said to Al, who sat next to her.

"He took an earlier shuttle. He said his messenger-service dispatcher was expecting him back this afternoon."

Shortly after takeoff they hit an air pocket. It shook the plane, but her stomach hardly noticed. It was already upside down from seeing Jack at the morning's press conference.

The pilot came on the intercom: there'd be initial turbulence in the Washington area, turning to tranquil skies over New York.

Exactly the flight plan she intended to follow once she was on the ground.

Sticks Dickey stood behind his desk with a telephone in hand talking to the Senate majority leader. Eli Graves paced around the office.

"I'm telling you," Dickey said, "this MacLeod press conference is as cheap as it gets up here. . . . I know, Jim, but how's it gonna look if we *don't* put it to a vote before we adjourn? . . . I know, I know, but can't you see what he's doing? This is your classic inside-the-beltway, bullshit stunt. MacLeod's got the press reporting that a judge who's been against abortion all his life took secret steps to get a woman an abortion! And what's his proof? Some goddamn envelope with a couple of fucking words scribbled on it! I'm telling you, if you let him and the press get away with this, you'll never see the end of it. Right . . . right . . . mm-hmm . . . I hear you . . . right." He hung up and flopped back into his chair, picked up a letter opener, and held it in front of his eyes.

Graves stopped pacing. "What's the deal?"

"He wants to see how it plays on the evening news."

Graves smacked his fist into his hand. "MacLeod again! That son of a bitch. That *son of a bitch!*"

"Take it easy," Dickey said.

"I'm taking him out!" Graves said, "I'm taking him out of the game!"

"Slow down. As my daddy used to say, a man in a rage is like a fool on a—"

"Fuck your daddy," Graves said, staring at the floor.

Dickey's cheeks burned. "Son, if you start actin' the way you're talkin', you ain't gonna make it to sundown."

"Oh, yes I will," he said. "MacLeod won't, but I will."

Dickey walked to the door to make sure it was closed. He pointed his letter opener at his friend. "Take off your pack and stand at ease, Eli." He walked back to his desk, barely controlling his anger. "You remember our little talk in my kitchen a couple of months back?"

"Yeah, I remember. What's that got to do—"

"Shut up and listen!"

Graves looked as if he'd just discovered someone else was in the room. Dickey let the moment build a cold frame around what he was about to say.

"Now, I don't know what these threats toward MacLeod are all about, and frankly I don't want to know. But if you're in over your head, son, you better break surface and tread water awhile. You hear?"

Graves cooled off. "I'm not in over my head. And you don't have to lecture me. An arrow's been shot into the air—"

Sticks raised his hands to stop him from saying more, but Graves kept talking.

"—and I did it so long ago I haven't got any idea where it is or when it's gonna fall. Which means nobody else knows, either."

Sticks gauged what he was hearing. As hot and crazy as Graves was, he also sounded as if he knew what he was doing.

"But," Graves continued, "that's just one arrow. I've got another one of my own, and I'm gonna use it myself." He clenched his teeth, rippling the muscles in his jaw. "MacLeod's life is so full of trash, you wouldn't believe it. If I'd already gone public with what I've got on him, he never would have shown his face to the press today." He went to the door and grabbed the knob. "I'm not waiting any longer."

Sticks walked over to him. "You do things your way, Eli, and I'll do things mine. Just make sure you do them right."

Graves opened the door and turned back. "That crack I made about your father—"

"Forget it," Dickey said, not forgetting it.

Graves stood still a moment, searching for something to say, shifting from one foot to the other. "I guess fathers just don't mean that much to me," he said, and closed the door.

Dickey returned to his desk. Scanning a bookshelf behind him, he removed a volume marked *U.S. Constitution Annotated.* After reading a moment, he said, "Damn! I knew there was a way to skin this cat!" He hit his intercom button.

"Get me the White House," he told his secretary.

"Who at the White House?" she asked.

"The president, June," he said impatiently. "The president."

Billy Bannister slept peacefully with a sheet spread across his body and a swath of yellow antiseptic painted on his abdomen. Latex-gloved fingers drew a long black line on his abdomen and deftly applied a gleaming scalpel. The skin parted smoothly, without resistance, as the steel cut through the fat, down through the bluish-white rectus sheath. Fingers pried apart the muscle, clearing a path to the thin, silvery membrane covering the abdominal cavity. The scalpel moved toward it and nicked it, deliberately. A small hole appeared, a tiny tear in a stretched balloon, revealing blackness beneath. No organs showing through. A safe point of entry. The tips of steel scissors entered the small hole and snipped the membrane the length of the outer incision. Fingers paused a moment—applied a retractor to the sides of the gash—and pulled the flesh wide apart.

Then they entered.

"Good God, look at that."

Silence.

"Looks like a field of cauliflower buds."

"Now we know where the stomach pain was coming from. Look at that, it's metastasized. It's everywhere."

"Must have been getting worse by the hour."

Silence.

"How long do you give him?"

"Couple of days at most." Silence. "Look at the pancreas."

Silence.

"Do you want to close and resuscitate?"

"I don't know yet. Let's explore some more." Silence. "Good Lord, look at this. You can't give him enough morphine to deal with a cancer that far gone."

Silence. A long sigh.

"Somebody sponge my forehead, please."

"Are you all right?"

"Of course." Silence. "Let's get on with it."

"Are you—sure?"

"Got a better idea?" Silence. "We're not in the business of torturing people. Hypodermic, please."

Silence.

"What will this do to the program?"

"Nothing. We'll have to move ahead without the benefit of this one." Silence. "There. It should reach his brain in a few seconds."

Silence.

Silence.

Silence.

"He's flat line."

A sigh. "God rest his soul. Let's close him up."

"I'll do it." Silence. "Hand it to me, would you? It's right over there."

"What is?"

"The doll."

"**E**xcuse me," he said, "I have a package for Mr. Graves that requires his personal signature." A young man wearing a Dodgers baseball cap and horn-rim glasses stood at the reception desk at the Red Rose Society headquarters in Queens.

"His office is at the end of the hall," the receptionist said.

The bearded delivery man walked down the hallway to the last door, which was open. The secretary's chair in the outer office was empty, the computer screen lit, papers strewn over her desk, an FM station playing music softly.

The delivery man ran the zipper on his jacket up and down nervously. Then he pulled it down to the bottom and withdrew a plain manila envelope. On a label were the words, *Confidential to be opened by Mr. Graves only.* As he started to lay it on the secretary's desk, he saw that the door to the office behind her was ajar. Holding the package, he moved to the door and looked in.

The room was empty. He walked to the uncluttered desk and placed the envelope neatly in the center of a brown desk mat. Pulling back his hand, he bumped a pencil tray, knocking a bright silver coin onto the desktop. He picked it up and examined it, front and back. It was a Susan B. Anthony silver dollar.

A door latch sounded outside.

He shoved the coin into his jacket pocket, turned, and saw Graves's secretary in the doorway, as surprised as he was.

"May I help you?"

"I have a package for Mr. Graves," he said.

He pulled his empty hand from his jacket and picked the manila envelope off Graves's desk, handed it to the secretary, and moved past her toward the hallway.

"Do you want me to sign for it?" she asked as he left.

"Not necessary," he said, squeezing the silver dollar in his pocket, not looking back.

Eli Graves dropped his suitcase onto the floor of his Queens office. Even when a trip to Washington went well, he hated the place, but when he had to deal with people like Jack MacLeod and stay overnight to do it, he sank into a mood from hell.

As he walked past his secretary's desk he saw the large manila envelope and his spirits brightened.

He carried it into his office, closed his door, and sat down at his desk, raincoat on. Handling the envelope tenderly, he cut the flap with a letter opener and withdrew a sheaf of green notebook paper.

Just what he was hoping for. A new delivery.

He laid the pages in the center of his desk and began reading, moving his eyes across each line, drinking in the words, concentrated, agitated.

When he finished reading the fifth page, he stopped—pulled out a yellow highlighter from his desk drawer—and read the page again, marking certain passages, shaking his head slowly. "Sweet Mary." When he turned the page, he found four color snapshots taped to the paper.

He finished reading and stared ahead, thinking. After a moment he opened the bottom drawer of his desk, pulled out a black three-ring binder, inserted the green pages, and snapped the rings closed. He lifted the receiver and called his secretary.

"The manila envelope," he said. "I don't see a postmark. Where'd it come from?"

"A delivery boy dropped it off around noon."

Graves's heart pounded. "Ask Jeremy to come in, would you?" He hung up and nervously tapped his fingernails on the top of his desk. He had no idea who this guy Greensheets was, but this latest stuff on MacLeod was dynamite.

Jeremy Hackett entered from his office down the hall.

"It's time to organize a clinic protest," Graves said.

"Okay."

"Something big. I want to send the Senate a message supporting Titus."

"Feeling better about him?"

"No, but that's not the point. He's good bait."

"For what?"

"The proabortion fanatics."

Hackett looked confused. "You *want* proabortion types at the rally?"

"All we can get. Congressman MacLeod in particular."

Hackett leaned on Graves's desk and checked the angry look on his face. Then he saw the empty manila envelope.

"You got something from Greensheets." Graves shuffled through his mail. Hackett licked his lips nervously. "What the hell is this guy saying about MacLeod, anyway?"

"What he's been saying all along. Plus something new. Something that's finally going to wreck the bastard."

Hackett straightened up. "Talk about bait—you don't even know who Greensheets is. How do you know he's not making this stuff up?"

"The guy's for real, Jeremy," Graves said. He stuck a letter opener into a piece of mail and ripped it open. "You just get the permits and the police. Let me make the decisions."

Standing in the bathroom next to a paper grocery bag, Molly examined each object before dropping it in. She picked up his toothbrush with the splayed bristles—exactly like hers—and imagined him standing in front of the TV set brushing his teeth. Amazing, the amount of junk you could accumulate in a seven-week affair. She dropped it into the trash. Next she picked up a tube of toothpaste, squeezed dry. Boy, if that didn't say it all. She dropped it in, too.

She sat on the toilet lid and pulled off her shoes. After leaving the shuttle at La Guardia, she'd gone to the station in midtown Manhattan and edited her report on Jack's press conference for the evening news. Now she wanted to edit him out of her life. It was hard to tell which had hurt more, seeing him, or seeing Victoria. Either way, she preferred a blank screen.

She stood up and sorted through the remaining inventory: a used plastic razor, good for shaving legs—should I keep it?—a comb, a rust-stained can of shaving gel, a free sample of men's cologne from Bloomingdale's, a plastic container of dental floss. She shook the can of shaving cream—nearly empty—and held it over the bag. Bombs away. She picked up the vial of cologne to toss it out. Lowering her guard, she opened it and raised it to her nose. Visions of Virgin Gorda danced in her head . . . white boat cushions reflecting the light of the moon, an enormous towel used as a blanket . . . the gentle rocking of the boat, rolling in rhythm to their . . . *Stop.*

She raised the trash bag to the side of the counter and swept everything into it.

Carrying the sack into the bedroom, she walked to the chest and opened the drawer that was, or rather had been, his. A ragged blue T-shirt with *Santa Fe* written on it rested on top. She tossed it out and lifted a pair of worn-out sweat socks and a pair of decaying sneakers. Wrinkling her nose, she held them by their laces like a pair of dead mice and let go.

She returned to the drawer for what else remained: a *Congressional Record*, a program from a B'nai B'rith dinner with speech notes on the

285

back, a half roll of peppermint Life Savers with its strip of aluminum foil trailing off to the side. All of it, into the bag. Gonzo.

She lifted the last item in the drawer, a cardboard insert from a laundered shirt, and saw Jack's father's straight razor lying beneath. She picked it up and opened it carefully. It was beautiful and lethal—an ivory handle with a scrimshaw harbor scene and a blade with a clean, sharp edge. An heirloom she'd have to return to him.

She closed the bottom drawer and opened the top one, placing the razor inside. While she was at it she decided to throw out other mementos that may have found their way into her lingerie. Exploring the garments by touch, she felt something hard—an iridescent oyster shell—the one from Cinnamon Bay where she'd fallen asleep topless on the beach, avoiding a burn when he'd thoughtfully covered her with a huge straw hat. Into the bag it went. Next, the cigar band from Tortola. The one that fit his little finger, and her ring finger, perfectly. She hesitated, then tore it in two and dropped it in.

She found a lost pair of manicure scissors—nothing to do with him—and a pair of plastic sunglasses with I LOVE NY on the temples. *Throw them out. Don't be silly, they're usable. Come on, you wouldn't wear these things in a hundred years. That's not true, you already did. But that was then and this is now. But*—PITCH THEM.

Thunk.

She lifted a silk camisole and found a matchbook cover from the Eleventh Street Diner. Opening it, she saw a line of Byron's that Jack had written to her: *She walks in beauty, like the night/Of cloudless climes and starry skies.* God. All at once it looked like fresh Iowa corn. Still, she read it again, remembering the evening. . . . She read it yet again, recalling love and affection . . . unable to let go. Suddenly a black thought: had he written the same lines for someone else first? Someone like Victoria?

She raised her hand over the trash bag, debating what to do. Such lovely poetry . . . written on such an unforgettable night. Still . . . She opened her fingers reluctantly and let the matchbook fall.

Time to stop the bleeding and finish cleaning out the goddamn drawer.

The final sweep of the chest yielded two ticket stubs, a credit-card restaurant receipt from Elio's, a blue pencil with his name on the side, all of which she dumped into the bag. As she was straightening the garments to close the drawer, she noticed something under a bra strap. Pushing it aside, she found an earring—a faux onyx half ball with a long black drop dangling beneath. One of those don't-remind-me souvenirs from a trip down the road of errant male sex, somewhere between the fishnet stockings and the trashy blue eye shadow.

She held it up as if it belonged to someone else—which, in a sense, it did—watching the long, dangling drop swing back and forth, smoothly. Just as it had the last time she'd worn it ... when she'd thrown her hairbrush at him for a crack he'd made, then jumped on him, pummeled him, and soon felt the long, dangling drops swinging back and forth, smoothly.

"Good God," she whispered, apologizing to herself.

She snapped out of it, searched through silk and nylon for the matching black earring and, unable to find it, tossed the one she'd found into the trash bag.

The telephone rang. She answered and heard Elliot Landy's voice.

"How are you?" he asked.

"Fine," she said. Her eye caught the remains of the large white candle she and Jack had burned so often.

"I haven't seen you for a while," he said. "I didn't scare you off, did I?"

"Not at all." She reached out to the candle's blackened wick, delicately. Despite the lightness of her touch, it broke off in her fingers. "What gave you that idea?"

"Nothing special, just your everyday normal male insecurity. Listen, I'm in New York for the National Medical Examiners' Conference. I know it's awfully late, but have you had dinner yet?"

"Thanks, Elliot, but I just got back from Washington and I'm in the middle of a badly needed housecleaning." She flicked the broken wick into the trash.

"Okay. If you change your mind, give me a call at the Westbury. I'll be here all evening. What are you doing for dinner tomorrow?"

She dropped the candle into the bag, too. "Tomorrow's Thanksgiving, isn't it? I haven't thought about it. How about you?"

"Me neither. I was hoping we could talk about it tonight."

"Afraid I have to finish my search-and-destroy mission. If I happen to come across an appetite, I'll give you a call."

She hung up, slightly irritated with herself for forgetting to ask if there was anything new with the baby-doll autopsies. She lifted the Playbill she'd carried home from an off-Broadway musical she and Jack had seen and dropped it into the bag.

And that was it. Finished. The room had been swept clean. Emotionally sanitized. Her life was once again hers and hers alone.

Especially alone.

She rolled up the top of the paper sack and placed it inside a large plastic trash bag, closed it with a twisty, and carried it to the hallway for the janitor. After coming back inside, she went into the kitchen for a cold glass of water. When she opened the freezer door, there on a tray of ice cubes was the missing black, dangly earring. *Oh, God.* Now she remembered. The night of the melting ice cubes.

She pried the bauble loose and examined it the way she had its mate—except, this time, without self-reproach. Finally her resistance broke and she gave up.

Sighing in resignation, she walked back into the hallway, opened the plastic trash bag, and found the twin earring halfway down. She disregarded it and kept pawing. *There it is.*

She lifted out the matchbook cover, opened it, and read Byron's line, lovingly, like a valentine. After dropping it into her T-shirt pocket, she threw away the matching earring she was holding, closed the bag, and went inside.

Back in her bedroom, she felt better. And unexpectedly hungry.

She picked up the telephone and called Elliot Landy for a late dinner.

Jack set his own dinner—an open can of sardines, a jar of dill pickles, and a bottle of Yoo-Hoo—on the table next to the bed. He patted the top sheet in search of the remote control. He had moved back into Victoria's house, and although the mortgage was half his and he had been gone for only two months, he still felt strange. And guilty. Molly was not disappearing from his mind. At least not as fast as he assumed he was disappearing from hers. He pulled a pillow out from under the sheet and stretched out on top.

You made your bed. Now lie in it.

He fed himself a sardine like a seal and began reading a pamphlet describing how men could become an intimate part of the "birthing process." What a reach. The more he read, the more pathetic and impotent he felt. When the time came, he'd be there for V, of course. But if ever there was a moment a woman endured on her own, this had to be it.

He looked at his watch. The eleven o'clock news was under way. He located the remote and turned on the set to see if he could find coverage of his press conference. On came Channel 6 news—with Molly McCormick reporting.

"Dave, in an unusual press conference here in Washington today, Congressman Jack MacLeod of New York produced an envelope found in the bedroom of a woman who died from a mysterious abortion and said that it ties Judge Abner Titus to the woman's death."

Jack watched her closely. The telephone rang.

"Hello?"

"Jack!" It was Victoria, sounding panicky. "I found Billy Bannister!"

"What're you talking about?"

"I found Bannister! He's dead!"

"Wait a minute, slow down. What happened?"

She took a breath. "I came down to the Capitol Hill Clinic after hours to talk to Rachel and Kathy Keenan. We were sitting in Kathy's office when we heard a noise, like someone was trying a door. Rachel went to the entrance, and Kathy went to the back. I waited a minute, thinking it was nothing, but when they didn't return, I went to see what had happened. When I opened the door to the lab, there was Kathy staring at this body on a table."

"Wait a minute. A body?"

Her voice shook. "Bannister. He was naked as a jaybird, with this huge slit down the middle of his stomach."

"Stay right there. I'll be right down."

"No, don't. The guy rattling the door turned out to be the security guard. The police are on their way and I want to come home." She took a breath. "Jack, I'm so upset. I don't like what's going on here one little bit."

"Me neither." He paused. "What does Rachel think?"

"It's another baby-doll victim, I'm sure."

"Is that your view, or hers?"

Victoria exhaled. "I—I don't know."

Jack thought a moment. "Smells like a setup, V."

"What kind of a setup?"

"Who else knew you were going to the clinic tonight?"

"Nobody, as far as I know. Just you and Rachel and Kathy."

He drew a blank.

"I'll be right home," she said. "Don't turn paranoid till I get there."

Jack placed the bottles of wine on the backseat of the car and sat behind the wheel, waiting for Victoria to come out of their Georgetown house. She joined him shortly.

"That was Rachel calling," she said, closing the car door. "She was right. Bannister was another baby-doll killing."

"How does she know?"

"She talked to the D.C. medical examiner this morning."

"The medical examiner is working on Thanksgiving morning?"

"Guess so."

Jack dropped the car into gear. "I know what we should do. We should forget the whole damn subject and enjoy the holiday."

Victoria laid her hand on his shoulder in agreement. "Good idea."

It was about one-thirty in the afternoon when they turned off Duck Paddle Road onto the long, elm-lined lane leading to Rachel's farmhouse. Jack wanted to like Rachel—she was incredibly bright, physically attractive, a doctor who saved lives, Victoria's best friend—but for a variety of reasons, some of which he understood, some of which he didn't, she pissed him off.

Except today. Her Thanksgivings were classic events, Norman Rockwell time capsules filled with friends, football, and food. He planned to enjoy himself.

The farm was set among the rolling hills of Maryland, forty-five minutes to an hour from George Washington University Hospital, depending on traffic. She had fallen in love with the place while living in nearby Poolesville, working at the National Institutes of Health in Bethesda, doing experimental animal-organ transplants. She enjoyed the space and the privacy, especially for walking, thinking, and fly-fishing in a sylvan stream. She also liked raising animals. In addition to her two big Labradors and a cat that never left the house, there were milk cows, horses, chickens, and wild ducks on a pond. None of the animals was ever sold or slaughtered, prompting friends to say that she lived in a retirement home for mammals more than a farm. Critics, less generous, said it was her way of atoning for the beasts who'd died in her experiments.

Rachel said nothing.

Jack's entry around the circular gravel driveway revealed the farm complex. The main house was a friendly old stone structure surrounded by huge oaks offering summertime shade and wintertime sculpture. Nearby was a red barn housing a modern dairy, and behind it, mostly hidden by trees and bushes, was an attached one-story cinder-block structure of some sort. At the rear of the building, enclosed by a chain-link fence and shrubbery, was a moat-encircled island with large boulders and a jungle gym at the top, apparently an outdoor area for experiment-bound primates when the weather was warm.

Next to the dairy was a barn housing farm equipment, a tractor, and the Jeep Rachel drove to work each day. Across the circular driveway was a modest frame house, at one time the live-in residence of the hired help, now a remodeled guest quarters.

Jack parked next to one of the guests' cars and lifted the bottles of wine off the backseat. He and Victoria would have brought food, except that Jack was a survival cook and Victoria pretended not to know how. "Never let them see you cook or type," her mother had advised her as a teenager.

They walked through the cold from the car to the kitchen door. The moment they entered, it was hugs and kisses, "Take off your coats," "What smells so good?" "Don't eat that yet!" and "Make yourself useful, Jack." Two minutes later he was out of there with a plate of stolen oyster stuffing, heading for the study.

Sylvia Kingston-Brown, Victoria's elegant black codirector at The Law Clinic, inspected the silverware and place settings for eighteen while her husband tended a fire in the enormous dining-room fireplace. Kathy Keenan basted a twenty-five-pound turkey and chatted with Phoebe Chang and another member of Rachel's transplant team, all seven of whom were there.

Winston Jones was there too, sitting on the leather sofa in Rachel's walnut-paneled study, shelling peas and watching a football game. He had been a regular at Rachel's Thanksgiving dinners since Jack and Victoria had met five years before. It was one of the two times a year he was willing to leave New York and fly anywhere. The other was to a jazz camp in Chicago in July.

As dinnertime approached, the kitchen thinned out, leaving Rachel and Victoria alone. Rachel peeled apples for a Waldorf salad while Victoria positioned relishes on a tray.

"So, how is it?" Rachel asked.

"How's what?"

"Getting back together with Jack. Playing house. The honeymoon before the wedding."

"Good, actually."

Rachel kept her eyes on an apple, peeling it with a surgeon's deftness in one long curlicue. "So where does this leave the two of us?" she asked.

The two of them worked in silence. "This isn't exactly the time or place," Victoria said.

"You've been saying that for weeks now."

"Ray. I promised to marry him."

"Oh, for Pete's sake," Rachel said. She laid the apple on the counter and stuck the paring knife into it.

"Stop worrying about it," Victoria said. "It has nothing to do with us."

"It certainly does if you tell him." She checked the gravy, which was thickening like the air. "Are you still planning to?"

"Absolutely. I wouldn't marry him otherwise."

"I don't believe this." Rachel dropped her hands at her sides. "What do you think he's going to do? Say fine, go right ahead?"

"Maybe. I don't know."

"Vick—he's a *man*, for God's sake. If he knows what you're up to, he's going to *react*. Protect his interests."

"That's a risk I'll just have to take."

Rachel picked up another apple and began girdling it with a knife. "Please, Vick, listen to me. Wait and see if the vacation works out first. If it doesn't, he'll never have to know."

"But what if it does work? You know he'll find out sooner or later, and then what?" She put the last black olive in place. "I can't take the chance. It'd be too much of a betrayal." She stood back and looked at the tray. "When you get down to it, he probably has a right to know what's going on even if he wasn't marrying me."

"Oh, my," Rachel said with sigh, "you really are having trouble with this, aren't you?"

"But am I right?"

"No, you're *not* right. It's *your* life, not his. It's your body."

"Except that part of it that belongs to him now, too."

Rachel chopped the apples into small cubes. "I can't believe you said that."

"It's true. What I do here is my decision, but you have to admit he has something at stake."

Rachel heaved a sigh. "All right. Marry him if you want to, but for God's sake don't torture him with things that are none of his business— decisions that are strictly yours, or ours. I can't *imagine* that your telling him won't blow the whole thing. At least wait until you're close to the altar." She dumped the cubes into a large mixing bowl. "If getting married is pushing you to make this grand confession, maybe he'll get cold feet and you won't have to tell him after all."

"Not a chance."

"You never know. He's a man, isn't he?"

Victoria looked up and caught Rachel's eye. "It hasn't been *that* long since you've been with a man, has it?" Rachel didn't answer. Victoria continued filling the tray. "He likes living with a woman. Last few days he's been so happy he whistles."

"Whistles? You mean like one of the seven dwarfs?"

Victoria didn't look up. "Make all the fun you want, Ray, but you're missing the point. He's not the problem here. I am."

Rachel stopped mixing the salad and relaxed. "I know, I know. Christ, I'm sorry." She rested the wooden spoon on the counter. "I'm pretty uptight myself, aren't I? Just don't forget what I've said all along, because I mean it from the bottom of my heart. If you want out, I'll be disappointed, but I'll understand."

"I don't want out. When I stop and think about it, I've been headed in this direction for longer than I knew. It's just that now that we're there, I can't seem to take the last step."

Rachel reached out and pulled her into an embrace, rubbing her back. "I understand. Really, I do. If I were in your shoes, I'd be as nervous as you are."

The swinging door opened and Jack stuck his head in. "Am I interrupting something?"

"Raging hormones," Victoria said, backing away.

"Raging something," Rachel said. She quartered another apple.

"Rachel thinks I need a vacation," Victoria said, dabbing her eyes.

"I've been saying that for weeks," Jack said. Living together was like that: good advice from your spouse or lover was ho-hum, but from someone else, serious and objective. Unconditional love was the kind of love everyone wanted most, but once given, it became suspect precisely

because it was unconditional. He walked to her and held her head between his hands. "Are you all right?"

She nodded and forced a smile. He touched her cheek. "Where would
you like to go?"

"I don't know," she said. "Someplace warm and sunny. Want to go
with me?"

Rachel touched a potholder tensely, waiting for Jack's reply.

"I can't right now. Maybe I could catch up with you later."

Rachel opened the oven door to check the turkey, placed potholders
on the large speckled pan, and pulled it out. "What you ought to do is
go to René's Spa," she said to Victoria. "Wholesome food, Arizona air,
the right amount of exercise for you and the baby. Facials." She looked
up. "And lots of privacy. Except for one hour a day, there's no
telephone."

The door to the kitchen opened. Sylvia Kingston-Brown entered in a
black turtleneck and gold earrings, her trim Afro framing her high
cheekbones and finely chiseled features. The table was set, she said.
Rachel said that dinner would be ready in ten minutes.

Jack moved into the dining room and saw that the fire was dwindling.
Remembering the stack of wood next to the dairy barn, he went out the
door, coatless, and jogged fifty yards to the woodpile. After picking up
four split logs, he started to turn toward the house when he heard a
clanking noise—the sound of metal on metal—coming from inside the
barn.

He stopped and listened. All was quiet.

Cradling the wood in his arms, he walked to the barn door, pushed it
open with his foot, and entered. The cows stood in their straw-covered
stalls exhaling white plumes into the cold air. Stainless-steel milking
equipment, pipes, and gleaming milk cans lined an immaculate room.
He looked around a moment, searching for the source of the noise, hearing nothing. He turned to leave.

There it was again.

This time he could tell the direction it had come from—over by the
milk pumps. He looked to see what it might have been, but all he could
make out was a white wall with a large white door. His arms were aching from the weight of the wood, and his back was cold. He walked to
the door anyway and discovered a heavy wooden structure hung on
enormous steel hinges and covered with sheets of steel plating, its size
and strength camouflaged by the same white paint that covered the wall.
A thick wooden plank barred exit. Or was it entry? Wasn't the cinder-
block building behind this wall?

He placed his ear against the door and listened. Total silence. He waited a moment, tightening his muscles against the cold, wondering why a door in a barn was covered with steel plating. Another shiver told him it was time to get back to the house, kindle the fire, and enjoy a Thanksgiving dinner.

Instead, he laid the wood on the floor.

Looking over his shoulder, he saw an enormous pair of cow eyes warning him not to do it. *Fuck it.* He turned and lifted the brace.

The doorknob turned in his hand and the door opened—revealing another door a few inches away, a modern steel one with dead bolts at the top and bottom and a heavy brass lock that worked with a key. He tried the handle. No rotation. Placing his ear against the door, he could hear the faint sound of a radio playing. And the clanking metallic sound again—not randomly, but steadily, rhythmically. Then quiet. He pressed his ear tighter against the surface.

"Jack!"

He spun around and saw Phoebe Chang standing behind him.

"What are you doing?" she asked.

His cheeks flushed. "I came out for some firewood." He reached down for the logs. "I thought I heard something."

She pushed the heavy door closed and lifted the plank back into place. "There's work going on in there," she said curtly.

On Thanksgiving? "Shouldn't they knock off and join us?" he said.

"Soon as she can," she said, lifting two of the logs.

He lifted the other two and headed for the main house with Chang close behind. As they walked he deliberately allowed a log to slip to the ground. Bending to retrieve it, he looked back at the cinder-block building. It had no windows, only a frosted-glass skylight that ran the length of the roof.

They walked back to the house briskly, both shivering.

Virginia ham, roast turkey glazed with honey and basil, stuffing, peas, succotash, green beans, cranberry relish, whipped potatoes with giblet gravy, sweet potatoes baked in brown sugar and cinnamon, Waldorf salad, buttermilk biscuits. It was a Rachel Redpath Thanksgiving dinner.

Victoria asked for everyone's attention and toasted Rachel. Then Rachel lifted her glass.

"I think we should thank Jack for the job he did yesterday keeping Abner Titus from being confirmed." Everyone drank again.

Sylvia Kingston-Brown said, "Do you really think Titus was involved in Zenobia Davis's death?"

"His telephone number was on the envelope," Jack said. "What do you think, Win?"

"Personally, I don't think so," Winston said. "I don't like the guy any more than you do, but it's not the kind of thing he'd get involved with."

"Maybe we should put it to a vote," Sylvia said.

"Be interesting to see if there's a split between the men and the women," Victoria said.

"In case you haven't noticed," Jack said, "the men are seriously outnumbered here."

"That's irrelevant," Rachel said, helping herself to the cranberries. She replaced the spoon and looked at Jack. "After all, we're not in a battle of the sexes here, are we?"

"Not over this," Jack said. He lifted a large silver bowl and handed it to her. "Stuffing, Rachel?"

Everyone finished with a piece of pie for dessert—pumpkin praline, deep-dish apple with vanilla ice cream, mincemeat, or strawberry rhubarb—and slowly began to stretch and move. The four men helped clear the table, then, like oil separating from water, drifted back to the study to watch the second half of the Lions–Cowboys game. The process reminded Jack of his first seventh-grade dance—girls on one side of the gym, boys on the other, music echoing off the walls, PTA mothers trying to reverse the earth's sexual polarity and bring the kids together. From that night forward, getting boys and girls together required no help from the PTA—unless, that is, there was a kitchen and a football game on the premises.

Jack walked around the study trying to forget the amount of food he'd eaten, casually examining Rachel's bookshelf full of medical texts, novels, fly-fishing guidebooks, pictures, and mementos. A photograph of a softball team showed Rachel standing at the plate with a bat resting on her left shoulder, a woman behind her with a catcher's mitt. The rest of the all-female team stood behind her in a semicircle wearing sweatshirts, sneakers, and sunglasses. *NIH Kidney Busters* had been written on top, with the players' signatures and *Best wishes to Rachel* scribbled below.

Next to that was a photograph of Rachel sitting on the edge of a fountain somewhere in Europe—Paris, maybe, or if the other face in the picture was any indication, Rome. The woman with her arm in Rachel's was a classic statuesque beauty: mid-to-late forties, Mediterranean skin, sophisticated smile, slender neck, and brown hair as rich and shiny as an olive tapenade. He lifted the frame to read an inscription, but there was none.

He replaced the picture and looked at Rachel's Medal of Freedom. It was framed with a photograph of the first lady presenting it to her, shaking her hand. *With admiration, Maggie Clay*, it read at the bottom.

He lifted a photo of Rachel and Victoria standing on the steps of the Supreme Court the day Victoria had argued her first case there. The smiles on their faces made them look as though she'd already won, which, in fact, she had, although at the time she didn't yet know it. What struck him most was the confidence and good humor and optimism she radiated. It was a face he hadn't seen for a long time.

He wandered to a large leather chair with an ottoman, dropped into it, and laid his head back, watching bodies on the television set line up, hold still, and collide . . . listening to the comforting clichés of the announcers, "And what a day for football it is! . . . these guys came to play . . . don't go away, we'll be right back." The faint smell of fireplace smoke and the thick air turned his eyelids heavy, like his stomach. Soon the molecules in his body slowed to a normal pace . . . body and soul resting, safe and warm . . . swaddled in the humdrum contentment of a cozy Thanksgiving afternoon. . . .

"Jack?" A hand shook him—his ears came to life and his eyes followed. "Sorry to wake you," Victoria said, "but the president's making an announcement."

He pulled himself into a sitting position and blinked. Daylight had departed along with the guests, leaving Rachel, Victoria, and himself in the room. And the president of the United States, whose television face was literally larger than life.

". . . not only my concern for the *Costello* case, but all cases coming before a Supreme Court with less than a full complement of its justices. And so, after notifying the members of the Senate leadership, under the powers vested in me under Article Two of the Constitution, I am today appointing Judge Abner Titus chief justice of the United States. He will take the oath of office tomorrow morning."

Jack glanced at Victoria, who looked stunned. Rachel the same.

"Like all recess appointments," the president continued, "this one remains subject to confirmation by the Senate. While I have complete confidence this will happen when Congress reconvenes in January, if for any reason it does not, I have Judge Titus's unconditional promise that he will resign from the Court, in compliance with the Constitution, and remove himself from all cases pending before it. And that includes *Costello*."

"How can he do this?" Rachel said.

"Listen," Jack said, holding up his hand.

". . . aware of certain scurrilous, last-minute questions raised about Judge Titus, but as far as I am concerned, they are nothing more than a transparent attempt to delay the nominee's confirmation until after the *Costello* case is heard, disqualifying him from participating in the decision." The president leaned into the camera. "In the last few weeks this distinguished judge has been under the most intense, minute scrutiny imaginable—by the Senate and its investigative staff, the FBI, White House counsel, and the press—and not one whiff of credible impropriety has emerged." He eased up. "Some who've held this office would choose to let a man of Judge Titus's caliber and integrity be struck down by cheap accusations and press releases, but let me assure you of one thing right now—it isn't going to happen on my watch."

Victoria stared at the set in a catatonic gaze. Rachel walked to her and rested a hand on her shoulder. Without acknowledging her, Victoria said two words softly: "You win."

Jack couldn't tell whom she was addressing—the president, Titus, or Rachel. "Titus hasn't won," he said. "He still has to be confirmed in January."

Victoria stared ahead as if she hadn't heard him.

"V?" he said.

She stood up and turned toward the door. As she walked past Jack he reached out and took her hand, stopping her. She squeezed him lovingly, raising her other hand to touch his hair.

"What is it?" he asked, but she pulled away and left the room.

Keeping his eyes on Rachel, Jack rose to follow Victoria out the door—just as the telephone rang. Rachel reached for it on the mahogany desk, answered, and extended the receiver to Jack. He took it, irritated with the timing.

"Can you believe it?" his assistant, Ben Jacobs, said.

"Actually, no. Although it's a pretty neat trick if he can do it."

"I've got Professor Hall on the other line. Hold on a minute."

He could hear Jacobs in the background, conversing on another telephone. He looked up and saw Rachel asking in sign language if he wanted privacy, and shook his head no.

Jacobs returned. "Hall says it's been done five times before. Eisenhower did it three times himself—Earl Warren, William Brennan, and Potter Stewart."

"No shit." Jack sat down on the edge of the desk.

"A lawsuit's useless. How'd you like the subtle slam the president put on you and your press conference?"

"He can kiss my naked ass."

"I don't get it. Why's a moderate like Clay going out on a limb for a conservative like Titus?"

"I have no idea. Somebody must have a gun in his ribs, but I don't know who."

"According to Professor Hall, there's still a crack of daylight here. Apparently Chief Justice Titus will cast a preliminary vote on *Costello* right after it's been argued on December fourteenth, but the final vote on the case won't be taken until later, most likely not until next spring. If Titus isn't confirmed when the Senate comes back into session in January—whether because of the Zenobia Davis thing, or whatever—he'll have to quit the Court before the case is decided after all."

"Interesting. We'll talk about it in the morning. Happy Thanksgiving."

He hung up and looked at Rachel. She sat in her desk chair, glasses in hand, rubbing her face.

Jack stretched his arms toward the ceiling. "Where's V?"

"Upstairs in the guest room, I would imagine." She turned to her computer and began clacking away. "Tell her I'm here if she wants me."

He rotated his head on his shoulders like a boxer loosening up. "Top of the steps, to the left, right?" He walked out the door.

Victoria had pulled back the down quilt and top sheet and slipped into the huge, soft canopied bed on the second floor. Jack sat on the edge of the bed next to her. She lay on her side and snuggled her head into the pillow, eyes open. "I suppose it's possible," she said, "but if he can't be stopped now, what makes you think it's going to happen later?"

Jack drew his hand over her long brown hair. "Come on, sweetheart. Either way it goes, you can't take it so personally. He's still only one justice with one vote."

She turned onto her back and looked up at him, surprising him with a smile. "You know what I love about you? You never give up. Even when the odds are impossible. Even when you don't get it."

"What's not to get?" he said. "We're talking politics, not brain surgery." Her hand rose to his cheek. He said, "This is what's had you so depressed lately, isn't it?" His tone was hopeful.

She withdrew her hand and said, "I'm fine, really. In fact, in a way, I'm relieved."

Relieved? "Good. Get some sleep."

He placed his hands on her head and began massaging her hairline with his thumbs, working slowly down to her eyes and temples, under her cheekbones and the sides of her nose, around her mouth, jaw, and throat. By the time he'd finished, her eyes were closed and her breathing deep, resting on the edge of sleep. He leaned forward and kissed her lightly, then stood up, turned off the light, and left the room, closing the door quietly behind.

Jack stood in the doorway to Rachel's study with an unopened can of beer in his hand. She stopped typing and looked up. "How's she doing?"

"She's relieved," he said. He slipped his finger through the metal ring. "About what, I'm not sure. Last few months she's been downright morbid." He popped the can, sending a small mist of beer into the air.

Rachel hit the Save commands on her computer, removed her glasses, and swiveled her chair toward the door. "Well, for one thing, she's pregnant," she said.

He felt instantly pissed. How did she know how Victoria felt about being pregnant? He moved into the room. "It's more than that," he said. "She was worried about something before she got pregnant."

"Anybody who works as hard as she does is bound to burn out."

"Yeah, that's what she keeps telling me." He wandered to the bookshelf sipping beer. Dawdling, he straightened the pens and pencils in a malachite pencil holder—a felt-tip pen, a yellow pencil, a blue pencil—*A blue pencil?* He lifted it and saw his name on the side in white letters.

"These things turn up in the damnedest places," he said.

"What, a pencil in a pencil holder?"

He set his beer on the shelf and rolled the wooden shaft in his fingers. "Remember the news reports about how they found a broken piece of pencil inside the toy doll in Melvin Shivers?"

"Yeah?"

"What they didn't say was that it was one of mine."

She looked at him curiously. "What's the significance of that?"

"I don't know. What do you think?"

She raised her eyebrows. "Looks to me like someone who happened to have one of your pencils also happened not to be very fond of Mr. Shivers."

Jack smiled. "Either that or someone is deliberately trying to make me look bad."

"Oh, for crying out loud, Jack. Your pencils are all over the East Coast. Victoria uses them by the gross herself. Which I'm sure is where that one came from."

"During one of her rare visits here, I suppose."

She stared at him intently. "You're barking up the wrong tree, Jack. Believe me."

Like hell he was. He turned the pencil in his fingers and dropped it back into the holder. *Stay cool. Evidence counts, and you haven't got any. Yet.* "You're probably right." He took a deep breath through his nose. "I could use a short vacation myself." He picked up his beer can and turned it bottoms up, crushed it in his hand, and leaned on the edge of her desk, watching her over the computer screen, lighting his face from below. "Tell me something, Rachel. Who do you think is behind the baby-doll deaths, anyway?"

She wrinkled her forehead. "I have no idea. The only thing that makes sense so far is the vendetta theory."

"Yeah," he said. He tapped the crinkled-up can on the desktop and looked at his watch. "Think I'll make a couple of calls and hit it." He shoved himself away and walked to the door, and turned with a thought. "When you laid your hand on V's shoulder and she said, 'You win,' what did she mean by that?"

Rachel studied him a moment. "She was looking at the television set. I assume she was talking to the president. Or Titus maybe. Don't you?"

He assumed nothing, except that if Rachel said it, he doubted it. He turned to go.

"Jack?" He waited. "Victoria needs that vacation."

"I know." He headed for the kitchen telephone.

Jack heaved the bags into the cab's trunk, slammed the lid closed, and jogged back into the house. It was the day after Thanksgiving, it was cold, and as usual, he wore no coat. As Victoria pulled hers on he opened his briefcase and withdrew a copy of Anais Nin's *Henry and June*.

"Read this instead of briefs," he said.

She opened it to the title page, which he'd inscribed: *The greatest thing about life is its new beginnings. You and the baby are mine. Love, Jack.*

She broke into a smile and hugged him. "How'd you know I've never read this?"

"You told me once. Important details I remember." He kissed her ear. "Take care, sweetheart. Give yourself and our little pal a rest."

"Our little pal gets to rest no matter what," she said.

He drew her to him again. "I told you you'd be a good mother." She pulled back, her face slightly somber. He said, "Did I say something wrong?"

"No," she said, refocusing.

They walked to the cab and she climbed in and rolled down the window. "The only time the spa switchboard puts through calls is between six and seven at night," she said, "so I arranged a private line in my room. I'll call you with the number."

"They really do things fast out there," he said. He was surprised that she'd managed to get a reservation on a day's notice, particularly this time of the year, but Victoria had reminded him that she'd been there once before, with Rachel, and that the owner, René, was Ray's close friend.

Jack watched the cab depart. He returned to the house, found his coat, and headed back up to the Hill.

Ben Jacobs stuck his head into Jack's office. "Detective Norman Pulaski is here."

Jack checked his watch, surprised to see that it was already six o'clock. Congress was out of session until the New Year, but because of his press conference he had become the lightning rod for the anti-Titus campaign. Today he'd been so busy he'd forgotten to eat lunch.

"Send him in," Jack said.

Pulaski came in, shook hands, and sat in the chair across from Jack's desk, a rumpled Gorbachev in a wrinkled raincoat.

Jack said, "For a New Yorker you seem to be spending a lot of time in Washington."

"I love monuments," Pulaski said. He pointed his thumb over his shoulder. "All this commotion about the Titus nomination?"

"That's all there is these days," Jack said.

"I'm interested in something else, Congressman. The latest so-called baby-doll death."

"What makes you think that's something else?"

Pulaski looked surprised. "You mean you think Bannister's death is connected to Chief Justice Titus?"

Jack put his feet on his desk. "Pure speculation."

"Go ahead. Speculate."

Jack leaned back in his chair. "Let's look at this latest so-called co-incidence. I hold my press conference accusing Abner Titus of doing something rotten, and two days later Billy Bannister's body is discovered by the woman I'm planning to marry, who happens to be the leading witness against Titus's nomination. I know we're all paranoid up here, but this one stinks a little too much."

"The smell of things takes me only so far," Pulaski said. "Unfortunately, I got a DA who insists on evidence." He opened a notebook. "Mind if I ask a couple of questions?"

"Shoot."

"That's not the best thing to say to a cop," he said, deadpan. "Were you at the Capitol Hill Clinic the night Victoria Winters found Bannister?"

"No, I wasn't."

"Anytime prior to that?"

"I've been to the clinic before, sure."

"As a visitor?"

"Yes. I'm interested in what they do, and I'm acquainted with Kathy Keenan, the director." He watched the detective take a note. "I had my blood drawn there about a month ago," he added for no reason.

The detective looked up. "You were a patient at an abortion clinic?"

"It was for a cholesterol count. Kathy drew it as a favor." Stupid thing to volunteer.

The detective looked down and took another note. "So what else makes you suspect the baby-doll murders may be linked to Judge Titus?"

"Far as I'm concerned, the link is there. The only question is whether it's coincidental or deliberate."

Pulaski looked at him skeptically.

"Titus is a poker-playing friend of Senator Dickey's," Jack said. "One of Dickey's biggest financial supporters is Eli Graves. Graves and I are not on what you'd call the best of terms."

"You think he'd do something to embarrass you?"

Jack laughed. "Yes, I do."

"Including trying to implicate you in the deaths of three clinic bombers?"

"In Graves's eyes that would be too kind." Jack waited for the detective to taken another note, then continued. "He'd like to ruin me with a scandal."

"Has he got one?"

"Not in my eyes. But—" Why did he add *but*?

"But what?"

Shit. He'd stepped onto the slippery slope. "When I was a high-school teenager, I got my girlfriend pregnant."

"And?"

"And what?" Jack asked.

"That's the scandal?"

He smiled at Pulaski's surprise. "What strikes a homicide detective as scandalous and a newspaper as scandalous are two different things. Especially where a politician's involved."

"Was it in the press?"

"Recently, yeah. And apparently some eager beaver's still looking."

"Into a high-school *pregnancy*?"

Jack fidgeted. "Actually, there's more to it than that." Pulaski looked at him, waiting. "Unfortunately, the girl died."

"Sorry," Pulaski said. "How was that supposed to be your fault?"

"If you're Eli Graves, that's easy. Pregnancy by fornication leads to abortion. Abortion causes death."

"What abortion?"

"My girlfriend died during a cesarean operation in her eighth month of pregnancy. Apparently Graves considers that to be my fault."

"Did the child die too?"

"That's what I was told."

Pulaski studied him. "You don't sound so sure."

Jack dropped his feet to the floor. "Actually, I'm not. Look, Eli Graves wants to ruin me because I'm trying to stop Abner Titus. Who knows how far he's willing to go? He talks about this high-school tragedy as if there's more scandal to come, something dark and awful."

"Any idea what it is?"

"No, but I know he's a zealot with a hot head, he's threatened me before, and I wouldn't put anything past him. Certainly not lying about my past, including linking me to the baby-doll murders." He picked up one of his blue pencils. "It would explain how a piece of one of these showed up inside Melvin Shivers."

"I can imagine Graves trying to use your personal history against you politically, but isn't killing people to frame you going a little far? Especially when the dead guys are his political allies?"

Put that way, it sounded ridiculous. Jack needed to bolster his case. "Not if you look at what he says about abortion clinics."

"I have. He says he's against violence."

"Right. So does the Mafia."

"So complete the thought," Pulaski said. "You're saying he hires clinic bombers like Shivers and Moon and then gets rid of them?"

"It's not that impossible, is it? If they're dead, they can't finger him, and if he gets rid of them in a way that manages to implicate me, he's nailed two problems for the price of one."

Pulaski lifted his eyebrows. "Three, if you count Mr. Bannister."

Jack noticed that he was no longer taking notes.

Pulaski stared at him, rubbing the birthmark on his forehead. "Does Abner Titus know Eli Graves?"

"Senator Dickey would be your best source on that. As for whether Eli Graves knew the clinic bombers, the guy who might help you on that is a kid named Iggy Pitt. He knew Melvin Shivers and Harley Moon when they all lived at the same halfway house on Forty-third Street. You probably know the place. Wings."

"Where can I find him?"

"He works at a messenger service in the city. Ace, I think." Jack picked up the telephone, called long-distance information, and punched in a number. Pulaski stood up and wandered around the office looking at framed letters, stacks of papers, mementos of campaigns, and photographs of famous handshakes. Jack kept a wary eye on him until someone answered.

"Ace."

"Is Iggy Pitt there?"

"You just missed him. Hey, Irv!"

Jack said, "When's the best time to catch him?"

"He's a contract messenger, he don't have hours." Phones were ringing. "Put that on the shelf, will ya?" the man said. "He's usually here nights and weekends. Hey, Irv? Izzat Iggy out there? . . . Yeah, would you tell him he's got a phone call?" The voice returned. "Hold on a minute."

Jack watched Pulaski put on his glasses and focus on a photograph of a sailboat on the wall.

"Hello?"

"Iggy?"

"Yeah?"

"Jack MacLeod."

There was a long, heavy silence.

"Iggy, Detective Norman Pulaski of the New York police is here. He'd like to ask you a few questions about Melvin Shivers and Harley Moon. Do you mind?"

"What's he want to know?"

"Whatever you can tell him. What they did, who their friends were, things like that."

"Why me?"

"It's not just you. He's talking to everybody."

"I'm kinda busy. When?"

Jack covered the mouthpiece and looked at Pulaski. "When do you want to see him?"

"Tell him I'll drop by tomorrow afternoon."

"Tomorrow afternoon."

Iggy exhaled, exasperated. "Ask him to call first to be sure I'm here, okay?"

"Would you rather have him visit you at home?"

"No!" he said quickly. "I mean, I don't care who sees me talking to him. It's not like I'm a suspect or something, am I?"

"Until a few minutes ago he didn't even know who you were. Iggy?"

"Yeah?"

Jack started to ask about Molly, but changed his mind. "Thanks," he said, and hung up.

Pulaski was still examining the photograph. "Thistle. Seventeen feet length over all, mahogany planks, open hull, round bottom. Very fast."

Jack stood up. "You race sailboats?"

"Never been on one in my life."

"Really?"

"Can't swim."

Jack sat on the edge of his desk. "So how do you know so much about boats?"

"I like to read about them." He straightened the frame on the wall and walked back to his chair, standing. "When I retire, I'm going to put on a life vest, then I'm going to buy a boat and sail west until I find a nice, pretty island. Someplace where they think formaldehyde is some kinda fake leather."

"With your wife?"

"No." He touched his birthmark. "She passed away."

"Sorry."

Evidently Pulaski didn't want to talk about it. He closed his notebook. Then he talked about it. "Five years ago this April." He stuck the notebook into his coat pocket, preoccupied. Finally he extended an open hand. "Appreciate your time, Congressman." As they shook he pulled Jack toward him. "I think I'll keep your, uh, theories about Titus and Graves to myself for a while, if you know what I mean. See how they pan out before saying anything."

"Suit yourself," Jack said, walking him to the door.

"It's not me I was thinking about, Congressman. It's you. I wouldn't want anybody to accuse you of feeding the police some colorful suppositions about Judge Titus so's somebody in the department could leak them to the press and drop a little more chickenshit on the judge's shoes. If you know what I mean."

Jack smiled. "Happy to hear you have a strict policy of keeping speculation confidential, Detective," Jack said. "Makes me feel a lot better about my own situation."

Jack started go back into his office when he saw Faith approaching with a stack of pink telephone messages. "Victoria called with her telephone number at the spa. She said if she's not in, she'll be at dinner and you should call later."

He walked into his office, closed the door, and turned on the television set as Ben Jacobs entered through the side door.

"We're late," he said, reminding Jack they were due at a Leadership Coalition meeting.

"Give me one second," Jack said, punching the telephone pad.

Jacobs left as Victoria's phone rang at the spa. Jack changed channels on the TV set, looking for the six-thirty news. After a few more rings he was about to hang up when somebody answered.

"Hello?" a female voice said.

He was momentarily confused; the voice wasn't Victoria's, but still familiar. Like Rachel's.

"Rachel?" he said.

There was no answer, only the click of the receiver.

He dialed again.

"Hello?" a female voice said. This time there was no question: it was Victoria.

"How was the trip?" he asked.

"I'm feeling better already. What's happening there?"

"Ben's tapping his foot outside my door. I just wanted to catch you before you went to dinner."

"Everything's fine. Why don't you call me when you get back? I've already eaten, so I'll be here in my room."

Jack looked at his watch. "Isn't it two hours earlier there?"

"Yes, why?"

"You had dinner at four-thirty in the afternoon?"

There was a short silence. "I'm on what they call a health schedule. Up at six-thirty, salt-free lunch before noon, a low-calorie early dinner, bed by ten. Starting tomorrow morning you won't be able to reach me for three days."

"What's happening?"

"A rehabilitation crash. Exercise, sleep, organic food, and rose-hips tea. They're making me and the baby into whole new people."

"Tell them the baby's already a whole new person. I thought this was supposed to be a rest, not boot camp."

"It's what the doctor ordered," she said.

"Speaking of doctors, I called a few minutes ago and thought Rachel picked up the phone."

"You must have dialed the wrong number."

Jacobs opened the door and tapped his watch.

"Got to go," Jack said into the telephone. "I'll call you later."

He hung up and walked to the door—and stopped. "I'll be right with you," he told Ben.

After closing the door, he returned to his desk and found Rachel's Maryland farm number on his Rolodex. Hating himself, he dialed.

Someone picked up. "Hello?" It sounded like her voice, but he wasn't sure. Then the voice said "Hello?" again, and this time there was no doubt: it was Rachel.

He hung up, feeling foolish. And momentarily relieved.

Momentarily.

Pepper Loomis arrived at Abner Titus's hospital room carrying an armload of briefs and a fresh box of chocolate-covered cherries. Titus was in a bad mood. It was a peaceful Thanksgiving Saturday, yet here he was in the hospital, undergoing a checkup. Even with Rachel's explanation—"sympathetic pain," she called it—he didn't understand how a kidney problem could cause distress in the abdomen. Still, she was a world-class surgeon, she'd saved his life with a new kidney, and even if her politics were confused, her medicine wasn't. No one knew his anatomy, or medical history, the way she did.

He was sitting in bed reading a Justice Department memorandum entitled "Advice on Confirmation Hearings," which, despite its ten pages, could have been reduced to one sentence: say nothing before the hearing, say nothing during the hearing, and say nothing after. Pepper took off her coat and told him not to worry about confirmation, he was a shoo-in. He grunted and kept reading.

On his bed was the usual assortment of convalescent junk: a week-old magazine, a felt-tipped pen with the cap missing, two remote controls—one for the television set, one for the VCR—and the universal box of Kleenex. He policed the area regularly, reducing pollution to a minimum.

Next to the bed, within easy reach, was a credenza that had been pulled away from the wall to hold the gear he used most: his private telephone, the TV set and VCR, and various law books.

Pepper saw that *The Maltese Falcon* was playing from a videotape with the sound off. Titus claimed he was a Bogart fan, but his real hero was Sydney Greenstreet. She dropped the stack of briefs onto the bed with a bounce, forcing him to look over the tops of his glasses, as if finally noticing her.

"Forget the briefs and read my memos, Judge. Especially this one." She handed some papers to him. "It's my outline of your opinion in *Costello*." The case hadn't been argued yet, but the briefs had been submitted and he had read them. Besides, his mind had been made up long ago.

He turned the first page and sat up to read while she opened the box of chocolates, pulled one out, and dangled it disrespectfully before his eyes. He reached for it without acknowledging the taunt, glancing at it as if it were a nuisance that could be disposed of only in his mouth.

She wandered around the room as he read, checking her watch, straightening a pile of videotapes on the bedside credenza, fussing with the box of candy, making herself busy, nervously waiting for something to happen. When she'd returned from refilling his carafe of water, he'd finished reading her memo.

He said, "If you look at what I drafted in the Zenobia Davis case, I've practically written the *Costello* decision."

"I know. I assume you'll assign the majority opinion to yourself."

He drank some water. "Of course, but first I have to get out of here. Get Rachel Redpath in here, would you? I feel fine."

"The problem isn't how you feel, Judge, the problem is they still don't know what's causing the problem. Peritonitis can come and go in a minute. What if you have another attack?"

"Oh, for God's sake. With all the medicine she's pumped into me, I couldn't catch a cold."

Pepper picked up the telephone and told the chief resident that the judge wanted to see his doctor. The resident said Dr. Redpath was in preop preparing for a transplant and couldn't be disturbed. When Titus heard that, he became exasperated; Pepper calmed him down, picked up a stack of memos marked with yellow Post-it notes, and for the next half hour gave him the gist of her summaries of pending cases. He asked very few questions, trusting the quality of her work. Then he asked her to call Dr. Redpath again.

He reached for another cherry and froze. His face turned hard, as if he was trying to burp but couldn't.

"Judge?" she said, but he didn't answer.

She grabbed the nurse call button and punched it wildly, threw it onto the bed, and ran out the door toward the nurses' station.

"He's having an attack!" she yelled.

Everyone in the area shifted into high gear. Two nurses ran into the room and attached his monitors and oxygen. A resident examined him— pulse, pupils, breathing, pain in his abdomen. The orderlies grabbed the end of the bed and pushed it out the door on its huge rubber wheels.

"Get Dr. Redpath!" Pepper yelled, running alongside Titus as they rolled down the hall. They shoved the bed against the wall outside the operating room as Rachel appeared in surgeon's dress and gloves, a blue mask pulled down in front of her neck.

"Dr. Redpath!" Pepper said. "It's the chief justice!"

"I know who he is," Rachel said calmly, removing her gloves. She walked to the bed and bent over him. "What is it, Abner?"

"My stomach," he said. He was perspiring, and the lines around his eyes had deepened with pain.

Rachel called Phoebe Chang out of the operating room. "Tell everyone to stop what they're doing," she said. "We'd better see what we have here."

Chang turned and disappeared ahead of the orderlies as they rolled Titus's bed into the OR.

"What's wrong?" Pepper asked.

"You'll have to leave," Rachel said, and disappeared into the operating room herself.

Rachel stood at the lectern in the press room and pulled off her surgeon's cap, squinting into the lights as the cameras clicked away.

"The chief justice is stable and resting comfortably, although he hasn't regained consciousness yet. The other good news is that we finally found the culprit." She lifted her hand and held up a small stick of wood as the cameras whirred and clicked. "It's a toothpick," she said. "It had perforated the lining of his large intestine, causing an attack of peritonitis."

"How'd he get a toothpick in there?" a reporter asked.

"We're not sure, but we think it came from one of his martinis, which he has no business drinking in the first place. I'm told he's been known to gulp the whole thing down when he thinks he's about to get caught." There was a general stirring and a few guffaws as everyone recorded her words. "We've seen stranger things happen."

"Will he be back on the bench in time to hear the *Costello* case?" a reporter asked.

"Barring any unforeseen complications, yes."

"Did you X-ray him, and if so, why didn't you see the toothpick?"

"Vegetable matter doesn't show up on X rays."

"Aren't the intestines a little out of the way for a kidney-transplant surgeon?"

"The initial diagnosis was potential kidney failure. I happen to know he has only one kidney because I put it there. When that turned out not to be the problem, naturally we explored further."

"Did this operation take an unusually long time?" another reporter asked.

Rachel laughed. "Most of my patients prefer accuracy to speed, Bob.

And no, it wasn't especially long when you consider the ground we had to cover."

"Dr. Redpath? Isn't it a little ironic that someone with your political views, which seem opposite the chief justice's, just operated on him and saved his life?"

"I'm a surgeon," she said. "I leave the irony to you." She looked at her watch. "Now, if you'll excuse me, I have a patient to tend to."

The last camera was being packed into its metal box when Molly came bustling through the door, raincoat open, windblown hair all over the place. She hurried to the front row of empty chairs.

"What'd I miss?" she asked a lone remaining cameraman.

He looked up slowly. "Where *you* been, lady?"

"On the shuttle. What happened?"

"Chief justice had a toothpick in his gut."

"A what?"

"Martini toothpick." He snapped the locks on his case and lifted it onto his shoulder. Seeing he'd left a microphone clip on the podium, he reached for it and noticed a small plastic bag resting on the lip of the lectern. He held it up and saw the toothpick inside. "Matter of fact, here it is." He handed it to her.

She sprawled into a folding chair, kicked off her shoes, and stared at the toothpick as if she'd never seen one before.

Jack drove ninety miles an hour most of the way from Albuquerque to Santa Fe, which had no commercial airport. It was late at night and Interstate 25 was clear, but what pushed him most was Victoria. He missed her.

When he reached town, he followed the car-rental map to the adobe condominium they'd rented and parked on the garage apron. After grabbing his duffel bag from the backseat, he closed the car door and climbed the steps two at a time, wondering what the spa had done for her, how she looked, how she felt. He knocked—no answer—pushed the doorbell button and banged with the knocker. After a long moment the door finally opened.

It was Victoria, but not the Victoria he'd kissed good-bye three weeks before in Washington. She had lost weight and was pale, almost fragile, and her eyes showed the remains of ashen circles. But then she smiled a smile he hadn't seen for months, the one that mesmerized judges, comforted friendly witnesses, tricked hostile ones, and made his blood warm. Something about the vacation had been good for her.

She extended her arms and he grabbed her, lifted her off her feet, and closed the door with his heel. He asked her about the spa—"Too boring to talk about," she said—and the baby—"Doing fine." He got undressed and jumped into the shower and continued their conversation through the open bathroom door.

"Come on in," he yelled from the shower stall.

"I just got out," she said.

Soap and water wasn't what he had in mind. He stepped out and grabbed a towel, wrapped it around his waist, and walked to the bed. Victoria was already under the covers, propped up on pillows, thumbing through a magazine.

He ran his hand through his wet hair, pushing it back. "You haven't asked about Titus," he said.

She turned a page, detached, uninterested. "I know. Aren't you glad?"

He sat on the edge of the bed. If the spa had done nothing for her skin tone, it had been good for her state of mind. "He's still claiming he didn't call Zenobia Davis," Jack said. "A couple of Senate investigators and the press are still trying to discover the clinic where she died. The FBI's probably doing the same thing as part of his background check. The Leadership Coalition's still twisting arms and hoping for a bombshell before the Senate comes back into session. That's about it."

He stood up, dropped his towel onto the floor, and started to peel back the blanket to get into bed.

"Careful," she said, pulling the covers up. He stopped with a question mark on his face. "It's cold," she explained.

He lifted the covers cautiously and crawled under. She reached over and turned out the light. Strange, he thought. Unless it was the middle of the night, they never made love with the lights off.

Never mind. He drew her to him and proceeded patiently, whispering in her ear, telling her he'd missed her, feeling her expand and rise. Her eyes closed and her breathing became deep; her fingers told him where she was on the curve, when she was ready. He kissed her lips and ears, then moved his mouth down to her chin . . . down her neck . . . down through the shallow between her breasts . . . down to her midriff—

She stopped him.

"Come up here," she whispered, pulling him by his hair. "Make love to me."

He felt his scalp separating from his skull. "What was that I was doing?" he asked, moving upward.

"I mean like this."

She centered him on her body, rolled him onto his back, and opened her mouth to his. Then she began her own descent.

For a moment he wondered why pregnancy caused shyness. But then he lost track.

His eyes were still open, unable to sleep. He turned his head and looked at the dial. One o'clock. He lifted himself out of bed quietly, pulled on a robe, and slipped through the sliding-glass doors onto the wooden deck. The lights of Los Alamos cast a yellowish glow onto low-lying clouds, and the smell of pine and sage rose like smoke from a dying campfire. He flared his nostrils and drank it in, saturating his bloodstream.

Lying on the flat of the railing, near his hand, was a pine cone. He held it up, creating a silhouette against the distant light. *The perfect seed.* His mind did a quick inventory of the junk on its shelves—Abner Titus, the Supreme Court, congressional hearings, lobbyists, politics—and tossed them out, one by one.

His eyes began watering from the cold, so he returned to the bedroom and closed the glass door behind him, drawing the curtains to protect them from the morning light. Victoria was lying on her side, still asleep. He slipped under the covers and laid his arm around her. Then he closed his eyes and let the jet lag and fatigue pull him under.

Few places in the modern world rivaled the ancient Roman Colosseum for life-and-death decisions. The conference room of the United States Supreme Court was one.

It was ten o'clock on a Friday morning and the members of the Court were converging in the hallway, limbering up their thumbs to vote up or down on the cases that had been argued before them during the week. They assembled at an unhurried pace, chatting amiably about the weather and the morning's news, revealing nothing of the gravity of the decisions they were about to make. Still, casualness was not to be confused with callousness; like the Caesars before them, they'd simply become accustomed to their power.

For all its historic importance, the Supreme Court's conference room was more dignified than grand. On one side, near the chief justice's anteroom, was a sitting area with upholstered chairs and a sofa; on the other was the venerable conference table itself—a long, perfectly proportioned oak rectangle with green felt inlay, wooden book stands, individual pencil trays, and nine black leather chairs arranged on the perimeter. A table of character and weight, and yet, compared with the magnitude of the matters laid upon it, quite modest. On the floor was a burnt-sienna carpet; high above, in the center of the room, a crystal chandelier, too small for the room and a bit too fancy. Around the walls were tables, bookshelves, and paintings, and between the towering curtains, ceiling-high windows of bulletproof glass.

Doe v. Costello.

The case had been argued two days before. Following the preliminary vote they would cast this morning, the Court's provisional decision would be drafted by a justice who had voted in the majority. Dissenting opinions, if there were to be any, would be written by one or more justices who'd cast their lots with the minority. Drafts would then be circulated among all members over the next few months, allowing them to consider the reasoning and scope of the opinions, to redraft them and recirculate, and eventually, to sign on to one position or another. In *Costello*, the process would ultimately run its course the following spring—May or June, most likely—at which time a final, definitive vote would be taken and the

316

Court's decision announced to the public from the bench. The preliminary balloting this particular mid-December morning could thus be changed before the case was finally decided in the spring, although in a case of this magnitude, where votes were cast according to long-held views, a decisive shift was unlikely. All in all, the system was rational, deliberate, and civilized, even though in the end, of necessity, it would be reduced to a decision as stark and crude as the Roman games themselves: thumbs up or thumbs down. Affirm or reverse. Let live or let die.

Abner Titus sat in his wheelchair at the head of the table, flanked on both sides by the other justices. At the opposite end of the table, in the chair reserved for the Court's most senior associate, was Justice Michael Kelly—white-haired, liberal, Irish-Catholic, pro-choice—at seventy-eight a man whose convictions placed him at a far greater distance from the new chief justice than the length of the table allowed. The voting protocol was for the least tenured justices to cast their voice ballots first, ending with the chief. While in earlier times justices had routinely spoken their minds before voting, in recent years, given the press of business and the political divisions on the Court, preliminary votes were often tallied with little or no debate.

Which was how the first six votes were cast this morning.

Justices Julius Franconia, Constanza Castro, and Warren Handelman voted to reverse *Costello* and thereby overturn *Roe* v. *Wade*. Then Justices Kathryn Lamb, Matthew Forbes, and Paul Harris, the Court's only black justice, voted to affirm *Costello* and preserve *Roe*. So far, no surprises: three votes for, three against. Mother and fetus in perfect balance. Woman and egg in equipoise.

The next vote was cast by Justice Edmund Burke Little III, a former professor from Yale Law School and the neoconservative voice of the Court. Now it was four votes to overturn *Roe*, three to sustain, and Justice Kelly's turn to even the count.

Despite his age, Kelly was still a man of substantial presence. As a former U.S. senator from Massachusetts, two centuries earlier he might have been a minuteman. Which, in a way, he was about to become this morning. His oratorical skills were not what they once were, but he could still deliver a musket load when he had to.

He leaned forward with his eyes fixed on the table, as if he were about to jump three of his opponent's checkers. Once the room was his, he raised his head.

"I have never been pregnant. Nor have I been a black man. And yet, just as I cannot imagine the Court condoning slavery based upon race, I cannot imagine it condoning slavery based upon sex." He folded his hands in front of him. "We've heard a great deal of argument about when life begins, as if to answer that question—if it were possible—would settle all others. Well, with all due respect, I think not. I'm prepared to stipulate that human life begins at conception. For that matter, I'm prepared to stipulate that an unfertilized egg and an unejaculated sperm have the potential to create a child, too. I also agree with my conservative friends who keep pointing out that when a woman gets pregnant, she holds a person inside her, not a hippopotamus. While I appreciate this keen insight, I have difficulty with its relevance—not because of its kindergarten cuteness but because of its premise, which is that we should simply let nature take its course. As judges, we decide cases that protect people from the ravages of nature every day—disease, pestilence, hurricanes, earthquakes. With a single verdict of guilty, we even allow the state to end the God-given life of a murderer. We make these life-and-death decisions, which is as it should be, because, all humility aside, that is what we are here for. Until it comes to abortion. Then all at once we're supposed to go deaf and blind, or defer to the stars, or nature, or whatever else appears to justify the surrender of our wits.

"In all sincerity, I ask you, Why? What are we afraid of? What bogeyman stops us from being as decisive and honorable on this subject as we try to be on virtually every other?"

He unfolded his hands. "I think I know the answer. I think it's true that abortion is an enormously fearsome thing, so fearsome that even the normal comforts of precedent and analogy are of little help. What guides us on this question, regardless of how much we try to camouflage it with historical reference, is the value we place on human life. And that, my friends, is exactly what I believe the right to an abortion protects. It gives a pregnant woman the power to make a life-and-death decision during precisely that time when none of the rules or principles are simpleminded. It recognizes that if any human being possesses the wisdom and capacity to decide whether pregnancy threatens a mother's life, or the life of her family, or even the future life of the fetus itself, it is the mother. So, as a court of nine remote people, we are right to turn our backs on this difficult decision and acknowledge that we lack the necessary wisdom to make a single rule to do justice in so many different situations. Perhaps we are right, after all, to expect others to influence that decision—God, the stars, nature, religion, family. But if that's so, how can we possibly exclude the mother? How can we remove her from this complex, refined judgment and substitute the gross judgment of the state? Which, as my conservative colleagues so often love to remind us, is exactly who we are?"

He laid his hands flat on the table. "Because I cannot imagine being forced to remain pregnant against my will, I can't imagine a woman allowing that to happen to her, either. I *can* imagine her deciding to carry a child to term even though she would not have chosen to be pregnant in the first place. I *can* imagine her giving up a child for adoption. I can imagine her deciding to keep it, and I can imagine her changing her mind several times back and forth, exercising the one thing that distinguishes us from every other animal on the planet—our intelligence. In my view, that's what the abortion decision is all about, an exercise in human intelligence." He leaned forward in his chair. "Personally, if I were a pregnant woman forced to carry a child against my will, I would take up arms before surrendering."

"Oh, come, come, Michael," Titus interrupted.

"But I would," Kelly said. "In exactly the same spirit that justified taking up arms against King George's troops. Freedom of religion, habeas corpus, speech, petition—is the right of a woman to be free from state-imposed pregnancy any less basic? In my view, to deny a woman control of her own body would be a mistake as great as this Court's approval of slavery in *Dred Scott*." He pulled his hands off the table. "I vote to affirm, and I ask for a change of vote from at least one of you who's voted to reverse."

No one volunteered. The vote stood at four to four. All eyes turned to Chief Justice Abner Titus, the tiebreaker.

"They say never follow a banjo act, but since there's no one left but me, I guess I have no choice."

The justices shifted in their chairs and waited.

"In my opinion, nothing in the oath we take to support and defend the Constitution is of a higher duty than the protection of life. From Locke and Rousseau to the latest editorial in this morning's newspaper, no one can find a greater, or if my liberal friends will forgive an oblique reference to deity in this government building, more sacred duty than this.

"The issue, then, is what constitutes life within the meaning of the Fourteenth Amendment. As we on the Court should know better than most, the Constitution was not written in a vacuum, but with reference to the common experience and understanding of the framers. And in every respectable definition I can find that was customary then, and still prevalent today, the term *life* includes the unborn. Not merely from the moment of birth, or viability, but from the moment of conception.

"I have listened carefully to arguments that a woman should have a free and unsanctioned right to destroy life in her womb. And I agree that what's involved here is a balancing of interests between hers and the fetus's. After all, if children could be born without any adverse consequence to the mother, who would argue that a fetus should be killed gratuitously? Not even the zero-population-growth people would go that far. No, the controlling factor here is the burden an unwanted new life imposes on the woman who must bear it.

"I hear your eloquent description of it, Michael. Having spent many years examining the subject, I could even present a few arguments you've missed. But never have I found a single one of them, or all of them taken together, to justify the taking of unborn life."

He leaned forward in his wheelchair.

"Is there any of us of any political or philosophical or religious persuasion who can say that anything is more important, or vulnerable, or deserving of this Court's protection than the life of a newly conceived child?" He waited a moment and leaned back. "Once you reach that conclusion, you're forced to conclude that the burdens of childbearing, as painful and unwanted as they may be, simply cannot be lifted at the expense of innocent life."

He reached forward and lifted his glass of water to take a drink, giving Kelly an opening.

"Excuse me, Abner, but do I understand you to be saying you'd prohibit abortion even in cases of rape and incest? Or where the life of the mother is in danger?"

"Those facts are not presented here, Michael."

"I know that, but in the secrecy of this room, I'm asking anyway."

Titus pushed the glass forward, making room for his hands.

"Rape and incest are as vile as any violations I can imagine," he said. "And yet, once they've happened, killing the unknowing child is a punishment that has no relationship to the crime. In fact, it's worse than that. It relieves the male rapist of ongoing responsibility, moral and practical alike. I agree with your assessment that we have the obligation to make judgments, set standards, and draw lines. But *against* life? *Against* innocence and humanity itself?" He shook his head. "I can't imagine a greater betrayal of this Court's purpose. Counseling and compassion for a pregnant victim, of course. State assistance to the mother and child, naturally. Adoption services, foster homes, religious help, yes. But abortion? As normal and understandable as a rape victim's instincts may be to shed her pregnancy, they simply don't outweigh the life of the innocent child."

"I find that utterly barbaric," Kelly said.

Titus's face flushed and he raised his eyebrows. "According to historians, Michael, barbarians respected life in the wombs of their women and propagated fiercely, so I'll accept that as a compliment."

Kelly said, "It wasn't a personal comment, Abner."

"It wouldn't bother me if it were," Titus said. "Obviously, all of our opinions on this subject have highly personal roots." He allowed the perspiration on his forehead to remain untouched. "How many of us at this table can say with absolute certainty that we were not born against our mothers' wishes?" No one said a word. "Well, let me assure you." He paused. "I can't."

The room remained silent as he gathered up his papers. "I vote for the reversal of *Costello* and the explicit overruling of *Roe* v. *Wade*, and I assign the writing of the Court's opinion to myself."

"**M**ay I help you?"

The woman behind the perfume counter waited for Graves to answer, but he said nothing. She stood patiently, listening to chipmunks singing *Frosty the Snowman* for the twentieth time that day, driving her and the other salespeople one step closer to madness.

Graves set down a bag of ornaments and tiny blinking lights he'd purchased for the office Christmas tree and reached for a small glass vial sitting in a wooden rack. He'd come to the perfume department intending to purchase a gift for his secretary—a bottle of Jasmine Nights like the sample a girl had given him at the door—but seeing the mix-your-own perfume oils, he'd put his decision on hold.

He lifted the vial marked *Patchouli Oil*, removed the cork stopper, and raised the open tube to his nose. The aroma was momentarily sickening, a burst sewer pipe of bad childhood memories. Mini and Maxi, his "caretakers" . . . the ramshackle room reeking with patchouli. But the smell held a pleasant side, too: it reminded him of the recruit he'd found who always wore it, the kid with the beard, horn-rims, and Dodgers cap. The guy Detective Pulaski called Eggs Benedict.

The straight arrow.

Where had he gone after he and his pal had bombed the Atlantic Avenue Women's Health Center? Was he lying low? Was he stalking another clinic, with a pipe of dynamite in hand?

Or was Benedict on his original trajectory—aimed at Congressman John MacLeod?

"Patchouli is one of my favorites, too," the clerk said. "A real classic."

Focused, concentrating, he didn't hear her. Eggs Benedict was still out there somewhere, a straight arrow still in flight. He could just feel it.

He replaced the stopper. "I'll take a bottle of Jasmine Nights," he said, setting the vial in the rack. As the clerk wrapped the perfume and rang it up, Graves looked around the store, admiring the four-foot candy canes, listening to a chorus of "Silent Night."

•   •   •

"Feliz Navidad" floated out of the loudspeakers and through the evergreen-covered poles in the plaza in Santa Fe, where Jack and Victoria walked a path. They ambled to the sidewalk market filled with silver and turquoise bracelets, earrings and jewelry, Navajo and Beacon blankets, red-chili-pepper wreaths and *farolitos*—small paper bags with sand at the bottom holding a single glowing candle. Jack found a silver ring with a smooth red stone in the center and examined it. When he saw Victoria's eyes brighten, he handed it back to the Indian craftsman and moved on. Later, while she was browsing a bookstore with a mug of mulled cider in hand, he slipped away, returned to the market, and bought it for her.

It was that kind of a vacation. They watched skiers in Taos and took walks in the snow-spotted desert, Jack worrying about a miscarriage, Victoria unconcerned. They prowled galleries when Victoria felt up to it, watched Hopi dances, drank margaritas, and took long naps. They read and went to movies, and drove back roads with nothing but a gas-station map to guide them. Victoria seemed unpossessed by the pathos of her clients, her outrage at Abner Titus, and all the other coils in her angry mainspring. He didn't understand why, but it didn't matter. He liked it.

In fact, they were both so relaxed and happy, he thought they should get married then and there. She considered it—seriously, he thought—but preferred to stick to their original schedule. January 6, when a few friends would join them. He didn't press the issue, which she appreciated.

They extended their vacation through the New Year.

It was Friday morning, their last day in Santa Fe, and Ben Jacobs was on the telephone from Washington with his daily briefing. "The phone company confirmed to the Bureau that the call to Zenobia Davis's apartment was made from Titus's office, as her handwritten note seems to say."

"Can they tell what time it was made?"

"Eight-fifteen P.M."

"Any indication from the sign-in log whether someone else might have been in Titus's office that night?"

"Nothing."

"The security guard doesn't remember anybody unusual coming in?"

"Nope. And Titus hadn't signed out yet."

Jack summarized the situation. "The noose is a little tighter, Ben. He might hang yet."

"Maybe," Jacobs said. "Listen, I've contacted everybody we know in New York to get them to join the counter-demonstration at Graves's rally Saturday morning, and Winston and the district office are calling the troops. Are you still planning to be there?"

"Definitely. It's in my district."

The Red Rose Society's giant pro-life rally was being held outside the Park Avenue Women's Clinic, the largest facility in Jack's congressional district, an important constituent. The one to which he'd taken Molly in October, to interview the director.

Jack said, "I always show up when Graves makes a public appearance on my turf."

"I know. That's why I thought maybe you want to stay in Santa Fe."

Jack laughed. "It won't be as bad as the last time. If the turnout is half as big as it's supposed to be, Graves will never even see me. Besides, Victoria and I will be in town anyway. We're getting married that night, remember?"

"Who in the world wants to start out their wedding day protesting a Red Rose Society rally?"

"Who do you think?" Jack said. "Knowing V, she probably figures it'll be the most important thing she'll do that day."

Dr. Phoebe Chang opened the laboratory refrigerator door and placed a small key into a padlock, turned it, and pulled open a second door. She withdrew an unmarked bottle of clear fluid and handed it to Rachel. Without saying anything, Rachel stuck a needle through its synthetic cover and carefully withdrew twenty cubic centimeters into a syringe. She handed the bottle back to Phoebe, unscrewed the needle from the syringe, snapped on a cap, and placed the fluid in the side pocket of her white coat.

In the four weeks following his Thanksgiving weekend operation, Titus had recovered reasonably well, although there were still a few matters requiring a return visit. Symptoms that Rachel alone understood. There was also her usual concern for his transplanted kidney. She entered his room and found him alone, glasses on, reading a brief.

"Good morning," she said. She checked a clear plastic bag hanging on an IV pole. "How are you feeling?"

He removed his glasses and delayed answering, using his silence to balance the power in the doctor–patient relationship. "Fine, now that I know I'm about to get out of here."

She picked up his wrist and felt his pulse. "How's the nausea?"

"It's usually gone by noon."

"Any pain?"

"Not since the stitches were removed."

"Anything else?"

"Maybe a little something in the intestines now and then, but nothing serious."

"What's it feel like?"

"Like my stomach's turning over from being hungry."

"Maybe you are. Are you eating?"

He looked amused. "You're asking *me*?"

Rachel stood silently and made some marks on her clipboard. "You had a serious case of peritonitis, Mr. Chief Justice. I've seen patients' insides destroyed by the martini before, but never the toothpick."

Titus looked aggrieved. "I sure have been taking a lot of ribbing

about that, and I don't even remember when it happened. I'll have to tell
Daisy and Pepper to stop using toothpicks."

"They make your drinks for you?"

Titus closed his eyes. "Oh Lord, here we go. Another lecture."

"What do you mean 'another'? When did you hear the first one?"

He smiled. "There are lots of things about me that would surprise
you, Rachel."

"I certainly hope so." She picked up his half-full box of chocolate-
covered cherries. "What are these doing here?"

He lifted his body uneasily to another spot in the bed. "You know,"
he said, "if I were really smart, I probably wouldn't let you continue being my doctor."

"If you were really smart, you wouldn't let me in your room."

"Does that mean you're going to poison my apple juice?"

She placed the box of cherries under her arm. "Abner, if I'd wanted
to sabotage you, I would have done it *before* you heard *Costello*, not after. You're forgetting that I got you out of your bed before the argument
and postponed your monthly overnight until now." She finished taking
her notes. "Besides, it's not your body I want to change. It's your
mind."

"Well, if you ever discover how to do that, let me know. I have a few
candidates for that sort of thing myself."

"Not on the Court, I assume. From what I hear, you have five votes
anytime you want them."

"Votes are never that predictable."

"Not even in *Costello*?"

He looked at her, amused. "When you go fishing, you don't even use
bait, do you? You know I can't talk about pending cases. Now, when am
I getting out of here? It's almost Christmas."

"If you don't get impatient, you can leave tomorrow. Then I want you
back here for a checkup every two weeks and an overnight one weekend
a month. And I want you to meet with the dietician this afternoon."

"She's not going to take me off my martinis, I can tell you that right
now."

"Abner—"

"Any chocolates?"

"None. And absolutely no smoking."

Titus looked irritated. "I hate it when people mother me."

He picked up the brief and began reading. She walked to the IV
stand, set down the candy and clipboard, and fiddled with the tubes,
keeping an eye on him to make sure he didn't see what she was doing.

She removed the syringe from her coat pocket and quickly inserted it into the port that fed the tube running to his arm. As she pushed in the plunger he turned his head toward her, startling her.

"Rachel?"

"Yes?"

He turned back to his brief. "They tell me if you hadn't operated when you did, I would have died."

She relaxed and stepped to the side of his bed. "There are other good surgeons here, any one of whom would have saved you. Losing the chief justice of the United States is not a good item to put on a doctor's résumé."

He turned a page, speaking to her as if mildly distracted. "Nevertheless, I haven't thanked you properly."

"Don't worry," she said. "We'll have time to discuss our mutual contributions to life and the law later." She picked up her things and walked to the door. "Believe me, we will."

I t should have been a peaceful Saturday morning, but the moment he awoke he felt dark signals rippling across his consciousness. He opened his eyes and stared at the ceiling, trying to dismiss the free-floating anxiety that afflicts overly serious people. Victoria was lying on her side, stirring slightly. He laid his hand on her hip a moment, then climbed out of bed and walked to the window, opened it a crack, and bent down like a deer drinking from a stream, inhaling and sorting out the chemistry in New York's winter air: fumes from the all-night pizza parlor; automobile and bus exhaust; ozone from sunbaked oxygen— *Ozone.* Somewhere in the cosmic ether the sky was on fire, still a long way off but moving this way, sending its faint but unmistakable warning ahead of the flames:

Watch out, Jack. Today you could get fucked.

The taxi turned the corner behind Grand Central Station and stopped on Park Avenue behind a string of brake lights. Jack and Victoria peered out the window and saw the crowd spilling off the building's plaza into the street. By now the demonstration had assumed a carnivallike excitement—the sound of amplified voices reverberating off cement, the hand-painted signs moving up and down in rhythm to chanted slogans, police horses clopping sideways, tails whipping, flanks shivering. Even the people observing from across the street seemed to be participants as much as audience.

Jack paid the taxi driver as Victoria hopped out of the cab and walked quickly toward the crowd. The police had removed five pro-lifers who had chained themselves to the front door of the high-rise building that housed the women's clinic, and patrolmen kept the protesters divided into two groups on either side of blue sawhorses, forming a demilitarized corridor to the building's main entrance.

The larger antiabortion group had set up a wooden platform on the left, where Eli Graves sat waiting to speak, eyes roaming nervously and methodically over the crowd. Sitting on one side of him was the Reverend Gaylord Jenkins, and on the other, Bishop John Tracy. Three thou-

328

sand demonstrators stood before them in the plaza, signs in hand, red roses in lapels, listening to Senator Sticks Dickey boom his message through the loudspeakers.

"... *Doe* v. *Costello*, a case that could protect the lives of the unborn for generations to come. And I would just ask that when you say a prayer for the small and helpless victims among us, you pray for the justices of our Supreme Court, too. Ask God to show them that our great Constitution was founded on His law, and when critics say this is mixin' government and religion, well, pray for them, too, and all the others who ..."

Jack smiled. Sticks was amazing even for a politician. No shame whatsoever.

He and Victoria slipped between the sawhorses and worked their way toward Sally Feathers, the leader of the pro-choice counterdemonstrators. They stood behind the barricade waiting for her to raise a battery-powered megaphone and lead them in a chant. Off to Jack's right, leaning on a sawhorse, was Winston Jones; to his left, television cameras; next to them Iggy Pitt; and next to him ... Molly McCormick.

Seeing her shouldn't have surprised him, but it did. She leaned forward to say something to her cameraman and caught sight of him looking at her. He mouthed a silent hello and waited. She stared back a moment and responded with a hello of her own. It was their first personal exchange since they'd split up.

Senator Dickey's speech had ended, and Eli Graves was now at the microphone. "... which is why next week the Senate should confirm Judge Abner Titus as chief justice." Everyone on the pro-life side applauded.

"Now," Graves said, "what are the arguments the baby killers are making against the new chief justice? I'll tell you. Their case against him is that he is in favor of life! Their case against him is that he believes the Constitution protects the unborn! Their case against him is that he wants to end baby killing by overturning *Roe* v. *Wade*! And when they finally figured out that their case *against* him is America's case *for* him, what did they do?"

A man in the audience cupped his hands around his mouth and yelled, "They lied."

"That's right! They lied! They slandered and smeared a man who honors life with a story that he was somehow responsible for the death of a poor woman and her baby!"

A loud cry of "NOOO!" went up from the crowd.

"But you know what the answer is to this disgusting lie? The answer is, consider the source."

The audience applauded wildly.

"Consider Congressman Jack MacLeod! Consider his politics and his record. And if those aren't enough to convince you who's telling the truth, consider his life!"

Jack felt his blood rise, ready for a repeat of the sidewalk speech Graves had given in front of his office.

Graves continued. "As the Senate prepares to vote on the chief justice's confirmation, I ask how any senator can believe *anything* MacLeod says when you take into account who he is—a fornicator who slept with his high-school girlfriend, conceived a child by her, and tried to have it killed!"

Jack clenched his fist. Victoria reached out and touched his arm.

"Lord almighty," Graves said. "Thank God he failed!" He opened a black three-ring binder with green pages and photographs. "His girlfriend may have died, but—no thanks to him—at least his daughter was born."

His—His *what?* Jack's fist fell open first, then his mouth.

"That's right," Graves said. "A daughter was born and orphaned for twenty-five years, abandoned by the man who fathered her."

Jack felt his heart pounding in his ears.

"But he finally found her, and when he did, do you know what he did next?" No one in the crowd said a word, and Graves smiled. "I don't blame you," he said. "It's hard to guess, even harder to say."

He turned another page in his book and read silently. The crowd and Jack stood waiting.

"But there's too much at stake not to speak the truth," Graves said. "Because the only antidote to the lies about Chief Justice Titus is the truth about his accuser, Jack MacLeod." He turned another page in his notebook and looked up at the crowd. "Including his relationship with his daughter, Molly McCormick."

Jack looked over at Molly. She was staring at Graves, her lips parted, her face flat. As if she knew Jack was looking at her, she turned and found his eyes. Her hand rose to her mouth.

"Was he a good father?" Graves asked.

Jack found his feet moving toward the sawhorses.

"Not exactly," Graves said. "What he did was to—" He looked down and shook his head. "How can I say it, except just to say it?"

Jack leaped over a sawhorse and ran across the corridor toward the blue line bordering Graves and his audience. A policeman ran after him, but not before Jack had hurdled the next set of sawhorses and disappeared into the crowd, elbowing his way toward Graves.

A few yards away Iggy Pitt stood trembling. Then he jumped the sawhorse and ran toward Graves, too. Winston hopped over it and took chase.

Molly stood still, head swimming. Then she ducked under the sawhorse and followed.

Graves saw none of them coming, not even when he raised his eyes from the notebook and looked over the crowd. "What he did was to enter into an incestuous relationship."

Jack pushed past a man holding a sign and plowed toward the microphone. A few pro-choice demonstrators crossed the buffer zone and followed.

"And if that wasn't sinful enough," Graves said, voice rising, "he impregnated her with a child!"

The crowd was packed tighter close to the stage, but Jack pried his way through.

"And if *that* wasn't enough," Graves said, "he forced her to abort their child!"

Jack drove his body through a compressed group of demonstrators with signs reading END ABORTION NOW! and ABORTION IS MURDER!

"Right here!" Graves said, pointing at the sixth floor of the building behind him. "Right here, in this clinic!" He closed his binder and held it aloft like the Ten Commandments. "I have the proof here in my hands! I have pictures! I have reports! I have eyewitness accounts that prove it all!"

Jack clawed his way past the last demonstrators and jumped onto the platform. It was the first Graves saw of him coming. He dropped his notebook and backed away from the microphone, tripping over the bishop's feet and falling to the floor.

Jack stumbled toward him, reached down, and grabbed him by the throat. Except for a few startled gasps, the crowd went quiet.

A policeman jumped onto the stage and elbowed his way toward them. Demonstrators near the front climbed onto the stage and started to claw at Jack. A few pro-choice demonstrators fought back, and soon everyone lost track of who was who and what was what. The scene became a brawl, wildly out of logic or control.

In the midst of the melee, Jack continued wrestling with Graves on the platform floor. Graves tried to loosen Jack's grip on is neck; failing, he reached for Jack's throat and began strangling him in return.

The move took Jack by surprise, and in a moment the two of them were lying on their sides, choking each other, fighting for superior position, locked in a test of lung power as much as muscle power. Screaming people fell over them and onto them, scrambling to escape whatever was happening, which was not clear to anyone.

Jack felt his lungs burning and thought he was about to lose consciousness when Graves's grip unexpectedly relaxed. Jack sucked in fresh air and renewed his grip on Graves's throat. Now everything else was irrelevant: the crowd, the noise, the politics—nothing mattered except the destruction of this enemy.

Just as Jack thought he had the upper hand, a man standing over him with a sign reading STOP VIOLENCE TO THE UNBORN! lifted his stick in both hands, like Excalibur, and rammed it straight down. Into Jack's eye.

Jack thought he'd been shot in the head.

He released Graves's neck and smashed his palms against his face. Air roared into his throat and back out again. He curled onto his knees and elbows, compressed into a ball. Pain rocketed through his head and liquid oozed from his eye, thick and warm, like the white of a cracked egg.

Winston jumped onto the platform and lunged at the man with the stick, burying his shoulder in his midsection and lifting him into the air, over the edge of the stage, onto the cement plaza. The man landed on his back with an "Ooooff!" and the sound of popping ribs and the smack of his skull on concrete.

Pandemonium swept the area—people yelling, folding chairs collapsing, feet pounding on plywood—but Jack could hear only his own staggered breathing. He rolled onto his right side, still in the fetal position, hands pressed against his face. Suddenly it occurred to him that the worst was yet to come—any second now someone was going to rip away his hands and drive a red-hot poker into his right eye as well. Even in his mind-bending pain, he could hear voices in his head: *The left one is gone, protect the right!*

He pulled his knees up closer, elbows to his sides, and fought the chaos in his brain. A hand touched his, sending a bolt of fear into his chest, forcing him to grip his face tighter. Then he heard a voice.

"Oh, my God!" Molly said. "Somebody help!"

He felt her drop to her knees and cover his body with hers, nuzzling her cheek into rivulets of sweat and blood that covered the back of his neck. She placed her other hand on top of his head and rested her mouth by his ear.

"Hang on," she said, pressing the weight of her body on his.

By now police were on the platform in sufficient numbers to separate combatants and control the damage. A few feet away Graves was on one knee, coughing and holding his throat.

Bishop Tracy, Reverend Jenkins, and Senator Dickey were gone. Victoria and Iggy reached Jack and knelt next to him. Victoria looked up at a policeman and yelled, "We need a doctor!"

"Let's get him inside!" the policeman said. He and Iggy lifted Jack's shoulders; Molly and Victoria lifted his legs, and the four of them carried him off the end of the platform. Winston caught up with them and took Jack's legs from Victoria and Molly.

A policeman guarding the building opened the front door, let them enter, and locked it behind them. As Jack's litter bearers lugged him toward the elevators, a pair of doors opened and a doctor from the clinic stepped out. He saw Jack and motioned for the group to lay him on the marble floor. Kneeling, he said, "I won't hurt you," and tried to peel away Jack's hands. "Let me take a look." He might as well have been talking to stone. Seeing blood, he stood up. "Let's get him upstairs."

They dragged Jack into the elevator and laid him on the floor. The doors closed and the cab rose. Victoria punched the sixth-floor button over and over again, looking at the ceiling as if her line of sight would help draw the elevator upward. Winston and the doctor bent over Jack's head while Molly and Iggy stood at his side.

The elevator door opened, and across the hall a nurse opened the door to the clinic. She and the doctor had been there to keep the facility open in defiance of the rally, not expecting to see patients. The moment the nurse saw the group coming, she grabbed a wheelchair and pushed it under Jack's sagging body.

They wheeled him across the reception room, through the door to the interior hallway, and into one of the small examining rooms. The doctor switched on the light and walked to the sink. "Put him on the table," he said, washing up. To Winston he said, "I need you to stay here and help me get his hands off his face." To the nurse, he said, "Give him five ccs of Xanax." To the others he said, "Out of the room, please."

Iggy left first, followed by Molly, who paused at the door to see Victoria lean down and whisper something in Jack's ear. When Molly reached the reception room, she found Iggy pacing around, agitated, playing with the metal pull at the top of the zipper on his pile jacket. She laid her hand on his arm to calm him, but he yanked it away as if he didn't want her to touch him.

"He's going to be okay," Molly said, surprised at his reaction. He remained distracted, talking to himself as if he hadn't heard her.

The door from the hallway opened and Victoria walked in and sat down. She fished through her shoulder bag for a cigarette, lit it, and rested her neck on the back of the chair as she exhaled.

The front door opened and a policeman entered, assisting a wobbly Eli Graves. "I'm okay," he rasped, walking like a drunk. The policeman steered him to a chair across from Victoria and sat him down. He laid his head back and rubbed the front of his neck.

"Tell the doc to check him out, will you?" the policeman said to Victoria. "And tell him I may have one or two more." Then he left.

Seeing Graves made Molly's skin ripple. Unable to stay close to him, she walked back through the door leading to the examining rooms, leaving Victoria, Iggy, and Eli Graves in the reception area.

Victoria exhaled a lungful of smoke toward the ceiling. Leaning forward to crush out her cigarette, she saw Graves sitting quietly, still nursing his neck. Iggy continued pacing around the room, running his zipper up and down the top six inches of his jacket, walking in circles, slapping at the leather-backed chairs with his head down, lips moving, talking to himself.

Graves paid no attention to him the first time he walked past.

The second time he went still.

He lifted his head slightly, like a jackal catching a downwind scent. Then his eyes widened and his mouth opened with a look of horror, the expression of a passenger just before the plane crashes. He sprang from his chair and grabbed Iggy from behind, throwing one arm around his neck and the other around his chest, choking him and lifting him off his feet.

Victoria saw Iggy's eyes bulging and his tongue sticking out, his hands clawing wildly at Graves's forearm.

"What are you *doing?*" she yelled at Graves. She stood up. "Are you crazy?"

Graves swung Iggy around toward the wall, saying, "It's you!" in a gasp. Keeping an arm around his neck, he tried to reach under Iggy's jacket for something, but Iggy lifted his legs, found the wall, and pushed the two of them backward into Victoria, who was approaching from behind. Instinctively, she threw her arm around Graves's neck, applying the same choke hold on him that he had on Iggy, surprised at her own strength.

"Let go!" she yelled at Graves, and the three of them stood in the middle of the room—Iggy lifted onto his toes by Graves, Graves choked from behind by Victoria, Victoria having no idea what Graves was doing. "Let *go!*" she yelled again.

Graves didn't budge. "His guda key-us!" he said through his pinched windpipe.

"What?" Victoria yelled.

"His guda key-us," Graves rasped. "Datudie-al! Datudie-al!"

It didn't sound like "He's going to kill us!" to Victoria, and even if "Datudie-al!" had sounded like "patchouli oil!" it would have added nothing; she could already smell it on one of these two maniacs.

"Get-go!" Graves sputtered.

That one she understood. "You let go first!" She began pushing the three of them toward the clinic door like a bad vaudeville act.

They reached the door and stopped. Victoria felt Graves begin to weaken under her choke hold. She tightened her grip until he had no choice; he released Iggy, who fell to the floor, gasping. Using all her strength, she pushed Graves into the hallway, slammed the door shut, and turned the dead-bolt lock. Glancing through the wire-mesh window, she saw him feeling his way along the wall, coughing and stumbling toward the elevators.

She turned back to the room. Iggy was resting on one knee like a football player who'd had the wind knocked out of him, massaging his neck. Exhausted, shaking, she sat on the floor across from him with her legs out in front of her, back on her elbows with her head back, trying to catch her breath and come to grips with what was happening. After a moment Iggy rolled over onto the seat of his pants and sat on the floor facing her in the same position as she was, legs extended, elbows propping up his torso, head tilted back. She straightened her head and looked at him. "Are you all right?"

He didn't answer.

She saw that his jacket was unzipped. "Are you—"

She stopped in midsentence, entranced. Strapped around his exposed midsection was something resembling a vest, with vertical objects forming a tan fence of round pickets about eight inches long. She saw the green and red wires running from the tops of them to a khaki device on his belt. She'd never seen anything like it before.

Iggy brought his head upright and stared into her eyes. His face was drawn, his lips white, his eyes unfocused and distant.

"What is that?" she asked, knowing what it was. He didn't answer. "Who are you?"

He looked surprised, as if no one had ever asked him that question before. The answer had been bottled up for so long the words had become ossified, difficult to speak.

"You know who I am," he said. "Everyone calls me Iggy. Unless they call me Eggs."

"Eggs?"

He enjoyed the confusion on her face.

"What should I call you?" she asked in a tinny voice.

"Nothing."

She looked at him silently, assessing his power.

He said, "To you I am nobody."

"That's not true," she said eagerly. "Everybody is somebody."

He smiled the smile of one who knows better.

Her mind raced with the possibilities. Keep talking, she thought. Keep talking until someone arrives.

"You want to know who I *really* am?" he said.

"Who are you really?"

"A missionary."

"A missionary?" He didn't respond. "What kind of a missionary?" She hoped for a long-winded answer.

"A personal one."

His eyes searched hers for a sign that she understood, but she acted as though she understood nothing, least of all that he was a walking bomb wired to what looked like enough explosives to blow them out of the building.

"Tell me about it," she said.

He stared at the ceiling and chuckled. "It was beautiful out there today, wasn't it?"

"Sure was," she said, trying to recall the weather. "Very sunny."

"I mean the way they fell for it," he said, smiling. "Graves and MacLeod, a couple of puppets on a string."

She sat upright and crossed her legs in front of her like a Girl Scout at a campfire.

He brought his head forward and stared at her.

She picked at a dirty spot on the carpet.

He said, "I have to go see the congressman now."

"What for?"

"To give him a message."

"What kind of a message?"

"It's personal."

"You can tell me. I'll give it to him later."

He smiled. "I have to see his face when he gets it."

He rolled over and knelt on one knee, facing the door to the examining room where Jack was lying.

She leaned toward him and said, "We're getting married today."
He looked back at her, surprised. "Married? Why?"
She didn't understand his question. "We're in love."
His mouth turned up at the edges in a disbelieving grin.
"You don't think so?" she said.
"Maybe *you're* in love, but he isn't. He doesn't love anybody." He
turned back toward the room.
"I'm pregnant," she said, stopping him.
He turned. "By the congressman?"
She nodded.
"Good. Then you can come with me."
He'd almost drawn his other foot under his body when she sprang forward, knocking him back onto his hands and knees. He straightened up
and pushed her away, but she grabbed his jacket and pulled him down
onto her. He scrambled off and began crawling for the examining room.
She gathered her feet beneath her, leaped onto his back, and rode him
like a donkey, pulling his hair, yelling, "Stop it! Stop it!"
He reared up on his knees and grabbed her hands to pry them loose
from his scalp, eyes closed in pain.
She heard an elevator ding—someone was on the way!
He heard the sound too and stopped, as if making a decision. Then,
for no apparent reason, he released her hands and went limp.
With his resistance gone, she toppled backward onto the floor, pulling
him down on top of her, his back on her chest. Both of them rested
quietly, breathing hard.
Her nostrils expanded with the smell of something burning.
Her eyes widened. She pushed him off and rolled him onto his back.
Moving quickly, she straddled him, grabbed his hands away from his
chest, and pinned his wrists to the floor, above his head.
It was too easy. He'd made it too easy.
She looked at his right hand and saw the reason.
There, dangling from his fingers, was a metal ring with a pin
attached.
She looked into his eyes and saw two empty craters, the eyes of a
man whose soul had already departed. By the time the smell of the fuse
was fully noxious, the synapses in her brain were firing at the speed of
light, searching frantically for one last thought, one that was exactly
right, hidden in her memory bank, deep among the scars.
She found it a moment before ignition. *You prick*, it would have said
had there been time. *You fucking little prick.*

•   •   •

On the street below, the explosion rocked the building and reverberated between the skyscrapers like thunder rolling through a New York canyon. Chunks of skyline hit the street and bounced like hailstones, and when the rumbling finally stopped, a pink mist of powdered brick, drywall, and human flesh hung lazily in the air, like summer dust in a midwestern barn.

Spectators began filling the street along with siren-screeching, light-flashing vehicles—police, fire, emergency medical. The gawking crowd quickly found its observation points behind safe perimeters and watched the show, fire or water, blood or bodies, whatever chaos and mayhem were proud to offer. Everyone stood silently or pointed or talked in awed tones, passing along rumors that exaggerated or frightened, depending on which satisfied more.

A man in a sweat suit checked his watch and pushed his way through the crowd, bumping into another man wearing a sweater who was trying to extricate himself as well. They found themselves walking down the street together, away from the scene.

"You'd think they could pull this shit during the week and leave the weekends to us, wouldn't you?"

"Tell me about it," the other man said, and they parted.

PART THREE

The vice president of the United States, sitting as president of the Senate, read the final tally.

"Voting for confirmation, sixty-two; against, thirty-six. Judge Abner Jasper Titus is confirmed as the seventeenth chief justice of the United States."

A woman in the gallery wearing a purple headband yelled, "Keep abortion safe!" Two Capitol Hill policemen ran toward her as the vice president, gavel in hand, hit the large wooden plate on his desk, sending a loud reverberation through the chamber.

Abner Titus was sitting in his huge red leather chair in his chambers, telephone in hand, his face relaxed.

"Thank you, Mr. President," he said. "I appreciate your confidence."

He hung up and the group of staff around the desk applauded. Pepper Loomis gave him the biggest smile of all and held out a freshly opened box of chocolate-covered cherries. He reached for one and popped it into his mouth, unable to suppress a grin.

Sitting in his study next to the Oval Office, the president punched a button and spoke to his chief of staff. "I just talked to Titus, in case the press wants to know. It was congratulations, follow your conscience, the usual crap."

"Yes sir."

The president slammed down the telephone and stared at a news briefing on the explosion at the clinic. What in God's name were these maniacs doing? More to the point, what was he doing appointing their champion to the Supreme Court? *You got your pound of flesh, Barbara. Three hundred pounds of it. Blackmail's over.* She could send around her messenger boy Sticks Dickey anytime she wanted, but she wasn't getting anything more. Fuck her. Her eyeballs were bobbing in a cesspool, too: extortion, conspiracy, theft of President Stone's army records. He'd play chicken with her any day.

He called his chief of staff again. "I want to issue a strong statement against clinic violence," the president said.

"It's already being drafted," the aide said. He waited for the president to slam down the phone, as usual. "Anything else?"

"Yeah. Send the first lady two dozen long-stemmed roses."

"What should I say on the card?"

"Tell her—" He paused. "Tell her—" He paused again. "Just tell her they're from me."

"What color do you want?"

"Anything but red."

Now he slammed down the phone.

How could I have been so stupid? How, how, how?

It was after midnight, and Graves was still standing in the unlit front office of the A. J. Lyman Demolition Company, sweating like a thief, pawing through the *B*s in a file drawer lit by a penlight held in his teeth. *Bannicek, Bannister, Benton, Botnick.* No Benedict. Just as there had been no Iggy Pitt, no Anybody Pitt, no Ignatius Somebody, no Eggs Anything. Shit. He flicked off the penlight. *Shit!*

If he didn't find the green sheets before the police did, he was dead.

He stood tapping his finger on the drawer. Calm down, calm down. He'd been there an hour exploring a haystack of personnel folders, searching for a needle revealing where Eggs Benedict lived—a job application, a letter, a W-2, anything. So far, nothing. *Stay calm. Try to think what name he would have used.*

He flicked on the penlight and checked the *E*s again, looking for a name similar to "Eggs"—Egbert, Eggleston, Egmont. Nothing. He shoved the drawer closed with a bang, startling himself like a rabbit. Had anyone heard the noise? He waited. The only playback were the normal noises of the night—trucks passing by, the whoop of a police siren—sounds that made him jumpy but didn't scare him off.

Think, he told himself. Think the way he did.

That was the problem: he didn't know Benedict's mind. He'd launched an assassin deliberately *not* knowing who he was—no name, no traits—nothing that might link the two of them, even inadvertently. He rubbed the back of his neck and covered his face with his hands. *Think. There's gotta be a way to find where he lived.*

He stretched his memory back to their first meeting, the night he'd recruited Benedict as a demolition worker. No help there. He thought back to the meeting with the lawyer for the Baby Does who'd refused to give the police their names—*Who was that guy again?*—and the day he'd bailed them out of jail with a check. *Arnold James.* That's him. Maybe he had Benedict's name and address. He *had* to have it—Benedict was his client. Although . . . wasn't Benedict in jail precisely because he *wouldn't* reveal his name? Maybe not to the police, but he must have given it to his lawyer. Right?

He dropped his hands. What difference did it make? What was he going to do, break into a lawyer's office, too?

He leaned on the filing cabinet, tallying up the mistakes he'd made, how he'd placed a noose around his own neck. Bailing Benedict out of jail . . . recruiting him for a job . . . recommending him to a demolition site that used dynamite. All innocent moves—unless the police found a book of green sheets saying they were part of a criminal conspiracy. Even that wouldn't sink him if he hadn't waved the damn green sheets around for the cameras to see, calling them proof, telling the world they'd come from a golden source, making it look as if he and Benedict were bosom buddies. Sweet Mary. That's *exactly* how it looked. Here he was, Eli Graves, the brilliant archer, launching the ideal assassin, with no strings attached—and all the time the assassin was using him instead!

He took a deep breath. *Get a hold of yourself. Maybe the situation isn't that bad. Take it step by step.*

He pictured himself in a small room, talking to the police . . . denying a conspiracy . . . explaining he had no idea that Mr. Greensheets and Eggs Benedict were one and the same person.

He saw the detectives listening to him.

Regardless of what was written in the notebook, he'd say, he had no idea Benedict was going to steal dynamite and bomb two clinics.

One detective looks at the other. And asks more questions.

No, he'd answer, he didn't fake a windpipe problem so he could get into the clinic and help plant a bomb. Benedict got in by himself.

Yes, it was sheer, dumb luck that he escaped the clinic minutes before the bomb went off.

Yes, a woman smaller than he was had pushed him out the door, leaving herself behind to be killed. But he'd been choked, he'd been weakened.

Yes, Victoria Winters and Jack MacLeod were his sworn enemies, but that was coincidence, not a motive to kill them.

No, no—preaching that abortion clinics should be shut down was *not* inviting zealots to use violence.

Yes, yes— No, no— Wait a minute, you're not listening—

Shit. Back where he started. If he didn't find the green sheets before the police did, he could kiss his butt good-bye.

His butt. In jail. The thought of it swept over him like a wave, taking him back to the putrid moments of his childhood, making his cheeks burn. Damn Sticks Dickey and his straight-arrow bullshit. Even when you played the game by the rules, you still took an arrow through the skull. *How could I have been so stupid? How? How? How?*

Jack MacLeod. Ultimately, everything came back to Jack MacLeod. He was the fountainhead of all Graves despised, every miserable problem in his life. If he got out of this mess, he'd make MacLeod a target, all right. His own way.

He opened the first drawer again, stuck the penlight back into his mouth, and began riffling through the files. The drawers hadn't been cleaned out in years. Eggs Benedict had to be in here someplace.

He looked for a clue—a name that clicked, a photograph, a sheet of green paper, anything that said, "Here I am!"

Nothing.

He reached the last drawer, pulled a group of files halfway out, and riffled through them. Still nothing. Frustrated, he swung a fist and knocked the bunch of them—*Danielli, Demcik, Donaldson, Doerr*—out of the drawer. *I'm dead.*

He shone the penlight onto his watch. One-thirty. His jaw muscles rippled under his cheeks. He knelt down to reassemble the file folders, and as he was putting them in order, saw something interesting. A form filled out in pencil. Very small handwriting. Very similar to Greensheets'.

He lifted the folder carefully, laid it on the top of the steel cabinet, and turned on the penlight. Inside was a job application with the name *B. J. Doerr* at the top.

B. J. Doerr? What the hell kind of a name was B. J. Doerr?

He strained to make a connection. *Baby John Doerr? Baby John Doe?*

He studied the handwriting carefully under his battery-drained light. Doerr, Doe, Diddly-squat—the name didn't matter. The handwriting was definitely Greensheets'.

His eyes dropped to the address line: 616 Avenue B, Apartment 2. Lower East Side of Manhattan. He memorized it, stuffed the folders back into the drawer, and turned off his penlight, then stood perfectly still, repeating the address in a whisper, "Apartment two." He waited for a sign of trouble, someone who'd discovered him there.

Nothing appeared but black air.

*H*ss ... *whoosh* ... *gurgle. Hss* ... *whoosh* ... *gurgle.*

The diver peered through his face mask at a barracuda hovering in front of him, its tail fins waving a slow-motion good-bye. The sounds of the regulator mesmerized him—the hiss of his inhale, the whoosh of his exhale, the gurgle of bubbles wiggling toward the surface.

The sleek fish moved forward as if to see something behind the diver. Then it showed its teeth, grinning like a dog.

The diver pushed his hands and feet against the weight of the water, pirouetting to see what the fish saw. Above him was a woman—arms outstretched, facedown, eyes open—her body rising toward the surface like a hot-air balloon. Her lips were parted but no bubbles escaped her mouth. At first he couldn't see who she was. Then a tightness in his chest told him she was someone important to him . . . someone he loved. Someone like—

He ripped his regulator out of his mouth and extended it toward her, kicking his fins, unable to reach her. He tried to yell, but the cottony water muffled his voice. He moved toward her, but she continued floating away, out of reach. Finally, exhausted, suffocating, he stuck the regulator back into his mouth to save himself. Nothing came out. The hiss was silent, the air gone. He looked up and saw Victoria floating toward the sunlit surface. His heart pounded—compression, fear, panic—

Jack sat up in bed, arms flailing, gasping for oxygen. The rush of air in his throat echoed in his ears, confirming life. Whiteness appeared before his eyes. A covering on his face. Bandages. Plastic tubing taped to his mouth like a snorkel, seawater muting his wounds. He pawed the area around him. Cotton sheets. A bed.

A woman's voice. He felt someone take his hands and pull them away and hold them against a breast. *Victoria—is that you?* The voice spoke quietly, angrily telling someone that this was the second time the regulator had failed—get the hospital engineer up here right away. . . . The hands laid his arms gently back on his chest, and the metallic noises returned . . . the hiss of oxygen, the same hiss he'd heard underwater.

346

Then soft hands again, pushing his head down onto the pillow, stroking his hair lightly. . . . *V? Is that you? Are you all right?* The hands touching him said yes, everything's going to be all right. Then everything began moving in circles . . . merry-go-rounds and rusty Ferris wheels squeaking like a nurse's rubber soles on a tile floor . . . enormous pain in his left side . . . his left shoulder, left arm and leg . . . pain so intense a nurse's needle in his hip went unnoticed.

He gathered his wits and strained to remember. A crowd, a building, an elevator. Suddenly his memory began racing toward him like a sprinter with a torch, ready to illuminate it all. A few seconds more and he'd have it—*an eye—something in your eye—*

The Nembutal beat him to the tape. Gyrating circles closed the sky, swallowing him up and pulling him down into a whirlpool of deep, watery sleep. A comforting, rhythmic sound faded away on the surface, a sound he'd heard before and could almost, but not quite, place.

Hss . . . whoosh . . . gurgle. Hss . . . whoosh . . .

E

li Graves stood in the graffiti-splashed hallway, straining in the dim fluorescent light to see the numeral on the door. The tarnished number 2 hung crooked in the center. He looked over his shoulder, then slipped the credit card between the door and the jamb and jiggled it, hoping the lock was spring-loaded. The plastic slipped off the bolt—*crack!*

He took a breath. *Take your time. Do it the way you did in high school. Nice and easy.*

He tightened his surgeon's gloves and tried again. The hard plastic touched something; he wiggled it carefully and felt the bolt move. *Don't lose it.* The card achieved an angle, and—*click!* He turned the knob and the door opened.

He wiped the moisture from the worry lines above his eyebrows and entered the room, quietly pulling the door closed. Standing still, he let his eyes adjust to the nighttime shadows, listening to the clatter of a midnight garbage truck on the street. He felt the wall for a light switch, hesitating. Light meant trouble, but light would let him search. He had to take the chance.

He flipped on a bare bulb hanging over a round table, illuminating the room. A Murphy bed occupied the middle, with a kitchenette at one end and a bicycle standing in a space that led to a bathroom around the corner. He looked around and took it in. What a pigsty. He could tear the place apart and nobody'd even know he'd been there.

He started with the baker's rack next to the door: paperback novels, a Styrofoam coffee cup, detective stories, a pot of dirt without a plant, a pair of bicycle gloves. No green sheets.

Don't rush it. Be systematic.

He moved to a round table between the kitchenette and bed. On top was an envelope addressed to someone. *Bingo.* The handwriting was Eggs's. Spread over the tabletop were all manner of things—a dirty plate, an opened can of SpaghettiOs, a glass with dried amber in the bottom, a cereal bowl, a half tomato curling at the edges, a tin container lined with unpopped kernels of corn. There were miscellaneous papers, magazines, newspaper clippings, and scissors—the Dodgers cap and

348

horn-rim glasses Eggs wore—electronic tools and devices, wires, diodes, soldering iron, pliers, tape, screwdrivers, and an X-Acto knife as clean and sharp as a scalpel. Graves touched the things with the back of his latex-covered fingers, momentarily wondering how they fit into the puzzle of a life. Then he continued searching.

He stepped into the kitchenette and explored the area quickly—opening and closing drawers and wooden cabinets, looking under the cutting board, inside the broken wicker basket of unpaid bills and torn envelopes, under the sink, behind the empty box of powdered soap, inside the tiny refrigerator with a stalk of wilted celery. Nothing. *Take your time. You've got time.*

He stepped over to the Murphy bed and patted the graying sheets and a pilled wool blanket balled up on the stained mattress ticking. No papers there. He lifted the mattress and found a skin magazine resting on the springs. He held it up by its spine, disgusted, and shook it. Nothing fell out, not even a centerfold. He dropped the magazine and the mattress and looked around.

A club chair beckoned. He walked to it and touched a tuft of cotton in a hole on the soiled armrest. Moving aside a pair of jeans and a bicycle helmet, he lifted the cushion. A dulled nickel, peanut shells. No diary. He dropped the cushion halfway into place and stood up, red-faced, frustrated.

He stepped onto the braided rug in front of a chest of drawers. On top of it were a hardware-store receipt, an empty Domino's pizza box, a stack of Ace Messenger Service receipt forms, and a framed photograph of a small boy standing on a wooden porch between an unsmiling, rotund woman and a tall, austere man. American Gothic, circa 1979. *Is that him?*

He opened the top drawer and once again began chastising himself as he searched. Jeremy Hackett had told him not to trust the guy. A cigar box full of paraphernalia appeared—a set of keys, a broken Mickey Mouse watch. He saw a small velvet case and opened it and found a Purple Heart. After touching it respectfully, he resumed his search, still angry with himself for having been sucked in. Until the last batch of green sheets, everything had been so detailed, so accurate. So convincing.

He closed the drawer and searched the others—wooden dowels about eight inches long, a roll of brown paper, a bottle of Elmer's glue, an opened box of Quaker Oats. The stuff of fake dynamite.

He shoved the bottom drawer closed, bent forward, and laid his cheek on the rug to look underneath the chest. He couldn't leave until he'd searched every inch. If they caught him and threw him into the slammer—

The slammer. Suddenly being on his hands and knees thinking of a jail cell made his palms sweat. He rose quickly and squeezed past the bicycle in the hallway leading to the bathroom.

A closet door caught his attention. Opening it, he was hit by a pungent odor. He pulled a string hanging down and turned on a bare light bulb. On the floor was dirty clothing; leaning against the wall was a broomstick. He grabbed it and poked at the pile of clothes, lifting them like burning leaves, pushing them to the rear until only a T-shirt remained. He slipped the tip of the pole under it and felt it snag something. Pushing the shirt aside, he saw nothing.

He bent down for a closer look—nothing there—and ran his fingers over the smooth wooden floor. Weird. Nothing there. He pulled off a glove, drew his fingertip across the surface again and touched something—a nail head, flush with the floorboards but slightly loose.

He slipped his fingernail under it smoothly and popped it up, forming a tiny retractable handle. Pinching it between his fingers, he pulled, and up came a two-foot-square section of the floor. He pushed the clothes out of the way and propped the section against the wall, then bent forward to take a look.

Beneath the boards was a black three-ring notebook.

He lifted it out and stood up to bring it closer to the overhead bulb. Under the cover he could see green pages of notes in Eggs's small handwriting—newspaper clippings glued neatly in place, glossy photographs of people and buildings with explanatory notes, arrows, and dates, magazine articles, diagrams, and more handwritten notes.

Praise the Lord.

He wanted to page through it madly, looking for his name, searching for words that joined him in a conspiracy, but the light was bad, and he was a burglar, and what mattered most was that he'd found it. Better to get back to his rented room and examine it right.

He knelt down for one last look. Nothing evident, but beneath the floorboards was unsearched space. He reached under and felt something, a piece of fabric. Grabbing it, he pulled out a bag made of black parachute cloth.

He laid it on the floor, unzipped it, and withdrew a long, round object. At first he thought it was a wooden dowel like the ones he'd found in the drawer. Then he saw that he was wrong, it was the real thing. Holding it—merely touching it—made his mouth go dry.

He set the stick on the floor and reached into the bag and found three more just like it. And four dynamite caps, and a fake beard and a tube of spirit gum.

Thunk.

The sound of the downstairs door. Footsteps coming up the wooden stairs! He sat still holding his breath, praying for the angel of death to pass over.

The footsteps continued. Two sets of them.

He stuffed the things into the black bag and stood up. A man's voice in the hallway—shoe leather outside the door. He gathered up the parachute bag, his latex glove, and the black notebook and turned toward the bathroom.

Someone knocked on the apartment door.

He slipped into the bathroom, light switch off, and waited with the door slightly ajar.

Lowered voices, the jangle of keys, the sound of metal slipping into a lock.

Shit!

He looked around the bathroom and saw city lights filtering through a window above the toilet.

The door to the studio opened. "Anybody home?" a man's voice said.

He placed his gloved finger under the brass pull on the window, lifted, and stuck his head outside. He was two stories up, nothing below but a huge Dumpster across the alley, sitting beneath a trash chute.

The hallway door to the apartment banged closed. "Well, the lady was right about a light being on," a man's voice said. "Hello? Anybody here?"

He licked his lips, merging thought and action. He closed the bathroom door carefully—flushed his gloves down the toilet—and dropped the seat with a loud, innocent bang. With the toilet running, he held the black bag outside the window and shot it straight ahead as hard as he could, like a basketball. It formed a gentle arc and dropped into the far corner of the Dumpster—*poomp!* He turned around and took a breath. Then, holding the black notebook, he opened the bathroom door and walked out.

Rounding the corner, he stopped, seemingly startled. In front of him was a grizzled old man in a janitor's work clothes and a young policeman in uniform.

"Who are you?" the policeman asked.

"I'm a friend of Eggs's."

"Who's Eggs?" the janitor said. "Nobody here named Eggs."

Graves walked toward them with a forced smile, angry for having used a name.

"Hold it right there," the officer said. He unsnapped the leather strap that held his service revolver in place.

"But I'm a friend of—"

"Raise your hands."

Graves's shoulders slumped and he shook his head. "Look, I can explain—"

"Hands!"

Graves laid the notebook on the chair and raised his hands. The policeman patted him down from his chest to his knees. *Stay calm. Talk your way out of it.*

"You got some ID?" the officer asked.

Once he's got my name, I'm finished.

Graves moved his hand to his back pocket as if to retrieve his wallet, forming a fist behind him. He brought it out in a roundhouse swing, hitting the policeman squarely on the side of the head, knocking him to the floor.

Graves and the superintendent stared at the inert body. The superintendent looked up at Graves and took a step backward, frightened. Graves licked his lips and rubbed his forehead. Then he grabbed the three-ring binder off the chair and bolted out the door, down the wooden steps, and onto the sidewalk.

Toward a squad car that had pulled up at the curb.

Into the chest of the policeman who'd just stepped out.

Jack woke up seeing nothing but whiteness in his right eye and blackness in his left.

"Anybody here?" he asked in a gravel voice. No answer.

He lifted his right hand to his face—his left was still immobilized—and touched the gauze covering his eyes. His fingers found the lower edge of the tape and pried it upward, pulling back the patch and exposing a fuzzy view of a thumb. *I can see.* His neck muscles relaxed and his head dropped back onto the pillow.

He ran his hand along the side of the bed until it found a nurse's call button. He pushed it, firmly—not for a nurse, but for his wife. *Wife?* Had he and Victoria gotten married? Waiting, he searched his memory for what had happened. He remembered a demonstration, pain in his left eye, Victoria at his side—and nothing.

He heard someone enter the room and approach the bed. "Hello there," a man's voice said. Fingers lifted Jack's wrist and took his pulse.

"Where am I?" Jack asked.

"New York Hospital." The doctor let go and Jack could hear the click of a pen and writing. "You've had a pretty good sleep the last three days."

He peeled back the covering on Jack's right eye. Jack saw a tiny white light with an eyeball attached to it. The light went out and the room returned to dusk.

"What time is it?" Jack asked.

"Three in the morning. Can you see this?" The doctor held up two fingers.

"Two. Where's my—where's Victoria?"

The doctor pulled the gauze back down over his eye and pressed the tape onto his cheekbone. "I'm a resident here, Congressman. You want to talk to Dr. Stein."

Bad answer. "What happened? I can't remember."

"You had a piece of wallboard embedded in your scalp and you've got contusions along your left side and a broken left leg."

"From what?"

"A bomb."

Bomb? "What kind of bomb?"

"In the women's clinic, on Park Avenue. Where do you hurt most?"

"Left side. What clinic? Where's Victoria?"

"Hold on a second," the doctor said.

Another bad answer.

Jack heard the sound of glass and plastic on a steel tray. The doctor inserted a syringe in a medicine port and injected liquid into an intravenous line.

Jack heard the syringe laid on the tray and felt the morphine begin its cool flood. "Who else got hurt?"

"The man who helped carry you into the clinic, Winston Jones, is in critical condition, still unconscious."

Jack felt the circles beginning to descend on him. "Who else?" he said in a slight slur.

"A woman reporter was injured—"

"Molly?" For some reason the word *incest* prodded his temple, making no sense.

"She had a severe concussion. The doctor who was attending your eye injury died this morning. His nurse had a pair of forceps blown through her neck, but she'll recover, minus her larynx." He paused. "Congressman? Can you hear me?"

Jack lay perfectly still, trying to reject history, dissolve facts, make time stand still. Once again he felt the doctor lift his forearm to check his pulse, but this time he grabbed the man's wrist.

"I'm not going to ask you again—what happened to Victoria?"

The doctor remained still. "I'm sorry, Congressman. She died in the explosion."

Jack felt his throat close. "And the baby?" He knew the answer, but wanted to hear it.

"I'm afraid so."

He released the man's arm and let himself fall into the pool of morphine. Spirals carried him back to another time and place . . . a hot summer day in Brooklyn . . . a warehouse roof above the East River, blistering sun, fish-scented air . . . tourists chugging by on the Circle Line. He felt himself leaping off the parapet . . . Geronimo . . . stomach in the throat, body surrendering to gravity . . . down toward that magic moment . . . *Let me feel it once more, right now* . . . when he'd plunge through the cold, black surface into another world, leaving the hot, stinking, real one . . . far . . .

Behind.

Graves sat at a police-station desk with his wrists manacled, a telephone in one hand, the other cupped around the mouthpiece for privacy. As if the police, pimps, and prostitutes were actually interested in his conversation.

"What did he say?" he asked.

"He wouldn't let me discuss it," Sticks Dickey said.

Graves paused in disbelief. "He wouldn't—you didn't even talk to him?"

"When I told him why I was calling, he cut me off and said there was nothing he could do."

"That bastard!"

"Eli, listen. You don't wake up the chief justice of the United States in the middle of the night and ask him to bail somebody out of jail in New York City! That's not how Washington works!"

"Bullshit! You didn't even call him, did you?"

"Eli—"

"If he can take a call from a killer trying to avoid the electric chair, he can take a call from me! He wouldn't even *be* on the Supreme Court if it wasn't for me!"

"That's a bit of an exaggeration, Eli—"

"Like hell it is! He owes me!"

Dickey exhaled into the receiver. "How bad did you hurt the guy?"

Graves hesitated. "They say he's still unconscious."

"Jesus, Eli, I can't fix that with a telephone call. You need a lawyer. Where's Jeremy Hackett?"

"Out of town. Now listen. Call Titus back and tell him if he calls the desk sergeant and vouches for me, they'll release me on my own recognizance. Then we can deal with this when Jeremy gets back."

"Eli—"

"Listen to me! If I spend one minute in jail because Titus won't make a simple telephone call, there's gonna be hell to pay! He wants to make an enemy out of me? Let him try!"

The police sergeant tapped Graves on the shoulder. "Time's up," he said, reaching for the phone.

"Call him back!" Graves said into the mouthpiece as the policeman pulled the receiver away. "Tell him he owes me!"

The officer laid the receiver on its cradle and reached out and unlocked the handcuffs. Graves rubbed his wrists and surveyed the room, hoping to see someone who could get him out of there.

"Belt and necktie," the sergeant said flatly. He opened a large manila envelope, and Graves dropped in his personal effects—wallet, coins, his pocket calendar. He pulled off his necktie and dropped it in, too. "My lawyer will be here any minute," he said, stalling.

"I'm real happy to hear that. We'll make you comfortable till he shows up."

"Comfortable?" Graves stripped off his belt. "I haven't even got a toothbrush!"

He heard a single laugh and turned to see a tall man in a red satin cape and boots sitting at the next desk, staring through a haze of cigarette smoke, eyelids at half-mast. "Forget the toothbrush, chicken," he said. "Where you going, you gonna need more'n a little stick to keep the man off that cute little butt."

The mirror was heartless. The left side of his head was swathed in bandages running on an angle from his forehead down over his eye and ear; on his cheeks and neck were bruises and cuts—some stitched, some scabby. Every joint was swollen, every muscle bruised, even the bottoms of his feet. He leaned against the hospital sink to catch his breath and let the air bathe the dampness on his back through his hospital gown, waiting for the dizziness to pass and the pounding in his damaged left eye to subside. After a moment he looked into the mirror again. The unscathed right side of his face made the left all the more grotesque, the phantom of the opera's. The moment of explosion flashed through his mind—visions of Victoria's torn body—sickening him like his own image.

He looked away.

Leaning on a chair he'd used for a walker, Jack began inching his way back to the bed. Waiting for him at the foot of it was a black binder the nurse said Detective Norman Pulaski had dropped off earlier in the day with a request that he read it, when he felt up to it, so that they could discuss it later. Getting into bed was more painful than getting out. The morphine was wearing off.

He rested on his back for a moment, then dragged the book up to his side and propped it against his raised right knee. Opening it, he saw a sheaf of photocopied papers. What was this, a copy of Eli Graves's notebook? His eyes fell on a handwritten line at the top: *"There is no truth in him; he is a liar and the father of lies." John 8:44.* Who was he referring to?

At first the diary was so jumbled and disorganized it was difficult to read. Appearing between pages of newspaper clippings, newsletters, and magazine articles were bits and pieces of interviews with people who had known something about Jack's teenage life, and angry, stream-of-consciousness ramblings about a mother's death, a lost childhood, missing love. He read it curiously. He had no idea Graves had lived such a difficult life.

The handwritten notes appeared everywhere—in copies of pencil, pen, on scraps of whatever paper had been handy—all of them in one way or another condemning Jack MacLeod. He knew Graves hated him—but *this*? This was out of control.

He saw references to earlier events in Graves's life, like his being in the Army Corps of Engineers—funny, he didn't remember seeing that on his résumé—where he'd been tagged with the nickname "Eggs," which he hated. "Eggs"? Eli Graves was called "Eggs"? After arriving in New York, the diary said, he assumed the name of a friend he'd known in his first foster home—a fellow named Ignatius X. Pitt—

Ignatius Pitt? *This is* Iggy's *diary?*

He turned the page.

There were more newspaper articles about Jack. Between them, Iggy had written that he'd discovered the identity of his birth parents when he was fifteen, during a stay at his tenth foster home in East Syracuse.

Jack's head began to pound.

Iggy wrote that his mother had died in childbirth and his father had shown no interest in him, abandoning him at birth, never searching for him, never caring, treating him like so much human garbage.

Jack pulled himself up into a sitting position, oblivious of the pain it caused.

"He makes a virtue of baby killing," Iggy wrote. *"He crusades for legislation to kill the innocent. He should repent for his sins, but he doesn't. He makes them worse."*

Barely recognizing himself, Jack finally recognized himself.

Iggy? Honey gave birth to Iggy? *Iggy Pitt is my son?*

He closed his eyes and once again felt himself spinning on a tilted axis. Iggy Pitt, his *son*? The man who killed Victoria and her baby? Saying his father didn't *care* about him? Twenty-five years of worry, bewilderment and guilt—for this? What kind of insanity was he uncovering? What cosmic trick was being played?

His mind ratcheted backward, lost in a welter of questions. He lay back for a moment, then opened his unbandaged eye and turned the page.

Iggy explained how he'd set about his mission, tracking his father to New York, taking work as a part-time actor and construction worker, adopting two personas—the bearded Eggs, the smooth-cheeked Iggy—amused at how easy and useful the duplicity was. Researching back issues of the newspapers, he'd discovered a story about Congressman MacLeod and Winston Jones announcing the formation of a halfway house called Wings. He took a room and a part-time job there, ingratiating himself with Winston, patiently bringing himself closer to his prey. He learned that his father and Eli Graves were bitter, volatile enemies, which gave him strategic ideas about how to exact his revenge. He told of attending rallies given by the Red Rose Society—he liked those people because they tried to save people like himself from people like his father—and of feeding Eli Graves information about the congressman.

Then one day he caught a break: after he'd been arrested at a protest rally and booked as a nameless Baby John Doe, a lawyer named Arnold James had bailed him out of jail and told him the Red Rose Society was looking for qualified demolition workers.

His days in the army were useful at last.

He wrote about the night of the meeting to recruit workers, how he introduced himself to Graves and got a job with Lyman Demolition, how Graves had invited him to attend his sidewalk press conference and look for "targets of opportunity"—Graves's simpleminded, transparent invitation to target Congressman MacLeod. How funny. If only he knew. He loved what he'd felt that night—pursuing his secret quest, being in control of things, having power over people. Almost like the power he'd held over the puppets in Mrs. McFee's cellar, years before in his seventh foster home. He loved the feeling he'd had that night, staying up until dawn, excited and energized, sharpening his plans, aware that events were finally turning his way.

Jack turned the page.

Iggy wrote that with Winston's help he'd found a job as a bicycle messenger, which helped him uncover people like Jeanie Anders, his mother's best friend, who told him about Honey moving to Syracuse and Jack stealing money to send her to Harrisburg for an abortion. Of course his father would do that. He expected that.

He wrote about Angus Brody, who had been one of Jack's poker-playing buddies. Brody had been an especially good find, eventually confirming the kind of corrupt character Iggy had always suspected in his father, including how he'd gone berserk in the funeral home basement one night. Brody explained that he'd tried to stop him, but MacLeod had pulled a knife, put it to Brody's throat, and made his escape, leaving Honey O'Connor's body on the mortician's table, naked and defiled. Two other poker players who'd been there could confirm the story, Brody said, but Iggy didn't need to talk to them. He knew the truth when he heard it. He could just *feel* the truth about his father.

Jack closed his eyes.

The nurse entered with a tray of food, set it on a rolling table over his knees, and left. Nauseated by its smell, he pushed it away and turned back to the notebook.

Iggy wrote about Graves's sidewalk press conference, and how Winston had asked him to drop by Wings to answer a few questions from Congressman MacLeod, questions about Shivers and Moon. Imagine that! Being invited to meet the man you were stalking! If that wasn't a sign God was with him, nothing was.

He wrote about his anxiety as the day of the meeting approached. How he'd walked into the room and finally met his father—he was close enough to touch him!—surprised at how ordinary he was, so normal it had confused him, churning his stomach and making him numb. After answering harmless questions about Melvin Shivers and Harley Moon, he'd gone to the bathroom and vomited, calming his nerves.

Emerging from the bathroom, he'd joined MacLeod and Winston Jones as they headed out to listen to Eli Graves on the sidewalk next door. Walking with them, he'd experienced an insane urge to admit who he was—to embrace his father and forgive him and become his son, at last. The feeling was so intense it reminded him of the time he'd visited Niagara Falls and, mesmerized by the roaring water, felt an urge to leap over the railing. Feeling it again scared him, so he prayed for guidance and received it through scripture. *"Satan disguises himself as an angel of light,"* 2 Cor. 11:14, God reminded him. *"The serpent was more crafty than any other wild animal,"* Gen. 3:1. Evil loved to take the guise of the commonplace and the virtuous, but he wouldn't be tricked. By the time he reached the crowd that had gathered for the press conference, he felt stronger than ever. He'd survived his brief temptation in the wilderness and couldn't be led astray, not even by the pull of blood. *He killed my mother/He tried to kill me/He kills innocent life/Wherever it may be,* he wrote on the margins of a Congressman MacLeod newsletter. His father had tried to kill him when he was still in his mother's womb. If the congressman had his way, he'd pass legislation destroying millions of other babies, too. In the name of simple decency—in the name of all that was holy—for the sake of life itself, he had an obligation to take a shot back.

Breathing harder, Jack turned the page.

Iggy described his mission as if it were a secret courtship—everything exciting, everything possible. He wrote about the exhilaration he felt at the press conference as he watched Eli Graves using the green sheets he'd sent him, accusing MacLeod of fornication and teenage pregnancy and the sexual sins of youth. And then, most gratifying of all, watching his father peppered by reporters with the question Iggy loved most—*Where is the child? What happened to the child?* All while the child was standing right there *next* to him!

He wrote how he had run alongside the reporters as they pursued Congressman MacLeod, and how he saw a pretty woman reporter trip and fall, sprawling onto the sidewalk, skinning her knees. He'd gone to her aid, lifting her up and helping her to Wings for first aid, which had turned out to be another stroke of luck, allowing him to befriend Molly McCormick, who pulled some strings and got him an internship with her television crew. It had been sickening to see her fall in love with his father, and yet their love affair, coupled with revelations Molly had made about herself during the time they'd spent together covering stories, had given him vital grist for his green sheets. She was the right age to be Jack's child; her baby quilt had come from East Syracuse; she'd been orphaned at birth; the two of them had been photographed at the Park Avenue abortion clinic. With certain embellishments, these things had laid the foundation for a credible case of incest, teeing up an angry Eli Graves to make a wild, public provocation that would give Iggy his moment to strike. Molly's lust for his father would not only help him destroy the man, but do it with an indelible moral stain. After all, merely finishing him off, which he could do at will, was not enough. It had to be without a trace of public sorrow, or redemption, or martyrdom, even among baby killers of his own kind.

Jack's chest muscles tightened in pain.

Iggy wrote about his trip to Syracuse to interview Honey's senile aunt—how he'd introduced himself as Eli Graves, hoping she'd call the congressman and tell him about the visit, fueling his paranoia and making him that much easier to manipulate. *Just like one of Mrs. McFee's puppets.*

He wrote about his first crew assignment as a Channel Six intern, helping Molly cover an explosion at an abortion clinic in Queens—the very same clinic he and Billy Bannister had bombed the night before. Was Molly's request for his help a quirk of fate? Not a chance. It had to be deliberate, part of a plan. God's plan. Like bombing the clinic itself. "His will be done."

He explained how he and Bannister had executed the bombing, and how it was intended to prepare him for another one later. Stealing the dynamite, casing the target, unexpectedly finding the janitor's wife inside the clinic—these things had provided valuable lessons, proving that he could keep his head when the heat was on, proving that Billy Bannister couldn't. He was sorry about the janitor's wife's death, but compared with all the babies who would live as a result of closing down the clinic, clearly it had been a justifiable thing to do. "To make an omelette, you have to break some eggs."

Jack exhaled and turned the page.

Iggy wrote that he had met Abner Titus and obtained his autograph. Jack stopped reading. *Abner Titus? Iggy was in touch with Abner Titus?*

He read quickly, scanning the pages for more information linking the two of them. He found nothing more. On the other hand, there were chronological gaps in the narrative, pages that appeared to be missing. Who knew what their relationship had been?

The coin is good luck after all, Iggy wrote next. Whatever that meant.

Jack closed the binder on his finger and took a breather. His mind remained loyal to him, but his heart was fast becoming a traitor—pleading guilty to Iggy's indictment, bowing to his hatred. Anyone willing to give his life for a cause—even this one—revealed devotion too immense to be ignored.

With his throat tightening, Jack reopened the book and continued reading.

The final pages had been written the night before the bombing. The days leading up to the rally had been the most satisfying days of his life, Iggy said. Devising plans, adjusting to circumstances, being nimble, being *effective.* He had enjoyed drawing Eli Graves into his web—establishing the credibility of the green sheets, conditioning him for the false story of Jack and Molly—knowing that a lie fed to a receptive mind was the most powerful truth of all.

And then, Iggy's final summation, his true feelings about his father. Iggy had found it immensely satisfying seeing this Judas flounder and suffer, never knowing what accusation would hit him next, wobbling off balance and confused right up to the end. He didn't know precisely how the assassination would unfold the next day; he'd do his best to drop the bomb-laden vest next to MacLeod and make his escape before it went off. But if he couldn't engineer a time and place for that, if he had to, he'd use the friction fuse instead. Either way, he couldn't fail, because he was committed to do whatever it took to succeed. Regardless of the cost.

Jack turned the page and saw a photocopied document. A birth certificate. St. Luke's Hospital, East Syracuse, NY. *Be it known that on this thirteenth day of April, 1970, Baby Boy Smith was born to Mary O'Connor Smith and _____ .* He stopped reading at the empty space reserved for his own name, the space for the father. Instinctively, his finger touched the paper, as it would have the baby, had it been there. The creases where it had been folded were frayed and dirty, the sections between them puffed up like patches of a quilt, shaped by the curves of a human body. He looked down and saw a stamp marking the date the copy had been issued. November 14, 1982. His son had carried his birth certificate in his wallet since he was twelve years old.

Jack turned the page one more time.

The final passage in the diary was a eulogy to old Mrs. McFee and lonely days gone by. Days when she had told Iggy he was no good—she always said it twice—*"You good for nothing no-good"*—and cuffed him on the ears, exploding air into his head, deafening him before pushing him down the cellar stairs and locking the door behind. He remembered how he'd slink to his secret place behind the abandoned coal stoker, the place he'd hidden his puppets, the only place he'd ever felt safe in his whole life. He wrote that the blows to his ears didn't stop him from having his fun because the puppets talked *inside* his head, saying what he wanted them to say, doing what he wanted them to do—like giving each other hugs and kisses and make-believe hot cocoa at bedtime, and telling each other stories to the sound of an imaginary music box. Like kissing old Mrs. McFee good night, sweetly—then taking her by the hand, and leading her to the cellar door, and kicking her down the steps and holding her on the cement floor and jumping up and down on her and hitting her with their little fists and aiming a make-believe gun at her head and pulling the trigger and blowing it off—*koosh!* Like seeing her die.

Tomorrow, the bomb would be for Mrs. McFee as well as for his father.

Jack closed the diary and laid it on his stomach. Weeping, he closed his eyes and locked himself in a tomb until morning.

Eli Graves gripped the steel frame of his cell bed and buried his face in a pillow, trying to escape the pain that filled his body by imagining himself in another time and place. He pictured a sunny day in Golden Gate Park, running on the sod next to Mini and Maxi and their hippie friends, laughing as they rolled along a ten-foot ball of newspapers. . . . *Oh, God, I'm losing my breath.* . . . He imagined the soft feel of the grass under his feet, springy and cool, and the smell of fresh earth and the girl from Indiana who drew pictures of naked people on the sidewalk with pastel chalk—*Stop saying those words!*—the only time he could remember seeing naked people who looked harmless instead of disgusting—*No, no—don't think about naked—it'll push you into the pit!*

A pair of hands lathered the sweat on his skin and another pair pushed his face deeper into the pillow, breaking his concentration. He needed to find another image fast, or slide into the hole.

He pictured his first year in medical school, dissecting his cadaver, watching the other students turn pale and drop their heads between their knees, not him. He hated cutting flesh as much as the next guy, hated knowing that a few days earlier his corpse had been a living, breathing person, eating dinner and watching television with a wife or friend. Still, he made the cut, because he knew how to *concentrate.* He knew how to close out the world and blot out the extraneous, even what was happening to him right now. He knew how to survive, just as he would tonight. *Relax and breathe, relax and breathe. You're not here, you're someplace else. Don't grip the bed so hard . . . relax and breathe.*

The rocking motion of his body threatened to bring him into the present. Quickly, his mind warped time in a new direction . . . to a small sailboat outside the Golden Gate Bridge . . . huge, lazy swells towering over the craft before lifting it and passing beneath, lowering it into a trough and raising it up again, over and over. He counted forty waves without breaking his concentration—then reality loomed on the crest of the forty-first, promising to bury him in a mountain of filth and humiliation. *How much longer? . . . how long? . . . how long?*

Once again his imagination was failing. He needed a stronger antidote, a counterpain so lethal it would kill the one he was feeling beneath his belly button. He rotated his hand forward on the bed pipe and found the bent nail that had rescued him from the same fate only a few hours before. This time he dug it into the center of his other hand, piercing the flesh and sending a bolt of lightning up his arm into his head, momentarily blinding him. Fresh beads of sweat blossomed on his forehead—*Thank God, it's working*—giving him time to compose a new distraction. Memories of sunshine and good times were too soft now—he needed an image full of rage, something that would consume him and save him from the pit.

He'd already exhausted images of MacLeod, watching him standing in a lake of burning oil.

This time he'd use someone he hated almost as much. Abner Titus.

He pictured the chief justice striding down a Supreme Court hallway in a black robe, passing him by without so much as a glance, even though his wretched body was there to see, right in front of him, on his hands and knees as he was now, begging for mercy. *Oh, Christ, no more.* He pictured Titus on the witness stand in court—*Oh, God, I can't breathe!*—confessing that he was a merciless monster—*relax, breathe, relax, breathe*—admitting that, yes, of course he could have saved Eli Graves with a simple telephone call to a police station or with a signature on a bureaucratic form—*Hold on! Hold on!*—costing him nothing, sparing Graves the indignity, the hurt of—*Don't say the word! Don't say the word! Don't admit what they're doing to you! It'll throw you into the pit!*

He pressed his face down into the pillow and drove the nail half an inch into his palm, praying for one more image to set him free, one nightmare stark enough to stave off the one he was enduring.

He pictured Titus being led away to a jail cell just like this one, placed on his hands and knees—*What's that sound?*—held down the way he was being held down right now. *Sounds like an animal.* He imagined himself in the cell with Titus, walking toward the judge's naked backside with a stick of dynamite in hand—*like the howl of a dog caught in a trap*—nodding to the same men who were holding him down and assaulting him now, telling them to spread the judge instead—*a dog howling in pain*—then inserting the stick in his rear end and lighting the fuse and watching it burn down until—

A bolt of pain in his rectum broke the image and lifted his head from the pillow, opening his ears to the sound of the animal's baying. For a split second the sound belonged to someone else, then he recognized it for whose it was: his own. Tears and mucus vibrated on his face; his neck became streaked with veins and his voice turned hoarse and cracked as he continued howling against the pain—howling to reignite the imagined fuse he'd lit in Abner Titus's butt, howling to watch it burn down and erupt into a ball of heat, vaporizing the chief justice and everything around him—the cell, the prisoners, the iron bars—the whole filthy, disgusting, sex-crazed world—leveling it to a wasteland, silent, and flat, and *white!*—

He saw a tremendous flash inside his head, heard steel girders snapping in his neck, and as he imagined, watched the world turn silent and flat and white. Not from a maddened dream of Abner Titus exploding, but from a real, live fist that had come crashing down on the back of his neck, silencing the peculiar guttural screams of a man being raped and cracking his vertebrae in two places.

Jack fitted a pair of crutches under his arms and hobbled out the door and down the hall. Dizzy, perspiring, he found the room and peeked inside. Winston's mother sat next to her son with her elbows on his bed and her hands folded in front of her. Jack came up behind her and placed his palm on her shoulder, saying nothing. She glanced up at him and covered his hand with hers.

He looked down at his friend. Brain-wave monitors had been attached to his bandaged head, and his face was a rainbow of bruises. An oxygen tube, thin and inadequate, was taped into his nostrils. He slept as if he hadn't moved in days, which he hadn't; his lips were slightly parted and covered with Vaseline. The neurologist said that after three days in a coma, the longer it continued, the smaller his chances for recovery.

Winston Jones—the tough, sarcastic survivor, always helping other people—now fighting all alone. It seemed so unlikely. So unjust.

He gave Mrs. Jones's hand a squeeze and left.

He hobbled down the hall and knocked on Molly's door. Hearing no answer, he opened it and saw her lying asleep on her back, a large bouquet of flowers on the table next to her. He entered quietly and moved to the side of her bed. She had sustained cuts and bruises and a concussion that left her lapsing in and out of consciousness. He leaned his crutches against the table and sat on the edge of the mattress, feeling a painful knot forming in his chest.

She opened her eyes. And then her lips: "You look terrible," she said in a raspy voice. She tried to raise her hand. "You need a shave."

He took her hand and held it. Then he leaned over and embraced her, inhaling the stale smell of her hair.

"Are you really awake?" he asked, sitting up.

"I've been awake since yesterday, but I keep falling back asleep."

"No one told me," he said.

"They don't tell you anything around here. Not even how I got here. Except there was a bomb."

"Do you remember anything?"

She strained for memory. "I remember the clinic, waiting for Graves

367

to leave." She looked like a child about to open a report card. "You're not really my father, are you?"

"No," he said, shaking his head.

Her cheek muscles softened. "I didn't think so."

"Something worse," he said.

An alarm went off behind her eyes. "What? Tell me, Jack. Please. I want to know everything."

A nurse opened the door to Molly McCormick's room and stopped dead in her tracks, her face flushing with embarrassment. There, on the bed, were two people on their sides, holding each other closely, rocking back and forth gently, apparently in the act of making love.

And indeed they were, although not in the way the nurse assumed. Had she found them embracing in front of a casket, mourning vertically instead of horizontally, she would have understood at once what they were doing.

For the next week Jack visited Molly and Winston every day.

For the next month Victoria and her baby visited Jack every night.

"They tell me you're lucky to be alive," Detective Pulaski said.

"Yeah, that's me. Mr. Lucky." Jack hobbled back to the leather couch in the surgeons' lounge, which had been made available for the interview. "Either of you care for some coffee? There's a machine in the hall."

"No thanks," Pulaski said. His partner, "Bazooka Joe" Wilson, shook his head, too. "We just had lunch."

Pulaski waved at Jack to sit down. He dropped onto the sofa and lifted his plaster-covered left leg onto a coffee table.

Pulaski and Wilson drew up two chairs and sat. Pulaski reached out and gently removed Jack's collected newspaper stories about the bombing and Victoria's death from the top of Iggy's diary, then opened the binder and casually began turning pages.

"I take it you've read this," he said.

Jack nodded.

"Not exactly *Mary Poppins*, is it?" Pulaski rested an open notepad on his lap. "I'm looking for an angle on the baby-doll homicides, Congressman. Your son—"

" 'Iggy,' if you don't mind," Jack interrupted.

Pulaski pulled a felt-tipped pen from his pocket and removed the cap. "Iggy Pitt apparently knew all three victims. Shivers and Moon he knew from Wings, Bannister he met at an antiabortion rally, but he doesn't say anything about who kidnapped them or how they died." Jack wiggled his toes at the end of the cast. "Anything you can tell us to shed some light on this?"

"Such as?"

"Something about your fiancée? Victoria Winters?"

Jack's mouth curled into a wry grin. "Still grinding away on the prochoice vendetta theory, huh?"

"It's just a question."

"And I'll be happy to give you the answer. She wasn't involved."

"You sound pretty sure about that."

"I am. I knew her." He moved the cast into a more comfortable position. "The question I was hoping you'd be asking is who was behind the bombing that killed her."

Pulaski shifted in his chair. "You mean other than your s—other than Iggy Pitt?"

"Of course. You don't really think a twenty-five-year-old kid bombed two clinics without some help, do you?"

Pulaski shrugged his bushy eyebrows. "He had Billy Bannister the first time. Do you have someone else in mind?"

Time to get into it. "What about Eli Graves?"

"According to the diary, he kept Graves in the dark. Made him think he was dealing with somebody named Alfred Benedict, a.k.a. Eggs Benedict. Not Iggy Pitt."

Jack said, "Right. At least that's how it looks."

Pulaski scratched his cheek. "No offense, Congressman, but after twenty-five years in homicide, most things turn out to be how they look. You just have to know how to look."

Jack rolled his plastered foot from side to side. "Have you guys found Graves yet?"

"That's one of the things we wanted to talk to you about," Pulaski said. "First, any other ideas about who might have been behind the bombing?"

"What do you make of the diary's references to Abner Titus?"

"The chief justice? Iggy Pitt apparently met him at his confirmation hearing and got his autograph, but I don't see anything that suggests they had any further contact, do you?"

"Not in the diary, no. But Titus had a good motive to use the kid to stalk me."

"You mean, because you tried to keep Titus off the Supreme Court?"

Jack smiled. "Because I accused him of complicity in Zenobia Davis's death, yeah. Even a New York cop would have to agree that's a little rough."

Pulaski glanced over at Wilson, who had his ankle on his knee, rotating his sneakered foot the way he did when he wasn't buying something. Jack leaned toward the coffee table, struggling against his straightened leg, and picked up a ballpoint pen.

"All right," Pulaski said, "let's say the judge was provoked by what you did. What then? He hires someone to go after you?"

"Hires? No. This wasn't done for money."

"Okay, recruits someone."

"Maybe. It's extreme, but he might do it if he thought he could get away with it."

"How would he expect to get away with it?"

"By doing exactly what he did." Jack drew a tic-tac-toe board on his plaster cast. "He meets Iggy Pitt and gets to know him, discovers he's a crazy kid who hates me, gives him some help at the right moment, and boom. It's done."

"Wouldn't you expect to find some reference to that in the kid's diary?"

"Not necessarily. Titus is as meticulous as they come. Besides, there are missing pages, remember?" He placed an X in the upper left-hand box. Pulaski and Wilson said nothing. "I take it you don't agree," Jack said. He drew an O in the center box.

"I don't agree or disagree," Pulaski said, "but we are talking about a chief justice of the Supreme Court here."

Jack looked amused, and annoyed. "You think a bunch of senators confirming someone to the Supreme Court turns him into a moral virgin?" Pulaski said nothing. "I admit he isn't your typical suspect, but if you follow the logic of the thing, you've got to entertain the possibility."

Pulaski said, "Like I told you before, Congressman, I'm just an old-fashioned guy who likes to know if the suspect actually did the crime."

"No, you're not. You want *proof* that the suspect did the crime."

"Well, you got a point there. But since we're playing my game, we have to play by my rules."

Jack drew in another X in a box. *Like hell we do.* "There've been, what, three baby-doll victims?" he said, not looking up. "I think you should wait and see if there's a fourth. If this is a vendetta by a bunch of pro-choice maniacs, they'll do it again to get even with this latest bombing. But if it's somebody trying to make it *appear* to be a pro-choice vendetta, the kidnappings are finished."

"Why?"

"Because they've won. They've got Abner Titus on the Supreme Court, they've got people like Victoria and me dead or fucked up, they've got Eli Graves alive and well, the Red Rose Society rich as fudge. . . . Did I say they won? Fuckers made a clean sweep."

Pulaski saw a tattered sailing magazine sitting on the coffee table. He picked it up and rolled it into a baton. "We arrested Graves two nights ago," he said.

Jack looked surprised. "What for?"

"Breaking and entering Iggy Pitt's room, assaulting a police officer, theft of the diary. Were you aware that Graves was inside the clinic reception room with your fiancée just before the bomb went off?"

"He was?" The thought made his throat dry. "What was he doing in the clinic with Victoria?"

"One of our guys brought him up for the doctor to check out his windpipe." Pulaski set the magazine back on the table. "Which I gather you had more or less pinched closed during a fight with him."

"That's what I hear," Jack said. "I can't even remember being at the rally." He returned to his tic-tac-toe. "Tell me something. Where was Abner Titus at the time?"

Pulaski looked for an answer from Wilson, who shook his head.

"A few hundred miles away, I'm sure," Jack said, doodling an O onto his leg.

Pulaski watched. "Who's winning?"

Jack smiled as he doodled. "At the moment the bad guys." He looked up. "But the game isn't over yet."

Pulaski waited for him to continue, but Jack said nothing more. Seeing that he was fading, the detective stretched his locked fingers in front of him and turned his palms inside out, cracking his knuckles. "We'll pick this up again later."

Jack remained seated as the two of them stood up to leave. Pulaski put on his coat and fedora, started for the door, and hesitated.

"By the way," he said, turning, "I have something that apparently belonged to Victoria." He pulled an object out of his coat pocket and placed it in Jack's hand. "Do you recognize it?"

Jack held it up to his good eye. It was a silver dollar, the tails side scorched, the heads side showing Susan B. Anthony saying "V" as clearly as the day he'd had it engraved. If he'd been connected to a heart monitor, the detectives would have called a nurse.

"Where'd you find it?" he asked.

"At the bomb site, buried in the wall."

Jack hid his Adam's apple with his hand. "Yeah, it's hers. Can I keep it?"

Pulaski waved okay and left. When the door clicked shut, Jack lifted the coin to examine it. Victoria's? She'd never even seen the thing. It had gone from his own pocket to Abner Titus's the night of Sticks Dickey's poker game.

Obviously, it had gone from Titus's pocket to Iggy's.

He rolled the piece of silver between his fingers, feeling Abner Titus's complicity growing heavier with each turn, feeling his own blood turning hot and cold, like dry ice. *The coin is good luck after all,* Iggy had written.

Now he understood.

Jeremy Hackett walked ahead of the two uniformed hospital guards, one carrying a clipboard and a fat ring of keys, the other pushing an empty wheelchair. "I hate to rush you fellows, but if my client is late for his arraignment, he may as well not leave this place at all."

When they reached the hospital room, the guard knocked on the door with his knuckle, pushed it open, and saw his prisoner lying asleep on his back. He motioned for Hackett to enter, then checked his watch and made a note on his clipboard.

Hackett walked in and approached the bed. "Hey, Eli, get up. We're gonna be late." He reached out and shook him. "Eli?"

Leaning forward, he saw a young man about Eli Graves's age, with Graves's dark hair, wearing a hospital orderly's jacket and sleeping as peacefully as a drunk on a doorstep. An empty syringe of morphine intended for Graves lay on the table next to him, and attached to his coat with a hemostat was a hospital envelope that read, *To Jeremy Hackett. Attorney–Client Privilege.* He ripped it open and read:

> *Dear Jeremy:*
> *If I'd stuck around and the judge denied bail, I'd be back in jail before noon. No matter how unlikely that is, I can't take the chance.*
> *Don't try to find me. When the time comes, I'll find you. I have something to do first.*
> *Eli.*
> *P.S. I didn't hurt the orderly, I put him to sleep.*

Standing at the desk at the Paradise Hotel, a seedy flophouse on Manhattan's Eighth Avenue, a man with sunken eyes and bandaged palms was signing a register under a false name. Around his neck, cradling his chin, was an orthopedic brace made of white plastic with black foam lining.

"Where can I find a hardware store?" he asked in a strained voice.

The hotel manager sat on the hind legs of his poncho-draped chair, face unshaven, pushing a chewed-up toothpick around his mouth. "Down the block, cross the street."

The man in the neck brace laid his fifty dollars on the sign-in sheet and raised his bloodshot eyes, catching the stare of the clerk. The clerk dropped his chair onto all fours and stood up like an aching farmer, pushing a key across the scuffed wooden desk. "Second floor up, no cookin' in the room, no noise after eleven, no complaining when somebody else breaks the rules." He gawked at the injured man's face and stuck the dirty toothpick back into his mouth, forming a snarl as he played with his teeth.

Eli Graves stared back. "What are you looking at?" he asked angrily.

"Zero," the clerk said, sitting down. "A walking goose egg."

Jack hobbled on crutches out the Gothic door and lowered his hatless head against a January drizzle, hoping to escape with as few words as possible. Funerals were supposed to confer emotional release and finality, but he wanted neither. He'd find another way to deal with Victoria's death, even if he didn't know yet what it was.

He passed by the minister, giving her a nod, and thought he was home free until he saw Rachel standing on the sidewalk twenty yards away. She was talking to a woman in a charcoal-gray suit, a pair of sunglasses, and a narrow-brimmed black hat. The woman looked vaguely familiar—a lobbyist, perhaps, or someone he'd met at a political reception, he couldn't recall. There had been scores of mourners at the service, some of whom he'd met before, most of whom he hadn't, including many of Victoria's clients, friends from government agencies, lawyers, and court personnel. As he approached, the woman in the gray suit turned and walked away, leaving Rachel alone to greet Jack.

She touched his arm as a hello and the two of them started walking together. "Sorry I couldn't get up to New York to see you," she said. "Are you okay?"

"No, but that doesn't mean I can't act like it." They continued down the sidewalk in silence.

"Something on your mind you want to talk about?" He didn't respond. "Come on, Jack. If you can't be honest at a funeral, you never will be."

Put that way, he couldn't resist.

"I keep having this nagging suspicion that you know something about Victoria's death you're not telling me."

She stopped walking. "Whatever in the world made you say that? Victoria was my best friend."

Jack swiveled on his crutches and faced her. "Remember when she went to Arizona, after Thanksgiving?"

"Yes?"

"Did you go with her?"

She lifted her eyebrows. "To Arizona?"

He detected a small tightness in her voice. "Yeah, to the spa, in Arizona."

"No," she said. "What made you think I did?"

He stood up straight, putting his weight on his good leg. "I called her the night she arrived and thought I heard you answer the telephone."

She looked perplexed. "She left for the spa the day after Thanksgiving, didn't she? A Friday?"

"Yes."

"I operated on Abner Titus at George Washington Hospital the next day."

Jack nodded. "Guess that explains why I heard your voice when I called your number at the farm."

"Then why did you think I was in Arizona?"

"It occurred to me later that you might have had your telephone calls forwarded to the spa."

She stared at him a moment. "Take a few days off and find some sunshine, Jack. When you get back we'll have dinner and sort everything out. Okay?"

"I'll count on it," he said. They shook hands and parted.

He crossed the street and headed away from the church, replaying their exchange in his head. God. He'd accused her of something pretty bad. By the time he reached the corner, he felt the need to apologize, but when he turned around, she was gone. Couldn't have gotten far, he thought, and hobbled back toward the church.

As he approached the church from across the street, he saw Rachel standing under an archway at a side entrance to the building, once again engaged in conversation with the woman in the charcoal-gray suit. He stepped over the curbstone and waited. The woman's head was bowed and she was dabbing a tissue under her sunglasses; Rachel was holding her by the shoulders and talking to her earnestly, apparently comforting her. Placing her arms around the woman to embrace her, she accidentally bumped her friend's hat, knocking it askew. Reaching for it, the woman raised her face and caught sight of Jack standing on the sidewalk, watching. She appeared momentarily stunned, as if she were embarrassed to be seen crying—or perhaps to be seen at all. Quickly, she turned, opened the door, and disappeared inside the church. Without looking back, Rachel followed.

He waited a moment and turned back toward the corner—directly into a microphone held by Joslyn Brooks, a television reporter.

"I know this is a difficult moment, Congressman, but could you tell us who you think might have been behind the bombing?"

Good Lord. It was the perfect combination on a day of mourning: a woman reporter, a television camera, and words.

"Sorry," he said. "Not now."

He stepped around her and continued down the sidewalk, stabbing the ground with his crutches. His coat was open and the January drizzle drenched his unprotected bare head, but none of it mattered. He was where he wanted to be—alone, without telephones or well-meaning friends. Especially women. There was something about them that pissed him off—all of them, regardless of who they were or where they stood—left, right, or center. Like the way they claimed to be better nurturers than men, then got angry when men said maybe women were better suited to raise children. Or like women who said men ought to be more in touch with their "female" qualities, and then, when they saw a man cry, muttered "wimp" and found a fullback to fuck their brains out.

He was tired of women who railed against garter belts and corsets, but starved themselves to death trying to fit into a size six. He was tired of women whose greatest aspirations were to look like lipstick ads, having not a clue why they were so boring. He was tired of ladies who lunched, swapping stories over couscous about their extramarital affairs, wondering over decaffeccinos why men were not monogamous. He was tired of women who beat men at their own power games, then pulled up the ladder before their sisters got a grip on the bottom rung. He'd had enough of them all—Brooklyn mothers named MacLeod who died of cancer when their sons were only ten; teenage girls named Honey who fell in love with their boyfriends and got pregnant and died; lovers named Molly who got knocked silly in clinic bombings; wives-to-be called Victoria who got blown to bits; unnamed baby girls who died in their mothers' wombs; TV reporters named Joslyn who interviewed men at funerals, too dense to know that for men words were the *enemy* of grief, not their expression. He was tired of them all.

He stopped to look at some camping gear in the window of Sporting World and saw his face reflecting in the glass. His hair was stringy and overdue for a cut, his eye patch wet and soggy, slipping down. The scars on his face from the explosion were still healing and ugly, the old Mexican scar over his right eye more prominent than usual.

That's right, take it out on women. You're such a perfect specimen yourself: fair-minded. rational. equality loving. Christ.

He turned from the window and swung his crutches and feet down the street through the middle of a puddle, soaking his cast and shoes. It was cold but it felt good, stomping through water. It felt good being angry in a world where anger and violence were obviously so goddamn effective. It felt good being vindictive, shucking off pretense, reconnecting with the raw, honest instinct that made men the brutes of the earth. It felt good to be *uncivilized*. Natural and powerful. Good.

He pulled the door to the travel agency open, held it with his crutch, and hobbled to the counter. An attractive, fortyish woman making reservations on a computer keyboard greeted him with an enormous smile, showing no trace of curiosity or judgment about the grizzled heap he was. He requested his tickets, and as he watched her clack away on the keys, simply being near her lifted his spirits and calmed him down, reconnecting him to a different spirit. A female spirit. A human one.

"Have a safe trip," she said, handing him an open ticket to St. Thomas.

He saw a wedding ring on her finger. He said nothing, unaware that he was staring at her.

She looked puzzled. "Can I help you with something else?"

He blinked. "No, thank you," he said, and backed away from the counter.

He stopped in the middle of the room to place the tickets inside his coat, and found himself examining the back of his ringless left hand. *V's gone, forever gone. Get used to it.*

He stood quietly and put the torch to an emotional bridge. One among the many he would burn in the coming weeks, one day at a time. As the ashes turned cold and fell, he lowered his hand to his crutch and left.

The forest-green Dumpster sat in the alley under gathering snow, waiting for daybreak and the first load of wallboard and plaster to come rumbling down the chute into its belly.

Quietly, out of the snow-flecked shadows, a pair of bandaged hands appeared on the container's edge, followed by a human head cradled on a neck brace, rising slowly like a night periscope. Blood vessels strained on the man's forehead—a foot found its way onto the rim of the Dumpster—and the grunting figure hoisted itself up and dropped a short distance onto a pile of debris. The alley went silent, with snow falling between the tenements.

Five minutes passed before he stirred. Struggling, Eli Graves rolled over onto his hands and knees and crawled into the corner. Kneeling on pieces of sheetrock, he began lifting the trash one item at a time: a hunk of vinyl flooring; a push-button telephone pad, which he stuck into his pocket; a splintered joist. He laid each discarded piece on a pile at the side, careful to avoid fresh nail wounds to the palms of his already punctured hands.

Finally he found what he was searching for.

He reached down and yanked at a fabric handle and pulled free a black bag made of parachute cloth. Holding his head and torso erect, he patted it as if he were a blind man, then unzipped it, reached inside, and felt four cylinders about eight inches long. Lifting one, he examined its silhouette against the street lamp at the end of the alley.

For the first time in a long time, he was pleased.

Molly lay on the autopsy table in the D.C. morgue, eyes shut, hands folded over her chest.

Elliot Landy hung up the wall telephone and walked to the table. "Sorry to take so long," he said.

She opened her eyes and sat up, dangling her legs and shoeless feet over the side. The two of them embraced. "It's good to see you," he said. "How are you feeling?"

"I get tired about this time every afternoon, but if I lie down for a few minutes, I'm fine." She took his hand. "You came all the way to New York to see me, and there I was, unconscious. Your flowers were the first thing I saw when I woke up."

He pushed up his glasses for a closer look and lightly touched her face. "You're healing nicely. Any headaches?"

"Not since the big one."

He helped her off the table. She slipped on her shoes and walked to the counter, where he pulled up a stool and told her to sit. She complied gladly; having been in the hospital for eight days had done nothing for her sore feet.

"I'm back at work," she said, "back on the charming baby-doll murders. Homicides, excuse me. Anything new?"

He straightened a pile of medical journals on the counter. "Remember when we talked after Zenobia Davis's autopsy, and I had something I couldn't tell you?"

"Yes?"

"Are we still off the record?"

"Sure."

He pulled a manila folder from the shelf above the counter, opened it to a marker, and showed her a close shot of an incision and sutures. "This is the first victim, Melvin Shivers, before we opened up his previous autopsy sutures." He pulled two more volumes off the shelf and opened them. "And this is Harley Moon, number two." He turned another page. "And this is the third, Billy Bannister."

She leaned forward and saw the continuous suture—the baseball stitch—in all three. "Yeah?"

"Now look at this." He opened another folder of photographs. "This is Zenobia Davis's hysterotomy incision." He handed her a magnifying glass.

She took it and studied the photograph. "It's another baseball stitch." She looked up. "But you said those are standard procedure, didn't you?"

"They are, but that's not what I'm talking about. Look at the left side, where the suture begins."

She bent forward with the magnifying glass. "Looks like a knot."

"Not one knot. Two of them, about half an inch apart. Now look at where the sutures begin on the three men." He slid the photographs toward her.

"Hm. Same two knots." She straightened up. "Why would the person who sewed up these guys be sewing up Zenobia Davis?"

"You tell me."

She looked puzzled, and once again lifted the magnifying glass. "Who could have done this?" she said to herself, inspecting the pictures.

He looked over her shoulder. "Do you fish?"

"You're asking a girl from West Virginia?"

"Ever see an arbor knot?"

"A what?"

"An arbor knot. Something fly fishermen use, like a slipknot."

"Fly-fishing," she said softly, examining the photographs. "I was more into, like, bamboo poles and plastic bobbers."

"Whoever worked on these guys could have been a fly fisherman who tied the knots instinctively."

"What else do you see here? Any more black silk?"

"No."

"How about the size of the baseball stitch?"

"Nothing unusual."

She stared at the photo again. "They cross from southwest to northeast. Can you tell whether they were sewn up with a right hand or left?"

He shook his head. "I doubt it." Holding the magnifying glass in his left hand, he made stitching motions in the air with his right, first one way, then the other, pulling an imaginary suture back toward himself, and angling it forty-five degrees upward toward the imaginary cadaver's head. "I haven't closed in years, but that's how I'd do it." He examined the sutures in the photograph and saw that their angles were exactly opposite his own. "If I had to guess—you know how I feel about guessing—"

"Guess."

"I'd guess whoever did it was left-handed."

She hopped off the stool.

Her enthusiasm puzzled him. "There must be a million left-handed people in Washington, D.C., alone," he said. "Even if I'm right, what good is that?"

She pulled the strap of her handbag onto her shoulder. "As my silver-tongued producer so gracefully likes to say, 'Information to a reporter is like an enema to a dead man. It may not help, but it sure can't hurt.' "

He sat in the middle of the sagging flophouse bed with his eyes centered dead ahead, a Buddhist monk in prayer. Strewn around him were tools and electronic gear, *The Urban Terrorist's Cookbook*, an electronics manual, and a two-month old lawyers' newspaper article entitled, "All Work and No Play: The Lifestyle of Chief Justice Abner Titus." Certain passages in it—particularly the ones describing the judge's two-room suite at GW Hospital—were highlighted in yellow.

He lowered his head onto the pillow and rested. In his mind he could see all the pieces falling into place. All but one.

Time to put it where it belonged.

He lifted himself off the bed and slipped on his jacket and shoes, then walked to the dresser and unscrewed the cap on a bottle of painkilling vodka. Wasn't morphine, but it helped. He brought it to his lips, turned it up, and drained what was left. Eyes watering, he dropped the bottle to the floor, zipped up his coat, and swept a pile of quarters from the dresser top into his pocket.

Out on the street he walked with his neck brace hidden beneath a black scarf, no more conspicuous than the assortment of other derelicts and damaged people who walked Eighth Avenue. Still, he kept an eye out for the police.

He passed an automatic teller machine but didn't stop. When he ran low on cash, he'd have to travel a long distance from here to use his card, New Jersey or Brooklyn, maybe the Bronx. The cops would probably be monitoring his bank account every day.

He reached the pay phone at the corner and rehearsed what he'd say, the precise words, the inflection, the confident tone. He laid his quarters on the metal platform and lifted the receiver. After calling long-distance information, he dialed the number the operator had given him, dropped his coins, and waited. Two rings and a secretary answered. He introduced himself by his real name, certain that it was the visa that would give him passage to the person he was calling. The startled secretary asked him to wait, and sure enough, in a few seconds there it was—the voice he was waiting for, the mere sound of which heated his skin.

"Hello?" the voice said.

"Congressman MacLeod?" he answered.

"Yes?"

"This is Eli Graves. Case you haven't heard, I'm back on the street."

Jack paused at the entrance to the orthopedic wing at New York City Hospital and examined his reflection in the glass door—the splayed wooden crutches, the dirty leg cast, the black patch over his eye, the scabs and scars, mending but still evident on his face. He was somewhat deformed, but untroubled by it. They said he'd get his eyesight back in time—the stick jammed into his face had been deflected by his cheekbone—and as for the rest, he was getting used to it. In fact, considering his state of mind, he was beginning to enjoy it.

He pressed the rubber tip of his crutch onto the black rubber mat, opened the automatic door, and hobbled inside to a waiting room. Looking around, he was reminded of the saloon in *Star Wars*. There was a man with an orthopedic screw through a knee, a boy in a halo neck brace, a woman with a walker. There were collars everywhere—soft ones, hard ones, wide and narrow ones—a plaster cast on an arm, an amputee with an exposed prosthesis, patients in multitrauma devices, body jackets, plastic, aluminum, Velcro. Now he understood why Eli Graves had insisted on meeting him here.

Graves sat on a couch reading a magazine, pretending to be another orthopedic patient. Jack had to look twice to be sure who it was: the collar, the lost weight, the sunken eyes fixed in a POW's thousand-yard stare. But then he saw their signature glint, the menace. No question whose eyes those were.

He moved to the couch and leaned his crutches against the wall, preparing to sit, feeling his viscera recoil as if he were nearing a reptile. Settle down, he told himself. Flaring his nostrils, he sat next to Graves, careful not to touch him.

"Let's make this quick," Jack said. He picked up a dog-eared *Field and Stream* from a coffee table.

Graves turned a page of his *Sports Illustrated*. "You were onto Titus at your press conference," he said. "You just didn't have the whole story." He paused, milking Jack's silent curiosity. "His nomination was corrupt from the start. He wanted a seat on the Supreme Court, but with his conservative record, he knew President Clay wouldn't appoint him, at least not without some heavy-duty political pressure. That's what he got from Senator Dickey."

"What kind of pressure?"

"Sticks has something on the president. I don't know what it is, but the price for keeping it quiet was Titus's appointment to the Court."

Jack's skin began to crawl again. "Sticks Dickey is blackmailing the president?"

"He doesn't like to use that term," Graves said. "Anyway, getting Titus the nomination was one thing, but getting the Senate to confirm him was another. Sticks assumed Titus had plenty of political support on the right, including an endorsement from me, but when I met Titus I hated him."

"Why?"

Graves opened his bandaged hands, stared at his palms, and closed them. "That's my business," he said. "I told Sticks he could get somebody better than Titus appointed, but he didn't want to hear it. He said once I got to know the judge I'd trust him and like him more. He said he was hearing this case, the Zenobia Davis abortion case, and how he handled it would prove his true colors."

Jack turned a magazine page, and Graves continued.

"Confirmation looked like it was going to be close, which made Titus nervous, unsure how to play it. If he allowed Zenobia Davis to abort, he was afraid I'd sink him with the pro-lifers, and if he didn't allow her to abort, he knew he'd catch hell from the liberals. He and Sticks decided their chances were better leaning on me, so Sticks arranged a couple of meetings between us, including one on the shuttle to New York. That's when Titus came up with the solution."

"What solution?"

Graves turned the page of his magazine, taking his time. "The two of us were talking about how hard it is to dramatize the immorality of abortion—you know, with television and movies showing everything these days, nothing shocks people anymore. So Titus says, what if somebody videotaped a woman aborting in her third trimester? Not something staged, but the real thing? The murder of a live baby right before your eyes?"

"Jesus."

"After that, he delayed ruling on Zenobia Davis's case until she was big as a house. Then he called her up and told her he was going to rule in her favor the next morning. He said she could finally have her abortion, except for one problem—her husband might be able to stop it during an appeal. By the time the appeal was finished, he said, she'd be so pregnant she couldn't abort no matter who won. But not to worry. He had an answer. He'd arranged an abortion for her that night, before her husband had enough time to appeal, just like you proabortionist lawyers do for your clients. That way, when Titus's decision was announced in the morning, there'd be nothing left for her husband to appeal."

Was this real? "And she fell for it?"

"She went to the clinic that night, but by then the fetus was so big they had to take it out cesarean. Something went wrong and she and the baby both died."

"Who performed the operation?"

"I don't know. All you can see on the videotape are rubber-gloved hands and scalpels working on her midsection. Assuming you can stand to watch it."

"You have the videotape?"

"Of course. That's the whole point."

Jack laid the magazine on his lap. "What do you want from me, Graves?"

"The same thing you want. Abner Titus. I want you to take this videotape and shove it up his ass, have him thrown off the Court, prosecuted, humiliated, sent to jail—whatever you can do to him, I want it done."

"Jesus. What'd he do to you, anyway?"

"I told you, that's my business."

Jack drummed his fingers on the magazine. "A videotape without proof Titus was behind it is worthless."

"But I can prove he was behind it! All I have to do is get him on the telephone and I'll record him talking about it on tape. Put that conversation together with the videotape of the operation and he's finished!"

Jack opened the magazine again. "You don't need me to record a telephone conversation with Abner Titus. You can call him yourself."

"I've tried, but his secretary won't put me through. But according to this story the *American Barrister* did on him, there's one place he answers the telephone himself."

"Where?"

"A private line in his hospital room."

Jack closed his magazine and breathed in the overly warm hospital air. "Forget it, Graves. There's no way I can get his private number. And even if I could, why would I?"

"Because he had a hand in Victoria Winters's death."

Jack swallowed. "Come on, Graves. Cut the shit."

Graves reached up and pinched the bridge of his nose, grimacing. "I was with Titus the night he said he was helping your son track you down."

Jack sat still.

"Actually," Graves said, "you were there too. Remember the poker game at Sticks Dickey's house?"

Jack pictured it. "You were the fourth player?"

"While you were sitting at the poker table I was upstairs cooling my heels. If you don't believe me, I can prove it. After you left, Titus showed me a silver dollar he won off you. A Susan B. Anthony with the letter V engraved on it."

Jack felt a spear in his chest. He reached into his pocket and pulled out the coin.

Graves looked down at it. "Sweet Mary—that's it! How'd you get that?"

"They found it at the clinic. After the explosion."

"Mother of God. The kid must have been carrying it."

They both sat quietly. Jack turned the coin in his fingers, picturing Abner Titus and Iggy Pitt, Eggs Benedict, together.

"Help me out, MacLeod. You want to get rid of Titus as much as I do."

"What do you mean 'get rid of'?"

Graves's choice of words was too hot, too obvious. He backtracked and rephrased. "You know, embarrass him. Wreck his career."

Jack didn't like it, either the idea or the tone. "Forget it," he said. He closed his magazine and lifted the cast on his leg, preparing to leave.

"See this bulletin board?" Graves said. Above his head was a cork panel with notices of carpooling offers, lost pets, and used orthopedic equipment for sale. "Print the words *VCR for Sale* on an index card with Abner Titus's private hospital number written backward, in case somebody else sees it and tries to call. Stick it in the top left corner."

Jack stood up with his back to Graves, acknowledging nothing. He hopped up and down on one foot until his crutches were comfortably under his arms.

"MacLeod?" Graves said barely loud enough to be heard.

Jack stopped but didn't turn around.

"I hear she was pregnant when she died." Jack remained standing. "He raped us both, MacLeod. Before you decide what to do, take a look in the mirror and see for yourself. You'll do the right thing."

H e hiccuped.

Jack lifted the bottle to his mouth and turned it upside down—another dagger in the throat, another grimace—and lowered it, removing it from his lips too soon, feeling the cool, perfumey gin spill down his chin and neck.

Once again it was an endless February, the month that he'd discovered, waiting for Honey's return, was eight weeks long. This time it felt more like eighteen.

He closed his eyes and loosened his grip on the bottle, letting it slide through his hand into a standing position on the floor, a guard keeping the enemy inside the fort instead of out. Jack's face rested peacefully, his mouth open slightly, the flickering light of the silent television set blessing and cursing him for the simultaneously pure and loving, dirty and hateful thoughts that filled his mind.

He pictured the New York–Washington shuttle with Abner Titus and Eli Graves sitting next to each other talking about videotaping Zenobia Davis's abortion. He imagined a video camera mounted on the surgical lamp above the operating table . . . the glint of the scalpel drawn across an abdomen, over and over, slicing deeper into the flesh, down through the fat . . . down to the rubbery uterus. Down to the baby.

His eardrums vibrated with the sound of Pat Sajak saying, "No Love Lost," but it failed to disturb the dream he'd slipped into.

He saw a body on the operating table—now it was Victoria's, eyes closed, a nurse sponging her forehead. An enormous figure in a black robe moved toward her, silent and menacing, and bent over her, blocking all but her face from his view. Suddenly her eyes opened and she stared up at Jack with her mouth open in a silent scream. His heart pounded—the figure in the robe straightened up and turned around, black cap, black mask, holding a baby by its heels, like a wet rabbit. Victoria's operating table was now a casket, sliding away, over the edge of a platform—disappearing—*she's gone!* He reached for the baby . . . almost had it . . . when the figure in the robe flung it into the air, its tiny hands clawing the sky for safety—

Ring!

He woke up in front of the bathroom mirror, heart pounding, his face covered with shaving lather.

Ring!

He stared at the sweat under his eyes, the pulse in his neck, the peak of shaving cream on his lower lip fluttering in his breath.

Ring!

Entering the bedroom, he wiped the lather off his hands and picked up the telephone.

"Hello, Jack?" a voice said. It was Rachel.

He sat on the edge of the bed and rested his splitting forehead in his fingers. His left leg was extended; the cast had been removed the day before. "How are you, Rachel?"

"I'm fine, but you sound awful."

"Yeah, no, I'm fine—you just caught me napping." He glanced at the red numerals on the clock next to Victoria's side of the bed. Seven-fifteen P. M.

"Go back to sleep. We'll talk later."

"No problem. What's up?"

"Last time I saw you we talked about getting together for dinner," she said. "Want to come out to the farm one night?"

Yes, he did. He was still carrying questions on his shoulder like chips and wanted her to knock one or two off. "Sure, when?"

"I'm off to a conference in Rome till the end of the week—how about Sunday night?"

"Sounds fine."

He hung up and sat still, disoriented and depressed. The room was dusky, lit only by the cool TV screen. He looked up and saw a new puzzle on *Wheel of Fortune*: "E E T E SC RE."

"I'll solve it," the contestant said. "Even the Score." Music and applause.

He stared at the TV set, waiting for an omen to appear. A phrase, a laugh, a sign telling him what to do about the question that continued to stalk him. All he saw was a spinning wheel.

He reached for the telephone book slowly, as if under duress, and opened it near the middle.

If I'm within a hundred pages of the name, I'll make the call. If not, it's over.

He found the telephone number ten pages away.

He picked up the telephone and dialed. A switchboard operator answered, "George Washington University." He asked for his party.

If I get through to him, I'll go for it. If not, it's over.

The operator patched the call through to another telephone. A woman answered and asked who was calling. He gave her his name and waited. On the TV screen was "G   Z   ," and the hint, "Motion picture."

"Hello?" a voice answered.

"Hello, Mr. Chief Justice?"

"Yes?"

"Jack MacLeod calling." He could feel the receiver turn icy. "I hope I didn't wake you."

"No, you didn't," Titus said.

"Sorry to find you in the hospital. I know how much fun they are."

"So I've read," Titus said. "Sorry to hear about your fiancée and the baby, MacLeod. She was a fine lawyer. Has to be quite a loss."

"Yes, well. Putting a tragedy like this behind you makes you think about completing other unfinished business, too. Which is why I'm calling. There's a hatchet I've been carrying around that I'd like to bury, Abner—" He stopped talking. "Can you hold on a second? It's my other line."

He pushed the hold button and waited, tapping the receiver against his naked thigh.

If he gives it to me, I still don't have to use it. If he doesn't, that'll be the end of it. Definitely.

On the television was GODZILLA, music, applause.

He punched the line button. "Abner, I apologize but I have to take another call. Can I call you right back?"

"To tell you the truth, MacLeod—"

"Just give me one minute, would you? It's important."

An exasperated sigh. "All right."

"Trying to reach you through the hospital switchboard was murder," Jack said. "Do you have a direct line?" He waited, knee jiggling.

"Call me on 555-1788. If you get the answering machine, give your name and I'll pick up."

"I'll call you right back."

On the television set, the spinning wheel clicked past five hundred dollars and stopped on *Surprise.*

He hung up, feeling as if he'd just loaded a gun.

"THIS . . . IS JEOPARDY!"

Graves laid his needle-nose pliers on the Paradise Hotel's faded red chenille bedspread and glanced at the beat-up television set, listening to Alex Trebek through a pair of earphones. He looked down at his open electronics manual and put his latex-gloved fingers back to work.

In the bottom of the disassembled VCR was a flat, printed circuit board dotted with tiny transistors, capacitors, "pots," and diodes—the silicon that had shrunk the world's toys as much as they had its missiles and bombs. He pushed the ribbon of wires aside and gently placed the first stick of explosive into the space.

It fit.

He laid in two more and tried to squeeze in a fourth, but there wasn't enough room. It didn't matter. Wretched excess. The difference between kingdom come and smithereens.

He lifted out the three sticks and taped them together, pausing to touch the infrared receiver glued behind the VCR's air vents to make sure it was firmly in place. Sitting on the bed next to the video player was a brand-new telephone answering machine—a MessageMate 500 exactly like the one the newspaper had photographed in Abner Titus's fancy hospital room. He had rewired it so that when its microprocessor brain heard the three push-button tones normally used to trigger record-ed messages, the electrical pulse intended for the playback motor would be diverted to the infrared devices instead. And from them to a capacitor that would store up electrical energy, then in forty-five minutes send it to the blasting caps which were inserted into the sticks of dynamite. He memorized the answering machine's private code—three, one, six—and peeled off the label and threw it away so that no one else would see it, not even by happenstance. Then he screwed the cover into place.

Time to see if it worked.

He plugged the machines into an extension cord, took the wires ulti-mately intended for the blasting caps, and attached them for the moment to an old-fashioned photographer's flashbulb a clerk had found for him in the rattletrap hardware store nearby.

"I'll take Famous Lovers for one hundred," the contestant said.

392

"These two heads of state put their heads together on the Nile."

He pawed through the junk on the bed and found the pad of telephone buttons he'd stolen from the Dumpster and connected it to the answering machine. Everything appeared to be ready. He pulled off his earphones and imagined himself at the fateful moment, standing at a pay telephone late at night, after Titus was asleep, dialing his private hospital number and waiting for a recording to invite him to leave a message after the beep. Then punching in the playback code, three-one-six. And leaving the chief justice a message. The last one he'd ever get.

He repositioned himself on the bed. After triggering the tape to start rolling, he heard the beep and punched in the playback code, three, one, six.

The machine clicked softly and went silent. If he'd wired the system correctly, the infrared light was now beaming its energy to the VCR a few inches away, slowly charging up its capacitor with enough electricity to ignite the flashbulb's filament. A small flash of light tonight, a very big one when it counted later.

In forty-five minutes he'd know.

He placed the earphones back on his head and sat hunched over, staring at the TV set in a catatonic gaze, back aching with fatigue, eyelids drooping from alcohol and sleepless nights. A spider of sweat crawled into the hollow of his neck as he cleared the bed of gear, preparing to lie down. Particles of dust illuminated by the glow of the TV screen floated before his eyes—thousands of tiny specks, hovering and circling, organizing themselves for what his boggled mind saw as an attack. He tried to swat them away, agitating them into a frenzy, inciting a riot in his brain, losing control and lashing out and flailing wildly—accidentally smashing his fist into the collar around his neck.

His head felt like a piano dropped onto a sidewalk. Pain ran through his body the way it had the night he'd been raped, reducing his brain to a simple on-off switch. He could hear his voice rising, drowning out the TV sound in his earphones. He tried to give up, but his nerve endings refused the white flag.

After a few minutes he closed his eyes and laid his face forward onto the VCR, counting seconds, praying for the tide to ebb. Voices from the television set mingled with voices in his head. "The category is Famous Italians." He felt the piss in his pants starting to cool—"He was one of the physicists on the Manhattan Project"—*bong*—"Who is Fermi?"—its pungent smell mixing with the stench of sweat and dead skin from under his neck brace. "Ghosts and Goblins for five hundred dollars." *Breathe. Relax. Breathe.* " . . . trial by dunking." *Bong.* "What are witches? I'll take Animal Husbandry for six hundred." *Make the voices go away—bong.* "What is bull semen? Ivy Leagues for two hundred."

His mind slowly retreated from his body into a semiconscious netherworld where sound faded in and out like the drone of an airplane during a Sunday afternoon nap. *"What is a Roman soldier?"* he heard, no longer distinguishing television voices from the ones in his head.

He drifted slowly into other places: a field of stone . . . crossing on bare feet. A pinnacle high in the sky, where no one could touch him . . . where falling was fearsome but inviting, a blessing, an escape. A small, perfumey room—a little boy lying on a dirty mattress with a hairy man standing over him dressed like a Roman soldier in a chest plate, thongs, and a leather skirt—a *lifted skirt.* He saw the hairy man's spear piercing the little boy, blood trickling down his thighs. He saw the boy trying to dismount his spindle, held fast by nails in his palms—chest heaving, full of hate—the spear rising through him into the throat—*I thirst*—up through the belly, into the throat—*I do not forgive them!*—up through the belly, into the throat—*I want them dead—*

POP!

He opened his eyes and found himself staring down at the soiled flophouse bedspread. The pain was mostly gone, the separation of mind from body nearly complete. A laugh track from a TV sitcom filled his earphones. Pulling them off, he felt bits of hard confetti fall from his hair, a stinging sensation on his neck and a trickle of blood, warm and sticky to the touch.

He lifted his head and blinked at the flashbulb. It was gone, leaving nothing behind but a scorched rim of brass and shards of white-powdered glass that had exploded through the room, like shrapnel.

He stared in disbelief.

My God. It works.

Rachel sat with Dr. Delfina Rinaldi at a sidewalk café overlooking the cobblestones in the Piazza San Marco. The same midafternoon sun that for centuries had lit the burnt-sienna clay facades, flower boxes, and red wine lit them today, as if time ran in a circle.

Rachel was in a more linear frame of mind.

"Here it is," she said, handing a small sheaf of papers to her friend. "It's a schedule of every immunosuppressant cocktail we've used so far."

"Including the right dose of Leukenase?"

"I certainly hope so."

Dr. Delfina Rinaldi—tall and olive-skinned, wearing an elegant silk dress—paged through the report smoothly, completely focused on its contents, unmindful of her dignified sensuality. As she read, Rachel dipped a piece of bread into her wine and looked out over the square. A few blocks away the streets were filled with noisy little cars and Lambrettas and old trucks chugging around rotaries, but here the air was relatively quiet and fumeless, a comforting urban landscape. The swarm of tourists was gone in late February, leaving Rome to Romans and a manageable number of visitors like Rachel, who was there to deliver a paper on animal-to-human liver grafts before the International Conference of Transplant Surgeons.

It had been four days of seminars, speeches, and dinners, religiously followed each night by discussions in the hotel lounge with two brilliant Japanese surgeons from Tokyo, two extraordinary women doctors who were there to meet the extraordinary Dr. Redpath. Like members of Rachel's staff, they, too, had quickly become captivated by her charisma, daring, and expertise, and soon they were hearing what they'd come for: the problems they would encounter as they trekked into unexplored transplantation territory, the solutions Rachel had devised in her unprecedented work, the ones she had yet to discover. Cautious at first, Rachel became impressed by their technical acumen and seriousness of purpose. Without identifying any of her patients, she answered their questions and gave them as much information as she could.

As she set down her wineglass a street urchin about nine years old approached to sell her a red geranium he'd stolen from a window box, or perhaps a grave. His brown hair was cut straight across his forehead, his face tan and dirty, his scruffy shorts held up by a man's suspenders tied in a knot in back. On his feet were a pair of sneakers, reasonably new, noticeably too large.

Delfina shooed him away with the back of her hand and adjusted her glasses and examined the chart. "What about toxicity?"

"Doesn't seem to be a problem," Rachel said. She pointed to a column on the chart. "We've used FK 506 with no adverse effects. The hyperkalemia resolved itself within forty-eight hours."

The street urchin peered from around a column, looking at the table, trying not to be seen.

Delfina finished skimming the report and laid it on the table. "How far off to the critical moment?"

Rachel took a sip of wine. "We're only twenty-five days away."

Delfina lifted her glass of wine in a silent toast. As the two of them were about to drink, they heard the sound of footsteps and turned to see the boy approaching at a dead run. He grabbed Rachel's purse off the floor, only to have it instantly ripped from his hands, flipping him onto the floor like a tripped horse in an old western. Fast he was, but not particularly observant: he'd missed seeing Rachel tie the bag's shoulder strap to the leg of the cast-iron table.

A waiter in a black tuxedo and a white apron grabbed him by the back of the neck and raised him off his feet to throw him off the sidewalk. Rachel reached him first, explaining with her hands that everything was okay, she wanted the boy to stay. As the waiter collected the things from her bag and laid them on the table—coins, a lipstick, a compact—Rachel brought the frightened boy to her chair, stood him in front of her, and dipped her cotton napkin into a glass of Pellegrino and dabbed at his knee. She talked to him quietly, cleaning the scrape, telling him in broken Italian that if he was so quick and brave, he should become a doctor instead of a thief.

"You're without hope," Delfina said to her.

"I think you mean 'hopeless,' " Rachel said.

Delfina watched a moment, checked her watch, then stood up and leaned over to give her friend a good-bye kiss on the cheek. "So, this is it? Is that how you say it?"

"That's how you say it. This is it."

"I don't like it that we won't be talking to each other," Delfina said.

"Me neither, but don't worry, you'll do just fine. I'll be thinking of you every day." She gave her hand a good-luck squeeze, and Delfina turned away.

The boy stood still, watching and listening. As Delfina left, Rachel lifted him onto her lap and brushed his hair with her fingers, talking to him in English, which he didn't understand. A few minutes later she pulled his face into her neck and held it there. His eyelids moved up and down heavily until, finally, taking a deep breath, he closed them. She did the same, smoothing his sun-perfumed hair slowly, as if she, too, were about to nap. After a few minutes, her fingers stopped moving and the two of them sat still, a dozing pietà.

His eyes opened.

He leaped off her lap, grabbed her compact off the table, and ran toward the street—a wild bird, briefly captured, suddenly breaking free. She watched him run to the fountain with his oversized shoes flopping beneath him, splashing the water with his hand as he went, disappearing around the corner.

A couple at the next table shook their heads and the men at the bar laughed, but Rachel didn't notice. Not because she didn't care, but because she was preoccupied with thoughts of another wild bird . . . resting in another nest . . . and her friend Victoria, and what might have been if she had lived.

Catching herself, she drank the rest of her wine and stood up to leave, no longer thinking about what might have been, but the events that lay shortly ahead.

The hospital service elevator opened and the maintenance man pushed his equipment-loaded, four-wheeled cart into the hallway on the sixth floor. As a nurse passed by, her eyes seemed to remain on him a little too long, her interest too intense. He continued walking. What had caught her attention? he wondered. The false beard? The worried eyes? The stolen jumpsuit? The telephone answering machine sitting on the second shelf among cable connectors and tools? Maybe it was the way he held his head, straight up and immobile, as if he were wearing his neck brace which he needed desperately. Whatever, her curiosity made him nervous.

He approached a guard sitting outside Titus's hospital room, reading a magazine. The man looked up. "Yes, sir," he said without smiling.

"VCR repair," the maintenance man said. His head felt like a bowling ball on a bamboo stick, wobbling dangerously, causing a grimace.

The guard turned a page in his notebook, and another. He eyeballed the equipment.

"What kind of repair did you say?"

"VCR."

Eli Graves felt his skin itch under the fake beard. Beads of sweat sprouted under his jumpsuit and on his forehead. Better to wipe them off obviously, as if they came from exertion instead of fear. He pulled a handkerchief from his pocket, blew his nose, wiped his face, and scratched his prickly beard.

The guard looked back at his notebook. "I don't see anything on the list here." He reached for the telephone on the small table. Graves waited, holding himself together. This was not the time to show nervous eyes, lick your lips, or bolt for the exit. The guard set down the receiver. Graves saw the man's hand drop beneath the table and expected him to draw his service revolver. Instead, he rose to his feet.

"Wait here," he said, disgusted that no one had answered his call. As he started to walk away Pepper Loomis emerged from the hospital room wearing a coat and hat, on her way out. The guard stopped.

"Miss Loomis, do you know anything about a broken VCR?"

"No. Why?"

398

Graves raised his eyebrows. "Never mind. I'll come back later." He started to roll the cart away.

"What's the problem?" Loomis asked.

Graves turned his stiffly held torso toward her. "I got a call to bring up a new VCR. They told me the one he's got is busted."

Loomis tugged at her lip. "Must have made the call himself."

The guard said, "Could you ask him, ma'am?"

"Not now. He's sleeping."

At last, an up tick: Titus was taking his three o'clock nap on schedule, just as the newspaper article said he would be. "Not to worry, ma'am," Graves said, and once again pulled on the cart.

"Sorry," the guard said. "I can't let you in without approval or an escort."

Loomis mumbled, "He does love his movies." She checked her watch. "How long will it take?"

Graves paused. "Unplug the old one, plug in the new."

She questioned the guard with her eyes. He nodded his approval.

Signaling them to be quiet with an index finger to her lips, Loomis grabbed the large handle on the door. The guard held it open as Graves rolled in the cart. There was no threshold plate to run over, nothing to jostle or bounce the equipment, no noise except the quiet whir of well-oiled rubber wheels on tile.

Graves pushed the cart past the foot of the bed and around behind the credenza that had been pulled away from the wall, careful to keep his eyes forward, listening to the deep bellow of huge lungs feeding a three-hundred-pound body. He pulled the cart to a stop and immediately went into the routine he'd practiced so many times in his flophouse room.

First, the VCR.

Molly entered the house and stepped over a pile of magazines into the living room. There were crushed cans of beer and soda; sweatpants and socks lying like flotsam on a beach; books, pencils, papers, popcorn, things out of place, objects upside down. Jack saw a look of revulsion on her face.

"Needs a little picking up," he said.

"Save yourself the time, use a flamethrower."

He feebly lifted an empty soda can off the floor and tossed it into a trash basket, punctuating her point. Standing like a shipwrecked pirate— unshaven, uncombed, shirttails out, ragged jeans—he surveyed the wreckage as if he were seeing it for the first time.

"Now that you mention it," he said, "does look a little like the Pinn Island dump." She didn't get it. "Brooklyn," he said. "We used to hunt rats with flashlights taped onto twenty-twos."

She lifted an empty pizza box off an overstuffed chair and sat down.

He sat on the sofa and laid his stiff left leg on the seat cushions next to him.

"What brings you by?" he asked.

"You not answering the telephone. I got worried about how you were handling Winston."

He shook his head. "Hard to believe, isn't it?" The distance in his face faded. "You look good, Molly. How are you feeling?"

"I'm fine, back at work on the baby-doll murders. Although I won't be for long if I don't come up with something to report."

"Found anything new?"

"Maybe."

Jack smiled. "We're off-the-record, if that's what you want."

She slouched down in the chair. "Eliott Landy says whoever sewed up Zenobia Davis after she died also sewed up the baby-doll victims."

Jack sat up, bending his newly liberated knee in spite of the pain. "What are you talking about?"

"He found an unusual signature knot in the sutures on all four bodies."

"What kind of a knot?"

400

"It's called an arbor knot. Something fly fishermen use. Might have been tied by somebody left-handed."

Jack lifted himself forward to the edge of the sofa. "Jesus." Reaching out to a Chinese checkers set, he dropped a yellow marble into a hole, completing a long line across the board. "I think you've done it."

"Done what?"

"Found the missing link. The piece of evidence that's going to sink Abner Titus."

"How? What?"

"The arbor knot. It connects the baby-doll victims and Zenobia Davis, right? And I've found something that connects Zenobia Davis to Titus. Put the two connections together, and Titus is tied to them all."

"Wait a minute, wait a minute. What missing link between Zenobia Davis and Titus? You tried that in your press conference and got nowhere, remember?"

"Yeah, vaguely," he said, wishing he didn't. "But I'm talking about something else. A new piece of evidence."

She tucked her chin into her neck. "What evidence?"

"I think I can get my hands on a videotape of the operation that killed her."

She sat up. "A videotape?"

"Yeah. Whoever operated on her videotaped it."

"Why, for God's sake?"

"To show the world what the death of a third-trimester fetus looks like."

Her face fell. "That's *sick*. Who did that?"

"Titus. Or at least he helped set it up."

"Why?"

"As a favor to Eli Graves for helping get him on the Court." He had her attention. "Here's what I think happened. Titus delayed Davis's abortion until she was six months pregnant, then called her up and arranged the operation. That's why she wrote the words *clinic* and *midnite* and his telephone number on the envelope I found in her Bible. She went to the clinic for the abortion, as she was told, but something went wrong during the operation and she and the baby died."

Molly looked astonished.

Jack said, "You think this is off the wall."

"Actually, at the moment I'm thinking maybe it *isn't*. I know something that backs up what you're saying."

"What?"

"Still off the record?"

"Of course."

"Elliot Landy says Zenobia Davis's autopsy showed that she died of massive hemorrhaging during surgery. Something called a DIC. Happens during uterine operations, sometimes."

"Jesus, that's consistent." Jack got up and prowled around the living room with a slight limp. "This is it, Molly. I can feel it. I'm finally going to nail that fucker, and you're going to have the biggest story of your life."

"Where is this videotape?"

"Eli Graves has it."

Another surprise. "You're in touch with Eli Graves?"

"More or less."

"Good Lord, Jack, what are you doing getting involved with him? He's a fugitive, and a liar. He hates you."

"No more than he hates Titus."

"Titus? I thought he was his biggest supporter."

"Politically, yes. Personally, he hates him."

"He does?" Information was multiplying. "Wait a minute, let's take this a step at a time. Why would Graves cooperate with you of all people?"

"I have something he needs."

"What?"

"If I give him Titus's private telephone number at the hospital, Graves thinks he can record Abner talking about how he set up Zenobia Davis's operation. Put that tape together with the videotape of her death, and you've got Titus smack in the middle of the conspiracy that killed her."

She tried to digest it. "Jesus, Jack."

"What's wrong with it?"

"I don't know. Titus, for starters. I have a hard time believing he'd do this."

"Come on, Molly, at least try it on for size. You're a tough investigative reporter, remember?"

She bristled. "I am, but that doesn't mean I have to lose my mind." She crossed her legs and leaned forward, elbow on knee. "After the lies Graves told about you and me at the rally, how can you trust anything he says?"

"If he didn't have Titus in his sights, I wouldn't."

"He'd rather crucify you than Titus any day."

"He'd like to crucify me *and* Titus. He just can't do it in that order."

"What's his problem with Titus?"

"He won't say. My guess is that it's like any other conspiracy, sooner or later it falls apart. Picture it, Molly. Graves and Titus both have a hand in the Zenobia Davis operation. That means Titus has to be worried that Graves will blackmail him, which means Graves has to worry that Titus will get him first, which forces him to make a pre-emptive strike against Titus—"

"Whoa, wait a minute. Last I heard the Cold War's over."

"Yeah, but poker isn't." He leaned over his stiff leg, picked up a sweatshirt, and tossed it toward the kitchen door, in the general direction of a washing machine. "Any way you cut it, how would Graves know so much about Zenobia Davis's death if he wasn't part of it?"

"What's he know that hasn't been publicized?" Jack didn't answer. "Maybe he's making this stuff up as he goes," she said. "Weaving generally known facts with logical speculation is the most convincing lie there is. Did he tell you how Davis died?"

"Not exactly. He said something went wrong during surgery."

"Big deal. Anyone who reads the papers knows that."

"He's in this thing, Molly." Jack continued to knit together his case. "I wouldn't be surprised if he was in the operating room when she died. He went to medical school for a year."

"That doesn't mean anything. Can you tell from the videotape who performed the operation?"

"Graves says all you can see are rubber-gloved hands. But that's off the point. The question is, whoever did it, was Titus behind it?"

Molly tried to imagine it. "Could Titus's surgeon have done it?"

"Rachel? Not a chance. As far as she's concerned, Titus is the enemy."

"Some enemy. First she gives him a new kidney, then she performs emergency surgery to save his life. She's been helping this guy for a long time." She watched Jack lift two socks from the floor and toss them into a growing pile. "Don't you find it a little strange that a transplant surgeon operated on him for peritonitis?" she said.

"I've never thought about it. Far as I know, a surgeon's a surgeon."

"Not at all. Spending time with Elliot Landy has taught me a few things. I think there's something fishy going on between your pal Dr. Redpath and the chief justice."

"This is just a feeling, or do you have some facts?"

"Lord, you sound just like Elliot."

"Is that good or bad?"

She didn't answer. "Remember the press conference when Redpath held up the toothpick she said she'd removed from Titus's intestines? I arrived late and found it in a little plastic bag on the podium. I showed it to Elliot, and he said no way had it come out of someone's intestines. There was no discoloration from the digestive tract, no sign of bile or hydrochloric acid."

"Why would she make that up?" Jack asked.

"You tell me. Maybe she and Titus made it up together."

He stacked some newspapers. "Trying to fit Rachel Redpath into a conspiracy with Abner Titus just doesn't add up, Molly. She and Victoria did everything they could to defeat him."

"Isn't it possible your views about that are a bit clouded? Because of Victoria, I mean? A couple of detectives in the Hundred and Second Precinct still think she may have been part of a vendetta against abortion clinic bombers."

"That's horseshit." He sat back on the sofa and exercised his left leg. "With some hard evidence you might convince me Rachel was up to something like that, but Victoria?—" A thought interrupted him.

"What is it?"

"Rachel. I was just remembering something that happened at the funeral. I saw this woman dressed in a dark gray suit crying on Rachel's shoulder. When she saw me looking at her, she turned and walked away. Something about it made no sense."

"Maybe she was embarrassed that you saw her. Who was it?"

"I don't know. I've seen her someplace, but I can't remember where."

"What'd she look like?"

"Thirties, sandy hair pushed up under a black hat."

"Someone on Rachel's medical team?"

"I don't think so. She looked too tailored. More like a lobbyist, or a lawyer. Besides, I met Rachel's team at the farm at Thanksgiving." He positioned an empty can on the table. "Although, come to think of it, there was one person who never made it to dinner."

"How do you know?"

"I went outside to get some firewood and heard a clanking noise and some music coming from a building connected to the dairy barn. Phoebe Chang said someone was working there, she'd join us later, but now that I think about it, nobody did."

"What kind of music was it?"

"Elvis. 'Love Me Tender,' I think."

"I love 'Love Me Tender.' "

He gathered two empty cans from the table and floor and stacked them on top of the first. "I'm supposed to have dinner with Rachel Sunday night," he said. "Want me to ask her about the toothpick?"

She considered it a moment. "Why not?" Her eyes moved to a pot of yellowing philodendrons on the coffee table. She touched the leaves lightly. "Jesus, Jack. It takes a lot to kill a philodendron."

"I don't know why. I water it every day."

"Oh, Jack." She lifted the plant to prune the leaves.

"Don't throw it out," he said, his voice a bit too insistent.

She set the plant back on the coffee table and, sitting quietly, began pinching off dead leaves. "This was Victoria's, wasn't it?" she said. He didn't answer. She finished trimming it anyway.

"Molly, I—"

"No need to answer, really. Dumb question." She stared at him for a long moment. "Why don't you take a few days off and get some sunshine? You look like the underside of an oyster."

"I bought a ticket to St. Thomas after the funeral but never used it." He stacked another empty can. "Remember the fresh lobster and cold creamed corn on the beach at White Bay?"

"I remember you reading office memos while I went swimming."

They sat quietly as he continued building the empty cans. "I know you've got three good reasons to say no—"

"Jack—"

"—and a dozen *bad* reasons to say no—"

"Jack—"

"—but go with me, would you?"

"Don't, Jack. I can't. Really."

"Just as friends, no fooling around. We could take off tomorrow morning and come back Monday night."

"Tomorrow? Aren't you going to the funeral?"

He laid one more can on top of the wobbly tower. "What funeral?" he said, and the whole thing came clattering down.

Her face emptied. "Oh, God, Jack. I thought you knew. Winston died this morning."

He sat back, holding an empty can between his knees.

"I'm so sorry," she said. "When I asked how you felt about Winston, and you said, 'Hard to believe ... ' "

"I thought you were talking about his coma."

She stood up and sat next to him on the sofa.

He turned a can around in his hands. "When's the funeral?"

"Monday afternoon. Want to fly up together?"

He strained to stand up, then walked to an antique writing desk and looked at a black-and-white photograph hanging above it on the wall, a picture of himself and Winston resting elbows on a stack of precinct cards from Jack's first campaign. To no one in particular he said, "It never ends, does it?"

"What doesn't?"

He examined the empty can in his hand, turning it over and back again as if there was a message written on it. Finally he set it on the writing desk. "I'll have to meet you at the service. There's something I have to take care of here in Washington first."

She stood up and squeezed his arm. He gave her a hug and said good-bye.

He checked his watch and hustled stiff-legged up the steps and into the shower. If he hurried, he could still make the last one.

Dressing and packing quickly, he stuffed a few things into a bag, made sure he had his shuttle credit card, and limped down the steps. He walked to the small desk in the living room, picked up an index card, and with a felt-tipped pen wrote, *VCR for Sale. Call (202) 747-4555.*

The telephone number was written in reverse, exactly as Graves had told him to write it. Except that it wasn't Abner Titus's private line.

It was his own.

"What are you waiting for, Congressman?" Graves's telephone voice was urgent, as if he were selling a used car. "I asked for Titus's telephone number, not yours. He's leaving the hospital tomorrow, which means if I don't call him tonight, who knows if we'll get another chance."

"Problem is," Jack said, "once I give you his private number, I've given up my ace. I want something for it now."

"What?"

"The videotape of Zenobia Davis's operation."

The suggestion caught Graves by surprise. "Until I get Titus on tape talking about it, it's worthless."

"Cut the crap, Graves. I called a press conference in November and took a shot at Titus and all that happened was he got sworn in and I got egg on my face. I'm not going to accuse him of anything until I know I've got the goods."

"You won't get them with the videotape. I told you, all you can see are a surgeon's hands operating on a woman's abdomen."

"I'll take it. There are plenty of ways to tell if the patient is Zenobia Davis. The police have records, the medical examiner has photographs of her body. Same goes for Titus if you get him on tape. I'm not going public until I'm sure the voice is his."

Graves remained silent. "What have you got in mind?"

Jack tapped his finger on the receiver, thinking. "Forty minutes north of Washington there's a fork in the road called Arrowhead, Maryland. Take Exit Nineteen off the Beltway and go north to Route Twenty-Eight, then west till you come to Duck Paddle Road, then north to your first blinking light. Just beyond it you'll see a country store with a pay phone out front, one of those waist-high boxes on a pole. With me?"

"Keep going."

"I'll stop there tonight on my way to a nearby farm, around eight-thirty. I'll print the words *VCR for Sale* on the side of the shelter with Titus's private telephone number written backwards. You can hide in the bushes and watch, for all I care. After I've left, call the number and listen for his voice and you'll know you've got his direct line."

"What about the videotape?"

"Wrap it in a plastic bag and tape it to the top of the telephone shelter. I'll pick it up after dinner, on my way home from the farm."

"How long will it take you to drive from the pay phone to your house?" Graves said.

"To Georgetown? Forty-five minutes, an hour, maybe. What difference does it make?"

"Let's say it takes forty-five minutes." He paused. "You can pick up the videotape at twelve-fifteen. But not a minute sooner, got it?"

"What's so important about keeping me out of my own house till one o'clock in the morning?"

Graves paused as if he had to invent an answer. "I need time to make sure you've given me Titus's real telephone number."

"It's his. You'll know that the minute you call it—"

"Look, that's what I want! Take it or leave it!"

Jack groaned. "Sounds like you don't want me to see this videotape at all."

"On the contrary, I want you to see it real bad. But only after one o'clock."

Jack had another thought. "Tell me something, Graves. What's to keep this videotape from implicating you in Davis's death?"

"I told you, I had nothing to do with it. Titus arranged the operation and gave me the tape afterward."

"And you think a prosecutor will believe that?"

"Why not? There's nothing on it to prove otherwise."

Boy, does he not get it. Graves didn't know about the arbor knots, and he was naive as hell about the videotape. At a minimum, he'd have to admit receiving it from Titus; at a maximum, the police and the press would find evidence more damning.

Jack checked his watch. The deal on the table was like all deals: without time, there were no guarantees, only calculated risks. On the downside, Graves could take Titus's telephone number and run, refusing to give Jack the videotape, failing to get Titus on tape admitting he'd arranged Zenobia's operation. Nothing lost there; Jack had no more than that now. And the upside? The upside was a mother lode. If the videotape showed what Graves said it did, Jack could nail Titus *and* implicate Graves, avenge Victoria's death and Winston's *and* Zenobia's . . . make Molly a superstar, eliminate Titus's decisive Supreme Court vote and save *Roe* v. *Wade*, vindicating himself publicly. The potential payoff was far too big not to place the bet.

"All right, relax," Jack said. "I'll give you Titus's private number, and I'll pick up the videotape at a quarter after midnight."

"Not before. And MacLeod?"

"Yeah?"

"You're the one who can relax. Once I've got Titus on tape, believe me, he's as good as finished."

I t was quarter to nine when Jack turned off Duck Paddle Road onto the driveway leading to Rachel's farmhouse. The freezing rain in Washington had turned to snow in Maryland, and the elms that lined the gravel lane glistened and drooped with the weight of winter ice. As he neared the end of the driveway he saw a flash of light on the horizon, lightning or a snapped power line, he couldn't tell which.

He drove around the circular driveway to the tractor shed and pulled in, turned off his lights, and got out of the car. Floodlights mounted on the outbuildings lit the area. Limping toward the stone house, he saw that the snow was accumulating and quickened his pace.

The front door opened and Rachel appeared with a disarming smile and outstretched arms, appealing to his sense of civility, bleeding off some of his steam. She led him into her cozy, wood-paneled study where logs crackled in the fireplace and books, photographs, and memorabilia lined the walls. She had pulled a wooden extension from the front of her large mahogany desk and covered it with a linen tablecloth, candles, silver, and wineglasses. He looked around the room a moment, remembering Thanksgiving, and handed her his raincoat. Taking her cue, he sat in a leather club chair next to the fireplace, extending his stiff left leg on an ottoman in front of him.

She poured them each a scotch and sat on the leather couch.

"You're looking well, especially compared to the last time I saw you," she said.

He touched the patch on his left eye, which was healing but still black and blue. "Not as pretty as I used to be, but what the heck, can't have everything."

"I'm more concerned about what's going on *inside* your head."

Jack smiled at her. "I'm fine, Rachel. Really."

She took a sip and considered him from behind her glass. "Do you miss her?"

"A lot. How about you?"

"Every day."

Jack set his glass on the walnut table. "We were lucky we knew her. But when you think about it, she was lucky, too."

410

"How so?"

"Having two people love her deeply when most people are fortunate to have one." He watched for a reaction.

"Oh, she had far more than two," she said, sidestepping his insinuation. "Almost everyone who met Victoria loved her." She checked her watch. "Come on, let's have some dinner."

In the kitchen she dished up roasted game hen with mashed turnips, sliced beets, and green beans. He carried their plates back to the study, lit the candles, and poured the wine, then held her chair for her and sat on the other side of the table.

"Here's to V," he said, lifting his glass. She responded in kind, focusing on him over her glass, eerily . . . almost as if Victoria's eyes were behind hers. He chalked up the feeling to having had too little sleep.

For the next hour they chatted amiably, talking of nothing in particular—her work, his work, the Baltimore Orioles, the New York Knicks. After dinner and a dessert of hot apple crisp with fresh dairy cream, they settled in for coffee. Jack watched her across the table. "There's always been something unspoken between us, hasn't there?" he said.

"Yes, I suppose there has. What do you think it is?"

He shook his head. "Male–female stuff, competing personalities." She didn't react, so he decided to bump up the bet. "And Abner Titus."

"Titus? Why?"

"I keep getting this feeling there's more to your relationship with him than meets the eye."

"Well, I should hope so. I'm his surgeon."

"I don't mean that. I mean something else." He drank some coffee, admiring her cool. At the side of the table was a carved crystal shot glass holding a handful of round, wooden toothpicks. He picked one out and played with it. "I saw a reporter Friday," he said. "Molly McCormick. She's been trying to reach you."

"I'm not taking calls from the press right now. What did she want?"

"Apparently you left the toothpick you removed from Titus on the lectern at the press conference. She showed it to a pathologist who told her it couldn't have come from anyone's intestines."

She dabbled with her spoon and set it on her saucer, then rested her arms on the silk chair. "And?"

"I think she was looking for an explanation."

She stared at him coldly. "I don't have one. At least not that I care to give."

He wiped his mouth with his napkin and sat back. "Well, I'm glad we cleared that up."

"Look, Jack. This is the second time you've accused me of something sinister—first at the funeral, and now this. We can talk about our differences all you want, but I don't care for accusations."

He touched the crystal shot glass. "All I did was ask whether the toothpick came out of his intestines. I'm not accusing you of anything."

"Don't play cross-examining lawyer with me, Jack, I've been up against too many of them. It was a press conference, with television and photographs. I wanted to show what we'd found. Whether it was the exact same toothpick or a different one, I don't know and, frankly, don't care."

"Is that why you went to the trouble of putting it in a plastic bag?"

She shifted in her chair. "Jack, why don't we get to the bottom of what's really bothering you? I've known for a long time what you think about me and Victoria—I don't want to get into that right now—but what's this garbage about Titus?"

"I may be able to prove he engineered Zenobia Davis's death."

She put down her cup. "Are we back to that again?"

"It's different this time. There's a videotape of her abortion."

She paled. "A videotape?"

"Yeah. I understand it practically puts Titus in the operating room. I'll have it later tonight."

"Where? Where'd it come from?" Her voice wasn't as controlled as it had been.

"I can't say yet, but once I get it, I'll show it to you." He fixed his eyes on hers and twisted the knife. "Believe me, I intend to show it to you."

"Well, if you've never seen a DIC before, brace yourself. It's pretty awful."

"That's what I hear." He paused. "That's funny. I don't remember the press reporting that she died of a DIC."

"Yes, they did. Or else I heard it from the medical examiner's office. I don't know what you're driving at, Jack, but if you think my interest in Abner Titus is anything but professional, you're wrong." She saw a disbelieving face. "I detest his philosophy and you know it. As far as I'm concerned, the man is a danger to every woman with a womb."

"At least that's what you and Victoria always said."

"*Said?* Did you think we were kidding?"

He unwrapped an amaretto cookie. "Not at the time, but since the bombing, certain things I used to take for granted now seem"—he searched for the word—"curious."

"You mean suspicious, don't you? And threatening?"

"Maybe."

"Like me and Victoria."

Ah, so there it was, out in the open at last. Her countermove. As delicate as a battering ram. "Like you and Victoria, yes. Like you and Titus."

She uncrossed her legs and turned away a moment. And back. "Jack, I'm the last person in the world to throw psychiatry at anyone—"

"Jesus, Rachel—"

"—but you have to take into account what you've been through—"

"I don't believe this—"

"—the strongest person in the world would bend under the stress you've had."

Screw her. He was pissed off and tired, but not too tired to know he was being gaslighted.

The lights blinked once and went off, leaving them sitting in the flickering yellow of a candle.

"It's the ice," she said. "It's bringing down the lines." She pushed away from the table and walked to the window. "Good Lord, have you looked outside? We must have four inches of snow."

The lights came on again. She looked at her watch. It was eleven-thirty. "It's going to be a mess. Do you have to be in town early in the morning?"

"What's tomorrow, Monday? Not really."

"Good. I'll make up the guest room. Then I'm going to pour two stiff brandies and we're going to finish this discussion. All of it." She headed out the door into the hallway. "Break out some candles while we still have power. They're in the cabinet under the bookcase." He heard her climb the creaky wooden stair.

He found three candles in the cabinet. He lit one and, as he was setting it in an ashtray on the bookshelf, noticed the framed photographs he'd seen at Thanksgiving. The dark-haired woman sitting with Rachel at a fountain in Rome . . . the softball team gathered behind Rachel as she stood at home plate, a bat on her left shoulder . . . the Medal of Freedom— *Left* shoulder? Rachel was left-handed?

He picked up the frame. A face in the group of players looked familiar. He carried it to the desk lamp for a better look.

It was *her*—the woman in the charcoal-gray suit he'd seen at Victoria's funeral. A bit younger, but definitely her. Same hair, same eyes, same serious expression. Again he tried to place her, but couldn't.

He returned the photograph to the bookshelf and ran his finger along the edge, past the medical texts, past the photograph of Victoria and

Rachel on the steps of the Supreme Court. He stopped at a thin orange spine that caught his eye and pulled the book off the shelf. *Pumpkin Poems*, it said above a drawing of Old Mother Hubbard sitting in the window of a pumpkin shell.

He opened it to the first page and saw a handwritten inscription:

To Ray, whom I knew too little in the flesh, but will love forever in my heart.

It wasn't signed, but it didn't need to be. He knew Victoria's hand-writing as well as his own.

He felt his cheeks flush. He read the words again, looking for an escape from the obvious. The word *flesh* didn't allow it.

What a fool he'd been.

He had no idea how she'd done it, but from the moment he'd called Victoria at the spa and heard Rachel's voice, he knew that the two of them were together. No, that wasn't right; he'd known much longer than that. The cryptic chats, the looks they gave each other when they shouldn't have, the ones they didn't when they should have, the telephone calls, the closeness, the tension. They'd carried it off gracefully, discreetly, but still, he should have known. Detective Norm Pulaski was right. Things were exactly what they seemed to be, if only you looked.

He saw a small white triangle of paper edging out at the bottom of the book and pulled it out. It was a photograph of Victoria and Rachel standing arm in arm, wearing heavy coats. Behind them was a barn with a pile of firewood in front of it—the barn and firewood here at the farm. He looked at the lower right corner of the photograph and saw the date the camera had printed on it: *12-1*. Then it hit him: December first, when V was supposed to be at the spa. He finally got it. They were together here at the farm, not in Arizona. Of course. The telephone had been call-forwarded as he'd suspected—not from the farm to Arizona, but from Arizona to the farm. No wonder Rachel had answered when he called the spa—probably picked up the line by mistake, out of habit, then picked up her own line when he called back to confirm her voice. No wonder Victoria's skin had shown no trace of the sun when they'd met in Santa Fe. No wonder she'd been reluctant to make love. God. He hadn't been a fool, he'd been a total asshole. Stay the night? In this house? With Rachel Redpath?

He couldn't get out of there fast enough.

He grabbed his jacket and looked around the room for his raincoat but couldn't find it. *Fuck it.*

Heading for the front door, he passed the staircase leading up to the guest bedroom Rachel was making up. The same room he and Victoria had slept in Thanksgiving night. The same bed she and Rachel had no doubt enjoyed together. He looked up the steps in Rachel's direction. "Fuck you, too," he said, and walked outside.

The floodlights had been turned off, leaving the driveway and out-buildings in a sea of soot. His uplifted face told him the snow was still falling, heavily. He limped to the tractor shed, shoulders hunched and collar up, and climbed into his car. The engine started easily; he backed out too fast, spinning sideways in the snow.

He eased off the accelerator and drove down the elm-lined lane, slow-ing to turn onto Duck Paddle Road. He leaned forward over the steering wheel and peered through moving wiper blades, as if bringing his eyes a few inches closer to the road would help. He pushed the car as hard as he could; Arrowhead was only three miles away. At the rate he was going, in ten minutes he'd pick up Graves's videotape—if it was there—and be on his way home.

He maneuvered down the road's snow-covered center line, holding the car on track, holding his emotions in check. It wasn't his instincts that were to blame—it was his refusal to *listen* to them—his asinine, nit-picking lawyer's insistence on *proof* of everything. God, what an idiot. He'd made that mistake before. No more.

He held the road carefully, and after a few minutes saw the blinking stoplight at Arrowhead through a veil of falling snow. When the car was almost beneath it, the stop light suddenly disappeared. No blinks—just gone. He looked at the country-store window. The neon Live Bait sign had gone out, too.

There were no lights anywhere.

He swung the car right and faced the pay telephone where he'd stopped a few hours earlier and written Titus's private number for Eli Graves. Keeping his headlights trained on the pole and the engine run-ning, he got out, ankle-deep in snow, and walked to the shelter.

He laid his hand on top of it and searched for the videotape. Nothing there. He pawed the surface urgently. Still nothing. *Damn.* He waited a moment, imagining the possibilities, then ran his hand down the back of the box. A rise on the surface stopped his hand along with the crinkling sound of frozen plastic tape.

On the back was something stuck to the shelter. A bag. Carefully, he peeled it away, held it up in the headlights, and tore it open.

It was the videotape.

He slipped it into his jacket pocket and hurried back to the car, brushing the snow off his shoulders, knocking it off his shoes as he climbed in. He checked his watch. Quarter to midnight. He'd be home in an hour, a little longer if the interstates weren't plowed. Before one o'clock. As if that mattered.

He headed down Duck Paddle Road for Route 28 South, continuing to flog himself for having been so dumb about Rachel and Victoria. A slow-moving county truck, a salt spreader with a rotating yellow beacon on the cab, moved along in front of him. How could he have been so dense? If he were prosecuting himself for stupidity, he'd have a field day in court with himself— *In court.* The words bothered him. *In court?*

He stood on the brakes and spun the car into a half turn. *In court. The lady in gray. Abner Titus's law clerk. Pepper Loomis!* He'd seen her once before, sitting with Titus in the Senate caucus room during his confirmation hearing. Victoria thought she was bad news. *So what was she doing at Victoria's funeral? And what was Rachel doing embracing and consoling her?* He watched the salt truck's yellow flashing light disappear into the falling confetti. Rachel Redpath and Abner Titus. Linked in ways he could hardly imagine. Linked in one he could.

He headed back to the farm.

He pulled into the tractor shed and turned off the engine and headlights, surrounding himself with blackness. Combing through the glove compartment, he found a tattered pack of matches. He dropped them into his breast pocket and climbed out of the car. After feeling his way to the open shed door, he began groping through the snow toward the stone farmhouse. Squinting, he strained to find a light coming from a window—the glow of a candle, the beam of a flashlight. He saw nothing but midnight blue disappearing into black velvet.

He trudged forward, imagining how he'd conduct Rachel's interrogation—gloves off, to the mat—when off to the side something caught his eye: a small red dot, first on, then off. He stopped and peered into the pitch. He'd seen it over there, in the direction of the dairy barn. The light failed to reappear. He felt a rim of snow melting into his shoes.

He took two steps backward, retracing his path. The red light came on. A step forward, off—a step backward, on. It was visible only on a narrow line of sight; he must have been seeing it through a window, or a door. There was no electricity, no power, and yet—a light?

He altered course.

Working his way through the snow, he reached the barn door and found it ajar, as he'd guessed. He pushed it open wide and entered. Except for a tiny red light across the way, the room was black as a mine shaft. He stood and listened to his own breathing, smelling damp straw and cow manure.

A faint vibration shivered under his feet. What? He stood still and sensed it. It felt like a generator—maybe the red light indicated it was running, the power was on. Electricity to keep the cows from freezing, or to run the milking machines.

Or something.

He pulled the matchbook from his shirt pocket and struck one. There was no draft in the room, allowing the flame to burn straight up. He walked slowly toward the back of the barn, past the resting cows to the large door he'd found at Thanksgiving. The red light was now directly above it. The match began to warm his fingertips; he shook it out and struck another.

He lifted the heavy plank on the outer door and pulled it open by a steel handle, revealing the inner door a few inches away. Pressing his ear to it, he listened but heard nothing. He knocked and tried the knob. A dead bolt in the lock held fast. The heat of the match approached his fingertips again; he shook it out and lit another. Only two more in the pack. He ran his fingers along the edge of the doorjamb, hoping to find a key. No luck. He stood still and let the match burn.

What the fuck's going on?

He was being shut out of something important, manipulated by someone, or something, behind closed doors. He'd already taken enough of Rachel's shit for one night. He didn't like it.

The flame burned his skin and he shook it out. He lit the next-to-last one and retraced his steps to the outer door. As he neared it, the flame struggled against the wind and died. He stepped outside and headed back to the tractor shed, walking in blinding darkness.

He found his car, opened the door, and turned on the headlights, then straightened up and surveyed the room. There were plows and disks with summer dirt still caked on the blades. To the side was a snow-blower, shovels, a wheelbarrow, and a manure spreader with a coiled hemp rope hanging from the handle.

He walked to the machine, lifted the rope, pulled it around his shoulder, and continued searching. Against the wall was a massive workbench holding a motorized lathe. Next to it, with a pour spout inserted, was a half-pint can of motor oil. He limped over to it and lifted it off the bench. Beneath it, dirty and rusted, was a sheet-metal sign with a lightning bolt on it. He picked it up. The letters spelled ANGER. He rubbed the space in front of it, looking for the *D*. It had been worn off, like the *K* before EEP OUT, and the *H* and *E* bracketing IGH VOLTAG. *Voltage?*

He set it down, placed the can of oil in his coat pocket, and was preparing to turn away when he caught sight of what he was searching for: a crowbar. He lifted it off its wall hook and returned to his car to turn out the headlights. After pausing to his let eyesight adjust to the dark, he headed back to the barn.

He entered cautiously, lit his last match and, shielding it with his cupped hands, worked his way through the void back to the double doors. Before the flame died, he lit a piece of straw from the floor, quickly uncoiled the rope from his shoulder, and spread it over the top of the doorjamb, leaving its two ends dangling on each side. After pouring motor oil down both sides of the rope, he touched the burning straw to the ends, setting them on fire like two large flaming wicks. He had a minute, maybe two, before they'd burn out.

Working fast, he jimmied the end of the crowbar between the door and the jamb, then positioned his mended left leg at an angle, for leverage, and pulled back with all his might. The jamb bent away from the lock, but not far enough. He tried again. More bent metal, no exposed bolt. He repeated the move again—three times, four. Sweat on his forehead glistened orange in the flame, like a blacksmith's, and the hardened steel of the crowbar against the metal door filled the room with wrenching moans, waking the cows.

He pried harder, wildly, curling back the jamb until he'd finally exposed the brass bolt. The ends of the rope were burning close to the top of the door. He wiped his brow and watched plumes of his breath heave white against the air. Then he stood back, gripped the crowbar with both hands, and smashed the bolt with the tool's heavy, rounded end. When it appeared to be weakened, he dropped the tool and kicked the center of the door hard with the bottom of his foot—God help him if anyone was on the other side. Finally the lock gave way and the door opened, just as the rope flickered and died.

He stood in suffocating blackness, disconnected from everything but the sound of his own panting and the smell of burning, oil-soaked hemp.

He took a step into the black hole, felt the inside wall, and found a row of switches. He placed his knuckle under the first one, hoping the rumble beneath him was the generator he imagined, and flipped it up.

A row of ceiling lights lit up a workout room—barbells, exercise mats, a bicycle, treadmill, weight machine. A weight machine. *The sound of metal on metal.* On the walls were posters demonstrating weight-lifting positions, a large mirror, a gas-station calendar girl wearing nothing but red shorts and a smile. Beneath her feet the days of November had been marked off with large black *X*s.

He saw an entrance at the side of the room and walked toward it, touching the dust on the sports equipment as he went by. Opening the door, he found a small, shadowy hallway with closed doors on each side, their brass knobs glinting in shards of light from the room behind him.

He walked to the first door and opened it. The room was blind space, but the odor was instantaneous, powerful, and alien, making him slightly dizzy. Warning him of what he'd found.

He reached inside the door and hit the switch.

The operating tables stood a few feet apart, side by side, surgical lamps hovering above them like enormous bug eyes. Around the room were ominous devices—electrical equipment, gleaming pumps, coiled wires, stainless-steel counters, sinks, hoses—all the intimidating apparatus of the operating room, with monitors and telephones and speaker boxes attached. The place looked sinister, verging on haywire . . . so strange and unexpected he felt a surge of fear. He had opened a barn door, but instead of farmer Brown's pitchforks and hay he'd found the innards of a high-tech beast. A sleek Hydra, momentarily at rest. Lying in wait.

In the center of the room, clamped to the surgical lamps' armatures and aimed down at the operating tables, were two video cameras.

He took it all in and retreated to the interior hallway.

He tried the next door. It opened. He flipped on the light switch and saw what appeared to be a computer room. On the perimeter was a countertop desk with monitors and television screens, halogen lamps, external modems, electronic gear, and multiple-line telephones with squawk boxes attached. He stepped inside. Above the long desk were shelves with books, loose-leaf binders, medical manuals on anatomy, surgery, biochemistry. On one shelf was a long row of videocassettes, each box labeled and dated: S-1 through S-21, M-1 through M-15, a single B-1, and a single D-1.

He reached for a cassette and saw its label . . . partially obscured by a neon worm. Shit. What a time for a migraine.

He instinctively patted his pockets for an aspirin, knowing he had none, and stepped back into the hall in search of caffeine. He tried a door—it was a closet—and another door, which was a kitchen. Catch the headache fast, he told himself. The light from the hallway fell on a refrigerator across the room. He walked to it and opened the door. Vials of medicine, jars with labels, a carton of milk, but no colas. Above the refrigerator hung a round wall clock, its sweep hand jerking forward one second at a time. *What's so important about one o'clock?* he heard himself ask Graves on the telephone. The words played hide-and-seek in his stomach.

420

He opened the cabinets above the sink. No coffee, no tea. *I want you to see the tape real bad—after one o'clock,* Graves had said. He opened the cabinet below the sink and saw an empty garbage pail, a can of Lysol, but no soft drinks. *Once I've got Titus on tape, he's as good as finished.* He leaned his back against the counter and put his face in his hands. The neon worms were multiplying like amoebas. *What's so important about one o'clock?*

He stood still, replaying various memory tapes in his head: Molly's warning—*Why are you getting involved with Graves? He's a liar, and he hates you.* And Graves's tale about Titus—how he owed Graves something . . . how he'd arranged Zenobia's abortion . . . how he'd helped Iggy stalk his own father . . . all of it. He wasn't merely counting on Graves's complicated story. He'd constructed a fucking cathedral on it.

He pulled off his eye patch and held it over his heart like a miniature shield, but it was too late. The truth had already penetrated his breastbone and hit its mark.

He searched his splintering assumptions for a solid answer, a defense, a justification. *The tape! It's on the videotape!*

He stuck his eye patch into his pants pocket and limped back to the computer room, pulling Graves's videotape from his jacket pocket as he went. He found a VCR, shoved the videotape into the slot, followed the coaxial cable to a TV monitor, and turned it on. Fuzz appeared on screen.

He wiped his forehead and laid his finger on the Fast Forward button and pushed. Black-and-white snow appeared on screen. Then colored snow. He hit the Play button and waited, listening for sound. A picture formed on the screen . . . something familiar . . . a picture of—

The Road Runner? *What?*

His lips tingled with numbness.

He hit the Fast Forward button and watched the Road Runner climb a mountain at lightning speed—*beebeep*—Wile E. Coyote dashing off the edge of a cliff, screeching to a halt in midair, looking down between his legs, plunging to a tiny dot at the bottom of a canyon—*poomp!—beebeep.*

The tape turned to black-and-white snow again.

He continued racing ahead on fast forward, looking for Zenobia Davis—fast forward—looking for color—fast forward—looking for an operating table, a scalpel, a room—fast forward—a doctor, a clinic, *come on, be there*—fast forward—*there's nothing there*, fast forward, *it's blank*, fast forward, fuzz.

He stared at the screen as the tape continued to roll, refusing to believe his eyes. Watching the blank monitor, the truth slowly began emerging in small blips, like sonar images of an iceberg. *Ping*: there was no videotape of Zenobia's death. *Ping*: Titus had not arranged her abortion after all. *Ping*: Graves had lied about Titus helping Iggy to hunt him down. *Ping*: Graves had told the truth about enough things to make his lies work. Everything had been a ruse to obtain Titus's private hospital number. A ruse so Graves could . . . what? If he didn't want it in order to get Titus on tape, what did he want it for? And why did he use his worst enemy to get it?

Wait! Look! The static lines on the TV screen had disappeared. A flicker of something—and a picture! Moving feet . . . the video camera jiggling, someone holding it as they walked. The sound of shoes crunching in snow, heavy breathing.

The lens caught empty space, and then a light . . . illuminating a pole with a pay telephone on it . . . the telephone in front of the country store! The camera came closer, jiggled again, and stopped a few feet away . . . blurry, now focused . . . now zooming in on—a telephone number on the side of the shelter. Abner Titus's private telephone number, in reverse. The number Jack had written there only a few hours before. With his felt-tipped pen. In his own personal handwriting.

What the fuck?

The sound of breathing again . . . the camera light turned off . . . blackness. Then light and color again . . . the inside of an automobile— the camera jiggling wildly before settling down on the passenger side of the seat, aimed back at the driver. It was Eli Graves, leaning against the steering wheel, smiling at the camera, holding something against his cheek above his neck brace. A piece of— What was it?

An index card. The one with Jack's home telephone number on it. In his own handwriting. The one he'd printed at home, the day Molly told him Winston had died. The one he'd pinned to the bulletin board at the hospital. In order to get Graves to call him back. To arrange the video-tape swap.

He felt his hull take a gash, the chill of ice water pouring in . . .

Graves dropped the index card and lifted something. A Polaroid photograph of an electronic device. The metal housing of a stereo set—no, it was a VCR—filled with wires and gizmos and long, tan sticks. *Long tan sticks?*

"This is it," Graves's voice said. "Pretty nifty, huh?"

Graves dropped the photograph and stared into the lens and grinned. "Congratulations, Congressman. We did it."

We did it? *We* did what?

Jack stood still and watched it unfold in his mind. Eli Graves's videotape. Evidence of a conspiracy between the two of them. A perfect setup: pictures of tan sticks of dynamite in a VCR, the statement, *We did it.* Pictures of Titus's telephone number in MacLeod's handwriting—a coconspirator's handwriting. The telephone number Graves wanted so badly—*one o'clock*—the one he got from Jack, which made it look like the two of them were working together—*He's finished*—as if he and Graves were going to, were planning to, were plotting to—to—

Oh, Christ. What have I done?

The screen turned to snow and the tape stopped.

He raised his watch. Twelve-fifteen. He grabbed the telephone; it was dead. He heard a sound behind him and turned. Rachel stood in the doorway with a shotgun pointed at his chest.

"Jack!"

He hung up and looked around wildly.

"What in God's name is going on?" she said.

"I need a telephone!"

"What for? What are you doing?"

"I think there's a bomb in Titus's hospital room. Set to go off at one o'clock!"

She lowered the shotgun. "A bomb?"

"I think Eli Graves planted a bomb in Titus's room. If I'm right, it's going to go off in forty-five minutes." Another glance at his watch. "Forty-three."

She slumped and her hand rose to her chest. "Sweet Jesus."

The Jeep sat across the circular drive facing an oak tree. Rachel jumped in and started it. Jack climbed into the passenger seat. "Get on the car phone!" she said, throwing the gear into reverse, spewing snow and gravel. She stopped to put the jeep into forward.

A ghost appeared at the driver's side window.

Rachel rolled it down. "If the phones come on," she said, "call the hospital and tell them there may be a bomb in Titus's room!"

"Oh, my God!" a woman in a coat and nightgown said. Jack saw her face.

It was Pepper Loomis.

Rachel hit the accelerator and tore down the lane. She turned onto Duck Paddle Road, fishtailing the Jeep and knocking down her mailbox. Straightening out, she started the windshield wipers and accelerated.

"Get on the phone!" she said.

He dialed and waited for the line to connect. The telephone gave them the *dee-do* sound of empty space.

"Damn!" she said. "Land lines from the mobil cells are out. Keep trying! We'll be in range of one that works in a few minutes!"

She knew the road perfectly, but the snow made it difficult. Another five minutes and they'd be on Route 28, another twisty two-lane road. Not until they reached Interstate 270 would the roads be plowed. Maybe.

Jack hit the green Send button. Still no connection.

She downshifted, and the engine groaned. "What kind of a bomb is it?" she yelled over the noise.

"Dynamite. I think it's in his VCR."

"His VCR? What if we get somebody to unplug it?"

"I don't know. It might have its own power source, a battery. Could be rigged to blow up if it's moved. The only safe thing to do is get him out of the room!"

"Lord," she said. "He's all wired up to the support and monitoring equipment." The Jeep went into a skid; Rachel steered out of it skillfully and accelerated back to sixty. "How do you know there's a bomb there?"

He redialed. Nothing. "I found out from Graves."

"*Graves?* What's *he* got to do with it?"

"I got involved with him."

"What kind of involved?"

"I gave him Titus's private telephone number at the hospital."

She absorbed it slowly. "Good Lord, Jack. What in God's name possessed you?"

"I told you. I thought Titus killed Zenobia Davis."

"Well, he didn't."

She started into another spin, steered out of it, and accelerated.

"How do you know?" he asked.

"Because I know who did."

"Who?"

She downshifted and turned into a sharp curve. "I did."

"You?"

"Try the phone!"

"What do you mean you killed Zenobia?" The phone didn't connect.

They hit a bump and flew off the ground, landing on the Jeep's left tires. On a dry road the rubber would have dug in and flipped them into a sixty-mile-an-hour roll, but the snow allowed them to slide, bringing the right wheels back onto the surface. Jack lowered his hand from the cab's ceiling.

"Don't kill yourself," he shouted. "This is my problem, not yours!"

"*Your* problem? If Eli Graves has done what you think he's done, thirty minutes from now he's going to blow up everything I've worked for all my life!"

"What work? What the hell are you talking about?"

She pushed the fallen sun visor out of the way and pointed at the glove compartment. "I need a cigarette," she said. He opened it, lit a long, thin brown one, and handed it to her. She dragged on it and cracked the window. The snow rushed at them through the headlights. "Lord. Whether we save him or not, at this point there's no way you're not going to find out."

"Find out what, for Christ's sake?"

"About Abner."

"What about him?"

She took another drag and exhaled. "Do you know what an ectopic pregnancy is?"

"A fertilized egg growing in the fallopian tube?"

"Usually, yes. But sometimes an egg migrates into the abdominal cavity, attaches itself to the abdominal wall or intestines, and starts growing there. A few undetected cases have even gone to term and the babies delivered."

"What's that have to do with Titus?" He watched her.

"He has something growing inside him."

"What the fuck are you talking about?"

"He's carrying a fetus."

"A *fetus*? What kind of fetus?"

"A human fetus."

"But he's a man!" Suddenly he had doubts. "Isn't he?"

"Of course, but so what?"

"So *what*? Are you telling me you planted a fertilized egg inside a *man*?"

"Not exactly, but sort of."

"What's 'sort of'?"

She didn't answer. "Try the telephone."

He pressed the green button. Once again, static. He hung up and imagined Titus's belly. "Jesus. Does he have any idea?"

She looked over at him as if he were the one who was crazy.

All at once he was speeding toward the unknown with someone he didn't know. Suddenly he felt he had more in common with any man on earth—a Tibetan on a yak, an Eskimo in an igloo, a hunter on the Serengeti—*any* man—than he did with this woman. She was abnormal. A deviant. A mutation he'd never encountered or heard of anywhere.

"Why?" he asked. "How could you do this?"

She remained focused on the road, once again not answering.

"You don't want to tell me?"

"No, it's not that," she said. "It's just that if you have to ask the question, you probably wouldn't understand the answer. Keep trying the phone."

Another transmission, another signal lost in space.

He checked his watch. Twenty minutes to go. They were approaching Interstate 270, where they'd make better time in the slushy tracks of cars and trucks.

"Look!" Jack said. "A pay phone!"

She braked and went into a long, twisting slide that ended with the Jeep facing in the opposite direction. He jumped out and ran to the phone while she turned around and pulled up next to him.

He climbed back in. "Busted," he puffed.

The tires bit down. He hit the green Send button, heard an irritating *dee-do*, and hit the End button. Then again.

This time the static was overlaid with the sound of a ringing telephone.

"George Washington University, how may I help you?" a distant voice crackled.

"Hello!" he shouted. His answer was a field of white static. "Damn."

"We're getting close!" she said. "Try Titus's private line."

He started to dial, and stopped. "Shit, I can't—it might trigger the thing." He redialed the hospital, pressed the green button, the End button, and the green button in succession. "If we get through, maybe you should do the talking."

"About a bomb? Are you serious? That'll mean police interviews, hospital inquisitions, the press—I'll lose Titus to another doctor in two seconds. You'll have to do it. Tell them you're a congressman."

"How's that help? Soon as the police interview me they'll know about you."

He tried again. No contact. He held the receiver chest-high, hypnotized by the onrushing snow, trying to organize the questions that bombarded him like flakes against the windshield. "You still haven't told me how Zenobia Davis died."

"I don't intend to."

He pressed the buttons on the phone.

"Come on, Rachel, talk to me, tell me what the hell's happening here! I want to know how and why you make a man pregnant!" He wasn't asking, he was demanding.

She looked at her watch—seventeen minutes to go—and shifted in her seat. "A fertilized egg planted in the abdominal cavity of a man is no different from one planted in a woman. The difficulty is bringing the pregnancy to a cesarean delivery without a rupture and massive hemorrhaging. That's why ectopic pregnancies are so dangerous."

"Doesn't the fetus need female hormones or something?"

"Nothing that can't be administered IV. Titus is on progesterone, but that's more a precaution than a necessity. What the embryo needs is a rich supply of blood, male or female. Beltway coming up."

They turned onto the interstate and pursued a set of taillights in the distance.

"I still don't get it," Jack said. "There must be a technical problem with this thing somewhere."

"A problem?" She let out a small laugh. "There should be only one. The *biggest* problem is the placenta. Even after a successful cesarean delivery, you've still got the placenta rooted in the vascular system. That's why nature created uteruses. The decidua—the womb's lining—sloughs off at birth, bringing everything out fairly neat and clean, including the placenta."

"Where's that leave Titus? How're you going to keep him from bleeding to death?"

"I'd tell you, but at the moment I don't think you'd like the answer."

They sped by a station wagon and headed into the void, with no distant tail light as guide.

"Goddamn it, Rachel, *I want answers!*"

"I'm sure you do." She ejected the cigarette. "Look. If the biggest problem is the placenta, instead of transplanting an embryo, why not transplant an entire uterus? The whole reproductive package—the fetus, the placenta, the endometrium—everything but the vaginal birth canal?"

"Is that possible?"

"Of course it is. The Cincinnati Zoo's been transplanting the embryos of blue baboons and endangered species into cows' bellies and bringing them to term for some time now, completely normally. We've simply taken it a step further by doing the same thing with pregnant uteri."

"Uteri? You've done more than one?"

"Yes." She picked up speed. "Snow's getting slushier."

"You mean you've done it on animals?"

"Mm—animals, yes." A glance at him. "But not exclusively."

He and the receiver waited, both suspended in mid-air. "Jesus, Rachel. Are you telling me . . . *what* are you telling me?" He looked at the passing telephone poles, each one connected to the other by long strands of wire. "Are you trying to tell me the baby-doll victims—Shivers and his pal, what's-his-name, and Billy Bannister—that you . . . that they . . ." He waited for a denial.

She turned caustic. "You ask that question as if we're not at this very moment racing to save the life of someone you've helped target for a bombing."

He shook his head. "Good God, Rachel. You deliberately *killed* those guys?"

"Actually, we tried very hard not to."

"Then how'd it happen? I'll bet they didn't die laughing."

"Animal work and live organ transplants answer a lot of questions about tissue rejection, blood compatibility, and the like, but they can only take you so far." She turned off the Beltway onto Canal Road. "Don't act so shocked. At some point science always needs live subjects. Medical science included."

She turned for a second and found him mesmerized.

"Everyone has a killer instinct, Jack. Pushed far enough, people use it to protect themselves."

"Protect themselves? From what?"

She shook her head. "I'm not trying to excuse what I've done, I'm trying to explain it. You've seen scientific risks all your life. You're just not used to seeing them taken by a woman."

"Men, women, what's the difference?" They sped toward Chain Bridge. "The transplants didn't work, did they?"

"Actually, they *did* work. It was postop complications we couldn't control. But Titus has shown no indications of a rejection—although, as I say, taking a fetus to term and performing a successful cesarean is another matter." She wiped the corner of the windshield. "He'll be our fourth procedure."

He stared at her. She didn't *look* like a mutant—she had elegant features, clear eyes, a full head of hair. Christ. Maybe she wasn't a mutant. Maybe she was exactly the opposite—a normal, ordinary woman who was merely revealing the secret that made all women tick. The female X factor. A hidden, hardwired chip of female chromosomes, physiology, and logic that men had talked about, written about, and joked about for centuries, but after the laughter and bleeding had stopped, left them staring at each other as dumbfounded and mystified as ever. Maybe that's what he was seeing. Maybe he was the first man to see it. He hit the Send button. Make that the first *surviving* man to see it. Shivers, Moon, and Bannister must have seen it, too, before they died. Whoever, whatever she was, a few things about her were apparent: she was powerful, she was angry, and she was capable of doing anything.

No answer. "Damn!"

"Come on, Jack. We're in range!"

"I'm trying!"

"Trying isn't good enough! Are you doing it right?"

"Of course!" He hit the green button.

"Considering you can't see the butter dish when it's staring you in the face, you never know."

"Good God, is there *anything* Victoria didn't tell you about me?"

"Nothing relevant." She reached over, took the receiver, cleared it, and punched in the number. "Don't worry. She gave you good marks on the stuff men think is important."

"As if you knew."

"I know more about men than you think." She handed him the telephone. "Here. You must have been pushing Redial without Send."

"No, I wasn't." Patronizing son of a bitch.

"Try it anyway. Push the Send button." She slowed down behind a slow-moving truck.

"What are you waiting for?" he yelled. "Let's go!"

A huge semitrailer roared by a few feet away, rocking the Jeep. Rachel floored the accelerator, caught up, and cut through the truck's rooster tail of slush. "Good Lord," she said, "the way you backseat drive, you and Graves didn't need a bomb to kill Titus, you could have just taken him out for a ride."

No static—they were in range of a working land line. A steady ring. "George Washington University, may I help you?"

"Listen carefully, please!" Jack said. "I have information that a bomb may have been placed in Chief Justice Titus's room!" He wanted to get to the verb before he lost the connection. "You need to—"

"Just a moment, please." Silence.

He waited.

"Tell the operator he's on the sixth floor," Rachel said.

"Security, Wilkins speaking," a man's voice said.

"Mr. Wilkins, I have reason to believe someone may have placed a bomb in the chief justice's hospital room! Believe me, this is not a prank."

"Who's this again?"

"It doesn't matter who—the important thing is to get the chief justice out of his room immediately!"

"What kind of a bomb?"

"Dynamite. Most likely wired into the VCR."

"How'd it get there?"

"I'm not sure."

"Hold the line a minute."

"We haven't got a minute—"

"Hold the line, sir." Jack could hear the man talking to others, telling one of them to alert the nurses, get up to the sixth floor and call him on line two. "How is it fused?"

"I don't know anything about it except I think it's there and it's timed to go off at one o'clock." He waited, hot and frustrated. "Can't you get the chief justice out of his room and we can talk about this later?"

He could hear the guard having another conversation. Rachel said, "Tell them to alert the nurses' station!"

"He already did," Jack said. He lowered his voice. "Look, Mr. Wilkins. I know this sounds strange, but somehow someone got into the chief justice's room with a bomb, and it's going to blow up in—eight minutes."

"I understand what you're saying, but you'll have to bear with me a second. The chief justice is hooked up to some pretty complicated equipment. A phony threat that gets us to move him too fast could endanger him, if you see what I mean."

"I understand, but if you don't get him out of there immediately, there won't be anything left of him to endanger!"

Wilkins spoke to someone: "He's on line two. Pick up and tell me what's going on up there." Back on the phone: "How big is the bomb?"

"I think it's two or three sticks of dynamite."

"Will it blow if we unplug it?"

"I don't know—that's why you've got to get him *out!*"

Rachel said, "Tell him not to worry about disconnecting Titus's support lines!"

"Have you called the bomb squad?" Wilkins asked.

"There isn't *time* for the bomb squad!" Jack said. "Go ahead and disconnect his support lines. If you don't get him out of there right now, they're both going to be blown up!" Jack heard the word *both* and felt his skin turn cold.

"Say again?" Wilkins said. "Sorry, but did you say *both*? Both who?"

"Whoever is—you know, with him. His nurse."

"What nurse?"

Shit. No nurse. "Never mind, it doesn't matter. Just get him out of there!"

A pause. "Hold the line a minute." Another pause—static—then disconnect.

"I lost him!"

They sped down Canal Road. The snow was softer, and the Jeep moved faster. Two minutes to go.

He redialed the hospital and waited for another connection. They turned off the Whitehurst Freeway and raced the last few blocks. She gunned all four wheels toward the building's entrance and skidded to a stop. Jack jumped out and ran toward the entrance as fast as his limp allowed. He reached the glass door and grabbed the steel handle.

PART FOUR

The bomb went off.

The concussion rocked Jack backward; he slipped in the snow, caught himself, and looked up as bits of glass, wallboard, and debris rained down from a smoking, gaping hole. Rachel stood next to the Jeep, head tilted back, mouth open.

Jack ran with a slight hobble to the entrance. The lights on the elevator were still working, but he couldn't be sure; he took the stairwell instead, two steps at a time, pulling on the railing for support.

He opened the sixth-floor door. Cones of light from battery-powered emergency lamps pierced the dust and smoke. Down the hall he could see the outline of someone standing, a man, coughing and stepping around a door that had been blown off its hinges. Moving closer, he saw that it was someone coming to the aid of the security guard, who was on his knees. *Titus?* Not big enough.

He moved down the hall, stepped past the two people, and entered a room fogged with smoke and airborne grit. He extended his hand, choking, searching for a bed. Nothing was there except debris crunching underfoot.

He tapped his hands and fingers over the wall, a blind man feeling for the braille of a child. Sharp objects had been driven into the surface— bits of twisted sheet metal, wire, and glass. He felt something wet and sticky and brought his hand close to his eye. Black liquid . . . too dark to tell. He touched it with the tip of his tongue. The taste of iron. Blood. *Whose?* He felt flapping, scalloped flesh on his palm—new pain—and then light-headed relief. The blood was his own.

There was heavy breathing at the door. He turned and saw Rachel's silhouette.

"I can't tell," he said.

She ran down the hall toward a hazy glow where electric lights were still working. Jack followed. A few people appeared in the hallway; coughs and murmurs mixed with the sounds of sirens filtering in. Rachel saw a nurse from her surgical team standing guard at a door.

"Where is he?"

"Inside," the nurse said.
"Wait here," Rachel said to Jack.

Abner Titus was on a bed in his hospital gown, wide-awake, still rigged to oxygen and a stainless-steel pole with bags of saline and medicine ports. Two male hospital attendants were connecting the heart monitor, tightening C-clamps and taping clear plastic tubing in place while a nurse checked to be sure they were unkinked and flowing.

Gracefully, calmly, Rachel walked to his side.

"I hear you had a bit of excitement." She looked for the electrical jack leading to the fetal heartbeat monitor, but it was nowhere in sight. Wrong time to ask for a Doptone to hear the fetal thump. She picked up an ordinary stethoscope from the top of his bed, placed the ends in her ears, and slid the diaphragm under his gown, onto his chest. "How are you feeling?"

"I'd feel better if somebody told me what the hell's going on."

She said nothing, searching for the sound of two heartbeats. "What'd they tell you?"

"Nothing! An army of white coats came rushing into my room, pulled everything apart, and rolled me down here. Next thing I know I hear an enormous explosion. How'd you get here so fast?"

She moved the stethoscope onto his abdomen and strained to hear life.

He grabbed her hand. "What the hell are you doing down there?" She stood up. "I want to know what's going on, Rachel, or I promise you, I'll have myself another doctor in here in five minutes!" He let go of her hand and glared at her, citing her for contempt.

She played with the stethoscope.

"I'd appreciate everyone leaving the room," she said. As the nurse and orderlies left she patted Titus on the arm. "I'll be right back."

Jack waited in the hall.

"I've got a problem," she said. "We're in the wrong environment here—I haven't even got the equipment I need to find a fetal pulse. Not only that, Titus smells a rat. If I sound unconvincing to him, he'll bring in another doctor." She tapped her lips. "I think the only chance I've got is to tell him."

"You mean you were planning *not* to?"

"Of course not. Not until the fetus was mature enough to deliver."

She tapped her fingers against her cheek. "Damn it, Jack. Only three more weeks and we could have tried to incubate."

"Jesus, Rachel. You really want it all, don't you?"

She looked at him coldly. "I'd like to save the fetus, if that's what you mean."

"What for? As a monument to your scientific genius?"

"I won't dignify that with an answer."

"Come on, Rachel, this is sick. The fetus isn't the issue here, Abner Titus is. I don't like him any more than you do, but if he were a woman, you'd be calling this is an outrageous forced pregnancy. He'd abort and you know it. You'd be the first to give him a hand."

Her eyes narrowed. "Thanks for the advice, Jack. Now I've got to get back inside."

He stepped in front of the door, stopping her. "You're into something enormously wrong here, Rachel. If he wants to get rid of it, you've got to help, not stop him."

"And you'll still feel that way tomorrow?"

"Of course. Why wouldn't I?"

She hesitated. "It's like everything else, Jack. It all depends on whose ox is being gored."

He looked surprised. "Wait a minute—this isn't *your* child, is it?"

She smiled wanly. "At my age? I wish it were. It would make life a lot easier."

"Whose life?"

"Yours."

"Mine?" He was confused. "Why mine?"

She stared at him.

He stared back, watching the answer develop before his eyes . . . slowly but clearly, like a brand-new Polaroid snapshot.

"That's right," she said. "It's yours."

"**V**ictoria didn't go to Arizona," Rachel said. "She came here for the transplant of her uterus."

He remained motionless.

"Pull yourself together, Jack. I may need your help. This little bomb you've gotten involved with may have missed the judge, but it isn't doing much for your child's future." She disappeared inside Titus's room.

He sat on the floor with his back against the wall, his forehead resting on raised knees, hands behind his neck. The hallway was crowded with people now—police, firemen, electricians, hospital staff. And reporters. A fire official asked the press to remain behind a yellow police tape near the nurses' station, a few yards away. Jack was oblivious. His mind kept tripping over a simple message: *My child, Victoria's child, is still alive.*

A voice said, "Jack!"

He looked up and saw Molly standing with her cameraman, assuring a fire official that they were moving along as fast as they could go, okay?

"What are you doing here?" he asked.

"I was about to ask you the same question." Her cameraman pulled her arm toward the plastic ribbon. "We have to move over here," she said to Jack. "Come with me a minute."

He stood up—*Rachel's in there telling Titus right now*—and moved to the press area.

"What in the heck happened here?" she asked, uncurling her microphone cable. She tested for sound.

"Looks like somebody planted a bomb." *What's Titus going to do?*

"Give me one minute on tape, would you?"

His mind was elsewhere. *Obviously, he'll get rid of it!*

She cleared her throat and lowered the mike. The halogens lit up. "Congressman MacLeod, what happened here tonight?"

He woke up. "I'm not sure, but I intend to find out."

"According to one of the nurses, someone called in a tip about the bomb and that's what saved the chief justice's life. Do you know who it was?"

438

"I really couldn't say." He looked down the hall toward Titus's room and lifted the yellow tape. *What the fuck can I do to stop him?*

She held him with another question. "Do you think the bomb was planted by a pro-choice radical?"

Christ—Rachel's going to blow it! Molly's words reached his brain on a delayed feed. "No, I don't."

"You were the chief justice's biggest critic in Congress. What went through your mind when you heard he was almost killed?"

He looked at her, trying to play back her question. "What went through your mind?"

"*Your* mind, yes." She held the microphone in front of his face, waiting.

"Well, nobody wants to see this sort of thing happen, not even to an adversary." He looked toward Titus's room. "I'm sorry, but there's something I have to do at the moment, if you'll excuse me."

He lifted the ribbon. Molly watched him, concerned, and turned to face the camera.

"Well, there's one piece of the story, Dave. Congressman Jack MacLeod, who only a few weeks ago charged Chief Justice Abner Titus with being responsible for a woman's death, is here tonight trying to find out who made an attempt on the judge's life. Another case of politics making strange bedfellows, even in a hospital. This is Molly McCormick reporting from George Washington University Medical Center."

The crash came just as Jack opened the door. He saw Titus standing barefoot in a white hospital gown, gripping the metal frame of a bed he'd overturned, staring at Rachel across an upended mattress, heaving like a bellows, stoking his fury. She waited, a look of terror on her face.

"Close the door!" she said.

"What's—"

"It's nothing I can't handle! Just keep everyone out!"

Titus saw the monitor on the wall above the bed with its pulsating blips mocking him with his own heartbeat. Enraged, he reached up and seized the box, tore it off its moorings, and heaved it toward Rachel, missing her by inches before smashing it against a vertical support between the windows. The cable connecting him to the monitor went taut, jerking at his chest. He looked down at it dumbly, Frankenstein's monster discovering his stitches, and grabbed the wire and the other tethers—lines into his bloodstream, the oxygen tube in his nostrils. He yanked them away, ripping the suction cups off his skin and the IV shunts from his veins.

Rachel screamed, "Stop!"

Titus looked up at her through panicked, raving eyes.

A nurse opened the door. Jack closed it, but not before she had seen what was happening.

Titus was stalking Rachel with clenched fists and bloodshot eyes.

Jack left the door and moved toward Titus's back, trying to flank him from the rear. Off to the side, on a hospital cart, was the roll of adhesive tape the orderlies had used to jerry-rig Titus's equipment. He picked up the spool, tore off a yard, and stretched it between his hands like a restraining strap.

The nurse reentered the room holding something in her hand. Seeing her, Jack turned to stop her. "She's okay!" Rachel said. She held out her hand to receive something as the nurse edged along the walls toward her.

Titus stepped around the overturned bed.

The nurse handed Rachel a syringe and a bottle of clear fluid. With her hands shaking, Rachel held the bottle upside down, pushed in the hypodermic—a glance at Titus—and drew out the sodium pentothal. She cleared the needle with a snap of her finger and a squirt into the air and held it up like a weapon.

Titus pushed an intravenous pole out of the way, clearing the last obstacle between himself and his prey. She pressed her back against the windows. He took a step toward her—

"Abner!" Jack barked.

Titus stopped and turned around. Jack held the tape between his thumbs and forefingers, palms exposed, as if to say he came in peace.

Titus faced him, reddened, sweat dripping off his chin. His face looked puzzled, like a dog watching television. Then a trace of recognition flickered in his eyes. He stumbled forward and dropped onto his knees in front of Jack. "Help me," he wheezed.

Jack knelt.

Molly entered the room with her cameraman, camcorder on his shoulder, tape rolling. Rachel saw the halogen lights and yelled, "Turn those things off and get out!" but they paid no attention. The nurse started for them.

Titus reached up for Jack's shoulders and fell forward, exposing his bare buttocks through the back of his hospital gown.

"I want them *out of here!*" Rachel yelled at the nurse. She leaned forward—jabbed the needle into his left buttock—and mashed down the plunger.

Titus straightened up and let go of Jack.

The nurse stepped in front of the camera, arms raised. The cameraman continued shooting over her shoulder. She put her hand on the lens and pulled it down. Molly said, "All right, we're going!" and the cameraman said, "Don't touch the lens!" The three of them went out the door.

Titus rose to one knee, head down, grimacing. Rachel knelt next to Jack and held Titus's head.

"It's gonna be okay," she said, trying to calm him.

Titus looked at her with fearful, red-rimmed eyes, then turned to Jack, grabbed the lapels on his coat, and pulled his ear down to his mouth.

"Help me . . . get out," he whispered, man to man.

Jack pulled back and looked him in the eye. "I can't."

Titus's vacant face asked, Why not?

"It's mine," Jack answered softly.

Titus's eyes widened, and instantly, Jack wished he hadn't said that. He searched for different words, better words, a softer approach, but it was too late; his answer and the sedative had already taken their toll. Drool escaped Titus's parted lips and his head began bobbing like a newborn baby's. With his eyes rolling upward, his hands slipped down Jack's lapels and he slumped to the floor.

Jack rested his neck on the back of the leather chair. Phoebe Chang stuck her head through the lounge door.

"He's sleeping. Should we connect the monitors?"

"No," Rachel said. "Let's wait until he's awake."

"I've still got two heartbeats," Phoebe said softly, backing away.

Rachel smiled at her.

"You need some sleep," she told Jack. His eyes were shut and his body immobile, as if he were listening to a Walkman. She crushed out her cigarette. "I promised Vick I'd do my best to keep the fetus alive. Far as I'm concerned, her death doesn't change that."

He didn't open his eyes or move.

"Don't you agree?" she asked.

"How should I know? I don't even know who she was."

"I know there's a lot to choke down here, but don't let your imagination run away with you."

That opened his eyes. "My wife-to-be joins a criminal conspiracy to transplant her pregnant uterus into the chief justice, and you're warning me about *my* imagination?"

"Victoria wasn't part of this project until the last four months of her life. Before that she suspected something was going on, but she didn't want to know what it was. So she didn't."

"Sure, she didn't," Jack said. "Just like the piano player in a whorehouse doesn't know what's going on upstairs."

Rachel pulled her hair back. "News reports of Shivers's death set off her first alarm. Privately, she told me to stop doing whatever I was doing, but of course I couldn't do that. I did ask her for something, though."

"What, her left ovary?"

"A blood sample. I wanted to find out if she and Titus were a good tissue match." She didn't see Jack's face flush. "None of the staff was compatible with him. Vick said forget it, she'd never donate an organ. But I knew she might change her mind eventually."

"Why was that?"

"She listened to me." Rachel took a replenishing breath. "We did a

442

blood analysis, and sure enough, they were a near-perfect match. Heaven-sent."

"And just like that, she said here's my pregnant uterus."

"On the contrary, she remained opposed to the transplant for all the reasons you could imagine—major surgery, an outrageous criminal conspiracy. When she stumbled into Bannister's body at the clinic, I thought that was it, she was so upset."

"I remember her call." He rubbed the back of his neck. "What an act."

"It wasn't an act. Between that night and her concern for you, I thought she'd changed her mind completely."

"Me?"

"Absolutely. She thought if she made the donation, sooner or later she'd be identified as the biological mother, which meant you'd be suspected as the father. She thought that would be very hard on you, especially if the fetus died. You know, given the Honey O'Connor thing, a lost child, your burning desire to have a family."

"But it wasn't enough to stop her."

"In the end, no, it wasn't. But something else almost did."

"What?"

"The fetus. She thought if the transplant failed in the first ninety days of pregnancy she'd lose her uterus, but not a viable fetus, a child. But what if the transplant worked? What if Titus discovered the baby before it could be delivered? What if he chose to destroy it? That was her greatest fear." Rachel considered something. "Amazing. Despite all my predictions to the contrary, that's exactly where we are today."

"Tell me when to feel sorry."

She seemed genuinely surprised. "Victoria had a terrible time with this, Jack. Really."

"Then why did she do it?"

"If it hadn't been for a turn of events, I'm sure she wouldn't have." She opened an ice bucket on the counter, dipped her fingers into water, and drew them across her forehead. "Remember the night the two of you found Zenobia Davis's body? She was sure Titus was responsible—and then, an hour later, she found out he'd been nominated to the Supreme Court."

"I remember."

"When she realized Titus was about to become chief justice and put a few million other women in Zenobia Davis's shoes . . . well. That's when she decided she'd try to get pregnant after all. And did. If you recall."

As if he needed to be reminded. "But Titus wasn't responsible for Davis's death," he said.

"That's right, but she didn't know that."

"Why not?"

"Because I didn't tell her."

Jack stood up slowly. "So you were somehow responsible for Zenobia's death . . . which means you must have been the one who took her body back to her apartment, then called Victoria at the restaurant and told her to find Zenobia and get her to the clinic. Right?" Rachel offered no defense, not even a response. "Jesus Christ, Rachel. What kind of a buddy-fucker are you?"

Rachel paled. "This admittedly was not my finest hour. But obviously, I couldn't tell Vick the truth."

"Why not?" He held up a hand. "Don't tell me. Because then she would have blamed you instead of Titus for Zenobia's death, right? Which meant she wouldn't have been angry at Titus enough to get pregnant, or enraged enough to join your screwball plan?"

Her lips parted, but she didn't answer. Instead, she picked up the telephone and dialed Charlie Chadwick, her lawyer, while Jack paced, then sat down and cooled off. After apologizing for the hour, she arranged a meeting in his office.

"Don't stop the story now," Jack said. "The night we find Zenobia V gets pregnant, refuses to tell me, says she won't marry me, and we break up. That was all part of the plan?"

"She didn't want you to know of the pregnancy, or what she was contemplating doing with it. By the time she got pregnant, she'd concluded it wasn't inevitable that you'd find out after all."

"But I discovered it anyway."

"And pressed her to get married, and have the baby. Everything came to a head on Thanksgiving Day. She had decided to tell you everything—you know, the lawyer's answer to all problems, full disclosure. I knew the minute she did that the transplant was finished. But thanks to President Clay, it didn't come to that." Rachel touched the coffeepot to see if it was warm. "Remember when Victoria watched him announce he was putting Titus on the bench without Senate confirmation? When she said, 'You win'?"

"Yeah."

"Well, she wasn't talking to the television set, or President Clay, or the chief justice. She was talking to me."

She poured herself a cup of coffee and offered one to Jack, who declined. "The day after Thanksgiving, instead of going to a spa in Arizona, she came to the farm. That was the night I forgot which line was reserved for call-forwarding from out west and nearly blew it by answering your call." She took a sip of coffee and winced. "I checked Victoria into the hospital the next day, Saturday. We prepped her for surgery, arranged Titus's fake attack of peritonitis, and performed the transplant." She checked her watch. "Time to get moving."

Jack was lost in a black forest.

"Jack?" she said. He looked down at his wet and filthy clothes.

Rachel led him through a door into a scrub room. "Shower's over there," she said. "You can wear this." She tossed him a surgeon's light blue top.

He untied his shoelaces. "What about Pepper Loomis? What's she got to do with this?"

"What *hasn't* she got to do with it is the question. She loaded Titus's cherries with cassavathate, which gave him symptoms of peritonitis when we needed him in the hospital. One day in his office he became short of breath and she gave him mouth-to-mouth resuscitation. She helped Tara give him his vaccination and his first dose of Leukenase."

"Tara?"

"Our anesthesiologist. When I couldn't get Titus in for a checkup, Pepper brought him into the courthouse parking lot with a mob of screaming protestors. Tara knocked his keys under the car, which got him down onto all fours, and gave him the injection." Rachel opened her locker door. "In some ways, Pepper had the toughest job of any of us. She had to work with him every day, keep up appearances. She even had to help him write his abominable antiabortion decisions."

"And the toothpick?"

"It came from the crystal shot glass on the table."

Jack pulled off his shoe. "Who else knows about this?"

"The seven members of my team, plus Pepper Loomis and Kathy Keenan. Nine in all. The same people who've kept the project a secret for three years."

Jack leaned down to untie his other laces. "You know I'm going to have to tell the police about Eli Graves and the videotape."

She looked alarmed. "Why? You didn't commit a crime—all you did was give someone a telephone number. You didn't know he was going to try to blow him up."

"True, but they may not see it that way. Anyway, the police have to know who did it. Graves is still out there somewhere."

"But he's already a fugitive, and the police are looking for him anyway. Why do they need another reason?"

"That's not how it works, Rachel."

"Jack, listen—"

He held up his hand. "Okay, okay. I'll figure it out. Right now I want to take a shower and try to save . . ." He paused. "My kid."

"By the way, I know you think it's a girl, but it's not." He didn't get it. "I'm not sure Vick would have gone through with it if it had been," she said.

He felt his cheeks burn. "You trying to tell me she was willing to put a boy's life in danger, but not a girl's?"

"Actually, more like the opposite. Considering how Titus felt about women, she thought if he found out he was pregnant with a girl he'd terminate in a second, but a boy he might give a chance."

"Good God," Jack whispered. "You guys really cut the bullshit thin."

Rachel looked unapologetic. "Regardless of what you think, she cared about this child. She even gave him a name."

"What was it?"

"Ray."

Ray? He blanched.

Rachel said, "It wasn't my idea."

He wasn't listening. His mind had already leaped back to Rachel's study and the book of *Pumpkin Poems . . . To Ray, whom I knew too little in the flesh, but will love forever in my heart.*

Her son, in her flesh. A book of nursery rhymes Victoria had inscribed not to Rachel, but to her own child.

He stared at a drain on the locker-room floor and watched Victoria's love affair with Rachel disappear through the grating.

"What's the matter?" Rachel asked.

"I was thinking about a children's book I found in your study. The one with the inscription to Ray." He fiddled with his shoe. "I thought it was written to you. I thought you and Victoria were, you know . . ."

"I know what you thought. I've known for a long time. But you were wrong."

"Why didn't you say something?"

"Better not to. It helped keep you from seeing what was going on."

He ran his hand through his hair.

"Don't be so hard on yourself," she said. "Men's sexual paranoia has always been good camouflage for what women are really up to."

"Yeah, but Jesus, Rachel. I misread this one big time."

"Anyone would have. Vick and I talked in riddles and generalities all the time, trying to keep the project confidential. We called it our 'vacation.' " She closed her locker door and tried the latch. "Masters never understand the slaves as well as the slaves understand the masters, Jack. But cheer up, it won't be that way forever." She tossed a towel at him. "I'll be ready in five minutes."

Titus lay asleep on his back, lungs expanding and contracting, heartbeat steady, his consciousness submerged in a sea of phenobarbital. The room was dim, lit only by a crack of light slipping through the slightly open bathroom door. Suddenly something inside him stirred, waking him before the sedative had run its course.

He opened his eyes, groggy and confused. Where was he? He moved his hands. Sheets. He was in a bed—but whose? He searched the blank ceiling for bearings, a heartbeat, recollection, memory.

He raised himself onto his elbows like a punch-drunk fighter. Dizzy, bewildered, he groped his way to the edge of the mattress and dropped his legs over the side. How interesting. Something resembling a pair of feet down there. Possessing a mind of their own, they pawed the air clumsily—misjudged the distance to the floor—and lured him over the side, smashing his knees, stomach, and head against the tile.

He lay still. No pain. Utter confusion.

He lifted himself to his hands and knees, breathing hard, and examined the seams in the tile flooring. They were very straight. And long. And fascinating. His doped-up head was content to follow them endlessly, unconcerned about time.

Once again, something inside him stirred. This time the sensation felt vaguely familiar—something he'd experienced before. *It's coming to me. . . .*

His heart got it before his brain did. Pounding like a fist, it began pumping the sedative from his mind, clearing a path for his memory: the sound of an explosion . . . Rachel Redpath in his hospital room . . . standing beside his bed . . . telling him he was . . . telling him . . . telling him he was—

Oh, my God. *Oh, my God.*

He broke into an icy sweat, instantly sickened and shaking. His brain screamed *Expel!* and his body shuddered. Straining at the neck, he tried to vomit up the creature in huge, gut-wrenching spasms, turning his stomach inside out. Rotten hospital chicken and putrid carrots spewed from his mouth and nose. But no baby.

He gasped for air. Another gag, another eruption. More desper-

447

ate breathing. He opened his eyes and saw a thick line of slime sagging from his mouth to a puddle on the floor. Flooded with revulsion, he lifted his hand to swat the scum away, slipped, and crashed to the floor.

This time, pain. A numb cheek. Blood running from his nose.

He lay with his face in the goo, concentrating on the basics: air in the lungs, consciousness in the brain. Gathering his strength, he raised his head; a few feet away was a friendly object he recognized—a white porcelain toilet bowl glowing in the bathroom light behind the partly opened door. Water to clean himself off, shimmering like an oasis.

He tried to raise himself to his hands and knees to crawl to it, but nothing happened. His muscles were exhausted from vomiting and turning over beds and throwing monitors against walls. He waited a moment and tried again. Once again his body refused.

Panic rippled through him. He talked himself down: retreat, collect your strength, take refuge. Find your dignity. Clear your mind. You're in a hospital. Someone will be here any minute . . . they'll pick you up, clean you off, and . . . And what? What next? What will they do to you? What will they do to your—

His skin tingled and he began hyperventilating again. *This is not possible.*

He lay shivering and cold, struggling to contain hysteria. He saw no way out, no place go, nowhere to hide. He was a prisoner now, a captive of his own exhaustion and the beast that coiled in his gut, feeding off him, growing inside him, moving around like a—a—*cancer.*

He closed his eyes and prayed, promising whatever was asked of him. He wanted to cut a new deal with God, but so many things were happening in his abdomen he couldn't concentrate. As if heaven was listening, he felt a cool shroud descend upon him, easing his fears. Then it hit him: *a shroud?* Shrouds were for dead people. Was this—*it?*

A life-ending vision flashed before his eyes—not a corny montage of his past, but a clear, strong image of who he was at that very moment: the chief justice of the United States, the most powerful judge in the world, helpless and alone, raped by a surgeon's knife, impregnated with a tumor, lying in his own stench. Pathetic. Small.

Finished.

An enormous sadness overcame him. *I'm going to die.*

He lay still and wept, and in a few moments once again felt something rising in his throat. Not a physical substance this time, but a word . . . pushing through the distrust and anger and scars that had insulated him from his feelings since he was a ten-year-old boy who'd learned his parents hadn't wanted him.

"Mommy." The word emerged in a whisper, and a bubble of phlegm ballooned out of his mouth and popped.

"**H**o-lee shit, will you look at that!"

Dave Leeds, anchor for Washington's Channel 6 News, sat in the amber-lit control room in front of a TV monitor with Molly McCormick and Tim Benton, the show's producer. At five-thirty in the morning, they were getting punchy. "Look at that!" he yelled. On screen was Abner Titus on his hands and knees, hospital gown open at the back. "Supreme Court butt, right before your eyes!"

"Looks like any other big butt to me," Molly said. They watched Rachel plunge the syringe into Titus's hip.

The tape ended with the engineer in the control room freeze-framing Titus straightening up in front of Jack, his hands reaching out for help. "What the hell are they doing?" the producer asked.

"Who gives a shit?" Dave Leeds said. "The action's great!"

"But what's it say?"

"It says the chief justice of the United States went bananas and a Medal of Freedom surgeon jabbed a needle in his ass in front of a United States congressman! Jesus, Tim! What more do you want?"

"An explanation."

Leeds turned to Molly. "So give him one."

Molly shrugged.

Leeds said, "Why don't we air it this morning, feed the network, and smoke the whole thing out?"

The producer stood up from his swiveling stool. "It's not that simple." He saw Leeds's stricken look. "We're in a Supreme Court justice's private hospital room, for crissake!"

Leeds turned toward Molly. "Did anybody tell you not to enter his room?"

"Not exactly."

"What's that mean?" the producer asked.

"When we came into the room, Dr. Redpath told us to turn off the camera but we kept shooting."

"So?" Leeds said. "It's not her room, it's his."

"She's his doctor," the producer said, calling him an asshole.

Leeds put his forehead on the console and pretended to beat his brains

450

out. He looked up. "Tim, baby, you can't be serious. What's the problem here?" The producer didn't answer. "You want privacy?" Leeds said. "No problem. It's not like you can see his balls or something." He grabbed the intercom mike and looked toward the engineer's booth. "Jerry, run the tape back, will you? See if you can see the chief justice's balls." He looked up at the producer. "What else?"

The producer pushed a rheostat on the control panel up and down. "There has to be more to the story."

"Aw, come on, Tim. We can't sit on footage like this. Somebody else will hear what happened and run with it."

The producer walked toward the door with Molly following. "I'll get back to you."

Leeds shouted, "It's not every day you see a supreme court justice on his knees! Think of the ratings!"

The producer stopped in the corridor to talk to Molly. "I'll take this to the guys upstairs and meet you back here in fifteen minutes. We'll lay in your voice-over, and get it ready for air."

"It's too fast," she said. "This is the tip of the iceberg. If the networks see it, they'll take it away from us."

He raised his fist to his mouth and blew on his clenched fingers.

Molly said, "Nobody else has this tape, believe me. This is our Emmy, Tim. I can smell it."

He thought a moment. "I'll ask the lawyers to vet it, buy some time—"

"All I need is a day," she said, backing away. "Two max."

He shook his head, no promises. "Just find out what the fuck's going on."

"Tell me about the kidnappings," Chadwick said.

Charlie Chadwick sat in his well-pressed slacks and Harris tweed jacket with his feet up on his desk—brown loafers, ribbed socks— pouring himself a small scotch from a ship's decanter. His sixty-year-old face was thin and shaved, smelling lightly of the bay rum he'd used since he was a teenager. Drinking or not—and rarely was he not—he was still one of the best lawyers in Washington, even at six A.M.

"We agreed that the only subjects we'd experiment on were men who'd killed someone in the abortion-clinic bombing," Rachel said.

"You didn't think that would excuse you, did you?"

"Of course not."

Chadwick rested his glass on his lap. "Why the baby dolls?"

"Pepper Loomis and Kathy Keenan—she's director of the Capitol Hill Women's Clinic—the two of them felt that Melvin Shivers's death should be used as a deterrent to other clinic bombers."

"And you?"

"Honestly? If it had been up to me, I would have given him a decent burial in the north pasture and moved on to his partner, Harley Moon. But they felt strongly about it, so I went along. And who knows? Maybe they were right."

"Why do you say that?"

"There's been only one clinic bombing on the East Coast since."

Chadwick lifted his feet off his desk. "What about the autopsies?"

"We had to find out what had gone wrong, of course, and we had to conceal anything that might give us away. We flushed out their blood hoping the medical examiner's lab would have a more difficult time finding the immunosuppressants, and we excised a portion of the iliac artery that would have revealed our supply line to the uterus. I made my autopsy cut on top of the transplant incision hoping a busy medical examiner might not see the scar tissue, even though I knew it was unlikely. Then we removed their livers."

"Why the livers?"

"Livers are an excellent place to find the compounds we were using. We also hoped it would throw everyone off."

452

"What was the point of the broken pencil?"

"It was an accident. Tara picked up one of MacLeod's office pencils to puncture a hole in the doll's belly so she could insert the capsule with the note saying, *Keep it.* We didn't know a piece had broken off until we read about it in the newspapers."

"And Victoria Winters wasn't in on it?"

"No. Not until she donated her uterus. She never did know Pepper Loomis was involved."

Chadwick swallowed some whiskey, a bit more than usual for the hour.

"Why did you tell MacLeod that you killed Zenobia Davis?"

Rachel tilted her head back and spoke to the ceiling. "Vick and I did all we could to convince Zenobia to abort, but she wouldn't do it without the court's approval." She looked ahead. "Titus was grinding out his magnum opus on abortion law, which left her twisting. It was outrageous, but there it was. The more it dragged on, the more upset Victoria became." She straightened up in her chair. "At that point we had kidnapped Harley Moon and were looking for an organ to transplant into him. Zenobia couldn't stand the idea of carrying a rapist's child and couldn't stand the idea of killing it, either. She didn't want any more children, so the solution to her problem looked like the solution to ours. We'd harvest her uterus for Moon, save the fetus, and she'd end her pregnancy. Looked good, except for one small catch."

"What was that?"

"She wanted assurance that she wasn't violating the judge's court order. As it turned out, Titus had decided he couldn't legally stop her anyway, which Pepper Loomis, his law clerk, knew about, of course. So she called up Zenobia with the news two days before the opinion came out. Apparently Zenobia wrote Pepper's telephone number on an envelope and stuck it in her Bible." She smiled wanly. "It's always the little stuff you don't anticipate."

"Did you make the transplant?"

"Yes. It went fine for Moon, but not for Zenobia."

"What was her problem?"

"Massive hemorrhaging. An event known as a DIC. Rare, but it happens. It's all on videotape."

"You taped it?"

"We videotaped everything." She inhaled. "When Jack said he had a videotape of Zenobia's death, at first it really threw me. I couldn't figure out how he got it. Then I realized it wasn't my tape; he'd been sold a bill of goods by somebody else."

"If Zenobia Davis died of a rare complication that occurred in the middle of a consensual operation, I wouldn't say you killed her, Rachel."

"Maybe not legally, but it was still my fault. A few days before the operation, Victoria finally convinced her to abort, but by then I didn't want to lose the fetus. I couldn't say that to Victoria, so I had Pepper call the clinic, as Titus's law clerk, and warn us not to violate a court order. The call came just as she and Zenobia arrived. If I hadn't pulled that trick, Zenobia probably would have aborted safely and been alive today." She punched out her cigarette.

"My dear Rachel." Chadwick waited for her to say more, but she was quiet. Finally he leaned forward and asked the question he'd postponed for as long as he could. "Why?"

She placed both palms on her face, then lowered them and looked at him with flushed cheeks and watery eyes. She had spent most of her life waiting for this question, but hearing it now, she couldn't answer.

"If the time comes, Charlie, get me the right jury and I'll explain the whole thing."

It was the most he would get from her.

She checked the time. "Are you going to come watch?"

He shook his head. "I'm against this, Rachel. You're creating a witness to your crime." She stood up anyway. "Besides," he said, "I faint when anyone so much as spells the word *b-l-o-o-d*. I don't think I could take it."

"We'll know in a minute if someone else can."

She opened the door to the conference room, where an audience of one sat patiently, nervously, waiting.

Rachel pushed the rewind button on the VCR.

"The transplant is the moment when it all comes together—or doesn't," she said to Jack, who stood next to her. "What you won't see here is the enormous amount of preparation leading up to the surgery."

"Such as?"

"To start with, you need enough tissue compatibility between the donor and recipient to reduce the chances of an acute rejection. But even if you clear that hurdle, the recipient's immune system can still cause a rejection."

"Which is why you suppress it chemically."

"Yes, but it's not like tuning a violin. If you go too far, you cripple the body's ability to reject infections."

Snow stormed on the TV screen as the tape continued rewinding. She opened a warm cola and poured herself some caffeine.

"The trick is to tailor an immunosuppressant cocktail to fit the particular patient. With Melvin Shivers we didn't suppress it enough. He rejected the uterus and triggered a spontaneous abortion. It happened at the farm while I was at the hospital giving a speech to my students. On medical ethics, as I recall. One of our young surgeons opened him up and tried to stem the hemorrhaging with Phoebe helping on the telephone from the hospital lab. When I discovered that my beeper battery was low, I left the lecture to help, but it was too late."

"Same thing happen to Harley Moon?"

"The opposite. We suppressed his immune response too much. He died of pneumococcal pneumonia. Unfortunately, Zenobia's fetus died with him."

"Zenobia's?"

Nuts. She'd let it slip out. "Yes. I'll explain when we're finished." She took a swallow of cola. "Billy Bannister was our last effort before Victoria's transplant. We wanted to make dosage adjustments on him, but when we opened him up, we found a massive cancer. Because Victoria and Titus were a perfect tissue match, we went ahead with their procedure anyway."

"What's in the cocktail?"

"Steroids, FK 506, anticancer medication, anti-inflammation agents. And Leukenase, a compound we developed doing baboon kidney grafts to humans."

He imagined the baby swimming in a uterus filled with toxic drugs. "All that stuff doesn't poison the fetus?"

"No. Pregnant women have been undergoing kidney and liver transplants for years. With Shivers and Moon we simply missed the right combination."

"Who was Shivers's donor?"

She hesitated. "Kathy Keenan."

The screen lit up with an image Jack couldn't quite make out—light blue fabric with a wide slit in the center, beneath it a yellowish, wrinkled surface. Then something familiar: a belly button at the top, an abdomen below.

"Who's that?"

Gauging his reaction, she answered cautiously. "Victoria." No response. "Still with me?"

He didn't hear. He was imaging the Victoria he knew . . . the one in the bikini at the beach, stepping out from under a shower with a towel over her head and shoulders . . . a tanned, smooth abdomen glistening with rivulets of water, not the one he was seeing on the screen, shrouded and mummified, opened up in a sacrifice to a god he didn't know.

"There's a chair behind you," she said.

"What's wrong with her skin?" he asked quietly.

"Nothing. It's been scrubbed with Betadine and covered with clear plastic adhesive to help keep bacteria from infecting the incision."

Jack didn't understand why Victoria had voluntarily left the earth for this distant planet.

Gloved fingers adjusted the fabric around her belly. "The hands you see are mine," Rachel said. Her on-screen voice said, "Can I start?" A woman's voice answered, "Anytime."

"That's Tara talking, our anesthesiologist."

On screen, Rachel's hand held a scalpel with her index finger extended upward. She positioned the tip of the blade below Victoria's navel, half an inch to the left of center, and in one smooth motion drew it downward toward her pelvic bone. The skin parted easily, leaving two ribbons of red in its wake.

Jack's nostrils expanded in search of oxygen. On screen, hands dabbed the blood with sponges.

Rachel handed the scalpel to her scrub nurse and received a clean one in return, another precaution against contamination. She positioned the blade near the top of the outer incision and moved it downward once again, cutting through a half-inch layer of yellow fat.

Jack stayed on his feet.

She checked his face. "Are you all right?"

He nodded, and they both watched. She drew the scalpel one more time, exposing a silvery, thin layer of tissue. Using a forceps, she lifted it like a tent—then snipped it open the length of the outer incision.

Jack watched as a pair of beef-red muscles came into view running vertically in Victoria's abdomen.

Rachel's fingers moved the muscle to the side and applied two metal devices to hold the incision open. She saw Jack wince at the enormous size of the opening. "The key to successful surgery is exposure," she said.

On screen, another thin layer of fat revealed itself. Instead of cutting through it this time, her fingers spread it apart like soft pie dough, clearing the way to the final sheath covering the abdominal cavity: a resilient, whitish membrane as thin as a coat of paint. Jack had never seen anything like it. Despite its strength, it appeared to be delicate and tenuous, as if nature had gift-wrapped the important parts of the human body in gossamer tissue. Once again a pair of forceps appeared, lifted the membrane, and held it while she nicked it with a scalpel in order to see what was beneath. The small opening resembled the keyhole to a dark closet.

Seeing no bowel, Rachel inserted the tip of a scissors and extended the incision, opening up Victoria's interior.

Jack finally backed up to the chair and sat down.

Rachel's fingers examined the intestines for abnormalities. Finding none, she packed them out of the way with sponges, leaving a clear view of the pelvic cavity—a gently arched bone; a flaccid bladder, catheterized and empty; more blood vessels; and, finally, the object of it all, the human prize itself:

A smooth, pink uterus. The sacred cradle of life.

Jack leaned forward. The organ was about the size of a big tennis ball—for some reason he'd imagined it larger—nestled into a glossy spiderweb of ligaments and tissue. On either side at the top were two thin shafts of flesh—the fallopian tubes—with fingers at each end cradling almond-shaped ovaries, like tiny hands carrying miniature footballs.

"The uterus is actually anchored in the pelvis by very little," Rachel said. "Three paired ligaments hold it in place on each side, and some connective tissue encases the cervix in the top of the vagina. What we're going to do now is sever them all."

"Where is Titus at this point?"

"You'll see in a minute. First, we're going to dissect the ovaries from the uterus."

"It doesn't need them?"

"No. It needs the progesterone they produce but that can be administered by injection."

Jack watched as Rachel severed the pencil-sized cables of tissue holding the top of the uterus, first on the left, then on the right.

One pair of ligaments gone, two pairs to go.

Next came the hammocklike webbing holding the uterus along its sides. Hidden inside each side were large twin arteries and veins carrying blood to and from the fetus. "Nature gave the uterus blood vessels on both sides," she said, "but one side is enough. That's what allows us to make the transfer without interrupting the flow of blood to the organ. We leave one set of vessels connected to Victoria while we attach the other set to Titus. Once his blood is circulating in it, we sever the remaining set connected to her."

Starting on the left, she cut away the webbing—careful not to touch the tube that carried urine—until the first set of blood vessels were exposed. Normally the size of a drinking straw, they had been expanded by pregnancy to the diameter of a dime. She clamped, cut, and tied them off, leaving inch-long stumps. "Those are the ones we'll connect to Titus."

On-screen, she repeated the excision on the right side, this time leaving the uterus's artery and vein attached to the mother. Then she turned to the last set of anchors, the cardinal ligaments, and severed them on each side. Finally she clamped the vagina and cut away the cervix.

Except for the one set of vessels feeding blood on the right side, Victoria's uterus was now disconnected from her body.

Jack ran his hand over his face. "No offense, but this looks almost too easy."

"In an emergency, an experienced surgeon can remove a uterus in twenty minutes."

"Not if you're trying to save a fetus, I assume."

"No, of course not. Interrupting the flow of blood to the fetal brain is a serious problem."

"How long can it be stopped?"

"I wouldn't want to do it for more than a couple of minutes."

"But you can't complete a transplant in two minutes, can you?"

"No. But watch." She pointed to the side of the screen. "Behind me on an operating table is Titus with his abdominal cavity and groin opened up."

"Groin?"

"The vessels we'd ordinarily use to service the uterus were serving his new kidney. Next choice was to go to the femorals, in his groin. Phoebe Chang has already grafted Gore-Tex shunts into them, inserted two long plastic tubes, and clamped them off. We're going to attach the other ends of the tubes to the blood vessels I left on Victoria's uterus and establish blood circulation between her and Titus."

Jack slid down and rested his chin on his hands. Amazed.

Rachel's gloved hands disappeared from the camera's lens and returned with a long piece of half-inch-wide clear plastic tubing, closed by a clamp. "The tube looks empty, but it's filled with saline to remove the air. Injecting a bubble into the uterus could be lethal."

She laid the tube down and found the inch-long stump of severed artery on the side of the uterus. Holding it between her fingers, she clamped it and removed the suture. With the stump now open, she flushed it with blood thinner to prevent clotting, then carefully inserted the end of the plastic tube into it like a plumber fitting one pipe inside another. The match was good.

They watched as she wound a line of suture material around and around the stump, like a fisherman tying a fly, sealing the artery to the tube. Then she grafted a second tube to the stump of Victoria's uterine vein, just as she had to the artery.

"Nearly ready."

"What happens if it doesn't work?"

"Hypothermia."

"How's that?"

"We'd flush the uterus with icy saline until we'd cooled it enough to stop the fetal heartbeat. Then we would have removed it, placed it in ice slush to maintain its temperature, and finished the transfer to Titus."

"Stopping the heartbeat doesn't kill the fetus?"

"No. It starts up again as soon as it's warmed. Usually."

He thought she was kidding.

"It's a procedure used on newborn babies who require heart surgery," she explained.

"How do you know it would have worked here?"

She lit a cigarette. "We tried it on Harley Moon."

Once again he found himself staring at Dr. Jekyll, awed by her skill, horrified by her mission. He turned back to the TV screen. Her gloved hands were removing the clamps on the two tubes running between Victoria and Titus. A few drops of Victoria's blood backed up into the clear saline, turning from red to pink in delicate, fading strands.

Jack felt his throat tighten.

"Now for the big moment," Rachel said.

On tape they could hear her say, "I'm ready for flow." Everything was silent, and the tubes turned dark red as Titus's blood began circulating into Victoria's uterus.

Rachel's on-screen voice began describing what she was doing for the camera. She clamped, cut, and tied off the blood vessels that remained on the uterus, the last links between Victoria and her fetus.

"That's it," she said to Jack. "The fetus is completely free of Victoria. Now it belongs to Abner Titus."

They watched as she slipped her gloved fingers under the womb, cradled it in her palms, and lifted it out of Victoria's body. Jack remembered the papoose that had appeared in his dreams of Honey, dropping away from him toward a distant sea. He folded his hands on top of his head, opening his lungs.

Rachel walked to the VCR and ejected the videotape. After inserting a second cassette, she stepped back. The screen lit up, revealing a different abdominal incision recorded by another camera, an enormous belly held open by retractors. Now he knew where Titus was.

Rachel and her team talked to each other sparsely and professionally. Her hands came into view cradling the small uterus with the tubes attached. After inserting sponges to hold back Titus's intestines, she gently laid the organ into its new abdominal bed.

"Now the endgame begins," she said to Jack.

They watched as two sets of surgeons' hands, Rachel's and Phoebe's, went to work inside Titus's lower abdomen, attaching the uterus's left artery and vein to Titus's femoral vessels. Once circulation was assured, they removed the redundant plastic tubes from the second set of uterine vessels and tied off the stumps, turning them into cul-de-sacs.

Rachel's fingers appeared on screen with two thin, eight-inch-long wires resembling fishing-line leaders. At one end they disappeared into a tiny electrical jack; at the other, two small needles. Even in the midst of the bizarre, they seemed alien.

"What're those?"

"Electrodes."

He winced as she inserted the needles into the muscle of the uterus.

Moving delicately, she drew the attached wires up through the gaping incision and taped the jack to the surface of Titus's belly.

"We use them to monitor the fetal heartbeat, like an electrocardiogram."

"Didn't he wonder what they were there for?"

"First ten days they were hidden under the dressing. After that, I told him we were monitoring his intestines for peristalsis. He bought it." She stubbed out her cigarette.

"At this point everything is looking good," she explained. "The fetus's heartbeat is strong, no sign of irregularity indicating distress. What we have to do next is to anchor the uterus in place. Of course, since we don't have female ligaments in a man's pelvis, we had to improvise."

Rachel's on-camera hands went to work again, suturing the uterus's cervix to the thin, tough tissue covering Titus's pelvic bone. "What we're going to do is place the uterus in a position similar to the one it had occupied in Victoria. We anchored the lower end first. In a minute you'll see us anchor the body of the uterus to his abdominal wall."

"Where does the uterus go when it expands?"

"Same place a woman's goes, backward and upward."

"There's enough room in there?"

"Heavens, yes. More than you'll find in a woman who wears size six."

They watched as she ran a curved needle through the surface of the uterus. She drew a long line of black silk suture material through it, pulling both ends upward with the smoothness of a gifted seamstress, tightening the organ in place. Four times in all.

Jack watched as she sewed his child into the body of his enemy. He drove the image deep into his brain, dispelling the last, foggy veils that had until now provided the blessed comfort of ignorance, mystery, and disbelief.

Rachel began suturing up the original incision.

Finally something recognizable on screen—the familiar mantle that even doctors were willing to call by its ordinary name, *skin*. Seeing it drawn together at last relieved some of the anxiety he'd been feeling for Victoria.

Rachel turned off the VCR. "Once we closed, all we could do was wait."

"For what?"

"A rejection. The first two weeks are the most critical, but you can't be sure it won't happen at any time."

Jack contemplated her race against the clock.

She pulled the cassette from the VCR and held it up. "Seen enough?"

"Yeah."

"Good," she said. She opened a drawer and dropped in the two cassettes. "Because if things go the way I predict, you'll never see them again."

The door opened, spilling light and hallway sounds inside. Then it closed on pneumatic air, once again sealing the room tight.

Rachel stood unmoving, allowing her eyesight to adjust. The blinds had been drawn nearly closed, leaving tentacles of daylight creeping across the patient's bed and a chrome chair that had been drawn up next to it. She smoothed her starched coat with her hands—she seldom wore whites, but for this occasion there was no question she would—and positioned the stethoscope around her neck, beneath her neatly styled red hair. Overall, she looked as imposing and imperious as a chief justice of the United States. Which was precisely the point.

She walked on crepe soles to the chair next to the bed. Titus was lying on his back with a sheet drawn up around his neck, his forearm across his eyes, hiding his face. She sat down, crossed her legs, and leaned back.

Neither one spoke for a long time.

Finally she said, "Tell me how you're feeling."

She waited for an answer, but he didn't speak.

She leaned forward, crinkling the leather seat. "I'm going to take your pulse now. Do you understand?" She reached out, but before she could touch him, his hand sprang up, grabbed her wrist, and twisted it backward, forcing a grimace to her face.

A hoarse whisper escaped his lips. "Don't ever touch me—*ever* touch me—without my permission. If you do, I'll kill you." He tightened his grip for a second and let go.

Rachel leaned back in the chair, shaken. A long moment passed while she regained her composure. "There are certain things I have to discuss with you, Abner. As a surgeon."

"You're not a surgeon. You're a rapist with a scalpel." He removed his arm but refused to look at her. "We have nothing to discuss. All I want to hear from you is how you intend to remove this abomination from my body."

He rolled his head toward her, and their eyes finally met. Despite the shadows on his face, she could see a tic beneath his right eye.

"Do you hear me?" he said, trembling. "I want this thing out of me, *now!*"

She stared at him, savoring his malice, feeling her own rage heating the sockets of her eyes. "I can't do that."

"Why not?"

"Removing the fetus now would mean its certain death. To have any chance at all, it needs at least three more weeks of gestation."

He stared at her uncomprehendingly. "You're insane!"

"I know how you feel."

"You have *no* idea how I feel!"

She exploded out of her chair. "I know *exactly* how you feel! The whole *point* is how you feel!"

He closed his eyes and lay still, controlling his fury. "Every minute this—*thing* remains inside me, I am being raped all over again. Even in the privacy of this room, I'm being humiliated beyond belief by what you've done. If this monstrosity ever becomes public, you might as well have killed me on the operating table."

"You're not going to die. All I need are twenty-one days."

"That's *not* my responsibility!" he said. "I had nothing whatsoever to do with this!"

"That's true, you didn't. Just like millions of women don't. But now the fetus is there nevertheless. Remember how you feel about that? You can't simply let it die."

"As far as I'm concerned, it's dead already."

"It is *not* dead! It's as alive and well as it would be if it were still in its mother's body."

"Good God." He covered his eyes with his arm. "You have no idea what you've done, Doctor. You and the *mother*, as you call her, sentenced this fetus to death the moment you removed it from her." He lifted his arm. "Calling her a mother is obscene." His blood was rising again. "If you have any respect whatsoever for my life, or your profession, or the law—"

"Don't speak to me of the law!" She stepped toward him and he recoiled. Her legs touched the side of the bed and she loomed over him, tall and domineering, a thin sheen of dampness gleaming on her forehead. "In this room, *I* am the law! In this room, *I* will judge you the way you judge women. You have no choice here, Mr. Chief Justice. *I* decide what happens to your body! *I* decide whether you terminate or carry!" Her voice became taut, a quivering string, barely containing a lifetime of anger. "*I* decide whether you breathe or bleed!"

He closed his eyes and tried to keep himself from spinning out of control. He was as much a hostage as someone chained to a basement wall in Beirut. He told himself to stay calm, keep an avenue of escape open, even if only in his imagination.

"When did you intend to tell me?" he asked. "When I began hemorrhaging to death?"

Rachel sat down. "I planned to tell you once the fetus was viable, when you came to the farm to go fly-fishing with me. The cesarean section, your recovery, the incubation—it could all happen there. In private."

"Then what? Blackmail?"

"That was never even a consideration."

"It's all about collecting trophies, isn't it?"

"I already have all the honors I could ever want."

"No publicity, no extortion. For God's sake, what's the point?"

"*You* are the point! Who you are, how you think. What you don't understand. The way you wield your enormous power over people's lives."

He turned his head away.

She said, "Events went out of control a few weeks early, but the original plan is still possible. If you cooperate."

"Cooperate?" He was astonished. "You misjudge me badly, Rachel. I am not a woman, and I have no intention of lying down and taking this like one. If you don't remove this thing within twenty-four hours, I'll find another surgeon who will, regardless of the consequences. Disclosure, humiliation, the loss of my seat on the Court—I'll risk it all. Even my life. Do you understand?"

"Of course I understand," she said coldly. "It's the same thought a woman has before she chooses a back-alley abortion." She sat tapping her fingers on the arm of her chair. "Now I want you to listen to me. No one can perform this surgery as safely as I can, or as secretly. Surely you must know that's true. If you hold on for three more weeks, there's a reasonable chance everything will work out fine—the cesarean, removing the uterus, your privacy—maybe even the baby's survival. But if you call in another surgical team, there's no way to predict what will happen, except that the risk of publicity will increase."

"From who? You or them?"

She was pleased that he recognized the threat. "Both."

"If this is ever disclosed by anyone, you and your friends will spend the rest of your lives in jail. I promise you."

"It's a meaningless threat, Abner. I've known of that possibility from day one. I've already accomplished most of what I set out to do. What matters now is saving the child." She let the words sink in. "Considering your views on the subject, I would have thought you'd make the fetus's survival paramount to everything, your own welfare included."

He lay motionless with his eyes closed. "Considering your views on the subject," he said, "I would have expected you to let me make that decision."

"Both?"

"That's what the caller said. If we didn't move Titus out of his room, they'd *both* be blown up."

Molly stared at the hospital security officer and pondered what she was hearing. "Who did he have in mind besides Titus?"

The officer said the man mentioned a nurse, but seemed to change his mind. Maybe he was thinking of the security guard. He had no idea.

Molly opened her notebook, jotted down a word, and forced her feet into her shoes. She stood up and thanked him and walked down the hall to the hospital reception area. Finding an empty bench, she sat down, pulled off one of her pumps, and rubbed her toes.

Both?

"Is Titus bluffing?" Rachel asked.

"I don't think so," Jack said. "I've played poker with him, and it's not his game. As a matter of fact, he probably thinks *you're* bluffing and that when you seriously consider prison, you'll cave in and remove the fetus."

"Maybe he's convincing himself that another surgeon can do the job and keep it quiet."

"Too risky. Word would leak out."

"Maybe he's convincing himself that a leak wouldn't be as embarrassing as he imagines." She considered the possibility. "If he gets *that* into his head, we're finished. Fear of disclosure is the only thing we've got going for us."

"He has to know what the press would do to him if they find out. Pregnant men jokes, talk shows up the kazoo. And what about *Costello*? What's he going to do about that—announce the overruling of *Roe* v. *Wade* from the operating table where he's having an abortion?"

"He doesn't think of it as an abortion."

"Fine. Let him try explaining that to *60 Minutes*."

"It's a normal reaction, Jack. You know the argument—if God intended men to get pregnant, He would have given them uteruses."

467

"But that's exactly what He did. Same way He gave Titus a new kidney. Even used the same surgeon, for Christ's sake."

"I think that particular logic is escaping him at the moment."

"It is a little cute," Jack mumbled. He began pacing. "I'm telling you, he'd wait three weeks if he had any idea what the press would do to him."

"Maybe. But how do you convince him of that without giving away the story?" She dabbed a tissue to her forehead. "We just have to hang in there and let him twist."

"Right. Which is exactly what he's doing to us."

Daisy Gibbs, Titus's secretary, took off her coat and draped it on a hanger in the closet. After adjusting a few strands of hair, she turned toward the bed and halted, startled by the chief justice's appearance. His lips were dry and his forehead lined, and somber crescents cradled his eyes.

"Oh my, Abner. You don't look well."

He sought refuge under closed eyelids.

"What is it?" she asked. "Your kidney?"

He didn't answer.

"Your heart?"

"No."

She sat down in the chair next to the bed. "I know what it is. You sneaked yourself a martini."

"No, no, no, stop guessing. I'm fine. I just need some rest."

She positioned a stenographer's pad on her lap. "You're scheduled to announce the Court's opinion on *Costello* this Monday. Do you want a postponement?"

"Absolutely not. I'm having surgery tomorrow, but I'll be strong enough to be out of here in five days. Where the hell is Pepper, anyway?"

"What kind of surgery?"

"I don't know. Exploratory stuff. She should have been here by now."

"I'm sure she's on her way. My, you're wound up."

He rubbed his face and dropped his hands at his sides, staring at the ceiling as if appealing to heaven.

Daisy pulled the sheet up to his neck and smoothed out the wrinkles. She'd never seen him this way before, so tense and preoccupied. So quiet. Frightened, actually. She reached over and finger-combed his hair off his forehead with a mother's touch.

He lay still, unprotesting, absorbing it like a sponge. A little boy soaking up maternity, surrendering to the peace of an afternoon nap . . .

• • •

"Abner?"

He felt a hand gently shaking him . . . Daisy's hand. "Pepper's here."

He looked over and saw Pepper in her coat and black leather gloves setting a fresh box of chocolate cherries and a videotape of *Casablanca* on the table next to the bed.

"We need a few minutes alone," he said to Daisy. When the door closed behind her, Titus looked away, dreading the news he had to break.

"Sit down," he said. "I have something to tell you."

She remained on her feet with her coat and gloves on.

"I'm going to tell you something that requires absolute trust and secrecy," he said. She stood in silence. "Last night I discovered I've become the victim of the most shocking conspiracy you can imagine. Beyond imagination." He cleared his throat. "It's so hard to describe . . . I haven't actually said the words yet."

"What words?"

"That I'm . . ."

"Go ahead, Judge. Say the words." She stood tensely, as if waiting for a verdict.

"I'm carrying a child."

She let the words sink in, saying nothing.

He looked at her. "Did you hear what I said? There's a live fetus inside me." She remained still. "For God's sake, Pepper, don't you get it?" He pointed at the chair. "Now sit down."

"I can't."

He looked puzzled. "Why not? I need your help."

"I can't do that either."

He looked confused. Her tone was cold, her mouth set and her eyes unblinking. It made no sense to him. No sense at all.

Until . . .

It finally made sense.

His cheeks turned red. "Good God," he said, rolling his head away. "Get out."

Her face reddened like his. She waited a moment, then headed for the door.

"Wait!" he said, stopping her. "I want to know why."

She turned and faced him. It was a moment she, too, had long imagined, and yet she found herself unable to answer. Her eyes clouded.

He said, "This is all about Zenobia Davis, isn't it?"

"No." Her voice was barely audible.

"Then what is it?"

"Her daughter." She shivered as if she were standing in a draft. "It's about the survivors, all the people left behind after you've finished playing with their mothers' lives. I know who they are. I'm one of them."

"I didn't hurt Zenobia Davis or her daughter and you know it."

"That's not true!" She took a step toward him. "You frightened that poor woman to death! Why can't you see that? *Why?*" She pulled off a glove and raised a shaking finger to her eyes to wipe away a tear. Her face was slightly swollen, and a wisp of hair had fallen from under her hat. Slowly, she regained her composure. "We are not cows, Judge," she said shakily. "We're human beings."

He looked at her as if she were a favorite daughter gone bad. Then he raised his hand and brushed her away sadly, a tired old man shooing a fly off his ear.

"What's going on, Jack?"

"I can't say."

"You mean you won't say." Molly heard the rustling of the telephone receiver, Jack's muffled voice asking someone in his office to give him a few minutes. The sound of a door closing.

"Molly, listen to me. If you chase this thing down you're going to end up doing a lot of damage you don't want to do. Believe me."

"What kind of damage?"

"If I told you, I'd be doing it myself."

"How can I back off a story like this without knowing what it's about? I know you know something, Jack. Why else would you have been at the hospital so soon after the explosion? And how in God's name did the chief justice's room get torn up like that? Why was he so upset?"

"I can't help you, Molly."

"Whoever called in the bomb warning said if they didn't move Titus right away, he and another person would *both* be blown up. What does that mean, 'both'? Who else was in the room with Titus last night?"

"Come on, Molly."

"Come on yourself. I'm the one who's in a squeeze here."

"So am I."

"Ah-*ha*. Then you *are* in trouble."

"I didn't say that."

It made no sense. "What's going on, Jack? Are you in the middle of a scandal?" Silence. "What happened to all your theories? Titus and the arbor knot, and the videotape? And what did Rachel Redpath say about the toothpick?" No answer. "I wish I could see your face. You never could play poker with me."

"Molly, please. Leave it alone for a few days, would you?"

She thought about it. "There's a story here, Jack, and I'm gonna get it. I hope it's not about you. For your sake, I really do."

•   •   •

471

Jack hung up and rested in his leather chair, dizzy from lack of sleep. A baby? What in the world was he going to do with a baby? Reality was finally corkscrewing into his mind.

He leaned forward and opened his center desk drawer. Pawing through the junk, he found a water-stained photograph of Victoria sitting with him on two milk-painted chairs at a small hotel in Baja, Mexico. He set it in front of him.

So, it wasn't an accident after all. She'd deliberately gone off the pill to get pregnant. He wouldn't have found a diaphragm in the bathroom drawer because she didn't own one. She had no intention of aborting the day he found her in the clinic. She was there to be examined in preparation for the transplant. He'd surprised her, and she'd improvised perfectly, making up answers as she went along, offering to postpone the abortion he assumed she wanted, agreeing to consider changing her mind. *Just don't pressure me.* Bull.

If the child was born, how was he going to explain where it came from?

No wonder she'd been so calm and resigned in Santa Fe. The stress of deciding what to do was over, the deed done. No wonder she was physically weak and hid her surgical scar. No wonder she hadn't worried about miscarrying a baby that was no longer inside her. God-*damn.*

If they find out where the baby came from, will they call him a freak?

He rubbed his thumb against a smudge on the photograph. It had been taken only three years before, but it seemed like thirty. They'd been such different people then. Or was she? He held the picture closer and studied her face. What was she thinking the moment the shutter had clicked? Was she debating the transplant that far back? Planning a phony trip to Arizona? A private telephone line at the spa? Masking the fire in her belly with a Mexican tan and a beautiful smile?

Christ, he didn't know.

He moved his head and felt the room turn slowly on its side, like a capsizing boat.

All I know is I want this kid to survive.

He dropped the photograph onto the writing blotter. Victoria's critics had accused her of being driven by self-promotion and ambition—anything but love—but they were wrong. Hell, she'd virtually *brimmed* with love—as long as it was for women victims. At least Rachel thought men and women were separated by a curable disease. Victoria had seen them permanently, congenitally at war, as if the moment the first cell split, the X and Y chromosomes had fallen onto opposite sides of a great, yawning divide. Suckling babies, cooking meals, darning socks, nursing egos, molding children in their fathers' images—she wanted no part of being a foot soldier in an army commanded by men. She and Jack had bridged their differences gracefully and often, like two birds sailing above a canyon, momentarily touching wings. But nesting? Marriage? Family? If he'd been smarter, he would have understood from the start that for her these things were not closed questions; for her they were unconstitutional.

And yet, they had loved each other. And despite their differences, she'd given him a gift.

He massaged his forehead and examined the photograph. He remembered how they'd stowed their watches the day they arrived at their hotel in Baja, forgetting about Congress and battered women and time itself. He remembered the two of them lying in the sun and walking beaches, picking up shells and listening to animal sounds in the night, finding constellations in the Mexican sky. He remembered noticing things about her he'd never noticed before—the thickness of her hair, the size of her irises, the pores in her skin, the sunlit down on the back of her neck. And toes—how weird they looked—and the stretch marks on her hips running north and south like smooth, silt-filled arroyos. Antagonists glaring across a sexual divide? No one could have been more in tune with each other than they were on those quiet days and nights.

He also remembered when the vacation had come to an end. They had rented a car and driven to Tijuana to feed their growing appetites for lights and people, and after a dinner of steamed goat, fresh tortillas, and cold beer, had walked the back alleys, looking for one of the raunchy scenes that made the town infamous. It was shortly before midnight, and hearing music from a bar, they'd entered a roomful of men ogling a naked young woman—a raven-haired girl with a lithe figure and golden-brown skin, standing on a small stage in high heels, legs spread apart, stroking the coat of a donkey that had been raised onto its hind legs by a leather strap. He remembered seeing the girl wrap her arms around the animal and begin moving up and down on its black-and-pink-spotted organ, undulating to the catcalls of the laughing, drinking men who boozed and banged their beer bottles on the bar to the beat of bad rock music.

He took Victoria by the arm to leave, but she held fast and kept her eyes on the young woman. Finally, having conquered the animal, the girl uncoupled herself and walked to the edge of the stage where the men had gathered, all of them pushing and shoving for position, yelling and waving their pesos and greenbacks while she stood in front of them, exposed and dripping, looking them over, preparing to choose her next subject. She pointed with an arched finger, and a lucky man grinned and walked to the edge of the stage as his friends slinked back to their chairs. Standing barely out of reach, she milked the moment for the benefit of the crowd, then stepped forward and snatched the money from his hand, grabbed him by his hair, and buried his face between her legs. The place went wild. She closed her eyes, writhed in a fake orgasm, and pushed him away and walked off stage, counting her money.

At that point Victoria had walked away, too—not to the exit, but to a door next to the stage marked CABALLEROS Y CABALLERAS. He remembered watching the crowd calm down . . . and the sinking feeling in his stomach when he saw Victoria walk out onto the stage, dragging the young girl by her wrist. The perplexed crowd watched as she held up the girl's hand. *"Esta es su niña!"* she shouted at their dumbstruck faces. *"Esta es su madre! Esta is su esposa!"* Someone turned off the music and the room fell quiet. "What you do to this girl you must do to your mother! What you do to this girl you must do to your sister! Do you understand? What you do to this girl you must do to your daughter!" They looked completely befuddled. "What you do to this girl you must do to me!"

To— Jesus Christ. Did he hear her say, *"To me?"*

At first no one moved and he thought she'd gotten away with it. But then one man stood up, then another, and in a few seconds the whole fucking place was on its feet pushing toward the stage.

He remembered feeling himself moving on someone else's rubbery legs . . . jumping onto the platform, grabbing Victoria by the hand and pulling her off to the side . . . the glint of bottles in the air, glass breaking around his feet . . . the flash of something before it hit him in the face—a thud, no pain . . . a flimsy door knocked off its hinges, Victoria still in tow . . . shoe leather on the street, hoarse breathing, warm liquid in his eye, everything turning the color red.

He remembered the silence in the car as they drove through the desert back to the hotel and Victoria's teary gaze turning to a cold, dry stare. He'd offered her the handkerchief from his split eyebrow, but she hadn't taken it and didn't speak. Finally, an hour later, she uttered the only thing she'd say at all, the same words she'd spoken to him the night Zenobia Davis died, in the same resigned, flat voice.

"It's going to take a thousand years."

Jack caught himself staring at the photograph. The telephone rang. He picked it up and Faith put through a call from Rachel.

"Better come over to the hospital right away," she said.

"Why, what happened?"

"It's Titus. He's made his move."

Jack entered Rachel's office on the sixth floor. She swiveled around in her chair and motioned for him to close the door. "Abner's upped the ante. He's got himself a lawyer, someone who knows how to get a client an abortion and keep it quiet."

"Who?"

"Victoria's partner. Sylvia Kingston-Brown."

He stared at her, dumbfounded. "Christ, that's brilliant."

"There's more. He's called Dr. Gerald Benson for a meeting tomorrow morning at nine."

"Who's that?"

"A world-class gynecological surgeon. I've known him for years. He's an egomaniac who dislikes women surgeons generally and me in particular, but he's as good as they come. Titus hasn't told him why he wants to see him yet. He says if I operate before nine o'clock tomorrow morning he won't have to, and if I don't, he will."

"Even at the risk you'll go public?"

"He doesn't believe I'll do it. And even if I did, he says it wouldn't be as bad as being pregnant three more weeks."

Jack went to the desk and picked up a pencil.

"He's desperate," she said. "It happens."

Jack was in high gear, twirling the pencil, searching for a way out. "Wait a minute," he said. "How large is the fetus?"

"At this point? About twenty centimeters."

"How big is that?"

"Including the uterus, about the size of a cantaloupe."

"I've got the answer. If the fetus is still too small to be incubated, why don't you take it out of Titus and warehouse it until it's big enough?"

"Warehouse it? Where?"

"In me."

They stared at one another. Jack began perspiring.

"I don't know what's involved," he said, "but I'm healthy, and I'm the biological parent, which means my immune system won't reject it, right?" He swallowed reflexively and touched his belly. "There's enough room in here for a cantaloupe."

She extended her hand toward him. "Come here."

He walked to her, expecting her to examine his abdomen, but she laid her hand on his cheek instead. "It can't be done. You and the fetus are an incompatible blood match. You're type A, the fetus is type B."

"How do you know?"

"We did an HLA typing before the transplant, when we were working up a genetic profile. Remember when Kathy Keenan drew your blood for a cholesterol check?" He looked blank. "It went to our lab at the farm."

Jack backed up and sat in a chair. She stood up and approached him. "But I'd call that a very brave offer, Jack."

"Not if you'd felt my pulse."

She reached down and squeezed his hand, surprising him with a moment of genuine affection. Then she returned to her club chair. "I'd take the whole story public and open myself up to prosecution if I thought it would save the baby, but I can't tell whether the publicity would shame him into following his pro-life philosophy or drive him straight over the edge."

"As long as he's willing to see another surgeon, it's a moot question."

She sat with the silence of a trapped animal. Jack sensed it. "You're not giving up, are you?"

"Letting another surgeon operate is the worst thing that could happen. We lose the child, increase the danger to Titus's life, humiliate him for no reason . . . expose my team to prosecution."

"There's an angle here, Rachel. I just haven't found it yet."

She looked at her watch. "Only a few hours left." Leaning back, she said, "Somewhere along the way, he must have seen me break the first rule of warfare."

"What's that?"

"Never let them see you sweat."

An amber-haired young woman wearing a nurse's white smock, plain skirt, and brown pumps stood in front of the filing shelves rubbing her eyes with the back of her hand, continuing her tedious search. She looked up at the next stack of patient reports, certain that they, too, were filled with the indecipherable Sanskrit that passed for doctors' handwriting. Opening her palm, she read the patient number she'd written on it with a felt-tipped pen: *961143*. The patient's name she hadn't needed to write down: *Judy Smith*. Perfect cover. Simple and phony. Question was, why would they use a *woman's* name to disguise the file of a male chief justice? It smelled like more than routine security.

She had nearly finished checking the files named *Smith* when the rubber-stamped number at the bottom of a manila folder suddenly appeared: 961143. She pulled it out, careful to mark the place it had come from with a pink piece of paper, a medical form of some kind that had apparently slipped out of a file.

She checked the folder in her hand and saw the name: *Smith, Judy*. Below it was a typed message that read, *All progress notes on this patient have been transferred to the attending physician, Dr. Rachel Redpath.*

She opened the folder. It was empty.

Her shoulders drooped again.

She looked at her watch and lifted the pile of reports above the pink form she'd used to mark the place in the stack. The weight of the files on top of the form was crumpling it, so she pulled it out and began smoothing it with her hand when something caught her eye. Two words, upside-down: *Laboratory Report.*

She turned the form right side up.

Next to the word *Patient* was *Smith, Judy*, and down the left side were printed medical abbreviations, all unintelligible to a reporter accustomed to covering cheese fairs. Her eyes stopped at the only handwriting on the page—*110,000 i.u.* Next to it were the printed letters *HCG*.

"Hello there," a voice said from behind.

She turned and saw a handsome man in his thirties wearing a lab smock and a smile.

"Hello." She dropped the pink slip into the *Smith, Judy* folder, hoping he hadn't noticed.

"Can I help you with something?" he said.

"No thanks, I'm all set."

"I haven't seen you here before. Are you new to the staff?"

"As a matter of fact, I just arrived today." She shoved the file folder into place and walked to the door. When she reached it, she turned and caught him staring at her. Were they the eyes of suspicion, or a conventional sexual leer? Hoping they were the latter, she decided to take a chance.

"You know, there is one thing you could do," she said, smiling.

"Sure, what?"

"You could tell me what HCG stands for."

"HCG? That's Human Chorionic Gonadotropin."

"A chemical, right?"

"A hormone."

He took a step toward her. *Damn. He's suspicious.*

"Really," she said. "What's it do?"

"Several things." He moved closer.

"Like what?"

"Best thing it does is ensure a continuous flow of progesterone."

Progesterone? All at once his eyes were undressing her. *Thank God.* She said, "Why would it want to do that?"

"For the uterus."

Her face fell. "The—*uterus?*"

Another step forward. "Yeah, you know—one of those things women like to keep handy when they're having a baby?"

She smiled. "I know what a uterus is, Doctor, thank you." *Hang in there.* "Just out of curiosity—is there any other use for HCG? Like, can you imagine any reason you'd ever find it in a man?"

He was practically on top of her now, one elbow resting on the files. "Sure," he said. "As long as he's pregnant." He looked amused. "Jesus, you really are new around here, aren't you?"

She pulled the handle on the door. "Never can know too much about the birds and the bees," she said, and left before he could give her a lesson.

After exiting the building, she maintained an inconspicuous pace down the sidewalk, jotting something in a reporter's notebook with the WAPL-TV logo on the cover as she went. When she reached the corner, she looked up, saw a red light, and bounced on the balls of her feet, waiting for it to change.

When it turned green, she pulled off her pumps and sprinted in her favorite mode—barefoot—for her car.

• • •

Jack left his house and walked to the taxi waiting at the curb. He got in, gave the driver the name of the restaurant, and sat back, feeling vaguely hungry for the first time since dinner at Rachel's the night before. The cab started up and disappeared into traffic.

Back home, his telephone rang.

Beep.

"Jack, it's Molly. Are you there? Pick up, Jack, please." Pause. "Jack, where are you?" Pause. "It's Monday night, and I'm at the studio here in Washington. We *have* to talk!" Silence. "Shit," she muttered. "All right, here goes. I found out what happened to Abner Titus, and I need to talk to you." The tape rolled quietly. "Jack, I've got a serious problem here. I saw a lab report that says he's"—her voice lowered—"God, I can't even say it on your answering machine. I know about his— *condition*. I just don't know what you have to do with it. I don't want to do something that will hurt you, at least not if I can avoid it. Without killing the story, of course. Lord, what am I talking about? Whatever, I can't sit on this much longer. I'm in editing, 555-6987."

Beep.

Jack asked to be seated in the center of the room at the most conspicuous table in one of the best restaurants in town. In Washington, the rule was simple: if you wanted to plan a robbery of the U.S. Treasury, do it in a public restaurant and no one would notice. And if you wanted to say "good morning" to the Senate elevator operator after the door had closed, do it, but be forewarned: you were now part of a vast conspiracy.

Jack wanted this one to stay secret.

He had hardly taken his seat when his rumpled guest arrived, a balding man who drew a yellow legal pad from a tattered leather briefcase and flopped it onto the white linen tablecloth. "I'll say one thing for you people," he said, looking around the room, impressed. "You sure know how to live."

Then Jeremy Hackett sat down.

Beep.

"Dr. Redpath, this is Molly McCormick, WAPL-TV. I'm the reporter who was in the hospital room with a camera last night. I hate to call you at three in the morning, but I've uncovered some information about the chief justice's—uh, condition. Before I go with the story, I want to give you a chance to comment. Please call me the moment you get this message. I'm here in Washington at 555-6987."

Beep.

A few blocks away from the TV station, Rachel showed her pass to the hospital guard, looked at her watch, and scribbled her name and "3:05 A.M." onto the sign-in sheet.

"Kinda early even for you, isn't it, Doctor?" the guard said.

"Sure is, Jimmy, but I need a head start."

"What kinda organ you putting into somebody this time?"

"This one's not about what goes in," she said. "This one's about what comes out."

"**A**bner Titus and I have a missile pointed at each other," Jack said. "I'm threatening to expose his pregnancy, and he's threatening to abort my kid."

He poured Molly a beer, popped a can for himself, and sat on the counter next to the sink at his Georgetown house. At three-thirty in the morning his taste usually ran to pickled herring. Not tonight.

"By the way, congratulations on finding out," he said. "The entertainment reporter from Rich Hill, West Virginia, has obviously moved beyond covering frog-jumping contests." She gave him an I-know-I-know smile. "If you tell the world he's pregnant," he said, "my threat is gone. He'll terminate in a minute."

"I'm not happy about that, but I didn't create the problem," she said.

"Neither did I. But there it is."

She walked to the sink. "Let me ask you something of personal importance to me, if you don't mind."

"Sure."

"What kind of a reporter do you think I'd be if I turned my back on a story like this?"

"Jesus, Molly. You don't have to leave tread marks on your grandmother's back to be a good journalist."

"Really. You sure about that?"

She reached out and touched a leaf on Victoria's philodendron, which was sitting on the counter. "Sorry, Jack, I can't do it. It's only a matter of time before the whole Washington press corps finds out he's pregnant, and then the story won't be mine."

Jack tilted his beer can upside down, viewing her coldly.

"Don't look at me that way," she said.

"What the fuck do you want me to do, wrap you in the First Amendment and give you a kiss?"

"This is my job."

"That's what the executioner always says."

Her face flushed. "That's not fair. This is my Pentagon Papers, a story

481

that could change everything for me." She found her shoes under the table and slipped them on.

"Are you sure this is about your career?" he asked. "Or is it about us?"

"What's that supposed to mean?"

"We broke up because of this kid, remember?"

Her lips tightened. "Do you really think I'd try to get back at you by hurting an unborn *baby?*"

"Deliberately, no." He crushed his empty beer can. "Subconsciously, who knows?" He tossed it into the trash. "I've been there myself." He pictured himself giving Graves the chief justice's telephone number. "Recently."

"Well, that's just great. Now that you're into confessions, tell me— did you leave me for Victoria or the baby?"

"Far as I knew, when you got one, you got them both." The transplant hit him, mother and child severed. "Obviously, I didn't consider the miracles of modern medicine."

"You know what I'm asking."

Yes, he did. "My relationship with Victoria had come apart before I fell in love with you, Molly. I went back to her when she became pregnant. I would have done the same with you."

"You would have done the same with anyone capable of giving you a baby." She was obviously stung.

So was he. "Jesus, Molly. Am I really that bad?"

Her face softened, as if she'd gone too far. She was angry with him, but anger was not a major chunk of her personality. For her, brooding about past disasters only victimized her long after the original reason for the victimization had ended. She liked herself too much to do that to herself. But neither was she a patsy. If emotional scars were not to be worshipped, neither were they to be ignored.

Standing close to Jack, she felt herself drawn to him by their original gravitational tug, as strong and natural as the pull of the moon on the tides. Sure it was, she thought. And as dumb and dangerous as black leather jackets and big motorcycles. She knew. She'd been there.

She put her hand behind his neck and began rubbing it gently. "I don't want to hurt you, Jack. If you can show me a way out, I'll take it. But don't ask me to give up everything I've worked for."

"You're right. I can't do that." He placed his hands on her waist respectfully. "There is a way out of this," he said quietly. "I don't like it, but it's a way out."

Molly didn't get it.

"Take out your notebook," he said. "If you hold the story on Abner Titus, I'll give you another one that's just as good."

"What story could be as good as this?"

"The one you've been chasing since you came to New York. Since the first time I saw you on television."

To the television-trained eye, the place could have been the bridge of the starship *Enterprise*. There were two surgeons, two assistants, two nurses, and an anesthesiologist, some in contamination-proof bubble helmets, all wearing jumpsuits, booties, and gloves. There were gleaming machines and digital displays, monitors blipping and regulators humming as the surgical team moved in synchronized grooves, focused and concentrated, as unconcerned about the mundane occurrences on earth as they would have been traveling at warp ten in hyperspace.

"Tell the orderlies we'll be ready for the patient in one minute," Rachel said to her scrub nurse. An incubator stood on the other side of the room, camoflaged by a blue drape. No one in the room held illusions that it would be useful.

Lying partially sedated on a gurney in his room, dopey but still anxious, Abner Titus sensed the electricity in the air: the tension, the professional cool, the unstated awareness that a life—two lives—were at risk. An orderly entered the room, said, "Hello, Judge," and checked to make sure that the tubes, lines, and connections were in order—oxygen flowing, monitor lines disconnected—ready for the move down the hall. After telling the chief justice to relax, "It's a short, easy ride," the orderly maneuvered the gurney toward the door.

Rachel was finishing her preop check list. "Tara?"

Her anesthesiologist set a clear plastic mask on the operating table and said she was ready for the patient. In a few minutes she would close the chief justice's eyes, fuel him with sodium pentothal and nitrous oxide, and launch him like a rocket into the blackness, somewhere in deep outer space. Then, like the team around him, he, too, would be impervious to the outside world: insulated from its petty hurricanes and wars, unaware of its fires and floods . . . cut off even from the earthquake that was about to unleash itself in just a few moments—a tremor that would come not from the earth's grinding

484

tectonic plates, but from something much mightier still—a few seconds of televised airwaves so ephemeral they couldn't be seen or felt in transmission, yet powerful enough to bend the needle on the government's best Richter scale.

It was on the seven o'clock morning news.

"Molly McCormick has the exclusive story live from Washington, D.C.," the anchorwoman said.

Molly appeared on the television screen with a pink nose and white puffs of breath around her microphone.

"Connie, earlier this morning, in an exclusive interview, WAPL-TV received a major piece of information on the mysterious baby-doll murders in New York and Washington. According to a well-placed source, three kidnapped men whose bodies were found with toy dolls inserted into their abdomens were part of a bizarre medical experiment involving the transplantation of live fetuses into their bodies. That's right, Connie—fetuses. Two of the men, Melvin Shivers and Harley Moon, were apparently, briefly, the first pregnant men ever. . . ."

The orderly was pushing Titus down the hall toward the operating room when a second orderly walked up to the gurney and helped pull it along.

"Did you hear that?" the second man asked.

"No, what?"

"Somebody got a man pregnant."

The words penetrated Titus's fog like a laser. He opened his eyes.

"No kidding," the second orderly said. "It was just on the news."

Titus struggled onto his elbows as they rolled the stretcher up to the side of the operating table. He saw multiple Rachels bobbing before his sedated eyes.

"They know!" he said in a slur.

"Know what?"

"It'sch on . . . the news!"

Rachel turned to the orderlies. "What's he talking about?"

Titus stretched open his eyelids and surveyed the complicated equipment and aliens in space suits. "Who are you people? What are you doing . . . to me?" He struggled to escape, face flushed, knees and torso rising.

Rachel and the two orderlies grabbed him and held him down. "Get the mask on him!" she said, trying to quiet him before he spilled the beans in front of the orderlies. Tara turned on a valve and placed the cover over his nose and mouth. He turned his head to escape it.

"Stop!" he said, his voice muffled by the clear plastic.

Tara increased the gas and held the mask tight. In a few seconds he was under.

Rachel removed her surgeon's mask and looked down at Titus. The orderlies and her team stood by.

"Obviously, we now have a problem with his consent," she said. "Under hospital rules, the operation's aborted."

BABY-DOLL VICTIMS PREG! the headline on the *New York Post* read.

The female disc jockey led into a commercial with, "Hey—women have been saying for years that men have menopause, but did you *ever?*"

". . . to which the French minister of culture responded, 'Of course I'm not surprised. Americans have understood nothing about sex since the Puritans landed on a rock.' "

"The first problem is what to call a pregnant man," Ellen Goodman said to her editor, reading from her computer screen. "Suggestions so far include *male host, male mother, futher,* and *mather.*"
    "Try *wuss,*" he said, and walked away.

The managing editor of the *World Star* looked up from a drawing of a Martian playing guitar and accepted a mock-up of the following week's front page that was being handed to him. He stuck a breath mint into his mouth and looked over the layout. Above WOMAN WITH TEN-INCH TONGUE! and to the right of JOHN WAYNE WAS GAY! was the lead: HOW THE BABY-DOLL CONVICTS *Really* GOT PREGNANT—AND WHERE!
    He shoved it back, rejecting it. "We've done male pregnancy a hundred times. Stick to Elvis."

The assistant editor of the *New England Journal of Medicine* handed a clipping from the *Boston Globe* to the writer. "Right now, this is a joke, but there are some important issues here. Take a look, would you?"

•   •   •

"... no official word, although observers familiar with the Holy See say that as soon as the pope is sufficiently well, he is likely to condemn the experiment not only as a criminal act but as a gross violation of God's natural laws, much as the Church has condemned genetic engineering, fetal tissue studies, and certain other medical experimentation. Meanwhile, according to the pontiff's aides, his recovery from his recent liver transplant is proceeding nicely, allowing him for the first time to ..."

Ralph Nader waited for the reporters to simmer down and continued his statement. "But just as other medical advances have been overused, such as X rays, silicone breast implants, and diet pills, we should not be captivated by reports of male pregnancy until we have measured the precise effects on the male anatomy of new medical technologies and therapies, including the administration of large doses of female hormones, the dangers of cesarean sections, the ..."

When the laughter stopped, Don Imus, WFAN radio, said, "If Raquel Welch wants to make me pregnant, it can be arranged."

"So, Michael, what brings you by?"

Justice Edmund Burke Little III, the most conservative member of the Supreme Court, sat in his favorite leather chair. The buttons on his vest bulged slightly, and a meerschaum pipe dangled from his teeth.

"Abner Titus," said Justice Kelly. He sat down in the red upholstered chair Little reserved for guests in his chambers. "He's still in the hospital, out of communication. And enormously depressed, I'm told. Maybe clinically so."

"Come, come, Michael."

"I'm preparing a motion to disqualify him from further participation in *Costello*, before we take the final vote."

"You can't be serious," Little said.

"I wouldn't be here if I weren't."

Little repositioned himself in his chair. "You know how the votes stack up, Michael. If Titus is disqualified from *Costello*, we'll be split four to four, which means *Roe* will be affirmed instead of overruled. Do you really want the constitutional definition of abortion rights in America to be decided by a last-minute, cheap-shot disqualification of the chief justice?"

"No more than I want them to be decided by the vote of a chief justice who's mentally incompetent."

"Michael, listen to me. Even if he were bonkers, at this point what difference would it make? He's already heard the case, he participated in the preliminary conference, and he voted to overrule *Roe*. He's even written the majority opinion."

"Not quite," Kelly said. "According to his secretary, he hasn't finished it yet."

"Poppycock! Last-minute editing."

"Fred Vinson had already joined in the printed opinion of the Court in *Fortney* when he died," Kelly said, "and the Court disqualified his vote because the decision hadn't been issued yet. The same for Abe Fortas's vote in *Mendenhall*, when he resigned shortly before the decision was announced."

Little tapped the ashes from the bowl of his pipe. "Your motion stinks, Michael. It's pure politics!"

"It's no such thing. Although, frankly, it wouldn't make any difference if it were. It takes five votes to disqualify a justice. I have only four. Unless someone on your side agrees he's incompetent, he stays. You're the one who holds the deciding vote on this, Ed. Not me."

"You know how I'm going to vote, so what's the point?"

"No, I *don't* know how you're going to vote, and neither do you. This isn't a gimmick. I want to know whether he's too sick to vote. And regardless of our philosophical differences, I expect you to take the question seriously."

Little relit his pipe.

Kelly stood up. "I suggest the two of us pay him a visit at the hospital tonight, see him for ourselves and talk to his doctors. If he looks fine, I'll withdraw my motion. If not, I'm convening the Court for a vote on his disqualification tomorrow morning."

Little stayed seated, puffing. "I'll take a look."

Rachel closed the door and walked to Titus's bedside. He lay on his back, dozing. When she looked down at him, his appearance startled her. His enormous girth was shrinking from lack of appetite, the skin on his face was slack and lined, his hair mussed and his eyes sunken, as if they'd been bruised in a fight. Most telling, given his fastidiousness, was something she'd never seen on him before: an unshaven face. Sensing her, he opened his eyes.

"I won't stay long," she said. "I just wanted you to know that I had nothing to do with this morning's news."

"You mean you had nothing to do with *leaking* the news. Dr. Chang already told me. As for how these three men got pregnant and died, I suspect that's another matter."

"Abner—"

He held up his hand. "I don't want to hear anything about it. Denials, confessions, nothing." His eyes narrowed. "My God, Rachel. What in heaven's name have you done?"

She sat down. "Have you seen how the press is covering this thing?"

"The male pregnancies? It's as bad as I imagined. Worse."

"It's still not too late to come out to the farm for three weeks, Abner. You could fish, take some time, and rest before we operate."

"And if I don't, what? You'll add me to the list of America's most pregnant men?" He closed his eyes, silent and exhausted.

She sat silently, too. For the first time she could remember, she found herself admiring something about him—his determination to save himself. As best she could tell, it was the same stuff women had been summoning from their marrow since history's first unwanted pregnancy.

She lifted his wrist and took his pulse, which was high, and sat back and considered the chess game they were playing. In the battle of inverted wills—hers to force his pregnancy, his to terminate it—they were both stalemating each other by playing each other's roles, each betraying, in the process, their deepest, most cherished principles. How much longer could she keep this up? Everything told her to keep trying—her promise to Victoria to save the fetus, her dream of taking the experiment to a successful conclusion, her recognition of Jack's interest as the father, her passion to alter indelibly Titus's thinking. Everything, that is, but the one thing that had brought her to this point in the first place: the right to choose. Maybe she should blink. If one of them had to lose a soul here, better him than her.

Unless, somehow, she could still have it both ways. Just this once.

She searched again for a way to save the fetus, but she couldn't find it. Titus had another surgeon. Despite the dangers that posed, victory over the fetus was assured. Choice would prevail in all its glory after all. It was time to accept defeat, cut losses, remember Hippocrates, do no more harm.

After sitting quietly a moment, she reached out and touched his arm. "You win," she said without bitterness. "No need to call in another surgeon. I'm rescheduling the operation for six o'clock tomorrow morning."

Daisy drew the razor up Titus's face and swished the blade in a pan of warm water. His head rested on a towel-draped pillow.

She rinsed his face and patted his once cherubic cheeks dry, then turned his head toward her. "You look perfectly healthy to me. Justices Little and Kelly are going to find you fit as a fiddle."

His expression turned sour. "This expedition of theirs is nothing but Kelly's ham-handed attempt to disqualify me before the vote on *Costello.*"

"Don't be such a cynic, Abner. If that's what he was doing, why would he bring along Justice Little?"

Unconvinced, he turned to the television set and listened. "Reports from Washington, D.C., this morning that three men were made pregnant late last year are bringing a variety of reactions from the sublime to the ridiculous. Today in New York, an enterprising plastics maker has already created a—"

He raised the remote control and turned off the sound. "I think I'd like to be alone for a while."

Daisy carried the pan of shaving water to the bathroom and emptied it. When she returned, he said, "Put in the *Maltese Falcon* for me, will you?"

She walked to the credenza next to his bed, slipped a cassette out of a box, and pushed it into the VCR. The tape rolled. WARNER BROS. PICTURES appeared along with a map of the continent of Africa. *A Hal B. Wallis Production* materialized over the sound of "The Marseilles."

"That's *Casablanca,*" he said.

"But that's your favorite. Don't you want Sydney Greenstreet?"

"He's in the *Maltese Falcon,* too."

She lingered a moment, waiting for him to change his mind, but he wiggled his finger to switch the tapes. Reluctantly, she did. "Anything else before I go?" she asked.

"Yes. Call Sylvia Kingston-Brown. Tell her to be on the lookout for MacLeod sneaking into court at the last minute. She'll know what I mean."

Daisy departed, leaving Titus in a blue funk. If MacLeod sued, it was nearly impossible to imagine a district court entering an order stopping him from terminating the pregnancy, but how could he be sure? Worse yet, what was to keep MacLeod from using a lawsuit to take the story public? Rachel he could threaten with prosecution, but he had no such leverage on MacLeod. And publicity aside, even if MacLeod lost a TRO at the trial court level, there were still dangerous games he could play in the court of appeals. Most of the appellate judges were pro-choice, thank God. Still, if an appeal caught the wrong panel—a colleague jealous of his appointment to the Supreme Court, someone looking to even an old score—who knew? They could put his operation on hold while they "deliberated" on some pissant point of law, and there wouldn't be a thing he could do about it, least of all petition the Supreme Court. And if the judges moved at their usual snail's pace—Christ, they'd push the pregnancy past the point of viability without even trying.

Exactly as he'd done to Zenobia Davis.

He shifted his weight to relieve the heat prickles on his neck. Bastards. The pro-choicers would love to stick him with that bit of poetic justice.

His adrenaline continued to flow, bringing worse possibilities over the dam. What if a lower court delayed the termination for a few days—just long enough for his decision in *Costello* to overturn *Roe*? Then what would he do? Termination of male pregnancy wasn't the kind of abortion his opinion was meant to prohibit, but still. Think how it would look. *Pricks.* He'd be the butt of every political cartoon in the country.

It didn't matter. He'd terminate regardless. *Except . . . wait a minute.* Would Redpath operate on him if MacLeod got a court order against it? Would Dr. Benson, or any other reputable surgeon, risk a contempt citation? Jesus, maybe not. And even if he found one who would, what about himself? The chief justice of the United States in contempt of court? Lord help him—contempt was an impeachable offense! Imagine being tried for that in the U.S. Senate, of all places. Sticks Dickey would be on his side, but what good was that? Even if he hadn't been politically neutralized by his publicized association with Eli Graves, the press would make it look like the Senate's leading pro-lifer was supporting an abortion, which, knowing Sticks's backbone, would send him running for the North Carolina hills. Damn. Without a powerful friend on Judiciary, he'd be a sitting duck.

He began feeling heat prickles again. Slow down. You're out of control. After all, how in God's name could a pack of liberals who made abortion the litmus test of political correctness impeach someone for *having* one? It was impossible. No way. Too hypocritical for words.

He sat up and burped, bringing tears to his eyes, and lay back on his pillow. Slowly, his paranoia continued to rise.

Like hell they couldn't impeach him. There wasn't anybody on earth who could dress up a lynching and make it look as high-minded and principled as a bunch of plastic-minded, mean-spirited, holier-than-thou liberals.

Breaking into a sweat, he opened a box of cherries and dug into the jungle of little brown paper cups, looking for help the way a heart-attack victim searches for nitro. He popped a chocolate into his mouth, bit down, and felt the soft cherry goo calm his nerves, like a blanket of foam on short-circuited wires. *Cut the paranoia.* Think about your strengths. You're losing sight of the single most powerful card you hold . . . the fail-safe that transcends the dirtiest politics the mind can imagine . . . the one, unbreachable bond you and nine out of ten judges and United States senators have in common, even liberals . . . the Teflon coating, the bulletproof vest.

We're all men.

"**C**ome on in, Eli. We'll get it straightened out." The telephone receiver was turning moist in Jeremy Hackett's hand. "Eli?"

"Can't be fixed," Graves said. His breathing was sporadic, labored.

"Everything can be fixed if you give it a chance," Hackett said. Silence on the line. "I did it," he said. He started to cry.

"I know that," Hackett said sympathetically. "The feds, ATF, NYPD—they're all looking for you. Sooner or later they're gonna find you."

Graves cried for a long time. Before he'd finished, he spoke in a cracked soprano voice. "I can't . . . go back. . . ."

"Tell me where you are, Eli. We'll talk it over." A telephone-company recording intervened, a pleasant faceless woman's voice asking for another quarter. "Give me a number where I can call you back!" Hackett said quickly. No answer. "Eli—"

He heard the sound of a quarter being dropped into the box.

Hackett said, "I'm your lawyer, Eli. Your friend—"

"I see things," Graves said. His crying had stopped; his voice had become clipped, and cold.

"See things?"

"I see things. I know what I was put here to do."

"What's that?"

"When you got nothing left, that's when you understand what you're meant to do."

"Eli—"

"Makes you free."

Hackett exhaled in frustration. He was losing him. He needed a new hook, words from Graves's own mouth.

"You want to talk about what you were put on earth for? Remember why you got into this business in the first place? Not the money, or the power, but the real reason? Do you remember?" Silence. Graves was listening. "It was to save the unborn." Maybe he was getting through. "You still have work to do, pal. Unfinished work." No answer. "Am I right?"

"For your sins."

A pause. "For my sins?"

"Christ died for your sins."

Hackett paused. "Listen to me, Eli. You're not well. You need help. Let me get you help."

A long pause, the rhythmic sound of breathing. No words.

Hackett waited.

"One more thing," Graves said.

"Yes? What is it?"

"One more thing . . . I have to do."

"What is it?" Silence. "Tell me what you have to do, Eli."

"God wants me to do it."

"God wants you to do *what?*" Silence. "Eli—tell me what God—"

Click.

Rachel closed her eyes for a final powdering, then swiveled around in her chair and carefully removed a Kleenex shielding her collar from the makeup, wadding it up. Pepper Loomis, sitting on the other side of the TV station's scarred enamel vanity, was concerned.

"Are you sure you want to do this? It's not too late to back out."

"Somebody's got to defend the science of this," Rachel said. "Who's a better candidate than I am?"

"But that's precisely the problem. If you look knowledgeable, you're going to make yourself the chief suspect in the crime."

"I'll be careful." She leaned closer to the mirror and fussed with her hair. "Phoebe called a few minutes ago with the latest report from the hospital."

"And?"

"Titus refused to see Justices Kelly and Little."

"Why?"

"He said it was a put-up job to have him disqualified from the case and had Daisy call the meeting off. What's the significance of that?'"

"It means Kelly will ask for a vote on his motion to disqualify Titus, but it won't carry. What about the message—did Titus see it?"

"Afraid not. Apparently he insisted on watching the *Maltese Falcon* instead of *Casablanca.*"

"Damn. I picked the wrong movie. I was *sure* he'd want to see *Casablanca.*"

Rachel tossed the wadded-up tissue into the wastebasket. "You don't know how he would have reacted even if he'd seen it. It was a far-out idea to begin with. You did all you could."

"All I did was deliver the tape to the room when I visited him," Pepper answered. "The hard part was Daisy's, trying to get it into the VCR."

"This . . . is *Nightline!*"

Trumpets, a commercial, and Ted Koppel:

"Poets have written about it, movies have portrayed it, comedians have joked about it, but until now, no one has actually done anything about it. No, I am not talking about the weather, I'm talking about male pregnancy. This morning three men, all previously involved in abortion-clinic bombings, were reported to be subjects of a grisly medical experiment in which two of them were implanted with uteruses containing live human fetuses.

"Tonight we're going to explore the subject of male pregnancy with Dr. Rachel Redpath—kidney transplant surgeon, author, researcher, and a recipient of the Medal of Freedom, the highest civilian award the country has to bestow. Joining us from our Boston affiliate is Dr. Herman Leonard, holder of the André Stavinski chair for bioethics at Boston University Medical School and author of *The Limits of Medical Intervention,* a book critical of recent trends in genetic engineering and medical experimentation.

"Dr. Redpath, before discussing who might have kidnapped these men and why, how is it medically possible to make a man pregnant?"

"In theory it's quite simple. Ectopic pregnancies have always existed. There have been recorded births of such babies."

"But they're very dangerous, aren't they?"

"Yes. In a normal pregnancy, the lining of the uterus detaches at birth. If the placenta is rooted someplace else—say, the intestinal wall—separating it can cause massive hemorrhaging."

"Meaning the mother could bleed to death."

"That's right. On the other hand, if a pregnant uterus were transplanted, which I understand from press reports may have been the case here, the risks of placental hemorrhaging would be reduced, perhaps to normal." She paused, censoring herself. "I have done this myself with male baboons."

"How is the fetus finally removed?"

"Same as it is in a woman. By cesarean section."

"Mr. Koppel?" Leonard interjected.

498

"Yes, Dr. Leonard."

"If I may, I'd like to interject something here. From a purely technical standpoint, I don't doubt male pregnancy is feasible, but ethically, there's absolutely nothing to justify an experiment of this nature. According to press reports, what we have here are men who were kidnapped and impregnated against their consent. Turned into human guinea pigs, if you will, and for what? What purpose is served by this dangerous male form of pregnancy when nature has created normal, healthy uteruses in women?"

"Dr. Redpath?" Koppel said.

"I can imagine several purposes, but first I'd like to say that male pregnancy is far more similar to female pregnancy than Dr. Leonard suggests. There are even a few advantages. Like the average size of the abdominal cavity."

"That's outrageous," Leonard said. "Even if the subjects had willingly volunteered, what about the risks of surgery? Twice no less—once to implant the uterus, once to remove the baby?

"Surgery poses additional risks, yes," Rachel said. "Except for that, there's very little difference."

"Saying 'except for that' is like describing the 1940s without World War Two," Leonard said.

"He has a point, doesn't he, Dr. Redpath?" Koppel said.

"It's a point, yes, but it's not dispositive. Medical advances have always carried risks."

"But that's precisely the problem," Leonard said. "Where's the advance? How is mankind bettered? The central principle of medicine is to protect life, not endanger it."

"Dr. Redpath," Koppel said, "that brings us back to the motive for this experiment. Why do you suppose this happened, and who do you think did it?"

"I can't address who did it, but I think it's possible that these experiments could change attitudes quite a bit. And on one subject especially."

"What's that?" Koppel asked.

"Abortion. As Florynce Kennedy said back in the sixties, 'if men could get pregnant, abortion would be a sacrament.' Slightly exaggerated, perhaps, but you get the point. Now that there's evidence that it can be done, that alone will cause men to stop and ask; Shouldn't we have legislation protecting the right to become unpregnant?"

"But is this really likely?" Koppel asked. "Men would presumably become pregnant only by choice, which means the circumstances that

cause women to choose an abortion—rape, incest, or simple mistake—
wouldn't be involved, would they?"

"Frankly," Leonard interrupted, "I'm not sure you're right about that,
Mr. Koppel. Who's to say that the band of marauders who kidnapped
and impregnated these poor convicts won't do the same to me?"

"Dr. Redpath?" Koppel said.

"It's not something that should keep you awake nights, Herman."

"How can you be so sure?" Leonard said.

"I'm not. I simply don't think it's something to become hysterical
about."

"Who's hysterical?" Leonard yelled.

"All right everybody," Koppel said.

"I find this unbelievable," Leonard said.

Koppel said, "We'll take a commercial break and return in a
moment. . . ."

Detective Norman Pulaski touched the Off button on the remote control,
laid his open *Boating* magazine on the ottoman, and picked up the telephone. He punched in a Washington, D.C., number.

"Wilson? Norm Pulaski here. You watch *Nightline?*"

"Yeah," said Det. Wilson. "What'd you think?"

"I think Dr. Rachel Redpath knows one hell of a lot about how to put
babies into men."

"No shit. But a Medal of Freedom winner? Kidnapping and
homicide?"

"After twenty-five years in this business, believe me, anything's
possible."

"I'm ready to go for it if you are," Wilson said.

"I'll take the shuttle down tomorrow morning and be in your office
at nine-thirty. We'll pull the file and map out how we're gonna do this.
If she's not our man, we gotta be careful how we treat her."

"And if she is?"

He closed his magazine. "Pretty nice case."

David Letterman grinned into the camera with his index cards in hand.
"The top ten reasons you don't want to undergo a kidney transplant in
Washington, D.C. Reason number ten." Drumroll. "Instead of a new
kidney you could end up with your girlfriend's illegitimate kid. Number
nine . . ."

•   •   •

Rachel and Pepper left the ABC *Nightline* studio on Connecticut Avenue and walked toward Pepper's car, which was parked on a side street. Despite the late hour, there were enough people on the sidewalk to camouflage the man in the midnight-blue ski parka, jeans, and black knit cap.

"The telephone calls started coming into the studio before you finished your first sentence," Pepper said. "Women fairly supportive, men generally against."

They turned off Connecticut Avenue onto a shadowy side street. The man in the parka followed at a distance.

Pepper said, "The telegrams and faxes are getting interesting."

"Such as?"

"Let's see. The American Society of Transsexuals wants you to speak at their annual convention next week. So far, they have twenty-eight candidates who've volunteered for transplants."

"Great. We can open a factory."

The man behind them walked faster, closing the gap.

"A group of women calling themselves 'Womb Power' are picketing you tomorrow."

"What for?"

"Robbing them of their unique power to give birth. The only real power women have. Or had."

"Mm. I should have known."

The stalker put his right hand into the pocket of his ski parka and came closer, walking quietly on sneakered feet.

"Then there are the usual number of threats against your life."

"I'm not surprised."

They reached the car. Pepper dug into her purse for the keys as Rachel stood waiting, lost in thought. "It's all turning to ashes, isn't it?" she said. "It's either an enormous joke or a threat beyond imagination."

The man in the ski parka was only a few feet away, but neither of the women saw him coming.

"You always said it wouldn't be easy," Pepper said, straining to see in the dark. "Where the hell are those keys?"

Rachel heard footsteps and turned, startled. The man was close enough to touch her.

"Are you Dr. Redpath?" he asked.

Pepper looked up from her purse. The gray figure was standing with his right hand in his pocket, his eyes focused and intent, a man on a mission.

"Yes?" Rachel answered.

"This is for you."

He pulled his hand from his pocket and extended it toward her, freezing her in her shoes. Then she saw a piece of paper.

She raised her hand and took it, and the man trotted away.

Pepper closed her eyes and collapsed against the car in relief. After a moment she unlocked the door and they both climbed in. They sat still, recouping. Then Pepper turned on the dome light and Rachel opened the paper.

The word *Subpoena* appeared in Gothic script at the top. She scanned the page for the key words: *You are commanded to appear . . .* John Doe I *v.* John Doe II *. . . emergency proceeding one o'clock* A.M.

Forty-five minutes from now.

Five hours before she was scheduled to operate on Titus.

"**B**efore we begin, I must tell you that I have read the petitioner's papers and find this the most bizarre, outrageous case I have witnessed in my twelve years on the bench."

Judge Francis X. McCarthy, district court judge for the District of Columbia, leaned forward and rested the leather elbow patches of his green cardigan on top of the desk blotter. It was one o'clock in the morning, in the study of his home, where the litigants in the incognito case of *John Doe I* v. *John Doe II* had gathered for an emergency hearing. McCarthy was taking his turn as the district court's motions judge, which obliged him to hear petitions at virtually any time of the day or night. It was a job all judges disliked, particularly when rousted out of bed for something like this. Except that he'd never seen something like this.

Holding the hearing in his home was permitted by the court's rules. Given the early-morning hour, the location was convenient to the judge, but that was a secondary consideration. Secrecy was the first. Even if Abner Titus had not been McCarthy's personal friend, which he was, allowing an embarrassment of this magnitude to become public knowledge seemed nearly as outrageous as the pregnancy itself. The judge had called in a court stenographer he normally used in national security cases, someone whom he trusted completely, and directed her to make a single transcript of the proceeding and give it to him with all her notes. He would hold the material in his chambers, under lock and key, along with the foreign embassy wiretaps, intelligence matters, and other sealed cases. Having read MacLeod's petition for a restraining order seeking to prohibit Titus from terminating the pregnancy, the first thing McCarthy told everyone when they gathered in the room—and this he said off the record—was that if he ever caught anyone leaking the story to the press, he would personally see to it that he or she spent the rest of his or her natural life in jail. Even if he had to invent a case to do it.

"Mr. Hackett," he said, "tell me why you are here."

Attired in a white shirt, red tie, and his favorite iridescent-green suit, Jeremy Hackett cleared his throat and stood up in front of a dining-room

503

chair, one of several that had been pulled into the room. Holding a yellow pad in his left hand, he ran his right over the top of his bald head, slicking back his thinning hair.

"Good morning, Your Honor. We appreciate your availability and want to assure you that if this petition did not present a matter of life and death, we would not presume upon you at this terribly inconvenient hour."

Sitting next to Hackett, Jack looked around the room like a lost automobile driver trying to figure out where he was. His disorientation was understandable. Here he was, the country's leading congressional proponent of the right to choose, suing to prevent the termination of a pregnancy with the help of Jeremy Hackett, counsel to the Red Rose Society and former lawyer for Eli Graves, the man who had helped destroy Victoria and who still wanted to destroy Jack.

And here was Hackett, New York's leading pro-life lawyer, the best advocate Jack could find on his side of the issue, preparing to make a case based on the testimony of Rachel Redpath, a leading pro-choice doctor, a recipient of the Medal of Freedom and, unknown to the rest of the world—so far, at least—a killer who nevertheless stood ready to jeopardize her freedom in order to save his child.

And there was Rachel, sitting pensively, preparing for a knockdown fight with her dear friend, Sylvia Kingston-Brown, a tough, honest lawyer who, if she had to, could elicit enough incriminating testimony from Rachel to send her to jail for a long time. And for what client would this pro-choice lawyer do that?

Chief Justice Abner Titus, the one man Sylvia Kingston-Brown hated more than any other, the would-be author of the destruction of *Roe* v. *Wade* and all that she held dear—the country's leading judicial opponent of the right to abort, a right he was now seeking to exercise on his own behalf to save himself from the threat of Jack's own flesh and blood.

And who was the one person who could stop it? The man at the desk, Judge Francis X. McCarthy, the severest antiabortion district court judge east of the Mississippi—a man whose philosophy Jack had worked hard for years to defeat. A man whose philosophy Jack now prayed would prevail.

It wasn't impossible to sort it all out, but it would have been easier if he'd been observing the room from the doorway, hanging upside down in his gravity boots.

Hackett was finishing. ". . . and so, Your Honor, there is nothing less than life itself at stake here, the life of a helpless, unborn child who sleeps in his mother's womb, waiting for Your Honor's decision to save his sacred, innocent life. Waiting for us in this room to recognize the very purpose of the law—to protect life pursuant to the will of God almighty." Jack had forgotten that Hackett always ended his arguments with an appeal to God. Ordinarily corny. Tonight a good idea. He could use all the help he could get.

Sylvia Kingston-Brown rose. She stood next to her chair, poised and erect, her gray-flecked Afro lending height and dignity to an air of natural authority.

The judge sat immobile, frowning.

"Your Honor," she said, and waited for the soft clacking of the stenographer's machine to stop. "Whenever I hear opposing counsel appeal to the laws of God, I get the distinct feeling that one of us is in the wrong place. Taking nothing away from the court's majesty, I believe we *are* talking about the laws and Constitution of the United States, not heaven. Which raises the only question in this proceeding that matters— does Chief Justice Abner Titus possess the absolute, unqualified, and unimpaired right to terminate this pregnancy? The answer, of course, is an absolute, unqualified yes. In fact, it is so clear I cannot imagine why we are here." She sat down.

Judge McCarthy shifted in his chair. "Mr. Hackett," he said. "Before you start, obviously, serious crimes have been committed here. I cannot explore them in this proceeding, but I certainly can ask whether your client's hands are clean."

"Your Honor, Congressman MacLeod had nothing to do with the implantation of the fetus into the chief justice. He didn't even know about it until two days ago."

"Well, that may be, but there is nothing here to explain how this happened. The way your petition is written, it looks as if the first male pregnancy is the second Immaculate Conception."

Hackett said nothing.

The judge nodded at him. "You and I have been on the wrong side of *Roe* v. *Wade* for more years than I care to count, Counselor. So, tell me. Aside from the unique fact that the respondent is a man instead of a woman, why is this case any different from all your others?"

"Your Honor, *Roe* v. *Wade* guarantees the right to an abortion until the child is viable, at which point the child enters a zone of protection. The Supreme Court used twenty-four weeks as a rule of thumb, not an ironclad rule. Even if the child residing in Justice Titus is not yet twenty-four weeks old, if it is viable, the threshold of legal protection has been crossed."

"Does this mean you are prepared to prove viability?"

"Yes, Your Honor."

"And how do you propose to do that?"

"By calling one of the world's leading experts on the subject."

Rachel raised her right hand, and as the stenographer swore her in, the bittersweet nature of the testimony she was about to give suddenly came home. All her life she had imagined a moment when she'd toss culture, custom, law, medicine, and religion into the air and explode them into clean, pure oxygen, changing people's attitudes forever. She hadn't known exactly where it would happen—inside a crowded courtroom, outside a bombed abortion clinic, writing for the *New England Journal of Medicine*—only that, eventually, it would.

She'd never expected that it would happen too soon. When she'd gauged the project's chances, for some reason she'd always pictured total success or total failure, not a no-man's-land between. And yet, that's where she was, her right hand in the air and everything in jeopardy—her work, her liberty, the fetus's life, Victoria's sacrifice, women's emancipation from the tyranny of the egg itself. Unmoved as she normally was by irony, the one she was facing now impressed her deeply: Hackett as her deliverer, Jack as her ally, Sylvia Kingston-Brown as her slayer, her own self-betraying testimony against choice. Lord. The only plus she could see was something she never dreamed possible: the judge deciding the child's fate was an unyielding, bull-headed right-to-lifer.

If that was the good news, Sylvia Kingston-Brown was the bad. From memory alone she could impeach Rachel enough to reduce her and the witness chair to a pile of fine, smoldering ash.

"I do." Rachel lowered her hand.

Hackett stood at his chair with a yellow pencil fluttering between his fingers, exactly as it had the last time she'd seen him, when she'd flippantly questioned his manhood and sparred with him at Zenobia Davis's hearing. He'd won the argument that day, preventing Zenobia's abortion and helping enrage Victoria enough to conceive the fetus whose life was now in question.

She prayed he'd win again.

"Dr. Redpath," he said, "in your expert opinion, is the fetus presently carried by Chief Justice Titus a viable child protectable within the meaning of *Roe* v. *Wade* and related case law?"

"Yes."

"I have no further questions."

Instead of asking her to explain in detail, Hackett chose to elicit a simple conclusion and hope that her well-known credentials, the ungodly hour of the day, and the informality of the proceeding would carry him through. That way, if her friend Kingston-Brown went easy on her in cross-examination, Rachel might at least escape a confession of criminal wrongdoing.

Sylvia Kingston-Brown rose from her chair.

"Dr. Redpath, I am going to be equally succinct. And if I receive the candid answers for which you are renowned, this will not be —*complicated.*" The way she emphasized the word constituted a clear warning that she'd bear down hard if she had to. She paused to let the message sink in, and for a moment the two of them studied each other as if they'd never met before, much less that they were old friends.

"You are familiar with *Roe* v. *Wade,* isn't that so?"

"Yes."

"And with the subsequent decisions such as *Webster* and *Casey,* which state that viability must be reached before the right to abort can be curtailed?"

"Yes."

"And isn't it true that you have testified on past occasions that you personally know of no instances in which a fetus has developed sufficient lung capacity to be considered viable prior to the twenty-fourth week of pregnancy?"

"I have."

"And you are aware, are you not, that counsel for the petitioner has stipulated that the child was conceived only twenty-one weeks ago?"

"Yes."

Kingston-Brown moved to the edge of the question Rachel was waiting for—the one that would ask her to explain why this fetus should be considered different. But believing she'd already carried the day, and preferring not to ask a hostile witness "why?" when she didn't know the answer, and not wanting to destroy Rachel if she could avoid it, she sat down. "I have no further questions, Your Honor."

Rachel was astonished. "Your Honor," she said turning to the judge, "there's information here which is essential to your decision."

"Objection," Kingston-Brown said.

Rachel looked at Hackett, telling him with her eyes to take the next step, even if it brought her closer to the edge.

"Your Honor," Jeremy Hackett said, "this is not a jury trial. Under *Harris* v. *Nelson* you have inherent power to discover the truth here." Judge McCarthy considered the matter and turned to Rachel. "Go ahead," he said.

Hackett looked at Rachel. "Please tell the court why, in your expert opinion, the fetus residing in Abner Titus is viable at this time."

She composed herself. "Recent literature indicates that a fetus born as early as twenty-two weeks after conception can survive under the right circumstances. While this is admittedly rare, too rare in the absence of special circumstances to overcome the presumption of nonviability, when special circumstances exist, viability can occur."

"And what special circumstances are present here?"

"The baby has had such an extraordinary amount of nourishment and support, in my opinion, its age is the chronological equivalent of a twenty-five-week-old fetus."

"Objection!" Kingston-Brown said. "There is absolutely no foundation whatsoever for an opinion like that."

"Sustained." The judge looked at Hackett.

Hackett saw Rachel standing on the steps of the gallows. If she explained the baby's "special circumstances," she'd risk disclosing her criminal role in the transplant, placing a noose around her own neck. There was a time when he would have enjoyed doing that himself. But not now.

He asked the question gently, as if inviting her not to answer: "Dr. Redpath, on what factual basis do you offer your opinion?"

Rachel sat up straight. "I am personally familiar with the gestation of this child in the abdomen of my patient, Chief Justice Abner Titus."

The air turned stone-cold. "Stop right there," the judge said, raising his hand. The stenographer's machine caught up with the testimony, and the room fell quiet. "You're in dangerous territory, Doctor. You're aware, I assume, that you have a right against self-incrimination?"

"Yes, I am."

"And that what you say here can be used against you?"

"Yes."

"All right. You're free to do as you wish, but I must warn you, if I hear testimony that incriminates you in possible crimes, I will refer the matter to the United States attorney for prosecution. Do you understand?"

"Yes, Your Honor."

The warning was expected but ominous, shaking her. The look on

Hackett's face asked whether she wanted to continue. After a moment she said, "Ask the question, Mr. Hackett."

Hackett licked his lips. "Would you please tell the court all the facts and circumstances leading you to believe the child is viable?"

Jack rose to his feet. "Your Honor, may I interrupt? As the petitioner in this matter, I'd like to confer with my lawyer before the witness continues."

The judge approved with an open hand in Hackett's direction.

Jack put his head together with Jeremy Hackett's, and after huddling a moment, asked Sylvia Kingston-Brown to join them. A minute later he and Kingston-Brown took their seats. Hackett, standing, spoke to the judge.

"Your Honor, with the court's permission, my client would like to withdraw his petition."

The judge looked almost as surprised as Rachel. "Permission granted," he said.

Rachel looked at Jack for an explanation, but he was busy pulling on his coat. "You'll make the call immediately, right, Sylvia?" he said to Kingston-Brown.

"Don't worry, it'll be done before you get there."

"What call?" Rachel asked. "Where are you going?"

"The only place that's left," Jack said.

Riding up in the elevator, he knew it required a weapon bigger than any he'd used so far, a weapon so devastating Titus would have no choice. He might have a few qualms about using it, but he'd use it nevertheless. The problem was he had no idea what it was.

The doors opened on the sixth floor and Jack began walking down the hall. The threat of disclosure obviously wasn't going to do it. As terrified as Titus was of public humiliation, he was more terrified of the fetus inside him. There was no other bluff Jack could see, either. Accusing the judge of being a hypocrite wasn't going to help; he would reject it as patronizing and insulting, one hypocrite lecturing another. The Zenobia Davis card had already been played, and badly. If there was something in the judge's background—a bribe, an embarrassment—he didn't know what it was and had no time to go hunting. In fact, except for martinis and poker, Jack had no idea what made Titus tick—his passions, his foibles, his wants, his needs.

He introduced himself to the security guard and waited, preparing to go into the most important shoot-out of his life wearing an empty holster.

The guard opened the door for him. He combed his hair with his hand, straightened his tie, and was preparing to enter when suddenly it occurred to him: *Going in with nothing is the point.* In fact, nothing was the most powerful thing he had.

He walked into the room. Titus was stretched out with his head propped up on two pillows. Next to him on the table was a gooseneck reading lamp casting shards of light across the bed, accentuating deep shadows around his eyes, turning the stress lines on his face into plowed furrows against the sun.

Jack sat in the chair next to the bed.

"I appreciate your seeing me." His voice was firm, but with none of the accusatorial tone he normally used with this man.

"Apparently, I have no alternative," Titus said. "According to my lawyer, this meeting is the price of your withdrawing your petition." His voice barely contained his contempt. "I'd appreciate your getting to the point."

510

Jack reached over to the gooseneck lamp and pushed the shade down, removing Titus's face from the glare. "I'm here to plead for my son's life."

Titus took a deep, impatient breath. "Of course you are." He raised his wristwatch. "Now, if you'll excuse me, I'm having surgery in a few hours and need some rest."

"Three weeks. That's all I'm asking."

"You're not asking anything. You're threatening. I don't give in to blackmail, MacLeod. Regardless of the consequences."

Jack's fingers drummed a nervous beat on the armrest. "I've done everything I know how to save this baby, Abner. I have nothing left. Not even the threat of publicity. I've given that up. All I can do now is plead."

Titus lifted a damp tissue from the table and drew it across his face. He folded it neatly and placed it on a stainless-steel tray by the lamp.

"Tell me something, MacLeod. If the situation were reversed and you were carrying my child, what would you do?" He'd become a judge who expected an honest answer.

"Two days ago, exactly what you're doing. I'd abort."

"And now?"

"If you wanted your child as much as I want mine, I'd give you the three weeks."

Titus shifted his body in the bed. "It's too late. Especially after you've pulled every trick in the book."

"That's something to hold against me, not the baby."

"You don't mean *the* baby, you mean *your* baby. You have no interest in speaking for other unborn fetuses. In fact, you're trying to pass legislation that would obliterate them."

"No, I'm not. I'm trying to give women the same power I'm sitting here recognizing in you. Which I acknowledge even if it means the end of my son's life." He didn't blink. "What else have I got to give?"

"Now that you're down to the bottom of the barrel, nothing."

Titus fell quiet, and Jack felt two lives being squeezed out of him, his own and his son's.

Titus said, "Doesn't it seem slightly unfair to you, MacLeod? That people like you, with no moral constraints about abortion, leave the rest of us with the burdens of unwanted pregnancies?"

"I've tried for years to relieve the burdens of unwanted pregnancies. And if there were any way I could assume the burden of this one, believe me, I'd do it."

Titus said nothing more, letting the weight of his silence crush Jack until there was nothing left to be said.

Abner Titus had won, and they both knew it.

Jack took a breath and stood up. "Thanks for hearing me out." As he lifted the gooseneck lamp back to its original position, he saw a video-cassette lying on the table with *Casablanca* printed on the side. He picked it up. "This must be the tape," he said to himself.

"What tape?"

Jack turned it over in his hand. "It's nothing, just a silly, desperate ploy. Rachel and her friends acting like a couple of right-to-life counselors."

He laid it down and walked to the door. As he reached for the stainless-steel handle he heard Titus's voice say, "MacLeod?"

He stopped without turning around.

Titus said, "I'm . . . sorry."

Jack held on to the door handle, wanting to believe that Titus was apologizing for something that didn't matter at the moment—past battles between them, Victoria's death, Rachel's transplant, Jack's begging—anything but the termination of his son's life. If he'd seen anything to support that interpretation, the slightest crack of daylight, he would have returned to his chair.

Instead, he opened the door and left.

Titus pushed the Play button and waited. On-screen, the Nazi officer emerged from a German airplane and walked along the tarmac with Claude Rains. "I've already heard about this café and Mr. Rick himself," the officer said.

A moment later the screen went blank—a snowy image appeared—and then a satellite picture of a continent or a river. He tried to make out a round shape at the bottom of the screen. It wasn't a ball—it was . . . what was it? A head? Looks like . . . His lips parted. *My God. It* is *a head! I'm looking at a sonogram! Of a baby!* The indecipherable was coming clearer: feet and hands, a torso, an umbilical cord. Instantly it nailed him. *It's not a baby. It's my baby.*

He closed his eyes and raised the remote control, preparing to turn off the set. Holding it in the air, he placed his thumb on the button and waited . . . unable to avoid one more look. The fetus was lying peacefully now, not moving. The thought of it inside himself made Titus shudder and his stomach turn, but this time he didn't panic or feel the urge to vomit.

Suddenly the baby in the sonogram moved, pushing against the sides of its pouch like a frog inside a balloon.

Titus lowered the remote control to his side and let the videotape continue running.

After a minute the screen blipped, and the fetus was gone, replaced by Sydney Greenstreet standing at the bar in a white suit and hat, talking to Humphrey Bogart as Sam played the piano behind him.

"What do you want for Sam?" Greenstreet asked.

"I don't buy or sell human beings," Bogart replied.

Titus tried to watch the movie and forget everything—the old Sydney Greenstreet vicarious escape that usually worked so well. But his heart wasn't in it, and neither was his head.

He turned off the TV set, resenting the tears that were spilling down his cheeks.

Exhausted, he closed his eyes and gave up, letting his mind remember what it wanted.

"**D**o it, son. Kill it."

Young Abner stood with a boulder raised above his head, his face lit by the headlights of his father's car at the side of the road—a twelve-year-old boy with tears streaming down his cheeks, mucus running over his lips, his face contorted in painful indecision. Lying between his feet in the center of the road was a beautiful striped cat, its head against the pavement, its eyes wide and shiny with fear. A small trickle of blood ran from its mouth, and its tail twitched and curled in the air.

"I can't!" Abner said.

"You have to," said his father. "It's in pain."

Fingering the stone with both hands, he raised his eyes up from the cat and looked at his father. "I can't! *You* hit him—*you* do it!"

"Who hit him isn't the point. You have to learn how to take the facts as you find them and make the right decision."

A small light appeared in the distance where the road disappeared on an invisible horizon.

Abner looked down at the cat and cried uncontrollably.

His father waited.

The light in the distance became two headlights accompanied by the faint rumble of a truck engine.

"Come on, son. Don't let him suffer anymore."

"I *can't!*"

"If you don't do it now, that truck coming down the highway is going to run over him!"

Abner's face contorted. "Good! I hope it does!"

"That's cheating!" his father yelled. "Now put the animal out of its misery and move it off the road before it's too late!"

The truck's eighteen wheels whined.

"I can't!" Abner looked at his father, pleading for mercy. "Don't make me do it!"

"Right now! We're standing in the middle of the road!"

Abner squeezed the boulder in his hands and looked down at the cat, oblivious to the headlights bearing down. A distant blast from an air

514

horn—"Abner!" his father yelled—another blast—the sound of air brakes grabbing—*"Abner!"*

Abner brought the rock down—crushed the cat's skull—and grabbed the animal's body just as his father yanked him off to the side of the road. The enormous rig slid by a few feet away—horn blaring, tires smoking—its trailer rocking back and forth against the moaning brakes.

Abner lay in the ditch, clutching the cat's body in his arms.

The road was empty and silent.

His father picked himself off the shoulder and stepped down the shallow embankment to see if the boy was all right. Seeing him coming, Abner scrambled backward on his hands and knees, still holding the cat against his chest.

"I hate you!" he screamed, crying. He got to his feet and moved backward toward a cornfield. "I *hate* you!"

"Abner—"

"And I know about you!" He pointed his finger as far as it could reach. "I know what you wanted to do to me! I *know* about you!"

Rachel lifted the pen and found the next blank line on the sign-in sheet.

"Another early morning, huh, Doc?" the hospital guard said.

"Afraid so." She looked at her watch and jotted 6:05 A.M. on the paper.

"I tell ya," the guard said, "between you and the chief justice's entourage, this place is a regular beehive this morning."

She stopped writing. "The chief justice?"

"Yeah, the CJ himself."

"What about him?"

"He and the marshals came through here just a few minutes ago."

She digested the words. "Abner Titus left the hospital?"

"Sure did."

"To where?"

"Don't know, but I know one thing. I been around long enough to tell the sick ones from the healthy ones, and let me tell ya, Doc. That man belongs in a bed."

She lifted the guard's telephone and punched in a number. In a second she heard a recorded greeting and a beep tone. "Jack, Rachel. Call me immediately. The pigeon's flown the coop."

The doors to the chief justice's conference room swung open and Titus entered in a wheelchair, enormous, scowling, and determined. Daisy pushed him under the crystal chandelier to the head of the felt-inlaid conference table where the eight other members of the Court were already seated. After handing Titus a manila envelope, she left the room, and the world's most powerful secret body began its deliberations.

"I understand a vote is about to be taken on my sanity," Titus said caustically. He glared at his fellow justices, saving his deepest condemnation for Justice Michael Kelly, who, as always, sat in the chair at the opposite end of the table. After a moment Titus's face softened slightly. "Considering the amount of time I've been in the hospital, I suppose I don't blame you."

His friend and mentor, Justice Edmund Little, said, "Michael and I tried to visit you last night, but we were told you were unable to see us."

Titus swallowed. The mere thought that they might have come into his room and discovered a clue to his condition—a fetal stethoscope, an inadvertent comment by Redpath's staff—dried his mouth.

"Abner," Justice Kelly said, "if you're here to tell us you're well enough to participate in the Court's business, that's good enough for me."

"I'll second that," Justice Little said. Titus looked around the table and saw everyone nodding, making the vote unanimous.

He opened the manila envelope and removed his completed opinion in *Costello*. "With that vote of confidence, I should probably wheel myself out the door and call it a day." He laid the opinion on the table. "But since I'm here and the printer awaits, I have something to say."

He scanned their faces.

"Being in the hospital has been what you might call a . . . learning experience." He thought he was ready to do this, but the words were coming slowly. "Last night I happened to see a sonogram of a twenty-one-week-old fetus." He glanced at a glass of water sitting within reach and pulled it to him. "While it might not have affected you the way it did me, it confirmed certain convictions I hold about the sanctity of life." He lifted the glass and held it a few inches above the table. "In fact," he said, staring at the clear water, "I concluded that if I were a pregnant woman, God forbid, I would find it impossible to abort."

Small beads of sweat began sprouting on his forehead. He set the glass down and reached into his vest pocket and withdrew a small, square envelope, tore it open, and removed a moist towelette, which he drew gracefully across his face. When he'd finished, he looked into the eyes of his colleagues and saw their curious, rapt attention.

He leaned back in the wheelchair in a small, last-ditch effort to escape what he had to do but it was too late. The silence, and the duty, were merciless.

"On the other hand, there's a problem here," he said softly.

He looked down at the surface of the table and raised his fist to his mouth as if he had indigestion. "The problem is that—"

He stopped talking, eyes watering. He reached out and took a drink of water.

Justice Little said, "Abner—are you all right?"

Titus set down the glass and waved him off, saying, "Hospital food." He caught his breath and rested his hand on his written opinion. Then, conquering his viscera, he summoned the words.

"The problem is that, while I myself would not abort a fetus, I can understand that others might feel—differently."

The other justices stared at him curiously, not yet understanding what he was saying. Justice Franconia glanced across the table at Justice Harris, whose eyes were locked on Titus.

Titus held the eight bewildered faces in his gaze and finished his statement.

"I am withdrawing my opinion in *Costello* and I am joining in Justice Kelly's opinion affirming *Roe*. Which makes Brother Kelly's opinion the majority opinion of the Court."

Justice Little was stunned. "My God," he said in a near whisper. "You really *have* lost your mind."

"I think we've already covered that, Ed," Titus said. He touched his pencil tray wistfully. His decision required him to give up so much, and to satisfy himself so little. Sadness and relief flooded him simultaneously, like the bittersweet exhaustion of a defeated general who must surrender his troops to save them.

Suddenly a wave of nausea swept over him. His hand rose to his mouth and his eyes became watery, his face bloated and white. "I've decided to take some time off," he said shakily, turning his wheelchair toward the door. "I'll be staying at my doctor's farm for a few weeks, but don't worry. I'll be back."

Justice Kelly, the oldest justice and the one seated farthest from the door, was the first on his feet. He reached the double doors and opened them wide as Titus rolled across the threshold.

Titus saw Daisy staring at him, alarmed.

The marshal grabbed the wheelchair from behind and pushed him into the red-carpeted hallway. As they reached the security guard's post a frazzled Jack MacLeod and Rachel Redpath appeared in front of him.

The three of them stopped, frozen in a triangle. Jack started to speak, but Titus held up his hand, saying, "Save it for the voters." He raised a handkerchief to his mouth and signaled the marshal to proceed. As they started up, he lowered his hand and spoke over his shoulder.

"I'm giving you your twenty-one days."

Rachel looked at Jack with a blank expression. Then she ran after the wheelchair.

Jack stood watching it roll down the hall on shuddering wheels, past a clerk and a bystander, around the corner, and toward an elevator that would lower it to an ambulance waiting in the Supreme Court's basement.

Jack walked into the reception area, gave a perfunctory wave hello, and entered his office. Knowing his body language, Faith buzzed him at his desk and said she'd hold his calls—the ten o'clock hearing was covered—the mail could wait—not to worry—buzz me when you're ready. She hung up without asking questions.

He loved that woman.

He lifted a business card and considered what to do. As long as Eli Graves was out there drawing a breath, he'd try to bring Jack, or someone, down. He was dangerous. He had to be found.

He tapped the card up and down on his desk blotter. He wanted to help, but if he told the police everything he knew about Graves and the bomb—the videotape, their telephone calls to each other, the meeting in the orthopedic ward—he'd be creating unknown trouble for himself. Would they believe he wasn't part of it? That he was gathering evidence against a guilty chief justice, or so he thought, rather than conspiring to blow him up? Could he keep himself out of the newspapers? Could he keep Rachel out of harm's way for three more weeks? Could he deep-six, forever, any mention of Abner Titus's *condition*?

Yes to that question, no matter what. As for the three weeks Rachel needed to comfort Titus and deliver the baby, he'd have to avoid telling them what she'd confessed to him about the baby-doll deaths. Could he avoid that for twenty-one days? Let's see: after telling them what he knew about Graves, he'd have to retain counsel for himself, schedule appointments with the prosecutor, negotiate Fifth Amendment ground rules. . . . The wheels of justice grind slowly, but exceedingly fine, the saying went. For once, perhaps, slow enough to do some good.

On the other hand, there were threats of news leaks, bad press, and an ugly, politically deadly scandal. The only way to minimize that was to shut up and let the police hunt for Graves on their own. Which they were doing anyway, so why butt in?

He tapped the card, weighing the alternatives, catching Victoria smiling at him in the water-stained photograph on his desk. *So near . . . so far.*

Lifting the receiver, he dialed the number on the business card. "Detective Norm Pulaski, please. Congressman Jack MacLeod calling."

"Give me your hand, son!"

Who's that talking to me?

A bearded man stood balanced on an I beam like an Olympic diver on a platform, hundreds of feet above asphalt and concrete. A few feet above him, lying on his stomach on a wooden plank, was an overweight construction worker in a dented hard hat and a checkered shirt, red-faced and grunting, extending his hand downward in an offer of help. Behind the worker were other anxious, wide-eyed faces—men in tin hats and leather gloves, unshaven, unfamiliar. As far as the bearded man was concerned, unfamiliar, irrelevant.

He took a step backward on the I beam, away from his rescuer.

"Come on, son," the hard hat said, "move forward and give me your hand!"

Who's that calling my name?

It was a startlingly beautiful New York morning—blue skies, yellow sun—high on the skeleton of a newly built skyscraper where there was no sound, no garbage, no earth. A place for birds and souls and sunlight as sweet as heaven. A place untouched by sex and violence. Unsullied by jail cells and convicts and nightmares. Unsoiled by vile human needs.

Two workers behind the rescuer strapped a safety harness onto his midsection, then snapped a carabiner onto a metal ring and drew back a safety rope which they tied to a steel column, quickly but well.

A splinter of sun struck the eyes of the bearded man on the I beam. He took another step backward, nearer the edge, and looked directly into the fiery ball in the sky. For a moment, before it blinded him, he could see the outline of its surface against the corona, white and swirling, a powerful, perfectly formed disk. Inviting him. Calling.

Whose voice is that? "Into Thy Hands, Father . . ."

The rescuer extended his body on the plank like a swimmer on a surf-board, inching a little more into the open air, moving closer.

The bearded man closed his eyes and marveled at the imprint of the sun on his retina.

The rescuer inched forward with his arm still extended. "Give me your hand, son. Reach out and take my hand."

The words penetrated the bearded man's ears, but his mind was elsewhere, dropping like a broken construction crane, accumulating debris and crashing down through the floors of the building like a snowball bent for hell.

The rescuer reached out for the bearded man's head, no more than a foot away. The man's mind continued its free fall.

That voice. "It is finished—"

He opened his eyes and stared at the rescuer's hand, now only inches away from him, fingers extended—

I know that voice—

—straining to save a life.

It's God's voice. It's my voice. It's God's. It's mine.

The bearded man reached up and unsnapped the collar from around his neck, tossed it away like a broken shackle, and crossed his hands on his chest as if he were about to be baptized by immersion. He tilted his head back slowly, wrenching a broken vertebra. Feeling nothing.

The rescuer stretched the ligaments in his arm to the burning point and grabbed the closest thing he could find, which was the man's beard. A piece of it parted from his face like a fistful of fur from an escaping fox.

The bearded man stepped to the side of the I beam as if he were hopping onto an adjacent, invisible platform. A small shuffle step, nicely executed. Into the clean, purified air.

Seven floors below, the corner of the skyscraper jutted out before making a vertical drop forty-two stories to the ground. A sudden gust of wind, the arms perfectly extended in flight, the sheer will to be reborn, innocent and unblemished—whatever the reason, Eli Graves missed the building and continued falling.

"Detective Wilson?"

"Yes?"

"Jim Fain, assistant U.S. attorney here in the District of Columbia. I understand you're working the baby-doll homicides?"

"Right."

"Something intended for your eyes came across my desk this morning. A note from my boss." Wilson heard rustling papers through the telephone. "Now, where the hell is it . . . ? One of these days I'm gonna have to defoliate this place."

Wilson waited. "What was the subject matter?"

"A call from Judge McCarthy . . . come on, show yourself . . . about a case. The record's sealed tight as a tick, so there's no way to get the pleadings or a transcript, but the judge names somebody he thinks knows a lot about fetal transplants."

"Remember who it is?"

"No, but . . . Christ, where the heck is it . . . ? Ah, here it is. Let's see. Blah, blah, yakety-yak . . . 'tell him he might want to interview Dr. Rachel Redpath.' "

"Dr. Redpath, right. Thanks for the call."

Pulaski held the telephone receiver out of the way of his egg salad sandwich, listening to Detective Joe Wilson tell him about the judge's letter naming Dr. Rachel Redpath. When Wilson had finished, Pulaski talked with his mouth full.

"Got a call from Congressman MacLeod," he said. "He's got a story about Eli Graves and a videotape you need to check out." He licked his thumb.

"Anything that ties him in with Redpath or the baby-doll murders?"

"Not that I can see." Leaning over the wax paper on his desk, he took the last bite. "But it wouldn't hurt to ask. I understand he's seeing the woman who broke the story. A reporter named Molly McCormick."

Wilson guffawed. "I'll waste my breath if you want, but if MacLeod's her source, he won't admit it, and if I ask her who is, she'll shoot me with the First Amendment." He could hear Pulaski finishing his dill pickle. "What else did MacLeod have to say?"

"He wanted to tell us what he knew about Graves's whereabouts."

"Anything helpful?"

"Might have been, but we already found the guy."

"No kidding. Where'd you pick him up?"

"Off the street." Pulaski wadded up the wax paper and brown bag into a ball. "Tried to fly off a forty-two-story building." He tossed his garbage toward a round metal wastebasket. It fell short. "That's the disappointing thing about gravity," he said. "It always lets you down."

"Mr. Chadwick?"

"Yes?"

"Detective Norm Pulaski, NYPD."

"Yes, of course. What can I do for you?"

"I'm calling about your client, Dr. Rachel Redpath. We'd like to have that talk with her sooner instead of later."

"How soon?"

"Tomorrow."

Chadwick fiddled with a painted stone on his desktop, a paperweight from his granddaughter. "As I mentioned last time we talked, Detective, Dr. Redpath is out of town and won't be back for three weeks."

"We'll go wherever she is. Especially if it's someplace warm."

"I'm afraid that still won't be possible."

"Come on, Mr. Chadwick." The tone was friendly; the message not. "You trying to run me to the trouble of getting a warrant?"

"On the contrary, I'm trying to save you the trouble. Even if you managed to get one, which I doubt, I'd advise her to take the Fifth."

"Pretty big step for an innocent person, wouldn't you say?"

Chadwick created a long silence. Pulaski waited him out.

"I need three weeks, Mr. Pulaski. If you sit tight and leave her alone for three more weeks, she's authorized me to make the following offer . . ."

"There it is."

"Will you look at that."

"Are you ready?"

"Ready and waiting."

Silence.

"Slippery little devil." Silence. "Okay, he's out. Cut the cord, Phoebe."

Tara Mayer flooded the cradling hands with oxygen as the scrub nurse carried the fetus to a warming bed, a device about the size of a busboy's cart, and laid him on a pad of blankets. Another member of the team cleaned him off with cotton and boric acid while others rigged him to the life-support system—an oxygen tube connected to a ventilator, an IV line in his foot, a plastic bag of liquid sugars, amino acids, vitamins, and minerals. Sensors on the baby's skin monitored its heart rate, respiration, and skin temperature, and television screens with squiggly red lines and pulsing green bars quietly signaled signs of life. Stretched across the top of the warming bed on foot-high Lucite panels was a piece of clear plastic kitchen wrap, holding in the heat of a radiant lamp's beams. Lights, tape, tubes, electrical cords, diodes, thermostats, valves, regulators—all the technology was there, and in the center of it, a tiny human being clinging to a whisper-thin breath of life.

Across the room at the operating table, Rachel and Phoebe were finishing Titus's hysterectomy.

"What does he weigh?" Phoebe asked through her surgeon's mask. She snipped free the two Dexon stitches anchoring the empty uterus to the patient's anterior abdominal wall.

"I'd say about a pound," Rachel responded.

"The whole package—fetus, placenta, and uterus—must have been close to nine or ten pounds, wouldn't you say?"

"Depends on how you weigh it," Rachel said. She lifted the severed uterus from the patient's belly. Except for closure, the procedure was essentially finished. "On a normal scale I'd say that's about right. But on Abner's mind, I'd say it was more like a ton."

•   •   •

Jack ushered Molly around the corner into the room and let her see for herself. On the warming bed was a tiny creature, too small to be called a baby, lying naked on its back—eyes closed, unabashed in a spread-eagle pose—a tiny Lilliputian tied down by life-sustaining wires, lines, and hoses.

"Oh, my God," she said, melting. "Look at him."

She walked to the bed quietly, fearing she'd wake him, and peered down through the clear plastic wrap. "I can't believe it. He's so *small.*"

"He has about a thirty-percent chance of surviving, but every day he lives, the odds improve."

She was smitten. "I may have blown a Pulitzer, but I'm glad I did what I did."

"I told you, reporters don't have to trample women and children to be good."

"Of course we do," she said, cooing, as if she were talking to the baby. "Have you named him yet?"

"He already has a name. Ray."

She raised her head. "Raymond?"

"No, just Ray."

The two of them stood like two proud parents, observing the infant. A few minutes later they left the room and walked down the hall toward the door to the dairy barn.

"I've been meaning to ask where you got the gorgeous tan," he said.

"Ten days in the Bahamas," she answered. They walked a few steps in silence. "With Elliot Landy."

He pulled the door open and led her past the cows to the barn door. "Serious or fun?"

"Both. The weather was great in the day. At night we more or less stayed in."

I'll bet. "What, no torch-lit limbos?"

"Nary a one."

"At least not on the dance floor," he said. Real smart, Jack. Make a wisecrack, show her you're jealous.

She walked toward the open barn door. "He's asked me to marry him," she said, crossing the threshold.

Jack followed and walked her toward her car. The air was fragrant with the smell of moist earth from a spring rain, fresh grass and animals, damp hay, crocuses and daffodils. Jack saw a single covey of geese flying northward in a check-mark formation and stopped to point it out. When they'd flown out of sight, he turned to her.

"So, what are you going to do?"

"I'm having dinner with him tonight to tell him," she said. She began walking along the gravel driveway. "Trouble is, I don't know what to say."

"I do. Tell him you're having dinner with a close friend who's helping you figure out the answer."

She laughed. "I think that would *be* the answer, don't you?"

They reached her car. He placed his hand on the door handle and they stood facing each other. "Tell him it's a friend who's completely objective and has nothing but your best interests at heart."

She said nothing.

"Someone who knows your heart—"

"Jack—"

"—and who's learned a few things about his own."

He fixed his eyes on hers, heating the space between them. Feeling it, she blushed slightly and looked away. "I have to go."

He opened the door for her, but before she climbed in he wrapped his arms around her and drew her to him. "Thanks for giving my child a chance to live, Molly. And since Abner Titus doesn't know what you did for his privacy, thanks for that, too."

She turned her face up to his; interpreting it as he wanted, he kissed her. Long enough to convey his feelings, not so long she'd have to break it off. He pulled her face into his neck and breathed in the fragrance of her hair.

She held on to him. Finally, exhaling in resignation, she pushed away and got in. Sitting in the driver's seat, she closed the door and started the engine.

He watched her through the side window. Instead of dropping the car into gear, she lifted a telephone, dialed, and began speaking, eyes dead ahead. He couldn't read her lips. After a few minutes she hung up and rolled down the window.

"I told him the truth and got a one-day postponement."

He smiled, but she didn't. "Something wrong?" he asked.

She touched the steering wheel. "He said regardless how things turn out, I'll always be . . . you know. The one for him." She looked up at Jack. "Except he said it much more . . . poetically."

Jack swallowed. True love was the toughest nut there was. He had his work cut out for him, assuming he had any chance at all.

"So," Molly said, "Where do you want to go for dinner?"

He leaned against the side of the car. After a line like Landy's, he had to choose the place exactly right. Blowing this one could blow it all.

A picture formed of the first time he'd lost his heart to her. A checkered tablecloth, sawdust on the floor, Elvis in the air, Molly dancing back to their table from a jukebox, smiling at him seductively, silently mouthing, *I love you*. Nailing him with those unspoken words the way Honey had nailed him with them since he was a kid.

"When's the last time you had vodka and oysters at a fish market?" he asked.

Rachel sat in front of the fireplace in her study, looking at her watch. "We have to hurry, they'll be here any minute."

She tossed a videotape marked *T-3* into a roaring fire—*T* for Titus, *3* for the third tape. The next cassette was marked *S-20*—the twentieth videotape of the Melvin Shivers transplant. This one she handed to Phoebe, who placed it in a large cardboard mover's carton. The two of them were destroying all evidence of Titus's operation and saving the evidence relating to the other subjects—*M* for Harley Moon, *B* for Billy Bannister, and *D* for Zenobia Davis. In another cardboard box, packed for safekeeping, were journals, notes, assays, lab reports, and other documentation of their first three procedures. The same research on the fourth one, Abner Titus, was burning in the fireplace.

"Have you heard from Delfina?" Phoebe asked, packing a set of photographs.

"No, and I won't. We agreed there would be no more communication after I saw her in Rome." She stoked the burning papers with an iron poker. "How are we doing?" she asked.

"We just put in the last of Abner."

Phoebe taped the boxes closed and sat on her heels on the floor, watching the fire burn. Sitting on the ottoman, Rachel prodded the red coals, keeping the heat high. The air turned warm as they watched the evidence of their work going up in flames, the videotape's chemicals blazing bright with peacock blues and greens, flaring and fading, refusing to pass into ash without offering a colorful salute.

They heard an automobile pull up and stop outside the front door. Without flinching, they continued staring into the lowering flames, their faces lit in the flicker of an expiring light.

The doorbell.

Rachel tossed on a log, stood up, and pulled the fire screen in front of the blaze, making it appear normal. Before going to the door, Phoebe opened her arms and embraced her friend. The doorbell sounded again.

Phoebe left the room for the hallway while Rachel pulled on her coat and set her suitcase on one of the boxes of evidence. In a moment her lawyer, Charlie Chadwick, entered the room.

529

Followed by Detective Pulaski.

"Everything is here," Rachel said.

Pulaski addressed her. "I take it from your attorney that you understand your Fifth Amendment rights?"

"I do, but as I assume he told you, I'm waiving them. I'll start providing you with details on the experiments as soon as you want." She gave Phoebe a kiss on the cheek and one last hug—not around her back, but, strangely, on her hips. Rachel turned to Pulaski. "Are you going to put me in handcuffs?"

"No, ma'am," he said, and picked up the first carton of evidence.

Phoebe closed the huge front door and walked back to the study to make sure that the fire had died. As she bent forward with the poker in hand she felt something bump her hip where Rachel had hugged her.

She straightened up, reached into the deep pocket of her loose-fitting skirt, and pulled out a videocassette. In the identification space was *T-4*, the last videotape of Abner Titus. The one that had captured him on the operating table, delivering the baby.

Stuck to the videocassette's logo was a small note with two words written in Rachel's unmistakable handwriting.

Keep it, it said.

The first lady swiveled her legs onto the double bed, leaned back against a set of pillows, and rested quietly, listening to the 747's jet engines burning holes in the ozone. After a moment she removed her shoes with her toes, but lacking the energy, left her Geoffrey Beene gown on. She turned her head and peered out the cabin window at the enormous full moon sitting on the tip of a silver wing. As if Air Force One had finally reached heavenly orbit on its own.

Not hardly, she thought.

She donned her reading glasses, picked up her book, and opened it to a red Chinese silk marker.

The president entered their quarters from the forward salon. Wasting no time, he pulled off his black tie, tossed it onto a soft, taupe leather chair, and sat on the bed next to her, exhaling with satisfaction.

"What are you so pleased about?" she asked, not looking up.

"I finally beat Sticks Dickey in a game of showdown."

"Mm," she said, turning a page. "Sounds like a game with a lot of wild cards."

"It wasn't the card game I was referring to."

She looked up.

He yanked off his shoes without untying the laces and leaned back and placed his warm, black-stockinged toes on hers. "He's been leaning on me the last few months. Tonight I made it clear it's time to lay off, he's gotten all he's going to get from me."

"Funny. I always thought Senator Dickey was just a water boy for someone else," she said, and turned a page. When he didn't respond, she added, "You *were* referring to Titus's Supreme Court appointment, I assume?"

He waited, and said, "More or less."

"So . . . does this mean it's finally over with?"

A thin smile formed on his lips. He was proud of his wife in equal parts—half for her empathy, half for her brains. Although he had never admitted it to her, obviously she knew that the rumors were basically right: he had accepted President Stone's stolen "Mockingbird" files from a blackmailer and thief, and worse than that, had denied knowledge of the crime under oath. She knew that the extortionist's price had been the appointment of Abner Titus. This, she was now saying, she knew most clearly.

So, she knew. So what. If he'd asked her advice at the time, she would have told him not to submit to blackmail—it was wrong, he'd never see the end of it—that sort of thing. And in most cases she would have been right, but this wasn't most cases. Politics at his level was more like those in the Mafia: once you paid your marker, chances were you didn't have to pay it twice. Anyway, it was useless speculation. If he wanted to hold on to the presidency, which he did, and make a difference for his country, which he did, and avoid disgrace, which he did, he had no choice.

That's why he hadn't told his wife. He always confided in her on matters where she could be of help—trust was not the issue—but to lay something on her she could do nothing about struck him as self-indulgent, a waste of the precious resource she was. As a husband, that's how he saw it. Of course, when it came to the subject of ideal marriages, the White House was not exactly where *How To* manuals were written. All he really knew was that a president needed the guts to shoulder certain problems alone.

He decided to keep the lid on it. "Is it finally over with?" he asked her question aloud. "If there ever was something to be over with—I said *if,* dear heart—then yes, it's over with. Now, do you want to drop the subject or do you want to become too informed for your own good?"

"Or yours," she said, and returned to her reading. Two paragraphs later she said, "So what's the senior senator from North Carolina think about the chief justice's vote in *Costello?*"

"He was surprised as hell."

"Who wasn't?"

"Me, actually."

She closed her book on her finger. "Get out, John. You had no earthly idea Titus would vote to save *Roe* and you know it. You were just plain lucky."

"Lucky, yes, surprised, no." He wiggled a toe peeking through a hole in his sock. "Presidents don't control the Supreme Court any more than they control the rest of the world. Hell, some of us can't even control our own bladders. When it comes to the Supreme Court, all you can do is appoint someone who's reasonably smart, shows some humanity, and hasn't been caught fucking a sheep. Lately." He saw her scowl. "I was assuming you were talking about a *male* justice."

"Obviously." She laid the book down and took off her glasses.

"That's the problem. Come here." She pulled his head into her lap and rested her own against the headboard and stroked his hair, remembering their days at the Cape, lying on a dune, eating potato chips and hot dogs, drinking brown-bottle beer. She looked down at him. "I'm spending a day with Rachel Redpath next week."

"Really," he said lazily, eyes shut. "What for?"

"I figure since I presented the Medal of Freedom to her, I'm kind of responsible for her. Do you mind?"

"If her felonious intent isn't infectious, doesn't bother me at all. As long as you love me, I'll support anything you want."

"I do love you," she said, and stopped stroking. "You know why?"

He opened his eyes and looked up at her. "You want me to answer that honestly?"

"Of course."

He closed them again and got comfortable. "I haven't the foggiest idea."

She leaned back and rested in a moment of harmony.

"Neither do I."

Titus turned the corner in the Supreme Court hallway and saw Justice Little approaching him a few feet away.

"Abner!" Little said, stopping. "Good to see you back. How are you feeling?"

"Fine, Ed. Fine." He looked at his watch and pointed down the hall toward his office. "I'm late. Mind if I catch up later?"

"Stop by after lunch," Little said. He lifted a folded newspaper and pointed at a headline about a Medal of Freedom winner being arrested for the baby-doll deaths. "I want to hear what it's like having a mad scientist as your kidney surgeon."

"No skin off my nose," Titus said with a smile. "As long as she knows the difference between a kidney and a uterus, she can do all the transplants on me she wants."

"I'm sure she's good, but can you believe what she did to those guys?" He lowered the newspaper. "Anyway, glad to see you had a successful rest."

"Does it show?"

"Sure does. Looks like you may have even lost some weight."

Titus turned and headed toward his office, and once he was out of earshot, answered Little under his breath. "Nine pounds three ounces in one day."

Everyone was there, from the serious, to the trashy, to the seriously trashy: *Times*es and *Posts*, *News*es, *Dispatch*es, *Tribunes*, and *Gazettes*. Network reporters and talk-show producers littered the courthouse steps, with foreign correspondents and documentary film crews adding to the pile. And circling them all in tabloid heaven were the black holes of the modern media age: *Hard Copy, First Edition,* pulpy magazines, and a constellation of newspapers with names ranging from *Suns* and *Stars* to *World*s and *Planet*s. As if they weren't spacey enough without announcing it on their mastheads.

Off to one side, at a measured distance from the "riffraff," a network news reporter spoke into the camera with a touch of aloofness, an air of mild amusement, describing the scene for his audience—the souvenir vendors, kitsch hawkers, and publicity seekers, who, he said, were threatening to make a circus of the criminal justice system. Not that he was wrong: behind him were bumper stickers reading, THE MARLBORO MAN SMOKES VIRGINIA SLIMS; buttons saying *I'd rather be drafted;* bottles labeled, *Pine Sol, for those special days of the month;* sweatshirts that read FREE THE BABY-DOLL NINE and posters that read SOYLENT GREEN WAS A KINDERGARTEN PARTY. The newscaster finished his report with a paternalistic shake of the head, as in What'll-these-kids-think-of-next, then handed his mike to an assistant and headed for the courthouse door. Not, however, before he'd stopped to purchase a T-shirt that read, *Okay, okay, but I won't do windows.* Stuffing it under his serious reporter's safari jacket, he entered the halls of justice.

"They say that on a brightly lit night on the African plains, monkeys can be seen climbing trees, trying to reach the moon."

It was the last day of the trial, and Rachel was making her own summation to the jury. She stood before them like a force of nature, commanding their attention with the earth's most basic elements: gravity, weight, energy, magnetism. Her red hair, normally askew, was full but composed, not sprayed or stern but under control, as she was. She wore

534

a plain linen jacket over a silk blouse that presented her suitably. No pompous dress-for-success, no ballsy I-am-woman-hear-me-roar, no flouncy beneath-this-is-a-sex-kitten, no cloying little-girl lace. Nothing to distract from her essential self, the timeless dignity of Eve.

"We've come a long way toward achieving harmony between the sexes, but when you consider how far we have yet to go, we are still little more than monkeys in a treetop, reaching for the moon, trying to imagine how to come close enough to bring it within our grasp."

She touched the railing.

"Members of the jury, all that I have done is to take the next step."

Much of the trial had been as unorthodox as the crimes for which Rachel stood indicted. Insisting on representing herself, with Charlie Chadwick as her legal adviser, her first move was to offer a partial deal to the prosecution: if the government gave her an immediate trial, she would not only hand over all the material evidence of her crimes—videotapes, journals, medical records—but cooperate fully with explanations, eliminating the government's need for lengthy, adversarial pretrial investigation. Defendants were often required to admit to key elements of an indictment as a condition of pleading guilty to a reduced charge, but handing the prosecution an airtight case, pleading *not* guilty, and going to trial? It made no sense, but it was too good for the prosecution to refuse.

But that wasn't all. Assuming that the defendant preferred an all-female jury, the prosecution used pretext and guile to select as many men as possible, expecting defense counsel to invoke Supreme Court case law and stop them. Instead, to their surprise, the defense seemed to fumble the ball until an all-male jury had been impaneled. It was only then that their success made the government nervous.

Having agreed to waive her rights and take the stand, Rachel testified at trial to all the relevant facts: how Shivers, Moon, and Bannister were kidnapped; how the transplants were executed; how the men died. In fact, her testimony was so fulsome that, by the time the chief prosecutor had made his closing argument, he felt compelled to warn the jury not to be misled by the truth. With the defendant having established the prosecutors' case for them, they now feared that she was going to pull a rabbit out of a hat.

And establish their case she had, answering all their questions truthfully and fully. All, that is, but the one the prosecution hadn't asked, which was the one the jury wanted most to hear: Why? Why these crimes, and why by her hand? That answer she hadn't given to anyone, not even her lawyer.

She walked in front of the jurors gracefully, measuring their concentration, reading their minds as if they were patients in her office. She stopped and stood straight, hands at her sides.

"I stand here not as a woman, or an aberration, or a representative of a strange criminal species. I am here as a human being. As one of you."

She began moving again.

"The reason I am content to be judged by a jury of men is that, at its heart, this trial raises a question that can be answered only by men. And that is, What would you do? What would you do if you were forced to bear children against your will? What would you do if you were unexpectedly pregnant with someone else's child? What would you do if you had decided of your own free will that you couldn't have a baby, yet were told that you must? What would you do if you had been taught for thousands of years that you had no decision in the matter? What would you do if you were told that your pregnant body belonged to someone else—another man, a husband, a father, a rapist, a fetus, a court, a church, a government—anyone but you? What would you do?"

She touched the railing.

"Fortunately, because you *are* men, we don't have to guess at the answer. We know what you would do because you've already done it—not once, but many times, throughout history. When you were taxed without representation, you grabbed your muskets and rebelled. When you were prevented from praying as you wanted, you killed your oppressors. When you were enslaved, you fought a civil war. When a Nazi tyrant threatened your homes, you burned his towns and smashed his bunkers. When a Japanese emperor bombed Pearl Harbor, you vaporized his cities."

She pushed away from the railing. "If you lost the most basic freedom of them all—the right to your own body—is there any doubt what you would do? I don't think so." She leaned forward. "And let me tell you. Having put myself in your shoes, I believe anyone who says that men find killing easy and natural knows nothing about men or killing. Anyone who says all men are born predators, driven by the thrill of conquest, knows nothing about the price decent men pay to defend themselves. But I do." She considered her own admission. "I have learned much about how, and why, men defend themselves and the people they love, even at the cost of human life. I know about the power that lies in their paradoxes and inconsistencies. I know how they save many by killing a few, and how they protect communities of peace with acts of war. I know how they sacrifice themselves so that others might live." She spoke as if she were forgiving them. "To see men behave this way seems natural. Often we call it brave and honorable. But to see women behave this way feels bizarre. Unnatural. And fearsome."

She walked to the other end of the railing.

"I once had an aunt who prided herself on her ability to spot a man's toupee. She said she could always see something that gave it away—the hairline, the color, the artificial part across the scalp. It never occurred to her that she couldn't see a good toupee precisely because it didn't give itself away. Well, the same is true for women with the instinct and willingness to kill. We are not easy for men to see because men are trained to believe that we don't exist. There are no scarlet letters on our foreheads, no combat boots on our feet. We appear to be no different from other women, and in most respects, we aren't. But if you want to understand who we are, take a look at who we resemble, who we mimic. Because that is why you are here judging me. We are like you. I am a walking female version of the rage you feel when you see a woman beaten or raped. I am the incarnation of the anger that runs through you when you see a man killed for no reason."

She looked at each of the jurors in turn. Then she returned to the counsel's podium, giving herself, and them, some distance.

"But of course, there is more governing us here than principles of justice. There is also justice's distant cousin, the law. Even if women's lives are greatly improved by what my colleagues and I have done— even if many lives are saved by the three we have taken—these are not justifications recognized by the laws we live under.

"I have understood this since the day the idea of the transplant entered my mind. I knew then that I would not be considered a general on a battlefield, where killing is excused by a declaration of war. I knew then that my team and I were not splitting atoms for the Manhattan Project. I knew that I was not authorized to scorch the earth on a march to the sea. I realized that we were not injecting men with syphilis to see how they would die, or placing them in the Nevada desert and detonating atom bombs over their heads. Oh, yes. I knew that our experiments were different from these. I knew that ours were impermissible. And I knew that for this difference, no matter how irrelevant it might be, I would have to pay a price."

She stepped out from behind the podium. "And so, as you deliberate my guilt or innocence, I ask only that you answer one question, the only one that truly matters in this trial. And that is this. Draped in a woman's body, but otherwise remaining the men you are, what would you do?"

Once again she approached the jury box. "But I also know you are looking for the answer to another question. I have seen it in your faces from the start. And that is, of all people who might have done this, why me?"

She brushed her fingers lightly over the worn, wooden railing and felt a sense memory flood into her chest . . . the memory of herself as a six-year-old girl caressing the smooth, cool underside of her mother's arm, the safest, most comforting place she'd ever known, or ever would. The jurors watched raptly, waiting to see if she'd finish.

"Why me?" she said softly. "Well, gentlemen. Let me tell you."

"I was not raped by a madman. I was not spit upon or cursed for entering a church while menstruating. I was not held down while old women cut off my clitoris. My vagina has never been sewn shut or ripped open. I was not forced to burn myself to death on the funeral pyre of a dead husband. I was not drowned in the Yangtze River because I was born without a penis. I was not sold into a harem in Khartoum. I was not stoned for touching the Torah. My throat was not slashed for sleeping with a man not my husband. I have never been beaten by a pimp. I was not held prisoner in a closet for seven years. I was never made to bless the size of a whip before my husband beat me with it. I was not dismembered with a chain saw. I was not stabbed to death by Richard Speck.

"My nipples were not cut off with a razor blade. I was not sodomized by my father. My feet were not bound until my arches snapped. I was not burned at the stake in France. I was not suffocated to death by the removal of brass rings from my elongated neck. I was not hanged as a witch in Salem. I did not go blind from my husband's syphilis. I never found the need to feign hysteria so that I could avoid intercourse and the pregnancy that would kill me. I was not beaten or sent to an asylum for masturbating.

"I was not tried for a crime by dunking. I was not an Arabian princess executed for refusing to deny that I had teenage sex. I was not forced to kill my daughters to keep them from becoming concubines. My blood was never used to make mortar.

"I did not have to endure running sores from a chastity belt. I was not tortured to death for adultery by having my legs tied together during labor. I was not forced to watch my stomach slit open to save a child who'd forever be called a bastard. I was not required by a court to give up custody of a toddler to a husband who was a child molester. I was not beaten by a lover so badly I had to feed myself through a straw. I was not hanged by my hands and whipped for dropping my veil.

"I never had to nurse one of my husband's six other wives back to health. I was not filmed copulating with dogs. I never found it necessary to write my last words in excrement and menstrual blood on the walls of a windowless cell. I have not delivered a baby squatting in a bean field. My children were not taken away from me because I left home without permission of a rabbinical court. I was not raped before my execution so that my murderers could avoid the Koran's prohibition against killing a virgin.

"I was not sent into the desert as a demon for refusing to lie under my husband. I was never called a whore because I didn't have a hymen. I was not given in marriage at the age of nine to an eighty-year-old Nepalese man. I was not left to die alone because I became a widow. I was not a young virgin who was buried alive to appease someone else's gods. I was not doused with kerosene and set afire so that my husband could collect a new dowry. I was not fitted with iron rings on my feet and chained to a post and left to starve because I loved another woman. I did not go blind sewing small stitches in a sweatshop. I have never seen a crowd of men cheering for the Yorkshire Ripper. I was not freely raped by my prison guards because I had joined a women's union. I was not required to marry my older sister's husband when she died. I was not murdered on my wedding night for failing to show virgin blood. I have never serviced twenty Japanese businessmen in a Korean brothel. My legs were not severed and sewn on backward for having sex with a man other than my husband. The law never equated me with minors, savages, and the insane. My tongue was never cut out for speaking in the presence of my tribal chief.

"No court has ever forced me to marry my rapist so that he could receive a smaller sentence for the crime. I have never had to pay the tax collector with my body. I was not killed by having a stake driven through my vagina. I was never made to eat lice from my husband's head. The flesh was never cut from my body and fed to my grandfather to cure his incurable disease. I did not grind my teeth to the gums chewing leather to make my master's moccasins soft.

"I did not have to perform endless fellatio on an old husband who could not climax. I was not fired because I refused to give sexual favors to a boss. I was not rejected from medical school, or excluded from a club I wished to join, or deprived of the chairmanship of my department, or denied the Medal of Freedom. I was never forced to sew buttons on a man's shirt. I was not even sent to my room for conduct unbecoming a lady."

She stood quietly a moment, honoring the silence. She lifted her hands to her chin, index fingers extended in a church steeple.

"I didn't commit the crimes of which I am charged for any one of these reasons. I committed them for all of them. Because even though none of these things happened to me, any of them *could* have happened to me. And one, which I have not mentioned, did. And why? Because of the most heinous crime of them all. The one of which I am profoundly, notoriously, and undeniably guilty.

"I am a woman."

She dropped her hands to her side.

"When I was six years old, I watched my mother die on an abortionist's table. Although I didn't know it at the time, that was the moment I crossed over from your rules to mine."

"Has the jury reached a verdict?" the judge asked.

The foreman stood up in the jury box. "We have, Your Honor." He opened a piece of paper and pushed his glasses up his nose, waiting.

The clerk said, "On count one for first-degree murder of Melvin Shivers, how does the jury find?"

"Not guilty," the foreman said.

The spectators broke into applause, and the judge gaveled the room to order.

"On count two for first-degree murder of Harley Moon, how do you find?"

"Not guilty." More applause.

"On count three for first-degree murder of William Bannister?"

"Not guilty."

The audience settled down and listened as the jury began dismantling the prosecution's case one brick at time—multiple counts of conspiracy: not guilty. Multiple counts of kidnapping, aiding, and abetting: not guilty. Multiple counts of assault with a deadly weapon (a scalpel), mayhem, disfigurement, malicious disfigurement, asportation (the moving of a dead body), the kitchen sink: not guilty. Finally, only three final counts remained.

"On count twenty-six, for first-degree manslaughter of William Bannister, how do you find?"

"Not guilty." His cancer had caused the jury to nullify the charge.

"On count twenty-seven, for first-degree manslaughter of Melvin Shivers, how do you find?"

"Guilty."

Murmurs. And silence.

"On count twenty-eight, for first-degree manslaughter of Harley Moon, how do you find?"

"Guilty."

The room remained quiet. Less onerous than a murder conviction, certainly. Still, Dr. Rachel Redpath would surely serve seven to ten years in prison.

She faced the jury. And nodded with respect.

• • •

The courtroom began deflating as reporters ran and spectators drifted out the rear door. Jack worked his way up the aisle and through the swinging gates as the handcuffs were being snapped on.

"Are you all right?" he asked Rachel.

"Of course," she said. "Maybe now I can get back to doing basic research. Or something worthwhile for some women in jail."

She reached up to her neck and pulled a thin gold chain from under her blouse, wriggled it over her head, and held it out in her manacled hands. Dangling at the end of it was the crystal intaglio ring the old abortionist had removed from her mother's neck the night she had died on the woman's kitchen table. She laid it in his palm. "This is for helping change the world, Jack." She hesitated a moment, listening to the silence behind her.

The marshal pulled at her arm and led her to the door at the front of the courtroom.

And then she was gone.

Jack walked south along a path in Central Park with his raincoat collar up and his head down. The eye patch was off; his eyesight restored; the limp largely gone; his agility renewed.

Congress had adjourned for the Memorial Day weekend, leaving him with things to be done. After his daily visit to neonatology to see his baby boy, he planned to spend the rest of the morning with his campaign staff, reviewing the polls, meshing campaign appearances, hearing what his primary opponent had to say about him that day, going about the business of exuding confidence. Despite the advantages of incumbency, all elections were difficult, and he took nothing for granted.

Walking on the path paralleling Fifth Avenue, he noticed a crowd on the sidewalk across the street, in front of an innocuous building. Naturally drawn to political gatherings, he stepped off the path toward the wrought-iron fence. Through the drizzle he could see about fifty people picketing a women's clinic, circling the sidewalk like Joshua's trumpeters, chanting and praying for the walls to come tumbling down.

He had no time for this. Still, he gripped the stanchions, studying the protesters' faces. From a distance they appeared ordinary and uncomplicated, so certain of themselves that they made him slightly envious.

He was about to push back and continue down the path when he saw a woman demonstrator wander away from the picket line, cross the street, and sit on a stone bench on the other side of the fence. She lifted her THOU SHALT NOT KILL sign from her shoulder and laid it on the sidewalk, and after placing a Bible in her lap, watched her friends continue demonstrating across the street.

"Tired?" Jack said to her through the bars.

She turned and saw him. "Sure am. Want to carry it awhile?"

"No thanks. I'm on the other side."

The woman's expression changed. "Say, aren't you—aren't you Congressman MacLeod?"

"Every two years, if I'm lucky."

The woman stood up and walked over to the fence, clutching the Bible to her breast like the Statue of Liberty holding her tablet. "You were pretty hurt in that clinic bombing, weren't you?"

"Yes."

"That was a terrible thing."

"Yes, it was."

She studied his face. "But you're okay now?"

"Yes, I am."

The two of them continued examining each other. After an awkward moment she said, "I feel like I need to confess something."

"What's that?"

"I know the man who poked you in the eye."

"Really? Who was it?"

"A friend."

"What happened to him?"

"He had a fractured skull and two broken ribs, but he's all right." She hesitated. "Say, you're not going to press charges against him, are you?"

"I don't know. Think I should?"

She looked alarmed. "Oh, Lord, I knew I shouldn't have brought it up. He's got five kids and a mortgage and he's been laid off since he got hurt and—"

Jack held up his hand. "Whoa, slow down, I'm not going to sue anybody." She was relieved. "Who is he again?"

"My husband."

Standing in silence, they studied each other like two war-weary knights, visors lifted, swords temporarily sheathed. Two ordinary people momentarily, briefly, connecting.

"I have to go," the woman said, and started to turn away.

"Just a second," he said. Seeing the Bible reminded him of his father, sitting in his lumpy club chair, reading bedtime stories to his children. Stories of Samson and Delilah ... the baby in the bulrushes ... the child in the manger. It was the exact same book she held in her hands, the exact same moral compass. So what was it that made her think north was south?

For a split second he thought he saw the answer. He reached through the fence, but instinctively she drew the Bible back, away from his grasp.

"You've got it upside down," he explained.

Oh, her expression said. She loosened her grip and turned the book around. She started to say something to him, then turned her face skyward, squinting. "Sure wish the rain would stop."

Across the street, a man with a bullhorn saw her dawdling. "Hey, Elise! Let's get with it, what d'ya say?"

She left the fence, walked to the bench, and bent down to pick up her sign. As she crossed the street, she glanced back at Jack, then rejoined the picket line.

He backed away from the fence and walked down the path, eventually arriving at a preschool playground with slides, tunnels, and swings. He stopped at the teeter-totter and leveled it with his hand. His son had survived his tenth week of life, which meant the odds had finally turned in his favor. The little guy was on a streak now. Jack could feel it. He pushed the end of the teeter-totter that had been on the ground into the up position and moved on.

Crossing the Sheep Meadow, he noticed that the rain had finally stopped. He stopped too, and drew in a deep, nostril-flared breath. The air was filled with the same fresh fragrance of wet grass he'd smelled a few weeks earlier at Rachel's farm, with Molly.

Molly.

He wondered what they would do together Saturday night. Then he wondered what she and Elliot would do together Sunday. It wasn't an ideal situation, but like his son, the longer he hung in, the better his chances of surviving. Patience was what he needed now. Patience and doing things right. Those were the only ways to get a streak started, and he knew a lot about streaks.

He reached into his pocket and pulled out Rachel's intaglio ring. Begging the stars' indulgence—he didn't want to push his luck too far or get ahead of his game—he slipped it onto his little finger. Like the cigar band he'd slipped onto Molly's finger in Tortola. Like the band, it fit. Perfectly.

He pulled it off and continued down the path toward his office, whistling lightly.

EPILOGUE

Rachel opened the cigar box and took out a fresh envelope. The prison guard stuck her head through the door to the lounge, said "Lights out in ten minutes," and promptly left the room, allowing the inmates to finish what they were doing.

Rachel licked the envelope flap on a letter to Phoebe Chang. Like her other fellow conspirators, Chang had pleaded guilty to a single count of manslaughter and was now serving time in another institution. She and Rachel wrote every week.

Opening the cigar box again, Rachel laid her correspondence inside, lingering for a moment over an English translation of an Italian newspaper article. She wanted one more look at the photograph of a woman standing at a bank of microphones making an announcement. The story itself she'd already read several times: Gianni Cardinal Cantini had undergone emergency surgery to correct complications stemming from a spleen transplant he'd undergone two years earlier. The woman in the photograph, the cardinal's chief surgeon, Dr. Delfina Rinaldi, was quoted as saying, "Today's operation went extremely well. Cardinal Cantini will be confined to private quarters in the clinic for several weeks, but I believe in a few more months, everything will come out fine."

Everything will come out fine. Despite the poor quality of the newsprint, Rachel swore she saw the twinkle she was looking for in Delfina's eyes.

She slipped the letter and news clipping into an envelope, showing no sign of emotion, no hint of satisfaction. Even in the privacy of her mind, she wished Cardinal Cantini no disrespect for his postoperative physical pain or, certainly, for the spiritual agony he would soon be suffering as he learned something of importance about a woman's heart. That is to say, the human heart.

She tapped her finger against her lips, stood up, stretched, and headed back toward her cell with the cigar box in hand. Her room was not a particularly cheerful place, but for the first time in weeks there was a touch of lightness to her step.

547

As she entered, only one thought troubled her.

As one might expect of a doctor, she had been a model prisoner for the last year—complying with the rules and regulations, conducting modest research, advising inmates, contributing to the general welfare of the prison. In fact, her behavior had been so impeccable, she'd earned all the privileges the penal system allowed.

Including her share of visitors. Which raised the problem at hand.

Should she refuse to see tomorrow's guests, insulating herself from the suspicion that was sure to arise if and when the news of their work finally broke? Or should she at least meet with them and explain why she couldn't be of help?

Or ... should she give her two friends from Tokyo, the brilliant female surgeons she'd met in Rome, exactly the technical information and instruction they had come halfway around the world to learn from her?

She turned out the light to make her decision. Prison walls had eyes. In the dark, no one could see her face. Or read her mind.

ACKNOWLEDGMENTS

I wish to thank Dr. Thomas E. Starzl, Director of the Transplantation Institute at the University of Pittsburgh Medical Center, for allowing me to interview members of his staff and observe organ transplants and immunosuppressant research at the University Hospital. I am particularly grateful to Dr. Andreas G. Tzakis, formerly of the Institute, currently codirector, Transplant Program, University of Miami School of Medicine, Miami, Florida, for his help, imagination, and good humor.

Equally invaluable was Dr. Harvey Rutstein, recertified diplomate of the American Board of Obstetrics and Gynecology, and director, New York State Society of Obstetricians and Gynecologists. His interest in the book was extraordinarily generous, and his instruction in gynecological anatomy and surgery is deeply appreciated.

Indispensable assistance was also given by Dr. Kari Reiber, Forensic Pathologist. Her explanation of how investigations into the causes of death are conducted, her rigorous professionalism, and her patient good nature made her an excellent teacher. Any deviations in the book from the practices she would normally follow are mine, not hers, a caveat that applies equally to all professionals whom I have consulted.

I'd like to thank my editor, Sam Vaughan, for the skillful exercise of his craft, his unrelenting civility, and enjoyable conversation having nothing to do with this book. In addition, I am indebted to Joni Evans for her encouragement; my agent and ally, Ed Victor; and my friend, Susan Lee Johnson. For taking time to read in draft, I want to thank Anne Abbott, Gloria Bunze, Diane Dennis, David Frohnmayer, Lisa Hedley, Barry Kingham, and my three children, Paul, Katie, and Matt Pottinger.

There have been others whose technical help was important in the writing of this book. Among these were Dr. Tim Monaghan, assistant medical examiner, Armed Forces Institute of Pathology, Washington, D.C.; Dr. Mindy L. Aisen, Burke Rehabilitation Center, Westchester County, New York; Dr. Spencer Sherman, ophthalmologist, New York City; Catherine LeRoy, former legislative assistant to Congressman Don Edwards of California; Jim Spalding, former administrative assistant to Congressman Guy Vander Jagt of Michigan; Peter E. Holmes, legislative consultant, Groom & Nordberg; Washington, D.C.; Dr. Alfred

Krauss, director, Department of Neonatology, New York Hospital; Dr. John Train, psychiatrist, New York City; Dr. Charles Steinberg, Cornell Medical Center, New York City; Dr. Katherine Hammock, neurosurgeon, Washington, D.C.; Dr. Janet Kennedy, psychiatrist, New York City; Lt. Walter Boser and Det. Michael Murray, Bomb Squad, New York City Police Department; Prof. Robert O'Neil, University of Virginia School of Law, Charlottesville, Virginia; Janet Benshoof, president, The Center for Reproductive Law and Policy, New York City; Peggy Brandenberg, National Institutes of Health, Bethesda, Md.; and Wanda Bond, United Network for Organ Sharing, Richmond, Virginia.

About the Author

STANLEY POTTINGER is a graduate of Harvard College and Harvard Law School. He practiced law in California and served as Director of the Office for Civil Rights at the Department of Health, Education, and Welfare, and as Assistant Attorney General of the Civil Rights Division, Department of Justice, in Washington, D.C. He has argued four cases before the Supreme Court. Mr. Pottinger has three grown children and lives in the New York City area. *The Fourth Procedure* is his first novel.